Perdition

BOOK V OF THE MARTYR SERIES

By MC Hunton

DEDICATION

For everyone whose trauma has made their
life a living hell.

I promise, it can get better.

CONTENTS

ACKNOWLEDGMENTS

To Talia, without whom the biggest twist in the series
wouldn't be nearly as twisty.

To Greg, for putting up with my incessant need for
immediate gratification upon every finished chapter.

To my beta reading team, for always encouraging me to
dig deeper.

And to the man who inspired Ace Rodfield –
may a woman actually break your fingers so
you might learn some manners.

CHAPTER ONE

An ocean of blood-red leaves washed over the asphalt, coating the street in crisp, autumn decay. Downtown Philadelphia glowed outside of the car. A fall festival had taken over the whole of Penn Square and made the drive through the city hell on four wheels. Pedestrians in sweaters and gloves sipped on steaming mugs of apple cider with no concern for the cars crawling through the intersections. Darius Jones stared out the passenger window, watching each happy face as it passed by. He rarely saw happy faces anymore. They felt fabricated, like he was moving through a simulation.

"So…" Chris Silver's voice dragged his focus into the car. She sat behind the wheel, slim body tense, hands perfectly placed at ten and four. Her blonde ponytail lay flat between her shoulder blades and stood out against the black Tactical Unit turtleneck. "Have you figured out what you're going to say?"

Darius sighed and ran a hand across his mouth. Stubble scraped his palm and the pads of his fingers. "No," he murmured. "Not yet."

"We're less than five minutes away," Cain Guttuso said, like Darius needed a damned reminder. He caught the older man watching him in the rearview mirror. Cain sat alone in the back seat, his ankle crossed over his knee, which made his tight-fitting slacks seem more constricting. Thanks to Envy ripping his soul apart and subsequently abandoning his body centuries ago, Cain was the only person in this whole city without an aura, and he'd been so quiet for the trip that Darius almost forgot he was there. Cain's Familiar, a large, longhaired tabby named Crescendo, curled up on the rear deck beneath the window. The cat's orange gaze met Darius's, too.

"I'll figure it out," Darius said.

The vital warmth of Chris's soul, a sharp contrast to Cain's emptiness, shifted as she looked at him. Her green eyes narrowed in an expression that could have just as easily been pity as sympathy, but she didn't say more. Instead, she turned back to the road, and her grip tightened.

Darius had signed up for this months ago, so he'd had time to prepare, but it never seemed to make it further up on his massive list of shit to do beyond the vague category of "Future Darius's Problem." Well, Future Darius was here and still completely unprepared. All he'd done since they'd climbed into the sedan an hour and a half ago was watch the country pass by while he relived the unimaginable—the most consequential loss the Martyrs had faced in nearly one hundred years—and tried to boil it down into something easy to comprehend.

Was such a thing even possible?

"Start simple," Cain suggested. His silky voice drifted through the cab. The setting sun caught his expression and cast a yellow glow against the white peppering his dark hair, lacing it with gold. "Answer her questions openly and honestly."

Darius considered him for a second longer before focusing on the street outside. Decorations for the upcoming holiday adorned every establishment and hung from tree branches like bodies. Zombies, ghosts, and skeletons danced in the wind, caricatures of death teasing a culture that did whatever it could to pretend death was so far on the horizon that thinking about it was a waste of time. Darius supposed this watered-down, cartoon version was better than the real thing. His stomach twisted.

"I still think we should've called her," Chris said, shaking her head. "Instead of just… springing it on her like this."

When they reached a red light, she flicked on her blinker. As things wrapped up and festival-goers headed back to their cars, a wave of warm energy flooded through the intersection. The individual auras from each human soul blended so seamlessly that instead of being separate entities, they felt like a river—simultaneously one and many.

"Correct me if I'm wrong," Cain ventured. He leaned forward, brows pinched over his bright eyes. "But I was under the impression that her program was no-contact?"

"They have a line for emergencies," Chris said, "and I'd argue this counted as an emergency."

The light flashed green, and Chris turned the corner. Darius watched people pass by on the sidewalk. Most of them probably lived peaceful lives… generally speaking. Concerned about things like love and money and what the hell they were going to eat for dinner. Sometimes, Darius wished he could go back to a time when those were the worst worries on his plate, too. A bitter scoff bulged in his throat. He swallowed it down.

"If we'd called her," he said, "she would've come home."

A tense quiet sank over the car, and it stayed stubbornly in place until they reached the bus station. Chris parked in the front lot. Darius unlatched his belt, opened the door, and stepped out.

Philadelphia's October felt different from New York's. The climate was similar enough, both brisk and breezy, but the city's towering high-rises gave the illusion of a darker day. Here, Darius squinted in the low-sitting sun, raising a hand above his brow to more easily see the front entrance to the bus station in the glare.

The people stood out, too. New York City was the single most populated metropolitan area in the United States, which meant no matter where Darius went within the city proper, he was always surrounded by hot human life. Somehow, though, Philadelphia felt hotter. He knew it probably had to do with the fall festival cramming so many together in such a small space, but part of him—an angry, jaded part—wondered if it was because the Sins' corruption wasn't as thick here. The souls were less tainted, less cold.

"Here she comes," Cain said. He'd gotten out of the car behind Darius and joined him on the sidewalk. Where Darius's Virtue power allowed him to feel the positive energy mankind let out, Cain's connection to the Sins gave him a cold sense of the negative side. His eyes tracked a point inside the building, and Darius focused in that direction. The familiar aura was so fragmented to Darius that he almost didn't sense it within the throng of travelers.

Suddenly, Darius's phone pinged with an alert, and he glanced down at the notification peering up at him from the screen.

"Finally got my phone back, bitches!"

Chris's buzzed, too, and her face paled when she looked at it. Cain's forehead furrowed curiously until he stole a peek at her screen. The text had been sent to a group chat of all the Martyr leadership. Or… the previous Martyr leadership. For five months, this thread had been dead.

"Oh, *no*," Cain said.

Darius groaned, pocketed his device, and ran a hand through his hair. He hadn't gotten it cut in a while, and the shaggy, brown locks snagged around his fingers. Cain's gaze flashed back to the station, this time tracking instantly to a set of glass double doors thirty feet down the brick wall. They opened, and a vibrant woman burst through. A duffle bag almost as big as she was tugged her down by the left shoulder. She hoisted it up as her bright blue eyes darted around the crowded sidewalk.

The last time Darius had seen her, she'd been sick and

skinny, just days out from a heroin overdose that had nearly claimed her life on the floor of a nightclub bathroom. Now, her heart-shaped face flaunted fuller cheeks and a healthy flush of pink as she fought to catch her breath. Soft yellow hair swept over her forehead, long enough to hide the piercing in her eyebrow. Her expression knitted nervously, as though concerned they'd forgotten about her in the six months she'd been gone.

Back then, Darius had been dreading her leaving. Now, he was dreading her return.

He forced a smile and raised a hand.

"Mackenzie!" he called.

Her face snapped in their direction, and a massive grin stretched across her mouth. She thrust her hand into the air with a squeal.

"Darius!" Mackenzie McKay shouted.

She rushed toward him, running as fast as the lumpy duffle and her short legs would allow until she was less than fifteen feet away. Then, she abandoned the bag entirely, sprinted the rest of the distance, and leapt into Darius in a crushing hug. The instant her arms wrapped around him, the knot of anxiety in his chest loosened—just enough to let the gratitude in—and he lifted her from the ground.

God, he'd missed this kind of energy in the Underground.

"What the hell are you doing here?" Mackenzie practically shrieked in his ear. Subtle hints of an Irish accent colored the words. "I thought the plan was to send a Recon unit to pick me up!"

Darius laughed, maybe the first genuine laugh he'd had since May, as he lowered her. "Plans change."

"Obviously," Mackenzie said. She squeezed him one last time before pulling back to look at his face. "Long trip? You look like you haven't slept since I've been gone!"

Pain smothered Darius's smile, and he glanced over her head at the massive transit station window. Did a reflection add ten years? Based on the shadows darkening the olive skin beneath his eyes and the way his green irises felt cold and colorless, he hoped so. Otherwise, this summer had taken a heavier toll on him than he wanted to admit. He'd just turned thirty, but god, he felt so much older.

"It's been really long, yeah," he managed to mutter with a cold chuckle. Mackenzie's lips twitched downward, and her eyes narrowed, but movement over Darius's shoulder distracted her. The smile filled out again.

"Chris!" Mackenzie practically shoved Darius aside to hug her, too. "Wow, our senior Virtue *and* the TAC director are escorting me home? Either I qualify for the VIP experience, or I *seriously* fucked up."

She met Darius's gaze, like she suspected something else entirely, but Cain saved him from having to say more.

"Perhaps we simply missed your penchant for quick wit," the Forgotten Sin said. He'd gathered her duffle, and while the bag had been cumbersome for Mackenzie to carry, Cain lifted it with such little effort the thing might as well have been full of feathers. He flung it behind one shoulder and gestured the other hand toward her head. "Blonde is a rather tame color for you. I think I preferred the blue."

Mackenzie laughed. "Me, too," she agreed as she ran her fingers through the strands for a dramatic side part. "But the grown-out roots were driving me insane. I sneaked away to buy some box bleach and dye from a corner store down the street, but they didn't have any fun shades, so I was stuck with this." She gave a sheepish grin followed by a shrug. "It was technically against the rules, but what were they gonna do? Kick me out on the last day?"

Cain offered a smile. "It sounds like you had a lovely trip."

A slender brow arched high into freshly-yellow bangs. "Is that what we're calling rehab now?" Mackenzie asked. "A trip?"

"Would you rather I call it a quarantine?" Cain suggested, a twinkle in his voice. "A detention? An *incarceration?*"

The bridge of Mackenzie's nose wrinkled, drawing attention to a new splattering of freckles peppering her cheeks, and she stuck her pierced tongue out between her teeth. "Ugh. No. Okay, we can go with 'trip,' then. And you're right. The 'trip' was amazing!"

They made their way back to the Martyr sedan. Cain opened the trunk and tossed Mackenzie's bag on top of a secret weapons compartment full of guns and armor before closing the door and walking to the passenger side. This time, he sat shotgun beside Chris while Mackenzie and Darius took the back seat. Darius wanted to look her in the face when he broke the news, but after they got situated, he found he couldn't easily look at her at all.

Minutes passed as Mackenzie recounted her experiences—the people she'd met, the lessons she'd learned, and the tools they'd given her to prevent another relapse that could make her spiral back to square one... or worse. The rehab program she'd selected was all about "reconnecting with your roots," which seemed to be more about disconnecting from everything else so you could figure out what those roots were to begin with. For the last six months, she'd been deep in the mountains without access to her phone, the internet, or other high-tech amenities.

Darius sat listlessly, vaguely listening to the stories about hiking part of the Appalachian Trail, paddle boarding the Lehigh River, and skinny dipping in crisp mountain ponds. Despite multiple complaints about bugs, dirt, and the sheer amount of sunscreen she had to apply to keep her Irish complexion from freckling more than it already had, she spoke with such joy and clarity that it made a guilty weight grow in his stomach.

"Do you think it helped?" Chris asked. They reached the highway, a vibrant setting sun retreating at their backs. Chris glanced up to the mirror, and Crescendo peeked at Mackenzie from between the front seats. "You're feeling better?"

"I mean, yeah," Mackenzie said, shrugging. "Jumping naked into the water aside, it was a lot of hard work, and it really showed me how lucky I am. Most of the people there don't have *anything* to go back to. All I thought about was how glad I was to come home. Can you imagine that? I missed you people and this stupid, bloody war we're fighting."

She laughed, glancing around the car. Darius caught her eye and forced a smile. Mackenzie's faltered again. She cleared her throat.

"Well, enough about me," she said. She lowered her hands back to her lap, where her nails tapped on her faded jeans. "What's been happening back at the Underground? Is R&D falling apart with Wolfe ruining the show? Did Verrette decide to stick around after all? Have we been planning a strike against Lust, or does Alan still have a stick up his butt about playing it safe?"

She tried to chuckle again, but the oxygen in the cabin seemed to disappear. Darius couldn't breathe. His lungs seized in his ribcage, refusing to open, as sweat broke out along his spine. Mackenzie's attention darted around them all—from Chris to Cain and finally to Darius. Her smile vanished.

"Okay," she blurted out when none of them replied. Darius, at last, met her eyes. They were wide and terrified. "You three have been acting cagey as *fuck*. What's going on? What happened?"

Darius swallowed hard, forcing himself to inhale a deep rush of stale air before he spoke.

"Alan is gone."

Mackenzie's mouth dropped open, and her pupils contracted. "Gone?" she repeated. Fingertips froze against her thighs, digging into the denim. "Gone where?"

Darius's jaw tightened. "He's *gone*, Mackenzie."

Neither Cain nor Chris turned back to watch her, but Crescendo's head was still peering around Cain's seat, his orange eyes focused intently on Mackenzie's face—a face drained of all color.

"*What?*" The word stammered out, barely louder than

the drone of their tires on the asphalt outside. She grabbed the sides of her head and twisted her fingers into her hair. "You're *joking.*"

Darius shook his head. A panicked rush of tears glistened behind Mackenzie's lashes.

"How? *When?*"

"Wrath shot him," Darius said. "May Seventh—"

"*May?*" Mackenzie interrupted. "*Five months ago?*" Darius nodded, and Mackenzie gawked. When she went on, her voice was tight. "Why didn't you call me? Why didn't you come *get* me?"

Chris's aura shifted as she and Cain exchanged a tense look. "Mackenzie," Darius managed to get out, "your recovery is *important.*"

She waved the concern away with a wild, trembling hand. "I can't believe you let me talk about this bullshit rehab program for ten fucking minutes when *Alan is—*" She stopped abruptly and drew a shaky breath. Her eyes slammed closed, crinkling her entire face as though she was fighting hard to keep from screaming. She opened them again and glared at Darius.

"Tell me *everything.*"

He did.

Mackenzie watched in stunned silence, for once in her life at a loss for words, as Darius spoke. He explained how Lamar Verrette, the Virtue Consent, *had* decided to join the Underground, how he wanted to destroy Connor Amoretto not just to remove Lust from the picture for good but to make New York City safe for his family again. He explained the planned strike and how that strike went south when Lamar had a panic attack. Then, the Sin escaped, Thorn was captured, and Alan…

Alan Blaine took a bullet to the head.

Mackenzie's face blanched. Her fingertips had migrated between her teeth, where she chewed her nails down to tender nubs. "Fuck," she muttered. Then, louder, "*Fuck!* This is so bad! What about the Underground? What about his

Influence?"

"The Underground is safe," Chris said, "but his Influence is gone." She didn't move her eyes from the road as she spoke. They carried the same drained look everyone else in the Martyrs wore right now. "All the protective Programming he installed to make sure we can't expose the location of the Underground has worn off, as well as anything else he's done over the decades. Alan was alive for almost one hundred and eighty years."

A blustering, incoherent sound stuttered from Mackenzie's mouth. "What… what do we *do?"*

"Holly already implemented an alert system for suspected threats, and her team's been running drills to make sure the Martyrs are ready if anything happens," Chris said. "As for the Programming… we're still fixing what we can."

"Fixing it?" Mackenzie asked. "How?"

Cain cleared his throat. "That, I'm sorry to say, is where *I* come in."

Mackenzie gaped at him. "You're *sorry?* What does *that* mean?"

"It means that Alan was not the only Forgotten Sin in the Underground," Cain said. "Though I am not as proficient in Programming as he was. It takes longer and may have some… uncomfortable side effects."

"What kind of side effects?" Mackenzie asked, her face pale beneath her freckles.

"Nothing permanent," Cain murmured. "At least… we don't believe it's permanent."

Mackenzie's eyes darted from Cain back to Darius, so wide that he could see the whole of her blue irises in the center of glistening, white circles.

"It's also non-negotiable," Darius said. God, he couldn't believe this was where he was now. When he'd first learned that Alan Programmed the Martyrs, he'd been appalled at the invasion of it. Now, here he was, demanding it himself.

A short silence followed, and then, Mackenzie nodded, just once, her jaw set.

"Close your eyes," Cain instructed her. "And relax."

The Programming took several minutes. Mackenzie wound her arms around herself, gritting her teeth. The Forgotten Envy sat properly in the passenger's seat, hands folded, forehead knitted.

Cain hadn't been lying when he'd complimented Alan's proficiency in the technique. The late Martyr leader could make it impossible for the Martyrs to communicate about the Underground and its location at all—whether they were calmly chatting about things over a cup of coffee in the courtyard or screaming under duress while their fingers were broken one by one. Mackenzie had once told Darius that this made the Martyrs "torture proof." The thought made his stomach squirm then, and it did the same now, but she was right. Alan's Martyrs hadn't been able to expose any information about the Underground's location. Not in words, in writing, or even in action by pointing at a map.

Losing that Programming had been devastating, and rebuilding it was a monstrous task.

Soon, Cain's shoulders relaxed, and Mackenzie let out a groan that turned into a curse on the way from her mouth. She touched her temples with a wince.

"My apologies," Cain said. He spun in his seat to offer Mackenzie an apologetic smile. "Alan developed his process well over a century ago and hadn't written the method down. I knew the basics of it—I was one of the people who helped fine-tune the original concept in the first place—but it still took us months to work out how best to get it done. Alan had nearly one hundred and fifty years to test and tweak his methods. I only had a few weeks. You may experience migraines, minor memory lapses, irritability…"

"It's fine," she said, but she didn't sound fine. "Has everyone been Reprogrammed?"

"Not yet," Darius replied.

"We're stretched thin," Chris said, "so we focused on the essential units first: TAC, Recon, and the Gray Unit. Most of the Martyrs who rarely leave the Underground still haven't been touched. We don't want to risk Programming them there."

Mackenzie's eyes widened, and she threw Cain a horrified look. "Has Envy repossessed?"

"Not as far as we can tell," Cain said, "but we didn't know about Lust's new host for months, and we can't take any unnecessary risks at the moment. Should the Sin complete possession, it would easily feel me using my Influence, so it's safest to stick to exercising that power away from our home base."

All Mackenzie seemed to be able to do was nod. Her head bobbed up and down, over and over again. Her hands wrung together in the gap between her legs, fingers pulling at one another until her knuckles were cracked and spent. Her gaze wandered into the encroaching twilight, where the sky was a dusky shade the color of bruised skin, but her focus was clearly elsewhere—somewhere darker. After a moment, she swallowed hard and turned back to Darius.

"How is Thorn?"

She asked it like she was afraid of the answer.

A stone tumbled in Darius's stomach, all its rough edges carving deep gouges in his gut. From the corner of his eye, he caught Chris checking the rearview mirror, and he had no doubts she was looking at him. Crescendo, too. The cat's head twisted further around Cain's chair until his bright, orange irises zeroed in.

"She says she's fine," Darius answered, voice low and colorless, "but she's not."

Mackenzie's eyes glistened again, and at last, a tear escaped her lash line. It sprinted a hot line down her cheek before she frantically brushed it off. Then, she turned away from him, from *all* of them, stared out the glass, and didn't speak the remainder of the drive.

By the time they made it home, the horizon was dark

and empty, even the moon hiding its face. The yellow glimmer of artificial lights broke through distant trees. A gas station materialized ahead of them, tucked a mile off Highway 9 in a rural, wooded area. The locals knew this place as a convenient stop to fill their tanks or buy snacks for the road, but to the Martyrs, it was so much more.

Before they even reached the building, warm energy sprung to life like a hundred candle flames flickering deep beneath the soil. Chris pulled them into the lot, which was empty except for a few stragglers pumping gas on the northern edge of the station. They circled to the far side, where an attached, drive-through car wash waited, tucked safely away from bright lights and prying eyes. Chris rolled her window down, slid a card through the credit slot, and waited for the door to open. When she drove inside, the wash shut around them. Instead of the massive brush rollers and water sprayers coming to life, the ground rumbled, and soon, they descended a steep slant into the Underground.

The vehicle spiraled deeper and deeper, the turns so tight that Chris hardly had to move the wheel to keep them on track. The auras beneath them grew in strength and size as they drove. Soon, Darius could identify them individually and get a sense of their location. The majority, he wasn't surprised to find, were downstairs.

"Welcome home," he said, looking at Mackenzie. She watched the glass doors with an empty stare. Her teeth clenched together, and she glanced at him. Without a word, she stepped into the garage. The rest followed suit. Cain moved to the back of the sedan to grab her things.

"I can take this to your room," he began, but Mackenzie stormed over and ripped the bag from his hands. She swayed under the weight.

"I've got it," she snapped, the first words she'd uttered in over an hour. Chris and Darius exchanged a quick look as Mackenzie turned on her heels and stomped away. The glass double doors swung shut behind her.

"Well," Cain said at last, "all things considered, I think

that went rather well."

He tried to smile, but Chris chewed her lip while Darius pinched the bridge of his nose. "I guess it's the best we could've hoped for," he said.

The three of them started clearing the vehicle—opening every secret hatch and hidden compartment until they'd emptied all the weaponry and armor they'd brought along. It was a lot, probably too much for this sort of day mission, but with everything that had happened, no one in the Underground took chances anymore. The main doors opened to a waiting room beside the hospital ward, a bright white space with equally white chairs and blinding white lights overhead.

From here, two hallways branched out. The one to the right headed to the elevator, and the one directly ahead led to their workspaces. Chris started in that direction, but as she paused to unlock the tactical room, Darius's attention drifted beyond her. His brows pulled together in a soft, concerned frown.

"Go ahead," Cain said. "We can handle this."

He adjusted a rifle case and opened a spare hand to take the ballistics vests Darius carried. Darius glanced between him and Chris, nodded once, and handed the gear over. As he walked further down the corridor, he heard Chris murmur a question to Cain that he couldn't quite make out before they disappeared into the tactical room, and their voices vanished behind a reinforced door.

Past that, past the R&D headquarters and the conference room, Darius followed the turn in the corridor to the alcove of leadership offices. Five doors dotted this shorter hall. Four of them, which lined the walls two to a side, had name plaques belonging to the lower directors: Jones, Wolfe, Silver, and McKay. These rooms were empty, devoid of the warm signature of human souls.

But the one at the end was not.

This door was bare, and Darius paused when he reached it. A faint, fragmented aura waited, still and quiet, on the other side. He drew a deep breath, wrapped his hand around the knob, and twisted it open.

The lounge was dark—it always was now that so few people had any reason to come back here. A soft rectangle of light stretched across the room as Darius stepped inside. Mackenzie didn't lift her head to acknowledge him. Her duffle bag lay forgotten on the creamy carpet like she'd discarded it the second she'd arrived. Instead of taking the couch across from where Darius stood, she'd sat right on the ground in front of the door to his left. Her lower back pressed against the wood while her shoulders slumped forward. She'd propped her elbows onto her knees and crossed her forearms between them to hide her face in the gap they made. Darius's chest ached at the sight of her—and ached more as he glanced at the name etched into the metal plate high over Mackenzie's head.

"She's not here," Darius said. He'd spoken quietly, barely a murmur, but in the silence, his words boomed like a bass drum.

"I figured." Mackenzie's voice was muffled from speaking directly at the ground between her legs, but all the same, it felt heavy. "I just had to make sure."

Darius hovered in the doorway before joining Mackenzie on the floor. He lowered himself at her side, sighing as he gazed across the room. The other door stared back at him, Alan Blaine's surname upon it, a brazen reminder of the gaping wound his loss had left behind.

They sat there for a while, quiet, lit only by the streak of golden light pouring in from the hallway. Mackenzie didn't move except for the shallow rise and fall of her shoulders. Darius was tempted to wrap an arm around them, but something about the way she held herself told him it wasn't the time. At last, she shuddered in a breath.

"I'm trying to be understanding," she started slowly, still not lifting her head, still refusing to look at him. "I really, really am. But I am *so* fucking mad at you."

Her grip tightened on her arms, and her fingertips

crushed deep dimples into her skin. A twinge pinched at Darius's heart. "I know."

"No," Mackenzie said, sharper now. "No, you *don't*, because *you* were here, Darius! You were *all* here! You got to help each other through it!"

Her face snapped up, bright blue eyes glistening with furious tears as she glared at him.

"Mackenzie," he began, "it wasn't like you were on vacation. It was *rehab*…"

Her nostrils flared. "And *this* wasn't just a god damned cold!" Mackenzie leapt to her feet, dragging one hand through her yellow hair while the other swung toward the opposite office. "Alan is *dead!* The goddamned *leader* of the Martyrs! This is *huge!* Fucking *insane!* There is only *one* other person in this whole fucking building who would be this hard to lose, and—"

Mackenzie's voice broke, cutting her off with a swell of emotion in her throat. Her neck tightened, and her attention flashed away from Darius to the door he still sat against. He slowly stood, as though the weight of his decision was fighting hard to keep him down and out in the face of Mackenzie's grief.

"And now she's probably spiraling," Mackenzie got out at last, but she wasn't shouting anymore. Instead, the words clawed from her mouth, scratching and high-pitched. Her eyes fixed on Thorn's name for a moment longer before they slashed at Darius again, piercing him, wounding him with just a look.

"That woman dragged me out of *hell*," Mackenzie said. "She didn't give up on me when everyone else would have, and where the fuck was I when *she* needed *my* help? Dicking around in the woods? Singing bullshit, stupid songs and bonding over board games while this place was on fucking fire?"

"Mackenzie," Darius tried to say, but Mackenzie spoke past him.

"I wasn't there for her!" She was shouting again, but

now, it sounded more like sobs. A trembling hand pressed against her heart, like she was mustering the power to keep its broken pieces together. "You robbed me of my chance to be there for her. For you. For everyone I care about!"

And as abruptly as she began, she quieted. Mackenzie stood opposite of Darius, tiny body shaking with all the volatile emotion locked within it. Darius wished he could reach inside, use his Virtuous healing abilities to mend emotional wounds, but it didn't work that way.

"You're right," he said. "We did do that—*I* did that. Chris wanted to call you, but I worried this might push you into another relapse, and we had too many other problems to deal with without dealing with that, too."

Mackenzie's jaw clenched. "You didn't even give me a chance," she hissed.

A lump formed in Darius's chest, remnants of the stale pain from a similar argument, years ago, where *he* was standing on the other side. Alan's voice echoed in his mind with a lesson he hadn't been ready to hear back then:

Sometimes, being a leader meant making difficult decisions… not because they were popular or fair or even honest, but because they would prevent the most bloodshed.

"I didn't think I could risk it," Darius admitted, "and if I had to go back, I'd do the same thing." A fresh wave of tears glistened behind Mackenzie's lashes, and he sighed. "I'm sorry. I never wanted to hurt you, but from where I'm standing, it was the safest call—for *you* and for the rest of the Underground."

Mackenzie said nothing. Her eyes sharpened on Darius, never moving, hardly blinking, as her chest rocked in heavy breath. Soon, though, her body began to relax, and the anger on her face faded into a deeper, purer grief.

Then, she nodded.

"In my program, we talked a lot about taking accountability," she said through a sniff. An errant tear escaped her lash line, drawing a dark, mascara-streaked line down her cheek. Mackenzie wiped it away. "We had to write out the shitty things that happened because we were using and recognize that those consequences are on *us*. I guess this is one of mine." More tears now. Mackenzie pressed the heels of her palms against her eyes and drew a breath before letting it out in a thin stream from tight lips. "Maybe I'm the one who should be saying I'm sorry."

Darius approached her and placed a hand on either shoulder. She spread her fingers open just enough to peek through as he leaned down to look her in the face.

"I know this isn't easy," he said, "and it's not what you want to hear, but staying at your program was exactly what we needed you to do. Now that you're at one hundred percent, I'll be leaning on you to help me keep this thing together. Can you do that?"

Mackenzie scoffed, her brows rising, as she moved her hands away to wave Darius off. "C'mon, give me a challenge." She forced a smile, and even though it hardly matched the fervor he was used to, it was a start. Darius's chest warmed.

"It's good to have you back, Mackenzie," he said.

"Happy to be back," she said. "Ugly crying and all." She opened a palm and widely gestured to her entire face. Darius laughed, and Mackenzie's smile stretched further. Her eyes flicked back to Thorn's door, and she breathed a sigh. "I should get to bed. Something tells me tomorrow is going to be a fucking mess."

She grabbed her duffle bag and hoisted it onto her shoulder, ignoring Darius's offer to carry it. They made their way back into the hallway. Darius paused in the doorframe one last time, looking back at Thorn's name. A band tightened around his heart—a chain forged of grief and loneliness and concern that hadn't released its hold on him since the day Alan Blaine had died. Memories of that afternoon crashed against him.

Sparkie, Thorn's Familiar, the ejected part of her soul, unconscious in his arms.

Alan, broken and bleeding at the losing end of a fight

with his only niece.

Thorn, consumed by so much fear and fury that she'd completely lost control. The bloody pipe in her hands turned toward her throat. The warehouse full of bodies under her feet. The pain in her eyes when she saw it all, as though seeing it for the first time, as though she had no idea how any of it had happened, and she'd rather *not* know because the truth might eat her alive.

Part of Thorn was still locked in that warehouse, still being tortured by the Sins. The woman who'd come home didn't feel the same. Now, she was trapped behind walls of her own making, rejecting any hand that reached in to help her climb above them.

"Darius?"

Mackenzie's voice pulled him back. She waited in the hallway, a sympathetic pull in her brow. He shut the door, and they walked toward the elevator. As the lift pitched them deeper into the earth, he grabbed his phone from his pocket and navigated to Thorn's contact.

Even though she never responded, Darius wasn't about to stop trying.

CHAPTER TWO

Someone was screaming.

It might have been Thorn.

She didn't know. She didn't know *anything*. The room swam with sensation. Cold energy buzzed, and people cried out. Their voices echoed like they were all trapped in a tomb together. No, not together. Like they were trapped in a tomb with *her*.

She couldn't breathe. Couldn't *think*. Couldn't make sense of what she was seeing, hearing, feeling. Figures warped, colors muted, and words garbled into horrific white noise. It came at her all at once, closing in, cutting off any chance for her to escape, and *fuck*—

Thorn was going to die here.

Fury and fear battled in the pit between her lungs—in that empty spot where her soul used to live—until fear won. She was surrounded, and every motion, every sound, every *glance* struck her like a bullet to the chest. Arms flung out. Faces contorted. Something came screaming toward her, aimed right between her eyes. Thorn caught it.

A pipe.

It was her sanctuary. Her liberation. Her deliverance from the grips of hell. The cool metal at her fingertips, the dull weight in her palms, the whoosh it made as it flew through the air, followed by the crunch of skulls splitting beneath it. Heads popped like fresh eggs, shattering into pieces, letting the life burst out in a viscous spray that coated her arms, her chest, her throat in raw, red splatter.

Thorn screamed, and she sobbed, and she *swung*.

It came at her in flashes. Bits and pieces of carnage rained down only to be shut away again, her psyche's desperate attempt to shield her from damnation. Autumn Hunt's laughter roared in her ears as Thorn caught glimpses of dead faces. Nameless men in black armor, civilians, Caleb Claytor. He was tethered to a chair, slumped back, his fingers shattered, mouth agape, and blonde hair caked in red. Bodies sprawled around him, laid out like some ritualistic sacrifice to a vengeful god who exchanged blessings for blood.

She sifted through time like broken glass. It was slivered and sharp, with missing pieces and dangerous edges. Everything tumbled out of order. Puppets clawed closer as Sins disappeared and mercenaries ran—not at her, but *from* her. Thorn felt wrung out, reduced to nothing more than panic, terror, and a violent need to protect herself at any cost. She needed to stop.

God, she *wanted* to stop.

But she couldn't. It was like being possessed by Wrath all over again. She watched in horror as a woman's neck snapped in her palms, as a merc dropped his weapon and ran howling, as Mayor Bently shrieked and begged for mercy. Pleaded. Cried. Until he couldn't speak at all anymore. His lower jaw came clean off in a single stroke, leaving a red-painted splash across the dusty ground. He stared at her, eyes wide, tongue lolling down the front of his throat. The pink flesh lapped against his Adam's apple.

Then, he was gone. They were *all* gone. The world went black before a distant voice called out to her. Thorn opened her eyes to a new room, full of new horrors, and stared into a brand new face.

Her heart stopped beating as the pipe clattered to the ground.

"It's okay!" Alan choked out the words, his voice raw and ragged. Blood coated his face, his clothes, *everything*. It congealed in his goatee, matted his shoulder-length black hair, poured from cuts healing on his cheeks. He caught her in his sight, and those eyes, black like hers—god, *exactly* like hers—filled with relief. He smiled. *Alan smiled.* "Everything is okay, Thorn. You're—"

Glass shattered. A red sunburst exploded from the back of Alan's head, canonizing him in a halo of death.

Thorn screamed again, and she kept screaming until the sound rang in her ears, in her chest, and in the fresh darkness around her. She gulped in gasps of air, her heart pounding so hard against her ribcage that she was sure it would break her bones and pierce itself upon them. Her cheeks were wet—no, her whole body was—soaked and sticky and slick with blood. Thorn's stomach buckled, threatening to heave.

A hard knocking startled her. She froze, muscles tense, pulse racing, breath caught in her throat.

"It's three in the morning!" a man yelled. *"Shut the fuck up!"*

The sensations of New York City filtered past the adrenaline coursing through Thorn's veins. Traffic honked, sirens wailed, and tenant auras dotted the space above and below her seventh-story apartment in floating orbs of icy, human essence. She flung a hand out until it collided with a lamp, scrambled for the switch, and turned it on. Bright, painful light flashed against her eyes.

An empty room came to life.

Thorn was already sitting up, staring at a blank, white wall. Damp sheets tangled around her, so she tore them off to reveal pale, shaking legs. Her loose nightshirt was so thoroughly drenched in cold sweat that it clung to her body like a second skin. A light weight thudded against her chest, smooth scales pressing to the bare flesh on her collar, and a pair of red, leathery wings enveloped her. Sparkie let out a keening cry as he nuzzled his head below her jawline. The neighbor pounded on Thorn's wall again, and again, she ignored him. She drew her knees up, propped her elbows upon them, and dipped her face into her hands. Her palms slid against a stream of tears on her cheekbones.

"Fuck," Thorn whispered.

The nightmares were getting worse. They taunted her almost every time she closed her eyes, and every time, they were more vivid. More cohesive. More *real.*

It was getting harder and harder to pretend that they weren't.

Thorn swung her legs off the edge of her mattress and planted her bare feet on the cold floor. Goosebumps sprouted along her arms, following a straight path down her spine until they covered every inch of her skin. The apartment had only the barest necessities: a lonely bed, a single dresser, a barren kitchenette. Thorn walked across the studio in four strides, reached the bathroom door, and pulled it open.

A shadowy silhouette loomed across from her, hovering in the mirror above the sink like a twisted caricature from a horror movie—a ghost that vanished whenever she turned on the light.

But Thorn didn't turn on the light. She'd already learned that this ghost wouldn't vanish, and she couldn't bear to look into its haunted face again.

Instead, Thorn showered in the dark. Sparkie leapt to the top of the frame while she stripped her sweat-soaked clothing away. The fabric dragged along the tangled mess of acid scars dripping down the inside of her forearm, and when the sleeve snagged on the *Peccostium* below her wrist, a dizzying chill sank into her nervous system—a chill that renewed her nausea if only because it reminded her of how closely she was linked to Wrath.

And how alone she was now that Alan was gone.

Thorn's breathing picked up, and her heart followed suit.

She stepped into the shower and turned it on, hotter and hotter and hotter, until even her Forgotten Sin healing powers weren't enough to stop the stream from stinging from the crown of her head to the soles of her feet. Steam wrapped around her, filling her mouth, her throat, her lungs. She sighed, tilted her head back, and closed her eyes.

This time, it wasn't bloody images from her nightmares that assaulted Thorn's mind—not Alan or Caleb or a room full of people Thorn couldn't remember if she'd killed or not. It was something far, far worse.

Darius.

His face was all she could see, warm and worried, with bright eyes the color of fresh-cut grass against earthen skin. Thorn's heart hurt, deep in the hole Wrath had carved out of her soul all those decades ago, and a new sting of tears pushed against her lashes. Sparkie let out a soft cry.

"Come back, Thorn," Darius's voice echoed in her head, so crisp and clear that he might as well have been standing in the shower beside her, close enough to touch, to hold. *"Come back. I'm here. You're safe."*

Thorn wound her arms around herself.

He was wrong. She *wasn't* safe.

And neither was he.

Drizzling rain misted New York in a haze. Open umbrellas created an undulating landscape of black nylon hills as the denizens of this godforsaken city rushed off to bullshit jobs for bullshit pay in a bullshit capitalist hellscape that had somehow convinced them that purpose came from profit.

Thorn Rose stood against a brick wall in Central Harlem, watching the early morning commuters go by like an uninvited lurker on the outskirts of a funeral procession. The building pressed to her back provided just enough cover to keep her out of the rain but not out of the cold. There was no escaping that, not in a place like *this*. The bulging population let out such an oppressive fog of human corruption that Thorn could hardly find herself within it. Frigid energy leaked out of every soul and seeped through Thorn's sweatshirt, her leggings, and her long, fingerless gloves. In nearly a century of living this way, she'd gotten used to it… or so she'd thought. In the last few months, the incessant cold had started to gnaw at her, digging its teeth so deep into her flesh that it tore to the bone.

She took a drink of the steaming coffee in her hands. It seared her tongue, burned her throat, and opened a painful bloom of heat all the way down her chest where she could pretend, if only for a second, that she wasn't so *achingly* empty.

But a second was all she got. Thorn's esophagus tingled as it healed, following the same path through her body that the scalding liquid had until all that remained was that constant sense of loss nestled between her lungs… a sense that had only grown heavier in the months since Alan had—

Thorn's jaw clenched, and her fist tightened around her cup as though she were holding that metal pipe again. The paper walls caved beneath her fingers, and the plastic lid popped off. Its contents gushed onto her hand and soaked into her glove in a scalding wave.

All she wanted to do was throw the damn thing—pitch it to the sidewalk with a scream that had been stuck in her skull since she woke up in that warehouse all those months ago. Instead, she pressed her eyes closed and forced herself to breathe, just *breathe*. Her fingers worked a familiar pattern, thumb tapping from her pointer to pinky and back again, as she tried to ground herself in an exercise Darius had taught her.

It backfired. Thoughts of *him* flooded her mind, and somehow, that was worse. Her rage gave way to regret.

Thorn furiously tossed her wasted coffee into a bin and grabbed a pack of cigarettes from her satchel, trading caffeine that didn't work for nicotine she couldn't feel. She lit one and drew a mouthful of toxic air deep into her lungs, but just like the coffee, the pain was a temporary relief.

A stream of smoke furled into the rain in front of Thorn's face as she sighed. Then, she pulled her hood over her head and made her way into the thick of the city.

The Martyrs had been around since the 1950s. While Thorn had been a child, having her soul cleaved out in pieces by Wrath so it could move in and make her life hell, Alan, Cain, and the other founding *Oblitus Peccatum* had built the Underground. By the time construction had completed, they'd amassed hundreds of recruits, and their war on the Sins was in full swing.

Nearly one hundred and forty years had passed since then, and Thorn herself had been a part of the organization for over ninety. When she'd accepted the role of Alan's second-in-command, she'd known, logically, that she was agreeing to take over his position, but she'd never thought it would actually happen. *No one* had. Like all other Forgotten Sins, Alan had been immortal outside of serious wounds that could kill him before his rapid healing prevented it. Since Alan rarely found reason to leave the Underground, Thorn had assumed he would be around forever.

Now, he was gone, and the organization was scraping to piece together everything he'd done to keep it up and running for damn near a century and a half.

Thorn's phone lit up with more alerts than ever before. Reports on every department, from TAC to maintenance, the hospital to R&D, funneled right to her inbox. As she made her way south on 5th Avenue, ignoring the pedestrians pressed in around her and the precipitation pattering onto the crown of her head, Thorn glanced at her device.

God, the sheer volume of *shit* she had to sort through now was overwhelming.

She scrolled the notifications numbly, like she did every morning, and marveled at how much her uncle had done that she never once stopped to think about. There were inventory lists, budget approvals, financial statements, patrol schedules, R&D summaries, personnel complaints, maintenance claims, security reports… She hardly had the time to read it all, let alone the mental bandwidth.

And that was only the *official* Martyr business.

Thorn's inbox clogged with a whole slew of *other* communications, too. Since Mackenzie's return to the Underground the previous night, the Irishwoman had sent Thorn no fewer than forty-seven texts, ranging in tone from concerned to offended. Chris reached out with the guise of providing an update on the status of their Tactical units in the city, but Thorn could read the worry between the lines—asking when she'd be back, if they could grab dinner to talk over all of it, which Thorn was *sure* was just an attempt to make sure she was fucking eating.

And then there was Darius. Thorn's stomach caved out.

"Just checking in."

Three words. Darius Jones just had to say three *stupid* words to unravel a full spool of dread in her belly. They came beneath dozens of other texts, nearly all left unanswered over the last several weeks. The weight of them, of *everything,* draped upon her, like she was sinking to the bottom of the East River all over again. All she knew was pressure and pain—cold water filling her nose, her mouth, her lungs. Sparkie whimpered in the satchel cinched to her thigh as Thorn's eyes moved to the photograph of Darius's face above their chat. His eyes stared deep into hers, as real and alive as if the man himself were standing before her.

God, she wanted to talk to him, but what the fuck should she say? What *could* she say?

"I feel like I'm drowning."

Her thumb hovered over the send button. Thorn chewed the inside of her cheek.

Then, she deleted the whole damned message.

Before she had the chance to slip her phone back into her pocket, a hard shoulder slammed into her, and Thorn stumbled to the side.

"Watch it, bitch!"

A sudden swell of rage filled her lungs, hot and toxic. She spun around just in time to see the asshole's back retreat—a broad-shouldered man, his blazer speckled with rain, his thinning hair slick with it. He threw a contemptuous look over his shoulder. Thorn's vision blurred until he was the only thing in focus, and the grays of New York began to darken. Sparkie writhed against her leg, a hiss rumbling in his throat.

It would take nothing—*nothing*—to ruin this man. Ten seconds. Five steps. One blow. That was it, and he'd be done. Thorn's fist wrapped around her phone until the metal casing groaned—

The device buzzed, and Thorn blinked. Harried pedestrians split around her, like something about the very person she was had been enough to tell them to stay the fuck away from her—that she was dangerous.

She *was* dangerous.

The fury stalled out, mingling with fear until the familiar, noxious feeling stole Thorn's breath. She took a step back, then another, and soon she was up against a wall. The brick pressed along her spine. Thorn drew a deep breath.

Then she realized her phone was still vibrating, and she looked down at the screen. Part of her worried it was Mackenzie, or Cain, or even Darius, but the name blinking up at her was much, much worse. Alexis Claytor.

Thorn's eyes pinched closed.

God, Alexis. No one in the Underground had walked away from the failed mission last May without a new scar to show for it, but Alexis's ran deeper than most—and Thorn had no illusions that *she* was responsible for all of them.

She tapped the answer icon. "Claytor."

"There's been an incident reported in Lenox Hill," Alexis said. Her tone was short, as though it were tethered to a tight leash to keep it from snapping at Thorn's throat. The typical clamor of the dispatch center didn't berate Thorn's ears like it usually did. Alexis must have stepped outside.

"An incident?" Thorn frowned. "What kind of incident?"

"Dunno," Alexis said. She didn't bother with pleasantries or small talk. She never had, but Thorn had noticed an even less friendly attitude lately. "Wasn't my call."

Thorn sighed, and her fingers gripped harder around her device. "What the fuck, Claytor. I need *useful* information."

"You told me to let you know if anything high profile happened within four blocks of where Hunt was last spotted," Alexis hissed. "At least six squad cars have been sent over, and the operator is still on the line with our caller. It sounds like an all-hands-on-deck kind of 'incident.' Is that *high profile* enough for you?"

Thorn's jaw clenched. Five months ago, it would have gashed open, spewing furious orders that Alexis watch her tone and never speak to her like that again, but things were different now.

Now, the Sins were gaining power, Alexis's job had been reduced to nothing more than a call center spy, and she was completely alone. Ever since her brother had been tortured and killed back in that warehouse, Alexis had never been the same. Thorn couldn't blame her. She knew how hard it was to lose the ones you loved in this war—what kind of person it could turn you into. When Thorn's son had been killed, she'd become so obsessed with revenge that she'd left a trail of bodies in her wake on the journey to find it.

If Alexis's grief manifested as a shitty attitude, Thorn could deal with that. It was better than blood.

"Send me the location," Thorn answered at last. Her attention moved toward the southeast, in the general direction of Lenox Hill. "And text me any updates."

"Understood." Alexis hung up without a goodbye. Seconds later, an address pushed through to Thorn's device. She read it, and a swirl of anxiety writhed like a wounded animal in her gut. 69th Street.

Seven days ago, Autumn Hunt's face had triggered the Martyrs' facial recognition software just south of there.

What Wrath was doing was anyone's guess, but considering how close she'd been to the 19th Precinct, Thorn assumed she was planting even more Programs deep into the heart of the NYPD. Just two blocks separated the locations... Maybe it was a coincidence.

Thorn doubted it.

Drawing a shallow breath, she slipped her phone into her pocket and made her way south, pulse pounding like a ticking bomb.

69th swarmed with police.

Squad cars blocked the street, parked along the intersections at Lexington and 3rd to prevent vehicles from driving in, but pedestrians weaseled along the sidewalk across from a towering high-rise. Sparkie circled in the sky, giving Thorn an aerial view as she pulled her hood lower over her face and pushed her way through the pack. Adrenaline pumped through her veins.

She had never loved crowds. They were clumsy, callous, and *cold*, but now they felt unbearable. Too many people pressed too close together. It was the perfect environment for the Sins to cause mayhem, and she couldn't help but imagine what would happen if Autumn Hunt showed up here. Two decades of possession made imagining all too easy, and memories of similar situations assaulted Thorn's mind. Parties, parades, peaceful protests, becoming so volatile that blood flowed in the streets. For a moment, Thorn couldn't breathe.

But she had to. She forced her lungs open, straightened her spine, and scanned the scene. A convoy of first responder vehicles lined up in a wall of gleaming steel and flashing lights as officers patrolled outside the building. Thorn kept back in the throng of civilians to avoid being spotted. The NYPD was more dangerous than ever now. With the Martyrs grounded for the last several months,

Wrath had wormed her way into the precincts, and Thorn had no doubt every damned cop in the city was Programmed to recognize her. Today, though, they weren't looking at the crowd. All around her, the gawkers of the city whispered, talked, and shouted.

"Do you see him?"

"There! Fuck, that's at least the twentieth floor."

"Jesus, is he gonna jump?"

Thorn's focus flicked toward the sky, and her heart plummeted.

The concrete face of the apartment complex blended in with the background, gray storm clouds casting the whole thing in a monochrome light that made the man's dark suit stick out like a black ant climbing a mound of salt. He stood more than two hundred feet from the ground, balancing on the edge of a balcony railing. He shifted, and a synchronized gasp rattled through the hundreds of bodies on the sidewalk below. Thorn's jaw dropped.

From the street, everything personal about him disappeared. She couldn't see his face, his build, even the color of his hair.

But she knew him—she knew the *feeling* of him. The loathing. The terror. The desperate need to make it all stop, just for a second, a second that lasted a lifetime. She knew what it was like to stand on that ledge.

Thorn pushed right up to a temporary barricade along 69th. Her hands wrapped around the bars, and she tilted her head back. Rainwater pattered against her cheeks as she stared up the side of the building.

"What's going on?" she asked aloud.

"That guy's been up there for half an hour," a woman to her right responded, eyes wide in horror. "The police are trying to talk him down…"

They were doing more than that. Thorn couldn't see the officers in the apartment at the man's back, but she could sense their auras hovering just behind his. There had to be at least six people in that room, but it was hard to differentiate them all, especially from this distance. Another team was preparing to rappel from the terrace above and force him back to safety in a less peaceful way when talking inevitably failed.

But they weren't fast enough. Thorn could tell they were losing him. Instead of calming down, he grew more agitated. His arms flailed out, and he wavered perilously. Another synchronized breath echoed around Thorn as the crowd reacted in a unified stroke. Sparkie dove in, risking getting closer to see the man more clearly. Tears poured down his cheeks, soaking his face as the storm drenched his hair and sports coat. He cried out a desperate, agonizing sob. "You don't understand! I've lost *everything!*"

Thorn's stomach swirled with an old, familiar pain, just as potent today as it had been one hundred years ago. An officer climbed onto the railing above as the man turned back to the street. He lifted a leg. Leaned forward—

Fuck, Thorn didn't know what else to do, so she reached for him.

A thread shot from Thorn's mind into the space between worlds, through the sky and the rain, and latched onto the cold energy above her head. Her Influence pierced into the man's consciousness and held like a harpoon, embedded so deep into his gray matter that she felt a sudden shock of horror and helplessness pass between them. It stung in her eyes and tightened her throat, but she pushed forward. A trickle of energy grappled in the link, her will and his fighting for the upper hand.

Thorn told him to stop.

Begged him to stop.

Asked him to think about the ones he loved. His friends. His family. His fucking cat, if he had one. It didn't matter. There had to be something—there was always *something*— worth living for. Even if he couldn't see it... even if *she* couldn't.

He hesitated. The officer got into position, ready to swing down and knock him back onto the terrace. Thorn just needed one more second…

She lost.

The man pushed around her Influence and leapt into the sky. The cop dove to catch him, but he was too late. His fingers grasped uselessly at a fluttering sports coat.

Thorn tried to gasp, but a bubble of air as hard as a stone lodged in her throat and choked her instead. She watched in slow motion, as though the world itself was trying to stop this tragedy from happening. He tumbled, turned, tore toward the earth. While the crowd around Thorn screamed, she herself stayed silent, the rushing in and around her ears stealing the breath from her lungs.

She knew this feeling, too.

The fall that lasted forever.

Suddenly, she felt far away, like the ground beneath her feet was made of water, and she was slowly sinking into it. Part of her wondered if he regretted it. If he wished he hadn't jumped or that he could sprout wings and spread them wide enough to catch the wind beneath him. She had.

But bodies don't grow wings. Only souls could do that.

It took him five seconds to hit the ground. He smashed into the asphalt driveway with a sickening crack that Thorn could feel in her bones more than she could actually hear, and his cold energy vanished. She couldn't see the spectacle from the far side of police barricades, but Sparkie had a view from the sky that made her stumble.

A sunburst of red from the back of his head.

The city roared to life. The sounds of screaming, sirens, and shouting over loudspeakers woke Thorn up. All around her, people cried and held onto one another as the officers demanded they leave the scene. No one did. Thorn stood still, the soles of her shoes cemented into the sidewalk as she tried to catch her breath, and Sparkie circled high above.

Then, just blocks away, something tugged at her core.

Wrath's Influence came to life like a sudden winter wind.

Panic snapped in Thorn's lungs, forcing them open and shut in rapid succession. Her face turned to the north, where her link to the Sin's essence let her know that Autumn Hunt was on her way *here*, right now, drawn to Thorn using her power. Thorn scrambled backward, colliding with other New Yorkers who had packed in tightly to watch a man plummet to his death like it was just another seasonal sport. People shoved her, swore at her, and Thorn's body contracted. Her eyes tracked each and every face as though she expected them to transform—to be a monster in human skin, a Sin beneath the surface, ready to rip her to pieces and feed her to the rats shuffling in the sewers underfoot.

But there were no monsters today—not beyond the ones living in Thorn's skull. She forced herself away from the crowd and found the nearest subway entrance. Sparkie dove from the sky and disappeared down the back of her motorcycle jacket just as Thorn hit the first step and descended into the earth. He pressed close to her spine, shaking so hard that it rattled Thorn to the core.

Wrath's Influence careened closer.

Thorn didn't care what train she took as long as it got her far away from here. She tapped her metro card against the reader, pushed through the turnstile, and hurried down the platform. When she reached the far end, she forced herself as close to the tracks as she could get. A bustling crowd of morning commuters pressed around her, their cold energy suffocating, and she peered over the edge as roaring sound barreled down the tunnel. Wrath's Influence flashed again, nearer this time—near enough that it made Thorn nauseous. Her head swam in the sensation.

The subway's front light came to life moments before the train squealed to a stop. Thorn pushed through the door as other passengers made their way out, ignoring the dirty looks and hard shoulders. When she was safely in the car, she hurried to the far back, next to the emergency exit, and braced herself against the wall. One hand wrapped firmly around the stanchion, which quieted the shaking in her fingers. Sparkie shuddered between her shoulder blades, and Thorn's heart hammered against her sternum.

Then the doors slid shut, and the subway jolted. Cold energy dashed around her, the auras of people on the street flowing in an ice-cold river over her head as Thorn darted away from Lenox Hill and the hell descending upon it. The pull of Wrath's power fell away. Instantly, like a valve had been released, Thorn's body relaxed. She closed her eyes.

Shame quickly overshadowed the relief, and she wanted to scream.

What the hell was wrong with her? She knew better than to go looking for a fight but running like a kicked dog with her tail between her legs was a new low, and she didn't know how to reconcile it. Her teeth clenched so hard that her jaw ached.

Quiet voices made their way to her through the chaos in her brain.

"…Oh man, I figured out why there were so many pigs out today. Check this out. The CFO of InvestX just jumped off his fucking balcony…"

Thorn's eyes snapped back open. Two teen boys sat on the bench across from her, leaning forward in their seats to watch a phone screen. A video flashed up at their faces—shaky footage of a building Thorn recognized because she'd been standing in front of it ten minutes ago. A numb chill settled over her shoulders.

Jesus fucking christ, news traveled fast.

"Holy shit," the other boy said as a dark figure dropped toward the ground. His eyes went wide. "Good riddance. Drain the swamp, one millionaire at a time. Think it was actually a suicide, or do you think he was pushed?"

The first boy shrugged. "Who knows? I'm sure they'll come up with some convincing story, just like they do with all the other weird shit happening in this city."

His friend scoffed. "Right," he said. "There's definitely something going on, but they'll do whatever they can to keep the sheeple nice and distracted."

They broke into snickering laughter and rewound the footage to watch it again. An indignant spark flashed to life in Thorn's chest. She turned away, staring out the window on her other side.

"You should send it to RebelTruth," the second boy said. "He'll debunk it."

"Aw, fuck yeah, that's a great idea. Did you catch his latest episode on LymeLite? The interview with that reverend down south?"

"Nah, not yet. What's it about?"

"The guy says he can explain it all—the deaths, the cover-ups, everything. Apparently, there's some crazy, supernatural war going on. He's seen it."

Thorn's heart skipped, and her focus shifted back to the boys as the second one arched forward. "A war against *who?*"

The first kid's eyes lit up.

"The Seven Deadly Sins."

CHAPTER THREE

The man in the video wasn't real, but god damn, he was a good imitation. AI overlays were nearly impossible to detect, and if Holly hadn't run the footage through some expensive program to prove his image had been computer-generated, Darius never would've spotted it. He was picture-perfect—unnervingly so. Flawless skin. Smooth hair. A smile that looked like it had been carved onto him by Michelangelo himself. The only real clue was in his eyes, which gleamed a bright shade of yellow that wasn't natural but could have been achieved with contact lenses. He had no name, of course. Like most social media "influencers," his entire persona was designed to appeal to the people who hung on his every word like he was preaching gospel. His platform was called "RebelTruth," so his followers simply called him "Rebel."

"So, what are you trying to say, Reverend Cunningham?" Rebel asked with an indulgent frown. The screen split down the middle, and he took up the right half. "That the Seven Deadly Sins are *real?*"

A ripple of apprehension shuddered through the conference room. Mackenzie swore under her breath as she pulled her legs up beneath her, blue eyes locked onto the drop-down display at the far wall. Nicholas Wolfe ran a hand down the beard roughing up his cheeks and chin. Chris hardly moved, but a muscle in her jaw twitched as a man they all recognized nodded to the left of Rebel's camera feed.

"Yes," Weston Cunningham said in a pointed, southern drawl, "and others like them. New York City has been inundated with demonic forces, Mr. Rebel, and you can bet your boots those forces have made their way elsewhere, too."

Cunningham looked different than Darius remembered. When he'd first come to the Underground over a year ago, he'd been thready and thankless after weeks traveling with Leroy Khoury searching for the Martyrs. He'd leapt out of the car, spitting hellfire from his mouth, and tore the Virtue Temperance apart for "unholy" behavior, unsuited for someone who had once led a God-fearing parish alongside him.

Now, he was thicker, his stringy body fleshed out with healthy weight, and he wore what looked like pale orange pajamas that made his blonde hair especially yellow under bright, clinical lights. A white robe draped around his shoulders. For a moment, Darius thought he abstractly resembled a dollar-store prophet.

"And these forces are demons?" Rebel pressed. "Or Sins?"

"I don't see there's a difference between the two, Mr. Rebel," Cunningham said. "Demons, Sins, devils… whatever you want to call them, these malignant spirits have descended upon the world, and they are bringing us all closer to damnation."

"Mmm." Rebel nodded. "And you say you've *seen* these demons yourself?"

"Yes, sir, I have," Cunningham replied. At that point, he shifted awkwardly in his chair, glancing over his shoulder at a beefy man wearing white scrubs in the background. The man didn't move, so Cunningham continued. "I've seen what these demons can do up close, and it is worse than you can even imagine."

"Would you mind telling me and the rest of the Truth Seekers out there what happened?"

The reverend grinned like he'd been handed a new congregation. "I'd be honored."

For the next few minutes, Darius was thrown into a past so horrific he'd never be able to scrub it from his mind. Weston Cunningham talked about his time at Reflection Farms, a small Christian community just outside of Sandersville, Georgia, and the brutal massacre that burned it all to ashes. Darius's body buzzed at the memories. Humid air. Hot auras. The horrifying, gut-churning sensation of those auras vanishing as Gluttony and Lust picked them off, one by one. Of the forty-three residents, only five had made it out alive.

Weston Cunningham was one of them.

"So, after you managed to escape, you ended up traveling with one of these 'Sins?'" Rebel asked.

"Yes, I did," Cunningham said. "A man named Leroy Khoury, though he wasn't really a man. He tried to say he'd been freed from possession, but he was sick with wickedness. He had all the same demonic powers as the others. Immortality. Quick healing. Mind control. I only stuck around to try to protect the girls he'd taken with him, but they were seduced by his evil and couldn't see him for what he truly was—a monster."

Darius's heart hurt, and he glanced up at Thorn. That made the hurt worse. Unlike the rest of the room, she hadn't taken a seat at the table, instead standing off to the side of the door. Her arms wound around her chest, and her nails dug deep into her arms. Sparkie had disappeared down the back of her shirt, but Darius could see the lump shivering from beneath Thorn's veil of pin-straight, black hair.

"And this man, this Leroy Khoury," Rebel went on. "You said he brought you somewhere north. New York City?"

"No, I don't reckon it was in the city proper, but that was where he said we aimed to go," Cunningham said. "The girls and myself rendezvoused with some of Khoury's associates, and Khoury went off on his own to distract the demons chasing us, but I now know he was leading us like holy lambs to the slaughter. We were taken to this place they called 'The Underground.' I couldn't tell you if it was actually underground or not. They brought us in blindfolded, like criminals."

Chris tensed, and Holly Andrews swore under her breath.

"Who are 'they?'"

"They call themselves 'The Martyrs,'" Cunningham answered. "They see themselves as some kind of salvation, but I was physically assaulted, spiritually *tortured*, as soon as I entered the damn building. Ah, excuse my language…"

Nicholas barked a cold laugh, and his hands balled on the table. "I'd like to assault that asshole again…"

"Me, too," Mackenzie agreed.

She held out a fist, which Nicholas bumped without looking away from the screen. Chris shushed them as the reverend kept talking.

"Then, one of them pulled me aside to explain this war they're fighting, and you wouldn't believe, they were *run* by these Sin Demons! Two of them! Like the Good Book says, the Beast out of the Earth and the Beast out of the Sea. Each had the Mark of the Beast, one on his head, the other on her right hand, just as the scripture says."

Thorn's jaw clenched. She touched her fingertips to her left wrist, where her *Peccostium* sat beneath her glove.

Rebel's eyes widened, and Cunningham scoffed. "This is what we've been warned about, Mr. Rebel. Satan and his Antichrist are coming, speaking their wicked lies in many tongues, making us believe their ungodly drivel. These so-called 'Martyrs' are only the beginning. Make no mistake, the elect among us are about to be tested. Plagues and pestilence are coming—"

"Shut it off," Chris cut in. "I can't listen to this any-more."

Thorn clicked a remote in her hand and killed the video.

"Fifty-seven minutes," she said. Her voice was low, tight with effort, like she was trying not to scream. She walked to the chair at the head of the table and gripped its back. "This *shit* goes on for fifty-seven fucking minutes. How the *fuck* did this happen?"

Her focus slashed to Holly, who sat in the chair nearest to her. The security lead's mouth dropped open, and she adjusted her thick-rimmed glasses beneath boyish, brown bangs.

"You mean, how did they manage to interview him?"

"I mean, how does he know *any* of this shit!" Thorn lost the battle, shouting as she tossed the remote onto the table. "You're supposed to be tracking down all the people we need to Reprogram, Andrews—the people who could be security risks. That's your number one priority! How the fuck did Weston Cunningham slip through the cracks?"

"Do you have any idea how many people Alan Pro-grammed?" Holly scoffed. Thorn turned away, walking back toward the exit while she ran a hand through her hair. Holly spoke louder. "Hundreds, maybe *thousands*, and it's not just about tracking them down. We have to determine how big of a threat they are, and this guy—"

"Is clearly a bigger threat than you realized," Thorn snapped. She spun back around, and her black eyes glittered furiously. Darius leaned forward on the table, hoping to catch her attention, but Thorn was singularly focused on Holly. She threw a hand to the far side of the room, indicat-ing the black screen. "He should have been the *first* person we—"

"He's locked in a state-run psych ward!" Holly defended, shooting to her feet. She was tiny compared to Thorn, standing at five feet even where Thorn was five-nine with-out the added lift of her boots, but Holly glowered at her with the ferocity of a dog that knew its bark was deadlier than its bite and wasn't afraid to use both. "After Alan masked his memories, Weston Cunningham went back down to Georgia. They ended up blaming him for the attack on his farm, but because he couldn't remember anything about what happened, he was institutionalized instead of thrown in prison! He's protected by miles of bureaucratic red tape *and* one thousand literal, physical miles. As far as viable threats go, he was one of the lowest on my list!"

Thorn glared at Holly, the air around her seething in rage, before she twisted away again and propped her hands on her hips. A low, keening hiss sounded from beneath her hair as Thorn's shoulders drew up in a sharp breath.

"There really wasn't any reason to think Cunningham would be this kind of a problem," Darius ventured as Holly slammed back into her chair and crossed her arms around an oversized hoodie.

"Seems like it was just really fucking bad luck," Mackenzie agreed.

"It's not just luck," Nicholas said. The former Diligence's bright, blue eyes homed in on the back of Thorn's head, and he frowned behind his beard. He'd grown it out over the last few months, and the blonde strands were nearly overrun with white at the edges. "Even if we had pegged Cunningham as a problem, we just don't have the time or resources to fix it all. You're the one who doesn't want to use your Influence to—"

"It would attract Wrath's attention," Thorn interrupted. She didn't turn back to face them, still glaring at a blank wall, but the muscles in her arms went more rigid. "We can't risk it."

Chris and Darius exchanged a quiet look as Nicholas sighed.

"I'm not arguing with you about this again," he said. "But if you won't help, you need to understand that it's not going to be perfect. It can't be. Cain is *one* man, and between Reprogramming our own people and getting to everyone Alan ever Influenced in the city, we've stretched him really fucking thin."

Thorn glanced back at last, and a shadow fell over her expression. God, the shame in her dark eyes made Darius want to wrap his arms around her, made him wish his Virtue healing abilities were worth a damn for emotional wounds… or worked on her at all. She must have sensed that because her attention landed on him for the first time since she'd walked into this room half an hour ago. He tried to offer a comforting smile, but she looked down at her feet instead.

"Is there anyone else we need to worry about?" Thorn asked. She came back to the table and pulled out the head chair, but she still didn't take it. "Anyone we haven't Programmed yet?"

Holly sighed. "I wouldn't say we have to worry, but there are three people who still have a *lot* of information about the Martyrs because they used to be one." She held up a hand and counted off on her fingers. "Noah Montgomery, Abraham Locke, and Simon Reed."

Thorn's eyes went wide, and her mouth slipped open. "Simon Reed is *alive?*"

"I don't actually know," Holly said. "There's no record of his passing out there—no obituary, no death certificate—but there aren't any records that he's still kicking, either. After he left the Underground, he founded a nonprofit hospital called The Reed Medical Foundation, where he worked until his retirement in 2064. Since then, there hasn't been any sign of him. If he *is* alive, he's one hundred and three."

Thorn's expression softened, just enough for Darius to notice, and she finally lowered into the chair. Mackenzie glanced at her, then to Darius, and shook her head. "Not exactly a high-level threat," the Irishwoman said.

"Exactly," Holly agreed. "As for Abraham and Jeremiah's son, I've reached out to both of them. Abraham moved to Florida with his dad a couple of months ago, and he hasn't responded to any of my messages. I don't think he wants to be involved, and I'm happy to leave him alone.

Noah Montgomery got back to me last week."

Chris nervously pulled a loose strand of blonde hair behind her ear. "What did he say?"

Holly shrugged. "Just that he has questions. We're setting up a time next week for one of our guys to pick him up and bring him in."

A soft blush reddened Chris's cheeks, and she nodded absently. Thorn cast her a quick look but said nothing as Nicholas cleared his throat.

"So, all these people were former Martyrs," he clarified. When Holly nodded, he smoothed a hand over his beard. "Then I'm not too worried about them. They don't have a reason to talk about the Underground the way Reverend Dickbag does, but that brings up another concern I have. It's not a surprise that he'd *want* to talk about the Martyrs, but what I want to know is why the fuck anyone would care what he has to say."

Mackenzie nodded. "That's a good point." Her blue eyes swept the table as she clattered her tongue piercing against the back of her teeth. God, Darius hadn't realized how much he'd missed hearing that sound in meetings. "If he's locked in a psych ward, his word is fucking garbage, right?"

"Normally, yeah," Holly said, "but there's been an uptick in people talking about strange things in New York, and it's not just because Alan's Programming wore off."

Chris frowned. "What do you mean?"

"People always post about the weird shit they see online," Holly said, "and we tend to cause a *lot* of weird shit. I try to clean up anything related to incidents involving the Martyrs, but there are a ton of people in that city. I have a small team, and this isn't our only priority. Hell, it isn't even our *biggest* priority. We can't possibly take it all down."

Thorn shook her head. "What the fuck does that have to do with Cunningham?"

"Because people have noticed us, Thorn," Holly snapped, "*and* the Sins, and they're looking for answers. Ever since Mayor Bently was killed, the city's been freaking out."

Darius's heart skipped, and he glanced at Thorn. Her expression immediately slackened, as though her mind had stepped away from the present and found itself in colder company. He, Nicholas, and Chris looked at one another, tense and concerned.

Mackenzie missed this look entirely. "Freaking out how?" she asked with a frown. "I thought the 'official' story was that his death was due to gang-related violence?"

"Under suspicious circumstances," Holly said, "but since no one really knows what happened, it's been the perfect breeding ground for insane rumors. It's like Roswell, JFK's assassination, and the 2066 siege on the Pentagon. Guys like this—" she gestured blindly to the screen "—are profiting off of it. They're tracking down unexplained stories or weird videos and making ridiculous claims about what might be going down, trying to connect it all in some wild conspiracy theories. I've seen everything from a giant government cover-up to a secret race of reptilian people to an alien invasion."

"And now, they're onto us," Darius said.

Holly turned to him and drew in a shallow breath. He noticed for the first time how tired her brown eyes looked behind her thick lenses. "Looks like it. This RebelTruth account isn't the first one we've run into. They're all over this new social media app." She reached into the center of the table to grab the remote and turned the screen back on. Cunningham's smug face reappeared, and Thorn seemed to come back to the table, her distant gaze focusing on him with a scowl. Holly navigated to a separate homepage, where an elaborate grid of moving video thumbnails stood out like an overloaded sensory mosaic. In the top corner, an icon resembling a slice of green citrus in the shape of a light bulb drew Darius's eye.

Nicholas squinted at the display. "What the hell is this?"

"LymeLite," Holly said. "It's been gaining traction for a few months now. The platform is all about building a following by blending short- and long-form content. Most of it's free, but accounts with enough followers can create subscription-only plans with less... restrictive content. There are a lot of thirst traps on here that are one wardrobe malfunction away from being classified as porn. Pretty sure most of the subscription plans *are* porn."

Mackenzie snorted a laugh. "That's the internet for you."

"But there's plenty of other stuff, too," Holly went on, "and people spouting out these kinds of crazy plots are a huge part of the market right now. As I've said, my team's on the lookout for anything the Martyrs have been involved in. So far, we've taken down accounts sharing things about the big incident with the police that killed Jeremiah, the protest Wrath made a mess of in 2092, and the nightclub shooting last spring, but we're running into a new problem..."

Thorn crossed her arms. "What kind of problem?"

"Taking down the accounts is actually generating more interest in these incidents," Holly said. She scratched the back of her head, ruffling her hair. "People just create new profiles as soon as they get shut down, and now they're starting to believe someone is trying to silence them. Every damned time I remove a video about us, three more pop up to take its place—like a digital hydra from hell."

Mackenzie's nose wrinkled in a grimace. "Well... they've got a point, don't they? Someone *is* trying to silence them... That someone is us."

"What other option do we have, though?" Chris asked. "We can't let any of this out, especially not now that Cunningham has attached our name to it."

"If it makes you feel better," Holly said, "just like with any conspiracy theory, ninety-nine percent of people think it's a load of bull. Hardly anyone takes these things seriously. I'd say more than half of RebelTruth's followers are there to argue with him."

"Still, millions of people live in New York City," Chris said. "Even if only one percent of them believe this, that's a big problem."

"Is it?" Nicholas asked. The room spun to him, and he shrugged. "I say we let them talk."

Darius shook his head. "You think we should just ignore it?"

"Absolutely not," Nicholas argued. "But I do think it's time we stop hiding out in the shadows and fight fire with fire."

An uncomfortable movement made its way around the table in a wave, everyone shifting in their chairs. Everyone but Thorn. Her eyes sharpened on Nicholas with a surgeon's precision.

"How?" Chris asked at last.

"If people are using this platform to learn about what's going on here, why don't we use it to get them *real* information?" Nicholas tilted his head toward the screen. "We could talk about how to identify Influence, how to resist it, what to do if you encounter a Puppet..."

Mackenzie snorted. "Wolfe, you didn't even know what LymeLite *was* five minutes ago, and now you want to jump onto it?"

"Not me," he corrected. "*Us.* Imagine the good we could do if—"

"No," Thorn cut in. The word fell like a guillotine, slicing Nicholas's argument in half. "We need to shut this shit down now before it gets out of hand."

Nicholas frowned, wrapping his arms around his chest. "It's *already* out of hand," he argued. "Come on, Thorn. What do we have to lose?"

"What do we have to *lose?*" She scoffed. "Our anonymity doesn't just protect us—it protects everyone around us! If people knew we were out there, if they were *looking* for us, how easily do you think the Sins could weaponize them? How long would it take them to manipulate civilians into dangerous situations by imitating our people just for a chance to get at *us?*"

"The Sins are *already* weaponizing civilians," Nicholas shot back. "They have the media, the NYPD, and an army of Sentries Programmed to report on us all over the damned city, not to mention the Puppets they throw in front of our bullets to avoid taking any themselves."

"It's out of the question, Wolfe," Thorn snapped before she turned to Holly instead. "Keep doing what you're doing. Shut down these accounts. Remove the videos. I want Cain sent to Georgia to Reprogram Cunningham as soon as—"

"Jesus Christ," Nicholas interrupted, "will you just listen to—"

"I said no!" Thorn slammed her hands onto the table as she sprang to her feet, spine arched like a spitting cat. Dark hair glided around her shoulders, framing her pale face in dark curtains. "We are *not* going to start broadcasting our existence all over the goddamned city!"

"Thorn—"

"Alan managed to keep the Martyrs a secret for over one hundred and fifty years," she said, screaming now. "I can do it for more than five fucking months!"

The room stilled with a sudden, static breath, like all six of them had plunged beneath the ice on a frozen lake and couldn't find the surface again. Thorn's shoulders trembled in a fury she was barely holding back.

No, not just fury. Pain sharpened her expression, wrinkling the bridge of her nose and glittering behind black lashes. Her eyes flashed up to Darius's, and the instant they connected, she spun away from the table—away from him. Not even Sparkie peered back. His entire body lay flat against Thorn's spine, quivering behind her hair.

Holly moved first. She cleared her throat as she leaned forward in her chair.

"If we're going to shut this conspiracy shit down, I need more help."

Nicholas nodded slowly, and Darius glanced at him, half-surprised he hadn't kept pushing, but the Former Diligence watched Thorn with a look that blended compassion and concern. "Okay," he said with a sigh. "Let's move our resources around. Get more people on security."

"What do you have in mind?" Chris asked. "Research and Discovery?"

She and Nicholas faced one another, seemingly grateful to have a new thread to follow, but Mackenzie gaped at Thorn as though she'd peeked behind her mask and found the face beneath it mangled and bloody.

"Seems like the best option," Nicholas agreed. "Keeping the Underground secured is more important than looking for Virtues right now. My researchers can track down problematic videos and accounts. Not sure what we'll do with the Recon units in the meantime. Mackenzie?"

He glanced at her, but Mackenzie didn't seem to hear him. Her focus held to the back of Thorn's head, and Darius worried she was about to break down. Nicholas gently laid a palm on Mackenzie's shoulder. The Irishwoman jumped as she twisted to the table again.

"I'm sorry," Mackenzie muttered, hastily dabbing at the corners of her eyes. "What were you saying?"

"If we put the Virtue search on hold, where could we use your Recon agents?" Nicholas asked.

Mackenzie chewed on her bottom lip. "Mmm… Well, if we're trying to keep an ear out for what people are saying about us, why not place them in New York City?"

Darius frowned. "Like Gray Unit agents?"

Thorn glanced over her shoulder.

"Yeah, exactly," Mackenzie said. "But instead of getting intel on the Sins, they'd be on the lookout for this shit." Mackenzie opened a palm toward the display screen, which still flickered with silent thumbnails on LymeLite's main page. "Thorn overheard a couple of kids talking about it on the subway. Other people have to be talking about it, too."

Nicholas nodded, impressed, but Darius's gaze moved back to Thorn. Her expression muted, no longer quite as volatile as it had been minutes ago, and her brows drew uneasily together. "What do you think?" he asked her.

She didn't answer right away. Her void-like eyes swung back to Darius, and she took a breath that slowly expanded her chest beneath crossed arms. Finally, she approached the head of the table.

"Putting more people in the city is dangerous," she said.

Now, Nicholas groaned. "God damn it, this is impossible," he said, throwing a hand up. "You don't want to use your Influence. You don't want to expand the Gray Unit. You don't want to take advantage of this new platform to educate civilians on the Sins. Here's an idea, Thorn. Why don't you tell us what you *do* want to do so at least we have a place to start?"

Thorn cast him a venomous glare, and her lips pressed together. Chris pinched the bridge of her nose. "Nicholas," she began, but Thorn cut her off.

"I want to make sure we do this *right*, Wolfe," she snarled. "If we rush into this half-cocked and hair-triggered, it will be a disaster."

"I understand that," Nicholas fired back, "but we can't stand still, either. TAC is at full capacity, all of our critical people have been Reprogrammed, and we've got our entire leadership circle back together." He gestured to Mackenzie, whose blue eyes flashed between him and Thorn with the shock of a rabbit in a steel trap. "We need to get back out there, and if you want to put all our focus on shutting this conspiracy shit down, getting more men on the ground will help us do that."

Thorn's fingers gripped tighter to her biceps, nails pressing crescents into her skin. At last, she nodded.

"I'll start prepping apartments tomorrow morning," she said. "McKay, I need a full profile of all your Recon agents so I can set them up in the best areas for their specific skills. Get that to Andrews, too. We may need to orchestrate jobs in the city."

"You got it," Mackenzie said.

Thorn nodded again, this time quicker. Less certain. "Okay. Let's get moving."

She headed toward the door, and Darius leapt to his feet to follow her.

"Hey," he said as they stepped into the hallway. Thorn didn't stop for him, didn't even hesitate at the sound of his voice as she made her way toward the garage. "Is there anything I can do to help? I know you have a lot on—"

"I've got it," Thorn said. Then, she swept through the doors while he stood alone in the center of the waiting room. Her hair shifted, and Sparkie's head peeked out between strands of silky black. His eyes met Darius's as Thorn put on her helmet, threw her leg over her motorcycle, and disappeared up the garage.

A strong aura pressed beside Darius as Chris wrapped an arm around his shoulder. He let out a sigh. Mackenzie's energy fidgeted in the hallway behind them.

"What the *fuck* was that?" she breathed.

"That," Nicholas said, and Darius turned to see him standing beside her, "is what we've been dealing with for the last five months." He cast Mackenzie a dark look. "Welcome back."

Her mouth slipped open, fingertips gently pressed to her lips. She stared at the spot where Thorn had disappeared as though she'd just seen a ghost.

CHAPTER FOUR

Shadows draped Washington Heights like a cool sheet. It was nearly 5:00, evening traffic already in full swing. The sidewalks flickered with movement as people bustled between bus stations and apartment stoops. Vehicular cacophony echoed between the buildings: horns honking, brakes squealing, tires grinding against the gritty, potholed asphalt. Normally, the city noise didn't bother Thorn, but right now, it grated on her nerves like chewing on a wad of tin foil.

The days since seeing Cunningham's interview had blown by in a whirlwind. While Cain headed to the Georgia State Mental Institution to Reprogram the zealous fucker, Nicholas and his researchers were drowning in the deep web, dredging more video evidence. Thorn had been buried beneath paperwork and technicalities, managing all her other duties on top of establishing their ten Recon agents in Manhattan proper. She'd never had a force of fully-fledged Martyrs this large living in New York before. The thought of it made her stomach squirm. Worries and work kept her wired, and she'd slept even less than usual in the last ninety-six hours. She felt pulled thin, half-translucent, like all it would take was a bright enough light at just the right angle to see through her bullshit.

Thorn paused outside a colorless brick building along 161st Street. A bottlebrush bloom of crisp, orange leaves clung to a couple of listless trees planted carelessly in small plots. The building hadn't changed much in the decades since the Martyrs had purchased one of the flats inside, but the trees certainly had. Every three or so years, they'd fail—starved and parched to death in an urban environment that valued them solely for their aesthetic beauty without putting much concern into the stunted existence it provided them. When they inevitably withered, the city simply put a nearly-identical substitute in their place, as though making a statement that nothing that lived here, not even the goddamned foliage, was so special it couldn't be replaced, and the rest of the world wouldn't notice.

But Thorn had. Live long enough, and you couldn't help but notice that kind of shit. She glanced at the branches clawing into a cloudless sky as Sparkie alighted on one at the center, landing so quietly that not a single leaf rustled. As soon as he was settled, the little lizard wrapped his red, leathery wings around his blue body to better blend into the autumn colors. Thorn looked up the street, then back the way she'd come, before she strode to the front door, typed an access code, and slipped into the foyer.

Silence greeted her.

Thorn walked down the hallway, took her first right, and stopped at the second apartment. Everything about this door was exactly like the others down the corridor: navy paint, golden numbers, brass fixtures.

Well... not *exactly*.

Thorn wrapped her hand around the knob and pressed her fingertip to a hidden sensor at the base. The biometrics lock scanned her print before unlatching with a soft *click!* The door opened inward, swinging with an unusual weight thanks to the fortified steel concealed beneath a wood veneer. It thudded shut behind Thorn's back, and she took a moment to breathe in the stale, untouched air.

She hadn't placed an agent here in years. She hadn't had

a reason to. None of the Sins had been frequent enough visitors to Washington Heights since Sloth's host three iterations ago. After that, this place was kept on standby as an emergency safe house for any Martyr in the city.

Clearly, no one had needed it. The spacious entry room was furnished as a den, with a musty pair of couches in an L-shape facing the adjacent wall. A flush-mounted monitor that functioned as both a television and a communication system was coated in such a thick layer of dust that the screen looked gray. Cobwebs draped from every corner, grime lined the floorboards, and through a bulletproof glass door, Thorn could see that the narrow strip of a rear yard lay scattered with trash that had blown in with the wind. A wrought iron staircase directly in front of her spiraled to the second floor, where a kitchen and bedroom boasted the same banal level of neglect. Thorn walked to the back exit, boots clicking on the laminate, and looked out at the sliver of a darkening sky barely visible between neighboring buildings. Beyond the composite perimeter fence, an alley let out at 162nd Street.

This was one of the best things about this location. Ground floor access. Multiple exits. Easy escape. In the unlikely event that the Sins did track it down, her agent wouldn't be stuck on the fourth floor without a lifeline to hold onto, hoping backup got there before the Sins or their militarized Puppets battered down the front fucking door.

Bitterness sank into Thorn's chest, and she sighed through it. Then, she heard something—not with *her* ears but with the senses she shared with her Familiar. A voice she knew.

"All right," Mackenzie McKay said. "Looks like we're almost there."

A pinch of panic jolted Thorn's stomach.

This was the final apartment, the final person she had to establish in the city, and Mackenzie hadn't shown up for any of the others. Why the fuck was she here tonight? Now that Thorn was paying attention, she could easily feel her. Her stark, cold energy was one of the most potent on the street outside, standing out amongst everyone else by several degrees.

God damn it. Thorn would have noticed Mackenzie's aura way earlier if she hadn't gotten so lost in her own head. The room went gray as Thorn focused on Sparkie's senses.

Mackenzie strode in from the east, choppy, yellow hair ruffling in the breeze. A man walked between her and the road, one hand lazily wrapped around a single backpack strap at his shoulder while the other shoved deep into his jacket pocket. He looked tall beside her, though Mackenzie made everyone look tall, and he flicked his black hair out of his face as he surveyed the apartment building with a frown.

John Waters, one of the senior Recon agents. Typically, he spent more than fifty percent of his time outside of the Underground, which suited Thorn just fine. She could do without his dirty looks and short attitude. The last she'd heard, he and Mackenzie hadn't been speaking after Mackenzie had pushed him into a bet that revolved around his ex and another man. It looked like her six-month stint in rehab was enough to clear the air. Thorn swore under her breath as Sparkie swiveled on his branch to watch them.

"Why am I all the way out in Washington Heights?" John grumbled. They reached the far end of the block, but his voice carried to the tree where Thorn's Familiar sat. "It's so out of the way."

Mackenzie flicked a wrist. "We've gotta spread you all out to cover more ground."

"Westmorland and Porter are both in the Financial District," he argued.

"The Financial District has a fuck ton more people," Mackenzie said. "If you really want a new assignment, talk to Thorn."

John scoffed. "Why bother? Thorn hates my guts. That's probably why she stuck me way the hell out here in the first place."

Thorn rolled her eyes as Mackenzie laughed.

"She doesn't hate your guts," the Irishwoman insisted. "Maybe that swooped-back thing you do with your hair, but definitely not your guts."

She elbowed John playfully. That turned up the corner of his mouth, but he didn't truly smile. Instead, he fished his phone out of his pocket.

"Well, she never *liked* me," he said as they stopped in front of the building. From his perch, Sparkie could make out a file on John's screen—the information document Thorn had sent about his assignment. "She made it pretty clear that she never approved of me when Chris and I were dating."

Mackenzie blew a mouthful of air between pursed lips. "Not *approving* of you and *not liking you* are different things, and what did you expect? Thorn practically raised Chris. She'll never approve of anyone dating her."

John's shoulders tensed. "She seems to approve of DuPont just fine."

As he typed in the code, Mackenzie stood, mouth agape, like she was at a loss for words. Thorn could remember every time someone had reduced Mackenzie to silence. It happened so rarely that the moments stood out. As the lock clicked open, John sighed.

"I'm sorry," he said. "This isn't even about Chris and Gabe..." He hesitated for a moment and glanced into the building with a furrow to his brow before he looked at Mackenzie again. "It's just... do you think Thorn's... good?"

Thorn's stomach dropped, and Sparkie bristled. Mackenzie shook her head. "What the hell are you on about?"

"I mean, is she okay?" John asked. "Ever since Alan was killed, she's seemed off, and no one else in the leadership will tell any of us what the hell is going on. People are starting to talk—"

"What are they saying?" Mackenzie cut in.

A shallow breath hitched in Thorn's chest as John shrugged.

"Just that she's lost it and shouldn't be in charge—"

"Fuck, I don't wanna hear this right now," Mackenzie hissed, interrupting him again.

"You asked me what they were saying!"

"John, I need you to listen to me."

Mackenzie hedged closer, but instead of peering into the building or down the street, her bright eyes started scanning the skies. They flashed by the tree, lingering where Sparkie sat, frozen in place. Thorn held her breath, but Mackenzie turned to John again.

"Alan wasn't just the Martyrs' commander. He was Thorn's *uncle*," Mackenzie muttered. Back in the apartment, the corners of Thorn's eyes stung. "We lost a leader, but she lost so much more than that, and from what I read in the reports, it was *awful*. Right now, she doesn't need a bunch of us talking shit about her behind her back. She needs support and maybe a little bit of fucking grace."

John's mouth tightened, but he said nothing.

"You're worried that Thorn assigned you an apartment in Washington Heights because she doesn't like you," Mackenzie went on, "but it looks like you're willing to believe the worst in Thorn because *you* don't like *her*."

A hard blush darkened John's face, and he looked at the ground. Mackenzie laid both palms on his shoulders, a sympathetic smile tugging on her painted lips.

"I know you and Thorn have a rocky history," she said, "and I *know* that's not all on you. But the Sins have done enough to rip us apart. Let's not make their job any easier by tearing each other down from the inside, all right?"

"Yeah," he muttered. "You're right. I'm sorry."

"Don't be sorry," Mackenzie said. "Be better. Lead by example. More platitude bullshit. Blah, blah, blah." She whipped her hands back and clapped them together. "Now, c'mon. I'm sure Thorn's waiting for us. If you hadn't made us late…"

She winked, and the rest of John's dour mood dissolved with a laugh as he walked into the building. Mackenzie paused in the entryway, looking to the sky one last time. Her gaze hovered near Sparkie for a second before she went inside and closed the door behind her.

Thorn's eyes opened, and her heart thrashed against her sternum. The room around her came back muted, and a lump lodged in her throat, forcing her to take short, choppy breaths. Two auras made their way down the hall, and Thorn stared into the rear yard. She half-considered walking out, vaulting the six-foot fence, and vanishing before they reached the apartment just so she didn't have to stare into their faces and pretend this was all fucking okay.

But that would just prove John right, wouldn't it? Just prove that she had lost it. Thorn's teeth ground together.

The lock clicked, and Mackenzie's voice carried through the swinging door.

"Here it is. Home sweet home. Hey, Thorn!"

Thorn forced her shoulders down, drew a deep breath, and unclenched her fists before she turned around. Mackenzie stood grinning by the entrance while John locked it back up.

"What are you doing here?" Thorn asked. "It won't take both of us to get Waters set up."

She tried to keep her tone neutral, but it bit from her mouth anyway. Mackenzie's expression remained unchanged, as though she hadn't noticed, but more likely, she chose to ignore it. John, however, threw Thorn a cold look as he dropped his bag off by the door.

"No," Mackenzie agreed, "but I figured I should learn how to do it. We may need to move people around, and it would be nice if you had help, wouldn't it?"

Her smile extended, crinkling the corners of her bright blue eyes. God, it had been too long since Thorn had seen those eyes and the vibrant light shining out from them. Her absence had stung like a knife wound and pierced just as deep. Thorn ached to throw her arms around Mackenzie, but she crossed them over her chest instead.

"It's not complicated," she said. "Andrews could walk you through it over the phone."

Mackenzie waved a hand. "Holly's busy as fuck. This was easiest."

She brushed past John and made her way straight for the television. A dusty remote lay on the coffee table. Mackenzie swiped it up. "Now, how the hell do you work this thing?"

While Mackenzie struggled with the com system, Thorn showed John the rest of the apartment. Like all other Martyr-owned units in the city, it came with more than a reinforced entrance, biometric locks, and bulletproof glass. Several emergency buttons were hidden around the apartment—embedded into the molding by every door and window, tucked beneath counter lips in the bathroom and kitchen, and on the wall behind each bedside table. Because this apartment featured two floors and multiple rooms, John also had access to three discreetly stored handguns. Thorn opened one of the drawers in the bedroom and indicated a fingerprint scanner tucked inside the front panel.

"Your information has already been added to this particular unit's infrastructure," Thorn said as she touched her thumb to the reader. A false bottom popped open, revealing a loaded Glock. "There are additional firearms behind the medicine cabinet in your bathroom and in the table downstairs. Whenever these compartments are triggered, an alert will automatically be sent to security, so don't go showing them off."

Thorn shot John a look, and he glared from where he leaned against the doorframe. His dark blue eyes shared the color of the sea on a stormy day, and that storm seemed to be alive and well in him right now. She thought he was going to argue with her, to snap back with some shitty comment and bad attitude like usual—and, fuck, maybe she was hoping he would—but instead, his shoulders rose and fell in a sigh before he simply said two words.

"Yes, ma'am."

Her upper lip curled. John had never called her "ma'am" before. Not without dripping sarcasm. Jesus, she'd give anything for the sarcasm.

Thorn clicked the gun case shut and left the room, desperate for some distance from the eggshells that seemed to be scattered around her feet. "The rest of your things will be brought by tomorrow morning," she said. John's aura followed as she headed toward the staircase. "Let's see if McKay's smarter than the machine."

They made their way back to the first floor. Before Thorn's feet hit the landing, Holly's voice rang across the room.

"Are you sure you turned it on?" she asked. Mackenzie's phone lay face-up on the table with the security lead on speaker.

"Of *course* I turned it on!" Mackenzie answered. "What kind of moron do you think I am?"

"A pretty big one," Holly quipped. "This is literally a three-step process, and step *one* is hitting the power button."

"Well, then we're a third of the way there, aren't we?"

"At this point, you're being difficult on purpose."

Mackenzie chuckled and tapped another button. The television flickered to some kid's program. Poorly animated 3D characters ran back and forth and bashed one another over the head with oversized bats. The volume was muted, so when they laughed, it looked like screaming. Thorn's stomach twisted. She snatched the remote out of Mackenzie's hands and hit the input button. The display went black.

"I've got it, Andrews," she said. "Standby for a system check."

Thorn tapped the cancel button on Mackenzie's phone before Holly could respond.

"Log into your Martyr communications app, Waters," Thorn said. While John dug out his device, Mackenzie stared at the side of Thorn's face. Thorn ignored her. "When it prompts you to sync, use your access code."

Within sixty seconds, John was logged in, the system loaded, and Holly's face filled the display. A discreet camera in the screen caught the three of them in its frame, evidenced by a small thumbnail in the corner.

"About time," Holly said, adjusting her thick-rimmed glasses. The lenses magnified her brown eyes. "Remind me to never send you on an assignment like this, McKay."

Mackenzie laughed as Thorn tossed the remote onto the couch.

"We're good to go on this side, Andrews," she said. "You can take over from here."

Without saying or waiting for a goodbye, Thorn walked out the door. She expected to hear it slam shut behind her, but Mackenzie's aura leapt up and erupted into the hall. Thorn's teeth clenched so hard that her jaw pulsed.

"Hey, wait up!" Mackenzie shouted. Thorn didn't, and Mackenzie scurried to her side. As they turned toward the foyer, she swiped a brush of yellow bangs out of her eyes. "It's been a while since we've hung out. I figured we could grab something to eat and—"

"I can't," Thorn cut in. She threw the door open and walked onto the dimming street. The lamps overhead flickered to life, blending cool dusk light with a warm yellow glow. "I'm busy."

Sparkie vaulted from the tree and disappeared down the back of Thorn's jacket. Mackenzie paused, her eyes cutting from Thorn to where her Familiar had been hiding, but she glossed over it with a shake of her head.

"Busy with what?" the Irishwoman pressed.

Thorn kept walking, and Mackenzie kept following. "McKay—"

"No, really, what's so damned important you can't stop to just *talk* to me for half a bloody second?"

Her tone had teeth, and it nipped at Thorn's consciousness sharp enough to twist her around. Mackenzie propped her hands on her hips, and her tongue piercing clicked behind tightly closed lips.

"I was gone for *six months*, Thorn," Mackenzie went on, hurt pooling between the syllables, "and it's *really* shitty that you haven't even bothered to say hi since I've been back."

Thorn's heart skipped a beat, scraping itself on the ragged walls of the hole in her chest. She nodded as she forced a sigh.

"You're right," she muttered at last. "I'm sorry, Mackenzie. You're right. A lot has changed, and I…" Thorn raised her palms, opening them up to nothing, which was exactly the justification she had for all of this shit. They fell limp at her sides. "I fucked up."

And she had. Right now, five months ago, and every goddamned second in between.

Mackenzie's eyes glistened as her shoulders sloped toward the earth. She inched forward.

"I know I wasn't here for you when… when it happened," she said, voice cracking.

Thorn's stomach swirled. "Mackenzie…"

"But I am now. You said it before, Thorn. We can get through this together." Mackenzie took another step and reached out her hands. They trembled. "Alan wouldn't want—"

"Stop," Thorn cut in. She shook her head. Backed away. Alan's voice swam in her skull. "Please—"

"It's okay," Mackenzie insisted.

"Everything is okay, Thorn."

Thorn pressed her eyes closed, but then she could see him, too. Alan's face filled her vision, broken, bruised, and bloodied. Her hands were red with it, and so was the warehouse—an ocean of death and decay rotting away beneath her feet. Nausea burned up Thorn's esophagus. Mackenzie came even closer, her icy aura pressing in like a wall.

"Mackenzie, don't."

"I just want to help—"

"Jesus, McKay, leave it alone!"

Mackenzie froze, mouth gaping, face a ghostly shade of white. Thorn's heart thundered—she felt it in her chest, in her neck, and in her clenched fists. Her body hummed like it was ramping up to an explosion, and the results would raze this whole neighborhood to the ground. Thorn fought to stop it.

"I don't *want* help," she went on. Her eyes stung, and her throat constricted as she forced out the words, "I don't want to talk about it. I don't even want to *think* about it! I *can't*. So just leave it alone."

Thorn's voice died, and silence followed as though the entire street had stopped to listen. No wind rustled the leaves, no birds chirped from nearby branches, and pedestrians hesitated, their auras lingering as they leered in this direction. Mackenzie stared at Thorn, and Thorn jutted her chin forward as though asking, *begging* Mackenzie to ball a fist and strike her. Instead, a single, wet tear trailed down Mackenzie's cheek.

"All right," she managed to get out. Her head bobbed in a tight, frantic nod that seemed to loosen the rest of her tears. More followed the first, glistening against her skin. Mackenzie didn't bother hiding them. "I'm so sorry."

Thorn wished Mackenzie *had* struck her. It would hurt less than this. Her jaw clenched as Sparkie let out a soft sound at the base of her neck, his body vibrating between her shoulders. Mackenzie stood there like she was waiting for Thorn to throw more blades into her chest. She tossed her gaze to the ground at Mackenzie's feet.

"It's fine," Thorn said, but it was a lie, and she knew Mackenzie knew it. "I'll see you later."

That was a lie, too.

Thorn strode down the street, ignoring the stares that burned against the back of her head. Mackenzie didn't follow this time, but she didn't walk away, either. Her soul, cold and alone, stood still as stone until Thorn rounded the corner. Then, she kept walking without any idea where the fuck she was going to go but knowing she couldn't stay *here*, and she didn't stop until she'd found herself on the Macombs Bridge over the Harlem River.

A column of filthy water stretched before her. Its dark depths rippled under violent New York lights. The sun had fully set now, turning the river and the sky the same bleak, black color. Thorn leaned against the suicide barrier along the walkway, her fingers wound into the chain link above her head, and stared at the silhouette of Manhattan in the distance.

She ached for some kind of relief, something better than terrorizing this fucking city with her short fuse and shitty attitude. Thorn considered calling Darius just to hear his voice, but she couldn't bring herself to do it. Every time she thought of him, she saw the look on his face in that warehouse—remembered the horror in his eyes when he'd realized what she'd become, what she'd *done*. The shame made her sick.

What kind of monster did Darius see lurking inside of her now?

That monster swirled in Thorn's gut and burned her throat like acid. She dipped a hand into her satchel, scrambling until she found a crumpled pack of cigarettes. Her fingers shook as she drew one out and struck her lighter. It took her three tries to get the tip to catch. It glowed orange like the glare of headlights, and that glow only brightened as she drew a deep breath of smoke. Thorn closed her eyes.

John Waters was right. They were all right. She *had* lost it.

For a few minutes, she stood on that bridge, nursing one cigarette, then two, then three down to used nubs that she crushed beneath her heel. The night grew deeper, cooler, and more lonesome the longer she stared at the water. She couldn't stand the idea of going back to her apartment, but returning to the Underground was out of the question. Thorn wouldn't be surprised if Mackenzie had already called the rest of the directors to fill them in on this latest outburst.

But she didn't want to be alone. She felt starved for company… company that wouldn't ask questions. Company that wouldn't expect answers. Company that wouldn't know about the horrors screaming inside her skull.

She didn't have company like that. Not anymore.

Thorn's eyes eased toward the east, to the opposite bank

of the Harlem River, where The Bronx waited like an old friend she'd fallen out of favor with. She swallowed against a dry throat. A thin film of smoky residue coated her tongue.

God, she could use more than company… She could use a drink.

———

The decision was made before Thorn even pulled out another cigarette—a decision she damn well knew was a mistake, but, fuck it, what else did she have to lose? She crossed the bridge, headed south, and half an hour later, Thorn stood across the street from an old, repurposed church. Intricate, stained-glass windows flickered, splashing a mosaic of multicolored fractals onto the sidewalk at its feet. A neon sign shaped like a crucifix flashed the words "The Cross."

Thorn took a deep breath as she looked up and down the road. It was empty: no people, no lurkers, nothing except two glowing orbs from a cat hiding beneath a parked sedan. She opened her jacket, and Sparkie took to the sky, landing on the streetlight overhead. With a quick snap, he ripped through the wires to a camera Holly had installed years ago.

No one needed to know she was coming back here.

Her Familiar dove back into the safety of her kevlar bike jacket. Thorn zipped it to her throat, walked across the street, and opened the door.

A wave of gruff voices, cold energy, and the comforting smell of old oak pews flooded her. A handful of faces spun her direction: grizzled men playing billiards, women prematurely aged by toxic marriages and nicotine habits, and other down-on-their-luck types. Some were new, but most Thorn recognized from the years she'd spent drowning her sins here.

"Well, would you look at that," a particularly bear-like man growled. His voice wheezed like an old set of smoky bellows, and he smiled beneath a bushy, gray mustache that made his tobacco-stained teeth seem more white than yellow. He grinned as he chalked the tip of his cue. "If it isn't Teagan Love. We thought you'd moved on to greener pastures."

Warmth pulsed through Thorn's chest. Fuck, she hadn't realized how good it would feel to disappear inside this particular identity again.

"Hey, Sully," she said with a smile. "Missed you, too."

Sully chortled like a grandfather who'd been caught with his hand in the cookie jar. Thorn didn't know much about him, just like he and no one else in this building knew much about Teagan Love, but she did know he'd spent time behind bars for accidentally killing a man in a brawl. The rumor was that the other guy had beaten Sully's husband until he'd been put on a ventilator, and Sully returned the favor a little too well. He'd gotten out of prison thirty years later to find himself divorced, homeless, and alone.

Alone, at least, until he stumbled upon The Cross and found a new faith—and a new family.

Like Sully, others who knew Thorn waved or smiled or spoke to her as she made her way through the bar. For all that The Cross lacked in glitz and glamor, it made up for in its congregation of devoted parishioners. They didn't have much, but they had each other, and they were happy—or at least relieved—to see her here again.

Except for the bartender.

Jay Coons watched her from behind the counter, frowning as he dried a glass with a white rag. She took her regular stool across from him, and his blue eyes narrowed. He glanced over her head as though making sure no one else was in earshot before he murmured, "What the hell are you doing here?"

He threw the rag over his shoulder and stored the glass beneath the counter. His face was cool and colorless beneath his auburn hair, betraying the dread Thorn's sudden appearance in his bar must have stirred inside of him. She couldn't blame him.

Jay was the only person in this room who knew who she really was—*what* she really was—and he'd made it crystal clear he didn't want anything to do with her or the war she was fighting.

"Things have been hard," Thorn said.

"I don't want to hear about it," Jay replied.

"And I don't want to talk about it," Thorn snapped. He blinked at her, and she sighed. "I have nowhere else to go, Jay."

Jay's jaw hardened, and he crossed his arms around his navy button-up. Thorn didn't know what he saw in her, what this man had *ever* seen in her, that made it hard for him to tell her no, but he must have seen it again tonight. At last, he shook his head and moved to the wall of liquor behind the bar. It glittered like a heathen's altar to a court of false deities, full of empty promises and pretty deceptions.

Seconds later, Jay snapped a scotch onto the counter just within Thorn's reach before he walked away. She lifted the alcohol, brought it to her lips, and breathed it in.

This wouldn't work, either. It was a temporary solution, a bandage she'd slapped over a gaping, gushing wound, but it would have to do.

For now

Thorn shot the scotch. It hit the back of her throat like a bullet.

CHAPTER FIVE

Darius read Mackenzie's email for a third time, his stomach in knots.

This wasn't an official record—not something that went into a report that the rest of the Underground had access to—but he and the Martyr directors all got the same note. Well, most of the other directors. Darius had immediately noticed that Thorn hadn't been included.

Because it was about *her*.

His teeth clenched as he considered the message—the *meaning*. Thorn's breakdown outside John's new apartment didn't surprise Darius as much as he wished it had. Neither did the others' responses. Nicholas and Chris bounced ideas back and forth on what to do, all ideas Darius had heard them share a dozen times in the last few months. An intervention. A conversation. A consequence.

Darius didn't say anything to this. He didn't know what *to* say.

So instead, he'd buried himself in other work. Checking in with the Recon teams in their new apartments. Researching RebelTruth and watching his LymeLite videos. Calling Samira Khoury—no, Samira *Nasser*, now—to let her and Leroy know that the video was removed and the reverend

Reprogrammed. But the distractions were short-lived. His mind kept wandering back to this—back to *her*.

He sighed and reclined in his chair, throwing his hands behind his head as he considered the office around him— an office that had once belonged to Abraham Locke. In many ways, it still did. The only thing Darius had done was fill the shelves with his own research binders and books. Otherwise, the blue carpeting, beige couch, and glass coffee table were exactly the same. Sometimes, it felt like their old counselor was still here. Still offering bits of advice and tools for healing.

Darius wished he could access those tools now—and that he knew Thorn would be willing to take them instead of sinking into old habits. *Bad* habits.

A knock interrupted Darius's thoughts, and he glanced at his door. Chris's aura hovered outside, and she cracked it open to peek inside. "Hey… Can I talk to you?"

Darius's heart flipped, but he nodded and got to his feet. Chris stepped into the room, closed the door behind her, and drew a shallow breath. She didn't meet Darius's eye, and he frowned.

"Is everything okay?"

Chris made a motion that seemed to be a blend of nodding her head, shaking her head, and shrugging all at once, which told Darius the answer was no. Then, with a sigh, she drew a strand of long, blonde hair behind her ear.

"Noah Montgomery is on his way to the Underground," she said. "Gabe picked him up. They'll be here any minute now."

"Oh," Darius said, but a bubble of relief burst between his lungs. He'd been sure she was here to discuss Thorn. "Isn't that… a good thing?"

"Yes," Chris said, pinching the bridge of her nose in a way that still said no. "It's complicated."

"Yeah, I kind of figured."

Chris groaned and sat on the couch.

"Noah and I grew up together," she started. "He was my

best friend… and eventually more than a friend."

"Ah…" Darius nodded as he took the plush armchair perpendicular to her. "I see what you mean by complicated."

Chris chuckled. *"That's* not even the complicated part," she said. "We were the only teenagers in the Underground, both of us had lost a parent, and we didn't have anyone else to talk to about all of this." She gestured around them. "It was bound to happen."

Darius's mind flashed back to Juniper and the similar situation they'd been in. Hormones, proximity, and shared trauma were a dangerous mix that had landed the two of them in trouble—and led them to the Williamsburg Bridge Street Market, looking for a way *out* of trouble. Ever since the Supreme Court's decision to revoke reproductive rights decades ago, illegal medication was the only option a lot of people had… and it was harder and harder to find.

"Fair point," he said. "So, what happened?"

"Well," Chris said, "Martyr kids are given a choice at eighteen. They can join the war, or they can leave. If they decided to leave, Alan would hide their memories, fill in the gaps with a fake childhood, and send them off with enough money to start their new lives…"

She paused and looked down at the glass table, chewing on her cheek as she considered how to continue. Darius leaned forward.

"Noah was a year older than me," she went on, "but he promised to wait until I was of age. We'd always said that no matter what we decided to do, we would be in it together.

"Then my mom was killed," Chris said quietly, "along with the TAC director at the time and over a dozen other Martyrs. It was the largest casualty event either one of us had ever seen. Jeremiah got promoted shortly after the funeral, and one night, we overheard him and Thorn talking about how they were worried the Martyrs would run out of people and how fucked we'd be if that happened. I started to think Noah and I needed to stay."

Darius nodded slowly. "But Noah didn't want to."

Chris shook her head. "He turned eighteen a couple of months later and didn't tell me he'd decided to go until Alan already had his new life sorted out. I was… *so* mad at him. We got into a huge fight. I said some *awful* things, things I didn't even believe, but I was seventeen and scared. We never talked again. He was Programmed and sent off before my senior year started."

She stopped there, still watching the reflections in the coffee table as though they held some kind of solace. Abraham had once told Darius he set his office up this way on purpose—that the calming colors and soft lights helped people feel more comfortable so they would open up. He wondered if that was what their old counselor had done—listened to the outpouring of trauma from Martyrs who had lost family, loved ones, everything they knew, while fine-tuning those lights between sessions to see if it might help them cope a little bit better.

Then, Darius said the most therapist-like thing he could think of: "How do you feel about seeing Noah again?"

Chris's eyes flicked up to him, and she sighed.

"This was fifteen years ago," she said. "It still hurts, but I'm not mad anymore. I haven't been for a long time. I understand why he did what he did, and I don't fault him for it. In a way, I'm happy he left. Otherwise, I could have lost him, too. I probably would have."

Her voice caught, and she cleared her throat.

"But for *Noah*, all those memories just came roaring back. It's not fifteen years old for him. It's still fresh. I called him a coward and a traitor, Darius." She laughed, but the sound was more like a defeated scoff falling out of her mouth. "And now I have to go in there and tell him that his father's dead."

Chris wilted into the couch, pressing her fingertips against closed eyes. Darius watched her for a moment before his focus glossed over the part of his office wall where he could feel Martyr energy in the Research and Discovery headquarters, in the tactical lockers, and in the conference room. Two people walked that way now: one Darius recognized and one he did not. He drew in a long breath.

Noah Montgomery had just stepped foot into the Underground for the first time since he'd been eighteen.

When Darius looked at Chris again, her eyes locked onto him as though she knew what he'd sensed. The color drained from her face. He smiled, stood up, and held out a hand.

"We'll tell him together."

A smirk softened Chris's face, and she allowed Darius to help her to her feet. As they walked down the hallway, he tracked Noah's movements. The man sat at the conference table and shuffled with nervous energy.

"How did Jeremiah feel about it?" Darius asked. Chris paused outside the room and glanced at him with a frown. "Noah leaving, I mean."

"Sad," she said, "but relieved. Jeremiah was the one who convinced him to go in the first place."

Darius's brows went up. "Really?"

"Really. All Martyr parents hope their kids decide to leave," Chris said, "because they love them too much to want them to stay."

That sank into Darius's stomach like a block of ice, and suddenly, all he saw was Thorn and her son looking back at him from a seventy-year-old photograph. She laughed as Donovan wrapped his arm around her shoulders just days before he was supposed to escape the war that ended up claiming his life.

Chris opened the door.

The second she walked into the room, Noah Montgomery leapt up. He'd been in the chair nearest to the door, and he was less than three feet away from Chris as she froze in the frame. Gabe DuPont sat beside him, wearing a tactical uniform that matched Chris's. He got to his feet and caught Darius's gaze with sharp, amber eyes.

At last, Chris cleared her throat. "Hey, Noah. It's been a

while."

"Chris." His voice constricted around her name, and tension shuddered from his body in a choppy laugh. Darius was stricken by how much he resembled his father. While Noah was shorter and didn't carry the bulky muscle that had made Jeremiah so intimidating, he had the same kind, dark eyes; deep, brown skin; and broad smile that filled his whole face. He took a step toward Chris, his arms raised, before that smile faltered. He stuttered to a stop and glanced at Darius before he focused on her again.

"When I remembered this place, I—" He cut off and adjusted his gray blazer with shaking fingers. "I didn't know what I would find."

Chris chuckled and lifted her palms with a shrug. "I'm still here."

"I see that," Noah said. He indicated her clothes. "And you joined TAC."

"Yeah…" The strained smile on Chris's face fell. "I was actually promoted to director two years ago."

Noah's brows went up, creating a range of creases on his forehead. "Two years?" he repeated. "I see…"

Neither of them spoke for a moment. Gabe and Darius exchanged another quick look as Chris and Noah sat with that—with all it meant—before she swallowed hard and shook her head.

"I'm so sorry, Noah," she murmured. "Jeremiah is—"

Noah lifted a hand to stop her. "I know. I knew the moment I read that letter from Holly. If Dad had been alive, he would have shown up at my damn door the day Alan died. I can't believe I missed him by just *two years*…"

He paused to draw a trembling breath, and his eyes glittered with fresh tears.

"But I didn't miss you," Noah went on. The words struggled from his mouth, high and throaty. "God, I am so glad you're okay."

Chris choked out an emotional laugh. The space between them dissolved as she rushed forward and threw her arms around Noah's shoulders. He accepted her without hesitation, curling down as he held her close. Warmth bloomed in Darius's stomach. He glanced at Gabe to see him watching the pair with his signature crooked smile bright upon his face.

A few seconds later, Chris pulled back and wiped the corners of her eyes.

"Noah," she said, clearing her throat to loosen a pinch in her voice, "you've already met Gabe DuPont. He's the second in command of the TAC unit… and my partner outside of it."

Chris turned to Gabe and laid an affectionate palm at the crook of his neck. His smile deepened before he held a hand out to Noah.

"DuPont…" Noah said with a frown as he took Gabe's palm. "Weren't you one of those SWAT officers killed in action a couple of years back?" Then, he scoffed. "The Sins were behind that, I take it?"

"You got it," Gabe said. "In some ways, I'm grateful. It got me on the right side of this fight."

Noah nodded, slow and thoughtful. Chris watched him with an eager gleam in her expression as she moved toward Darius and touched his arm.

"And this is Darius Jones," she began. "He's a Virtue."

Noah's eyes shot open, and he stepped back, like he needed to be able to see all of Darius all at once to trust that he was really there. His fingers moved over his open mouth, barely covering his shock.

"Nah," he said. "You're playing with me." But before Chris or anyone else could speak, he laughed, came forward again, and reached for Darius's hand. He shook it with so much vigor that Darius's whole arm rattled. "A Virtue. No way! Which one?"

"Kindness," Darius said with a chuckle.

"Kindness," Noah repeated, breathing it out in a whisper like he was praying to an old god he longed to believe in again. "I never thought I'd live to see a Virtue."

"Neither did I," Chris agreed. "And now, we have *two.*" Noah spun back toward her, and she opened her arms as though to hold the whole Underground within them. "A lot has happened since you've been gone, Noah. A lot of impossible things."

They finally sat at the conference table, diving into everything that had changed in the last fifteen years. Gabe excused himself, kissing the crown of Chris's head, while she and Darius shared stories of heartbreak and tragedy, of friends lost and hopes shattered.

But they also shared stories of triumph—of Teresa Solomon destroying Pride and proving once and for all that it could be done, of Sloth's fall and Nicholas Wolfe's sacrificed soul, of Samira Khoury breaking Gluttony's hold on the NYPD. Darius talked about life as a Virtue, and Chris bragged about how the Martyrs had grown more than ever, *thrived* more than ever. Noah listened in rapture, clinging to every word.

Darius, though, was suddenly reminded of every incredible, indelible victory the Martyrs had claimed these last few years. A bittersweet sting clenched his jaw. This latest death had overshadowed all of it, and Darius let himself forget how far they'd come.

He wasn't the only one. When Chris talked about Alan Blaine and how Noah had even come to remember this world at all, she visibly crumbled. A somber frown settled over Noah's face.

"I suspected it was bad, but *damn,*" he murmured. "I knew it had to be Wrath. No one else could've gotten to him. How's Thorn?"

Chris and Darius exchanged a look, and he sighed. "We're all just doing what we can to keep moving," Darius said.

Noah considered him, his expression sharp, making it clear he read beneath the subtext and understood what Darius really meant. Chris cleared her throat.

"Well, that pretty much covers everything on our end,"

she said, her tone short and high as she changed the subject with absolutely no attempt at subtlety. She leaned onto the table. "What about you? What have you been up to all these years?"

Sympathy softened Noah as he leaned back in his chair and crossed his arms. "Nothing as exciting as you, that's for damn sure. Five Virtues found and three Sins destroyed." He chuckled like he still couldn't believe it and shook his head. "I guess you could say my life took a pretty straight-forward path. College, marriage, career. My 'scholarships,' generously provided by the Martyrs, paid my way through Columbia for my undergrad and law degree. Now, I work at a major corporate law firm in New York and represent some of the biggest companies in the country."

Chris raised her brows. "You're a *lawyer?*"

Noah laughed. "You can't tell me you guys didn't keep a file on me after I left."

"I'm sure Holly did," Chris admitted, "but I never read it."

"Wow," he said, feigning offense. "That's cold."

Chris's mouth pulled into a smirk. "You chose to forget I even existed. I think I get a pass."

She tried to chuckle, but Noah's face fell, and he glanced down at his hands. A pink tint warmed Chris's cheeks, and she shook her head. "I'm sorry, that wasn't fair—"

"No," Noah said. "No, you're right. I did choose that, and I got fifteen years where I didn't have to think about the consequences of that choice. You didn't, and *that* wasn't fair."

The muscles in Chris's throat tightened. Noah sighed.

"I wanted to come back sooner," he said. "When I suddenly had all those memories of my childhood, I knew I had to. Your boy Gabe's right. This *is* the right side of the fight."

He paused, glancing at his hands as he clasped them together. Chris frowned.

"Then why didn't you?"

Noah looked back up. "Because it's complicated, Chris.

My wife had our baby girl a month before all this happened. I'm a father now."

He fished his phone out of his pocket and turned on the screen. The locked display showed a stunning woman with a head of tight, black curls and a smiling six-month-old in her arms. Chris reached for the device and drew it closer, admiring Noah's family.

"She's beautiful," Darius said. "Congratulations."

"Thank you," Noah said, but his tone was hard.

"Does your wife know?" Chris asked, handing the phone back. "About any of this?"

Noah shook his head. "I didn't want to worry Simone if I didn't have to. She's been struggling with postpartum depression since Zuri was born. This would only make it worse."

Chris's eyes glistened again. "You named your daughter Zuri? That's your—"

"Mother's name," Noah finished, laughing. "Yeah. I guess some things still slipped by Alan's Programming."

They both smirked—a small, sad gesture—before Noah drew a deep breath.

"Chris, I had to reconcile a lot of things before I was ready to face this war again," he went on. "I had to make a lot of tough decisions. I know how traumatic it was being a Martyr child, losing one parent, constantly terrified you're going to get that call that the other isn't coming home. The Underground doesn't exactly offer a stable life. I can't do that to my daughter."

Chris nodded, jaw tight, as she laced her fingers on the table. She held her composure, as professional as she always was, but a shadow of emotion pulled at all her fine lines.

"I understand," she said. Despite the tremble in her hands, her voice held firm. "Cain Guttuso has been Reprogramming everyone. He's not as adept as Alan was, so you might experience some temporary side effects. Headaches, memory problems—"

"Wait," Noah cut in. "That's not what I meant. I want

to help, I *want* to remember, but I can't do it here." He opened one arm toward the door, indicating the Underground beyond it. Chris stared at him as he asked, "Is that possible?"

Her face broke into a smile so wide that it revealed a line of gums above white teeth. "Of course it is," she breathed. "We can get you a secure phone line, all of the information on the current Sins, and access to—"

Darius laughed and laid a hand on Chris's shoulder. "Let's just get him Programmed to protect the Underground first," he said. "We can figure out the rest of it later. We have time."

Chris nodded, her cheeks flushed and eyes full, and Darius saw in her the open wound of a seventeen-year-old girl who'd never had the chance to say goodbye to her best friend—a wound that was finally beginning to heal.

"You're right," she said, dabbing at the corner of her lash line. "We do."

CHAPTER SIX

Darius had never seen the hospital ward *this* empty before. The lack of energy unnerved him.

He sat at the nursing station, Lamar Verrette in the chair beside him with a marker in hand. The young Consent anxiously doodled abstract patterns across a bed of scars on his forearm. His mahogany eyes flicked toward the doors.

"How many people did they bring out this time?" Lamar asked, tilting his head in Darius's direction. Blue eyeshadow adorned his lids, striking against warm, umber skin.

"Everyone who hadn't been Reprogrammed yet," Darius said. "All of Stevie's maintenance crew, the entire hospital staff, half of our researchers. That makes…" He closed his eyes, doing the math. "Twenty-seven, twenty-eight, twenty-nine… Oh, and Kenia, so thirty."

Lamar's brows pushed up toward a stylish mop of tightly kept locs. They'd grown out in the last few months, swooping over his forehead, and he brushed them back with the end of his marker. Blue nail polish caught the light, a welcome splash of color in this white, sterile space.

"Great," he said. "And more than half of them will come in puking or feeling like their head is going to explode. No wonder it's taking them so long…"

He glanced at his phone, and Darius saw the name Naomi Mori at the top of a chat window. Naomi was one of the researchers included in this group, which explained the nervous tapping of Lamar's toes on the tile beneath the large, crescent desk. Last year, the kid's life had been completely upheaved: the Sins had shot up the club he worked in, framed him as the gunman, and come after everyone he loved. The Martyrs placed his family in protective hiding with Samira, but Naomi stuck with Lamar. Now, all they had left was each other. Darius knew what it was like to cling to those shreds.

And he knew how hard it was, worrying they'd be torn away from you, too.

"It has been a while," Darius mused aloud. "I thought they'd be back by now..."

He grabbed his device and opened the Martyrs' tracking app. Every piece of personal tech assigned to their agents included a location tag that linked to Holly's system. Over thirty individual green dots snaked down the map in a line headed south on US 9: their returning Reprogramming group. Darius zoomed out a little further. Twenty-four other TAC officers spread out among Manhattan, along with ten Recon agents and two Gray Unit operatives. They'd never had this many people placed in New York at once, and the whole situation made Darius uneasy. He continued to toggle around the streets until he found Thorn's marker in Mott Haven, just north of the Harlem River. He frowned. What was she doing out there at six p.m. on a Saturday?

Lamar's eyes flicked to Darius's screen and then to his face again, sympathy written out on his expression. Or maybe it was pity. They felt the same to Darius right now. He cleared his throat as he slipped the phone away.

"They're almost here," he said. "With everyone Reprogrammed, things can finally get back to normal."

Lamar snorted. "Define 'normal.'"

They both gazed out at the hospital ward—desolate,

devoid of sounds and souls. Darius's stomach spun in knots.

"Fewer Programming side effects," he murmured. "More violence. Now that TAC is fully operational, we should expect more run-ins with Sentries… Puppets… Sins."

Darius's voice wandered off, and the color drained from Lamar's face. The next few minutes passed in tense quiet, Lamar resuming his doodling while Darius stared at the far wall in thought. Soon, a cluster of auras came to life in the distance. Both Virtues looked toward the ceiling as Martyrs approached on the road to the gas station. When they began their descent into the earth, Darius got to his feet, and Lamar snapped the lid onto his marker before he stuck it into his breast pocket.

Elijah Harris burst through the main doors. His wife and younger son were absent, but his oldest, green-faced and sullen, trailed behind him.

"Julien," Elijah said, jutting his chin down the ward. "Take a bed. I'll be there shortly."

Julien did as he was told, not looking at Lamar or Darius as he flopped onto the nearest cot. Elijah watched him go before turning back to the two Virtues, approaching the nursing station, and breathing an exasperated sigh.

"Is he okay?" Darius asked.

"Yes," Elijah responded, crossing his arms. He'd worn slacks and a t-shirt instead of his typical scrubs and lab coat, which made him feel older, like the casual look made the gray at his temples and the lines on his face more pronounced. "He has his SATs tomorrow morning. I think he's… *embellishing* his symptoms to bump the test back."

Darius chuckled as he glanced at the kid, though he wasn't sure "kid" was the right word. Julien Harris had shot up in the last couple of years. Now, he stood at the height of a full-grown man, though the rest of his body hadn't filled in past the gangly teenager phase.

"SATs, huh?" Lamar asked. "What university is he looking at?"

"He doesn't know yet," the doctor said, "but he's talked about going to med school eventually. Says it would be nice to help out here."

Elijah laughed, but the sound felt surface-level, like a shroud to hide a deeper feeling. Darius thought back to Noah Montgomery. Jeremiah had convinced his son to leave the Underground to spare him from a life in the Martyrs. Darius wondered if Elijah might try to do the same.

"Anyway," the doctor said, clearing his throat. "Thank you for your help. I know we're a bit behind schedule…"

"It's no problem," Darius said.

"Yeah," Lamar tacked on. "It's literally our job."

Elijah gave a quick, unconvinced nod. Other Martyrs filtered into the Underground, listlessly plodding through the double doors. One of them, an Asian woman with vibrant crimson hair and a vomit bag clutched to her chest, caught Lamar's eye and forced a miserable smile.

"Yes, well, with so many other problems in the Underground, I want to waste as little of your time as possible," the doctor said, "and I worry I've asked for too much of it already. These side effects seem to be harmless and temporary, but still, I *do* appreciate it."

Lamar shrugged. "I never saw much of a point in letting people suffer, harmless *or* temporary."

The doctor's bright, gray eyes crinkled in a genuine smile. He laid a paternal hand on Lamar's shoulder. "And *that* is what makes you such a valuable addition to my team." Lamar grinned and glanced at his feet, scratching the back of his head at the compliment.

Then Elijah slapped his hands together. "Now, let's get started." He walked around the desk and grabbed a couple of medical pads. "About forty percent of the people we worked with today didn't report any problems, but they might have lingering side effects down the road. The other sixty are dealing with the same things we've already seen: nausea, headaches, tinnitus, fasciculations… We'll need to document everything. Darius, could you take the odd beds?

Lamar, you're with me…"

They moved through the ward, but today wasn't just about healing. Ever since the first TAC units reported strange symptoms after Cain's Reprogramming, Dr. Harris had taken it as an opportunity to study how Influence affected the nervous system. They recorded every detail: every minor headache, every upset stomach, every twitching muscle.

"How would you describe it?" Elijah would ask. "Sudden? Intense? Shooting?"

Lamar followed and typed out responses. Elijah explained the nature of his questions and the kind of information he was most interested in, and occasionally, he let the new Virtue take the lead.

Meanwhile, Darius worked alone. Or… he tried to. He'd just finished healing Naomi and filling out her chart when the doors swung open.

"All right," Mackenzie announced as she stormed in. Half the Martyrs startled in their cots. "Someone's fixing this goddamn migraine before I punch Nicholas Wolfe in his obnoxious, bearded face."

A chorus of uncomfortable chuckles echoed throughout the room. Naomi leapt off the cot and tossed her vomit bag into a biohazard bin as Mackenzie took the now-open spot in front of Darius.

"Mackenzie," he said, "I've still got half the room to heal."

"And I've been buried in bullshit LymeLite videos for *ten hours,*" Mackenzie argued. "I think that's earned me a teeny, tiny cut in line. Besides, if you don't do something soon, you'll be healing both my headache *and* Nicholas's broken nose."

She didn't wait for him to answer as she flung herself backward with a groan. Naomi hesitated beside the mattress, pulling her vibrant red hair into a clip at the back of her head. "Still bad, huh?" she asked.

"We're *fucked,*" Mackenzie confirmed. "There's just too

much of it out there."

She didn't look at either of them, still lying on the bed with her eyes pressed shut. Her complexion went pale beneath bright yellow bangs. Darius's heart gave a nervous flutter.

Mackenzie had been off since she got back, not that he could blame her, considering what she came back *to,* but her mood seemed even worse after setting up the Recon units in the city. A pulse of fragile faith soured in Darius's stomach. He placed a palm across her forehead and opened the gates for his healing energy. Her migraine hit him like a right hook, pounding through his skull, but that was all he felt. No other symptoms, no other aches…

No remnants of drug use or withdrawal.

Shame warmed Darius's cheeks as he pulled away. "How's that feel?"

"Loads better," Mackenzie said with a sigh. She sat up, color rushing back to her face, and caught Darius's eye. A tiny smile lifted her expression. It was a shadow of the grins Darius expected from her, but he'd take it. "Thanks. Now, back to hell."

She hopped off the cot, high-top shoes landing on the tile with a quiet *tap-tap!* Darius put a hand on her shoulder.

"Hell can wait," he said. "Those videos aren't going anywhere. You need to eat and get some rest, or that migraine will come right back. "

Mackenzie scoffed. "Wish I could, but we've got to get ahead of this before it becomes an even bigger problem."

Darius crossed his arms, glancing at Naomi. The defeated look on her face mirrored the sentiment Mackenzie had shared so bluntly.

"It's really that bad?" he asked.

Naomi let out a frustrated sigh. "Even with the video of Reverend Dickbag down, clips from it keep popping up all over the place."

"It's exactly what Holly said was going to happen," Mackenzie added. "RebelTruth keeps opening new accounts and posting parts of the interview, and it's getting traction. The tag is in the spotlight now, and other people are trying to get in on it. Getting rid of it is like holding back a hurricane with a couple of two-by-fours."

Darius shook his head. "Spotlight? What the hell is a spotlight?"

"It's what LymeLite calls the top trending topics," Naomi said. She pulled her phone out of a cross-body bag, tapped around, and held it out. A bright yellow floodlight icon sat at the top of the LymeLite homepage. Naomi clicked it and opened a drop-down list. The third item from the top made Darius's mouth run dry.

"The Seven Deadly Sins," he murmured.

"Yep," Naomi said. "Tags in the spotlight have a ton of videos and views, so LymeLite promotes them, trying to get other users to check them out and make content of their own. Usually, that's just reposting things from popular creators and adding your spin on it. Thousands of videos are being added to this tag every single day."

"What are people even posting about the Sins?" Darius asked. A huge collection of thumbnails populated the screen. Naomi selected one, turned her volume on, and the phone burst with sound.

"These demons have many unholy powers bestowed upon them by Satan himself," Weston Cunningham's voice said. "They have superior strength, superior intelligence… The people they possess become abominations, corrupting the masses through deception, temptation, and even manipulation… They can actually control your body, mind, and soul to do their bidding…"

While he spoke, the phone flashed with footage of young adults wandering down a busy New York street like zombies, not stopping for other pedestrians, cyclists, or even vehicles. Cars slammed to a stop and laid on their horns.

Darius frowned. These people didn't seem like Puppets. Their eyes were too clear, their faces contorted into forced caricatures, like a theatrical production. Every once in a while, someone broke character, giggling in the background.

He shook his head. "This isn't real."

"Of course it's not," Mackenzie confirmed. "People are just taking the piss out of it. Most of 'em, anyway. For every ten fakes, AI videos, and other bullshit like this, there's one of a terrified citizen convinced a malevolent spirit took over their nana."

Darius held his hand out, tilting his chin at Naomi to ask if he could see her phone. When she dropped it into his palm, he started flicking through more content. Nearly every item under the Seven Deadly Sins spotlight was just like this—wanna-be influencers scratching at the bottom of the barrel with bad CGI and worse acting—but others were so convincing that Darius would have a hard time knowing they were altered if he didn't have intimate knowledge of the Sins already. People lifted statues in Central Park, bent rebar in their bare hands, or sprinted up Broadway, running faster than was humanly possible.

And then, something flashed on the screen. A place Darius knew. He stopped scrolling.

"Was Richmond Bently kidnapped and killed by an extremist, far-left gang," a woman said. Her upper body was cut out of another video, overlaid on a crime scene photo of the warehouse in Hunts Point. A professional headshot of the late mayor suddenly popped up in the corner, and she gestured toward it with an open palm. "*Or* was it an underground terrorist group called the Martyrs?"

Darius's jaw dropped, and he looked up to see Naomi shrug while Mackenzie's mouth set into a scowl. The Martyrs still seated on cots craned their necks, as though trying to steal a peek. Even Lamar and Dr. Harris paused to tune in.

"Bently's death isn't the only strange incident in New York City that the media has glossed over in the last few years," the video went on, "and even social platforms are hiding the truth and banning creators that expose—"

"Fuck." Mackenzie swiped Naomi's phone out of Darius's hands. "Security has to scrub this one…"

She tapped away, brows knitted together. Lamar called out from the far side of the ward. "Did I just hear someone call us a *terrorist* organization? What in the fake news is going on over there?"

"Just losers with stupid, boring lives jumping on the conspiracy bandwagon," Mackenzie grumbled.

"This isn't really a conspiracy," Naomi added. "They're not entirely wrong…"

"Well, they're not right, either," Mackenzie snapped.

"Right or wrong doesn't matter," Darius said. "Cunningham didn't paint us in a good light. He practically implied we were the same as the Sins."

"There was no implication about it," Mackenzie said. "The fucker shouted it with his whole chest."

Suddenly, Naomi's phone pinged, and the spotlight icon spun. A notification scrolled across the top of the screen. Darius gestured to it. "What's that mean?"

"A live broadcast under this tag just reached over ten thousand viewers," Naomi said, "so LymeLite is spotlighting it."

Mackenzie smashed her thumb onto a blinking "join now" button. The video shifted, and a dissonant chorus of city sound blared from the speakers. People lined the streets, illuminated by blindingly bright lights flashing down from nearby buildings. Darius couldn't get a good sense of the location, but if he had to guess, it was somewhere in Midtown.

"Why is everyone wearing masks?" he asked.

"Halloween," Naomi said. "There are events going on all over the city. It's why Programming everyone took forever."

"Today's Halloween?" Darius asked, shocked he hadn't realized. He glanced at Mackenzie. "What, no decorating this year?"

She snorted. "If you hadn't noticed, we've got more

important shit to worry about than putting stupid pumpkins around the Underground."

A pang twinged in Darius's chest, and he shook his head. "Or maybe it's the most important thing we need to worry about right now."

Mackenzie passed him a wan smile then focused back on the phone. The camera person ran down the sidewalk like they were tracking someone or something through the crowd. All the while, comments scrolled at the bottom, so many that Darius couldn't keep up with them.

"Did anyone else see that?"

"She went toward Times Square!"

"This shit ain't real, dumbass."

"What the hell is going on?"

"Look for a chick in a bird mask."

The scene blurred with dizzying movement and jumbled noise before the footage suddenly switched to portrait mode. A young man's face filled the display. He was painted like a frog, and green makeup rolled down his forehead in beads of inky sweat.

"Holy shit, you guys," he gasped. His eyes flashed from the street ahead to his camera, and he let out a dry, manic laugh. "We were just outside The Town Hall Theater, and—ah!—and this woman behind us stopped a pedicab with her bare hands. Her bare fuckin' hands!"

He laughed again. Darius and Mackenzie glanced at one another. Her tongue ring clattered against the back of her teeth.

"Can't believe we caught it live," a different person said off-screen.

"Yeah," the frog-faced guy said. "Yeah, no joke! Just insane. We're... we're trying to find her. She might be one of those *Sins*. Possessed or something!"

"Oh, *now* you fuckin' believe me?" the other person snapped.

The cameraman grinned, his teeth bright against the green, and turned the footage back around. The street came to life. Times Square pulsed with people, as it always did, but tonight was worse than usual. The sun had set, so the only light came from car headlights and massive, digital billboards with flashing colors, creating even more chaos. More than half of the crowd dressed in costumes, some simple, others so elaborate that they hardly looked human at all. They kept coming into the frame, walking directly in front of the man with the camera and forcing him to slow down. A cold chill plunged down Darius's spine.

"Influence," he whispered, and then, he shouted. "That's… that's Influence! Watch! People are getting in his way like they're doing it on purpose."

The three of them huddled in even closer, and the room curved inward, too. Warm energy from Martyrs across the ward arched in this direction. Now that he'd recognized it, Darius couldn't see anything else. There was an unmistakable pattern. Civilians stopped abruptly, turned around, or even rushed in from behind to block the way. Darius didn't see the tell-tale giveaway of Puppets—that blank, emotionless stare—but he did recognize the signs of crowd-control Influence he'd seen Thorn use.

"There she is!" one of the men filming finally shouted. "Hey, you! Lady! Stop!"

They'd left Times Square, and the pedestrian traffic began to let up. A woman wearing a black cloak shuffled toward a brightly lit Subway station on the corner of 50th and 8th. She turned. An intricate raven mask obscured the top half of her face, adorned with sleek feathers and a pronounced beak that protruded several inches from her nose. Darius could see nothing but her chin, and even that was hard to make out in the shaky footage. Dark mesh concealed her eyes, but still, her focus snapped right to the cameraman and caught him in that dead gaze.

"What are you—"

But he stopped mid-sentence, and suddenly, the feed shook harder, like an insurmountable weight was dragging his arms down. As the view sank toward the ground, his friend shouted, "Man, what the hell are you doing? Keep record—"

The livestream ended.

Darius looked at the ceiling, sick to his stomach. He knew the names of all Seven Sins—their faces, their profiles, their histories. He'd studied them over and over again. With what little he'd seen here, he knew, without a doubt, that something supernatural was at play.

But the options for what exactly that was were terrifying.

LymeLite redirected to another video, and Darius's attention drifted back to the room. Mackenzie stared at him as though she had stolen a look inside his head and come to the same conclusion. He still asked, "What do you think?"

"I think that's the first time there's been *any* real Sin shit on this stupid app. I gotta talk to Wolfe."

She spun away, rushed down the ward, and burst into the waiting room. Her lukewarm aura didn't stop until it reached the R&D Headquarters down the hall. Darius handed Naomi's phone back. Now, it blared with a different creator's voice, talking about how the Sins were involved with her local PTA. Darius shook his head and looked up to Elijah and the still-wounded Martyrs throughout the ward.

"I'm sorry," he began, but the doctor quieted him with a raised palm.

"Go," he said. "Lamar and I can handle this."

Darius nodded. "Thank you."

Then he followed Mackenzie. As he stepped into the hallway, he grabbed his phone and sent a quick message.

"We might have a Sin situation on our hands."

The device rang instantly in his palm. Thorn's contact photo filled his screen, a radiant shot of them dancing at Raquel and Skylar's wedding eight months ago. His heart simultaneously stung and soared at the sight of it.

"Darius," Thorn said when he answered, and god, just hearing her voice made his stomach swirl. "What's going on?"

CHAPTER SEVEN

A man in frog face paint talked at the camera. No, Thorn couldn't even consider him a man. The kid had to be younger than Lamar Verrette, hardly old enough to drink legally, and she was half-convinced he was plastered right now. The frame shook in unsteady hands as he walked through Times Square and spun in a circle with his arms flung out like he could capture the entire goddamned neighborhood in a single swoop.

"They say there's *demons* in New York," he said, mockery thicker than liquor in his voice. "It *is* Halloween night, so maybe we'll run into something strange or *spooky…*"

A flicker of anger lit up Thorn's cold chest as the guy barked a piercing, draining laugh. Someone shouted beside him. "Fuck you, Rio!"

The view swiveled to another grown fucking child, this one shorter, a little less put together, with his face painted like a bear with a bad attitude.

"Mitch over here is one of the tin-foil-hat-wearing weirdos convinced all of this 'sin' shit is real," Rio narrated. Mitch threw him the middle finger.

"There!" The video paused, and Mackenzie leapt from her chair and ran to the far side of the room to point at the footage. She was so short that even on her tiptoes with her arm fully extended, she didn't come close to reaching the top edge of the screen, where the red brick facade of The Town Hall Theater faced 43rd Street. "Check out the woman in black!"

A figure wearing a long cloak and elaborate raven mask walked along the sidewalk. Dozens of pedestrians pushed around her, obscuring half of her body and making her details even more difficult to discern than the costume did.

"Who is she?" Cain asked. He'd joined them in the conference room, seated beside Darius on the right-hand side of the table while Nicholas, Chris, and Mackenzie were on the left. Thorn stood near the door so she could easily see the footage… and because her whole body simmered beneath the surface of her skin, and she needed the space to fucking breathe.

"Our person of interest," Mackenzie said.

She hurried back to her spot and arched over the table, where a tablet lay, and she smashed a finger onto its display. The video began again. While the kids continued to fuck around in the foreground, Thorn's eyes tracked the woman. She searched for *anything* recognizable in her—the way she walked, the way she stood, and even the way her masked face swiveled to take in the street. Nothing. Anyone could be shrouded behind those hooded eyes and glossy feathers. After a few seconds, the raven woman turned toward the camera. For a flickering moment, her entire body was visible over Rio's shaking shoulders, standing perfectly still. Fuck, she *looked* like a goddamned demon lurking in the shadows, waiting to strike. A chill trickled down Thorn's spine, and she crossed her arms, nails driving into her bicep.

Then, the woman stepped off the curb just as a pedicab zipped in from the far side of the frame. The driver screamed for her to move, but instead of leaping back to the sidewalk, she looked at him.

Quick as a breath, as a gasp, she grabbed the pedicab's handlebars and jerked to the left. The entire thing—bike, cart, and squealing passengers—cascaded to the asphalt in a screaming arch.

"Holy *shit!*" Mitch shouted off-screen.

Mackenzie paused the footage again. "Eh?" She stood up straight, throwing her hands into the air like this was something worthy of fucking celebration. "What do you think?"

Her focus landed directly on Thorn, and everyone else followed. Five pairs of eyes locked onto her made Thorn's stomach squirm.

"I think we're supposed to be shutting this shit down," she hissed, "not getting sucked into it."

Mackenzie's jaw dropped, and her arms followed with a defeated slump. "We're *trying* to shut it down," she defended, "but that doesn't mean we should ignore *this.*"

She pointed at the screen again, but no one followed the motion this time. They still watched Thorn, fixated on her like she was an unstable nuclear reactor. Her grip tightened, and she felt Sparkie stiffen behind her hair.

"*This* isn't anything," Thorn said. Her head tilted toward the footage. "It doesn't take superhuman strength. All you need is the right timing, the right leverage, and some goddamned luck."

Mackenzie's mouth pressed closed, and she swallowed hard. Darius cleared his throat.

"It wasn't just stopping the cab," he said. "Watch."

He gestured to Mackenzie, who hit play, and they all watched the remainder in silence. When the woman paused outside the subway station and turned around, Thorn's lips slipped open in surprise. She knew that stop.

It was the one Wrath had chased her and Darius into last spring, where she'd cornered them underground and caught Sparkie, *nearly* caught them. Thorn suddenly felt Autumn Hunt's fingers coiled around her body. She'd still be wrapped in those fingers if Darius hadn't been there. His voice drew her back.

"It looks like there was Influence at play," he said. "Why

don't you come sit down?"

Thorn's gaze flicked down to his. It was the first time she'd properly looked him in the eye since she'd stormed into the room, and she regretted it immediately. He twisted in his chair, and he smiled. He fucking *smiled*. She didn't know how to feel about it, what to *do*, but she did know she hated the way it made her stomach wind up in knots. Thorn's teeth gnashed together as she turned back to the screen and, finally, moved to the head of the table. She was an imposter here, a wolf in sheep's clothing desperately trying to protect a flock that would just run screaming if they caught a glimpse of the fangs beneath her fleece.

But they knew already. Of course they knew. They'd met the beast before, and, god *damn* it, the way they all watched her now made her want to scream. Instead of taking a chair that never should have belonged to her, Thorn stood at the front of the room and drew a deep breath. "Who would be using Influence?"

"No clue," Mackenzie said, shrugging. She was the only other person still on her feet, and she propped her hands on her hips as she watched Thorn from her place between Nicholas and Chris. "That's why we wanted to talk to you two."

She gestured to Thorn and Cain, who sat with feline poise and polish. Like Darius, he'd hardly taken his eyes off of Thorn. She did her best not to look at him, either, but she sensed his attention like an ant beneath a magnifying glass. Now, though, he considered Mackenzie with a silky stare.

"You suspect Envy might have repossessed?" he asked.

"Maybe," Nicholas said. "Or it could be Autumn Hunt hiding in plain sight."

"It's not," Thorn snapped. "I went down and scoped the scene out last night. Hunt didn't use her Influence anywhere near the area while I was there *or* before."

"She's not Envy, either, I'm afraid," Cain added. "I haven't sensed the Sin's power since its last host was killed three years ago. I don't believe it's taken a new one yet. I assure you, the first inkling I get that Envy is embodied, I will come to you immediately."

Nicholas swore, glancing back at the screen while Mackenzie's tongue piercing clicked impatiently. Chris and Darius exchanged a quick look, and she pulled her lower lip between her teeth.

"Then what's happening here?" Chris drew the tablet toward her and dragged the footage backward. She muted the sound, pressed play, and handed the device to Thorn. Both the screen across the room and the one in her palms burst with movement. "What about the other people walking right into the frame, or how the man filming dropped the camera at the end? It's too consistent to be a coincidence. Maybe she's a Forgotten Sin?"

Thorn considered what Chris said, trying to ignore the gnawing anxiety clawing its way up from her gut, a rankled monster in her chest. She couldn't deny that there was something intentional about the way people interacted, but that just pissed her off more.

"I suppose it's possible," Cain murmured with a thoughtful shrug, "though Forgotten Sins tend to *avoid* the spotlight, not seek it out. Consider Leroy Khoury—"

"She's not a Forgotten Sin," Thorn snapped, slamming the tablet onto the table with a bang that made the room startle. "She's a fucking *hoax.* "

Nicholas scoffed and crossed his arms. "That would be a pretty elaborate hoax," he countered. "This was *live*, so there's no way the original video was an AI fake or altered beforehand—and I had Holly check for signs of tampering anyway. She couldn't find any."

"Technology isn't the only way to generate false media, Wolfe." Thorn thrust a finger down at the screen, still silently running the footage in front of her. "This isn't Influence. It's goddamned *actors.* "

Nicholas opened his mouth to argue, but Mackenzie silenced him by touching his shoulder. "How do you figure that?" she asked.

"Because shit like this is all over the fucking internet already!" Thorn spat.

"Just because it's all over the internet doesn't mean that's how *this* one was made," Mackenzie interjected. "What else here says it's faked?"

"I was *in* Times Square," Thorn exclaimed. "I didn't see a *single shred* of evidence that anything supernatural was there. But do you know what we *do* have plenty of evidence of?" Her eyes cast a net around the room and were met by silence. "People on this goddamned app pretending they've been Influenced, acting like brainless drones, and outright *lying* for any scrap of attention. I can't believe we're wasting our time and resources taking this seriously."

"It's our job to take it seriously," Nicholas argued. "I know we've been focusing on damage control for almost half the goddamned year, but the whole point of the Martyrs is to track down the Sins and do whatever we can to stop them, right?"

A coil of rage twisted ravenously in Thorn's gut. She threw her hands up to release some of that pent-up energy. "This *isn't* the Sins!"

"You have exactly as much proof of that as we do that it is!" Nicholas stood now, too, like he refused to look up to Thorn anymore, and shouted at her over Mackenzie and Chris's heads. "Jesus, Thorn, this is all it is with you anymore! You come in here and yell at us about the shit you don't want to do!"

Thorn glared at him, all too fucking aware of everyone staring at her. Mackenzie shifted in front of the Former Diligence's torso, her heavily corrupted aura almost masking the fact that his torn soul didn't have one at all, as though she aimed to protect him—*from Thorn*. Chris remained seated on Mackenzie's other side, but Thorn could sense how tightly wound she was, ready to leap up if things got out of hand. Even Cain and Darius glanced at one another, speaking a secret language that Thorn didn't need to know to understand.

Her jaw clenched, and she wound her arms around her chest, horrified at the swirl of shame and anger searing up her windpipe.

Why the *fuck* was she like this?

"So it's not Wrath or Envy," Nicholas went on, this time more evenly. "Fine. But there are two *other* Sins out there. Maybe this raven woman is one of Greed's or Lust's Puppets. You said all it takes is timing, leverage, and luck to flip a pedicab, so it stands to reason that the Sins could have Influenced her from afar. Can you tell me *that's* not true?"

Thorn still didn't speak—still didn't know if she *could* speak without burning down every single bridge in this room. Nicholas raised his hands with a placating, pitying gesture.

"You could be right. It *could* be bullshit. But it also could be something real, and we can't ignore that."

They all went quiet, watching, *waiting* for Thorn to start screaming again. Sparkie buzzed between her shoulder blades, his tail a rigid line down her spine.

Darius broke the silence first. He cleared his throat as he leaned forward on the table, and the shift of focus toward him felt like a weight lifted off Thorn's lungs.

"If it's Claytor or Amoretto, we have a different problem," he said. "A Sin getting caught on camera by mistake is one thing, but if this woman was Puppetted, they were clearly trying to make her *look* like one of them. Why?"

Cain let out a sigh. "We're certainly not the only ones who have noticed what's happening on LymeLite," he pointed out. "If we've been paying attention, so have the Sins, and they *love* to take advantage of the chaos humanity creates."

"That's a good point," Nicholas said, nodding thoughtfully. "They could be feeding this beast without putting themselves in direct danger. It's not a bad strategy…"

He lowered back into his chair, and Mackenzie cast Thorn an uncomfortable look before she did the same, leaving Thorn the sole person standing. Her nails dug deeper into her arms.

"But the Sins usually cover up anything that might expose them," Chris argued. She drew a strand of blonde hair behind her ear as she looked at everyone seated around the table. "They've done just as much as we have to keep this conflict a secret, maybe even more. Why would that change now?"

"Because the Martyrs have been exposed," Darius said. "By *name.*"

Mackenzie's face paled. Her bleached bangs made her look washed out and highlighted a new speckling of freckles along her nose that Thorn hadn't noticed. "And if everyone in New York City is on the lookout for us…" she began.

"Our job just got a *lot* fucking harder," Nicholas finished.

For a moment, no one responded. Nicholas and Mackenzie looked at one another while Cain slowly shook his head. Darius glanced at Thorn. She saw him move from her periphery and caught the gleam of his eyes landing on the side of her face. At last, Chris clasped her hands—gripping so tightly that her knuckles went bone white—and sighed.

"What do you think we should do?"

Thorn's heart sank—not because of what Chris asked, but because of *who* she'd asked. Thorn turned to watch Darius just as his head swiveled in Chris's direction. The entire table followed suit, everyone looking to *Darius* for the answer, to *Darius* for guidance in moving forward.

Suddenly, Thorn felt far away, like the walls were getting closer and she was destined to be crushed within them. Her mouth slipped open as she sucked in a short, shallow breath.

Darius blinked at Chris, glanced at the others, and finally landed on Thorn. Her pulse leapt, fluttering madly in her fingertips. His lower lip dragged between his teeth.

"I think," he said at last, "we keep doing what we're doing."

Thorn's stomach flipped as Nicholas groaned and threw

a hand into the air.

"*What?* But Darius—"

"If the Sins are trying to use this situation to their advantage, this *won't* be the last time we find content like this," Darius interrupted, gesturing to the screen on the opposite wall. "And if we're digging through these videos to take them down anyway, we're more likely to catch something suspicious as soon as it goes live. We need more information *and* more time, two things we don't have right now, but holding out for more proof can give us both."

The argument on Nicholas's tongue died, and he relaxed back in his chair. The rest of them nodded together, all parts of the same machine—a machine Thorn was gumming up by simply existing in the same space as them, breathing their air and breaking their concentration. She stared at Darius, awed by how he always managed to keep a cool head, no matter what kind of hell she dragged him through. Just like Alan.

He turned back, his eyes capturing hers before she could look away.

"How's that sound?"

Awful. It *all* sounded fucking *awful.*

She didn't know how to articulate her feelings on the matter. *Darius's plan* was fine, but the consequences of learning that Nicholas could be right, that the Sins were willing to expose themselves just to bleed the Martyrs a little further, were so horrifying that she didn't even want to take the chance to find out. How much more dangerous could this city get?

But she couldn't say any of that, so instead, she nodded. Short and choppy.

"Great."

Without another word, from her, from Darius, from *anyone,* Thorn strode from the room. Five faces turned to follow her, but Thorn didn't look at them, and even Sparkie refused to come out from behind her hair to steal a final glance.

The door opened silently, gliding on its hinges like the wind into the room, where darkness swallowed it whole. Thorn flicked on the lights, and Alan's office came to life. A knot lodged in her throat.

Stepping over the threshold felt like walking into a time capsule. The Martyrs hadn't touched this place in the months since he'd passed. As far as Thorn knew, the only people who had even set foot in this room were Cain and Nicholas, slipping in to retrieve paperwork, forms, or other administrative documents before immediately slipping out again. Everything else remained exactly as it had before, a shrine to a man no one had expected to lose, not so soon… not so violently.

Visions of Alan's final moments assaulted her with blood-red intensity, and Thorn had to stop to catch her breath. Sparkie hissed on her shoulder as she grabbed the back of one of the plush chairs in front of Alan's mahogany desk, closing her eyes against images of his bloated face and broken body. Her fingers felt cold, like they were wrapped around a metal pipe instead of upholstery, like that pipe was pressed against a caving trachea, and her heart beat upon her sternum.

She was safe, she reminded herself. She was home, in the Underground, in control and alone, where she couldn't hurt anyone else.

After breathing deep for several seconds, Sparkie wound around Thorn's throat, and she stood up straight, opening her eyes again. This time, different memories flooded her—bittersweet and biting.

She stepped between the chairs, thinking back to all the midday fights and late-night talks until the comforting drone of Alan's voice practically vibrated within these walls again. When she reached the desk, she ran her fingertips along its surface. Thorn had never seen his desk dusty before, but now a layer as thick as ash after a forest fire coated everything upon it: his sleek keyboard, his razor-thin monitor, his reading glasses. Thorn lifted them, turned them around in her fingers. How many times had she watched her uncle put these on—prop them on his strong nose so he could more easily read the reports handed to him, especially *her* reports in that tight, tiny cursive? They'd been a reminder of his humanness, of the man he'd been without Wrath at the reins, a man Thorn had only met as a toddler before his falling out with her mother and subsequent deployment to Korea. They were evidence that the Sins' power couldn't touch everything—couldn't *change* everything.

Thorn opened the glasses and cleaned the lenses on her shirt. Gray patches marked the black fabric, which she didn't bother to brush away as she folded them again, now shining like Alan had always kept them. She carefully set them back into the delicate silhouette they'd left in the dust.

Her eyes traversed the room. Beside the desk, a circular imprint sank into the plush red carpeting. Thorn imagined his Familiar curled up there, watching her with those piercing blue eyes, stunningly contrasted against black fur. A closed closet door stood on the nearest wall, a casket now for Alan's coats. Behind the desk, floor-to-ceiling bookshelves and display cases towered as catacombs to thousands of years of Martyr founder history.

She walked around the desk to stand beneath those shelves. Thorn raised a hand toward a small glass box, lifted the lid, and drew out a Revolutionary-War-era pistol—the one Alexander had used in his infamous duel, the last elaborate death he'd faked before finally agreeing to join Cain in his mission to fight the Sins. It was heavy in her fingers, the metal cold, wooden handle smooth and polished.

Thorn had never met the other Martyr founders, but she remembered them all—remembered the way they'd fought to free her from Wrath, even if it meant dying at her hands. She remembered every sliced neck. Every broken skull. Every punctured heart.

And she remembered mourning them in the solitude of

her own mind while Wrath reveled.

She had been freed from the Sin for exactly one hundred years—to the *day*.

But was she truly free?

Because now the bitch was reveling again, forcing her to revisit memories long buried, deaths long put to rest. Thorn was once again left with palms coated in blood that, in a merciless stroke of irony, was never her own.

The door opened behind her. Thorn's lungs seized with a gasp as she twisted around, and Sparkie arched, spitting on her shoulder. Cain froze in the doorway, fingers still wrapped around the knob. His bright eyes flicked to the gun before landing back on her face.

"If you intend to shoot me, my dear, may I recommend a more… modern weapon?"

He smiled, and Thorn tried, god, she *tried* to return it, but her muscles seemed to have forgotten how.

"What are you doing here?" she asked, turning her back on him again to place the pistol in its case. The lid closed with a *snap!* Sparkie settled and watched Cain so Thorn didn't have to. The old Forgotten Envy slipped into the room and quietly closed the door. His Familiar pranced ahead of him and leapt onto one of the chairs. The cat's keen, orange eyes fixed Sparkie in their gaze. The lizard disappeared behind Thorn's hair.

"Looking for you, naturally," Cain said. "I must admit, this was the last place I expected to find you."

He walked between the chairs, following the same path Thorn had taken. She glanced over her shoulder as he considered the trails her fingers etched into the dust on Alan's desk. The dark wood glistened, bright and shining, wherever she had touched. He looked up to her again. His lips pulled down.

"Why *are* you here?"

Thorn's throat tightened, and she swallowed hard. Cain didn't move, standing just on the far side of the desk—exactly where *she* had stood so many times over the decades.

He squeezed his hands into the front pockets of his gray slacks casually, like this was just another day, just another conversation, but Crescendo's flicking tail betrayed his concern.

At last, Thorn sighed. "Trying to figure out how he did it."

She turned back to the wall behind her—back to the books and relics and mementos. One stood out to her. An old, black-and-white photograph of a young soldier fresh out of World War II. It was tucked between an ancient Chinese vase and a volume of Indian fables. She picked it up.

Alan was barely recognizable here, wearing his US Army dress uniform, his black hair cropped short, and his young cheeks freshly shaven. The only thing that looked like the man she knew at all was his eyes—deep and haunted, but not because of the Sins. Because of the *war*.

Most of the items in Alan's office hadn't belonged to him, but instead to the other founders. He hadn't had much to bring to the table. No wealth. No status. No *power*.

But he'd had *drive*. Ambition. That had been enough.

Thorn stroked a thumb against the glass, clearing the dust from Alan's face. Without his signature goatee and shoulder-length black hair, his resemblance to Donovan was striking. Heartbreakingly so. The older her son had grown, the more he looked like her uncle. Thorn had always suspected Alan grew it all out to help ease the pain of losing him, so she'd never turn the corner and look into those dead eyes, but she'd never actually asked. Now, she'd never have the chance.

"How he did what, my dear?" Cain asked quietly.

"How he did *this*." Thorn spun around and opened an arm to the room. "How he ran the Underground. How he kept the Martyrs together. How he kept *himself* together." Her voice cracked, and she clenched her jaw. She placed a hand on the back of Alan's desk chair and closed her eyes as her aching, empty chest flared.

Cain did nothing more than watch her, mouth pressed

firmly shut, like he was afraid that he would spook her if he spoke—like she was as fucking fragile and delicate as a wounded doe fighting for her life on the side of the road after being struck by a car. She shook her head and forced her teeth apart to say, "He had it *all* figured out. I thought, maybe, just being in his space, I could figure some of it out, too."

More silence. Cain's head dipped into a nod. His eyes never left Thorn's face.

"Well…" he began, "did you?"

Thorn scoffed. "No. There's nothing in this room but ghosts."

She looked down at the old photograph still clutched in her hand, into Alan's young, hallowed eyes, before she placed the frame onto the shelf again. This time, she kept it at the front where it wouldn't be so easily overshadowed.

"That may be true," Cain said, "but even ghosts are known to share their secrets every now and then."

"Not this one," Thorn muttered.

"Don't be so sure."

Thorn glanced over her shoulder, frowning as Sparkie considered Cain, too. He hadn't moved, but Crescendo's tail continued to flick back and forth. At Thorn's confused look, Cain tilted his head toward the desk.

"Bottom right drawer."

Her eyes dropped down. Alan had always kept this one locked, but now a pair of tiny, silver keys dangled from the handle. It opened with the thunk and heavy glide of a filing cabinet. Inside, binders and folders were organized in an immaculate, color-coded pattern, but sitting at the top, laid out flat, was an envelope. Thorn's name was neatly written in Alan's old, familiar script. Her stomach dropped as she lifted it.

"What's this?"

Cain shrugged, his nerves more apparent now—not in him, but in the way Crescendo craned his neck, alert on Thorn's face.

"A letter for you," Cain said. "I found it when I was collecting personnel forms for the security team."

Thorn's brows drew together, and she swallowed a mouthful of nothing, like maybe it would calm the swirling in her gut.

"Why didn't you tell me?"

Her voice shuddered with fear, with fury… Honestly, Thorn didn't know which. Cain hesitated before he took a small step forward. The desk separated them, but he was still close enough that Thorn could have reached out to wrap a hand around his throat if she'd felt so inclined. The thought unsettled her, so she took a step back.

"I suppose I was worried you weren't ready," Cain answered at last. "I'm sorry. That wasn't my place."

Thorn looked at the envelope, felt the texture of it in her fingers and the weight in her palm. It was thick, as though Alan had stuffed his entire life's story beneath the fold. There was no seal, and it opened easily, hungry to be seen. A knot wormed its way into Thorn's gut.

"Did you read it?" she asked.

Her eyes flashed up to Cain. He shifted awkwardly, and Crescendo crouched down, like he could somehow blend into the chair's burgundy upholstery.

"I did."

Thorn nodded, the motion stiff. "Will it help?"

Cain sighed. "There is nothing Alan could have told you, Thorn, living or dead, to prepare you for your role leading the Martyrs now." He pulled a hand free from his pocket and indicated the envelope held tightly in hers. "But it *will* answer some of your questions."

For several long seconds, they watched each other, Cain as patient as ever while Thorn's nails tapped against the paper. Sparkie slithered behind her hair, pressing against her spine as he tried to shrink into something small and untouchable. At last, Thorn drew the letter free. It was longer than she'd expected—pages upon pages of Alan's bold script, handwritten perfectly in jet-black ink. She unfolded it, and her heart ached at her name written at the top of the first line.

Thorn,

> *I do not know the circumstances that have led us to my passing and you reading this letter. It unsettles me to think that I will be gone if this ever reaches your hands. There is so much I need to tell you, but first and most importantly, I must express one thing: I love you. I know I said it far too infrequently in life, but perhaps saying it once more in death can ease the pain of this moment.*

Those circumstances rocked through Thorn like an earthquake. She smelled the metallic stink of blood, felt the vibration of a metal pipe striking bone rumble up her arms, and heard Alan screaming her name. Practically crying it. Praying for salvation. Sparkie screeched as her breath whisked out of her lungs, and her hands began to shake so badly that she hardly managed to fold the message and shove it back into the envelope.

Cain rushed around the desk as Crescendo leapt upon it, closing in on Thorn, cornering her between the past and present without a way out. She backed away, her spine aligned with the shelving, and lifted a trembling hand. They both froze, staring at her. She forced a short laugh that didn't stop the corners of her eyes from stinging.

"Looks like you were right," Thorn said, her voice low and seedy. She threw the letter back into the drawer and kicked the thing closed so hard that a thin layer of dust fluttered from its surface. "I'm not ready."

To read the letter. To run the Underground. For any of it.

CHAPTER EIGHT

Darius hadn't expected the woman in the raven mask to create so much chaos, but in the days that followed, that's all it was.

Within twenty-four hours, clips from the LymeLite footage took over the internet, the tabloids, and even the mainstream media. Despite the Martyrs' best efforts to take it all down before things got out of hand, their team of twenty just couldn't get ahead of millions of viewers. Influencers leapt on the trend, whether to denounce the supernatural or support it. News anchors laughed about this latest unhinged fad ripping through the city. And civilians? They couldn't stay away from the fun. More videos surfaced—with more lousy editing, more AI fakes, and more bullshit. Soon, their feeds were clogged with shitty copycats in cheap costumes. Black birds popped up on the subway, strode through Central Park, and even struck poses in front of New York's most overcrowded tourist attractions. It started to look like Thorn was right: the raven woman was nothing but an elaborate hoax.

Then, exactly one week after that first encounter, she appeared again.

She'd been spotted in Foley Square by the Triumph of

the Human Spirit. The granite monument pierced into the air like a towering, black blade, and the woman stood rigid in her elaborate mask and hooded cloak. She was easy to differentiate from her copycats. Her disguise matched the first video exactly, and unlike most of the fakes, this one had been a live stream, which meant there was no fancy editing, no artificial intelligence, *nothing* to explain the strange behavior—not just in *her* but in *other people*. New York's crowds completely avoided the Raven, walking in a perfect, twenty-foot circle around her as though they were afraid to approach... or were being Influenced not to. The closer they got, the less they'd look at her, sometimes looking *through* her like she wasn't there at all. A sinking feeling made Darius's stomach heavy.

But she did nothing more than turn, stare ominously at the camera, and take off running in the opposite direction. Just like the first time, the Raven moved through bustling pedestrians without any resistance, and again, people moved in to slow any attempt at following her. That night, Nicholas had cornered Thorn, still reeking of cigarette smoke on her way through the parking garage with this new evidence, insisting something supernatural was at play, but she still demanded "more proof."

Seven days later, in the dreary monotony of the Research and Discovery Headquarters, a gasp broke the silence.

"There she is!" Parker Boseman's voice rang throughout the room. She looked over her shoulder, eyes wide, tight ringlets wild around her tawny face. "Nicholas, I got her again!"

Everyone leapt to their feet, abandoning their workstations along the wall or the circular tables in the center of the room to crowd in around Parker's computer. Darius and Nicholas took up two desks at the back—Nicholas at his own and Darius using the one Mackenzie usually worked at—and they glanced at one another before Nicholas stood up.

"Cast it, Parker," he called. He'd mounted a large display

onto the wall beside the door for moments like this, and he turned it on as Parker tapped a few keys. The screen filled with panicked movement, like something you would expect to see in some crappy, found-footage horror movie.

The noon sun blared overhead on a street corner. A nagging familiarity itched at the back of Darius's mind with long, painful nails, but he couldn't quite place where he'd seen that location before. As the camera view zoomed in toward busy traffic, speakers on either side of the screen crackled with erratic noise. Nicholas winced as he muted the sound, and his team settled back into their chairs to watch. The entire room held its breath.

A black-clad figure stood in the middle of the road. She was unmistakable. The iridescent feathers on her mask glistened like a fresh oil slick on the blacktop, and dense mesh covered the eyes, making it impossible to get any sense of the person behind them. The sun shone off the black beak like it was carved from volcanic glass.

"What the hell is she doing?" Nicholas murmured.

The Raven didn't move, didn't so much as tilt her head. Vehicles drove around her like she wasn't there. They cut into other lanes or onto the concrete walkway in the center of the sprawling intersection, tires hopping the curb to get enough space to pass without touching her. The cloak billowed at her ankles with every near miss.

Then, her head turned, just an inch, barely enough to count as turning, and those blank eyes connected right with the camera.

And she ran. Cars slammed on their brakes in a synchronized motion as she darted through them. Before she vanished on the far side of the road, her hood slipped, revealing a head of yellow-blonde hair pulled into a French twist above her slender neck.

The screen flickered, but the Martyrs stopped watching. Faces swiveled around to stare at Nicholas and Darius. Nicholas shook his head, mouth set into a firm frown behind his beard.

"Dan," he said, baby blue eyes slashing to Daniel Park, his research lead. "Get me anything you can on who posted this. Name, address, goddamned birthday. I want to look into them. Parker, send the source to Holly, then get me the location. Everyone else, track down other videos or photos from this incident. Someone else might have caught something. They'll start uploading any second, and I want to see *every* angle we can."

The room fluttered to life. Nicholas fell into his chair again, but instead of getting to work, he leaned back. His eyes narrowed as he stared at the ceiling, perturbed and thoughtful. Darius got to his feet, walked over, and leaned a hip against Nicholas's desk.

"What are you thinking?" he asked as he crossed his arms.

Nicholas chewed on his cheek for a moment. "I'm thinking two times is a coincidence, but three's a pattern." He looked at Darius and breathed a frustrated sigh. "There's *clearly* something going on here, and I need Thorn to take this fucking seriously."

Darius's stomach dipped. "She will," he said. "Give her time."

Nicholas's expression sharpened. "We don't *have* time, Darius. Right now, she only sees what she wants to see, and *this*—" he gestured to the screen, now replaying the footage "—is *not* something she wants to see. I need more than weird behavior and assumed Influence. I need concrete fucking evidence connecting this to the Sins."

He groaned, turning back to his computer, and Darius watched him with a frown. Parker's energy approached them. She cleared her throat.

"I sent the link to Holly and found the address. Broome and Allen Street, Lower East Side."

The memory hit Darius like a runaway vehicle, punctuated with the sounds of gunfire and screaming. His heart lodged in his throat as he murmured, "Oh, man. That's where Eva died."

Nicholas froze as though he, too, were suddenly thrown two years back in time. Guilt darkened his expression. Eva Torres had bled out on that street corner because Darius had gotten hurt, and Nicholas focused on healing him first, despite Thorn's insistence that Eva wouldn't make it. The former Diligence opened his mouth to speak, but Parker cut him off with a gasp.

"That's it," she said, almost to herself. "That's it! I thought it might be, but this latest attack didn't fit the pattern… well, I didn't *think* it fit, but it does! I—"

"Parker," Nicholas cut in. He raised a hand to catch her focus, and her jaw snapped shut. "What the hell are you talking about?"

Her cheeks flushed. "Right. Sorry. It's just… I think I found the proof you're looking for. All these locations—the subway stop by Times Square, Federal Plaza, *that* intersection…" She pointed at the large display behind her back. "They're *all* places we've run into the Sins!"

Nicholas's eyes shot wide. *"Are* they?" He swiveled back to his computer and typed madly. Seconds later, he swore under his breath and got to his feet. His face was pale beneath a splattering of freckles across the bridge of his nose. "Holy shit. I think it's worse than that. Dan!" Nicholas turned to the room, and Daniel's head popped up. "Can you pull up an image of the subway stop on 8th and 50th?" The street view filled the screen, and Nicholas passed Darius a bleak look. "What can you tell me about *this* location?"

Darius frowned. "That's where Thorn and I went when Wrath was—"

Nicholas snapped, pointing a finger at the center of Darius's chest. "Exactly! These aren't just locations of Martyr and Sin conflict… They're locations with conflicts that involved Wrath and *Thorn.*"

A numb wave poured down Darius's spine, and he laid a hand on Nicholas's desk to keep himself steady. Everything he knew about Thorn's history with Autumn Hunt sat like a lump of coal in his gut. Nicholas watched him, concern echoed in his expression.

The second Thorn disengaged her motorcycle's electric engine, a voice in the darkness made her jump.

"You're back late."

Thorn twisted around, left hand instinctively reaching for a knife in her thigh pocket. Nicholas walked toward her from the loading area outside the glass double doors. Even before he'd sacrificed the Virtuous part of his soul to destroy Sloth, Nicholas had been one of the few people in the Underground without an aura she could sense, but Thorn wasn't used to him being so goddamned stealthy. She swore under her breath.

"Jesus Christ, Wolfe," she snapped as she pulled her helmet off and locked it onto her handlebars. "Haven't you learned your lesson about sneaking up on people in the garage?"

He raised a brow. "Are you going to smash my face into your bike's dash?"

"I might," she grumbled, "if you're going to wait around in the dark for me to show up."

She slid off the seat and threw him a hot look. Nicholas crossed his arms.

"I didn't wait around in the dark," he said. "I had Holly track your phone's location and let me know if you started heading this way. I didn't expect it to be after midnight, but I guess I should just be glad you came home at all."

He didn't budge, his expression a solid wall of irritating tenacity that made Thorn want to both hit and hug him. The condescension curled her fingers into fists, but at least he wasn't fucking afraid of getting on her bad side like everyone else.

"So you're stalking me," Thorn replied, striding past him as she made her way into the waiting room. Sparkie peeked his head out of her satchel to watch Nicholas slip through at her heels.

"I'm doing my job," he said.

"Keeping tabs on when I come and go from the Underground is *not* your job, Wolfe."

"No, but figuring out what the Sins might be up to is. Your office or mine?"

They'd reached the hallway to the directors' offices, and Thorn turned around as Nicholas paused outside the door with his name upon it. He had a hand on the knob already, as though he was prepared to make the decision for her. At this hour, the lights were dimmed to barely brighter than a full moon on a cloudless night, so Thorn couldn't make out all of Nicholas's expression, but even so, she could tell it was serious. Her throat ran dry.

"The Raven?" she asked, her voice suddenly loud and brittle.

Nicholas nodded.

Thorn stood still a moment longer, her legs leaden beneath her, and Nicholas waited—just fucking waited—until she finally took a step toward him. His door opened, and he turned on the light, extending an arm to welcome Thorn ahead of him.

Before Nicholas became the director of the research portion of "Research and Discovery," the job and this office belonged to Lina Brooks. Then, just over a year ago, the Sins had found their memorial garden. Decades of Martyr memories had been burned to the ground, reduced to ash. They'd destroyed Cain's greatest artistic masterpiece, desecrated Donovan's grave, and ended Lina's life in a plume of fire and smoke. Thorn remembered that day vividly. The nauseating smell of charred human flesh saturating the back of their SUV. Lina's skin, melted and mangled, slipping not against but *through* Thorn's hands. Her energy blinking out, that comforting, cold sensation of a human soul disappearing seconds before Darius had been able to heal her.

Of all the losses Thorn had experienced here, that one had filled her with more guilt than any other. She thought nothing else could ever compare.

Until Alan.

Thorn stepped into Nicholas's office like a specter. Her body felt distant from her brain as she paused in the center of the room, and Sparkie climbed to her shoulder. When Lina had claimed this space, it had been cramped and cluttered, boxes and piles and shelves of papers, binders, photographs, and artifacts giving the warm, passionate air of a historian hard at work.

Nicholas changed everything. Lina's beloved books had been moved to the R&D Headquarters, her files digitized and archived, and her wooden furniture replaced with early-twenty-first-century minimalist pieces. A sleek, glass desk sat in front of the back wall, which was lined with floor-to-ceiling shelves. The chairs before it were firm and uncomfortable, the decor sharp and angular, and an abstract blue and white rug made Thorn feel like she was standing on an iceberg.

The warmest thing in the room was a photograph beside Nicholas's computer monitor, showing a much younger, clean-shaven version of himself with his sister, who may as well have been his clone with the same blonde hair and blue eyes. They sat on either side of a much older woman, who had no hair at all beneath the sky-blue scarf wrapped around her head. Thorn stared at the picture as Nicholas's door clicked shut behind them.

"Have a seat."

Thorn didn't, instead crossing her arms as he walked to his desk and grabbed a file from its surface. She watched him flick open the folder and leaf through the pages until he found what he was looking for. He glanced back, saw her still standing, and sighed. Without a word, he flashed the paper toward her. Thorn snapped it out of his hands and began to read.

By the time she finished, the weight of every word, every *sentence*, dragged her down until the backs of her legs hit one of the chairs. Her lungs stuttered, and she shook her head.

When she looked up, Sparkie's eyes remained glued to the report, his body still and rigid. A grim look settled into the lines of Nicholas's face.

"Is a connection to *Autumn Hunt* proof enough for you?"

Thorn shook her head. "It *can't* be Wrath," she said, furious at her fear response to that name. Then, she was *just* furious. Her nose curled. "I haven't felt her use her Influence in *any* of these!"

She gestured toward the sheet, where Sparkie reread the section tying the Raven's appearances to battles Thorn and Wrath had fought. She remembered all of them. The blast of rifle fire as she stopped the Sin from blowing her people to pieces. The wailing crowd at the bottom of the courthouse steps. The packed subway, with Wrath's fist closed so tightly around her Familiar's ribcage that Thorn hadn't been able to breathe. She could barely breathe now, and she took a moment to steady her nerves, willing the fire burning up her throat to calm down and recede into her chest.

Nicholas threw his arms up in an exasperated shrug. "I don't know what to tell you," he said, "but this can't be a coincidence. Influence or not, Autumn Hunt is *clearly* involved."

"But *how?*" Thorn exploded to her feet again, one hand tight around a crumpling paper while the other pulled through her hair so hard it hurt. "And *why?* Who the fuck *is* this woman?"

"Thorn—"

"It doesn't make sense!" she cut in. Thorn spun away from Nicholas, pacing at the far end of the room. Nicholas came toward her, but she ignored him, and Sparkie let out a cry. "If she's trying to send me a message, why not just do it herself? Why use this fucking stranger? Why play these goddamned games? Why—"

"Thorn!"

This time, Nicholas laid a palm on her shoulder. The contact startled her. She twisted toward him, and he grabbed her again, with both hands this time. Thorn tore out of his grip, glaring at him, as Sparkie's wings quivered behind her head.

"*This* is why," Nicholas said. He gestured toward her. "Wrath is under your skin. Don't let her do this to you."

Thorn's hands curled, clenched so tightly that her nails pressed deep into the palms of her gloves. After a moment, Nicholas pointed at the page bunched up in her left fist.

"There is an obvious pattern," he went on, like Thorn's little outburst had never happened. "Not only is she showing up in places relevant to you and Wrath, every appearance happens exactly seven days apart. We ran the information through our computer system and found a list of potential targets from incidents over the last few years. Did you get that far?"

She had, but by the time she'd reached the end of the report, everything had been gray and fuzzy. Thorn forced her grip to loosen, stretched the paper flat, and looked at the bottom again.

A handful of locations stared up at her, begging Thorn to relive every bloody moment, and she did. The attacks on the Williamsburg Bridge Street Market after Wrath had learned Darius was still alive. The bomb beneath that car in a housing authority parking lot. The garage in Queens, full of smoke and soot and screaming.

The warehouse in Hunts Point—

"Her first three appearances were in Manhattan," Nicholas said. His voice sliced through the fog in Thorn's mind. She glanced back at him, her heart lodged so high in her throat that she felt like she was choking. "So I think it's safe to focus there first. That narrows us down to two locations. If we narrow further, only looking south of 59th, there's one."

Thorn drew a shallow breath. "Darius's market."

Nicholas nodded. "I want to send people down there next Saturday to keep an eye on the place. See if we can't figure out what's going on, or maybe she'll be somewhere else or not show up at all and prove my whole theory is a load of shit."

Nicholas crossed his arms, watching Thorn with every ounce of confidence that his theory *wasn't* a load of shit. She considered the report again, smoothing the wrinkles she'd crushed into the paper. Her stomach felt just as mangled.

She wanted to refuse, to tell Nicholas to fuck off and that they weren't going to feed this delusion more than they already had, but it was getting harder and harder to deny that *Thorn* was the delusional one. Strange behavior. Signs of Influence.

And strings tying this whole thing to *Autumn Hunt.*

"Okay," she said at last. Nicholas visibly relaxed. "Organize a meeting first thing in the morning, and we'll start making a plan."

Nicholas smiled, but Thorn felt like she'd swallowed a vat of hot, rancid oil, and she rushed out of the office before it all surged back up. That night, Thorn lay wide awake, battling a plague of memories and horrors that burrowed deep into her consciousness and refused to let it rest.

Thorn was awake for nearly seven days. Sleep came in bursts, bits and pieces sneaking in just often enough to keep her from feeling completely strung out by the time she walked onto the market Saturday morning. Bustling crowds pulsed around her, and Thorn's aching eyes narrowed as she looked out at the sprawling landscape of slipshod stalls, tattered tarps, and frazzled faces. Though the sun was high, the Williamsburg Street Bridge cast a long shadow that the masses huddled under, collecting into a thick, writhing organism. Vehicles droned by above their heads, an icy river of never-ending human auras that was completely unaware of the sea of less fortunate souls beneath it.

She paused at the edge of the underpass. Smoke and smells and sounds filled the area with a disjointed blur of sensations. The community here was just as distinct. All ages. All ethnicities. All stuck in this hell together. Thorn spotted tired old men missing teeth, exhausted women with empty carts and emptier stomachs, and children, barefoot and broad-smiled, bobbing between booths. People just like Darius, guilty of the unforgivable crime of being born poor, as far as the eye could see. For a moment, Thorn was struck with a surreal sense of déjà vu—like she'd traveled back three years and stepped foot into this world for the first time.

It was *so* fucked up.

Despite being deeply aware of the evils facing humanity, and the evils instilled by humanity itself, even Thorn was privileged enough that she could completely forget places like this existed. But then again, wasn't that the goddamned point? Out of sight, out of mind. The rest of the city was so caught up in its own battles, fighting against an impossible cost of living, dwindling support services, and laws that threatened their most basic human rights, that they ignored the market entirely. It was too fresh, too close of a reminder of what would happen to *them* if they didn't play the game right.

This was where people went when everything else had finally failed them—when the world finally got sick of pretending it cared long enough to hold them above water. Instead, it forced them under, face-first, hoping their lungs filled quickly, not out of mercy but because a floating body was one it didn't need to feed.

New York City was corrupt, abandoning the market long ago, leaving it to sink or swim with a concrete weight strapped around its feet.

Thorn's teeth gnashed together, and she closed her eyes to calm the beast raging at the injustices she was powerless to stop. The ebb and flow of human souls washed around her. Anxiety tickled up her spine.

"Three TAC units in position." Gabe's voice crackled through the com piece in her ear, practiced and professional. "We have people placed at Pitt, FDR Drive, and Columbia. Thorn, where are you at?"

"I'm already in," she answered as she pulled her phone out and loaded her map. Seven dots blinked from the screen: a larger blue one, marking where she was near the center of the market, and three green pairs highlighting the Fourth, Fifth, and Twelfth Response Units. Sparkie flew in circles above them, but the bridge obscured most of his vantage point and made it hard to see where her people were located. Her stomach swirled, unsettled. "Everyone ready?"

"Ready as ever," Conrad Carter said, his voice gruff. Thorn could hear the subtle, lopsided cadence to his speech caused by the pinch of chewing tobacco he had perpetually jammed between his lower lip and gums. "What're we lookin' for exactly? Some bitch in a bird mask?"

"A *woman* in a raven mask," Deidre Cummins corrected, eliciting a scoff from Carter that Thorn knew was accompanied by a melodramatic eye roll. "Other people will probably notice her first, so keep an eye out for weird behavior."

Carter snorted. "What classifies as *weird* down here? I mean, look around! This whole goddamned place is full of weirdos…"

A spark filled Thorn's mouth with fire as she glanced across the market again—at the unwell, unhappy, and unaccommodated masses. "Shut the fuck up, Carter," she hissed. "We're not here for your social commentary. We're here to work, so *work*, and keep your shitty opinions to yourself."

He grumbled some bullshit apology before the line went quiet, and Thorn shook her head. She'd wanted to handle this alone, but Chris insisted on sending her three most experienced TAC teams—Gabe's, Carter's, and Cummins's—not only to cover more ground but to make sure Thorn had backup close at hand. On top of that, additional units patrolled the nearby neighborhoods. They couldn't take chances, Chris had said. Not if all of this could be connected to Wrath.

But that was exactly why Thorn *hadn't* wanted to take

chances. More Martyrs meant more opportunities for Hunt to hurt someone and more people Thorn had to protect. She drew a breath.

"Our goal today is reconnaissance," she said. "Wrath's Influence has not been associated with this person, so if there *is* Sin involvement, it's either Greed or Lust pulling the strings. Keep an eye out for Anton Claytor and Connor Amoretto. If you see them, *do not engage*. Is that understood?"

A chorus of "yes, ma'am" sounded in Thorn's ear, but no amount of confirmation would make her feel safer here. She silenced her mic and put her phone away before her hands went through a quick inventory pat—touching the gun strapped to her back, the folded knife pressed inside her thigh pocket, and a sonic disruptor device in her satchel—before she zipped her kevlar bike jacket up to her throat, swallowed hard, and headed deeper into the market.

Normally, when Thorn moved through the city, all it took to go unnoticed was lifting her hood, sloping her shoulders, and avoiding eye contact. That wasn't true in the Williamsburg Bridge Street Market. Thorn drew attention by simply *existing*. Faces flashed in her direction as Thorn walked between stands, each full of suspicion at this *stranger* in their space. They recognized her, not personally, but as a concept. She was too healthy. Too clean. Too put-together. It didn't take long for the community here to walk around her, like they were afraid of catching whatever she carried.

The morning slowly shifted to afternoon. Thorn wandered through the market crowds, searching for something even more out of place than she was. Somehow, this was more difficult than looking for a Virtue. Three years ago, Thorn at least had a name to go off of. A vague idea of what the man she was searching for was doing here. And a motivator—to reach him before the Sins did.

Now, though, she didn't want to be here, and she hoped, god, she fucking *prayed* they came home empty-handed.

Thorn sighed as she reached the same intersection she'd

initially walked in from, shoving her hands into her pockets. She'd circled the whole market three times now, drawing more ire from the locals with each loop until Thorn was positive none of them would even notice a woman walking around in a goddamned mask because they were too busy focusing on her. The rest of her TAC teams weren't quite as obvious. Thorn had crossed their paths a handful of times, and even she hadn't immediately noticed they weren't a part of the fabric here.

She wanted to believe it was the oversized hoodies they wore to obscure their bulletproof vests, but part of her knew *she* was the problem. An ink stain on a vibrant quilt of multicultural pattern. Whispers and stares chased her down the street. Even the city rodents, who feared neither Heaven nor Hell, seemed leery of her. Rats scurried from her path, pigeons fluttered away, and a giant, black bird peered at her from the orange leaves of a nearby tree. It let out a throaty caw, and Thorn wanted to laugh. She *had* come looking for a raven, hadn't she?

Suddenly, a tickle raced up her back. She turned around and glanced at a nearby fruit stand. A Middle Eastern man spoke in Urdu to a customer, but the moment his eyes met hers, his voice stuttered to a stop, and he stared with the full-face shock of a gazelle spotting a lioness lurking in the grass. A woman approached him, and he gestured in Thorn's direction. Her mouth ran dry, and she hurried across the walkway.

"It's about time," a chilly voice said, the very sound of it pouring ice water down Thorn's spine. "I was starting to think you'd stand me up."

She twisted around, and she froze.

A woman leaned against a light pole not five feet away— short, slender, simple, wearing an off-white blouse above black slacks and closed-toed flats. Her yellow hair wound into a French twist behind her head, so perfectly pinned that not a single strand frayed out of place. She drew a large tote across her shoulder and pulled it open, revealing an intricate, feathered mask and velvety black cloak.

Thorn's lips slipped open, not because she'd found the Raven…

But because she didn't have an aura.

The woman gave a placid, idle smile.

"Hello, Thorn."

CHAPTER NINE

All Thorn could do was stare, acutely aware of the shock tightening her expression. The woman's smile claimed more of her face. Her eyes crinkled, and lips cracked to expose two rows of too-white teeth. A voice in the back of Thorn's mind tried to reason with her—tried to tell her not to panic, that Chris had been right and this could be a good thing—but even as that voice whispered, warning sirens drowned it out. Thorn reached for the pistol behind her back.

The Raven's crystalline blue eyes snapped to her hand, but that porcelain smile didn't fade.

"Oh, there's no need for that," the woman said. She twisted slightly to the right and hiked up her pant leg, confirming something Thorn already knew.

The *Peccostium* stood out against the woman's ankle, sharp black against pale, rosy skin.

Thorn finally found her voice. "You're a—"

"Walk with me," the woman cut in before the words had escaped Thorn's mouth. "People are starting to stare…"

She glanced to the side, where the man at the fruit stand was completely fixated on Thorn. The Raven passed her a shrewd look, tilted her head in the opposite direction, and turned away. For a few seconds, Thorn was caught, captivated, her mind scrambling to catch up. Finally, she tapped the coms piece in her ear. "I found her," she murmured to her team. "Close in on my location, but keep your distance. I don't want her to know I'm not here alone."

Gabe's voice crackled through. "Wait, *what?* Are you talking to her?"

"I will be," Thorn answered. "I'm muting my speakers, but keep the line open and record *everything*. Got it, DuPont?"

"Yes, ma'am."

Thorn touched her earpiece again, silencing all feedback from the attending TAC units, and rushed after the Raven before she disappeared into the crowd. Thorn kept at a distance as the woman led her toward a food court at the center of the market. Once she'd started walking, the blonde didn't even glance back to make sure Thorn followed, as though she *knew* Thorn would be incapable of doing anything else. They reached an open parking lot, one of the few places not tucked beneath the bridge above, encircled by food trucks and stalls, blustering lines of starving people, and an elaborate mosaic of mouth-watering smells. The woman found a free table and took a seat. The metal bench groaned under her weight. Thorn didn't join her, content instead to stand six feet away.

"Who are you?"

The Raven considered her for a patient moment before clicking her tongue against her teeth and gesturing to the seat across from her.

"Sit down, Thorn," she insisted. "We have a *lot* to talk about."

Thorn hesitated for a second longer. Sparkie spiraled overhead, keen eyes searching the masses for familiar faces. He soon spotted six: all three TAC teams set up on separate ends of the lot, far enough that their energy was lost in the swarm of cold souls but near enough that Thorn would have been able to make eye contact with any one of them had she dared look away from the Raven. Her gaze never left the woman's face, not even as she finally lowered herself to the table.

The second her thighs hit the bench, the Raven beamed.

"Ooh, I am so excited we finally have a chance to meet," she said with girlish glee. Her feet tapped on the blacktop. An old German accent flowed from her tongue like the aftertaste of something that once held a much stronger flavor. It reminded Thorn of Cain—of age and experience and years upon years of life. "I feel like I'm in the presence of royalty. The way you and your Martyrs are taking on the Sins is… extraordinary."

The Raven's eyes sharpened, and Thorn drew her shoulders back.

"You know a lot about me," she stated, trying hard to keep the nerves in her belly from crawling out of her mouth and weakening her words, "but I don't even know your name."

The woman scoffed, flicking her wrist like she was swatting a housefly.

"Names are so much less important than legacy," she said, but all the same, she took the hand she'd just used to wave Thorn's worries away and reached across the table. "Edith Froschlin." Thorn grabbed her palm. Edith's fingers tightened with a bone-grinding grip, and she grinned. "It's a pleasure."

Thorn shivered. She wasn't sure that's the word she'd use. Her arms wrapped around her chest.

"How *do* you know so much about me?"

Edith's eyes glistened, and she pressed her lips together in a smug smirk—the kind one might share with a close friend who was in on a joke the rest of the room didn't understand. A smirk that simply said, "You know the answer already."

Thorn's stomach churned like she'd swallowed an ashtray of spent cigarettes. She rose back to her feet, but they felt distant beneath her.

"You work for them?" Thorn breathed.

"Sit down," Edith said. "If you don't *control yourself*, you'll draw the wrong kind of attention." She threw a look around the food court before settling on Thorn's face again. "I don't know about *you*, but *I'd* rather Autumn Hunt never find out we spoke today. That self-indulgent cow likes to think she's in charge, and it's better for us all if she *continues* to think that. I don't need to deal with her incessant *whining*."

She rolled her eyes, her head tilting back dramatically as she raised one hand and mimed a blabbering mouth. Thorn continued to stare, tongue dry and tacky.

"You know Autumn Hunt?" she managed to ask.

"Sweet girl," Edith said with a smile, "I know everyone. *Sit.*"

She indicated the bench again by dipping her chin so slightly that she may as well have not moved at all. Thorn got the distinct impression that this wasn't a request so much as it was an order—from a woman who *expected* her orders to be followed. The part of her that hated being told what to do wanted to throw punches instead, but violence had a nasty habit of stifling conversation, and Thorn had a lot she needed to learn. So, her heart thrumming against her sternum, her hands balled into fists, Thorn sat.

Edith's expression brightened. She leaned onto the table, fingers laced in a delicate cradle beneath her chin. "And I was told you were uncivilized…"

Thorn's teeth gnashed together. Edith went on as though she didn't notice.

"Now, to answer your question, no, I don't work for the Sins. I am an independent agent. They do their business, I do mine, and for the most part, we leave one another alone."

Thorn frowned. "That's impossible. They kill their discarded hosts."

"Not always," Edith countered, her blue eyes moving down Thorn's body hungrily before snapping back to her face. She sighed and sat up straight again. "Though I will admit, Greed *did* try. After we had both immigrated to the United States, it tracked me down with full intentions of eliminating me. I managed to… convince it that I could be an asset. Hence, a partnership was born.”

Needles prickled up Thorn's spine, and she fought to keep her lip from curling indignantly. *Partnership?*

“Yes,” Edith said without acknowledging the venom in Thorn's voice. “They allow me to do as I wish, unobstructed, and I offer my services whenever they need them. I have flourished over the decades, building my *own* empire, much like the one you and that poor uncle of yours built.” She flashed Thorn a smile, but Thorn's jaw was too tight to return it. “Those idiots got the short end of the deal and have never once stopped to question it. So much for wisdom of the ages!”

Edith threw her head back and laughed, the deep, hearty sound pouring straight from her chest. Thorn swallowed a lump that had grown in her throat and glanced at Gabe, who was watching from the other side of a long line by an empanada stand. His face had drained of color.

When Edith settled, Thorn looked back to her and asked, “What kind of services can you offer the Sins?”

“Personnel, primarily,” Edith said, shrugging. “You are not the only liberated vessel to have built your own militia. When they need more manpower than they can collect with their Influence, I'll offer a handful of highly trained men. For a fee, of course.”

Cold shock cracked over Thorn's skull, and her eyes widened. “The mercenaries… They were *yours?*”

Edith smiled, fangs out. “They *were*. I lost many good men that fateful May afternoon. Seventeen of my best. I saw what you did. It was… incredible. Artistic, even.”

That dangerous smile flickered, and a shadow stole the light from Edith's expression. Sparkie swirled lower, now hunting through the dense market crowds for faces he *didn't* know, but he couldn't spot anything suspicious in the sea of people. How many men did Edith have lurking here? Nerves tightened Thorn's throat. She shifted where she sat, and Edith shook her head.

"Don't worry," she said, but her tone did nothing but make Thorn worry more. "I'm not seeking *revenge*. It's simply a cost of doing business—well, a cost of doing the kind of business *I* do. Those men are paid handsomely for their service, and they understand the risks when they agree to work with me."

Thorn's eyes narrowed. "If you're not here for revenge, why *are* you here?"

Edith paused before she drew a deep breath and held her head high. "Because the Sins have hired me out again…"

A moment stretched between them, Edith watching calmly while every atom in Thorn's body flared a bright red warning. Her left hand wandered back toward a weapon. Edith noticed, and she sighed.

"I'll be completely upfront with you, Thorn," she said, brushing her palms together before clasping them on the metal tabletop. "Until a few weeks ago, I had no idea you or your Martyrs even existed. That's one of the drawbacks of associating with this horrid group. They have *no* respect for the terms of our agreement. They were content to let me live my life, not knowing that *someone* was out here ripping them to shreds. They were probably afraid I'd seek you out… want to work *with* you…"

She eyed Thorn again, and Thorn's fist wrapped around the knife in her thigh pocket.

"Is that what you've come to do?"

Edith didn't answer her.

"But recently, news of your organization popped up online. When you've reached a certain age, you start to pick up on what's real and what's an illusion. I'm sure you can relate to that." She smiled, but Thorn took the compliment like a piece of spoiled meat, curling her nose. "So, I met with Anton Claytor and demanded an explanation. The next thing I know, Autumn was on my doorstep with a new proposal: kill the Martyrs. Payment for every single head. I don't even want to tell you how much. The number is so high that even I lost my breath."

She giggled, but Thorn's mouth slipped open in horror. Overhead, Sparkie tracked the TAC teams as they drew in a little tighter.

"They gave me everything they know about your organization," Edith continued, "to make the job easier, *but* the contract comes with one crucial stipulation… I am *not* allowed to kill *you*."She paused again, frowning at Thorn from across the table. "Naturally, this piqued my interest. Why in the world would Wrath want this *one woman* alive? A *previous host*, no less. I knew, then, that I had to meet you. I *had* to know what makes you *so special*…"

Thorn scoffed. "I'm not special."

"Oh, but Thorn, you *are,*"Edith insisted, and for the first time, Thorn sensed a genuine emotion in her: awe. She took Thorn in like she'd found a holy grail, opening her hands in reverence. "Look at *you*, at all you've accomplished! You've destroyed… what is it? Three of them now? These all-powerful, timeless beings are *scared* of you, as they damn well should be! But even still, Wrath wants to keep you around. You clearly have more value to her alive than dead…"

"Can you get to the point?" Thorn hissed.

"The point is," Edith said, "I like you, Thorn, and I especially like that *they* don't like you. It's *fun* for me."

She paused, and Thorn's muscles toyed with relaxing, but instinct kept them tightly wound. Then, Edith sighed with a sound like a knife against steel.

"However, it's come to my attention that Greed's destruction would present a… conflict of interest for me."

Thorn frowned. "What kind of *conflict?*"

"A… loss of investment, in a way."

"What investment?"

Edith scoffed. "My powers, of course. My *legacy*. Once you've lived as a god, how can you *possibly* go back to being merely… human?"

Thorn's jaw clenched, and her fingers tightened around her blade.

"I have worked far too hard to let that go," Edith went on. "So, I wanted to offer you a… counter deal, if you will."

She waited a few seconds for Thorn to respond. When no response came, the Forgotten Greed simply said three words:

"Call it off."

Thorn's eyes shot wide. *"What?"*

"Stop fighting this war. Before it's too late."

The corner of Thorn's lip jerked in a snarl, and she bristled, anger charging around her and raising the hairs on her arms and the back of her neck. "Is that a threat?"

"Oh, no!" Edith laughed, waving away Thorn's concerns. "It's an opportunity to finally put all of this behind you. You've already lost so much. Are you really willing to lose *more?*"

The aching hole in Thorn's chest opened further, her rage quieting for a dense moment of pain as she thought about Donovan. About Alan. About *Darius.* His face flashed across her mind, olive skin warm and welcoming, green eyes full of worry. For a second, Thorn had to remind herself to breathe.

"I will handle *all* of it," Edith pressed on. "I will fabricate our battles, fake your casualties, and tell the Sins you're all wiped out. They will never, *ever* bother you again. Then, you'll be free."

"Free to do *what?*" Thorn countered. "Live forever with this curse—"

"This blessing!" Edith interrupted. "This gift! This *miracle!* Thorn, *you* are a miracle. You've tethered yourself to these *cattle,* but they are not your equals. They are *dust* compared to you."

She gestured around the food court, indicating the market, the city, the entire *world* in a grand, sweeping movement. Thorn glared at her.

"They are *everything,* especially compared to me."

Edith snorted. "They should *worship* you. But instead, they have *limited* you. Forced you into a box that you outgrew the second you were free from Wrath. They want to keep you small, keep you *contained*, because they know they could never hope to own you if you reach your full potential."

A dangerous, boiling mix of anger and fear spun in Thorn's stomach. She stamped it down. "My full potential as *what*? A monster?"

"Monster. Hah!" Edith crossed her arms, leaning against the table, drawing closer to Thorn. "The only monsters here are those who want to destroy us because they do not understand us… *appreciate* us." She lifted one hand and pointed a finger at the center of Thorn's chest, right at the spot where her soul had once lived. "You are not a monster. You are a god. *We* are gods, Thorn, sisters, cut from the same cloth, claiming the same *birthright*, and it's time we *embrace* our divinity."

Thorn frowned. "We?"

Edith tilted further forward until she took up Thorn's entire frame of view. Her breath danced against Thorn's chin as she said, "Join me." Awe snaked back into her tone, and her expression flushed with hopeful light. "Abandon this thankless war, this life of death and pain, and live the way you were *meant* to live. This immortal existence can be so lonely, but it doesn't have to be. Not if we do this together."

She reached her hands out, palms facing the heavens, eagerly waiting for Thorn to dip her fingers into them. But Thorn didn't see salvation. She saw two pale, deadly traps with sharp teeth waiting to ensnare her, break her, and skin her alive as they dragged her to perdition.

Slowly, Thorn rose to her feet.

"I can't do that."

Edith's eyes sharpened into icy points, slender face stiffening with forced calm. "Don't waste this incredible existence you've been given. Don't waste *good* lives. It would be such a shame to see your sheep slaughtered where they roam…" Thorn's teeth clenched, and Edith smirked. "*That* is a threat."

"The answer is no."

Every ounce of poise, of peace, of pleasantry burned away, leaving Edith cold and callous. Thorn drew her blade free. Flicked it open.

"So be it," Edith murmured.

She raised her hand above her head and snapped.

A gunshot blasted through the market.

Screaming echoed around Thorn's skull. Hundreds of people bolted, the swirling miasma of cold energy churning in a tumultuous storm. Edith's mercenaries seemed to materialize out of the civilians. A half dozen men in plainclothes wielding pistols sprinted toward the table. TAC met them before they arrived, forcing hand-to-hand combat to keep stray bullets from flying into the mob.

While Sparkie tracked the fighting, Thorn lunged across the table, her knife held backward so the blade ran along her forearm. Edith ducked to the side only to be immediately swallowed by the frantic crowd.

Thorn dove in after her. Bodies bombarded her, screaming, sobbing people desperately trying to escape. Another shot boomed nearby, and the screaming grew louder. Thorn shoved against the flow—against men dragging women, mothers carrying children—until she exploded into empty space. Her chest burned.

Edith had disappeared.

And the Raven rose before her.

Just as she had in all the livestreams, she stood perfectly still, a statue in the chaos, her black beak glistening, long cloak rippling, as she watched Thorn through empty eyes. The force of her Influence tapped Thorn's temples as she pushed out a blanket command to the mob around her. Thorn's teeth gnashed together, and she attacked.

Edith was quick. With every punch, every slash, every goddamned *glance*, she slipped to the side, moving just enough to avoid the blow. It was like she could sense Thorn, see her from more than one angle, to anticipate each strike.

Thorn flew past her *again,* her blade biting empty air, and she exclaimed a throaty cry that vanished in the noise around them. Her black hair tangled in a web in front of her face. She furiously swiped it away.

All the while, Edith just fucking *stared* at her.

As a third gunshot rocked the lot, as more people howled in fear, as bodies slammed to the pavement only to be trampled beneath a stampede of terrified feet, Thorn felt herself spiraling. Hot rage coiled around her throat, constricting her airway, and a gray tunnel pin-holed her vision until all she saw was that goddamned raven mask.

A jolt of panic pierced the rage, and suddenly, Thorn was back in that warehouse. Her lungs hitched.

She couldn't do this. Not again. Not *here.*

Thorn took a step back, drew a shaky breath, and tapped her thumb against her fingertips to ground herself in the moment, but the moment was so fucking chaotic that all it did was spin her up more. She saw terrified faces, smelled the sharp stink of panicked perspiration, heard frantic voices calling for loved ones in the din. Edith still didn't move, standing like a ghoul in the center of the food court. Thorn's hands trembled, and Sparkie torpedoed toward her.

A mass of black feathers struck him out of the sky.

Searing pain ripped along Thorn's shoulders, down her spine as something attacked her Familiar high above. Thorn threw her head back, a gasp strangling her throat, and gazed helplessly into a bright, blue expanse. Her jaw dropped.

A *raven.*

The bird croaked, its voice sharp in Thorn's skull as it grappled with Sparkie mid-flight. A blustering, frenzied battle of wings and teeth, scales and feathers consumed her focus. She peaked, plunged, and plummeted, her stomach and ribs howling at the phantom sensation of talons piercing through her flesh—of a pointed beak plucking at her eyes and nose and mouth. Thorn screamed and stumbled backward.

Another blast rang through the market, and Sparkie

screeched. Thorn sucked in only to realize that she could hardly breathe. It felt like her lungs had been replaced with stones—or crushed beneath them. She placed a hand against her sternum, trying to force her chest open and draw in more air. The sweet, metallic taste of blood coated her mouth on the exhale. Oh, shit. She recognized this sensation.

A collapsed lung.

Cold dread pitched down her body.

Thorn's shaking fingers explored her torso until they found a hole ripped beneath her armpit, tearing through a weak point in her jacket. Hot blood soaked her clothing, streaming down her waist. Fuck, she hurt so much from the raven's assault on her Familiar that she hardly felt this new pain.

Bang!

Another bullet slammed into her back, thudding against the kevlar on her shoulder blade without passing through. The bone cleaved with a disorienting *crack!* Thorn flew forward, her knife falling from her grip as she landed on hands and knees, the blacktop gritty beneath red-stained fingertips. Sparkie went limp in the sky. The raven released him, circling above as the lizard careened toward the street and crashed onto the ground beside Thorn. She jolted with the impact and cried out, coughing a lungful of blood between her palms.

A cold energy drew up on her side. Thorn clenched her teeth, found her knife again, and turned, ready to slash—

Deidre Cummins grabbed her wrist.

"Back up's almost here," she said, helping Thorn to her feet. The motion made Thorn's oxygen-deprived brain swim. "We've got to—"

A crisp, curved knife no longer than Thorn's pinky stabbed into Cummins's throat just beneath her jawline. She gargled a horrifying scream as the knife was pulled clean out. Arterial spray gushed from the wound, splattering Thorn's face in a crimson shower. It was in her eyes. Her nose. Her *mouth.* Thorn gaped as Cummins slumped to her knees, her cold energy flickering to dust.

Edith, in her haunting masked and hooded glory, stood before her. The massive raven drifted to her shoulder, clutching the velvet cloak with long, dangerous talons, and let out a throaty caw. Thorn reached for the gun at her back, but Edith backhanded her, slashing her cheek with the blade and cutting a deep incision in her skin. Thorn nearly fell again, but Edith grabbed the front of her jacket and drew her closer, dragging Thorn in until her face pressed against the smooth, black beak on her feathered mask. Blood dribbled from her wound, flowing down the smooth surface and dripping off the point. This close, Thorn could barely see the outline of Edith's expression behind mesh eyes.

"One down, Mourning Dove," Edith whispered.

She brushed a thumb against the healing gash in Thorn's cheek, pulling it open again, smearing blood to her hairline. Then, she thrust her away. Thorn, her chest still heavy, shoulder still screaming, mind still on fire, stumbled backward until she tripped over Deidre Cummins lying lifeless in a pool of blood. She slammed onto the pavement. Piercing pain shot through her back until Thorn felt like she'd been impaled upon a spike in her spine. For a breathless second, all she saw was an empty sky, broken briefly by a large, black silhouette.

The food court cleared. Civilians vanished, mercenaries retreated, and sirens wailed in the distance. Martyrs closed in. Backup had arrived in full body armor, and soon, Thorn was surrounded by familiar faces. Sparkie clumsily climbed to her chest as Thorn tried to stand, but her head spun. Dizziness crept in as she struggled for air. Her heart pounded fervently, desperate to get oxygen back to her brain from lungs that couldn't fully open. She hacked again, filling her mouth with bloody spray.

Gabe's hand wrapped around the back of Thorn's arm to lift her. He looked no worse for wear, a little bruised and beaten, but his cognac eyes narrowed with concern. She tried to draw a deep breath, but her chest felt like it was full of fluid. She coughed. Wet, red droplets speckled Gabe's hoodie.

"The Raven," she gasped. "Where is she?"

"Gone," he said, "and we've got to go, too. We have people wounded… including you. Come on." He pulled Thorn's arm around his neck. She winced as the movement made her broken shoulder blade scream. Behind them, Conrad Carter lifted Cummins. His bulk eclipsed her, making her look like a child draped from his arms. Edith's voice echoed in Thorn's mind.

One down.

CHAPTER TEN

Footage from the market made its way back to the Underground before their TAC teams did.

Darius sat at the nurses' station with Raquel Hernandez, Lamar, and a handful of other medical staff. They huddled around a single computer monitor, watching the LymeLite feed. Frantic faces flashed by as screams crackled through tiny speakers. Darius's eyes darted from one person to the next, looking for someone he knew—not from the Martyrs, but from his life before.

"There she is," Lamar murmured.

The camera broke through the crowd at last and caught a glimpse of a dark figure. The raven mask gleamed in the light, black feathers glistening metallic violet and beetle green. Thorn stood opposite of her, back to them, face hidden, identity preserved. She raised her left hand to reveal a blade held tight against her forearm.

Then she attacked.

Running bodies blocked the view, so they caught the fight in glimpses. Thorn lunged and slashed, punching at that raven mask over and over again. Every time she came in, the Raven swept out of harm's way like a shadow, like she anticipated every single strike the second Thorn thought to make it. Seeing her so evenly matched, maybe even *out-matched*, made Darius's mouth run dry. He swallowed hard.

The footage suddenly lurched to the side and then up to the sky. A gravelly scream that sounded chillingly like Thorn poured from the speakers before the screen faded to gray and restarted from the beginning. Darius shook his head as he muted the feed.

"Was this another live cast?" he asked.

"Yeah," Lamar said. "Naomi just found it. It took a lot longer for this one to gain traction."

"Probably because of the location," Raquel said. Her wavy, brown hair fell in fuzzy wisps from a messy bun at the back of her head. She swiped a strand away from her cheek. "Part of how LymeLite decides what kind of content to spotlight is by how many other users are nearby. A lot of people in this neighborhood don't even have phones…"

Darius's jaw tightened. Even as Thorn flashed in and out of sight, her face was never visible. "That might be a good thing," he said. Fewer phones meant less footage from this incident and a lower chance that Thorn could be recognized. Raquel caught his eye, and he knew by the anxious pull to her mouth that she was thinking the same thing.

They rewatched the same footage loop back to the start a third time. It wasn't any better without sound, and Darius felt sick. When the view jolted back to the sky, he made out a burst of movement in the corner, like the wing of a large bird mid-flight.

The door to Elijah's office flung open.

"Get prepped in triage," the doctor called as he strode into the ward. "Our teams are fifteen minutes out."

The nurses leapt to their feet, and Darius followed. He went through the motions on autopilot, his mind still back at the desk, echoing with Thorn's screaming.

They returned in waves. Darius reacted to the sight of blood like a Pavlovian response. The second injured Martyrs poured into the hospital ward, filling the triage room with flurried activity, frantic energy, and that distinct, sickly-sweet metallic scent, healing power flowed into his finger-tips, hungry for release.

Elijah and his hospital staff brought the wounded in, determining who needed urgent care and a Virtue's touch and who could wait a little longer before being seen. After hell had broken loose on the Williamsburg Bridge Street Market and backup had swarmed the scene, a total of fifteen of their people had been involved. More than half of them reported injuries, ranging from minor to severe, but they'd only lost one. Thank god there had only been one.

Darius hated that this was something worth celebrating. As he helped Amelia Chan lie back on the cot, her black hair drenched in blood from a gash along her hairline, he numbly resented that he'd gotten to the point of feeling *good* about "only one" death.

They worked in tandem, Lamar examining a patient to his left, Dr. Harris to his right, while nurses sorted through the final rush. Darius's mind was in a thousand places all at once as he listened to the whispers circulating the room: of Forgotten Sins and ultimatums, raven masks and fired bullets. While shaken Martyrs took to cots or chairs, Darius wondered how many other casualties had been left behind in the market. Jalal. Mrs. Miller. Miguel…

The doors opened one last time, and Gabe's energy strode in, drawing Darius's focus back to the present. He glanced up, and his heart plunged.

"Thorn!"

She stood on the threshold, ashen and bloodied. Gabe hovered just behind her shoulder as though making sure she was safe to stand at all. Darius ran over. Thorn held up a palm to stop him from drawing too close.

"I'm fine," she insisted, but she didn't look fine. Her pale skin had even less color than usual, and the color that did remain concentrated in her dusky lips and the dark circles beneath her eyes. Red streaks coated her face, throat, and the sliver of her chest visible through her open jacket. Sparkie clung to her left shoulder, his tiny ribcage heaving with belabored breath.

"You told me your lung collapsed," Gabe said.

Thorn glared at him, but before she could argue, a deep, wet cough erupted from her mouth. She covered it by dipping her face into the crook of her elbow. When she pulled her arm away, Darius spotted a fresh, crimson coating on her tongue.

Adrenaline coursed through his veins, and healing power surged to the tips of his fingers. He ached to touch her, to lay his hands on her bare skin and pour all of himself into her just to take this pain away, but Virtue power didn't work on souls corrupted by the Sins.

"Operating room," Elijah called without looking up from his patient. "Raquel, escort Thorn to the OR, get an x-ray, and prep a chest tube."

Raquel stepped away from where she was working with Conrad and hurried toward Thorn, who glared at Elijah over the nurse's head.

"Harris—"

"If you hadn't noticed, my hands are full," Elijah snapped. He threw her a scalpel-sharp look, gray eyes glinting above his medical mask. Darius knew by the tone he was scowling. *"Go to the operating room."*

Thorn's nostrils flared, but her gaze fluttered to Darius before she stormed through the hospital ward. Raquel scurried behind her, and Darius watched the doors swing shut in their wake. He released a bubble of held breath in a sigh. A firm hand landed on his shoulder, and Gabe offered a sympathetic look.

"Darius," Elijah said. The doctor watched him with weary patience. "Tend to the more seriously wounded. You have more experience and know your limits better. Lamar, take the minor injuries. They can be healed to completion without draining your energy." Lamar and Darius nodded.

Within minutes, the chaos of the triage room settled. Four TAC agents had been wounded enough to require immediate healing, and Darius and Dr. Harris managed them promptly while Lamar made his way through the rest of the patients. Once the heart-pounding pace of moving from body to body finally slowed, the ward filled with uneasy silence. Darius and Lamar set up at the nursing station, where they sipped on a couple of juice boxes to replenish their strength. Darius's attention kept wandering toward the operating room doors, where he could feel Dr. Harris and Raquel. The second those two auras began walking this way, Darius's spine went straight.

Raquel returned first. She made her way through the double doors, pushing a medical trolley covered in tools, supplies, trash, and—Darius's guts turned to mud—a bundle of bloody clothes and a single metal slug rolling inside a plastic dish, trailing a little half-circle of red. Raquel caught his eye and smiled before disappearing toward the supply closet on the far side of the room. Darius's gaze moved back to the OR.

Minutes later, Elijah stepped out.

"How's Thorn?" Darius blurted the second the doctor appeared.

Elijah heaved a sigh like he'd been holding it in for the last half hour. "You'd think I was trying to murder that woman," he grumbled as he leaned his forearms against the nursing station's tall countertop. "About the only damn time she's ever in that room and *not* complaining is when she's actively dying."

Lamar let out a tiny, uncomfortable laugh while Darius shook his head. "It's not that bad?"

Elijah shrugged. "She was shot beneath the arm, which broke a couple of ribs and caused a pretty severe hemopneumothorax, but we've placed a chest tube to drain the blood and allow the lung to reinflate. The second bullet hit her in the back, but all it did was crack her scapula. That should resolve on its own by the end of the day."

"That *sounds* bad," Lamar said, his eyes so wide they were practically full circles.

"For you or me, it could be," Elijah said. "But thanks to

those Sin powers of hers and the tube I shoved into her ribcage, her lung should heal in half an hour or so, which is much better than the *days* it would have taken if she sulked in her room to heal alone."

"Is she going to recover in the OR?" Darius asked.

Elijah nodded. "We have no need for it now, thanks to your hard work, and it keeps her well away from *me* for the time being..." He cleared his throat and stood back to his full height. "And away from the rest of the Martyrs, whom I must attend to. If you'll excuse me."

With that, Elijah walked away, heading to the line of occupied cots down the ward. Darius watched him go before his eyes swung back to the operating room. He sighed.

"It's hard," Lamar murmured.

Darius turned around to find the other Virtue considering him with soft, mahogany eyes. "What is?"

Lamar tilted his head toward the doors. "Not knowing how to help someone who's clearly hurting so badly."

A breath escaped Darius's mouth. "I think I *could* help," he murmured, "if I could just get in."

Lamar nodded, slow and thoughtful. "Well, I don't think the door is locked. Just closed. Maybe you should give it a try." A mischievous twinkle lit up his expression. The meaning jolted Darius like he'd touched an exposed wire, and his heart fluttered.

It couldn't hurt to try, could it?

Darius rose to his feet. "Thanks, Lamar."

He passed the young Consent a smile, which Lamar returned.

"Any time, honey," he said. "And if she slams it in your face, I'll have an emotional support pink lemonade waiting for you." He held up a juice box, wiggling it with a wink. "Don't worry. It's virgin."

Darius laughed harder than he had in months, and god, it felt good. Healing, almost, like Lamar had tapped into some secret ability to mend the human spirit.

After tossing his empty juice box in the trash, Darius

walked to the operating room and laid his hand on the door. He hesitated for only a moment to steady his nerves before gently pushing it open.

He'd only been in the operating room twice before, both in his earliest months with the Martyrs: first when Eva had nearly died and he'd initiated Kindness, and again after Thorn had taken a couple of bullets for him, exposing herself as a Forgotten Sin. A single cot sat in the exact center while all kinds of impressive medical devices rested against each wall. They had x-ray machines, ventilation systems, massive ring lights, and robotic surgical aids. The only thing pulled close to the cot now was a single lamp, shining down on Thorn.

Darius hesitated.

He wasn't sure what he'd expected. In the past, no one besides Alan had been allowed to see her after a procedure. She reclined back, staring up at the ceiling with a dark look across her face. A white medical gown draped her torso, and a drainage tube extended from the base. It was full of deep red liquid as it drew blood from her lungs into a receptacle on the ground. Darius's face went cold.

He'd seen Thorn go through hell—had dragged her from beneath the wreckage of a blown-up car, helped clean her up after a man buried a pitchfork two inches into her belly, tended to her wounds when she'd been stabbed in the *Peccostium*—but somehow, *this* was hard to see. Something about Thorn being in the hospital, tethered to machines, made her seem vulnerable and reminded Darius that her immortality wasn't bulletproof.

Reminded him that Thorn *could* die.

As though she could read his mind or sense him staring, Thorn's eyes snapped down, looking past the lights, the equipment, and landed right on him. Her lips slipped open, and she shot up on the mattress. Darius stared at her. He didn't know what else to do.

For the first time in six long months, Darius and Thorn were alone.

"What are you doing here?"

Thorn's voice filled the room with a cold wind, which Darius walked through anyway, determined not to show her he felt the chill.

"Just checking in." He paused at the foot of her bed. "Elijah said you should be good in half an hour."

"Thank god," Thorn replied. She looked away, busying herself with the hem of her medical gown. She lifted it at her hip and up her side to examine the plastic tube poking between her bottom ribs, like she was impatient for the damned thing to heal so she could get out of this situation. Her pale skin had been hastily wiped clean, remnants of blood barely visible in tinted streaks along her toned stomach and the curve of her waist.

Heat bloomed across Darius's cheeks, and he averted his gaze. He'd seen more of Thorn's body before, during workouts when she wore nothing but a sports bra and leggings or when he would meditate while she swam, but something about it felt invasive now, so he focused on her face. Somehow, that made him feel worse. Like her torso, she'd been cleaned from her hairline to her throat, but grungy, red patches still stuck at her temples and jaw. As she smoothed her gown down, she winced. Darius breathed a sigh.

He still ached to heal her, but more than that, he wanted to hold her, feel her pressed up against his chest, and comfort her.

Or maybe he just needed to comfort himself.

"How are you doing?" Darius asked. Even though he'd spoken quietly, this sterile room amplified the sound.

"I'm pretty sick of answering that question." Thorn's response came short and irritable.

"Maybe if you answered honestly, people would stop asking."

Her glare slashed up to where he stood like she was ready to fight, but Darius didn't flinch. For a tense few seconds, Thorn looked at him the way she used to: steady, piercing, and ardent. Her focus wandered from his eyes to his mouth to the arms he'd wrapped around his chest. Sparkie peered out around her hair, fixed on Darius, too.

And the door to her soul cracked open.

"You want to know how I'm doing?" she asked, pinching the bridge of her nose. *"Honestly?* Not fucking well. Harris just dug a bullet out of my body, some psychopath Forgotten Sin is on the streets of New York City with a bounty for Martyr heads, and the *market…*" Her attention snapped back to him. Pain pulled her face together. "I'm so sorry, Darius. That market is so important to you. If I had—"

"Thorn," he cut in and, without stopping to think, moving on pure instinct, he laid a hand on her arm just below where the cuff of her medical gown draped loose around her bicep. "There's nothing you could have done. It sounds like she came in ready to hurt people. She was probably waiting for you to give her an excuse."

Thorn's body gently tilted toward him, the weight of her firm against his palm. Her eyes locked onto his, lingering as though she'd been wanting this—*needing* this—for weeks. His heart skipped, and Darius gently grazed his thumb against her skin. Thorn's lower lip slipped between her teeth.

"That's just it," she said quietly. "I *could* have done something. I panicked, Darius, and if I hadn't, maybe it wouldn't have been as bad. Maybe she wouldn't have done so much damage. Maybe Cummins—"

Thorn cut off abruptly, throwing her head to the side with a hiss like the name burned her tongue. Darius let go of her arm and settled onto the cot beside her without saying a word. She didn't draw away from him but instead leaned in, just slightly, just enough for their shoulders to touch. This close to her, Darius could just make out the smell of sandalwood and vanilla beneath the mask of antiseptic.

They sat like that, quietly, thoughtfully, for several long minutes before Thorn cleared her throat.

"What have you heard about Edith?" she asked.

He frowned. "Edith?"

She turned to him. A darkness settled over her expression. "The Raven."

Darius breathed air into his cheeks, releasing it in a slow stream. "Not much. Gabe sent Chris the recordings as soon as you were out of the city. She, Mackenzie, and Nicholas are in her office listening to them now."

Thorn nodded, a slow, solemn gesture, and her expression glazed over as though she were revisiting the market in her mind. "She's delusional," she murmured, barely above a whisper. He caught a chill of fear in her voice. "And dangerous."

"I noticed." Darius glanced toward the hospital ward, where the energies of wounded Martyrs sat along cots down the hall.

Thorn's eyes sharpened on him again. "You don't understand. She *knows* the Sins, Darius. She knows about this war, about us, about *me*... Fuck, she doesn't even realize that they're using her..."

Her voice drifted off, and Darius's stomach flipped. "How do you mean?"

"Wrath hired her to hunt us down, and Edith is convinced she's got her outsmarted—that she has all of them fooled. But what's really happening here?" Thorn's jaw clenched, and her focus caught on some distant point. She drew in a short breath and held it hard in her chest. "Edith will kill our people, and we'll kill hers, while the Sins sit back and watch until there's no one left to die."

Silence stretched between them as Thorn tumbled back into her thoughts. They must have been troubling. She wound her arms around her chest with a wince, and her neck and shoulders went so taut that Darius could see every tendon, every muscle straining against her skin. Behind her hair, Sparkie squirmed, making the silky strands ripple like dark water. At last, Thorn spoke again, so softly that Darius was sure he misheard her.

"She wanted me to come with her."

He blinked, narrowing his eyes. "She what?"

"Wanted me to leave the Martyrs," Thorn said. Her face tilted in his direction. This close, she looked sick. The color had begun to return to her skin, but dark circles stubbornly clung beneath her eyes, making those half-empty, black depths seem haunted. "She said she would leave my people alone if we stopped hunting the Sins, and I joined her."

Darius shook his head. "Join her in *what?*"

Thorn blanched. "Being a god."

His mouth dropped open, but before he could ask any more questions, an aura moved toward the doors. Darius and Thorn glanced up as someone knocked before swinging one open, and Raquel peeked her head into the room.

"I'm sorry," she said, offering an apologetic smile that was half-grimace. She held up a phone. "I found this in your jacket pocket as I was prepping it for sanitation. It just buzzed."

Thorn's brows drew in. Sparkie suddenly appeared on her shoulder, head up, wings flared. "It's not mine."

She pulled her medical gown up to reach the thigh pocket in her leggings and drew out a cell. Raquel glanced at the one in her palm. It didn't match Thorn's—didn't look anything like the rest of the Martyr-issued devices. It was smaller. Simpler. One of those cheap burners that could do nothing more than send texts, receive calls, and access a simple browser.

"I thought it might be for your contacts in New York," Raquel started, but her tone made it clear she was unsettled by the fact that Thorn didn't recognize the thing. She looked at it like it might explode in her hands.

"Let me see it." Thorn reached out, and Raquel practically forced the phone into her fingers. Thorn turned on the screen, which immediately showed a notification. When she opened it, her eyes went wide, and Sparkie let out a sudden cry from her shoulder that made Darius's heart jump into his throat.

"What's wrong?" he asked.

Thorn answered by handing him the device. One message displayed upon the screen. Just three words.

"Hello, Mourning Dove."

"She slipped a *phone* into your pocket?" Nicholas asked indignantly. "Why the hell aren't we on red alert or some shit? She could have tracked you all the way back to the Underground!"

They gathered in the conference room, Chris and Darius on the left side of the table, Mackenzie and Nicholas on the right, while Thorn paced behind the head chair. Cain had joined them, seated on Darius's other side with his hands folded neatly in his lap. Nicholas crossed his arms, and his mouth curved into a severe frown behind his beard as he glared at Thorn.

"You think we're fucking stupid, Wolfe?" she snapped, swiveling to the table with her hands on her hips. Sparkie's spine arched, and his wings flared behind her head. Despite having healed and washed up over an hour ago, she still looked like she belonged in the hospital ward, if not for her physical health, for her mental well-being. A manic glint sharpened her eyes, only made more intense by the shadows below them. "All of our vehicles have disruptors specifically designed to identify suspicious tracking signals and block them before they even make it out of New York City. Andrews got into the damned thing to disable the GPS chip, too. I'm not concerned about her following me. I'm concerned about her *contacting* me."

Thorn pulled the burner out of her pocket, brandished it like a weapon, and tossed it onto the table. Mackenzie swiped it up.

"'Hello, *Mourning Dove?*'" she read aloud, her nose wrinkling in a grimace. "Eww. Don't like that."

Nicholas opened his palm, and Mackenzie dropped the device into it as Darius turned back to Thorn. "Did you message her back?"

Thorn glanced at him, jaw tight, and shook her head.

"Good," Nicholas said. "She's clearly trying to rattle you. Don't give her the satisfaction of a response."

"It's more than that," Cain said, his silky voice cutting into the tension of the room. "She wants *access* to you, which is far more troubling. You could very well be the first of her kind Edith Froschlin has seen in decades."

Something in the way he said the name snagged Darius's attention. It was familiar, like a name Cain had said often once upon a time. Darius wasn't the only one to notice. Thorn's eyes narrowed while Nicholas and Mackenzie exchanged a curious look. Chris tilted around Darius, swiping a strand of blonde hair behind her ear.

"Did you know her, Cain?" she asked.

Cain sighed and tapped his fingers against the table like he was itching to wrap them around a glass of wine. "Not personally, no, but I know *of* her. Edith Froschlin was Greed's host during the Second World War. It's certainly in our records, buried beneath decades of dust..."

Nicholas's brows shot up. He put the burner phone back down, swapping it for his own, and started digging through the server. Thorn shook her head.

"Why the hell haven't I heard about her?" she asked.

Cain responded with a scoff. "Because we thought she was *dead*. This was ages ago, well before the Martyrs existed. At the time, the Sins were divided between the United States and Europe. Greed and Wrath had both moved to Germany to take advantage of the evils happening there, and Yin was abroad, trying to eliminate them. Wrath was a general, nearly untouchable except, it seems, by lucky shots from American snipers..."

His voice cracked, and Thorn's face paled. Her head jerked to the side, as though to hide her expression from the rest of them, while Sparkie shrank behind her back. Cain cleared his throat before he went on.

"But Edith was involved with the head of the German

Tank Commission in Wolfsburg. We suspected she played a significant part in the development of German weaponry. There is great profit in war if you're willing to get blood on your hands…"

Chris leaned forward. "What happened to her?"

"Yin eventually tracked her down and killed her." Cain opened his palms, breathing a frustrated sigh. "Or so we thought. I don't know the specifics, but it *did* include a steam engine and a deep gorge. Nothing *anyone* should have been able to come back from. The next time we found Greed, it had possessed some government agent in the States with ties to nuclear development. After those bombs dropped on Japan, all seven Sins made their way here. Following power, as they were known to do before they joined forces and created a power of their own."

Mackenzie's tongue piercing rattled against her teeth. "It's been almost one hundred and fifty years since that war ended," she said. "What has she been up to since then?"

"Building a legacy," Thorn said. Everyone turned to her, but Thorn didn't move. Her black eyes were glassy and disconnected, somewhere far away from this room and these people. Darius and Chris exchanged a dark look as Mackenzie snorted.

"A legacy?" she echoed. When Thorn did nothing more than nod, Mackenzie threw her hands up. "What the *fuck* does that even mean?"

"Who knows?" Nicholas said. "But we'll see if we can find out. Thorn, do you recognize any of these?"

He turned his phone around, displaying a collection of photographs. They looked like clones—dozens of petite white women with sharp features and bright eyes. Thorn swiped the device out of Nicholas's hands and scrolled through the thumbnails for less than three seconds before she froze.

"Where the hell did you find this?" she asked.

Thorn passed the phone back, now with a single headshot filling the screen, and he placed it flat on the table. The woman looked like a porcelain doll: perfect complexion, crystal blue eyes, and blonde hair pulled into an elegant bun so immaculate that it appeared to be carved rather than brushed smooth. Something in her cold expression made a shiver crawl down Darius's spine.

"There were a couple of old photographs in the archives," Nicholas said. "I ran them through a newspaper database using Holly's AI facial recognition software for matches. That yielded a ton of false positives, but when I cross-referenced the results with the name Edith..." He tapped his knuckles against the screen. "Voila."

"She used the same name?" Mackenzie asked. "What an idiot."

"Just the first name," Nicholas said. "Here she's identified as 'Edith Fischer.' She was apparently the warden of the Falkenrath Incarceration Center."

"Falkenrath?" Chris frowned. "The medium-security prison north of Hawthorne?"

"That's the one," Nicholas confirmed. "Looks like she was involved when it first opened in the 2040s, but she stepped down after less than a decade."

"She would have to," Cain said. "It's the standard pattern for *Oblitus Peccatum*. We can only stay in one place for so long before our immortality forces us into a new life. The only examples I have otherwise are those like us..."

He and Thorn glanced at one another, the look they shared sharp with worry. Darius frowned.

"You think she's built something like *the Martyrs?*" he asked.

"It's possible," Thorn muttered. Her attention slipped back toward Nicholas's phone. "All the mercenaries are hers. They could know what she is. Fuck, they probably do."

Thorn's teeth gnashed together, and she shook her head as she wound her arms around herself.

"Let's not get ahead of ourselves just yet," Chris said. She laced her fingers as she looked around the table. "What do we know about Edith? She works with the Sins and has been hired out to kill Martyrs, but she's willing to lie and let us live if we stop trying to eliminate them. She also seems pretty fixated on Thorn…"

Thorn's expression hardened, and Sparkie quivered behind her hair.

"She has grown weary of being alone," Cain said.

Faces swiveled in his direction. Nicholas's contorted with skepticism.

"How do you figure *that?*" he asked.

Cain scoffed. "She said so herself, or did you miss that part of her monologue?" When Nicholas raised a brow, Cain offered a quaint shrug. "'*This immortal existence can be so lonely.*' It was more than an attempt at emotional manipulation. It's true. Without others to share this long life, it becomes very isolating *very* quickly." He drifted off, his gaze slowly wandering back to Thorn. She didn't meet his eye—didn't meet *any* of their eyes—content instead to glare at the ground by her feet. "It's not you that she is fixated on, my dear. It is the *idea* of you. The idea of having someone who can persist just as long as she has. It must have fascinated her."

Thorn's focus snapped up to him, hot and violent, as Sparkie sprang back to her shoulder with his tiny teeth bared. "If she's so goddamned lonely," Thorn hissed, "then she should be *happy* we're trying to eliminate Greed. *She should want to join me!*"

"Just because you want to be free from your link to Wrath doesn't mean all Forgotten Sins feel the same," Cain said, but it seemed to be the wrong thing *to* say. Thorn's cheeks flushed an angry red.

"It's *hell*, Cain!" she snarled. Sparkie screeched alongside her. "Who the *fuck* would want this?"

Thorn pressed a hand flat against her sternum. A static quiet stilled the room. Darius's stomach plunged while Chris exhaled a sigh beside him. Across the table, Nicholas mirrored Thorn's motion, touching the gaping wound in his soul with distant and empty eyes. Mackenzie glanced at him, her lip pinched between her teeth, before she turned back to Thorn.

Cain shook his head.

"I agree with you," he defended, quiet and earnest. "Why else would I be here today? I am not saying I think she's right, or even that I understand her, but Edith Froschlin is not the first of our kind to enjoy the powers provided to her by the ruining of her spirit, and she certainly won't be the last… Not unless we do our job and remove the Sins from the map entirely."

For another few aching seconds, no one spoke. Thorn's jaw clenched, the muscles flexing back and forth like she was grinding gravel into grit between her teeth. Finally, Chris cleared her throat.

"Cain's right. We need to keep an eye out for what Edith is up to, but we can't let her distract us from our main priority: destroying Greed, Lust, Envy, and Wrath."

"We can't exactly ignore her, though," Mackenzie pointed out, pulling her legs beneath her until her tiny body all but balled up on her chair. "She's getting *paid* to kill us, and something tells me she's not going to stop if we just ask nicely."

Nicholas leaned back. "I agree. We can't *do* our job if she's making the city less safe for us. I'll see what else we can dig up on her. Maybe figure out how we could track her down."

"I don't think tracking her down will be a problem," Darius said. "She *wants* attention… The question is why."

"If attention is what she wants," Thorn growled, "attention is what she's going to get… and I'll make sure it's fucking miserable."

He glanced at her, and Thorn made a point not to look back. Sparkie did, though. The Familiar fixed on Darius with black, beady eyes.

CHAPTER ELEVEN

After the market, Edith Froschlin didn't wait seven days to make another appearance.

She waited two.

Darius woke up Tuesday morning expecting to go for a run in the gym, eat some scrambled eggs, and head to R&D to help the research team look more into the Forgotten Greed's history. Instead, he was bombarded by a slew of messages from Chris, Holly, and even Thorn about a new Raven sighting at the High Line Park over Chelsea.

This time, it was more than just unsettling. It was violent.

The LymeLite live stream shook with frantic movement as a black-shrouded figure ran past trees and through panicked pedestrians with a couple of men at her heels—men with guns. Darius watched in helpless horror as the packed pathways erupted in screaming. People hunted for an exit only to find themselves trapped thirty feet above the ground while bullets loosed into the crowd. A sixteen-year-old girl bled out in her father's arms while Edith vaulted over the railing. The drop hardly slowed her down. She sprinted east up 17th without missing a stride.

Two days after that, it happened outside the Bowery Electric, landing a handful of tourists in the hospital with critical wounds. Two more, at a bookshop near Union Square. Every time, she texted the burner a location stamp minutes before the live streams started rolling, and every time, TAC was too late to do anything but watch the aftermath from a distance as police secured the areas, forensics draped sheets over bodies, and passers-by leered behind crime scene tape.

Nicholas swore into his cereal.

"This has to be staged," he said, voice muffled around a mouthful of frosted wheat squares. He and Darius sat at one of the wrought iron tables in the courtyard, watching and analyzing each horrific incident on a laptop between them. Darius couldn't believe the man still had an appetite after all they'd seen. "Look at the people attacking her. What do you notice?"

It was the incident in Bowery, where Edith had sprinted down a walking path, cloak furling like a black flag. Her followers kept close, handguns up and ready, bulletproof vests around their chests, and beneath them, they wore—

Darius gasped. "Holy shit. They look like *us.*"

Nicholas slapped a palm onto the table, making his bowl rattle and a couple of nearby nurses jump. "Exactly!" He zoomed in, and it became even more damning. Beige cargo pants. Black turtlenecks. Even the same style of armor their TAC department wore. "I checked out the videos from all three incidents, and every one of them had guys like this. Never the same two, but always dressed *exactly* like Martyrs. They have to be her mercs."

Darius's stomach twisted. "She's framing us."

"She has to be," Nicholas agreed. "She flat out told Thorn she's out for Martyr blood, and thanks to Reverend Dickhead, our name has been outed to the general public. Now, she wants to make *us* look like the bad guys. Think about these four incidents."

Nicholas shoveled another bite into his mouth and tapped a few keys. The laptop divided into quadrants: one with the fight with Thorn at the market and the other three with these fresh attacks. Darius leaned closer to the computer.

"Every single one of these has two things in common: people got hurt, and Edith comes out looking like a victim."

Darius scoffed. "A victim? How? She *killed* someone!"

"Did she?" Nicholas challenged. "This is the *only* footage of that attack, and we don't see her touch anybody. But you know what we *do* see?"

He navigated that feed until the screen filled with a still image of Thorn's back as she dove in, blade drawn, slashing at that black, beaked face. Darius's heart sank.

"I don't know about you," Nicholas said, "but if I saw this without any other context, I wouldn't think the *Raven* is the instigator here."

Nicholas pressed play, and the footage rolled. Thorn attacked again and again, relentlessly coming for Edith Froschlin with a violence Darius hadn't seen in her for six months. His mind flashed to that dingy warehouse in Hunts Point, a metal pipe clutched in her hands, Alan on his knees…

"Fuck," he breathed.

"All the other videos are like this," Nicholas went on. "With people who look just like *us*. She's minding her own business when a couple of assholes with guns start shooting. This is a fucking trap. Give it another week, and someone will link this to the Martyrs. I wouldn't be surprised if she's pulling strings behind the scenes to make that happen."

Darius threw himself back in the chair and glared at the screen. "We *have* to find her."

"I know," Nicholas said, "but she's good at covering her tracks. Holly tried to trace the number texting that burner, but it's impossible. Skylar says she's probably using a system similar to what they've set up with our phones."

"Damn it," Darius grumbled. "What about her background? Is there anything we've dug up that could help us figure out where she might be now?"

Nicholas barked a laugh. "We haven't dug up *anything.*

For one, my team is still spending most of their time helping security find and remove videos about all this shit, which has only gotten *harder* since the market fiasco. I'm looking into Edith Froschlin in my spare time, and there's not much to see. Other than the Falkenrath thing, she hasn't done much to draw any attention. That's *fifty years* unaccounted for. There may be some evidence tying her to a couple of factories that boomed after the war, and I suspect she was involved in the for-profit prison system way before Falkenrath opened, but I can't prove it. All I know is that she has a whole militia of trained operatives, so she has to be using them *somewhere.* I want to do some research into who might hire out muscle for private security, but there's a good chance it's all black-market shit."

Darius frowned. "Like what?"

"Blackmail," Nicholas said. "Coercion. Assassination." Darius's eyes widened, and Nicholas nodded. "You see my point, then. That kind of thing will be a *lot* harder to find, and the people involved probably have money or power."

Darius sighed. "Like the Sins."

"Exactly. If she's smart, and I hate to say that it looks like she is, she's hiding all of that under a dozen layers of protection." Nicholas lifted his spoon and used the end to gesture to the screen. "We could have one of her clients strapped to a chair with Cain Influencing the truth out of their brains, and we'd still never be able to connect them to Froschlin."

After that, Nicholas slurped the rest of his way through his now-soggy bowl of cereal while Darius took over the laptop and compared the four videos still on the screen. The Raven's bleak, black mask looked at him from every frame, those empty eyes cold and dangerous. He took in a short, shallow breath.

Then, a strange rustling caught his attention.

Across from the dining area, the door to the break room stood wide open, and every aura nestled within—easily twenty people—suddenly moved toward the nearest wall, the one with the television. Darius glanced up.

LymeLite alerts began to ping.

The Martyrs seated around him pulled out their phones, and before Darius knew what was going on, they were all more engrossed in their devices than their half-eaten meals. A nervous tickle ran up his back.

Then his and Nicholas's phones sounded, too, but from the leadership group chat. They looked down at the same time to a text from.

"The Raven is back again."

Darius clicked the attached link. A LymeLite video filled his screen.

"Thank you so much for flying me out for this interview," the AI-masked host of the RebelTruth podcast said. He sat beside an unmistakable masked figure. She somehow seemed larger, more formidable, seated on the mustard yellow couch.

"Thank *you* for agreeing to have me on your show," Edith Froschlin crooned in a voice thick with dangerous intention.

"Oh, shit," Darius breathed. He leapt to his feet, and Nicholas shot up after him. They sprinted across the courtyard, Edith's voice following them through tiny speakers on smaller devices until they burst into the break room, where she was life-size and full-volume on a massive screen mounted into the wall. A room full of Martyrs, dozens of sets of eyes, stared in silence: Raquel and John, Elijah's boys, even Conrad and Alexis. They'd come over from the pool table in the back, cues still in hand.

Mackenzie stood at the front, a thumbnail jammed between her teeth. Her attention flashed to Darius and Nicholas. She wildly waved them over.

"So," the host was saying, "you're claiming you're *not* responsible for the violence following you all over Manhattan?"

"You've seen the videos, Rebel," Edith replied. "I'm not sure how anyone can honestly watch them and think I *am* responsible."

"What the hell is happening?" Mackenzie blurted out. "I thought we shut this fucker's channel down *weeks* ago!"

"We did," Nicholas said, not looking away from the live LymeLite feed. "He keeps opening new accounts."

Mackenzie swore under her breath. "Thorn is going to be *pissed.*"

And at that moment, Thorn ripped into the room.

Fury sizzled off her body until the very air around her seemed to shimmer in a rage that threatened to overwhelm the rest of them. Darius felt it sink into his spine. Her obsidian-sharp eyes slashed right to Nicholas.

"What the *fuck* are you doing?" she snarled.

———

Thorn's entire being hummed with rage. It sank into her muscles, settled in her bones, and shivered within each and every atom, from the soles of her feet to the gray matter inside her skull.

Jesus *Christ*, she wanted to fucking scream.

The room stared at her, two dozen faces gawking with wide eyes and gaping mouths, but Thorn focused only on Nicholas. A roar bulged in her throat.

"We need to shut this down!" A hand lashed out toward the television, where Edith's cloaked shoulders rose and fell in a dramatic sigh. The display was so large, so crisp, that every detail on every feather glistened. Sparkie cringed at the sight of that big, beaked raven mask and quietly tucked behind Thorn's hair. She felt him quiver between her shoulder blades. "Now!"

"This isn't a goddamned movie, Thorn," Nicholas said as the rest of the Martyrs whispered behind his back. She glanced up, half-registering some of them as Nicholas argued. "Shutting it down would take time, and maybe we shouldn't anyway! Just listen!"

He jutted his chin forward, and Thorn barely caught the

tail end of Rebel's last statement.

"…one does hear rumors, and you can't blame people for jumping to conclusions," he said with the air of a man who liked to tell women to calm down, no matter how justified their anger was. His digitally masked face turned into what many would consider a beguiling frown. The AI filter was less effective at this angle, giving him an uncanny valley appearance, where the lines of his false face didn't quite align with the rest of his head, shimmering as he shook it. "There have been theories about you floating around since October, almost a *month* ago."

Edith laughed. Her disguise obscured all visual aspects of her identity, but her voice, soft and sweet and fucking *fake*, grated on Thorn's nerves. She crossed her arms, lodging her breath in her chest to stop the vitriol from boiling into her throat.

"Ahh…" Edith replied. "You mean the accusations that I am one of the Seven Deadly Sins?"

Thorn's spine went rigid. She took another step into the room, barely, consciously keeping far enough back that not a single person was near enough for her to touch because, god damn it, she was terrified of what she would do, what she was *capable of*, if any one of them came too close.

Rebel nodded, and then, he frowned. "Well? Do you claim to be one of these Sins?"

Edith's head tilted back in a way that made it clear she was beaming beneath that beak. "Yes. I do."

Mackenzie uttered a soft curse followed by the rattling of her tongue piercing against her teeth. Behind her, the Martyrs exploded into a murmuring chorus that hardly had the strength to punch through the ringing fog within Thorn's ears.

"And these supposed abilities," Rebel went on. "Mind control. Superior strength. Immortality. All of this is true, too? You *have* these powers? You can *prove* they exist?"

Thorn could practically see the cold smile stretching across Edith's face as she uttered a low, sinister chuckle.

Every vein in Thorn's body rippled with cold adrenaline and a helpless sense of dread.

This couldn't be happening.

"I can," Edith said.

Fuck.

She raised her hands again, letting the cloak fall away to reveal slender forearms. Edith pulled her sleeve up, opened her wrist to the air, and grabbed the same small, curved knife that she'd stabbed into Deidre Cummins's throat. In a quick, velvety motion, she pierced the blade into the base of her wrist and dragged it up her arm. A shallow, seven-inch cut divided her skin, the high-definition feed showing every layer of flesh and fat tissue seconds before the blood poured.

A quiet gasp rustled around the break room. Darius swore under his breath while Nicholas did so loud and clear. "Jesus *fucking* Christ."

"There are over twenty *thousand* people watching this livestream right now," Mackenzie said.

Rebel gaped, lost for words, as the wound began to close. It pinched together like someone had drawn an invisible needle and thread through the edges and pulled them tight again. Thorn's body went numb, and her shattered soul buzzed within it.

"Shut it down," she hissed. Her eyes flashed to Nicholas. "Call Andrews. Tell her to shut it down!"

"No," Nicholas argued. "We need to figure out what she's up to! Let her show us her hand!"

"What she's *up to?*" Thorn echoed indignantly. She flung a hand toward the screen, where Rebel was now standing and shouting—in shock and elation. "She's exposing herself and *us* in the process!"

"She hasn't named us at all," Nicholas challenged. "But she *is* giving us insight we can't get anywhere else! If we want to find her, we need to learn more about her."

Thorn opened her mouth to argue further, but Edith spoke again, and her focus snapped back to the feed.

"The name 'Sins,' I think, is unfair," Edith went on, watching her arm as the slash faded to a fine, pink scar. She ran her fingers down the area, smearing a thick swatch of blood across pale skin. Rebel still stared, mouth ajar. "It's full of preconceived judgment, prejudice, and hate, when really, all it is, all it has *ever* been, is a word to vilify our most basic, human natures."

The break room stilled, and Thorn crossed her arms again as Sparkie let out a low hiss behind her back. She was torn between two conflicting needs: to cut the broadcast and protect their anonymity or to watch this disaster unfold—to know what Edith would say and do next.

"In some societies," Edith continued when Rebel still didn't speak, "it is a 'Sin' to ambition for success… to desire recognition… to kiss the one you love. But I'm here to ask you, if that's *sin,* is it really such a *bad thing?*"

Nicholas let out a snort while Darius shook his head. He glanced at Thorn, but she didn't look, *couldn't* look back.

"My kind has existed for centuries," Edith said. "Eons. When your ancestors sprouted legs and crawled out of the primordial ooze, mine were already thriving. We're not *enemies* of humanity. We're *assets.*"

"What do you mean?" Rebel finally asked as he retook his spot on the couch, this time a little further away. His voice was quieter, like Edith's blade had left a cut in his wrists, too, draining the bravado from his body in thin, red ribbons.

"We bring out the best of you, Rebel," Edith said. "That's all. We make you *more* of what you were always meant to be."

Rebel shook his head. "Weston Cunningham called it corruption. You're saying he was wrong?"

"I'm saying perhaps we take the words of a man who believes the earth is six thousand years old with a grain of salt," Edith replied, her tone a tickle of amusement. "Weston Cunningham is a zealot and a fearmonger. He and men like him can't help but see the world through the only lens they've ever been given. Tell me, if you were born blind, how could you comprehend what real sight was?" She traced her nails along her bloodied arm again before pulling the sleeve down at last, hiding the gore behind black cotton. "Weston Cunningham simply can't help what he doesn't know."

"Well," Rebel began cautiously, like he was afraid Edith might reach out and choke him if she didn't like what he said next, "it looks like he doesn't know much of *anything* anymore." Edith's head tilted curiously, that raven mask peering back with a malicious glint. Rebel continued. "We reached out for a follow-up interview, but he didn't remember me or any of the incidents we talked about before. Were... *your* people behind that?"

Edith chuckled. The sound sent fire ants crawling across Thorn's skin.

"No, we were not," Edith said, "but I do believe we share a common adversary with Mr. Cunningham who would benefit from his silence..."

Thorn's heart skipped as Rebel asked, "You mean the Martyrs?"

A bustle of murmurs filled the room as Thorn growled, "Fuck."

"The very same," Edith said. "You asked who was responsible for the violence that has stalked me through New York City. Well, Rebel, I think you just got your answer."

"Wolfe!" Thorn snarled. Nicholas was already on his phone, typing madly.

"Are you saying the people who attacked you," Rebel asked, "that woman on the Lower East Side, and those men with the guns... They're part of this group?"

"That is precisely what I am saying," Edith said.

Mackenzie scoffed and cupped her hands around her mouth. "Bullshit!" she shouted at the screen. A volley of voices echoed agreement.

"From what I know," Edith went on, "that woman is their leader, and the others follow her word like *gospel.*"

A shiver ran down Thorn's spine, and she tightened her arms around her chest until every muscle, every joint trembled. Darius looked at her again. Thorn still didn't look back, but Sparkie peeked between strands of black hair. The concern on Darius's face made Thorn's lungs ache.

"Do you know her?" Rebel asked.

Edith shook her head. "I had never seen her before she attacked me."

"According to Weston Cunningham, the Martyrs are run by these Si—" Rebel caught himself. Cleared his throat. "By beings like *you*. Is she…"

His voice drifted off. Edith tilted her masked head curiously. "One of us?" she offered.

"Yes."

Edith paused as though searching for a satisfactory answer. Thorn's nails dug into her bicep.

"She's not *aligned* with us," Edith said at last, "but as for whether she has supernatural abilities of her own… I suppose time will tell. It always does. Eventually."

Rebel leaned in slowly. "You say she's not aligned with you… I assume you mean these Martyrs as a whole."

"I do, Rebel."

"You seem to know a lot about them," Rebel pressed. "More than anyone else, at least." When Edith nodded, he frowned. "What can you tell us?"

"I can tell you that they're dangerous," Edith said. The break room went deadly silent, like time stood still. Even Mackenzie's tongue piercing stilled behind her teeth. "Like so many others over the centuries, they believe we're an evil that needs to be wiped off the face of the earth. This is *genocide*, and they will stop at *nothing* to see it through. These incidents prove that civilian lives do not matter to them, and it is not the first time they've spilled innocent blood in an attempt to wound us." Edith's shoulders rose and fell in a humble, placating sigh. "Just in the last few years, they have been responsible for bombings all over Manhattan, for violence within the police department, and even for the kidnap and murder of Mayor Richmond Bently…"

Thorn's breath caught, and her lips slipped open. Memories from months ago flashed by in blood-red succession. She saw Bently again, heard his stunted cries for mercy, watched his jaw come clean off his face. She was so entrenched in her own mind that she almost missed Edith's next words, but they drew her back to the present with a sharp, icy snap.

"Like all cults," the woman behind the raven mask crooned, "the Martyrs work by isolating their followers from regular society, indoctrinating them into their extremist views, and convincing them that they are working under a righteous cause when what they really are, what they have always been and will always be, are terrorists."

Nicholas swore again while Mackenzie violently threw her arms up. Darius stood by Thorn's side, eyes dark and jaw set.

"And that's what this is about, then?" Rebel said, gesturing to Edith again. "This get-up. This crow persona—"

"*Raven*, Rebel."

"That's what you're after? You want to scare the Martyrs?"

"No." Edith's voice was so chilly that it sent a shiver through Thorn's chest from fifty miles away. "I want to *stop* the Martyrs. My brothers and sisters and I, my *people*, have the right to exist, and this beautiful city deserves to finally have *peace*. We are not the monsters these Martyrs would have you believe we are, and enough is enough. I cannot stand by and let some vigilante *G.I. Jane* come in here, guns blazing, and ruin innocent lives because of her own twisted prejudices and lust for power."

Thorn's eyes shot wide, and she suddenly felt thick and heavy, like another bullet had crashed through her ribcage and collapsed her lungs again. Sparkie let out a sharp cry before Thorn could compose herself. Again, Darius glanced at her. Again, she ignored him.

"How do you intend to stop them?" Rebel asked.

When Edith spoke, Thorn heard the smile in her words. "How do you stop any radical group? Expose their lies, drain their resources, and never let them sleep."

Rebel frowned. "Resources? What resources can—"

The screen froze, Rebel's AI-generated face devolving into a blocky, pixelated mess. Suddenly, the display went white, and a tiny LymeLite logo materialized at the center. A scrolling line of text appeared around it.

"Uh-oh! We're experiencing technical difficulties. Please check back later!"

Thorn stared at that stupid text, watching it orbit the goddamned logo like rings on a planet. The room was silent around her, but inside, she was screaming.

Nicholas finally huffed out a breath. "Looks like Holly managed to shut it down."

Rage tore up Thorn's throat. She spun away from the crowd, pulled back a fist, and smashed it into the wall beside the open door. The sheetrock atop the concrete backing bent, but the concrete itself didn't, and her bones splintered up her hand. Needles of pain moved from Thorn's fingers to her wrist. Her ears were already ringing, so she hardly heard Sparkie let out a shrill cry from her shoulder.

"We should have shut this shit down the *second* it went live!" she snarled. "What the *fuck* did we gain from any of this?"

Thorn twisted back around, flinging her broken hand at the empty screen. The Martyrs stared, still and silent, like they were all fucking scared of her. All but Darius. He stepped forward and caught her eye, holding it like they were alone, and when he spoke, his voice was steady.

"Getting insight on what she's trying to do is helpful," he reasoned.

"Trying?" Thorn barked a laugh as she turned around and walked away from him, from *everyone*. "She's not *trying* anything. She's doing it! She believes she's a fucking *god*, Darius! And this fucker makes a living off of spreading mindless bullshit to rabid fans who will buy anything he says!

There will be people out there who *believe* her!"

"And there will be people who don't," Darius said.

"We couldn't have gotten this insight any other way, Thorn," Nicholas added.

Thorn stood on the outskirts of the room, body buzzing with a wave of anger she didn't know what to do with. The Martyrs stared at her—Darius, Nicholas, Mackenzie, and *so many* others—like they didn't know what to do with her. Murmurs whispered from ear to ear, and gazes flicked from her face to the crack she'd punched into the wall. A wash of cold shame doused Thorn's head.

She wasn't an asset here. She was a liability. The Martyrs deserved more than this. Than *her*. The bloodbath flooded back, but this time, she soaked in it.

Thorn was the one who should have died in that warehouse.

Mackenzie cleared her throat. Thorn's stinging eyes darted to her. "We still need to decide what to do about Froschlin," she murmured.

"I say it's time we go on the LymeLite offensive," Nicholas said. He crossed his arms and glanced at Mackenzie—and then to the rest of the room beyond her. "We've tried to remove all of the content for weeks now, but this thing is getting too goddamned big. I say we start telling people the truth of—"

"Jesus, Wolfe," Thorn cut in. Her core swirled with a new fire.

Nicholas let out a frustrated groan. "Won't you just *listen*—"

"No!" Thorn shouted. The room flinched beneath her voice. "I won't! I already told you we are *not* going to add fuel to this fucking fire! We need to put it *out*."

"How the hell do you want to do that, then?" Nicholas asked, rising to meet her tone. "Because what we're doing *now* isn't fucking working! Security is stretched to the max, and that's with my entire research staff helping out. This *isn't* sustainable."

"Then *make it* sustainable."

Nicholas's eyes narrowed, and his jaw clenched, but he didn't say more. Thorn knew from the look on his face that he wasn't going to bring it up again—not because he'd stop believing in it, but because the embers of the bridge Thorn was burning between them were getting too hot to touch. The shame swelled deeper.

Suddenly, it wasn't just Nicholas she noticed, but all of them. Every single person, all watching her unravel. She looked from one to the other, ricocheting like a bullet. Raquel's wide mouth, Carter's shock, John Waters—and all she could hear was his voice in her head, telling her she'd lost it.

Then Alexis Claytor. Thorn caught on her. She hadn't seen Alexis in person for months. Her ice-blue stare, pallid face, and short, platinum hair. It tugged on her subconscious…

And all Thorn saw was her little brother dripping in blood.

Fuck, she needed to get out of here.

Thorn spun away and ran out the door. She stormed across the courtyard, and the attention of all the Martyrs gathered there felt like fire upon her skin. They tracked her until she reached the stairwell, where she climbed the steps two at a time, and flew into the foyer outside with a gasp. The garage waited on the other side of a set of double doors. Thorn pressed her fists against the glass, closed her eyes, and tucked her head between her elbows.

God, she couldn't do this.

"Where are you going?"

Darius's voice echoed through the tiny entrance, and Thorn twisted around with a jolt. He stood in the open stairwell, one hand still on the handle, his ribcage pulsing with labored breath like he'd sprinted after her. Thorn gritted her teeth.

"It doesn't matter," she growled.

"It does to me."

Thorn's heart pounded against her chest as Darius stepped into the foyer. His expression settled into a firm, unyielding conviction. He drew closer still, and Thorn let out a short, shaky breath.

"I'm not doing the Martyrs any favors by staying here," she said at last. "I'm no good… to anyone."

Darius's green eyes softened. God, Thorn hated that look—hated knowing she was the cause of it.

"Thorn," he began.

She cut him off.

"But if I'm in the city, maybe I can get this bitch the next time she strikes. She won't catch me off guard again."

Thorn turned back and strode into the garage. As she threw her leg over her bike, Sparkie watched Darius. He hovered in the doorway like he wanted to run out and stop her. Hold her close. Tell her they needed her—*he* needed her.

Part of Thorn wished he would. She moved slowly, giving him the chance, waiting for him to burst into the lot…

But he didn't.

CHAPTER TWELVE

Thorn's world was consumed by crows.

Edith dominated New York City. Even though Holly had cut off the live feed and removed the original recording, RebelTruth's interview ripped through the boroughs like a deadly virus. Clips, quotes, and full-length transcripts popped up within minutes of the broadcast ending, and before the Martyrs could catch their collective breath, it was fucking *everywhere*. Wherever Thorn went, whispers of the Raven fluttered: beneath every dripping scaffold, on every street corner, and in every dark cafe. She couldn't escape them. Not even at The Cross.

It was busy for a Monday night. Every pool table was occupied, every pew taken, and the raucous sound of rough laughter stoked Thorn's frustration. She lifted a tumbler of scotch, but her phone pinged before she took a sip. A message from John Waters.

"More of them," he typed. *"These guys are all over the damn place."*

She froze, the glass pressed against her lower lip, as a picture filled her screen. A group of people in black cloaks and bird masks circled a bus stop.

"Fuck," Thorn murmured.

Her Gray Unit inbox was full of this shit. While Alexis Claytor and Peter Mulligan were still doing what they could to track the Sins through Manhattan, all ten of Mackenzie's Recon agents had been added to Thorn's roster. In the three days since Rebel's interview, every single one of them had flooded her feed with photographs of people dressed like Edith all over the city.

A string of texts immediately followed John's—other Recon members commenting on the cheaply made replica masks or joking about this phenomenon they'd universally agreed was called "The Cult of the Crow," despite Mulligan's insistence that Edith's theme was technically ravens.

Thorn's teeth gritted. The way Mackenzie ran her team was so different from what she was used to. This camaraderie, this *sociability*, was foreign. The Recon team was more than just coworkers. They were friends. Close friends.

But none of them asked the right fucking questions. Thorn typed back.

"Where?"

She took a sip to wet her tongue, watching John's reply come in.

"Amsterdam and West 138th."

Thorn frowned, placed her scotch on the counter, and opened a mapping app. She input the location, and a yellow marker joined dozens of others, all indicating different places where these raven rip-offs had been spotted. This was the first in West Harlem. Thorn had hoped to see a pattern, a clue as to what Edith might be up to or where she'd show up next, but so far, it seemed random.

Fuck, Thorn needed something, *anything* to follow.

She set her phone down and pulled the burner out of her satchel. A string of messages from Edith populated the screen, all coordinates for the attacks. She'd sent them all too late for the Martyrs to do a damn thing but watch them explode online. Thorn checked this stupid phone every couple of hours, coming back to it like a bad habit she couldn't drop, just *hoping* for a text to come rolling in, but it had been suspiciously quiet since that interview went live.

What was Edith up to now?

The anticipation of waiting for the next body to hit the floor made Thorn's skin itch. She was tempted to respond, to prod at Edith and prompt some kind of reaction just so she didn't have to wonder anymore, but Nicholas's voice droned in her conscience like a dickhead angel on her shoulder, reminding her that it was a bad idea.

With a sigh, she tucked the burner away and raised her drink again. Jay appeared as soon as she'd drained it, like all it took was an empty glass to summon the man from bartender hell. He tilted another shot of scotch into her tumbler. The amber liquid splashed refracted light against her hand, and when she brought it to her lips, the sweet, woody aroma touched her nose and made her mouth water.

Thorn glanced up to thank him, but Jay moved down the bar without sparing her a passing glance. A knot tightened her throat.

Jay might not have kicked her out of The Cross, but he certainly hadn't welcomed her back with open arms. Not even an open hand. He spoke to her as little as possible whenever she walked through that door. Thorn considered herself lucky he was willing to fill her glass at all.

She went to take another sip when a male voice she didn't recognize said, "So, what do you think about that crow lady, huh?"

Thorn went numb, and her vision grayed out as all her focus moved to the conversation behind her. Jay's energy paused at the far end of the bar like he was doing the same thing. Outside, where he kept watch from the old church's retired bell tower, Sparkie petrified into a tiny, blue gargoyle in his perch.

Sully chortled a deep, rumbling laugh. "The *Raven?*" he corrected. The sound of billiard balls clattering together punctuated the question with a racket of clicks and thunks. "I *don't* think about the fucking Raven. It's some bullshit conspiracy and a waste of my goddamned time. Don't tell me you're buying into it?"

A handful of regular patrons chuckled. Thorn slowly lowered her drink to the counter, tilting her head just enough to open her ear to the room.

"Hey, fuck you," the unfamiliar voice said with a laugh meant to temper the line, but hints of a wounded ego bled through. So did alcohol. It smoothed the space between each word, softened every syllable, to create a sloppy, wet cadence. "I'm not *buying* into it, but I'm not fucking ignoring it, either. I just think it's a little weird."

Thorn chanced a glance at the pool table in the opposite corner of the bar. Sully's big, bushy mustache obscured half of his grin, and his eyes twinkled as another man chalked the tip of his cue. He was a new face here, someone who had started coming to The Cross sometime in the months Thorn had been away. The guy seemed younger than the typical crowd but still older than Thorn—well, older than she appeared, at least. She pegged him for forty, maybe forty-five. He'd buzzed his hair short and wore a pair of sunglasses reversed on his skull, making it seem like the back of his head was staring at the patrons drinking behind him.

"Weird's one word for it," Sully said. "Don't believe everything you see on LymeLite, buddy. No one with any common sense is taking that shit seriously."

Backward Sunglasses scoffed. "I think it's common sense to think that the things happening in New York City have been happening for a reason," he countered. "Have you seen that feature on FXN? They're saying this terrorist group, those… Martyrs or whatever? They've been behind almost every crazy attack that's happened since 2030 or some shit. I mean, they killed the fucking *mayor!*" He paused, lining up to take a shot. "Trust me, it's all just one big scam, a fuckin' cover-up, to keep the sheep from panicking…"

Thorn's teeth clenched, and she glanced at Jay. He quietly caught her eye, his face pale beneath ruffled, auburn hair, and shook his head as though begging her *not* to make a fucking scene. Backward Sunglasses flicked his stick forward, but the dull thud that followed made it clear he'd missed his target. He swore.

Sully snorted. "Funny, isn't it?" he said as he moved around the table. "The men who call other men sheep are the same guys who don't have two brain cells to rub together to think for themselves."

He lobbed an amused but critical look at the new guy. Instead of digging through his drunk brain for a comeback, he muttered something incoherent, his neck and face flushing hot red—from humiliation or alcohol, Thorn didn't know, but she'd bet Mackenzie ten bucks it was both. Sully wheezed another smoky laugh as he struck the cue. The new guy, if possible, burned even brighter as the eight ball landed in the side pocket.

"Good game," Sully said. The newcomer grumbled and tossed his stick to the table. Thorn turned back to the counter, raised her drink, and poured the rest of her scotch right onto the anxious knot worming in her throat. Again, Jay was there to fill it immediately.

A cold aura flopped onto the stool beside her.

"Rum and coke," Backward Sunglasses said the second Jay lifted the bottle from Thorn's tumbler. "Make it a double."

Jay nodded. "You got it." He threw another warning look Thorn's way before he headed to the prep station on the far side of the bar. The new guy tapped his fingers on the sticky countertop while he waited, glancing after Jay, back toward Sully, and then, finally, at Thorn. His fidgeting stilled, and Thorn resisted the urge to roll her eyes as he took a slow, invasive inventory of her, from her face to her body, lingering well past the point of polite.

"Don't take this the wrong way," he said gracelessly, "but you don't look like the kind of girl to come to a shithole bar like this." He thrust his head toward the back corner where Sully and a couple of other guys were setting up for another game of pool. "It's a little… rough for a wellbred girl like yourself, don't you think?"

Thorn lifted her scotch. "No. I don't."

She took a sip, and the guy grinned, brandishing a set of bad veneers and receding gums. Jay returned, slid the double rum and coke across the counter, and headed off again. The man took a deep swig before swiveling in his stool to face Thorn entirely.

"Name's Ace." He held out a hand. "Just moved up north from Brooklyn."

Thorn cast Ace a look from the corner of her eye. A nagging impulse to tell him to fuck off nearly overpowered the common sense that drove her in-town personas, but she managed to gag it down with another mouthful of liquor.

The last thing she wanted to do was give Jay a reason to kick her out for good. She had a feeling he was looking for one.

So, resisting the urge to shove him off his barstool, Thorn took Ace's palm in one quick, definitive motion. It was clammy and wet with a tacky mix of condensation and sweat.

"Teagan."

She immediately let go and returned to her drink.

Or... she tried to.

Ace clicked his tongue. "Oh, no," he said, leaning toward her like they were sharing some personal moment, in on the same joke. "That's not how ladies shake hands. You've got to be nice and soft. Like *this.*" He grabbed her palm before she could wrap it back around her glass and loosened his hold until his wrist was limp and powerless. Thorn's lip curled. "Men don't like it when a girl's got a stronger handshake than they do. Don't want to embarrass your boyfriend, do you?"

He barked a laugh that struck a match against the rough edges of Thorn's rage, and the whole damn thing ignited in a plume of fire that reduced her common sense to ashes. Her grip constricted until Ace's laughter squeezed into a scream. He toppled backward off his stool and would have coiled to the ground if Thorn weren't holding him up by his bruised and battered fingers. She leaned in, spitting words at the top of his head with a snarl.

"What makes you think I give a *fuck* what men *like?*"

"Hey!"

Jay's voice brought the room back into focus, and Thorn became suddenly aware of a pulse of cold auras rushing toward her.

Fuck.

She released Ace, letting him fumble to his knees while she turned back to the counter and her drink. Sully's energy hulked just behind Thorn's back while Jay materialized in front of her.

"Is everything all right here?" he asked. One of his hands pressed flat against the bartop, but the other tucked beneath it. The Cross went silent around them, all the souls in the room reduced to quiet, church whispers.

"This *bitch* tried to break my fingers!" Ace growled from the ground. He clambered to his feet, simultaneously stepping back from Thorn as he did, and cradled his hand to his chest. His spine collided with Sully's round belly, and he yelped in surprise. Sully's eyes, usually kind and carefree, narrowed as he looked from Ace to Jay and finally to Thorn before rounding on Ace again.

"What'd you do to *her?*"

"*What?*" Ace hissed. "Nothing! We were just talking!"

Thorn responded by pouring a splash of scotch over her tongue. As it trickled down her throat, Jay's mouth pressed thin.

"Is that true?" he asked.

"If you want to call casual sexism talking," Thorn said, "sure."

Ace scoffed. "Fuck you, cunt! Real women *enjoy* the attention. It was just a joke!"

Thorn didn't look at him as she said, "Jokes are supposed to be funny."

Ace's face scalded, and he made to take a step forward. Before his heel landed back on the floor, Sully wound a thick fist around his shoulder.

"All right, bucko," he said, "let's go cool down."

He dragged Ace away from the counter, but Ace ripped out of his grip.

"Get your hands off of me, cock sucker," he hissed. He stumbled from the room, throwing a glare and two middle fingers over his shoulder as he opened the heavy door. A beam of sunset spilled across the old wood, stopping at Thorn's feet, before a slam echoed through the bar. The parishioners inside The Cross slowly gazed back toward Thorn, Jay, and Sully. The old man snorted.

"He says that like it's a bad thing." He chuckled, releasing a pressure valve, and the rest of the bar laughed with him. When Sully turned to Thorn, his expression went more serious. "You okay, sweetheart?"

Thorn lifted her scotch. "I can take care of myself, Sully."

He nodded slowly, eyes soft. "'Course you can. Doesn't mean you have to."

Sully nudged her gently, threw her a wink, and went back to the game of pool he'd abandoned. Thorn breathed a sigh and shot the rest of her drink into her mouth, relishing the burn. She snapped the glass to the counter for Jay to refill. He didn't.

Instead, he asked, "Can I talk to you?"

Thorn's stomach swirled around the alcohol, and she pressed her teeth together as she rose to her feet. Jay came around the counter, propping the metal bat he kept for emergencies against the wall before he led Thorn into a hallway. Here, two bathrooms, a storage room, and the door to the back exit broke up the brick walls. Jay opened the storage room and allowed Thorn in first.

She stepped over the threshold, and a parade of memories greeted her, good, bad, and bittersweet. When she and Jay had been… more than whatever the fuck they were now, they'd found themselves here often. The metal shelves would dig into Thorn's naked back, and the wood floor had been rough beneath her knees. They'd filled this tiny space with heat and passion in their desperate attempt to use one another's body to fill a need or escape their problems.

But Thorn had also dug a shattered cell phone out of the meat on her thigh right here, leaving a pile of bloody shrapnel and all the evidence Jay needed to finally see her for the monster she really was. She swallowed hard.

"Jay," she began, but he cut her off.

"You *can't* assault people in the bar," he said, his voice quiet and tired. He propped one hand on his hip while the other ran down his clean-shaven face. "Not even if they're dickheads who deserve it."

"I know," Thorn said. "I'm sorry."

Jay peered at her from over his fingertips, heaved a sigh, and flopped his arms to his sides.

"What the hell is going on?"

An old, familiar affection warmed the question, and Thorn started, taken aback. Something fluttered in the emptiness in her chest. Nerves? Gratitude? *Fear?*

"I thought you didn't want to know," she said at last.

"I don't," Jay said. "I *really* fucking don't. But I'm starting to think I have to." He lifted a hand, gesturing in Thorn's direction. "I was *never* supposed to see you again, and then you show up out of the blue saying shit's been hard right before this psycho raven lady starts talking about the Sins and the Martyrs and…" His train of thought sputtered out, and his throat tightened. "That video from the Lower East Side… that was *you*, wasn't it?"

Thorn's gut twisted, and she nodded. Jay's face turned to stone. He inhaled a shaky breath.

"What's going on, Thorn?" he asked again.

At first, Thorn didn't speak. She wasn't sure if she *should*. Jay had asked not to be involved, had explicitly told her he wanted nothing to do with this war she was fighting.

But whether he liked it or not, this war was on his front step. No one in this city was safe from it. Most of them were just ignorant of the battles happening around them. Not Jay.

Not anymore. He'd clearly seen the signs.

Finally, Thorn said, "She's after us."

"Who is?"

"The Raven," Thorn answered. "The Sins hired her to kill my agents, and she doesn't care who else she hurts along the way."

Jay crossed his arms. A deep frown settled across his features, making him look older than his mid-thirties. "Is she trying to lure you out?"

"I don't know what she wants," Thorn said, the admission sour in her mouth. "But whatever it is, she's way ahead of me. This whole damned thing is spiraling out of control. I can't stop it."

They stood in silence for a moment before Jay said, "Well, I'm here to—"

Thorn shook her head. "No."

"I'm not talking about joining your group," he clarified, raising his hands, "but… you have a safe place at The Cross, okay? For as long as you need it."

A sudden, unexpected surge of emotion wound around Thorn's neck like a rope, strangling her breath and her thoughts deep in her throat. She nodded. That seemed like enough for Jay. Thank god. It was all she could give him.

"I don't know what resources Froschlin could *possibly* have access to," Chris said.

Darius's breathing came in deep, heavy pulses, matching the smooth cadence of his feet pounding the treadmill's track. A layer of sweat along his shoulders and chest made his shirt cling to him, and his hair plastered against his forehead. He wiped it away with the back of his hand as he glanced at Chris on the neighboring machine.

"Me, neither," he said between breaths. "Do you think… she has a way to get info about the Martyrs?"

"You mean a mole?" Chris shook her head. Her blonde

ponytail swung behind her, crossing back and forth over the scar cutting from her left shoulder to right hip. "I doubt it. If someone were feeding her information, she could do a *lot* more damage... Remember Jacob?"

"Yeah, I do," Darius panted. "But we didn't realize what he was doing... for years."

Chris grimaced and nodded a reluctant agreement. "That's true..."

A chime rang on both of their watches, and they lowered their speeds for a cool-down walk. Darius heaved a breath from deep within his lungs, throwing his hands behind his head to open his chest cavity and accommodate more air. Chris tapped on her watch to check a couple of notifications before she heaved a sigh.

"If Froschlin knew more about us," she went on, "why resort to taunting us? Why not do something more damaging?"

Darius's jaw clenched. "Because that's less fun. Why make us run when she can make us jump?"

And they *were* jumping. Just that morning, there had been *another* incident in Manhattan with the Raven and her team of Martyr lookalikes. Once again, she had texted the burner to let Thorn know, and once again, they hadn't been able to get there in time to stop it. Civilians were wounded, Edith escaped, and the Martyrs—the *real* Martyrs—were left doing damage control.

"So, she's trying to rattle us," Chris said. "Throw us off our game."

"Looks like it," Darius muttered.

They fell into a quiet rhythm, with nothing but their steady breathing and the sounds of the gym to keep them company. Conrad, Seth, and a couple of other TAC officers were working off their frustrations with more brutal than average deadlifts while Charlotte Davis and her brother Andre took turns on the punching bag in the corner of the room. When Darius and Chris hopped off their treadmills, the door to the men's lockers swung open, and Gabe walked through. Water slicked his dark hair back, and his amber eyes lit up the moment they landed on Chris. He smiled and met her outside the women's room. The smell of chlorine sneaked through the woodsy scent of his shampoo.

"Hey." Gabe adjusted the gym bag on his shoulder, leaned down, and caught Chris's lips in a tender kiss.

"Hey," she echoed, smiling against his mouth. "How was your swim?"

"Good," Gabe said. "Still think you should join me sometime. It's way easier on your joints, you know."

He passed her an affectionate, teasing smile. Chris laughed.

"But a less practical skill," she said. "I'll stick to solid ground. You and Thorn can have the water."

The mention of Thorn's name strained Chris's expression, pulling at the corners of her eyes. She busied herself with adjusting the elastic in her hair. Darius's workout-weary lungs exhaled a slow breath. His mind wandered back to the last time he'd seen Thorn, when she'd headed back into the city again, running from the hard conversations rather than sitting down and getting them over with. He'd wanted to chase after her, grab her tight, and beg her to stay. He wished he had.

Thorn wasn't the only one hurting. They *all* were. He wondered if she saw that.

Chris cleared her throat. "Anyway," she said. A notification blinked on her watch, and she glanced at it. "I need to go take—"

She froze, her green eyes huge, shocked circles. The pink flush of exercise wiped clear from her face, leaving her pale and petrified. She patted her thighs, hunting for a phone she didn't have, before she twisted toward the women's locker room.

"What's wrong?" Darius asked as she pulled the door open.

Chris ran inside, where Darius couldn't see her anymore, but she shouted back. Her voice echoed down the narrow, tiled room.

"Noah's in trouble!"

She returned seconds later, a shirt haphazardly thrown over her sweat-glistening torso, and sprinted from the room with Darius and Gabe right behind her. She found Noah's contact and smashed her thumb against the call button. The second he answered, she asked, "What happened?"

The three of them rushed across the courtyard. Chris cut a line through the dinner crowd right to the stairs, ignoring the elevator, like climbing four flights of steps would take the edge off her panic. Darius couldn't hear Noah's voice from the phone crushed against Chris's ear, but her gaunt face told him enough.

"You got a picture?" Chris asked as they stormed down the hallway to her office. Her fingers quaked as she tried to slide her key into the lock. Gabe snatched it and opened the door. Chris burst into the room. "Send it to me."

She didn't bother with the light, moving through the dark by muscle memory. Darius flicked the switch, and Gabe shut the door with a snap that resounded like a gunshot. This office had once belonged to Noah's father, and the reality of that hit Darius hard enough to catch his breath. Jeremiah Montgomery had kept it clean and tidy, almost military minimalistic. Two wooden chairs sat before a desk, and a bookshelf to the side of it stocked dozens of firearm and gear manuals. The only personalized decor sat on the top shelf: an old photograph of Noah, freshly eighteen, standing in a purple graduation cap and gown. Darius's attention hovered over the young man's smiling face for a haunting moment.

Suddenly, present-day Noah's voice reached his ears. Darius spun around to see Chris settling behind her desk, the phone on speaker, while her computer screen flashed to life.

"My boss told me this high-profile client requested to work with me *specifically*," Noah said. Panic quickened his tone, filling the room with a sharp static of anxiety that crawled into Darius's bones and made it impossible for him to relax. Gabe stood behind Chris, and Darius joined at her side as Noah continued. "Said he wanted the top attorney in the agency. When I walked into my office, he was just… waiting there for me. Chris, what the hell am I going to do? I have a family now! I—"

"Noah, *breathe*," Chris cut in. "Did Claytor do anything to indicate he knew you were associated with us?"

She clicked a notification on her desktop, and a photograph filled the display. Noah had clearly concealed his phone behind his arm to get the shot. His dress shirt's deep, navy fabric cut a line across the screen. Beyond it, Darius could make out the trappings of a massive, high-rise business suite. Floor-to-ceiling windows opened to spectacular Manhattan views, the urban landscape looking nearly science fiction, glistening in sharp light and deep shadows as the autumn sun sank lower in the sky. A man loomed on the far side of a sleek, ebony desk. He wasn't particularly tall or intimidating, but the sight of him made Darius's body go numb anyway.

Greed.

Even from a candid photo like this, the Sin seeped of cold, calculating malice. His platinum hair and icy eyes would have stolen the warmth from his sharp features if there had been any left to steal. The gunmetal suit, perfectly tailored to fit his slim stature, gave him the appearance of a man carved from stone. Somehow, he made even his canary yellow tie feel frigid.

"Noah," Chris said when her old friend hadn't spoken. "*Noah,* did he seem suspicious of you?"

"I don't think so," Noah answered at last.

"Did he ask you anything strange?" she went on. "Like he was digging for information?"

"No. No, he didn't," Noah said. "H-he just talked about some accounts he had that are tied up in a massive series of fraud cases we're working. He showed me his numbers, and then I felt the pressure of Influence and—*fuck.*"

Noah dissolved again, a series of quiet, staccato gasps against the mic pulsing from Chris's speaker. She pressed her palms together in a mimicry of prayer, closing her eyes as she rested her lips against the sides of her hands.

"Okay," Chris said, her voice a drone of calm that didn't align with the rigidness in her body. A shaky breath exhaled between her fingers. Gabe took her by both shoulders, holding firmly, and the tension ebbed as she went on. "Okay, so it was all about business. That's good, Noah. Where are you now?"

"Still in my office," Noah replied. "He left five minutes ago. I can't go home, Chris. What if he has people watching me?"

A strangled noise crackled through the speaker, and Chris opened her eyes and navigated to a map of Manhattan. Over a dozen green dots moved slowly through the streets—markers of her units' locations. She tapped a couple of keys until Noah Montgomery's name populated the top corner, and the display automatically centered above a building in the Financial District.

"Noah, I have Darius and Gabe here," Chris said. "We're going to get a TAC patrol to escort you home, and Gabe will send another to guard your family, too." She threw Gabe a quick, worried look. He nodded, immediately sweeping from the room. Chris spoke again before the door closed behind him. "I can have someone positioned at your apartment twenty-four seven, but if Claytor *does* have people watching you, you need to act as naturally as possible, okay? You can't do anything that would sound alarm bells."

Noah made an incredulous sound that could've just as easily been a laugh as a scoff. "That's a hell of a lot easier said than done."

"I know," Chris said. "But it's important. Our Gray Unit agents—"

"I know damn well how it works, Chris!" Noah snapped.

A tense silence fell. Chris froze in her chair, and Noah breathed with percussive rattling on the other side of the line. Darius laid a hand on Chris's arm in Gabe's absence to offer a fleeting attempt at comfort that he knew would be appreciated, even if it didn't help a damn bit. After a moment, Noah sighed.

"Look, I know you're just trying to help," he murmured, "but Chris… I'm freaking out. He's *never* been here before. Or, shit, maybe he has, and he just wiped my memory of it. I didn't remember how to resist Influence until a few months ago. God *damn* it…"

His voice petered off again, and Chris's body softly raised and lowered beneath Darius's grip. "I appreciate that you're really worried, Noah, but you *need* to listen to me if we're going to keep you, your wife, and your daughter safe. You're also welcome back here, or we can relocate you."

"I can't do that. How the hell am I supposed to explain that to Simone?" Noah groaned. "But thank you… Thanks for everything."

"Of course," Chris said. "Anything for you. Even if it *is* a coincidence, running into any of the Sins is terrifying…"

Noah let out a huff of air. "To put it mildly…"

Chris's expression softened into a small, meek smile. Darius drew his hand off her arm at last, but not before he felt her tense again, as though steeling herself for a difficult conversation.

"I know this might sound insensitive," she began.

Noah cut her off before she could finish the thought. "You want to know more about why he was here," he stated plainly, as though this were old news to a Martyr kid.

"Yes," Chris admitted. "Our Gray Unit agent following Claytor is relatively new to the job."

"And you need all the information you can get on him." Noah heaved a sigh into the mic. "I'm not at liberty to discuss confidential client details with you… but what the fuck does that matter now?" He choked out a desperate, humorless laugh. "I'm sure you've heard of InvestX?"

Chris shook her head. "No, I haven't."

"Really?" Noah seemed shocked. "They've been all over

the news. Their CFO, Orlando Manson, committed suicide a month or so ago, but their PR team tried to cover it up as some freak accident."

"Why? What's going on?"

"They're a huge crypto conglomerate based in New York," Noah said. "They started a couple of years ago, and they've completely blown up. Thousands of other companies have billions of dollars tied into their instruments—Collatorized Cryptocurrency Consolidation Credits, or C4s for short, which are a blend of some of the most powerful cryptocurrency units on the market. I can't express just *how much* money is tied up in this conglomerate, Chris, and a couple of months ago, an anonymous whistleblower accused them of mismanaging investor funds. Our agency is currently overseeing almost two dozen cases of private investors, banks, and other entities that are saying they can't get their money out. When those cases go public, it's going to be *bad.*"

Chris frowned at her phone. "And Greed wants to hide the fraud?"

"No," Noah said. "I… actually think he's *behind* the fraud. He tried to Influence me to see the wrong numbers in his accounts, but it didn't work. Anton Claytor started short-selling InvestX and their C4s days before the whistleblower report came out. In other words, he was betting that the company and its instruments would collapse. He knew it was coming. In fact, I think *he* may have leaked the fraud to the public and Influenced some of my clients to start pulling their money out."

Darius and Chris exchanged a troubled look. "Then… what's he doing?" Darius asked.

"He's suing on behalf of some of the corporations he owns that had money tied up in this mess," Noah said, "basically, not only is he invested in the company's collapse, but he's trying to drain as much of the remaining cash before any other wronged parties can get their hands on it. He wants me to bump his case to the highest priority, which guarantees he gets compensated before anyone else can even get a foot in the door… And I have to fucking do it! I've got to go along and act like a brainwashed idiot while he screws my other clients over, or he might realize I can see through his charade and come after Simone and Zuri!"

He let out another groan, but this one was less hopeless. More defeated. On Chris's desktop screen, one of the green TAC markers approached Noah's location, blinking a block away. A suspicion tickled at Darius's consciousness, a nagging feeling that they were close to something important. Something dangerous.

"What's going to happen with those clients?" he asked.

"Once the fraud becomes public, the company's instruments, its assets, and its stock will all flatline," Noah answered. "They'll lose everything. Those accounts will be completely drained, and depending on how the investigation goes, there's a good chance they won't get a dime back. It won't just affect them but the people they serve, too. Millions will get hit."

Realization cracked like an egg on Darius's skull. He heard Edith Froschlin's voice in his head.

"How do you stop any radical group? Expose their lies, drain their resources, and never let them sleep."

Drain their resources… The words lodged like a stone, grinding against Darius's brain. What was the biggest resource the Martyrs had?

"Oh *shit*…" he breathed.

Chris glanced up, frowning at him. "What?"

He racked his brain, thinking back to the night, over three years ago, when he'd sneaked into Alan's office and found those financial statements. What had Alan told him when he asked where the money had come from? That they'd made wise *investments* over the years…

"Where are the Martyr accounts set up?" Darius asked, meeting Chris's eyes. They widened at the question—at the *implication.*

"We need to talk to Holly," she breathed. *"Now."*

CHAPTER THIRTEEN

Holly flipped through account statements, one after the other, her face pale.

"Zero… Zero… Zero… Another fucking zero!" She dragged her fingers through her hair, pulling the short, brown strands into a mess at the top of her head. "God *damn* it!"

She stood at the head of the conference table, hinged at the waist as she leaned over a laptop, and toggled a wireless mouse to navigate the display. On the far side of the room, the massive screen stared back at them with a collection of completely fucked financial reports. Holly's eyes darted from left to right behind her thick-rimmed glasses, reading frantically while the rest of the room shifted in tense silence. Nicholas and Mackenzie sat side by side, his arms crossed while she clacked her tongue piercing against the back of her teeth. Across from them, Chris flushed nervously, and Darius's stomach swirled at the sight of someone so strong appearing so shaken. Cain had joined them late, and he settled on Darius's far side, pinching his fingers as if to hold the stem of a wine glass. Unlike the rest of them, who watched Holly, his bright eyes considered the numbers on the screen.

"If what I'm seeing here is right," Holly murmured, "and it looks like it is, seventy percent of our investments are just *gone.*" She strangled her mouse with a crushing grip and opened another document, causing the far screen to flicker again. She scanned this one, too, her cheeks losing the rest of their color. "This is *so* bad!"

She straightened up and stepped away from the table, as though she needed to move to loosen some of the furious energy building in her tiny body. While Holly paced, swinging back and forth with a pendulum beat, Nicholas leaned over, grabbed her laptop, and started clicking through the reports. His blue eyes narrowed, and a deep frown settled behind his white-speckled beard. Darius pulled his phone out of his pocket. He'd tried to call Thorn, but she'd sent him to voicemail and hadn't responded to the follow-up text explaining the situation. His teeth clenched, and he put the device away as Mackenzie arched over the table.

"I don't know much about the Martyr finances beyond the R&D budgets I would write up for Alan," she said, chewing on a cuticle with a guilty grimace. "Well, okay, the budgets Lina would write and I'd sign off on. This guy, too." She nudged Nicholas with her elbow. He didn't look up from the screen. He'd leaned so close to it that the bright light cast deep shadows on his face, making his expression more manic than thoughtful. "How fucked are we exactly?"

Cain drew a shallow breath. "When we pooled our resources together to build the Martyrs, Judith was *insistent* that we diversify our finances to protect us from events exactly like this one… Yet somehow, many of them managed to get tied up in the same time bomb of a company. May I?"

He indicated the laptop in front of Nicholas, and the former Virtue nodded as he passed it across the table. For a few quiet minutes, Cain read through the reports in more detail. All the while, the fine lines in his forehead knitted together.

"Judith organized our funds into three separate categories," he murmured. "Savings accounts, international holdings, and liquid investments. Each of these categories served a different purpose."

He clicked around, opening a selection of account summaries. The numbers on the screen were so large they made Darius balk.

"First, savings. She wanted a handful of high-yield accounts where a large chunk of our money would go with the intention of providing enough dividends in the form of interest returns to pay for the Martyrs' base expenses." Cain glanced up to find the rest of them watching him. "In other words, these accounts keep the lights on. They pay for our power, our food, and all the other needs we must maintain to survive. Every year, we would audit these needs, and if we had to, we would add more money to the accounts to guarantee we received enough interest returns to support the Underground. These, you can see here, have not been touched."

He returned to the laptop, toggling the mouse to open a separate collection of reports.

"After establishing this basic safety net," Cain went on, "Judith funneled another large portion of our money into international banks. Offshore accounts offer a separate level of protection and privacy, are much less likely to be accessed by malicious third parties, and provide a certain… distance from the Martyrs themselves. Judith intended for these accounts to be accessed in emergencies, like when sudden, unanticipated expenses crop up."

Chris leaned forward, lacing her fingers on the table. "Those are the funds we used to rebuild our TAC fleet last year."

Cain held a gracious palm in her direction. "Precisely. That's what these accounts are meant to handle, or… it may seem, in a case like the one we've found ourselves in *now*, where we lose our largest resources… Which leads us to these accounts."

He whispered a sigh, cleared his throat, and closed their international account statements to open several portfolio documents. Darius recognized them as the ones Holly had initially been sifting through. She still stood behind Alan's empty chair, brown eyes narrowed.

"Liquid investments," Cain said. "Judith believed… oh, what was it that she always said? 'Cash is trash?'" He waved the thought away with a lazy hand. "The point was, cash is too easily impacted and devalued by inflation and other such financial nonsense Judith cared much more about than I do. Investments, she insisted, offered more protection *and* an opportunity to grow. So, under her guidance, the Martyrs invested large sums of money in various industries across the country, relying on investment banks to help us navigate and trade the markets. Nearly half of our money is in these investments, and, as Holly has already so succinctly pointed out, seventy percent of them have been impacted by this InvestX scandal."

Darius shook his head. "Why did they invest so much?"

"Because investments, while higher risk, offer a *much* higher reward," Cain answered. "Most of what we deal in is stock accounts and bonds. Our portfolio is quite extensive and spread across a handful of different investment groups, which should offer protection to market fluctuations. In a situation like this, however, such a huge number of our managed investments had money wrapped up in InvestX or its instruments…" He shook his head, his voice wandering away with his thoughts.

"Unbelievable," Darius murmured. "So, you're telling me it just took *one* failed company for the whole thing to collapse?"

Cain sighed. "It appears so."

Nicholas shook his head, rubbing his temples with the pads of his fingers. "What are the dividends from these investments used for?"

"Typically," Cain said, "this money handles all other expenses above our bare necessities and below sudden, emergent needs. Ammunition, vehicle repair, replacing equipment, travel costs, feeding into our accessible debit accounts for external units…"

Nicholas's jaw flexed. "So… everything TAC, Discovery, and Gray handle."

"Unfortunately," Cain said with a grim nod, "yes."

Nicholas swore, unwinding his arms from around his ribcage to drag his hands down his face. Beside him, Mackenzie's tongue piercing rattled more rapidly until she jammed her nails between her teeth and chewed them instead.

"This isn't just going to affect the Martyrs," Darius said. "Noah said thousands of other people will be impacted by this."

"More like millions," Chris corrected.

"And I'd bet the Sins themselves will be, too," Darius said. "Greed included! Even if he did short-sell his stock, the market crashing will have long-term consequences. Why would he want that?"

"To hurt *us*," Holly said. Her voice growled from her throat in a furious hiss.

"What do you mean?" Chris pressed.

"It's like chemotherapy," Holly said. She walked to the table, her hands gripping the back of the head chair. "It's a poison, and it could kill the healthy cells your body needs to function, but the whole damn point of it is to kill the cancer first." She met Chris's eyes, her jaw tight. "*We're* the cancer in this scenario. This InvestX bullshit has affected nearly *every single* investment agency in the city. He's clearly willing to take some serious hits as long as he can strangle us in the process."

"Son of a *bitch*," Mackenzie muttered around the nub of her thumbnail. "What can we do?"

Holly shook her head. "Nothing. Unless Noah's firm can recover the money InvestX stole, we're fucked."

The room sank into an uncomfortable silence. Darius shifted in his seat, glancing from Cain to Holly to the rest of the table. "So… we just have to let this happen?"

"Noah is one of the best," Chris said. "If anyone has a

shot at recovering our assets, it's him."

Darius frowned. "Wouldn't that lead the Sins right to us?"

"No," Holly said. "Every single account we have is owned by a shell corporation, and we have dozens of them. They're all differentiated from one another to prevent connections from being made between them *or* us."

"But even so," Chris said, "Noah said the case could take *months*, and there's a possibility we won't be able to claw back any of the money. Then, it won't matter anyway."

A breath of silence stretched between them before Nicholas swore. "I can't believe we didn't catch this."

"I can't believe it happened in the first place," Holly said bitterly. "InvestX started up a couple of years ago, and I told Alan it looked like a fucking disaster waiting to happen and to make sure to keep our investments away from it! He must have signed off on—"

Holly suddenly froze, and her face flushed an even more dangerous shade of red. She dipped back to the laptop and typed madly. Darius watched as the drained investment accounts flashed on the screen again. The more she looked through, the angrier Holly appeared to become.

Cain cleared his throat. "Whatever the reason may be, it's irrelevant now," he said. "We should focus on how to move forward. Whether we like it or not, we are about to find ourselves in a perilous situation. You should all look at your departments and get a budget report of current expenses and potential areas to cut."

Chris and Nicholas nodded. Mackenzie's eyes widened into fawning circles, and Nicholas sighed as he said, "I'll help you out."

"Oh, thank god," she muttered.

"Darius," Cain went on, "can you speak with Dr. Harris about the hospital?"

"Absolutely," Darius replied.

Cain nodded before he turned to Holly. "Is it possible for us to pull *any* money out of these impacted accounts?"

Holly's mouth pressed into a fine line. "There's still technically money in a couple of them, but anything related to InvestX is zero at this point. Gone."

"Well… Just do what you can, I suppose." Cain rose to his feet, rubbing his hands together in a way that betrayed his lack of confidence in this arena. "Let's be on our way then…"

The others stood, too, and one by one, they filed out of the room. Chris, Mackenzie, and Nicholas all moved toward their offices while Holly turned in the opposite direction to head back to her domain in the basement. As Cain reached the door, Darius touched his shoulder.

"Hey," he said. "Thank you. I know you didn't want to get wrapped up in the Martyr leadership, but I really appreciate your help."

Cain offered a patient nod. "Ah, yes. I'm not relishing the idea, but let's just say it was never truly the *role* of leadership I resisted."

A glint of old, bittersweet resentment flashed across his expression, and Darius frowned. Before he could ask, though, Cain opened the door, and sudden shouting thundered down the hallway.

"How the *fuck* did this happen?"

Thorn.

Darius's heart flipped as he and Cain bolted toward the entrance. Holly's voice met them the moment they burst into the waiting room.

"What do you mean *how did it happen?*" she exclaimed, throwing her hands up. The two women stood six feet apart, Thorn a tower of stark white against sharp black while Holly glowered up at her beneath a messy fray of boyish hair. "Greed's pulling his Influence behind the scenes!"

Thorn's lip curled into a snarl. "And we've lost *half* of our money?" Hair fanned around her head in windswept tangles, and Sparkie clutched the kevlar bike jacket. He loomed over her shoulder and uttered a low, dangerous hiss as Thorn shook her head in a violent jerk. "What are we supposed to do now? Starve to fucking death?"

Darius hedged further into the room, Cain on his heels, while a pull of Virtuous energy approached the double doors to the hospital ward. Lamar's face peered through the narrow window. He met Darius's gaze with an ashen stare.

"We're figuring that out!" Holly snapped. "Not that you'd know—"

Cain coughed, loudly. "Ladies—"

"God *damn* it, Andrews!" Thorn's hands landed on her hips with a bruise-cutting grip. "You should have caught this!"

Holly balked, her eyes and mouth both wide and gaping. *"Me?"*

"Yes, *you!* Who the fuck else is in charge of our security?"

"Hah!" Holly took a step closer to Thorn, bristling with the energy of a fearless house cat challenging a Doberman. "This isn't a security problem! It's an *accounting* problem, and I've *never* been in charge of accounting." Her jaw clenched, and she shoved her phone screen in Thorn's face. *"Alan was.* And would you look at that? 'Alan' signed off on these InvestX shares… two months *after* he died."

Thorn froze. Her thin lips slipped open in a sudden, horrifying realization, but nothing more came out of them. Not even a breath.

Holly glared up at her, glowing red with joyless vindication. "Don't you *dare* come at me and say I should have caught this," she said. *"You* should have!" She thrust a finger at the center of Thorn's chest. Darius was sure Thorn would slap it away, but she simply stared as Holly went on. *"You* took over Alan's responsibilities after he died. *You* insisted you didn't need any help handling them. *You* are the one who hasn't been doing your job."

Holly's volume slowly grew louder and louder until she was nearly screaming. Thorn didn't move, her expression carved into an alabaster canvas of shock and shame. A liquid, crystalline gleam flashed behind her lashes. After a moment, Holly took a deep breath, pressed her fingertips into the bridge of her nose, and exhaled a sharp sigh.

"Thorn, I *know* his death was hardest on you," she continued. The forced calm sounded fake and placating. Thorn's lower lip quivered. "And we have *all* been patient… but we can't keep cleaning up your mess on top of everything else we're already killing ourselves over."

Thorn's eyes darted to Cain and Darius, standing just outside the hallway. A hot, humiliated flush colored her cheeks as she ripped her focus back toward Holly.

"You're killing yourselves?" Thorn repeated, but she was no longer shouting, and her hands moved away from her hips as she wrapped her arms around her chest instead. Sparkie disappeared down the back of her bike jacket. The sudden shift, the weaker stature, made Darius take a step further into the room. Thorn didn't look at him again. "I'm out there trying to stop a psychopath from killing people in New York City—a psychopath who wants to kill us. Stopping *her* is my top priority!"

"Jesus, listen to yourself!" Holly scoffed. "How do you plan to stop her if we run out of money? How do you expect to replace damaged armor? To stock up on ammunition? Or replenish our medical supplies?"

She threw a hand toward the hospital doors. Lamar startled and ducked beneath the glass window. Thorn glowered at her.

"*This* problem needs a solution," Holly went on. "More than *anything.*"

Thorn's nails dug into her biceps. "Then find a solution."

"So once again, it's *my* responsibility to un-fuck the things *you've* screwed up!"

"If you don't like the way I'm handling things, Andrews," Thorn snapped, but before she had the chance to finish, Holly laughed again.

"How you're *handling* things?" she repeated, shouting again. Thorn's pale cheeks darkened another dangerous shade of red. Sparkie let out a strangled growl Darius could barely hear from across the room. Holly didn't seem to notice, or care. "Jesus, Thorn, you're not *handling* anything! You're just—"

"Stop!"

Darius's voice cut through the waiting room, startling everyone—including himself. Holly spun on her heels to face the hallway, the look in her lens-magnified eyes making it clear she hadn't realized he and Cain were standing there. Thorn didn't look at him, instead casting her gaze to the ground at her feet. Darius shook his head.

"Arguing about whose fault this is won't help us," he said. "We're on the same goddamned team."

"On the same *team?*" Holly hissed. "So, because we're on the 'same team,' I have to shut my mouth, and Thorn won't be held accountable for her actions? Fucking *awesome.*"

Darius didn't reply, caught with his mouth wide open but painfully empty. Holly took off down the corridor without a second glance back. Thorn's sharp eyes finally landed on Darius with a cutting glint. Above them, though, her brows dipped into a soft curve. Neither spoke, and Cain shifted awkwardly from one foot to the other. Darius drew a deep breath, pulled his shoulders back, and touched Thorn's arm.

"I'll take over the budget."

The air went cold and still. Thorn shook her head. "No," she began, but he raised his hand to stop her.

"I'm not asking," he said. "You're both swamped. I'll handle it."

Thorn moved like she was about to speak again. Her mouth slivered open just enough to show a flash of her tongue pinched between white teeth, but nothing came out. Darius offered a smile. "You're welcome."

Her jaw snapped shut again, narrowing eyes implying that a thank you had been the furthest thing from her mind. Without another word, she tucked her chin to her chest and walked toward the elevator. Sparkie squeezed from the neckline of her jacket, poking his nose through long strands of black hair to watch Darius until Thorn turned the corner and vanished entirely.

As soon as she was gone, Cain cleared his throat.

"Well," he said with a silky blend of sarcasm and relief as he ran a hand through his salt and pepper hair. "I'd say this is a… creative solution. Have you ever *done* a budget before?"

Darius crossed his arms. "Nope."

"I'd thought not," Cain murmured. "I take it back. This isn't a creative solution. It's a *stupid* one."

Darius chuckled, landed a palm on Cain's shoulder, and turned back toward his office. Maybe Cain was right, but this was the first concession he'd gotten with Thorn—the first time she'd allowed him to help her in six months.

He was going to take it.

CHAPTER FOURTEEN

The Underground slept, but Darius didn't.

He held a thermos of fresh coffee in one hand and stifled a yawn behind the other as the elevator dragged him upward. Beneath his feet, a field of warm souls grew slowly distant. All the lights in the common areas had dimmed to something resembling the glow of moonlight shining down from a clear sky, and the Martyrs were either tucked happily into their beds or relaxing in the recreation room.

Not a soul stirred way up here.

Darius's tired body begged to join them—to collapse onto his mattress and melt into the blankets—but he had a feeling Dream Darius would be even worse at figuring out this budget problem than Conscious Darius was.

And the budget was all he'd thought about for three agonizing days. He'd buried himself in research, talked with all the directors, and combed through Alan's archives to get a feel for what their finances were *supposed* to look like so he could find the best places to cut. Hell, he'd even sunk so low as to search "how to manage a budget" on LymeLite to make sure he understood the basics. Logically, he knew he'd made progress, but it sure as hell didn't *feel* like it.

Darius wouldn't say he regretted offering to take over,

but he'd definitely underestimated how complicated this was going to be.

The elevator hit the top floor with a ping. He headed down the hallway and through the empty waiting area, as dark and silent as the night outside. Darius maneuvered his way by the murky glimmer of dull bulbs until he passed the conference room and turned down the short corridor into the leadership alcove. He paused.

A golden bar of light shone from beneath the door to the lounge between Alan's office and Thorn's. Darius's breath stuttered in his throat.

Maybe he wasn't the only one working late tonight.

He stood poised at the far end of the hall while his heart and mind battled for control of his body. He wanted to burst in, to find Thorn sitting at her desk, to hear her voice and see her smile. But Thorn had made it clear she wasn't ready for that—wasn't ready for him.

Darius picked up his feet again. Every step echoed loud against the tile, like the Underground itself was trying to make her as aware of *him* as he was of her. His office was closest to the lounge, and the light washed against his shoes as he slipped his key into the lock. It opened with a click that sounded more like a bang, and when he shut the door behind him, he was sure the walls themselves rattled.

Darius breathed a sigh and turned on the lights.

His desk sat exactly as he'd left it fifteen minutes ago: chair out, screen on, and an empty coffee mug beside his mouse. Darius sat down and stared at the spreadsheet filling the display. A financial breakdown of the TAC department.

Though Darius had talked to everyone with purchasing power, including all the department heads, team managers, and adjacent personnel, his meeting with Chris and Gabe had been the most intense by far. TAC was a beast, with more manpower, more equipment, and more needs than any of the others. They'd discussed the situation for hours, considering ammunition costs, added expenses for maintaining their fleet of electric vehicles, and cash outflows for the patrolling units in the city. Ultimately, they'd decided to scale back more than fifty percent of their operations until further notice.

That also meant no more side quests to catch Edith Froschlin. They couldn't risk losing equipment… or people. The decision didn't sit well with any of them, especially Thorn, who had taken her frustrations out on a punching bag until she spilled its sandy guts all over the gymnasium floor. Edith's latest stunt had taken place in Central Park that very afternoon, resulting in another critically injured civilian and a LymeLite hunt for the two Martyr knockoffs who'd opened fire on her in the crowd. Men and women in crow masks flocked to the scene in the aftermath, screaming about justice and Judas, demanding the Martyrs be caught and crucified.

Guilt swelled heavily in Darius's throat. He glanced at the wall his office shared with Thorn's. His body buzzed at the idea of her being so close, just a couple of layers of concrete and sheetrock away. If *he* felt this helpless, he could only imagine how crippled she was right now.

The urge to get up and go in there tugged at him again. And again, he stamped it down. Instead, Darius opened the thermos and refilled his mug. Steam spiraled upward as he closed his aching eyes and pressed his lips against the rim to take a tentative sip. It stung. He blew across the surface, casting ripples to the opposite edge.

A sudden knocking made Darius jolt so hard that a surge of hot coffee gushed over his mug and singed his hand. He hissed as he set it down, shook his fingers with a wince, and glanced up. A pale face peered through the narrow gap of his opening door. His cheeks flushed.

"Thorn."

It was all he said—all he felt safe to say, like uttering the wrong words in the wrong order might spook her back into hiding. He clumsily wiped his coffee-soaked hand on his jeans, hoping she wouldn't notice, but of course, she did. Thorn's sharp eyes caught on the motion before wandering to the mug ringed in a dark pool on the wood. Darius lifted it and wiped the spill with his sleeve.

"No coaster?" she asked.

Darius hesitated, not sure if this was a dig or dry humor. God, it had been so long since they'd interacted that he'd forgotten *how* to interact with her.

"I… don't usually need one," he said.

A quiet nod tilted Thorn's chin. "You're working late." Even though she'd spoken quietly, her deep voice reverberated like a plucked guitar string, melodic and lonely.

Darius shrugged. "That makes two of us."

Thorn slipped inside. The door clicked shut, and Darius wondered if the increased heat was in his imagination or if the furnace had kicked on. She walked across the room with a lithe, effortless grace, past the brown suede couch, glass-topped coffee table, and plush armchair to stand at the corner of Darius's desk. When she leaned forward to look at his computer, her hair cascaded in dark, silky falls around her shoulder. Sparkie peered over the curve of her neck, his chin cresting her bare skin just enough for Darius to spot his blue head. Thorn's eyes darted down the spreadsheet columns, taking time to consider every line item, every number, before they glided to him. The second her gaze caught his, Darius's mouth ran dry.

"It's the budget," he offered stupidly.

"I see that. How's it going?"

"We're figuring it out." Darius rubbed his eyes. "I've had so many meetings… This has to be the most activity this office has seen since Abraham left."

He chuckled, and Thorn smirked in response, with a curve on the verge of a real smile. She walked further around the desk to stand at Darius's side and stopped just far enough to where they didn't touch. The intoxicating scent of vanilla and sandalwood warmed his face as Thorn arched toward him. Though she didn't have an aura, Darius imagined the heat of her body, the draw of her soul, pulling at his anyway.

"And… what have you figured out?"

He sighed and crossed his arms. It felt like the safest place for them to be right now. "That Alan ran a really tight ship."

The second he said it, he wished he hadn't. At Alan's name, Thorn's body hardened, and her expression settled into a statuesque facade.

"There's not a lot of room for us to cut," Darius went on hastily. "Except maybe Nicholas's bulk cereal orders. That stuff looks *and* tastes like cardboard anyway…"

He threw Thorn a smile, but she didn't reply. Didn't even look at him. When she finally did speak, she simply murmured, "Alan was efficient."

Darius's jaw ached from the pressure of clenching it shut. Sparkie's head tilted in his direction, and the movement made Darius realize he was staring. He pointed to the screen with a nod. "Yeah, if you look at what we've done historically, departments like the hospital and maintenance only order exactly what they need to sustain themselves… and since they're critical in keeping the Underground and its people healthy, I don't feel comfortable cutting them. The kitchen, too, though Kenia did have some ideas for how to save on our food expenses." He let out a mirthless scoff. "Man, I've come full circle."

Thorn swiped a strand of hair behind her ear. "Full circle? What do you mean?"

"Worrying about medicine, money, and food," he said. This time, Thorn was the one who stared. Her focus made his cheeks burn anew. Darius cleared his throat.

"Anyway," he went on, toggling to the R&D budget sheet. "The Research department doesn't have a lot of extra costs since they're Underground-based, but our Discovery teams need access to funds for public transit and basic living expenses… same with the Gray Unit. Nicholas recommended some solutions here."

From his periphery, he caught Thorn finally tearing her gaze away from him to look at the screen, too.

"I also told Cain his art classes have to be put on hold," Darius said. "Can't really justify buying paint, canvas, or clay…"

"I bet he didn't like that," Thorn said.

"No, but he understood. He *did* ask if we could still get wine, though…"

Thorn laughed—a real, genuine laugh—that made Darius's head whip around. "Maybe if Cain didn't drink so much, we wouldn't be having this problem."

She tossed him an amused, sideways glance. A glisten of familiar humor gleamed in her expression, tugging at the corners of her mouth and making her dark irises glitter. God, Darius had missed that, missed this… missed *her*. Thorn never had an aura, but she had a presence—a steady, undeniable *something* that made her the most impressive person in whatever room she stepped into. Even now, despite the sick pallor to her skin and exhausted shadows carved beneath her eyes, she commanded that power. He wondered if she knew just how brightly her light still shined or if she mistook the shadows she cast for her own battered soul.

The longer he watched her, the clearer the answer. Thorn's smile withered beneath his gaze, her focus moving from his eyes to his mouth before she took a small step away and looked at the computer again.

"I heard you grounded nearly half of TAC," she said at last, severing the silence and tension with razor-sharp words.

"Yeah," Darius said. "It's our largest department and the biggest drain on our resources."

"It's also our most *important* department," Thorn replied, voice rising. "It's why the Martyrs were founded in the first place. We *can't* stop going after Edith."

Disappointment settled deep in Darius's lungs, and he forced a shallow, muddled breath between his lips. He should have known.

Thorn hadn't come in here to *see* him. She'd come to *fight* with him. Darius's pride stung—his *heart* stung.

"No," he countered, surprised at the sensation of a fist wrapped around his throat while he spoke. *"We* are the most important department: the leadership. And we'll fail *everyone* if we can't figure out how to make it through this without starving to death." Thorn's eyes widened, but Darius shook his head without giving her a chance to interrupt. "I understand your concern, but taking down Froschlin comes second, third… hell, it might not even make our top ten."

"She is *hurting* people," Thorn said as she crossed her arms and glared at him. Sparkie tucked behind her hair, disappearing from view.

"And TAC will be useless if we run out of the means to fund them," Darius said. His hands buzzed, threatening to ball into fists on his desktop, but he forced his fingers to open wide. "Look, Thorn, I have work to do. If you're just here to argue with me, you need to go."

He turned back to the computer and slammed his pinky onto the enter key harder than he'd intended, jolting his cursor to a new row in his spreadsheet. Thorn stood stone-still beside him, a dark shape in the corner of his eye. Darius scrolled back up to the top of his document, but nothing on the display made its way into his brain. He was too clouded with thoughts of her and all too aware of her focus on him, sharp enough to scar. When she did finally shift, he glanced up, expecting her to walk away.

But Thorn drew closer.

"I'm sorry."

Darius blinked, stunned, as a wounded, repentant glint darkened her eyes.

"Andrews was right," she went on. "The budget is *my* mess."

Thorn sighed, turned around, and leaned against his desk. Darius shook his head.

"You couldn't have predicted this, Thorn."

"I *literally* signed up for it," she countered. "And signed *off* on it. I *fucked* up, Darius." Thorn threw a hand into the air. "And I just *kept* fucking up. Our accounts started dipping weeks ago, not that I was paying any attention, and the investigation was all over the goddamned news! And let's not forget the InvestX CFO who committed—"

Her voice suddenly broke off, and Thorn pressed her eyes closed, covering them with a hand. Darius rose to his feet, unsure of what to do, how to help, so he gently touched his fingertips against her shoulder. She peered up, catching his gaze in those black depths. Darius held his breath in the seconds between her pulling away or accepting him.

She relaxed, lifted her hand, and grabbed his fingers in an urgent grip.

"I let them get in my head, Darius." The words were a whisper, and her jaw flexed as though she had a bitter taste trapped in her teeth. "Alan would have caught this. He could have stopped it from happening. All I'm good for is fucking fighting." She looked away. Bit her cheek. "And now that TAC has been cut, I can't even do that."

The muscles along her throat shifted, swallowing down the admission.

"I don't think that's true," Darius said. Thorn threw her gaze to the ground, and he leaned down to catch it before it landed. "Not about Alan, and not about *you.*"

Thorn's chin slanted up, her brow knitted. In a breath, she tilted toward him. Darius's heart leapt into his throat. They were so close, closer than they'd been in months, close enough that it made his entire being burn beneath the surface. It would take nothing—a step, a stroke, a *sigh*—to hold her.

But she released him, severing their connection. Darius withdrew his hand in a clenched fist, as though he could capture some of Thorn's essence in his palm.

"Anyway," she said. "I didn't come here to wallow in self-pity *or* yell at you. I came to help."

Darius scoffed. "It's almost midnight!"

"So?"

"So... go to bed," Darius said.

One of her brows arched in a delicate curve. God, how did even *that* expression highlight her exhaustion? "Are *you* going to bed?"

"Well, no—"

"Then neither am I," Thorn cut in. "How can I help?"

For a moment, Darius stared, and Thorn stared back with a stubbornness that reminded him of who she'd been before Hunts Point. Underneath the weariness and worry, he saw a foundation of will and want that made it clear she knew he couldn't turn her down.

So he smirked and opened the top drawer in his desk to grab a tablet. "Look for places we can cut costs," Darius said as he navigated to the budget document on their server and handed it to her.

Thorn's fingers brushed his as she took the device, sending an electrifying current up his arm, down his spine, and deep into his core. Then she walked back around his desk to sit on the couch. Every inch of distance she put between them felt like a gulf, every step an ocean. When she settled onto the cushions, legs folded neatly to one side, she adjusted her fingerless gloves and started to read. Darius watched her. He couldn't help it. Abraham had removed the bulbs from the overhead lights, instead relying on a couple of table lamps around the room. These provided a soft, comforting glow, which cast Thorn's face in shadows reminiscent of warm fire radiating from the hearth.

But they also highlighted the dark halos beneath her eyes and the sharp contrast of her cheekbones. Whatever Thorn did when she avoided the Underground, sleeping wasn't it. A pang of guilt that she was here now made Darius's stomach uneasy. She drew a liquid sheet of black hair behind an ear to reveal her Familiar peering across the room. His beady eyes landed on Darius, caught him staring, and Thorn's cheeks flushed a subtle shade of pink. Darius hastily sat at his computer again, but the values on the screen suddenly felt like a foreign language.

They worked until the room settled around them, and

the clock at the corner of Darius's display ticked into the new day. While he crunched the numbers for what they had lost in frozen assets, he could see a tiny, red marker indicating Thorn logged into the same sheet, reminding him that he wasn't alone in the room anymore. She highlighted rows and left notes, words flashing across his screen with recommendations, which he read in her voice. He avoided glancing up and drawing attention to the fact that her very presence here, breathing the same *air*, sent his heart racing and mind reeling. More than once, Darius wished he could have a Familiar, too—maybe a mouse or a dove—quietly watching Thorn without the clumsy awkwardness of human eyes so he could know if she was stealing looks at him the way he *wanted* to look at her. Every time the temptation struck, he drowned it with a sip of coffee until his mug was empty and thermos half-full.

But soon, even that ache faded, and the tension gave way to something close to comfortable. Darius's mind became more focused on facts and figures than the dark form sitting on his couch. Thorn made herself at home, discarding her boots and setting them beside the glass coffee table to pretzel her legs beneath her. Sparkie lay across her opposite shoulder, his wings sloping down either side of her body like a blanket.

At two in the morning, Darius's coffee was gone, and his brain couldn't stand the thought of focusing on their money problems for another goddamned second. He let out a sigh that sounded more like a groan as he leaned back in his chair and ran his hands down his face.

"All right," he said into the stillness. "I think I've got to call it."

He glanced up at Thorn, but she didn't move. Her back was to him, one arm raised to rest along the top of the couch, and Sparkie curled into a ball of blue scales and red webbing, hiding his face from view.

"Thorn?" Darius asked.

Silence answered. Thorn didn't so much as lift her head

from where it tilted into the curve of her wrist. The line of her neck extended to her shoulder, slowly rising and falling in a smooth, rhythmic pattern. Darius stood up and walked around his desk. When he reached the opposite side of the coffee table, his heart skipped.

Thorn's eyes were closed, lips gently parted, and her breath flowed in and out like the pull of the tide. She'd set the tablet in her lap, where it had gone untouched for long enough that the screen went black. Her body melted against the cushions, muscles softened into something mimicking peace, but somehow, an anxious knit still tightened her expression. Even in sleep, Thorn could never truly rest.

Darius hovered there, wondering if he should wake her up and tell her to go to bed, but he knew she wouldn't. Part of him considered moving her into a more comfortable position or grabbing the pillow and blanket she kept in her office, but he worried touching her at all would ruin this. As Darius watched her, taking a bittersweet moment to consider Thorn's features—her shadowed eyes, parched lips, and hollow cheekbones—he realized all he wanted now was to let her sleep for as long as she could.

God knew she needed it.

So he returned to his desk, closed out of all programs, and shut down his machine. He'd turn off the lights, leave the door unlocked, and give her this space, this *peace*. A couple of years ago, she'd done the same for him. How had she felt back then? Had she taken the time to watch him sleep? To really detail the exhaustion he'd tried to hide in his waking hours? Had her concern felt this deep? Hurt *this* much?

Warmth rose to his cheeks as Darius quietly crossed the room, opened the door, and reached for the switch.

Thorn shifted.

Darius froze over the threshold. The shadow of serenity dissolved, bit by bit, starting in her breath, which hitched in her throat. Her expression followed, eyelids tightly shut, nostrils flared, jaw clenched. A frail, strangled noise filled her mouth and squeezed its way from gnashed teeth.

Darius's heart thrummed against his sternum.

"Thorn?"

She jerked to one side. Then the other. The delicate curve of her spine suddenly spasmed into a violent arc, sending her head flying back. The motion forced her mouth open, and a chest-deep sob poured from it. Sparkie let out a shrill cry as he writhed, lost his grip, and tumbled to the cushions. He fell like a board, webbed wings stiff and rigid. Silent tears streamed down Thorn's face and coated her cheeks in a wet, glistening slick.

"Thorn!"

Darius tore back into the room and fell to one knee on the couch beside her. Her whole body trembled, and when he grabbed her by the shoulders, he found her skin damp with cold sweat and ridged in goosebumps. He gently shook her. Those black eyes shot wide open, and her lips parted in a stuttering gasp.

"Thorn, it's okay," he said. "I'm—"

"Don't touch me!"

She yanked out of Darius's grip and shoved away from him—shoved *him* away from *her.* His calves slammed into the edge of the coffee table, and he fell.

Thorn screamed as Darius crashed into the glass top shoulder-first. It shattered beneath him, and suddenly, the room reeked of the sweet, metallic stink of blood.

He didn't move as he put his senses back together. His body draped over the metal table frame, legs held off the ground with the deep, bruising pressure of a bar digging into his thigh. A thick, pounding ache at the side of his skull made him think his head had crashed into the opposite side. But all of that seemed to disappear within the searing pain tearing through his arm and the disorienting sensation of blood cutting a path to his elbow. It dripped from his skin and landed on the carpet with a wet pitter-patter that made his vision swim and his stomach buckle.

"Oh my god…"

Thorn leapt from the couch and poised by Darius's feet,

yet her voice reverberated like it was far away. Her mouth gaped in a scream without sound. Somewhere in the room, Sparkie let out a piercing cry.

"What happened?" she gasped. *"What did I do?"*

"It's okay," Darius said. He tried to crawl from the mangled table, but the moment he did, shards of glass sliced into his skin. He braced against the metal frame instead and climbed over the wreckage to flop onto the carpet. The sudden change in position made his head swim. "Thorn, it's okay."

"No, no, no," she whispered. A fresh gleam of unshed tears clung to her lashes. As she shook her head, one clawed free to trail a line down her cheek. Thorn walked backward until her spine collided with Darius's doorframe, and gravity dragged her to the ground. She stared at him, harrowed and distant, like she wasn't there at all but instead still standing in that lifeless, blood-splattered warehouse with a metal pipe in her hand and a plea to spare a life in her ear.

"Thorn, breathe," he murmured. "I'm here. Just breathe."

She did—in great, gulping gasps—and as Darius came closer, she pushed further against the frame until she nearly tumbled into the hall. He lowered back down and held out a hand. Thorn didn't take it.

"It was just a nightmare," Darius went on. "I've got you. You're safe."

The rapid rise and fall of Thorn's ribcage evened out, but the horror in her expression didn't fade. Her eyes traveled from his face to his arm, and she covered her mouth with trembling fingers.

"I'm fine," he said. "It's just a little—"

He glanced down. His voice crashed against his windpipe.

Blood.

He was *covered* in blood.

Thorn lurched forward, onto her knees. "Fuck, Darius," she rasped. *"Fuck!"*

A sudden chill settled over his brain as he stared at his arm. The gash cut through his skin and muscle. Darius wound his hand around it, trying to apply pressure to stop the bleeding, but the gaping mouth of his flesh devoured his fingers—attempted to swallow them whole.

"Thorn." Darius reeled, trying to keep his eyes open, as he swallowed down an anxious, nauseous rush. "Get Lamar."

Now, the wound poured faster, vomiting out a viscous, red stream. Darius was vaguely aware of the pain—of the feeling of his feet and fingers and face going colder. He stood, but his muscles sat heavily inside his skin, like they weren't accustomed to holding his weight.

"Lamar," he repeated. His office went fuzzy, and then, it went gray. He thought Thorn got to her feet, but maybe it was him, lowering back to her level to stop the room from spinning.

Jesus, it was spinning so fast.

Suddenly, Darius was weightless. Cold, aura-less arms hooked beneath his armpits and tilted him backward. He floated in a hazy current, gaze to the ceiling. A blue and red blur flashed above him. He thought he heard Thorn say his name as his body began to convulse and his eyelids fluttered closed…

When he opened them again, her face filled his view, so all he had to focus on was the concerned look in her dark eyes.

With a groan, Darius tried to sit up, but Thorn laid a palm flat to his heart and forced him back down. Something soft pressed against his back. His couch?

"Don't move," she said, but her voice lacked the strength usually attached to such orders. "Lamar's on his way."

Sure enough, the young Virtue's magnetic sensation sprinted across the courtyard beneath them. Thorn sat up straight, and one look at her made it clear how Darius had gotten here. Red streaks painted her collar and arms to where her gloves began. She removed one of them and leaned over him again as she tied the length of it around his bicep. A grimace flickered across her expression. "Shit…"

Darius stole another look at himself and immediately regretted it. A splatter of swirling, gray dots occluded his vision, threatening his consciousness again. He covered his face with the crook of his opposite elbow.

"I've healed worse than this," he said. His mouth stung with the sour build-up of saliva right before sickness. He swallowed it all down. "I can't believe I'm getting dizzy *now*. I guess it's different when it happens to you."

He tried to laugh, but Thorn's mouth set into a finer seam. She removed her other glove, exposing her scarred arm and *Peccostium*, and pressed it directly against the gash to staunch the bleeding. Though her makeshift tourniquet had slowed the flow, it still came heavily enough to saturate the fabric. As she adjusted, her fingers came back painted red.

Thorn began to tremble. It started in her hands, vibrated up her arms, and her breathing picked up. She'd already turned ghostly white, but somehow, she seemed to lose even more color. Darius's blood on her hands stood out in bright, horrifying contrast. She stared at it.

Darius moved to sit again. This time, Thorn didn't stop him. He grabbed her hands. Her skin felt unusually warm.

"Hey," he murmured, brows drawn deep in concern. Thorn looked up. "I'm—"

Sparkie tore around the corner with a cry. He bounded against the open office door and leapt over the threshold. Thorn ripped out of Darius's grip and sprung to her feet. Her Familiar landed on her shoulder, wings frazzled, tail rigid. Darius stood, too.

Lamar burst into the room.

He'd clearly been asleep, wearing nothing but a pair of gray sweatpants and a navy silk bonnet that tucked all of his locs neatly out of view, and his wide, mahogany eyes carried that distant look of someone who was jolted awake at two in the morning. His toned chest heaved in and out as he took in the state of the place—of the shattered table and blood-soaked carpet, Darius's bandaged arm and Thorn's red-streaked skin.

"Good *god*," he blurted out. "What the hell happened in here?" Before they had the chance to answer, Lamar rushed over, gingerly stepping around hunks of glass, and grabbed Darius by the elbow. When he sat on the couch, he dragged Darius down with him. One look at the cut made Lamar's nose curl, and he sucked in a sharp breath. "What were you trying to do? See what your insides looked like?"

Lamar's palms warmed with Virtue healing heat. That power coursed into Darius's body, tingling a little in his skull, his hands, and the backs of his thighs, but primarily focusing on his arm. The flesh crackled, nearly itching, as it pulled back together.

"I fell," Darius said.

Lamar cast him a dubious look. "…And almost turned your whole ass body into Swiss cheese?"

"It was a rough fall."

He tried to smile, but Lamar's eyes narrowed. Above them, standing exactly where she'd landed when she leapt away, Thorn shifted from one foot to the other and wound her arms across her chest. Lamar glanced between her and Darius, as though collecting pieces of evidence and sorting them into something resembling the truth. When he looked back at Darius, a knowing glint sharpened his expression.

"I guess so," he said at last.

Thorn drew a short breath, took a small step backward, and forced her clenched jaw apart to say, "I'm… going to put in a maintenance request to get this cleaned up." She didn't meet their gazes as she grabbed her boots and darted from the room. Instead of turning toward her office, she disappeared down the hallway and, Darius suspected with a twinge, from the Underground entirely.

Lamar watched the vacant door frame as his healing power wrapped up. When Darius's arm was back in one piece, Lamar untied the glove tourniquet and bundled it with the other, considering them with a frown before catching Darius's eye.

"You didn't fall."

He laid the bloodied, black mass of cloth on the couch's arm, which was already splattered with red. Darius massaged his fingertips into the freshly mended muscle, biding time because he knew he couldn't lie.

"It was an accident."

Lamar raised a brow. "Pretty big accident."

Darius's mouth ran dry, and he pinched the bridge of his nose. As the adrenaline wore off, exhaustion settled down his spine, and all he wanted to do was coil to the couch and pass out. "Thorn had a nightmare," he admitted at last.

Lamar motioned to the ruined table and glinting glass. *"This* is not a nightmare. It's PTSD." He tipped his chin. "And wait… She was *sleeping* here?" Lamar shook his head. "You know what, I'm going to table *that* for a minute. You didn't try to wake her up, did you?"

Darius blinked. "I—well, yeah! She was thrashing around—"

Lamar interrupted with a groan. His head rolled back in a dramatic arc. "Oh, honey, *no*. There's a *big* difference between a nightmare and a night *terror*. Waking her up won't work. Hell, it can be dangerous—*obviously*."

He once again indicated jagged shards swimming in a bloodied swamp of carpet. Darius's stomach twisted.

"How do you know that's what it was?"

Lamar uttered a sad laugh—a half-scoff. "Because I spent two years in therapy for PTSD," he answered. "Those nightmares throw you straight into a flashback that forces you to relive your trauma. I wasn't just assaulted by Connor Amoretto once. That man visited me every damn night for months."

Gentle fingers ran along the inside of Lamar's left arm, tracing the intricate, black ink patterns doodled over a devastating bed of self-inflicted scars. A numb grip pulled Darius out of this room and thrust him into another, where he watched Thorn perform this exact same ritual, nails gliding over her own mangled flesh, face flush with memory.

"I'm sorry," Darius murmured. "I don't know what else to say."

Lamar smiled. Despite the somber topic and late hour, warmth filled the expression. "You don't have to say anything. Just being here is enough. For me *and* for Thorn. That woman's been through hell, Darius. She's *still* going through hell. She's going to lash out, isolate herself... maybe even find relief in other self-destructive behaviors..."

His hold on his scars tightened, and he stretched his hand open before lacing his fingers on his lap. Darius's pulse leapt, and his heart stung with sharp, helpless pain.

"The scary thing is that there's not much else you can do," Lamar went on. "Healing takes time. Just don't give up. Be there for her. To talk, to listen, to just sit in the damn silence together, if that's what it takes to make sure she knows she isn't as alone as she feels."

Darius drew a slow, deliberate breath, like maybe a chest full of air would soothe the ache. It didn't. "What if she doesn't want us there?"

Lamar laid a hand on Darius's arm. "She does. She just doesn't think she deserves it. She probably feels too broken to be saved. It's our job to show her how full of crap that is."

He grinned, and Darius couldn't help but allow himself to laugh. "Aren't I supposed to be the Virtue mentor here? How'd you get so wise beyond your years?"

"Two things," Lamar answered, thrusting a pair of fingers into the air. "Therapy and a good night's sleep. This... hot mess can wait til morning."

He flourished his hands over the remains of Darius's coffee table before getting to his feet and tip-toeing back to the hallway. The light beneath the far door had been extinguished, and as the two of them passed through the waiting room, Darius peered into the garage. He'd expected Thorn's motorcycle to be gone, but his heart still sank at the empty space. As he walked to his quarters, Lamar's advice rattled around Darius's tired skull, and when he finally changed out of his ruined clothes and flopped onto his bed, he was already halfway through a text.

"Thanks for your help with the budget and on renovations. I hated that table. Are you free for coffee tomorrow?"

For a couple of minutes, he stared at it, eyes drooping and mind fading. Not even a series of three blinking dots coming to life beneath the message could keep him awake. By the morning, he thought he must have dreamed them because Thorn never responded.

CHAPTER FIFTEEN

Her lungs caught fire, but not enough. It was *never* enough.

Thorn lit another cigarette. The cherry glowed bright in the morning light, a sun in its own right, dawning over a tobacco ash and linen fiber cityscape. Scalding air stung down her throat, but the tenderness transitioned too soon to a tingle as her tissues healed faster than she could harm them. The pattern of exhaling smoke into the open air, sucking more pain into her chest, and feeling that pain wither away, used to calm her. Like a ritual. Or a prayer. When she reached the end of one invocation, she'd begin the hymn again until the demons in her gut were sated.

It wasn't working now, though. Thorn's ruined soul coiled like a cornered serpent, twisted and ready to strike. With a sigh, she flicked her spent stub over the edge of the fire escape, just as she had with a dozen matching sacrifices, and pulled a brand-new victim from the box.

December wind delivered a frigid current across Thorn's face. She sat below her open window in nothing but lounge pants and a sweatshirt, feet bare and hood up. Sparkie perched on the railing above, wings folded and tail twisted in a delicate loop around the wrought iron. He peered down as Thorn swapped the cigarettes for a lighter. She flicked it to life, but instead of breathing it against her latest smoke, she watched the newborn flame suffocate in the breeze.

Morning commuters bustled along the sidewalk below, buried beneath layers of thick jackets, warm hats, and flowing scarves that hid their human shape but not their human *nature*. Auras just as cold as the air around them tugged at Thorn in a never-ending flow. Fragile auras. Auras that could shatter at one wrong choice, one bad decision, one mistake. Hell, it didn't even have to be *their* mistake. All it took was a careless driver, an anxious cop, a sleeping weapon…

Thorn leaned her head against the brick wall at her back and opened her left palm toward the sky, the fresh cigarette dangling between two fingers. Though her hands were clean now, the memory of Darius's blood coating her skin made her want to wash them again and again, as though scrubbing her flesh might simultaneously scour her mind. But it didn't, and every damned time she closed her eyes, Darius was all she saw. Sparkie unwound himself from the fire escape and dove onto Thorn's shoulders to wrap around her throat instead. She laid a hand on top of him.

What the *hell* had she been thinking? She knew better than to take this chance, to get this close, but she'd ignored all of that because she'd missed him—*she missed him*—and what had that led to?

Shame swelled in her throat, and her eyes stung as tears caught in their corners. A tremor shuddered down her spine and jolted her into a shaking fit that had nothing to do with the cold. Thorn threw the unsmoked cigarette over the railing and stood up. Winter condensation coated the sill in damp beads, and her bare hands slid across it as she climbed back into her apartment. Once her feet landed on the wood flooring, she slammed the window shut. Glass panes rattled in the frame, and Thorn's arms, braced hard against the base, rattled with them. Her breath came in shallow gulps as Sparkie let out a strangled cry.

She wanted to scream. To sob. But mostly, she wanted to fucking *stab* something—something that *deserved* to get stabbed. But thanks to this goddamned drain on their assets, she couldn't do that, either. Until further notice, all TAC attempts to stop Edith Froschlin were put on hold. There was nothing Thorn could do about it.

…Or was there?

Her body went rigid and then, all at once, as fluid as the water in the East River, steady with purpose. She stood up straight and looked around the room. This studio offered little in terms of tech and tools, but it *did* have a laptop, a printer, and a box of markers. Her teeth clenched as she lowered her hood.

They couldn't risk sending *TAC* after Edith… but Thorn wasn't part of TAC. Not technically.

Since smoking had done fuck all to soothe her nerves, Thorn opted for a scalding shower before rearranging her studio. She shoved her dresser to the end of her bed to free up the widest wall in the room, and one by one, Thorn tiled the entire goddamned thing in maps. Manhattan, The Bronx, Staten Island, and the rest of New York City's boroughs came to life in single-sheet swatches until every square inch was covered. The sun rose as she worked, melting baby blue and pastel pink clouds into tobacco orange wisps and then cold, clear skies. Thorn moved to her nightstand, where two phones lay face up.

She hadn't touched her Martyr-issued device for two days, not since the text Darius had sent after she'd tried to impale him on his own goddamned coffee table. The thing buzzed constantly, and names flashed on the screen. Nicholas, Chris, Cain, and, of course, Darius again. Every time, her heart jolted, but she couldn't bring herself to read what they had to say.

But the other device, the burner Edith had slipped into her jacket, practically lived in Thorn's palm. Unlike her personal phone, which wouldn't stop going off, this one had been radio silent since the Raven's last public appearance.

That didn't stop Thorn from checking every sixty seconds. She picked it up again, her fingers itching for an update.

There wasn't one.

Sparkie grumbled a frustrated hiss from his perch atop her open bathroom door. With a sigh, Thorn flicked through two weeks of unanswered messages until she landed on that first one:

"Hello, Mourning Dove."

Those five syllables rang out in the chaotic space between Thorn's ears with a grating howl. She heard them with Edith's inflection, Edith's accent, *Edith's fucking voice.* Thorn's grip constricted until the device groaned in her palm, and she glared at that restricted number with a venom that could burn through skin.

"Where the hell are you?" she murmured as she walked back to her brand-new wall of makeshift maps. For a moment, she considered the streets, the landmarks, the history...

Then, she vandalized them.

First, Thorn added Edith's original appearances in four stark X's: the subway stop at 50th and 8th, the corner of Broome and Allen, the Triumph of the Human Spirit, and right at the center of Darius's market. Her hand hovered here, and she glanced at her phone. Sparkie let out a soft whine as Thorn marred the food court in blood-red ink.

After that, she scrolled through the messages again, adding additional marks for each location the Forgotten Greed had sent her. Unlike a normal goddamned person, Edith hadn't provided addresses, cross streets, or even GPS markers, but instead latitude and longitude coordinates, like she got off on making things as cryptic as fucking possible. Thorn bounced between the texts and a digital map, painstakingly finding the precise location for every one. When she was done, she stepped back and considered the pages with a frown.

For all the thought Edith had put into getting Thorn's attention with the initial incidents, the following seven seemed completely arbitrary. Thorn's eyes narrowed as they flicked between each new point, trying to recall if these places held any relevance to her—if she'd lost someone, or maybe hurt someone, on those grounds—but her memory came up blank. Besides sticking to Manhattan itself, there was no obvious pattern. She chewed on her lip, crushing it so hard between her teeth that she felt the vessels rupture and restore beneath the surface.

Nicholas would be able to figure it out. Hell, he probably already had. Diligence was more than the Virtue attached to his soul: it was a goddamned compulsion that hadn't left when the magic burned out, or maybe the very thing that seeded such a magic in the first place. She lifted her phone and tapped her nails against its titanium casing.

Instead of calling him, though, she opened her texts. A slew of unread messages assaulted her, and she flicked through them without pausing until she reached her Gray Unit feed.

Between Mackenzie's Recon and her Gray operatives, Thorn had over six dozen reports of creeps in crow masks stalking the streets of New York City. She marked all of these in purple ink, peppering her paper mosaic map with more scars. Like Edith's appearances, her little fan club was relegated to Manhattan, too. Clusters popped up in and around the areas the Raven had made big scenes, but that was hardly a surprise. What was that stupid quote everyone always got wrong? Imitation is the sincerest form of flattery? Thorn had a feeling this wasn't exactly what Oscar Wilde had in mind.

Teeth clenched and body tight, she shrank to the ground, with her back against the wall beneath her window. Sparkie sat perched on the bathroom door, and he stared at the top of her head. Thorn had the sudden sensation of seeing herself from a distance that should have been disorienting but somehow just felt like her fucking life right now.

Something buzzed. Instinctively, she glanced at her Martyr device, but when she looked down, she noticed the burner had lit up. Thorn's heart dropped so quickly that her breath followed with a hiss, and she grabbed it. A new message blinked at her.

"40.7312126, -73.9971330."

Thorn's skin, her spine, her *soul* quaked. For a deafening moment, her senses dissolved, all but that of touch, and the phone felt like fire at her fingertips. They hammered out a response all on their own, the first two words that popped into her head, words she'd been dying to spit in Edith's face since the day they'd met:

"Fucking coward."

Edith began typing the second Thorn hit send. She stared at the device while Sparkie vaulted to her window and paced in front of the glass. His shadow stretched out on the floor, the stature of a dragon with unfurled wings and sulfur breath.

"I was starting to think you hadn't gotten my gift, Mourning Dove."

A second text appeared just as quickly.

"You have half an hour…"

Thorn leapt to her feet and shoved the window open. Sparkie dove through, colliding with a punch of air so cold that it slammed against Thorn's chest, too. By the time he'd scaled the building and took to the sky, Thorn had finished lacing her boots. She pulled on her fingerless gloves, her bike jacket, and equipped herself with every goddamned weapon she could reasonably fit on her person: a blade sheathed at her ankle, another folded in her thigh pocket, and her pistol holstered and hidden at the small of her back. Her helmet hung from a hook on the door, and she grabbed it as she put the coordinates into her phone.

Washington Square Park.

Thorn slammed her apartment shut, locked it behind her, and sprinted down the hallway. According to the map, it would take her thirty minutes to arrive—barely enough time to get there—but Thorn knew how to navigate this city well enough to shave off a few precious seconds. Her footfalls sent thundering echoes up the stairwell, and once she hit the landing, she bolted into the lobby. Her motorcycle was parked in a paid lot around the corner, and Thorn slammed her helmet over her head as she flung her leg across the seat. The motor came to life with a hum, and her smart visor displayed the fastest route to her destination.

It also showed her texts.

Oh, fuck.

In the panic to get out the door, she hadn't felt her phone buzz inside the satchel cinched to her thigh, but now that the messages were staring her in the face, she couldn't avoid them. The top one was from Alexis Claytor, sent directly to Thorn… and Chris.

"NYPD is responding to an anonymous tip about a threat at Washington Square Park."

Thorn's mouth ran dry, and she sucked in a furious breath as she twisted her bike in a sharp turn and pulled onto the street. The afternoon traffic streamed past her, but Thorn squeezed between two bright yellow taxi cabs with the purpose and patience of a rock slide. One laid on its horn. Thorn ignored it.

Chris's response scrolled at the top of her visor. *"What kind of threat?"*

"Unknown," Alexis responded. *"Someone just called to report it and hung up."*

A bitter taste saturated Thorn's tongue. She merged onto Harlem River Drive before tapping the voice-to-text icon on her dash.

"I'll check it out," she said aloud. The words materialized inside the conversation chain, and Thorn thought that would be the end of it—hoped it would be—but a new alert pinged in her ear seven seconds later.

"I have a unit patrolling nearby," Chris replied. *"They can back you up."*

"No," Thorn shouted into her mic. "I can handle it."

She flew south, her bike's tires droning against the asphalt as she zipped in between lines of gridlocked cars. Her hands gripped the handlebars as though they were wound around Edith's throat, and her heart counted down the seconds in erratic thumps until Chris's third and final message came through.

"You need backup. Unit Twenty-Three will be there in ten."

Thorn turned off the voice-to-text feature and slammed the heel of her palm against the dash.

"Fuck!"

Her mind roiled as she calculated just how much damage Edith Froschlin could do before she got there. Sparkie, unburdened by things like winding streets and rush hour traffic, was already halfway to Washington Square Park, but Thorn still had twenty minutes to go.

She opened the throttle and needled through vehicles, weaving a thread of rage in her wake. All the while, Thorn expected the guillotine to fall and heads to roll—for TAC to call because they were under attack or for Sparkie to be struck out of the sky by a meteor of black feathers—but what she *hadn't* expected was Nicholas Wolfe chiming in to the conversation.

"We've got LymeLite reports of crazies in crow masks gathering at Washington Square Park," he sent privately to Thorn. *"Chris says you're headed that way now?"*

Thorn's stomach turned on itself, devouring her from the inside out. She didn't even bother with voice-to-text this time. She just called the man. Nicholas answered without a hello.

"What the hell is going on?" he barked into the phone.

"I was just about to ask you the same goddamned question," Thorn snapped as she approached the exit for East 25th. She wedged between slower traffic and the concrete barriers at the shoulder of the road to cut the turn. Other drivers shared their displeasure with middle fingers and prolonged honks.

"Exactly what I texted," Nicholas shouted to be heard over the noise. "Or are you too busy to read now, too?"

Thorn's teeth clenched. "What's happening on

LymeLite?"

"Videos started popping up a few minutes ago," Nicholas said. "A ton of those copycat crows are meeting up at Washington Square. I didn't think much of it until Chris said someone called a tip to the NYPD for the same area."

"What are the videos saying?"

"Most of them are other people recording from a distance," Nicholas responded, "but some of these masked fuckers are getting on themselves and claiming that the Raven *told* them to meet up there."

That ringing filled Thorn's ears again, stealing the sound and substance of the city. Suddenly, despite ripping around the corner and onto 25th at nearly thirty miles an hour, the world felt as though it moved in slow motion—like Thorn was driving through a vat of crystal-clear syrup instead of thin, winter air. Nicholas spoke again—no, he *kept* talking, and Thorn realized she hadn't heard a damned thing he'd said.

"…digging through now, and we can't find an original source from Froschlin at all. It could be bullsh—"

"It's not," Thorn cut in. "Fuck. *Fuck!* I need to call Chris."

A second of hesitation breathed between them before Nicholas asked, "Why?"

But it wasn't just a question. It was a challenge—an *accusation*—and Thorn had no choice now but to come clean. She shook her head, her throat so constricted she could hardly force out a breath, let alone a sentence. But she managed. Barely.

"Because Edith Froschlin is going to be at Washington Square Park."

Nicholas paused again. Thorn didn't need to see the disappointment on his face to know it was there. It seeped into his voice in brittle, weary tendrils. "She texted you."

Once again, it was not a question.

"Yes," Thorn admitted.

Now, Nicholas sighed, but the sound felt more like a

slap—a slap she deserved. "Chris and Gabe are across the hall," he said. "I'll talk to them. You just… get down there and try to stop her from hurting anyone."

He hung up without giving Thorn the chance to say anything else, and for the thousandth time in months, she wished she'd screamed, "I'm sorry!" Instead, she bottled that up along with everything else and careened toward the mess she'd made in the middle of town, hoping it wasn't as bad as she suspected it would be.

She had no such luck.

Greenwich Village pulsed with peril. Two blocks away from the coordinates Edith had sent, the streets were so packed that even on her motorcycle, Thorn couldn't easily get closer. She parked up East 8th Street and walked the rest of the way, popping in a set of earbuds.

The closer she got to Washington Square Park, the thicker and more incensed the crowds became. Cold energy coiled around Thorn until she couldn't tell if her shallow breathing was borne from anxiety or newly developed claustrophobia. Pedestrians and police strode down the sidewalks, whispering and wondering. An officer glanced her way, and Thorn's spine tingled with anticipation. She pulled her hood over her hair.

Ahead, people packed in like plague rats. The murmur of voices carried the cadence of a chant, teasing at Thorn's subconscious, and though she couldn't make out the words, her stomach twisted in a corkscrew knot. She looked around, hoping, or maybe dreading, to catch a sight of gleaming, iridescent feathers, but there was nothing. Not yet. High above, Sparkie hunted for any sign of Edith's Familiar lurking within barren branches or atop grimy rooftop terraces. So far, the only birds he saw were those congregated on the ground.

Thorn felt their energy before she spotted them herself. God, there were so many. Their shrouded shoulders and hooded heads created a tumultuous black sea that made it hard to tell where one body ended and another began, but she would guess that over fifty people made up the flock. The Washington Arch loomed over them, its white marble etched with gritty, gray lines where the city's filth settled into every crevice. The whole thing was a practice in pride if Thorn had ever seen one—a goddamned testament to the Roman Empire America had always dreamed of becoming without ever stopping to consider what had happened to Rome in the end. Winged victories graced the spandrels as though paying tribute to the bald eagle roosting at the cornerstone. That symbol had always felt like some kind of counterfeit deity—a false idol—perched upon a stolen throne. Even the statues of Washington himself reeked of ego, framed by ancient gods and goddesses as though to claim he'd been gifted the same divine status. Thorn stared up at them, her jaw clenched.

There were no gods here. Only fools delusional enough to believe they were one.

The chanting grew louder, and Thorn's focus pulled toward the ground. A tense circle formed around the cult of the crow. Onlookers and law enforcement kept a safe distance, the former to avoid getting caught up in any ritual sacrifice that might take place in the middle of the square and the latter to jump in and stop the blood from hitting the pavement when it inevitably spilled. Among them, a man and woman in beige and black glanced up and caught Thorn's eye. At first, she instinctively reached for her weapon, but when the woman nodded a short acknowledgment, Thorn realized with a humiliating flush that this must have been the backup Chris was talking about. She didn't recognize them—didn't even know their names—but it was too late to worry about that now.

Now, she had to worry about the crows.

Edith's flock had formed a circle, too, centered around a single figure standing upon a box that gave him just enough clearance to hold a megaphone to his face. Like the others, a black mask obscured his nose and eyes, but his pasty, stubble-specked chin dropped open beneath the feathers as he shouted.

"You have all been lied to!" The words rang across the square, but a familiarity made Thorn's eyes narrow. His irises gleamed with fanaticism through the holes in his mask as he spoke not just to his parish but to the outsiders beyond them. "These 'Martyrs' are gaslighting this whole city! Telling us we can't trust what our own eyes have seen, what our ears have heard! They have destroyed our communities, committed acts of terrorism against our people, and I say *enough is enough!*"

The crowd howled. In unison, they spoke one word, like a mantra—like a threat.

"Nevermore!"

A couple of black-clad people approached the outer circle, handing out thick sheets of paper. Thorn snatched one: a manifesto in forced trochaic octameter titled "Quoth The Raven."

The megaphone lifted again, and her gaze flicked up.

"They tell you it's all an accident! Random acts of violence! Or worse… that nothing happened in the first place!"

Fists punched into the air, echoing with the swoop of four dozen cloaks.

"Nevermore!"

"The Martyrs need to be wiped off the face of the earth!" the man yelled, and all at once, with a cold shock of dread dripping down her spine with egg-white viscosity, Thorn recognized him. His voice, his silhouette, his conspiratorial fixations. Her jaw fell open.

Howard Poole… Her old barista from Grind House Coffee.

He kept spitting vitriol into his mic.

"They're killing our people and soaking our streets in blood!"

"Nevermore!" the crowd called back.

"They're leaving children without parents and parents without children!"

"Nevermore!"

"They're tanking our economy—stealing our future!"

"Nevermore!"

"And worst of all," Poole screamed, "they don't care! *Enough is enough!*"

"NEVERMORE!"

It was enough for Thorn. A furious, stricken sting pinched her throat as she tossed the manifesto to the ground and shrank back into the line of gawkers. The noise still reached her, berating her as she walked around the arch. Poole's soapbox speech slowly transformed until the fire coming from the megaphone chanted in a call-and-response hymn, back and forth, over and over, until the word "nevermore" sawed against her brain with diamond-edged teeth.

Thorn walked in a wide arc, searching the spectators. Every pale, slender face, every head of blonde hair, gave her pause. None of them belonged to Edith.

But that was the power of Edith Froschlin.

She didn't have to be here in person to cause a scene. Just the fucking idea of her could stir a wave of people into a tsunami. As the crows rattled and raved, others began to nod along, to agree, to join in on the goddamned chant. Soon, it walled Thorn in on all sides. She couldn't escape it.

Her phone buzzed within her satchel and snapped her from sensory overload. She pulled it out, expecting a message from the Underground or updates on incoming backup, but instead, she stared into an empty screen. The buzzing tapped again, but not from the device in her palm. From another, still lodged deep in her bag.

Cold panic doused Thorn as she withdrew the burner. Two messages from that same restricted number.

"You'll need more than a hood to hide from me."

"Try again, Mourning Dove."

A third buzz. The device lit up happily.

"Look at that," Edith had typed. *"You're learning."*

Thorn's head snapped around the square in wild, desperate circles. Her lungs squeezed the air from her chest and refused to open again, forcing her into rapid, short breaths.

The dread melted into an unstable blend of rage and fear, and the longer Thorn searched for Edith, the more that sensation threatened to combust. When she couldn't spot the woman on the ground, she turned higher, hunting for a different bird. A flash of black caught her eye, and her heart seized.

A massive raven peered out from behind one of the arch's statues. It was roughly the same size as George Washington's carved face, and it gracelessly leapt up from the monument's shoulder to sit upon its tricorne hat. The beast's black feathers were so dark it looked like a gaping wound within the marble—a gash that cut so deep into the stone that no sunlight could reach inside. The Familiar shuffled side to side, ruffling its feathers as it stared at Thorn from above the crowd. Thorn's teeth ground together, and she raised the burner again. Tearing her eyes away from the animal felt like turning her back on a sniper and daring him to shoot.

"I'm not the one hiding," she typed.

Three dots flashed to life as Edith said, *"No? My mistake..."*

The raven let out a horrible, croaking caw before spreading its wings. They spanned five feet from feather-tip to feather-tip and completely obscured the sculpted images of Fame and Valor on either side. The congregation of crows burst into a symphony of gasps followed by reverent quiet. Howard Poole gawked over the rim of his megaphone, eyes wide behind the cut-out holes in his mask.

The crowd around them did *not* settle. Nervous energy rattled through the bodies to Thorn's left and right, and murmuring rippled like an earthquake had rocked the sea floor and sent shock waves to the surface. Thorn forced her way toward the arch.

An awestruck squeal cut across the square.

"There she is! It's her! The Raven!"

Sound erupted again, air swollen with shouts. Thorn's heart flailed behind her sternum, exchanging blows with the monster consuming her core as she hunted for a sign of Edith Froschlin within the chaos, but she couldn't see a damned thing from where she stood on the ground, and Sparkie staunchly refused to come closer. The memory of razor-sharp claws ripping into her skin made Thorn glance back to the monument, and her breath snagged at the hollow of her throat.

Edith's Familiar had vanished.

Suddenly, the gathered crows moved as a single mass. The frigid force of their combined human souls pulled away from Thorn, beneath the arch, and deeper into Washington Square Park. The onlookers around them followed as though drawn by the undesired magnetism of deadly curiosity. Thorn tried to get to the front, but the pressure of shoulders tight against hers made it nearly impossible. Instead, she shoved her way in the opposite direction and broke through.

The moment her boots hit open space, she ran. While cultists, civilians, and cops pressed forward, Thorn arced around them. She leapt over chain perimeter fences, darted through overgrown garden beds, and weaved between trees and park benches until she reached an open courtyard around the fountain. Sparkie glided above, so high that his shadow followed her like a pinprick upon the pavement. The crows reached the basin, stretching out in a big, black ring to surround it.

The water had been shut off for the winter, leaving the feature dry and barren. Stone steps descended into the depths, where the concrete sloped in a graceful, inverted dome until it reached the middle. The raised platform at the base typically shot jets forty-five feet into the sky. Now, that platform functioned as a stage, and Edith stood directly in the center.

Thorn's stomach roiled at the sight of her.

Somehow, the bitch managed to materialize out of thin air, to be noticed if and when *she* wanted to. She stood ominously still, as though carved into the city itself and only now coming to life. Like every other goddamned time the Raven had made a public appearance, she hid behind anonymity. Her cloak shrouded the shape of her body and sheathed her slick yellow hair, which only made the gleaming mask seem more dangerous. Afternoon sun sent a stunning flicker of iridescent light dancing across every vane in every feather, and the black beak glistened like a wet blade.

As her parish tightened around her, coming in so close that shoulders brushed and hands linked together, Edith raised her arms at her sides as though she herself had wings to fly. She didn't say a word. She didn't have to. Her flock worshipped her without wasting time or thought on sermon.

A biting, bitter taste seared up Thorn's throat. She reached behind her back, slipped her hand beneath the hem of her jacket, and wrapped her fingers around her gun.

How quickly could she pull it out, pull the trigger, she wondered? How many casualties was she willing to risk for a chance to plant a bullet into the center of that mother fucking raven mask and crack the thing in two?

Before Thorn had the chance to decide, a shot blasted through the square. Ten feet to her right, a petite, black-robed figure let out a curdled, breathless cry and fell to their knees before collapsing forward. The mask slipped askew to reveal a young woman, eyes wide and horrified as a swell of blood gathered beneath her chest. Her aura fluttered out. Thorn's heart fluttered with it.

Then screaming filled the air.

The ring around the fountain shattered. Cloaked men and women broke formation, flying in every direction as another bang rocked the park. Civilians followed suit, and the courtyard transformed into a churning sea of hot bodies and cold souls. While everyone else turned and ran, the NYPD sprinted toward the fountain, where Edith was now darting away.

A Martyr followed.

Wait, no. *Not* a Martyr.

Thorn shoved through the stampede of people, focusing on the man in black and beige. A matching gunman kept pace with him. They both leveled weapons and shot. Bullets zipped so far off from Edith it was a wonder anyone believed they were aiming for her at all. People wailed and fell in the crowd, casualties of a cause that was never theirs to begin with.

Rage boiled up Thorn's chest. She ripped her pistol from its holster, raised it, and pointed it across the square, but she didn't pull the trigger. There were still too many people, too many civilians. Sparkie torpedoed from the sky and glided parallel to the first shooter. Thorn exhaled a breath, focused on her Familiar, and lined up her aim—

A mass of cold energy took a swing at her from behind.

Thorn ducked as an arm sailed through the air exactly where her head had been. She spun around and lifted her gun, expecting a pissed-off police officer or a merc in Martyr colors.

Instead, she found herself staring into a pair of brown eyes shadowed behind a cheap crow mask. She hesitated.

He swung again. A right hook arched at Thorn's face. She leaned back, and a draft of air kissed the tip of her nose centimeters from where his knuckles missed it. When he came in a third time, he didn't use a fist. He held a knife.

Thorn thrust an arm between them. The tip of the blade glanced off the kevlar embedded into her jacket sleeve, and Thorn twisted into a more defensive position. He followed her, slashing again. Thorn whipped her pistol up, caught the edge of his palm with the butt of the gun, and sent his weapon flying.

Then she wrapped a fist around the man's throat and lifted him into the air. He grabbed her forearm, but not wildly or frantically. His fingertips grappled for the space just under her wrist joint—the spot where her *Peccostium* would have been had she held him with her left hand. Thorn's eyes shot wide.

Fuck. He wasn't one of Edith's psychotic supporters. He

was one of her *soldiers*.

Fury clouded Thorn's mind and created a vortex of gray haze in her vision. Her grip tightened, cutting off blood from his carotids until he stopped fighting altogether. His pulse and hers mingled beneath her fingertips, pounding so erratically that she couldn't tell them apart. He gasped for breath as his lips turned dusk purple beneath the beak on his mask.

Thorn didn't let go—didn't *want* to let go. Everything Edith and her mercenaries had stolen from her, done *to* her, howled in her ears. She remembered each moment with crystalline clarity: the sniper sitting on top of that building who had landed a round in her thigh, the wave of men at the cemetery who'd helped Lust escape, the *fuckers* who had lashed Caleb Claytor, sobbing and scared, to that chair— who had watched Wrath break his fingers one by one.

Then, she remembered beating those men down, the twang of a metal pipe crashing into their skulls, and the beautiful, awful color their life had painted across the floor in glistening, red arcs.

A gasp ripped into Thorn's lungs. She opened her hand, fingers trembling, and the crow collapsed in a heap of black satin and dull feathers. The swell of panic in her veins brought time to a standstill, arresting the crowd while she paced unrestricted within it. Deep in her psyche, a vengeance clawed awake, yawning its gaping jaws, hungry to spill more blood tonight. Her fingertips buzzed, and the weight of her gun pressed into her palm. With a scathing cry, Sparkie flew frenetic circles high above.

A gunshot blasted. Thorn snapped back into sync with the rest of the city and twisted around.

Edith had vanished. After sprinting west through the park, she'd all but disappeared behind a row of naked trees and left chaos behind.

Police swarmed the area, finally spurred into action now that bullets had been fired, bodies felled… nothing left for them to do. The square churned with a disjointed mix of panicked civilians, incensed protesters, and uniformed cops. Stagnant figures peppered the open space around the fountain with bright, deadly color. Crows and casualties caught in the crossfire. One snagged Thorn's eye, a lump of black, beige—and red. So much red.

One of the Martyrs she'd seen in the crowd.

He lay flat on his back, spread eagle, staring at a blue sky with gaping eyes. A gun lay discarded on the ground by his knee. Thorn's heart sank.

He'd died here—for her, *because* of her—and she didn't even know his name.

An officer shouted.

"Drop your weapon!"

Thorn glanced up. On the opposite side of the plaza, a man in police blues tucked around an abandoned coffee cart. He held a pistol at arm's length, finger hovering delicately over the trigger, sight trained on a form ducked behind a pockmarked plinth at the fountain's edge. The other half of Unit Twenty-Three pressed her back against the stone. Her eyes darted up and caught Thorn's. Terror glistened against her dark irises as she reached up to her com device and tapped into Thorn's line.

"Help me!" Her voice crawled across the courtyard and screamed in Thorn's ears all at once.

"I repeat, drop your weapon!" the officer commanded again.

Thorn went cold. She started to move—one step, then another, slowly at first, before she was jogging, *running*, her boots clattering against the pavement with the beating of a war drum. A delicate ringing in her skull drowned out all other sounds, and her field of view tunneled around the trapped TAC officer until everything else faded into gray static. Sparkie flew overhead, watching it all from a helpless distance.

Thorn was halfway there when a massive raven descended onto the plinth. The animal's shadow fell over her agent. She glanced up.

And a high-velocity round ripped her chest wide open.

It exploded through kevlar, flesh, and bone in a gut-clenching red spray.

"No!" Thorn screamed.

She sprinted harder. The officer on the other side swore and disappeared behind the coffee cart, his focus flying to the buildings in the distance. Thorn stampeded around the fountain, fell to her knees, and pressed a hand against the gaping wound in the woman's sternum. Warm, sticky blood painted Thorn's palms and soaked into her fingerless gloves. The TAC agent grabbed her arm, drew a gurgling, gasping breath, and tried to speak.

Then her eyes went cold, and her soul blinked out.

Thorn could only stare. A harsh, howling tone bounced between her ears, so loud and disorienting that she hardly noticed Martyrs speaking in her coms and someone else crooning at the top of her skull.

"Three down."

The words didn't register. Not right away. Not until Thorn looked up to where Edith's Familiar perched atop the plinth like a morose memorial monument looming over a freshly dug grave. The bird's beady eyes locked onto Thorn's as it tilted its head. Its gleaming, black beak creaked open.

"Three down, Mourning Dove."

It croaked the message in a mockery of human voice, an uncanny imitation that was too close to be comfortable, too far to be familiar. Thorn's lips slipped open. The bird spread its massive wings and, with one mighty flap, took to the sky. Thorn got to her feet, raised her weapon, and pointed it at the beast's back as it lazily flew south. The glint of a sniper's scope flashed in a nearby church bell tower. Rage exploded between her ribs, tearing her up inside, and she started to run.

Chris's voice crashed against her consciousness.

"Thorn!" she screamed through the earpiece, directly into Thorn's skull. Her voice crackled—with distance, with command, with *fear*. "Can you hear me? An evac team is waiting for you up Washington Place! Get out of there!"

A grip of panic hardened Thorn's vocal cords. She looked around, suddenly aware of more sirens approaching, more police swarming, and more exits closing. Now she'd drawn attention, and a vortex of cold energy spun toward her. "But Froschlin—"

"Get the *hell* out!" Chris shouted.

Thorn took a step backward, then another, holstering her gun behind her jacket. She reached into that link she shared with Wrath and spread a wave of Influence to convince the approaching officers that she fucking belonged here, armed and fuming, while they secured the crime scene and gathered evidence once the threat of violence had finally subsided—a threat that Thorn had personally delivered in a neatly wrapped, blood-red package. Somewhere far to the east, Autumn Hunt responded, as though using her own power to wave at Thorn from across the city and remind her that she was never as alone as she thought she was.

Thorn ran through Garibaldi Plaza and exploded onto University Place. A TAC vehicle sat at the corner of Washington and Greene. Conrad Carter sat behind the wheel, window rolled down, both meaty hands crushed around the wheel. His partner, Charlotte Davis, sat beside him, long locs pulled back and a short-range rifle in her palms.

"Get in!" Carter shouted.

Thorn pulled the back door open and leapt onto the bench seat. Sparkie dove through just before the door snapped shut, and Carter pulled away from the curb. They fled the scene in silence, weaving through incoming police cruisers and wailing ambulances. Thorn watched them pass, abstractly aware that maybe she should feel *something*, but she couldn't tap into any emotion at all.

When they turned south on Broadway, a phone buzzed in her pocket. She went straight for the burner this time.

Edith hadn't just sent a text. She'd sent a LymeLite video. The preview distinctly showed a face Thorn hardly recognized as her own, gnarled into a freeze-frame of fury. Her blood-stained thumb trembled as she opened the link.

All at once, she was back at that plaza, watching from a third point of view as she wound a fist around the mercenary crow's throat and lifted him single-handedly from the pavement. The man stopped fighting. Thorn did not let go. A caption beneath the footage simply read: "Martyr Leader Kills Protestor."

"You can't hide," Edith texted. *"Not anymore… Jane."*

All the emotion Thorn hadn't had access to seconds ago flooded back in a tsunami. Everything she knew, everything she *was*, reduced to a swell of unfiltered wrath so pure, so deadly, that she could barely keep herself from screaming. But Sparkie did. The sound erupted from his throat as Thorn's fingers balled into a knotted fist. She struck the car window.

Her knuckles punched through the glass, creating a spiderweb of cracks that mirrored her reflection in a thousand tiny pieces.

"Fuck!"

CHAPTER SIXTEEN

Darius watched Thorn leap from the Brooklyn Bridge, completely helpless to stop her.

She plunged toward the water, black hair flying, the blurry form of her Familiar frantically trying to keep her aloft, but it was no use. Thorn tumbled and turned through the air for one hundred and thirty feet before crashing into the East River. Darius had expected her to splash when she hit the surface, to send up a spray like a meteor striking Earth, but the collision was deceptively anticlimactic. A thud where there should have been a boom. Then, her body floated for a gravity-defying moment, splayed out and shattered, until the waves engulfed her and pulled her to the depths of hell.

He'd seen it once, from start to excruciating finish, and once was enough. That was all it took for the whole damned thing to replay in his mind, over and over again, until his already broken heart ground to dust at the base of his ribcage.

Darius knew Thorn had survived this, but god, for the life of him, he couldn't see how.

"Holy shit… Is that *Mr. Blaine?*"

A group of TAC agents huddled in a beige and black

circle around one of the wrought iron tables in the courtyard as they watched the LymeLite video on a tablet laid flat between them. Chris's unit partner, Seth Graves, ran a hand over his buzzed head and let out a tiny, shocked scoff.

"It is," he said. "Standing on the bridge! Was he trying to stop her?"

"Well, he sure as shit wasn't trying to *push* her," Conrad mocked. "This was right after she escaped Wrath, wasn't it?"

The ring closed tighter, and Darius heard the distinct voice of a reporter long since dead overlayed on the century-old footage.

"And she has hit the water," the woman said in a featureless monotone typical for broadcast stations. "That was a hard fall. The recovery boats are moving in, but they'll have their work cut out for them. The East River is known for its dangerous, high currents, and this year alone, three people have lost their lives after jumping off the Brooklyn Bridge."

One of the agents tapped the screen. "Wait, go back a second, right when she hits… God, that is *so* fucked…"

Darius's gut twisted. He stormed up to the table, shoved his way between Conrad's hulking form and Seth's slender one, and yanked the device away. The news helicopter filming the whole fucked up scene arched in a slow, steady circle as the camera zoomed in on an older man with salt and pepper hair diving into the water. Before he pulled Thorn to the surface, Darius shut the screen down. All five TAC agents froze where they sat, eyes wide and mouths pressed shut with the guilty energy of teenagers caught with a joint hidden inside their sock drawer. Conrad tongued a wad of chewing tobacco pressed beneath his lower lip while Seth frantically offered a contrite shrug.

"Sorry, Darius," he began, but Darius quieted him by holding the device up.

"I'm taking this."

Seth quietly nodded as Darius stomped away, tablet in

hand, and headed to the elevator. While he waited for it to arrive, a hot ball of auras squirmed behind him. Whispers brushed at the back of his neck, but Darius refused to listen to them, to address this at all, until he'd met with leadership. He opened the door to the conference room.

And saw Thorn climb over the guard rail all over again.

The video filled the display at the far end of the room, massive and impossible to miss. Darius's teeth gritted as Mackenzie, Holly, Chris, and Nicholas stared at it.

"We should *not* be watching this," he hissed.

Even after his words rang through the room, no one moved. Darius's nose curled, and he slammed the tablet down.

They finally turned to him. Mackenzie went bright red, shifting her gaze to the table, while Holly adjusted her glasses with her typical pragmatism. Across from her, Chris looked like she was about to cry, though for anger or anguish was anyone's guess.

"Turn it *off,*" Darius demanded.

Holly paused the footage as Nicholas threw his hands up in a frustrated shrug. "What do you expect us to do?" he asked. "Thorn's whole goddamned *existence* is all over LymeLite right now. She's the top trending topic."

"Not just on LymeLite," Holly said. "Other social sites are tuning in now, and even local media outlets are starting to pay attention, though the more reputable papers are just calling her a person of interest at the latest incident."

"Jesus Christ," Darius growled, gripping the back of an empty chair before he jutted his chin toward the screen. "This has *nothing* to do with that latest incident. This was her *suicide* attempt!"

His voice caught in his throat. Guilty tension settled around them, and all eyes cast downward. The shame bouncing from one body to the next was palpable enough to leave a bitter taste in the air. At last, Darius sighed.

"We're Thorn's *friends,*" he said, "and we should *never* invade her privacy this way."

"Of *course* we're her friends," Nicholas said, "but what do you expect us to do? She's been here for decades, and no one knows shit about her!"

"We're not *entitled* to know anything about her," Darius bit back. "And maybe, if you *want* to know more, you could ask. Maybe, instead of watching her trauma play out on the big screen, you reach out to her. Call her. Send her a goddamned *text*. Have any of you tried that?"

The silence that followed was answer enough. Nicholas's mouth slipped open and stayed there while Chris tearfully looked at her phone as though realizing even she had failed in this most basic act of compassion. Mackenzie shifted in her seat, arms wrapped around her chest. Her vibrant nails tapped anxiously against her biceps.

"I've *tried* talking to her," she said quietly, "and Thorn didn't want to hear it. Darius, we just want to help, but we *can't* if we don't know what she's going through… and how the hell are we supposed to do that if she doesn't let us in? I mean, fuck, none of us even knew she had a son until shit hit the fan with Teresa Solomon a couple of years ago."

Nicholas threw an open palm to Mackenzie. "Exactly," he said with a sigh. "Look, I'm not saying it's right, but that woman's obsession with secrecy is causing problems. She had more than ninety percent of her personnel file redacted, for fuck's sake. No one but Alan even had access to it."

"I have access to it," Holly chimed in.

They all spun toward her, surprise rippling across their faces. Chris found her voice first.

"…What?"

"I'm the one who set up the system," Holly said. "I have access to everything."

"The fuck, Andrews?" Nicholas said. He propped his hands on his hips and tilted his head toward the display. "You knew about this?"

Holly snorted. "No. I said I had *access* to it," she clarified. "I never said I *read* it. I agree with Jones on this. It wasn't any of my business what Thorn didn't want the rest of us to know…" Gratitude trickled down Darius's back, loosening some of the tension, until Holly glanced at him with a grim expression. "Until now, and unfortunately, *now* Froschlin has made it *all* of our business. We need to know what they're saying about Thorn if we're going to do anything about it."

She turned back to the screen, and Darius finally settled into his chair. His eyes caught on the still frame of Thorn standing on the edge of the bridge. She didn't look any different than she did today, but seeing her frozen there, sobbing and screaming at a short-haired, clean-shaven man he hardly recognized as Alan, was somehow worse than what came next.

Holly closed the file, and the display filled with a menagerie of articles, posts, videos, and photographs featuring Thorn as the main attraction. The bloodied pieces of her long life laid out like a circus sideshow to be gawked at. A fleeting marriage to a car salesman in Detroit. Court-mandated community service after a slew of unpaid speeding tickets. Her birth in Baltimore in December 1946, exactly one hundred and forty-seven years ago—*to the day*. A sudden surge of guilt sobered Darius's anger for a moment.

But reading more flared it back to life.

The Martyrs' display was full of intimate and personal details about who Thorn was before her possession that Darius knew she didn't want the rest of the world to know, and each new piece of information added kindling to the fire in his stomach.

But the thing that stuck out the most were the two words printed over and over again, beneath every photograph, attached to every article, tied to every incident:

Jane Morgan.

Thorn's name before she'd been possessed—the one Wrath had stolen from her, tainted for her, and used against her. Thorn had never shared it before. Not with Darius. Not with anyone.

And now, the world knew.

Darius's hands curled into fists.

"Digging into her past *before* the possession is a clear attempt at character assassination," Holly said, "plus, it highlights that there's something supernatural at play. Froschlin is right about one thing: people fear what they don't understand, and someone who can live as long as Thorn has is terrifying."

Mackenzie let out a snort that barely managed to disguise the rapid clicking of her tongue piercing. "That's bullshit! Why don't they fear *Froschlin?* She's immortal, too!"

"They probably do," Holly said with a shrug. "But she's telling them the truth, or at least, they think she is. That makes her the better option."

Darius frowned, tuning them out as he scanned a headline on the screen. *"Missing Woman Presumed a Runaway."* An unflattering image of Thorn sat beside a block of text full of damning quotes and accusations from her ex-husband, former co-workers, and even her own mother:

"Jane was aggressive, not at all the kind of woman you want to raise a family with. Everything was always a fight, and she'd get physical. Can you imagine what would have happened if we'd had kids?"

"The girl had a bit of a rage problem and didn't make a lot of friends here. I haven't seen her since she got fired after throwing a cup of water in a customer's face."

"I love her. Truly, I do, with all my heart… But after her father died, she was never the same. I haven't seen or spoken to her in almost nine years. I'm not surprised she's disappeared again."

Darius wanted to scream, but Holly's voice drew him back to the table.

"But as bad as all this is," she said, "it gets worse."

She tapped her keyboard, and the content about Thorn's life pre-possession vanished, only to be replaced with glimpses of a whole new hell: Thorn's life after it. Articles and images linking her to a disturbing array of violent incidents made Darius's jaw clench.

"There is *so* much here," Holly went on, flipping through the items as though perusing a catalog of fucked up trauma.

"Riots or protests where she was caught in the background of some photo… Violent accidents with her visible in security cameras… A whole bunch of random shootings where a woman matching her description was drawn up by police sketch artists…"

Darius's blood ran cold as those pieces flitted by, all bearing dates in early 2025, the months after Donovan Rose had been killed.

"And that doesn't even include the incidents all of us already knew about," Holly continued. The display highlighted more familiar moments now: resurfaced footage of her snapping a man's neck at the gala in Spokane, body cam feeds of her cutting through cops at the protest in Foley Square, shaky videos of Thorn screaming at Mackenzie in a dark nightclub after Darius had healed her. "The court of public opinion is crucifying her thanks to this shit, and the Martyrs will go down as collateral damage."

Darius swallowed hard. "This is *all* being circulated online?"

Holly nodded. "And *more*. This is just what I can *prove* is linked to Thorn. There's also a ton of speculation about other things that probably have nothing to do with her… and a *ton* of completely batshit stuff that is so out of left field I can't even begin to understand why anyone would believe it, but here we are."

Mackenzie swore around the clattering of her tongue piercing. "How the hell did this happen so fast? It's only been two bloody days since that first video of Thorn went viral!"

"A couple of things," Holly said, popping up a hand with two fingers raised. She tapped each one as she listed them off. "First, I'm not the only person in the world with fancy AI facial recognition software, and if someone had access to news records for the last century and a half, they could dig all this up in a few hours. Second, the Sins. We know Lust has a hand in the media, and we know Wrath likes to make Thorn's life hell." Her brows raised behind thick-

rimmed glasses as she nodded toward the screen. "This looks like hell to me."

Chris cursed beneath her breath. "Why, though?" Her voice came out with a subtle squeeze, barely masking an anger ruminating below the surface. "If Wrath wanted to expose Thorn, she's had *decades* to do it."

"But never an opportunity to do it quite like *this*," Nicholas argued. "Who the hell would have believed it? With all this supernatural fuckery getting attention and Edith Froschlin making it worse, it's a perfect shitstorm for us."

"Plus, no one's talking about the Sins anymore, which is exactly what they want," Holly added. "It's all about Thorn and her Martyrs, especially since the agents we lost in Washington Square Park were cops."

She struck a key and pulled up another article. This one, from *The Times*. Two familiar faces looked out. Darius's teeth gnashed.

"Tamera Osborne and Paul Kwan were NYPD officers," Holly continued. "Their appearance among the dead is making waves, considering they've been 'missing' since we picked them up. Their families are claiming kidnapping, and the crazies on LymeLite are running with that, saying that Thorn brainwashed them. This makes us look *super* bad."

The room went quiet, that dense kind of quiet following a tragedy no one knew how to talk about. Darius groaned and ran a hand over his face. "We need to do damage control."

"I already have people working on it," Nicholas said.

"Deleting these videos won't be enough," Holly said. "Froschlin staged *another* attack this morning, and one of her followers was killed by a fake Martyr. We're taking the fall for this, and now that she's gotten a rise out of us once, she's not going to quit."

"There *has* to be something we can do," Chris muttered. She crossed her arms, tight muscles clearly visible beneath her black turtleneck. "I'll talk to Gabe, see if we can't figure out *something* that works within our budget..."

"Great," Holly said. She closed her laptop and got to her feet. "In the meantime, I'll keep an eye on our… illustrious leader. Make sure she doesn't get herself into any more trouble."

An anxious flutter twinged in Darius's chest. "What do you mean?"

"I mean," Holly said with a sigh, "that she headed into the city and hasn't been back since."

Darius's mouth ran dry. "With everything that's going on, is she even *safe* in New York right now?"

"I've been tracking her location," Holly said, "but she's hardly left her apartment, Darius. It's not *New York* I'm worried about."

Images of Thorn vaulting from the Brooklyn Bridge assaulted Darius's mind, and his stomach suddenly hollowed out as though he were the one tumbling toward cold water. He stood up from his chair, his hand a steel vise around its top rail. Chris glanced up at him, but he didn't have the heart to catch her eye. He was afraid to see his own panic reflected back.

The table emptied, each director making their exit until Darius was the only one left. He waited until the door shut at Mackenzie's heels before he pulled his phone out of his pocket. His call went straight to Thorn's voicemail, just like it had a dozen times before.

"Hey," he said. "It's me again…"

When Darius stepped into the hallway, he found Cain leaning against the wall.

"Ah, Darius." He came forward, and his hands migrated behind his back, gripping so tightly that Darius could see the pull in his shoulders. "Could I speak to you? In… private?"

Darius glanced around, where the empty corridors and closed doors indicated they were already alone, but Cain's expression made it clear that wasn't what he meant. "Yeah," Darius said. "Yeah, of course."

He headed to his office, but when he went to unlock it, Cain moved past him and opened the door leading to the dark lounge between Alan's and Thorn's. A cold weight dropped into Darius's chest, but before he could say anything, the old Forgotten Envy tilted his head into the room with an expectant nod. Darius had no choice but to follow… right into Alan's abandoned domain.

He stopped the second his feet landed on that plush, burgundy carpet. His body refused to go further.

Cain flicked on the lights, but even overhead bulbs did little to brighten the stale shadow of grief saturating this place. It hadn't changed at all since Alan had died, yet somehow, it was unrecognizable. Thick dust coated every surface—the backs of two upholstered chairs, each shelf lining the walls, and all the books and artifacts upon them. Even the desk was painted with it, lightening the mahogany finish to a dull, musty brown except for a splattering of cat paw prints and three uneven trails where a human being had recently run their fingertips along the top. Cain walked around it, standing where Alan had always stood. An old military photograph hovered over his shoulder, staring at the room with cold, dark eyes.

"What are we doing here, Cain?" Darius asked.

Cain sighed and took a knee, nearly disappearing from view.

"In light of recent… developments, there's something I thought you might want to take a look at."

Though Darius couldn't see, he heard the tell-tale click of a key entering a lock, followed shortly by the rumble of a filing cabinet drawer sliding open. When Cain stood again, he had a massive folder in his hands, so thick that the pages within threatened to come bursting at the seams. Cain held it out to him, and Darius finally walked the rest of the way into the room. The folder landed heavily in his palms, like it carried more than just sheets of paper. The second he opened it, his heart skipped.

An old, black and white photograph of Thorn sat at the top.

Wait. No. The resemblance was uncanny but not exact. She had the same dark eyes and black hair, but her cheeks were a little rounder, her nose softer, and her skin a shade darker. He lifted it, flipped it over, and read a line of text written in smooth, unfamiliar cursive.

Raelyn Blaine, 1942

Darius glanced at Cain with a frown. "Alan's sister?" When Cain nodded, Darius set the file on top of the desk and began to flip through its contents. He found letters, drawings, newspaper clippings, and more pictures, all dated to the early 1940s. Darius shook his head, awed. "I can't believe he kept all of this…"

"Yes, well, Alan was quite sentimental under that drab monotone of his," Cain said.

A soft smile turned up the corners of Darius's mouth as he tenderly turned the next few pages, revealing postcards, poetry, a wedding photo. That smile soured as he considered the ghosts within the frame: Benjamin and Raelyn— now a Rose—with their best man, Alan Blaine.

Darius couldn't stop looking at him—at that empty smile and haunted stare. He didn't have the trimmed goatee or signature veil of shoulder-length hair, but the strong nose and sharp jaw were the same. Darius turned the page again. This time, his stomach spun into a nest of knots.

A birth announcement… for Jane Margaret Rose. December 8, 1946.

His eyes slid up from the file and caught Cain watching from across the desk. Darius swallowed hard before he asked, "Why do you want me to see this?"

The Forgotten Sin shifted his weight from one foot to the other, wringing his hands.

"Inside this file," he began, "you will find things about

Thorn's life that the *'media'* could never uncover... things that will heal her reputation rather than ruin it... things about her only Alan ever truly got to know."

Cain flipped the page with the birth announcement, revealing an image of a baby girl. Darius's heart fractured, knowing what kind of hell she would grow up to live through.

"What you've seen come to light these last few days," Cain went on, "is a *fraction* of who Thorn is, of what she's accomplished. This will show you that... and so much more."

They fell into silence, Cain still standing on the far side of Alan's desk while Darius considered him and then the open folder between them. He couldn't help but wonder what he might find within these pages—how many questions would finally have answers, how many curiosities would finally make sense. Maybe, for the first time since meeting her three years ago, Darius could truly understand Thorn. He drew a long, slow breath that flowed down his throat and expanded deep within his chest...

And then, he closed the folder.

Cain's fidgeting abruptly stopped. He took a tiny step forward. "Darius—"

"I appreciate what you're trying to do, Cain," Darius interrupted, "but too much of Thorn's life has been exposed against her will already. I'll wait to hear the rest until *she* decides she's ready to share it."

He lifted the folder, measured the weight of it in his palms, and held it forward. Cain didn't take it right away, instead watching Darius with a concerned pull tightening his expression. At last, he reached out, and for a second, they held onto the records of Thorn's life together.

"What if there are things even *she* does not fully understand?" Cain asked.

Darius gave a somber smile. "Then maybe she's the one who needs to read it."

He let go and turned around, abandoning Cain on the

far side of the shrine that had once been Alan Blaine's office. When he got to the door, though, he paused and looked back one last time. Cain had opened the folder and was reading something about halfway through its contents.

"Besides," Darius said. Cain's head flicked up, and Darius tilted his chin at the folder. "Nothing in that thing can convince me of something I already know."

Cain frowned. "Which is what?"

"That Thorn isn't a monster," Darius said. "No matter what she or anyone else might think."

With that, he opened the door and strode out, but not before catching the glistening of emotion in Cain's eyes.

CHAPTER SEVENTEEN

December's icy teeth snapped at Thorn as she walked across the Third Avenue Bridge. A stretch of dark water flowed beneath her, the Harlem trudging toward the ocean, carrying filth and pollution the city had long since stopped trying to prevent. The river funneled wind north in a turbulent tunnel that whipped Thorn's hood around her head and threatened to drag her out of hiding. She pulled it tighter around her chin and squinted into the heavy winter night.

She'd met very few people out this late, but every time, a spark of panic ignited in her chest. How many of them had seen the video? Had read the stories? Heard *that* name?

A dizzying, disconnected sensation made Thorn stop, and a surge of air filled her lungs in a way that felt distressingly like *water*. She grabbed the railing at the center of the bridge and hovered there, staring out at the river like it might take this feeling away. Sparkie writhed in the satchel against her thigh, and Thorn's eyes pinched closed.

Fuck. She couldn't sink to these depths again.

Thorn drew out a pack of cigarettes. That first breath of burning smoke wrapped around her chest, where it suffocated her worries, or at the very least drowned out the sound of their screaming. She dragged that fucker down to a nub of tobacco embers, lit a fresh one, and finally, she started to walk again.

The four days following the incident at Washington Square Park dragged by like a body too heavy to carry, and Thorn had nothing to distract her from the hell inside her head.

Holly, with Nicholas in tow, confiscated Edith's burner the second Thorn's car arrived back at the Underground— something she fucking deserved—and ever since, Thorn had just sat in her studio, stared at her maps, and replayed every bad decision that had led her to this moment. God, there were *so* many.

She couldn't stand the thought of being alone in that room for one more goddamned second, but she couldn't go back to the Underground, either. Couldn't face the people she'd failed or the problems she'd caused. Which left only one alternative…

A stupid fucking alternative.

Sure, she could get herself caught—even killed—while she wasted more of the Martyrs' bootstrapped budget on a TAC rescue operation, but what the hell did she have to lose?

They'd taken everything from her already.

Thorn reached the far side of the Harlem and made her way east. Every inch felt like a mile, and every movement from the corner of her eye made her pulse leap—a man sleeping on a doorstep, an alley cat darting beneath a car, even the flash of apartment lights turning off above her. Her heart pounded against her sternum with the anxious rapping of a subconscious trying to ask her if this was another mistake. She ignored it.

The wooden church door beckoned with false promises of forgiveness and redemption. Echoes of memories she'd long suppressed teased her. Taunted her. Sunday mornings. Itchy dresses. Her father's broad hand wrapped around hers as they walked to mass. The last service Thorn had ever attended was his funeral. After that, her mother sought out

God at the bottom of a bourbon bottle, and the congregation responded with meaningless thoughts and prayers to absolve them of any guilt for not doing more to support a grieving widow and gutted daughter.

How would *this* congregation feel about her now?

Thorn's throat constricted around the dregs of her latest cigarette. She swallowed it down, flicked the spent butt onto the ground, and wrapped her fingers around the handle. The room opened with a gust of warm air as she walked in.

A chill breathed through the bar, and conversation whittled to nothing, a moment of silent prayer. Thorn tried to act casual, *normal*, with short nods and half-empty smiles. No one returned them, not even Sully. He watched her from beneath thick, furrowed brows. Thorn's belly filled with sand.

Less than half the usual crowd had braved the biting cold, and Thorn was relieved to see only familiar faces. She headed for the open counter. Jay stood by the tabernacle of spirits and barely managed to snap his jaw shut again as he readied an offering of scotch. He put it down at the same moment she settled onto a stool. Her fingers quaked around the rim as she lifted the glass and drank it all in a quick, painless gulp, like a mouthful of water around a pill to soothe her nerves.

A minute passed by. Then two. Jay poured Thorn another drink, which she nursed more tenderly this time. Jay hardly took his eyes off her, and he wasn't the only one. With her hood still up, Thorn couldn't see the other patrons, but she sensed the way their energy slowed, how it lengthened when people craned their necks in her direction. When her second glass was finally empty, one of those energies approached. Thorn's spine stiffened as a familiar body took the space between her and the exit.

"Is it true?" Sully asked.

Oh, *fuck.*

Thorn turned around, catching Sully's eye before spotting the phone he held at chest level. Her own face looked out at her, an old photograph, old name, old *life*. Thorn's heart climbed into her esophagus, where it would have cut off any argument she might try to make if her addled brain had been able to come up with an argument to begin with. Sully's expression gave little room for interpretation. His mouth set behind a gray mustache.

Jay's aura crept as close to the bar as possible. Thorn didn't look at him. Her eyes remained locked onto Sully's. Sparkie squirmed in her satchel, and she laid a hand over top to settle him—and hide him.

"Sully," Jay began, but Sully cut him off.

"Quiet, boy." The gravelly base of his voice rose to the high ceilings with the echo of a pipe organ. He thrust his phone forward a few more inches, forcing it into Thorn's frame, and repeated the question: "Is this true? Everything they're saying?"

Thorn drew a shallow breath, pulled off her hood, and managed to squeeze out two words.

"Not everything."

A new hush whispered around the room. The frigid shape of Jay froze, one hand poised beneath the bar where Thorn knew it had wrapped around his bat. Sully's jaw worked through what Thorn had said, and his lips pressed together. He tapped the screen with a single, tobacco-stained fingernail, right over her personal details: when and where she was born, her last known mailing address, an ancient criminal record, and that goddamned name she hated so much.

"But *this* is," Sully said. "*This* is you?"

Thorn's throat tightened, but she nodded.

"Yes."

This time, it wasn't a whisper. It was a roar. Gasps and gossip rumbled from wall to wall until Thorn's ears rang. Sully's face remained hard as ever as he slipped his phone back into his front pocket and shook his head. The disappointment in the motion punched her solar plexus.

"I can't fucking believe it," he muttered.

Jay moved toward him. "Sully—"

"We missed your birthday!"

A grin shattered Sully's stony facade and crinkled all his fine lines. At first, Thorn didn't believe it. Her mouth dropped open as she tried to work out what he'd said, what he'd *meant*. Sully let out a deep, chortling laugh and thumped a broad palm on her shoulder.

"Jay, pour the lady another drink. One for me, too."

Behind Thorn's back, the shape of Jay's aura slumped with measurable relief, and he breathed a sigh audible enough to be heard over the sudden chatter bouncing around the walls. Other patrons moved closer, the cold energy of their souls a disconcerting contrast with their warm expressions. This didn't make sense. Not unless—

The realization felt like a jolt of electricity, and Thorn twisted back to find a guilty blush across Jay's cheeks and a bottle of scotch in his hands.

"You told them," she breathed.

The blush extended to his ears, but as Jay opened his mouth to defend himself, Sully interrupted.

"Don't blame the kid." He plopped onto the stool beside her. All around, the other regulars took their tables again. "He heard us talkin' after the videos started coming and told us to keep our damned mouths shut. When we pressed him for details, he folded like an origami crane. He sucks at lying."

Jay rolled his eyes as he poured two glasses. "Fuck you, too, Sully…"

Sully laughed again, and the rest of the bar echoed the hymn. Thorn, however, shook her head.

"If you already knew, why go through all *this?*" she asked.

"I told him it was a bad idea," Jay said.

Sully ignored him. "Because if you don't laugh about it, what the hell else are you supposed to do? I have a feeling life's been up your ass lately, so you could use it." He grabbed his drink and held it up to the light. "Cheers."

Thorn still didn't move—didn't know what to do or

what to say. She stared at Sully for a moment longer in complete disbelief. "But I'm—"

"One of us," Sully cut in. Now, that cheerful, childlike smile flickered off his face, replaced with an earnest, serious frown. "That's all that matters."

A surge of sudden gratitude stung the corners of Thorn's eyes. Sully nodded, just once, before he cleared his throat, like he, too, was overcome with emotion.

"So," he began again. "What do we call you? I'm gonna assume Teagan's a cover and that *other* name's been dead for a long time."

"Thorn," she said.

"Thorn." He repeated it slowly, as though exploring the way it felt, how it sounded. "Mm. I like it. Nice and powerful." He lifted the glass again and flashed a smile. "Cheers, *Thorn.*"

Finally, she grabbed her scotch, and despite herself, she smiled, too.

"Cheers."

The Cross had always been a safe haven from the hell of a life Thorn lived, but the moment that door opened, it became so much more. Sully and the other patrons didn't hassle Thorn for information about her traumas and terrors but instead asked about the Sins, about her power, and about why she chose to spend her time *here*, of all places. After an hour or so, when Thorn's guard lowered enough to feel like this wasn't all going to fall down on top of her, Sparkie crawled from her satchel and perched on her shoulder to a chorus of gasps.

But by far, what the regulars of The Cross were most impressed by was Thorn's ability to drink. By the time she threw a seventh scotch to the back of her throat, the entire bar had gathered.

"So, you *really* don't feel it?" Sully asked as Thorn placed the empty glass back on the counter.

"I could," Thorn admitted, "but it would take a *lot.*"

Unless her *Peccostium* was damaged, but Thorn didn't

mention that. While the others laughed, memories of her last drunken night swept Thorn away. Suddenly, she was in her room at the Underground, Darius's arms around her waist, the clean, musky scent of his skin tempting her closer, *so close* that their bodies pressed together. Heat flushed across her face, invading her nervous system with an unwelcome need that made her feel suddenly lost.

Jay let out an amused scoff from behind the bar. "That explains a lot." He refilled her scotch with a smirk. Something about the look on her face must have struck him, though, because that smirk dissolved. Before he could say more, an older woman shook her head to Thorn's left.

"S'real shame is what it is," she slurred. The dregs of a third rum and coke lingered at her fingertips. Even though the glass held nothing but a cluster of half-melted ice cubes, she still spilled it as she waved her hands in a sloppy gesture. "What's the point of drinkin' if you can't get *drunk?*"

"Oh, I've always found that just the experience of savoring a good merlot is *always* worth it."

A familiar but distinctly out-of-place voice made Thorn's heart skip. Sparkie darted behind her hair as she twisted around and made direct eye contact with one of the few people in the whole goddamned world who could sneak up on her.

Cain smiled. "Hello, my dear."

Sully leapt to his feet and planted himself between Cain and Thorn, an absolute grizzly of a man who had no idea he was squaring up against a beast far more dangerous.

"Who the fuck are you?" he growled.

Cain hooked his thumbs over his pockets, leaning his weight onto one leg while the other hip popped out. "I was going to ask you the same thing…"

Sully blustered, chest puffing up, and Thorn laid a hand on his arm. "It's okay. He's a… friend."

One brow arced into a delicate curve on Cain's head. "A *friend?* Well, this is embarrassing. *I* always considered us family."

Thorn's jaw clenched, and she glanced at Sully, at Jay, and at all the others. "Can you give us a minute?"

At first, no one moved. The Cross stood at a standstill, Sully shielding Thorn while Jay's hand wandered beneath the bar again. Thorn cleared her throat. Sully shot Cain one more threatening glower before he walked away. As though waiting for that cue, the others followed. Jay left last, but Cain called out to him before he'd made it two feet down the counter.

"Excuse me," he said as he took Sully's vacated stool. "Could I see your wine list?"

The corner of Jay's mouth twitched. "Sure. White or red?"

"I would like to explore your options on both."

"Those *are* your options," Jay said. "White or red."

Cain curled his nose. "Red, I suppose."

Jay nodded, caught Thorn's eye, and disappeared into the back. The second he whipped behind the wall, Thorn faced forward, keeping Cain steadily in her periphery, and drew her scotch to her lips. "How did you know I was here?"

He huffed a short, irritated sigh. "Like I said, we're *family*. I know you better than you know yourself. And, it might surprise you to learn, destroying a security camera has little effect on actually *finding* you."

Thorn's fingers tightened around her glass. "God *damn* it, Andrews."

"Is *Holly* the one in the wrong here?" Cain pressed. Thorn didn't answer, tilting a splash of liquor onto her tongue as her Familiar peeked his head out from her hair. Jay rematerialized, slid a glass of wine to Cain, and strode away again. Cain lifted it and went on. "But *no*, it wasn't Holly. Need I remind you that you aren't the only person in this room with part of your consciousness incarnated outside of your being? Mine is just… much more subtle."

Thorn's eyes shot wide before she could catch herself. She glanced over her shoulder, looking for the silhouette of a cat outlined in the dark windows. Cain took a sip, and his face soured. "Ugh! If *this* is the kind of wine they have, what *is* the point of drinking?"

He pushed the glass away. Thorn glared at him.

"You've been following me?"

"Of course not," Cain said with a scoff. "I've simply kept an eye on this particular safe space of yours." He opened his arms to the room. Patrons watched the pair of them with narrow, suspicious eyes. Sully looked like he was ready to shove Cain's face through a stained-glass panel if he so much as sneezed in Thorn's direction. Cain shook his head. "I should be wounded that you would rather spend your time here than with your... *friends*, but I suppose it's better than wallowing in solitude."

Thorn's spine stiffened. "They're good people," she defended.

"Surely, they are," Cain agreed. "But they're not *your* people, Thorn."

She opened her mouth, but no sound came out, like the beating of her heart in her throat made it impossible for her to speak. Cain considered her for a moment, the pull to his brows a soft, repentant kind of concern before he sighed.

"Grief is a funny thing," he went on, more quietly now. So quiet that even the barest echo of his voice died before it reached the ceiling. "It makes us feel so... exposed... Reveals our insecurities, our weaknesses, and forces the rawest parts of who we are out into the open. Sometimes, that leaves us so tender, so sensitive, that we feel like our only option is to hide away, and so we grieve alone."

Cain's eyes narrowed, as though they were looking right through the bullshit mask Thorn wore for the rest of the world and peering into the depths of her soul. She drew in a short breath, and Sparkie slithered down the back of her jacket.

"I'm *not* alone," she said, but her voice was as strong as a sheet of corroded iron.

Cain arched a brow. "No? My mistake."

He turned back toward the bar, lifted his wine, and took another sip that curled his nose. For several minutes, they sat in silence. Thorn tried to drink her scotch just to give her a goddamned distraction, but suddenly, it tasted like gasoline in her mouth. Cain's voice pulled her back in a quiet hum.

"The people here may respect you, Thorn," he murmured, this time without looking at her. "They may like you, even care about you, as well as they can… but they don't truly know you. They don't expect anything of you, and they don't demand anything in return. That makes them *safe*. There is no chance of letting them down."

His gaze slid her way, caught the frown on her lips, and he exhaled a weary sigh.

"If they were to turn their backs on you, it might sting, but at the end of the day, it wouldn't matter. You would move on and fill that void with other superficial connections and low-risk company. But can the same be said for me? For Chris? For *Darius?*"

Thorn's pulse leapt, stealing her breath, her *backbone*. She pulled away from Cain, putting another inch of distance between them. He shook his head.

"You are so *convinced* we will abandon you that you aren't giving us the chance to prove you wrong," Cain said. "Grieve, Thorn. By all means, *grieve*. But *this* is not grief." He glanced around The Cross again—to Jay, to Sully—before focusing back on her with a tender but biting glint. "It's escape, and the further you run from the people who love you, the harder it will be to find your way back to them."

With that, Cain rose to his feet, downed the rest of his wine, and leaned toward her. His lips planted a soft, loving kiss at the crown of her head before he threw a hundred-dollar bill onto the counter and strode from the room, as sudden and silent as when he'd walked in.

Thorn stared after him, her gut a tangled mess of live wires. Emotion stung her eyes, and no amount of blinking soothed it. Jay's cold energy approached from behind the bar.

"Everything good?"

She nodded. Short and quick.

"I need a cigarette."

Before he could press further, Thorn grabbed her things and headed toward the back exit. She ignored the curious looks, Sully calling her name, Jay asking her to wait, and burst through to the alley. Hot rage inoculated her against December's icy grip, and she ached for that cigarette burn deep in her chest just to kill the feeling before it took over. Thorn tore her satchel open and dug past loose weapons and spare clothes until she reached the pack of smokes. Sparkie vaulted into the sky with a cry as she grabbed one out, stuck the end between her lips, and flicked her lighter. The flame came to life inches before her face. She closed her eyes, savoring the tiny warmth against her cheeks, and drew in that first, freeing breath…

Nothing happened.

The writhing in her core didn't quiet, the buzzing didn't fade, and Thorn realized with a sickening horror that it wasn't rage she was trying to smother. It was *everything else*— things she had never learned how to master, to even *manage*. Cain's voice echoed in her head while a parade of images made Thorn's heart sick. Donovan bleeding out in her arms. Alan standing over her hospital bed the day she woke from that coma. Chris rocking with sobs after learning her mother had been killed in action. Darius holding her tight as he laid a warm palm against her chest, planning to heal her but discovering instead that she was too damned to be saved.

In a sudden surge, her stomach churned, and the once-familiar comfort of nicotine in her lungs made Thorn want to vomit. She ripped the cigarette away from her mouth and threw the thing, still smoldering, to the concrete.

Then she stood there, grieving alone.

With a scream, or a sob, or maybe both, Thorn wrapped her fists in her hair and tugged until she pulled herself down to her knees. The city's cold corruption gripped her. For the first time in over a century, Thorn shivered.

And slowly, delicately, as though the damned thing were a toxin she could absorb through naked skin, Thorn pulled her phone from her pocket. A slew of unanswered text messages flooded her inbox, all from people who *weren't safe*. Thorn's eyes trailed down the list, and every name felt like a gut punch in waiting. Cain, Holly, Mackenzie, Nicholas— even Lamar Verrette and Elijah Harris. Reaching out. Offering support. Sending condolences. Thorn ignored them, flicked through the list to Chris and—her heart clenched.

Darius Jones.

Standing took more effort than Thorn anticipated, as though all her muscles had turned to sand, but she *did* stand and then began her trek back toward her apartment. Along the way, she closed her texting app and navigated instead to her speed dial list. Alan's number sat at the top because, apparently, Thorn loved to torture herself. She skipped past it, thumb hovering over the second name down, but she didn't work up the courage to call until she was halfway over the Harlem.

The phone rang once, hardly long enough for Thorn's pounding heart to decide if it wanted to burst through her ribcage or climb into her throat before the line connected.

"Thorn?" a familiar voice said. "Are you okay?"

"Yeah," she tried to say, but the word came out a ragged mess. She swallowed it down and tried again. "I'm fine. I just…"

Thorn glanced down. Her right hand strangled the pack of cigarettes she hadn't realized she'd been holding this whole time. She uncurled her fingers, one at a time…

And then she crushed the box in a violent squeeze before chucking the whole damned thing over the edge. It disappeared into the dark before it hit the water.

"Do you have a second?"

CHAPTER EIGHTEEN

Darius gazed out at the courtyard, alight with a disorienting blend of dizzying relief and sinking disappointment. The late morning crowd pulsed through the dining area in a hungry ebb and flow, their warm energy like a tropical tide washing toward the shore. He and Chris had snatched a spot on the outskirts to have breakfast, and Darius poked at his scramble with the tines of his fork.

"Well… I'm glad she reached out to someone. What did she want to talk about?"

He glanced at his phone, still glaringly empty of any new messages. Of course, Thorn would contact Chris first, yet a small part of Darius ached that it hadn't been him.

Chris sighed and raised her coffee, a crease wedged between her brows. Steam wafted against her face, and she drew in a deep breath, like somehow the vapors alone would carry enough caffeine to make the exhaustion a little more bearable.

"Not much," Chris answered. When Darius frowned, she offered a half-shrug. "She just asked if I had a patrol this morning, and when I said I didn't, she wanted to set up time to spar."

Darius's brows shot up. "No wonder you're so tired."

"Tell me about it," Chris said with a laugh. "I'm a little rusty. Thorn and I haven't trained together since Alan died."

Her voice caught on a barb of emotion, and she cleared her throat as she looked into her mug. Darius heaved a sigh.

"I'm just glad she called at all," he murmured, fully aware that his tone came out more defeated than elated. He'd gladly give up an entire night of dreaming, an entire morning of sleep, an entire *day* of peace, for Thorn to call him, to *need* him, too.

Chris laid a hand on his forearm, and when Darius met her eye, she passed him a reassuring, bittersweet smile. "Me, too. We talked more during training. Thorn has some thoughts about how we might be able to go after Edith Froschlin."

"Edith?" Darius frowned, and though he hated himself for even thinking it, he asked, "No offense, Chris but… should Thorn get involved in anything to do with Edith right now?"

A flush darkened Chris's cheeks, but she dismissed Darius's worries with a quick shake of her head. "Edith's dragging her name through the dirt, Darius, and there was *another* incident this morning. We can't blame her for wanting to be involved. Plus, Thorn's the only one who's faced her head-on. She mentioned something I hadn't realized about the incident in Washington Square Park."

Chris reached into her pocket and pulled out her phone without giving Darius a chance to protest further. After a few seconds of navigating through apps, she laid it flat on the table to reveal a screenshot of Thorn holding one of the crow people up by the throat.

"*This* isn't one of Edith's followers," she said, tapping a nail against the screen. "It's one of her *mercenaries.*"

Darius leaned closer. There was nothing identifiable about the man at all. A full mask obscured his face, and the black cloak and clothing made the rest of his body an indistinct shape. Despite the fact that Thorn had hoisted him off the ground in a single hand, he was clearly several inches taller and much broader than her.

"How do you know?" Darius asked.

"For one, he could fight," Chris said. "But more importantly, he knew where to look for Thorn's *Peccostium*. Only someone working for Edith would have that information."

Darius's eyes went wide, and she nodded.

"I know, but we really shouldn't be shocked. Edith is dressing her people in TAC uniforms. Makes sense that she'd put them in crow masks, too. It guarantees that she'll *always* have backup close at hand, hiding in plain sight."

"And that we can't do anything about it," Darius said with a sigh. "She knows we can't attack the cultists. Most of them are civilians."

"Exactly," Chris agreed, and a glint flashed in her eyes— an excited, eager shine that overshadowed the fatigue. "But there's nothing that says we can't *join* them."

"Join them?" Darius asked, but the second the words left his mouth, realization pulled his jaw toward the ground. "You want to dress *TAC* as crows?"

"I do," Chris said. "Our traditional uniforms have been vilified thanks to Edith's copycat Martyrs, so we shouldn't wear them anyway. Masks will hide our identities, and cloaks will disguise armor no problem. We'd have a chance to get close to Edith without planting a giant target on our backs."

Darius nodded. Slowly. "God, Chris, that's *genius.*" She beamed at him, a vibrant smile radiating off her face. A smile Darius immediately dampened. "There's one problem, though. Can we afford it?"

Chris chewed on her lower lip. "Well… we could buy things in bulk to cut costs, but then we'd run into the problem of all our team looking exactly the same." She picked up her spoon and stabbed it into her untouched oats, crushing a raspberry into a bright red smear. "I'd want each of the masks to be unique. It would be nice if we could integrate our communication technology into them, too, but that's even more complicated. Hiring someone to custom build—what?"

She cut off abruptly when she glanced back up to Darius. His mouth had slipped open, and he ran a hand through his hair.

"That's just it," he murmured. "Custom build. We have Holly to get the tech side of things."

Chris gasped and grabbed Darius by the arm. "And Cain! Cain can make the masks!"

Darius grinned. The muscles on his face ached with how little they practiced this expression anymore, but it was a welcome ache. A healing one. "C'mon. Let's go see if it's even possible."

They abandoned their table, dropped their uneaten meals off in the kitchen, and while Chris went into the basement to discuss this with Holly and her team, Darius turned back to the courtyard, hoping he'd find Cain in one of the art rooms they'd shut down.

It looked like it might be time to reopen.

"Wow, Cain," Chris murmured. "This is incredible."

They'd gathered in the center of what had been the pottery studio. While Cain walked in a slow, deliberate arch around the only table not draped in glaze-streaked white sheets, Darius and Chris stood off to one side. Taylor Simmons, their weapon and gear expert, sat at the edge, typing away at a laptop. A mannequin bust sat in the middle between them all.

Cain curled one hand into a delicate fist and pressed it against his lips as he considered the device strapped to the thing's plastic head. Around the back and crown, the innards of a tactical helmet stretched in a cybernetic net, its wires and circuitry exposed to open air. In the front, though, a beautiful crow mask made of paper mâché and faux feathers covered the featureless face from chin to imaginary hairline. Cain pinched one between his fingers and plucked it free like a mother preening its young.

"Not bad for just two days of work," he murmured, adjusting another feather. A subtle fringe of gold plumage, visible through the black, crested the top of the head, and he smoothed it down. "Though I could do without this... monstrosity."

He waved a chaotic hand over the exposed electronic bits. Darius smiled while Taylor let out a laugh.

"We'll hide it," she said, "as soon as we know things are working the way we want them to." She stood, walked around to the front of the bust, and lifted the mask until it came free. "Let's give it a try. Chris?"

The Tactical director stepped forward, and Taylor lowered the device around her head. It had to be heavier than it looked. From his spot behind Chris's back, Darius could make out the flashing of more electronic components fit into the exterior facade. Sure enough, the entire thing tilted forward the second Taylor released it.

"Damn, I was afraid of that," she muttered. She reached behind Chris and gently tugged an adjustment strap. When she was done, it didn't move again. "There we go. How's that feel?"

Chris shrugged. "Not bad," she said, voice muffled by the mask. "A little tight."

"Too tight?" Taylor asked. She tucked Chris's hair behind her ears, checked the position, and slipped a pair of tethered headphones into place.

"No, not at all," Chris replied.

"Perfect." Taylor stood directly in front of her to check the fit one last time before moving back to the laptop. Chris turned around, and Darius's eyes widened. The mask fit to the contours of her face, smooth and elegant, and thanks to a pair of tinted polyurethane lenses, even her eyes were difficult to see. If not for the blonde ponytail at the base of her skull and the vital human aura as distinct to her as a fingerprint, Darius would never have recognized her. Chris hesitated when she caught him staring.

"How's it look?" she asked.

"Even better than on the mannequin," Darius said.

Cain came forward, holding a bundle of black velvet aloft. "We mustn't forget the final touch."

He unraveled the cloak with the gravitas of a king, whipped it about her shoulders, and fastened the clasp into place at her throat. When he raised the cowl over her head, the rest of Chris Silver disappeared, replaced entirely by a stunning, black bird.

"I added hooks at the temples…" Cain spoke in a murmur as he focused, securing tiny fabric loops inside the hood to the mask itself. "These should keep it all together. We wouldn't want to risk another case of exposed identity…"

Chris laughed. "I don't *have* an identity outside of the Underground, Cain."

He offered a warm smile. "Well, aren't *we* the lucky ones? Still, the less your beautiful face ends up in the *LymeLite*, my dear, the better."

Chris laughed again, and though Darius smiled, he couldn't help the pit of anxiety crumbling open in his stomach. He crossed his arms. She wouldn't wear this costume to a masquerade ball. She'd wear it to a battlefield. They had to remember that.

"So," he said as he turned back to Taylor. "What other features does this thing have?"

Taylor shrugged, and when she shook her head, her poof of natural, black hair swished at the top. "Photochromic lenses, ambient sound amplification, hearing protection, tracking chips, and our com system, which is… working, I think?" She glanced up, brown eyes landing on Chris. "I'm running an audio test. Let me know if you can hear this."

She tapped her pinky onto the enter key, and Chris instantly returned a thumbs-up.

"Perfect." Taylor typed a few notes into her program. "The mic is embedded beneath the beak, so audio feedback should be crystal clear, and it will seamlessly sync up between all of our agents."

Chris nodded. "Incredible. Thank you both so much. Am I good?"

She indicated her face, hidden behind a crow. When Taylor confirmed she was done, Cain helped remove the cloak, and Chris carefully pulled the device over her head. Staticky strands of yellow escaped her elastic and danced around her skull like flickering beams inside a plasma globe.

"It isn't as impressive as it looks," Taylor said, crossing her arms around an ample chest. "I cannibalized one of our older helmets and stole the tech."

Chris placed the mask onto the mannequin and stepped back to admire it the same way Cain had before. Her stance mimicked his, as though measuring a priceless piece of art, or crucial tactical equipment, by the number of souls it saved.

"As long as it gets the job done, I'm not worried about how it came together." A pair of matching, vertical lines pinched between her brows. "Though, I'm just realizing… how will we recognize *each other* if we're all wearing masks? I can't believe I didn't consider that."

Cain grinned. "Then it's a good thing *I* did. That's what these are for." His fingertips again migrated to the thin filigree of gold feathers at the very crest of the crow's black skull. "All Martyr masks will feature some kind of golden highlight. The feathers, the beak, maybe a lining around the eyes… Something subtle that will make it stand out from the rest, but not *too* much. It's still a risk, to be sure, but we can always modify the masks after each interaction to keep Edith Froschlin on her toes."

Chris breathed out a sigh into a graceful smile. "God, that's brilliant. The next question is, how many of these can we afford to make?"

She glanced at Taylor, who raised a brow. "How many do you want?"

"I'm not sure," Chris admitted. "Thorn is talking to Holly now, trying to figure out a pattern to these attacks, but we do know there were over a hundred fanatics at the latest incident. That's way more than we saw at the conflict at Washington Square." Her gaze disappeared past Taylor's shoulder, irises darting side to side as though doing the math in her head. "I imagine that number will only increase as Froschlin's movement gains more traction, but we don't want to create a suspicious surge of new people… Maybe twenty? To have in rotation and for backup in case some get marked or damaged?"

Taylor's full lips curled into a frown. "I can probably swing it, but we've got a limited number of these older helmets in storage. I'll do a count and get back to you."

"Perfect. Thank you, Taylor."

As Taylor nodded, Cain cleared his throat. "As far as the *aesthetic* side of this equation is concerned, I can put together as many of these as your heart desires." He gestured to the mask with an open palm. "I created a base mold for this one, which will make crafting more as effortless as it is enjoyable. I may even get a class together to… speed up the process." He glanced at Darius, a twinkle in his bright, half-empty eyes. "Perhaps these extracurricular arts *are* an essential part of the Underground after all?"

Darius chuckled, shaking his head. "Let's start with the mask workshop and see how that—"

A piercing alarm shot through the courtyard in a single, wailing scream. All at once, the building filled with sound, and the overhead lights faded from daylight white to a shade closer to mustard gas. Darius knew what that meant.

Yellow alert. A potential threat to the Underground.

He didn't remember seeing a drill in the schedule.

Darius turned to Chris, and the look on her face made his guts turn to jelly. Even in the flashing, saffron glow, he could tell the blood had drained from her cheeks. Horror made her eyes wide and mouth tight. The alarm tapered off, but the lights maintained the sickly color. The four of them exchanged a tense look.

All at once, they exploded into action.

Taylor rushed into the courtyard and toward the stairs

while Cain grabbed the mask, ran across the room, and locked it away. Darius turned to Chris, but she'd bolted toward the door like the Sins were breathing down her spine. Above him, around him, everywhere, Martyr energy swarmed as people cleared the courtyard and rushed to their rooms. The warm chatter gave way to panicked shouting, like all the damned work they'd done in their drills to prepare for this exact moment had been whisked away by the inevitability of it happening for real.

Darius burst into the courtyard.

"You know the drill!" he shouted over the chaos. A few faces glanced his way. "Lock everything down, get to your quarters, and wait for further instruction!"

He was met with a rally of "yes, sirs" before he listened to his own damned order and rushed toward the eastern wing of rooms. Above him, warm energy swarmed toward the tactical lockers as officers got ready for combat.

Edith Froschlin's burner phone sat at the center of Holly's desk like a goddamned mockery.

Thorn's fingers tingled, hungry to wind around the thing again. While Holly typed away, prattling about Froschlin's latest incident at the fish market on Pier 17, Thorn glared at the device like it had whispered some veiled threat and expected her to take it quietly. The security office buzzed with servers and terminals, and an air-conditioned chill pressed around her, but the fire in Thorn's gut kept her red hot.

"Interesting…" Holly was saying, as though speaking to herself, and Thorn wondered for the tenth time why the fuck she had to be here for this "conversation" in the first place. "This is the second time Froschlin's sent a location marker an hour before her crazies showed up…"

Holly struck another key, and the six screens above her head flickered with video footage. A stretch of the East River provided a backdrop to the Raven's latest publicity stunt.

"She's *clearly* trying to give us time to get there," Holly went on, "now that she knows we're getting her messages."

Absently, without even looking at the damned thing, Holly tapped the phone. Thorn's heart vaulted into her ribs, and Sparkie let out a low growl from his perch on her shoulder.

"And I think she's trying to slow things down," the security lead went on, but her voice hardly registered anymore. The burner's dark screen called to Thorn with a force like possession. "Fewer people are getting hurt. Hell, last time, her crows chased off the fake Martyrs without much of a fight. She knows that drawing too much of the *wrong* attention could bring in the military or the FBI, and she's only trying to bait *us*."

God, Thorn didn't want to be here—didn't want to be discussing the *technicalities* of Edith's work. She wanted to be out *there*, hunting the bitch down. Just the idea of taking Edith Froschlin on a third time spurred a disorienting storm to life in Thorn's belly—a cumulonimbus monstrosity where an updraft of scalding fury collided violently with a cold current of panic. Lightning pulsed through her nervous system as a croaking voice ricocheted around her skull, horrifyingly human-like.

"Three down."

Thorn crossed her arms, nails digging into her bicep, while her teeth gritted together.

"Is she only sending coordinates?" she asked at last, finally finding her voice.

Holly glanced back. "Huh?"

"Froschlin," Thorn stated. "Is she still *just* sending coordinates?"

Holly hesitated, as though she didn't want to answer because she knew a lie would be insulting, but the truth would light a more dangerous fire. At last, after loosening a sigh, she simply said, "No."

That was answer enough. Thorn read the real meaning

behind that single syllable, and Sparkie's wings frilled by her ear in a distracting sensation of leather vibrating upon leather. The imagined threats and taunts and torments hiding on that little screen made the rest of the room hard to see, to hear, to *feel*. Thorn's eyes fixated on the device tucked beneath Holly's monitor grid, and for half a second, she *wished* she hadn't given it up. A prickling sensation ran up Thorn's spine.

In a sudden, deliberate movement, Holly grabbed the phone, opened the top drawer in her desk, and shoved it to the back. A spell lifted from Thorn's shoulders, and her face washed over with warmth. She glanced up at Holly, finding the other woman watching her with a dark, distrustful look. Thorn's teeth gritted together.

A brittle thread of wounded pride and resentment had stretched between them from the second she'd entered the security office. Now, it pulled so taut it felt like it was bound to snap, and god knew what would get whipped in the process. Before Thorn had the chance to speak and test that line, the lights dimmed. Every human soul in the room around her and the Underground above froze as a siren blared. Holly's screens flashed a bright, venomous yellow.

They stared at each other, Thorn's jaw set while Holly's eyes widened behind the magnification of her glasses, and they reached the same grim conclusion. Sparkie screeched in Thorn's ear, louder than the siren.

"Code Yellow!" Holly shouted, turning back to her setup as Thorn leapt to her feet. "I need eyes on all entrances, exits, the emergency escape routes—"

"Who sounded the alarm?" Thorn cut in.

Holly tapped a few keys and forced her screens to reset. "Brandt. Convenience store, terminal two—"

"Get me a visual!"

Another rapid array of clicks and each display filled with a different feed from the gas station above. The top right showed the view from a camera tucked behind the register. Stefan Brandt's back was to them, one hand resting on a pistol hidden beneath the counter, while his partner, Haley Green, quietly locked the entrance on the opposite side of the room. A man stood across from Brandt, speaking wildly, his hands moving in dramatic motions. Something about him prodded at Thorn with a distant sense of familiarity. Her mouth ran dry, and she pointed a rigid finger at his face.

"Can you zoom in?"

Holly nodded, and the magnification increased by two, four, eight. He was Latino, well-built, healthy. A trimmed beard covered his chin and cheeks, and his short, black hair swept back from his eyes, making the furrow to his brow more obvious. Holly slammed her pinky onto one more key, and audio bloomed in the speakers.

"—not leaving!" the man yelled. Even his *voice* tugged on some memory Thorn couldn't quite place. "I've been trying to find her for years! I *know* Thorn's here, and I won't go anywhere until I talk to her!"

It clicked—the pieces arranging themselves into a picture that shouldn't exist—a picture that had been stripped and shredded. Thorn's lips slipped open in a shallow gasp, and she watched for a moment longer, waiting for him to turn, to give her a look at the left side of his face, to confirm what she didn't dare believe.

"I told you, sir," Brandt said. "I don't know who—"

The man shook his head. Thorn spotted the tapered corner of a scar wedged between his eyelid and brow.

"Oh, my god," she whispered.

Holly glanced back. "What's going—"

Thorn threw the door open. Hot air breathed against her with the moist, mildewy pressure of a wet belch from a monstrous belly. Before Holly had even finished asking the question, Thorn was out of her office.

The basement stretched out in a dark, abyssal labyrinth of shadowy corridors and groaning pipes. Her feet hammered against the concrete, following white-painted arrows toward the stairwell on the exact fucking opposite side of the space. She ran so quickly that the motion-activated lights chased at her back rather than guiding the way ahead of her. Thorn slammed into the door. Flung it open.

The siren's scream roused again, ringing in her skull.

As Thorn vaulted up the stairs two at a time, noise echoed down the shaft. Boots pounding onto concrete steps. Gear rumbling against armor. Gabe DuPont shouting orders. A mass of TAC officers entered the stairwell from the first floor just as Thorn bounded past them. Their cold energy filed into a neat line until Thorn collided with it, scattering bodies as she forced herself to the front. Carter grunted as she shouldered past him. Gabe's cognac eyes caught her from behind the lead helmet.

"What the hell are you doing?" he shouted.

Thorn ignored him.

She spiraled up ten flights, never slowing, never stopping, all too aware of a nervous sweat glistening along her neck as Sparkie wound around it. Her mental awareness stretched above, counting three distinct auras. Two she knew as the TAC team assigned to the station, but the third she recognized more distantly, so distantly that part of her was *sure* she was imagining it.

The door at the landing was locked. Thorn typed her passcode in, fucked it up, swore, and tried again before it flashed green and opened with a mechanical click. She rushed out, leaving the hidden entrance wide and gaping as she moved through the storage room and into the hallway.

Voices carried to her from across the building.

"Hands where I can see them!" Stefan Brandt ordered.

And then, the distinct *click* of a loaded gun being cocked. Thorn's chest tightened.

"Hold fire!" she screamed.

All three souls froze, cold and still as ice sculptures. Thorn ran down the hall, exploded into the room from an ingress behind the counter, and stopped on the threshold. Brandt stood shocked at the register, his firearm pointed at the man's chest. By the door, Green's trained on his head.

"Lower your weapons," Thorn commanded. "Now!"

They did. Quickly and quietly. The whole time, Thorn didn't tear her eyes away from the man before her, taking in everything about him, from his warm eyes, curled fists, and the scar cutting from just above his left eye all the way to his ear. He stared at her, too, like he couldn't fucking believe he was finally seeing her face-to-face.

"I'm sorry, ma'am," Brandt stammered. "He's not in our system and didn't know our code words. Do you know him?"

Thorn swallowed a lump that had grown like a tumor in her throat.

"We've met," she breathed. "Just once."

CHAPTER NINETEEN

The yellow alert rose and fell in an instant.

No sooner had Darius gotten to his quarters, the siren lifted, and the lights returned to their standard color. Before he could wonder what the hell was happening, Holly's system sent an Underground-wide message to every Martyr device.

False alarm.

He shook his head, whiplashed and half-convinced that they'd all fallen into some strange group delusion. When he returned to the courtyard, the cavernous space echoed as relieved Martyrs shared theories of what triggered the alert. As he reached the tables outside the dining area, Darius's phone went off. His heart stuttered when he saw Thorn's name flashing across the screen. He answered on the first ring.

"Hey!" he said—practically shouted—drawing attention from a couple of nearby researchers. His face burned, and he cleared his throat as he started again, more levelly. "Hey. How are you doing?"

Thorn's breath rattled through the speaker. "I need you to come to my office."

Darius frowned. "What happened?"

"Just… come up here. Now."

He blinked, swallowing hard, and glanced at the ceiling. In the spot he estimated Thorn's office sat, he detected an aura he'd never felt before. His stomach twirled, but not in the way of danger. In a way of nerves.

"I'm on my way."

———

The elevator dragged Darius upward, crawling on its cables. He walked down the hallway, through a throng of TAC agents dressing down from the alert, and reached the lounge outside Thorn's office. This close, the person inside had a shape, a structure, larger than Thorn, and so… warm. Not as searing as Chris and Gabe, but more than most of the other people Darius interacted with, like the comforting embrace of a blanket by the fire. He took a deep breath and released it in a slow stream, letting some of his anxiety wash away.

Then he opened the door.

First, he spotted Thorn, poised at the edge of the coffee table in front of her red couch. She bent at the waist, smooth hair drawn around one shoulder while Sparkie perched on the other. In front of her, a man sat rooted to the center cushion. He was all stiffness, from the soles of his feet to the crown of his head. They glanced up as Darius walked in.

And he froze.

It couldn't be.

The man rose to his feet. He was the right height, just a *little* shorter than Darius's six feet, and had the same deep, brown skin and black hair, but all of it was cleaner, more well-kept than Darius was used to. He smiled, and his smile matched every other smile Darius had seen on that face before, the smiles between running successful heists for food at the corner market, tossing apples across the kitchen, and playing with kids on that dirty bar floor.

And the scar, the *new* scar, that drew a swift, violent line across the left side of his face. Darius's breath caught.

It *couldn't* be.

The man opened his mouth, and Saul Torres's voice spilled out.

"Darius?"

A gasp lodged in Darius's throat, choking the words he didn't quite have yet, but it didn't matter. Saul collapsed the space between them. He threw his arms around Darius's shoulders, pulled him in—

And Darius shattered.

The last three years collapsed against his skull and fell off his tongue in a laugh, then a sob, and before Darius fully knew what was happening, he was crying into the crook of Saul's neck. His hands splayed out and then dug into the fabric on Saul's jacket, as though making sure it was real— that the man beneath it was more grit than ghost.

He didn't know how long they stood there, embracing like they would never embrace again. They laughed and they sobbed until they had nothing left to give. Darius was aware of Thorn in the room, standing behind Saul, watching these feelings unfurl with the glisten of unshed tears behind her eyelashes, but Darius didn't care how raw or ragged he looked right now.

Saul was *alive*.

Thorn left them alone.

During the tearful reunion, she'd excused herself by saying she would get them all some coffee, but Darius knew she was giving them a moment alone.

A moment they desperately needed.

After she left, the two of them sat back on the couch and talked both like no time had passed at all and as though they'd lived entire lifetimes apart. They focused on the broad strokes—on the bigger picture rather than the little details, the things that were easier to talk about.

Well, mostly easier.

Darius broke the news of Eva's death, which Saul seemed to sense coming, and they shared a few moments of silence for his sister as though she'd passed just yesterday. Then, Saul provided brief updates on Lindsay and Juniper— and what had happened to them the night Pride and Envy destroyed their lives.

The three had escaped into the old prohibition tunnels, just like Darius and Thorn had assumed when they'd found themselves in those same tunnels three years ago. Lindsay had still been sick, so the first thing Saul thought to do was to track down the family Darius had found for her. See if they couldn't get her some help.

They did—and so much more. David and Michelle Cochrane brought them all to their doctor, who not only provided antibiotics for Lindsay but stitched up the wound on Saul's face. Saul had tried to insist Juniper let the Cochranes take Lindsay then, but she hadn't been ready to give the girl up, so instead, the three of them tried to carve out a new life for themselves.

That all came to a screeching halt when Saul's face appeared on the news. They'd needed to keep Lindsay safe, so they ended up back with David and Michelle, who not only adopted Lindsay but offered Juniper a job as a live-in nanny.

Saul didn't say what *he'd* been up to since then, and Darius was afraid to ask. Not because he thought he might not like the answer, but because Saul's sudden appearance had thrown up a debris field of loose ends and missing pieces, and he wasn't sure he was ready to navigate that.

But Thorn was.

She walked back into the room a half hour after leaving it. Getting coffee couldn't have taken that long, and Darius suspected she'd done more than make a quick pitstop at the kitchen. She held a large thermos in one hand and three ceramic mugs in the other. Sparkie sat upon her shoulder, draped beneath a curtain of silky, black hair. His eyes caught on Darius as Thorn quietly closed the door behind her.

Instead of sitting on the couch with the two men or pulling her desk chair around, she reclaimed her spot on the coffee table in front of them. The rigidity of the wood perfectly matched the rigidity in her body as she uncapped the thermos, filled the mugs, and passed them out.

"Thank you," Saul said as he brought the coffee to his lips. His eyes closed as he took a tentative sip of the steaming liquid.

Thorn simply nodded. When she handed Darius his, their fingers brushed around the handle, and she quickly drew her hands away. Her mug sat untouched on the table beside her.

"I know today has been… intense." She hesitated, tongue grazing the crest of her teeth. "And I'm sure you'd like to process it all, but we *need* to talk, and it can't wait."

Her expression steeled, as though preparing for a battle, but Saul set his mug beside hers with a sigh.

"You're right," he said. "We do."

Thorn's shoulders relaxed. Her hands migrated between her knees, where they clasped together. The palms of her fingerless gloves brushed with a soft hiss.

"First, how did you find us?" she asked. "How did you *know* about us?"

Saul's mouth turned up in a humorless half-smile. "Simon Reed."

Thorn's eyes shot wide, and she sat up pin-straight again. Darius blinked, glancing from Saul to Thorn and back again before he said, "Wait—the old Martyr doctor?"

"Yeah," Saul said. "The Reed Medical Foundation is where Michelle and David Cochrane brought us when we asked for their help with Lindsay, and I've been working with them ever since I learned Eva might be alive, hoping to find her."

His voice tightened as he cast a glistening gaze to the ground. Darius stared at him, then at Thorn, expecting her to look as confused as he felt, but instead, he found understanding written across her face. His brows pinched.

"This foundation knows about the Sins?"

Thorn's attention flicked his way, and she exhaled a deep, anxious lungful of air. "Standard protocol for Martyrs who leave the Underground is to erase their memories," she said. "There have been a few who haven't. Jacob Locke. Samira Khoury… Usually, that privilege is reserved for people who still have a use to the war and will maintain contact with us…"

She paused, her eyes flashing from Saul to Darius, lingering just long enough to make his heart skip.

"Simon maintained contact with the Underground?" he asked.

Thorn shook her head. "Not exactly. He requested to keep his memories intact, to remember *everything* that was going on. Said that he would find his own way to help. At least, that's what Alan always told me. I… wasn't there for that conversation."

Her right hand freed itself from the left and traced an absent line from her *Peccostium* toward her elbow. Darius imagined the pull of scarred skin beneath her fingertips, tethering Thorn to darker days and damning dreams. He touched her knee, just a gentle reminder that she was here, *he* was here. She glanced up, irises gleaming behind dark lashes, before she cleared her throat and drew up straight again. Sparkie's head peeked above the curve of Thorn's shoulder while Darius returned his hands to his lap, all too aware of Saul's attention on the side of his face.

"What I *do* know," Thorn continued, "is that Reed went on to found his hospital, which has been owned by his family ever since. Clearly, he's passed down more than just the Foundation. He's passed on what he knows about the Sins, too."

"That's exactly right," Saul said. "The entire Reed line has been trying to help people they suspect have been impacted by the Sins. They offer affordable healthcare, donate money anonymously, and even get people out of dangerous situations… when they can."

Darius gawked. "And they told *you* about all of it?"

"Not at first," Saul admitted. "Initially, they just fixed us up and sent us on our way. Then, my pretty face made the front page of News Six."

He held out a palm and gestured to his head, where the smile across his face was more ironic than joyful. Thorn offered a short, knowing nod. "They realized the Sins were looking for you."

"That's what Sonia suspected, yeah," Saul said.

Thorn frowned. "Simon's granddaughter?"

Darius glanced at her, shocked at first that she seemed to know this information, but he supposed it made sense. Simon was more than a former Martyr doctor. He and Thorn had been close. *Very* close. Of course, she'd keep tabs on his life to see that he was living it well.

"Yeah," Saul said. "She's the lead surgeon at the Foundation now. Sonia figured the Sins were trying to track me down. Said they might suspect me of being a… what did she call it? A Virtue?"

The air evacuated Darius's lungs like he'd been dunked in cold water. He and Thorn stole a look at one another, but not quickly enough. Saul caught it, and his lips curled downward.

"What am I missing?" he asked.

Darius pinched the bridge of his nose. "They weren't looking for you because they thought you were a Virtue…" he began. "They were looking for you because they know *I* am, and they wanted to use you to get to me."

Silence followed. Saul's brown eyes went from narrow to round in an instant, and he stared at Darius as though everything in the world suddenly made sense. Nerves scrambled Darius's guts, and they didn't untangle until his old friend let out a single, loud laugh.

"Of *course* you are," he said, almost reverently. He ran a hand down his beard. "God, I should've known… They came to the orphanage looking for *you.*"

Darius wanted to share the moment, enjoy Saul's

enlightenment, but it was all he could do to stay above his grief—not sink into the devastating truth that his family had been killed because of who he was.

Now, Thorn touched him. Her hand landed upon the crook of his neck, and the sensation grounded him in this room again. A thumb hovered delicately over the pulse point by his collarbone. His heart skipped.

Then, she pulled back and turned to Saul.

"So, Sonia knew the Sins were hunting you down," Thorn went on, veering them back on track.

"Right," Saul said. He tore his focus away from Darius and considered her again. "She said they wouldn't give it up unless they thought I was dead, so we started working out a plan to fake it. The string of bombings Sloth was setting off around the city gave us the perfect cover. We were going to stage our own explosion. So, we planted a lead to the NYPD about me being spotted out in The Bronx—"

Thorn released a quiet gasp. Her eyes widened only to narrow again immediately. "At the Mitchell Houses?"

"Where you found me, yeah," Saul said.

Thorn swore under her breath. "So the bomb I found— it was *yours?*" Her focus snapped to Darius, and he sat up straight as the realization crawled down his spine. That's why their signal blockers hadn't worked. They'd been targeting the wrong technology.

"Yes," Saul said, drawing both of their attention again. "That incident changed *everything*. When you mentioned Juniper and Lindsay, I worried the Sins were looking for them, too. Then, Wrath showed up."

The muscles along Thorn's jaw hardened, and Darius shook his head. "She'd be able to identify your aura," he said.

"Exactly," Saul said, "which made things a lot more complicated. If I wanted her to buy my fake death, she had to sense me before I disappeared. So, we changed gears and planned an explosion at a storage complex on Staten Island. We planted unidentified cadavers from Reed's morgue in one of the units, bought another under Sloth's name, and sent a video to the tip hotline showing the girls and me going into the unit. Then, they went back to the Cochranes, and I hung out on a speedboat at the docks behind the facility with two other people to stand in for them, to make sure Wrath sensed three auras—"

"Fuck." Thorn moved one hand toward her face, hiding her open mouth behind a gloved palm. "Fuck, I'm *so* stupid."

Saul frowned, and Darius shook his head. "What?"

"Three auras," Thorn went on. "There *were* three auras, but I *never* should have felt three." Her eyes reconnected with Darius's. "Lindsay's a *child*. I can't sense her. I should have known something wasn't—"

"Wait," Saul cut in. "You were there?"

Thorn caught Saul's gaze, sharp and stern. "I was the *first one* there," she said. "We followed every lead, every *rumor*, about you for months. From the minute we realized you were still in the city. Eva couldn't let it go. I can't say I blamed her."

Saul's jaw dropped. A glisten of emotion dampened his expression. He swallowed it down before he said, "I had no idea…"

Silence sank around the office, covering them in a funeral veil. Saul finally spoke again, barely above a mutter that felt like shouting in this quiet space.

"Well… that 'death' stuck better than I expected, I guess. My face stopped showing up everywhere, so I could focus on what I was really interested in. Finding Eva—finding *you.*" He glanced at Thorn, who watched with dark curiosity. "But no one at the Foundation had ever *heard* of someone like you. Sonia worried you may have been a new Sin host."

Thorn's eyes shot wide, a blend of wounded offense flashing across her face before she could mask it. Darius leaned toward her.

"Even though Alan let Simon keep his memories, he

probably installed some Programming to stop him from talking about the Martyrs," he reasoned. "Couldn't risk him getting caught and taking you down, too."

Thorn glanced at him, and her expression softened, but Darius couldn't tell if it was because she'd been comforted or if she'd just managed to bottle up the hurt again.

"That's exactly right," Saul confirmed. "The Foundation knew a lot about the Sins, but no one knew about another agency fighting them—not until a couple of months ago."

"When Alan died," Darius murmured.

Saul nodded. "Simon woke up in a panic and told Sonia about the Martyrs. She thought the woman I was looking for might be a part of it." He studied Thorn, lips pressed into a subtle frown. "But we still had no way of tracking you down, and Simon refused to tell Sonia where to find the Underground. For safety, he said. And then—"

"He saw *me* on the news," Thorn interrupted, her tone a sharp stone, cutting and callous all at once.

Saul didn't reply right away. "He couldn't believe you were still alive."

Thorn uttered a cold scoff. "I believe it. He tried to pull the plug on me himself."

She rose to her feet and walked away, the muscles along her neck and shoulders chiseled hard from decades of pent-up regret. Sparkie was barely visible down her spine, betrayed by rigid wings that occasionally peeked out from black strands of hair. Saul watched after her before glancing at Darius, like he wasn't sure if he should continue. Darius dipped his chin, and Saul drew a deep breath.

"Even after he told me, tracking this place down still took a while. He's old, and his memory isn't great, but Simon wanted me to find you and tell you…"

He paused, drawing Thorn back. She stopped by her desk, framed by a wide wall of wild maps and red thread, before she looked over her shoulder. Saul didn't stand, but he didn't turn away, either.

"That he was wrong… and he's sorry."

Thorn's lips slipped open, flashing a glint of white teeth. Emotion glittered behind her lashes in a sentiment that showed just as much shock as bittersweet relief. Darius's chest swelled with disorienting cold heat. He couldn't fathom how much it meant for her to hear those words— and how much they stung all the same. At last, after long seconds of staring, Thorn nodded. Darius let out a cough to change the subject.

"So," he said, turning to Saul. "What happens now? Do we reach out? Try to work together?"

Saul echoed a soft laugh. "The Martyrs have gotten some pretty bad press, and Sonia doesn't want to risk drawing any attention." He glanced back to Thorn. "She actually asked me to see if you could keep her involvement in all of this between us."

Thorn's brows twitched together in a bristling frown. "She doesn't trust me to keep my people in line?"

"It's not about trust," Saul said, "but the Sins have ways of getting information out of just about anyone. Right now, they have no idea about the Reed Medical Foundation, and she'd like to keep it that way."

Darius exchanged a quick look with Thorn, who didn't soften, before focusing on Saul again.

"So... *you* know about the Sins," he began. "Does that mean June does, too?"

Saul nodded. "Yeah, but the Cochranes have no idea. Sonia doesn't want to involve people who have no reason to know. It's easier that way. As it stands, June gets to live the normal life she's always wanted—the life she deserves."

Darius's mouth ran dry. "And what about you?" He paused, a sudden swell of anxiety tightening his chest. "Now that you found us... what's next?"

Saul sighed, the sound a slow wind dragging dark clouds in overhead. "Eva's gone," he murmured, "but *you're* not, and you're... the only family I have left. This is where I want to be. If that's okay."

The storm lifted, and Darius couldn't stop the weightless

relief that pulled his mouth into a smile. "Yeah. Yeah, of course," he said, turning to Thorn to find her nodding. "We have plenty of space. I'll help you figure out what department you'd fit best and—what?"

Saul had broken into a beaming grin, and he laughed. "You haven't changed at all. Same old Darius, the fucking *Virtue*… Always ready to take on another lost kid. Man, I've missed you." He reached around Darius's shoulders to pull him in for another crushing hug. "June is going to lose her mind when she finds out you're okay."

Darius blinked. "Oh, you're still in touch?"

"I visit when I can, but I haven't been by in almost six months."

Warmth flooded Darius, overwhelming him for a moment. He nodded, in part to buy himself time so that when he spoke, it might be more even. "How are they doing?"

Saul smiled. "Good. Juniper is grateful to be a part of Lindsay's life, and Lindsay is *thriving*. She's almost seven now, smart as hell, and so happy."

He fished a phone from his pocket, flipped through his photo reel, and showed Darius a selfie of him with a little kid. They made silly faces, Saul's tongue rolled into a straw while Lindsay crossed her brown eyes and kissed at the camera. A carefree mane of mousy, brown hair framed her cheeks, which were healthy and round in a way that spoke to a life with enough food on the table to keep her belly full. Darius would have smiled, *should* have smiled, but a strange, inkling sensation coursed through his mind and down his spine in a slow, sugary drip.

"Oh my god…"

He held out a hand, and Saul dropped the device into his palm. Darius drew it closer. The glow from Lindsay's image shone against his cheeks like rays from the sun.

A sudden urge struck him. A need. An understanding that he hadn't felt this intensely since he'd run across an article about Nicholas Wolfe's charity gala years ago. A blast of awe slammed into Darius's chest and caught a lump of air deep in his lungs.

Then, the awe melted and dragged him down with it.

A cold hand landed on his shoulder.

"Darius?" Thorn's voice crawled to him through the fog. He glanced up, finding her gaze sharp. "Are you okay?"

He handed her Saul's phone with shaking fingers. "No. I need to go see her."

Saul frowned. "Why? What's going on?"

"I think... I think Lindsay might be a Virtue."

Thorn's eyes shot up to catch Darius's, wide open in a pure reflection of the storm of conflicting emotions swirling through his being. "If she is, that would make her either Charity," Thorn breathed, "or *Patience.*"

CHAPTER TWENTY

Darius sensed that magnetic pull the second Thorn turned onto West 156th Street.

His feet tapped nervous rhythms against the floor on the passenger's side of the sedan, all too aware of the bile bubbling at the base of his esophagus. He couldn't tell which feeling was winning: complete euphoria that they'd found the *sixth* Virtue or abject horror at what that meant.

Anxiety cored out his chest, mimicking the hollow pit that would one day consume him when he destroyed Envy—the same pit Lindsay—*little Lindsay*—would be condemned to endure, too.

Looked like horror was winning. Darius dipped his face into his hands. "Fuck."

Thorn cast him a sidelong glance. "No luck?"

The hopeful undertone in her voice made it worse, confirming Darius's *second* fear: that the broken part of Thorn's soul hadn't felt healed by Lindsay's presence. Another Virtue down—another Virtue that *couldn't* help her. God, this couldn't get any worse. He sighed into the bowl of his palms.

"It's her," Darius murmured.

Silence settled. Thorn's grip tightened on the steering

wheel with a leather squeak, the rigid bones in the backs of her hands visible even through her fingerless gloves. Street-lights flickered against the windshield and cast her face in uneven yellow bursts.

Saul shifted in the back seat. "What are you going to tell her parents?"

Darius sighed and exchanged a look with Thorn—or, he tried to. She didn't look back, glistening eyes glued to the road as they pulled into the first parking spot available half-way down the block.

"I'm not sure," he responded at last. "What do they already know?"

Saul sucked in an uninspiring breath. "Just that we were attacked by some people looking for you, and that those same people ended up coming after me, too, which was why they had to take Lindsay, but we never told them what was really going on. They'd have freaked the fuck out."

"They're still going to freak out," Darius muttered. "But Juniper *does* know?"

Saul nodded. "She knows about the Sins and the Virtues, but she doesn't know about the Martyrs… and she doesn't know I found *you*." Darius frowned, earning a half-shrug in response. "When I called and said I needed to see everyone, I didn't mention you. I thought it would be a fun surprise."

His smile filled his face, crinkling the corners of his eyes and pulling tight at his scar. Instead of anything close to joy or relief, Darius just felt ill.

"I don't know that I'd call this surprise *fun*," Thorn said bitterly as she shut off the car. Her voice growled like an old, angry engine. "We're about to tell those people that their little girl has to rip her soul into fucking pieces."

She opened the door, and an icy burst tore through the sedan. A shiver zipped up Darius's back.

The three of them walked eastward, hands shoved deep into jacket pockets. Up here in Washington Heights, foot traffic was significantly less than in more central parts of Manhattan, but Thorn still hid beneath a heavy hood and thick scarf. Sparkie hadn't joined them on the drive, so Darius assumed the Familiar had flown to the city early to scope out the neighborhood. He glanced into the dark sky, but even if Thorn's reptilian soul had been hovering twenty feet above their heads, he'd never be able to spot him.

Saul stopped outside of an old, smog-stained building. "This is it."

A flicker of anticipation lit up Darius's nerves. He hadn't needed Saul to tell them they'd reached the right place. His eyes trailed a path up the brick facade to the second floor. Even if she hadn't had a Virtue attached to her soul, Lindsay was unmistakable. She radiated childhood: a small physical presence surrounded by such an intense aura that the three adults sharing her space paled in comparison. And, though Darius couldn't articulate how or why, it *felt* like Lindsay. He narrowed his eyes, focusing on the others instead, but nothing about them triggered anything familiar. The knots tangling his stomach pulled into a messier web.

"C'mon," Saul said. "I have a key."

He moved toward the entrance, but Darius held back and reached for Thorn's shoulder before she followed. Her body tensed beneath his touch.

"Hey," he murmured, "you doing okay?"

Something sharp glinted across Thorn's expression, but beneath the dim lights and red scarf covering her nose and chin, he couldn't tell if it was anger, pain, or something else entirely.

"No," she said in a short, flat tone. "I'm not. Let's get this over with."

He'd expected her to lie to him, to give the same avoidant answer she always did, so he hardly had the sense of self to say or do anything else as she gently pulled out of his grip and joined Saul in the lobby. Darius came in last. As Thorn looped a finger into her scarf and loosened it to free her face, he tried to catch her eye but couldn't.

Saul's key allowed them access to the elevator bay, and they squeezed into a cramped car that rattled the entire ride up. David and Michelle Cochrane's unit was the furthest back, and every creaky step through the narrow hallway felt strangely perilous, like this entire thing—the building, the conversation, the future—could come crashing down at any second.

By the time they reached apartment twenty-five, Darius was sweating through his coat. Saul knocked, and an energy moved toward them. Darius sucked in a short breath, his heart racing…

Thorn's hand wound around his.

Darius startled, and he glanced down, but Thorn didn't meet his gaze. She just held firm with a steady, reliable grip. Warmth filled his chest and soothed the nerves, just a little, just *enough* to make him feel like he could do this.

The lock clicked, the door swung open, and Darius lurched back in time to the first friend he'd made, the first girl he'd loved, the first *family* he'd found for himself.

Juniper Foster.

She stood slight on the threshold, just as petite as she'd been before, but her face was fleshed out with a new, healthy fullness. Her orange hair clung to the back of her head in a clip, and loose strands draped around her freckled cheeks.

"Saul!" Juniper smiled a tiny smile that felt lacking, one part joy and three parts melancholy. She reached around Saul's shoulders, hugged him like a sister might, and squeezed tight. Her loose-fitting, green shirt flowed around her torso, making her appear smaller. "It's good to see you! It's been so—"

Her blue eyes flicked up and caught sight of Darius. She froze as Thorn stepped back and Saul pulled away, leaving a breath of space between where Juniper stood in the doorway and Darius in the hall. He raised his hands in a gesture that was just as much a shrug as it was an invitation.

"Hey, June."

"Oh, my god!"

A sob erupted from Juniper's mouth, and she stumbled

back as though her legs didn't have the strength to stay standing. Darius hurried forward to steady her, and the second his hands touched her skin, Juniper threw herself into him. Slender arms wound around his center, clutching at the middle of his back as she cried into his chest.

"It's—I can't believe—*Darius?*" The words poured out in an uneven beat, punctuated by tiny gasps. She drew away, just enough to bring her hands between them, and touched his face. Her fingers traced old, familiar patterns in his skin from the curve of his temples to the corners of his lips. She choked on a new flood of emotion. "It's *you!*"

He nodded, eyes burning. "It's me."

She grabbed him again, nestling her face into the crook of his neck. Hot tears slid against his skin. "It's been so hard without you," she whispered for only him to hear.

A guilty sensation trickled down Darius's spine, and he let out a quiet chuckle. "I've missed you, too," he said as he stood back. Strands of Juniper's hair clung to his stubble, and he smoothed them off with a palm. A warm energy approached the open door.

"Saul?"

A woman stepped onto the threshold. Darius recognized her from their meeting at that abandoned Java Hut on the edge of the market. Her blue eyes narrowed in a curious but kind look as they swept from Saul to the rest of them. "You didn't mention you were bringing friends…"

Juniper's head swiveled around, looking Thorn up and down as though realizing for the first time that Darius hadn't come alone. Michelle smiled, but the second her gaze met Darius's, realization dawned, and that smile wiped clean. A hand pressed against her breastbone.

"It can't be… *Darius Jones?*" she uttered in a breathy whisper. "But… how? Saul told us you were…" She drifted off before she slapped a too-sweet smile upon her face. "We never thought we'd see you again!"

Michelle shuffled forward awkwardly, like she wasn't sure if she should hug Darius, shake his hand, or ask him to leave, and she ended up doing none of the three. He let out a strained laugh and scratched the back of his head. "I know how you feel."

Michelle cleared her throat. "Where are my manners… Please, come in."

She gestured to allow the rest of them ahead of her. Saul and Juniper entered first with the casual comfort of people who knew this space and these people. Darius turned to Thorn. She held further back, lingering on the boundary of the scene as though she felt like an intruder here—a soldier who'd accidentally stepped into a wake instead of a war zone.

Without a word, Darius held out a hand. Her eyes flicked to it before meeting his gaze. She drew a deep breath, and they walked into the apartment together.

David and Michelle's home was small, opening into a quaint kitchen that transitioned seamlessly into a living room with windows looking out onto West 156th. A short hallway to the left led to three closed rooms and one open one, which a flash of white tile revealed to be a bath. Michelle quietly closed the door as Juniper stepped to the side to give their visitors more space.

A tiny but powerful little Virtue barreled toward them. "Tío Saul!"

That voice, *just* her voice, healed a part of Darius he'd given up on fixing a long time ago, and a surge of joy, pure and whole, threatened to drag him to his knees. A little girl he hardly recognized as the orphan he'd taken care of all those years ago leapt up from the couch and flung herself into Saul's belly. He caught her with a groan that immediately morphed into a deep, whole-body laugh.

"*Ay, mi princesita!*" Saul lifted Lindsay into his arms and planted an affectionate kiss on the crest of her cheekbone. "How are you? Getting into trouble?"

She giggled, but instead of answering, she glanced at Darius. Her face shifted into a show of childlike wonder. Darius's heart somersaulted as he considered this child—this

Virtue—and it took all of who he was not to burst into tears on the spot. Lindsay had everything he'd ever dreamed of for her. A home. A family. A *future*.

And he was here to fuck it up.

The center of Darius's chest ached as he leaned closer to get on her level and look her in the eye. She tilted her chin down, but something gleamed in her expression—something honest and open.

"Hey, Lindsay," Darius said softly. "Do you remember me?"

She shook her head, but her nose crinkled, eyes narrowing as though there was *something* in him she knew. Michelle traced her nails down the little girl's spine.

"Darius is the man who helped us find you," she murmured.

Lindsay brightened with sudden understanding, and she sat up in Saul's arms. One of her hands let go of his shirt to drift toward Darius. She brushed her fingertips against his temple with a frown.

"You cut your hair…"

A laugh caught in Darius's windpipe. "Yeah, I did. A lot has changed, huh? I mean, look at you!"

Lindsay grinned, wide and full, showing off a row of teeth, some missing and others too large for her little mouth. Darius brushed a thumb against her cheek and looked into her face—a face he thought had burned up in a fire, a face he'd known would have found its way to heaven if he believed such a place existed—and he blinked away the sting of tears at the corners of his eyes.

A warm aura moved toward the door at the start of the hallway. It creaked open, and David Cochrane stepped out. Saul's jaw dropped, and Darius's stomach writhed.

When they'd met three years ago, David had been a broad-shouldered beacon of life and passion, so full of determination to see his wife become a mother that he'd been willing to commit a felony to make it happen.

Now, he was a fragile shell of that person. His full head

of hair had fallen out, leaving behind a pale, lumpy scalp of withered skin. His brows, his lashes, his stubble followed suit, and the body beneath it all looked more like the sick and starving on the market than that of a vital man.

But his eyes landed on Darius with a familiar intensity, maintaining that contact as though daring the room to challenge their strength.

"Darius Jones," David said with a fervor that didn't match his figure. He made his way over to them, holding out a hand. His grip lacked substance, like the bones beneath the skin knew they might break if he held any harder. "How've you been?"

"Good," Darius said, and though he knew better than to stare, he couldn't help it. His eyes darted down the length of David's body. The man let out a scoff.

"Pancreatic cancer," he said. "Stage four. Who's your friend?"

He changed the topic before Darius's pity had time to take root and tilted his chin at Thorn. She drew her hood back, revealing the whole of her face and long locks of black hair. Juniper's focus slashed to Saul as David's mouth slipped open. Michelle let out a gasp.

"You're..." she began quietly. Fearfully. Her focus darted to her husband and back again. "You're the..."

"This is Thorn," Darius cut in, placing a hand on her shoulder. "We work together. She's one of my closest friends."

"Thorn is the woman I've been looking for," Saul clarified, lowering Lindsay to the ground. Juniper's eyes went wide, and Saul shook his head sadly. That seemed to answer a question she hadn't been brave enough to ask, and tears swelled behind her lashes.

The little girl, meanwhile, considered Thorn with the same innocent curiosity she had with Darius. Her shoulder leaned into Saul's hip as she glanced at him and whispered, "She has a funny name..."

Saul chuckled, but Michelle flushed a mortified red.

"Lindsay!" she hissed. "Honey, we don't say things like that…"

Lindsay's cheeks caught fire, and she tucked behind Saul's leg. Darius glanced at Thorn, shocked at the warm smile lifting her lips. She tilted forward to meet Lindsay's eye.

"It *is* kind of a funny name," Thorn agreed gently. Lindsay relaxed, and Thorn shrugged. "But it's mine, and I like it."

"Me, too," Lindsay asserted, more confidently now. She stepped away from the safety of Saul and nearer to Thorn before propping her fists on her hips. "You're like a superhero!"

Thorn's expression faltered, the smile sliding into a more tender, touched look, like the idea that this young Virtue might see anything so valiant in her was beyond comprehension. Darius nudged Thorn's shoulder with his own.

"She *is* a superhero," he said. Thorn cast him an incredulous look. "She's saved my life. More than once. I'd be lost without her."

While Lindsay's eyes opened into perfectly round discs, Thorn's narrowed on Darius's face. She watched him for a moment, brow furrowed, lips parted just a sliver, *just enough*, for her to take in a shallow brush of air. Then, her head shook, the tiniest motion, as though she didn't dare believe what she heard, what she saw, standing right in front of her—like somehow Darius's faith in her was so unfathomable that it made her doubt that any of this was real at all. He smiled, hoping to assure her that it was.

Michelle cleared her throat. "I'm so sorry," she said, reminding Darius that there was a room full of other people around them. "Saul didn't tell us he was bringing guests. I feel… so unprepared."

Darius glanced back, where she and Juniper stood near the island. Both women's focus snagged on Thorn, Michelle's with a pull of concern contracting every muscle while Juniper's blue eyes glassed over, and the tip of her nose turned a traitorous shade of pink. She quickly turned away and headed into the kitchen, hands wound tight at her chest. Michelle followed.

"Can I get you anything?" she went on. "A beer? Soda? Water?"

"No, thank you," Darius said. "We're just hoping to talk…"

Michelle's spine stiffened. Her hand froze on the refrigerator door, poised to pull it open, as she exchanged a look with her husband. Darius's mouth ran dry. He knew that look.

Michelle turned back to the fridge. "Lindsay, honey," she began in a practiced calm as she grabbed a beer. Her hand shook around the can. "Why don't you go play in your room?"

"Aww," the little girl groaned. "But I want to talk to Darius and Thorn, too!"

A plastic smile distorted Michelle's face. "I understand, sweetheart, but it's going to be…"

She paused. David completed her thought.

"Boring grown-up stuff," he said. "Like taxes and road construction."

Lindsay put on an expert but melodramatic pout. "I *like* road construction."

David shook his head. "Lindsay…"

"You can go into our room and turn on a show," Michelle offered instead. "How's that sound?"

Lindsay's mouth opened in a broad, toothy smile, and she let out a squeal before scurrying away, her socked feet shuffling across the laminate floor. Instead of taking a straight path, she looped side to side, hugging her mother's legs, kissing her father on the hand, and skipping the rest of the way to the nearest bedroom. The door shut behind her with an overzealous snap.

And the silence that followed swallowed the apartment. The six adults didn't move, not an inch, like every single one of them was acutely aware that Lindsay's presence had been the fragile thread upholding the screen of normalcy. Michelle's fingers gripped dimples into the beer can, while David's eyes glided back toward the strangers in his doorway.

Finally, his voice rumbled from his throat with a wildcat growl.

"You have five minutes, *five*, to explain why the hell you're here."

A sudden flurry of subtle movement fluttered around Darius—Thorn's body contracting with the buzz of built-up tension, Saul shifting from foot to foot, even Juniper curling around herself—but he kept his focus on Lindsay's father. The man's jaw clenched as he thrust out a threatening finger.

Toward Thorn.

"The only reason I didn't call the cops the second that woman walked into my home is because of what you and Saul have done for us," David continued. "Her face has been plastered all over the damned internet! She's that… that Jane Mor—"

"Thorn," Darius cut in, so immediately and fiercely that even he was caught off guard by the force of her true name exploding from his mouth. Thorn stilled to his left, a flicker of fear and fury flashing through the depths of her eyes. Darius stepped in front of her. "Her name is *Thorn*," he went on, more evenly but with just as much strength. "You shouldn't believe everything you see on LymeLite."

Another stretch of silence stole the room. This time, Juniper broke it.

"But, Darius, she's… one of *them*." Her focus darted toward Saul. "Like Dr. Reed told us, right? If she's been alive for as long as they say she has been, that would have to make her a…"

The thought pattered off, like the word itself was cursed. Thorn's teeth ground together, her nose curling, but all the indignation barely masked the cracks of hurt fracturing the surface. "Why don't you ask *her?*"

Juniper blanched and threw her gaze to the floor, where it didn't have to face the menace in Thorn's. Darius stepped forward again.

"No, she's not," he said. "But she *is* in command of the last line of defense against them. If you've seen the other shit, you must've heard of them, too."

Juniper's chin snapped back up, and her thin lips opened in a quiet gasp. Michelle and David exchanged a confused look.

"Is anyone going to explain what the fuck is going on?" David asked.

Darius offered a halfhearted smile. "We can, but it's going to take a *lot* more than five minutes…"

David glanced at Michelle again, and she nodded, just once, before a sigh rocked through her chest. "Well, then make yourselves at home…"

The Cochrane's living room filled and settled. David made his way to a solitary armchair at the far end of the room, lowering into it like the very act of sitting used up all his energy. Darius took the middle of the couch, Saul to one side, Juniper pressed up on the other. Michelle joined her husband on the arm of his chair, draped around his shoulder as much to comfort him as to steady herself. Thorn didn't sit, instead standing in the front, pacing inch by slow inch, nails digging into the kevlar jacket on her biceps as she talked.

Darius watched her, entranced, remembering how Alan had approached this—calmly, collected, with the air of confidence that he'd known, sooner or later, Darius would not just believe him but join him.

Thorn had less practice but more passion. She fumbled over phrases, but she spoke with urgency, *agency,* more like a storyteller than a historian, to a completely captive audience. David and Michelle gawked, and even Saul, who knew significantly more than the others, nodded quietly, soaking in every piece of new information. When Thorn freed her pocket knife and cut her arm to prove her healing power,

Juniper wrapped her hands around Darius's arm like she used to do when she was nervous and held with a painful grip.

And all the while, as Thorn's voice locked Darius's body in this room, Lindsay's looming, magnetic pressure lured his mind into another. Muffled music from a kid's TV show occasionally sneaked beneath the door, breaking his heart with every canned laugh. When Thorn's story finally reached Darius's Virtue, her eyes met his… and then darted up to the bedroom behind him.

"Dr. Reed was right?" Juniper breathed. "You're *Kindness?*"

He nodded, and a devastated smile wrinkled the bridge of her nose, as though she had registered all of the incredible and horrible truths of it all at once. She wound a hand around his as Michelle shook her head.

"How did the Sins track him down?" she asked Thorn. "You implied Virtues are hard to find."

Thorn drew a measured breath. "They are. Without an Initiated Virtue, who would be drawn to them, Uninitiated Virtues blend seamlessly into the rest of society. That said, they do… leave signs." Again, her eyes flashed to Darius. "The Sins learned about Darius through a young man named Cyrus Murphy, one of the orphans he'd raised."

Juniper gasped, and Saul's spine went rigid on Darius's other side. "Cyrus?" he repeated. "But Cyrus was killed in a shooting…"

Thorn shook her head. "Envy was planting Sentries in the area where he worked when my team and I showed up to stop her. He got caught in the crossfire, but more importantly, he *resisted* her Influence. She couldn't fully control him, which rarely happens… unless someone has been around a Virtue for an extended period of time. She knew what that meant, and so did we. I brought Cyrus back to the Underground to find out who in his life might have Virtuous power. We learned about the orphanage, but he refused to give us any more information or a location." She met

Darius's gaze. Old guilt pinched her expression. "So, we returned him to the city. I was following him home, but Envy found him, and she forced him to give up Darius's name before she…"

Her voice escaped her, and Thorn's jaw snapped shut. Juniper's hold on Darius's fingers tightened. "She what?"

Thorn cast her a dark look and shook her head. Juniper's lips trembled open, a single tear escaping her lashes. A swell of old grief resurged, and Darius placed his hand over hers.

"What about Envy?" Saul asked, rage burning beneath his crackling voice. "What happened to her?"

"That host was killed months later," Thorn answered, "and it hasn't taken a new one. Not that we've found, at least."

Saul's teeth clenched as he sat back against the couch. Michelle frowned before she cleared her throat. "What does any of this have to do with *us?*"

Thorn hesitated, glancing at Darius before she committed to answering. David sighed, laid a palm on his wife's knee, and leaned forward.

"Listen," he began. "I have *terminal* cancer. I've been in a lot of rooms with people needing to break bad news to me in the last five months. I know that look." He gestured between the two of them. "So, just spit it out. You didn't come all the way out here for some fucked up story time. Are they after us now, too, like they were after Cyrus? After Saul?"

Pressure wound around Darius's throat as he shook his head. Lindsay's magnetic force bounced on the far side of the nearest wall like she was *laughing*.

"No." Darius pried himself away from Juniper to wrap his arms around his chest. "We have no reason to think the Sins have any idea I've ever spoken to you."

Michelle's face lost its color, making her blue irises seem exceptionally bright as she asked, "Then… why are you here?"

"It's… about Lindsay," Darius began.

"Lindsay?" Michelle shot to her feet. David grabbed her

hand. "What do they want with Lindsay?"

She looked from Darius to Thorn and back again, but suddenly, Darius found he didn't have the strength to say it aloud—to tell this family that the daughter they'd fought *so* hard to have was destined to rip herself to pieces, to give up *her soul* so humanity might stand a chance at healing. Soon, it wasn't just Michelle watching him. It was David, too, and Juniper and Saul. Their focus burned enough to make him sweat. Darius swallowed, and he turned to Thorn. Her eyes were the only pair in the room that didn't make him feel like he was stuck on the tip of a burning candle wick, and he sank into them. She nodded and gently, gracefully, took the reins.

"Your daughter is a Virtue," Thorn said.

The air grew thin, like they'd collectively plunged into a tub of ice water and forgotten they could breathe. Juniper's eyes widened, and her attention swung from Thorn to Darius. Michelle's, too. She took on a shaken, sickly hue.

"What?" she whispered. She pulled her hand out of her husband's to grip the back of his chair instead. "How do you know? Can you… feel her?"

Darius nodded, giving all his focus, all his attention, to David and Michelle. Where she'd washed free from all color but green, his complexion seared. "I suspected it the minute Saul showed me her picture," he said, "and meeting her here confirmed it. Lindsay is—"

"No," David cut in, quietly at first and then, with more power. "No. I don't want to hear it."

"David," Saul began.

"I said I don't want to hear it!" David yelled.

Saul's mouth snapped shut, and Juniper startled on Darius's other side. In the nearest bedroom, Lindsay's magnetic presence paused before inching toward the door. Darius's stomach dropped as she pressed against the wood.

"You're telling me our daughter is a Virtue," David went on, still shouting, "that she has these powers to heal the sick and destroy some great evil, but you're *also* saying she has to sacrifice part of herself that she can *never* get back!"

Thorn breathed through a sigh. "I know it's hard—"

David interrupted her with a scathing scoff that made Thorn's nostrils flare. "Hard?" His hands balled into fists. "It's criminal! Do you have any idea how much that little girl has sacrificed already? How much *more* she's going to have to sacrifice?"

He threw a look toward the hallway behind him, where Lindsay sat as still as a cornered cat, listening to every word. Darius opened his mouth, about to interject, but David kept going.

"I don't know if you've been paying attention, but I'm *dying!* And now you want Lindsay to—"

"No one wants this," Thorn cut in. Her tone matched David's blow for blow, just as loud and unforgiving. She propped her hands on her hips. "No one *asked* for this. But we can't stop it, either. No amount of denial will change what Lindsay is!"

A sudden energy crackled in the air. No. Not the air. In Darius's psyche, in the link that pulled him and Lindsay together. It tugged a familiar spot in his mind from the only time he'd ever felt anything like it.

Right before Nicholas accepted Diligence.

Darius's heart pounded. "Guys—"

"I might not be able to *change it,*" David barreled over him, "but I *can* protect her from it!"

"She deserves to know who she is," Thorn argued. "What she's capable of!"

"And she will!" David countered. "When she's old enough to understand it! To *choose* it!" He'd moved to the edge of his chair, perilously close to tumbling from it. "For Christ's sake, Lindsay's not even *seven* yet! It's hard enough that she has to worry about her sick father! She's too young to worry about a goddamned *war,* too!"

The electricity in Darius's chest intensified until his pulse raced. He glanced back at the hallway, where Lindsay huddled behind the door. "Let's try to keep it down…"

"Don't tell me to keep it down in my own home!" David snapped.

Darius shook his head. "David, please—"

"*You* should know better than *anyone* how important it is for kids to have a childhood," David shouted, an accusatory finger trained at the center of Darius's chest. "The world is going to try to rip that away from her even without this Virtue shit, and I will *gladly* die to let her keep it!"

A pulse of invisible, Virtuous power exploded all at once. Darius pulled in a shattered gasp as a scream pierced the apartment.

"Lindsay!" Michelle exclaimed.

She sprinted to the bedroom, David on her heels and Saul and Juniper quickly behind them. Thorn dropped to a knee in front of Darius. Her hand clutched the crook of his neck. A sudden sweat clung to him, and her cold palm felt soothing against his skin. The look in her eyes made it clear she understood what had just happened. He grabbed her fingers, squeezed them tight.

Lindsay screamed again.

"What's wrong?" Michelle cried. "What happened? Saul, call 911!"

"Don't!"

Darius climbed to his feet and rushed to the doorway, where David knelt on the ground with his daughter's arms flung around him. She sobbed, pearly tears wetting her cheeks in giant, warm droplets as she pressed her face against David's throat. Darius's lips slipped open. When he'd initiated his Virtue, every touch had felt like fire, the sensation so scalding he could hardly handle it. Why on earth would Lindsay—

And it hit him all at once, a crushing blow to the chest. David's eyes were wide and glistening, his mouth gaping like a man who'd seen God. While Lindsay clutched him, David sat frozen, his spine rigid, head bowed in reverence, and his entire body flushed in a warm, healthy glow.

Then, suddenly and completely, Lindsay thrust herself

away and scrambled back toward the bed, holding her arms out like they'd been burned. David stared at her.

"Are you okay, Daddy?" the little girl asked, voice broken and weeping. "Do you feel better?"

Michelle gasped. David's expression twisted in a painful, aching joy as he nodded, once, twice, over and over again.

A haggard sound burst from David's chest, and then, he was sobbing.

CHAPTER TWENTY-ONE

Convincing the Cochranes to come to the Underground after Lindsay had accepted her Virtue was easy. Convincing them to let Thorn bring their daughter in *alone* was not.

Darius remembered his own Initiation with vivid clarity—how much it stung, how even a touchless presence burned like the sun, how the heat of someone's aura set his body on fire—and he wanted to prevent as much of that as he could. Thorn was the only person with a soul fractured enough not to hurt her.

So, they'd driven in alone while Darius went ahead with David and Michelle. He parked the car, furious at the sensation of people lingering in the waiting room.

"God damn it," Darius muttered as he disengaged the engine.

No one was supposed to know about Lindsay, but of course, they all did. Darius had called ahead and ordered them to clear the upper level, and when he hadn't given a reason why, speculation spread. He'd already received multiple messages from Mackenzie, Elijah, and Lamar asking if he was bringing a new Virtue. Darius ignored every single one of them, but he knew how these things went. Rumors took root in seconds.

He burst through the double doors, David comforting a crying Michelle at his heels.

"Conrad," Darius called, making the TAC agent and a couple of his friends jump. "What part of 'everyone downstairs' wasn't clear to you?"

Conrad Carter's eyes opened in feigned shock. "I didn't hear that—"

"Downstairs," Darius interrupted. "Now."

A scowl turned Conrad's mouth into a haggard line, and he slumped toward the hallway, buddies in tow. Darius turned back to David and Michelle just as Thorn's lights came to life in the garage. "Come on," he said.

Darius brought them through the hospital ward. It was strange traversing this space in this kind of isolation. The main lights were off, but one of the private suites at the back glowed yellow through a cracked door.

"Go ahead inside," he said gently. "We'll talk more in the morning."

They disappeared into the room. As the door shut, stealing the last beams of light, Darius headed to the exit. A cluster of warm souls hummed beneath his feet, and he considered how exactly he was going to answer the questions they were sure to have.

Before he figured it out, Thorn walked in from the triage entrance on the far side of the ward. He paused beside the door.

"It's getting hot again," Lindsay murmured, muffled with exhaustion. "Is it going to hurt?"

She draped around Thorn, legs hooked at her waist. The effortless way Thorn held the girl made Darius's heart ache—effortless not because her inhuman strength made Lindsay all but weightless in her arms, but because those arms had never lost the muscle memory of how to carry a sleeping child off to bed. Sparkie wound around the girl's neck, and Darius couldn't help but wonder, how often had she held Donovan this way?

"It might," Thorn replied softly, "but it *will* get easier. I promise. This is just what happens when superheroes get their powers…"

Lindsay nodded against Thorn's throat. Her face turned inward and vanished beneath long strands of silky, black hair. "Am I going to be like you?"

Thorn chuckled. It was a gentle, loving sound. "No. You're going to be like Darius, and he's *much* stronger than I am."

Darius's eyes stung as Thorn walked by, unaware of him standing there in the dark. As she passed the nursing station, Lindsay glanced up. Her warm, brown eyes looked right at him as though the shadows weren't there at all.

But she didn't say anything, and minutes later, she and Thorn disappeared inside the private room. Darius made his way out, his heart pounding a wondrous rhythm against his ribs. A voice made him jump.

"So," Nicholas said. He lingered in the ingress to the back offices, arms crossed over a baby blue button-up shirt. "Which one is she?"

Darius hesitated just a moment before swallowing hard. "Charity," he admitted.

Nicholas nodded, just once, before he shook his head. "God damn."

The following day, they set the Cochranes up in the Underground.

Saul and Juniper stayed at the apartment that night, packing up any essentials the family would need, while David and Michelle joined their daughter. First thing in the morning, Thorn, Cain, and a handful of TAC agents brought them back into town to instill Programming while Darius stayed home and filled the Martyrs in on what was going on. David and Michelle arrived back just in time to meet with him for dinner and talk more about their next steps. They'd been up until almost midnight, and when

Darius finally lay down, he felt like he'd been run through a wood chipper, his thoughts strewn in disjointed pieces on the pillow around his head.

They hadn't pieced back together the following morning.

"Another Virtue," Chris murmured.

She and Darius sat at a table at the edge of the dining area, enjoying their breakfast. Well, Chris was enjoying hers. Her oats were nearly gone, while he only grabbed a cup of coffee and had hardly taken a sip.

"Another *Initiated* Virtue," Chris added with a reverent sigh. "Finding just one of you had always felt impossible… Now, we only have one more to go."

"Yeah," Darius agreed, glancing around the courtyard. Upbeat chatter bounced back with a mood he hadn't felt here in way too long. He saw more smiles. Heard more joy. Sensed more *peace*. "It's… incredible."

But it didn't *feel* incredible. He looked into his mug. From the corner of his eye, he caught Chris watching him, and the smile on her face waned.

"How did Thorn take it?" she asked quietly.

It should have been a crushing question, a jab to the heart to ask about Thorn amidst another Virtue who *wasn't* Patience finding its way to them, but the recognition that Chris understood the complexities of the situation gave Darius a dissonant sense of relief.

"You know how she is," he muttered. "Kept everything close to the chest, but she was disappointed."

God, that felt like an understatement.

"I imagine *both* of you were," Chris said. "It's got to be a lot of big feelings… good and bad."

He pinched the bridge of his nose. "Jesus, Chris, you have no idea. I thought Lindsay was dead." Darius let out a short huff that strummed on a string of emotion he hadn't realized wrapped around his voice box. "I thought they were *all* dead, and now, here they are, and Lindsay…" He allowed his thoughts to wander, and Chris simply watched him, her fingers laced around her mug. "I guess I'm still processing all of it," Darius finished at last.

"That's understandable," Chris said. "It's a lot for all of you. How are Saul and Juniper?"

Darius shrugged. "Saul's good. Last night, he asked when he gets a gun."

He tossed Chris an amused look, which she returned with a chuckle.

"He'll have to jump through all the same hoops as everyone else," she responded. "We can talk more once he's passed the TAC assessments."

Darius laughed, the first real laugh he'd had in days, and stretched back in his chair. "That's what I said, and Gabe already offered to get him started. They're down in the shooting range now."

Chris smiled, her eyes lighting up. "He seems eager."

"He is," Darius agreed, and then, he frowned. "Juniper, though… I don't know. We're hanging out today. Hopefully, I'll get a better idea of where she's at."

"It will be nice to reconnect, I'm sure," Chris said.

"Yeah," Darius said, but his stomach felt uneasy. Chris leaned toward him like she could sense it.

"Do you not *want* to reconnect?" she asked.

He exhaled a sigh, scraping a hand down his face. His stubble caught on the heel of his palm. "It's not that," he muttered, "but things with Juniper used to be pretty complicated."

"In that 'more-than-a-friend' kind of way?" Chris asked.

Darius let out a short laugh. "Exactly. It ended after we started the orphanage, and we moved on. Or, I thought we did, but these last couple of days, she's been really…"

He paused, unsure how to say what he meant to say without sounding like an asshole. The edge of Chris's lip pulled into an empathetic smirk as she offered, "Attached?"

"Yes," he said. "I worry some of those feelings sparked back up."

"Hmm…" Chris drew her coffee to her lips, taking a

thoughtful sip. "They could have, or *maybe* she's just in a new place with new people and a brand new life. You're one of the only familiar faces down here. Plus, she *did* just learn you're not dead."

Chris cast him a sidelong look, and Darius chuckled.

"My recommendation?" Chris went on. "Show her around. Make her feel welcome." Then, she glanced at her watch. "But be done by four. Cain's almost done with those masks, so Gabe, Thorn, and I are going to start planning how we'll engage with Edith's next publicity stunt."

A cold weight pulled Darius's shoulders toward the ground. God, the excitement around Saul, Juniper, and Lindsay had almost been enough to make him forget about Edith. Almost.

"Why do you need me?" he asked. "I'm not exactly a tactical expert."

"No," Chris agreed, "but you *are* an expert in magical healing, and if experience has taught us anything about Edith Froschlin, it's that there's a good chance we'll need it. I'm going to argue that we should bring you along."

Darius's chest constricted as names and faces flashed through his mind. Deidre Cummins. Paul Kwan. Tamera Osborne. From what he'd gathered, he wouldn't have been able to save them, but he nodded all the same.

"All right. I'll be there."

"Thanks," Chris said. "I'll add it to your calendar."

She grabbed her phone and started typing in the details. Darius watched her absently, feeling oddly distanced from this table, this room, as he imagined himself in the back of a camouflaged medical van surrounded by civilians in crow masks. For a moment, he lived there, and he didn't come back to the present until an aura he had never imagined he'd know the feeling of entered the courtyard behind him. He turned around.

Juniper paused in the egress leading to the western wing of rooms, orange hair pulled into a clip at the back of her head. She looked into the open space like a tourist in a new neighborhood after dark, considering the tall ceilings, closed alcoves, and busy tables with an uneven blend of awe and worry. Darius grinned as he thrust a hand in the air.

"June!" he called, garnering a few startled looks from the nearest tables. Juniper's chin snapped his way, and a wash of relief smoothed the anxious creases across her forehead. While she made her way toward them, Chris grabbed her mug and got to her feet.

"I'll leave you to it," she said, but before she left, she laid a hand on Darius's shoulder, just below the crook of his neck. When she spoke again, she did so more quietly, with a warmth that poured from her body into his like a Virtue's healing touch. "I'm really happy you found them again."

Darius smiled, but this time, a sting prickled at the corners of his eyes, and all he managed was a nod. Chris squeezed him once more and turned away. Then, she immediately turned back.

"Oh!" She snapped her fingers, a glint sparkling in her eyes. "You should ask Kenia to bring Lindsay some breakfast... I think she made it just for her today."

Darius's brows drew together, and Chris smirked before she returned her mug to the bussing tub at the edge of the counter and headed to the elevator. Her path crossed Juniper's just shy of the table, and Chris offered her a good morning, which Juniper returned with a half-hearted nod. Darius got to his feet, and Juniper's icy discomfort melted. The second she was close enough to hug him, that's precisely what she did. Her skinny arms wound around his neck and held tight. Darius closed his eyes as this sensation, familiar and foreign all at once, thrust him back to every other embrace they had shared in the sixteen years they'd known one another before it all came crashing down.

"I'm sorry I'm late," Juniper breathed against his ear. "I got lost finding my way here from my room." She drew back, and the smile on her lips twitched toward a frown as she fixated on a point—a person—behind Darius. "Who is she?"

"Chris?" Darius asked as he glanced at the black and beige figure disappearing through closing elevator doors. "She runs the Tactical Armed Combat Department—TAC."

"Ah." Juniper nodded, but the concerned lines between her brows deepened. "That's the department Saul wanted to join. Isn't it dangerous?"

Darius's stomach chewed on the question. "It can be," he admitted. "TAC deals with the Sins the most, but they have to go through a lot of training. It'll be a while before Saul's qualified to join the team."

Juniper narrowed her eyes. "Do you *want* Saul to join the team?"

"I don't think what I want really matters," Darius said with a short, awkward laugh. God, that felt like the story of his life right now. "It's Saul's decision, and ultimately, Chris has the final say."

That didn't seem to be what Juniper wanted to hear. She crossed her arms, jaw tight, but she didn't voice any displeasure. Instead, she looked back toward the elevator, as though imagining who Chris was, what her job entailed, and all the horrifying things that accompanied it. Darius cleared his throat.

"C'mon," he said. "Let's grab some breakfast. Kenia apparently made something special..."

Darius guided her to the long counter, where warming trays full of chocolate chip pancakes sent an alluring aroma into the air. The sentiment touched his heart with two distinct sensations: the light weight of gratitude alongside a heavy curtain of dread. He plated a couple for himself and asked Kenia to take some up to Lindsay. The cook beamed at the request, and as Darius and Juniper returned to the dining area, he caught her happily carving two pancakes into cat shapes, complete with chocolate syrup whiskers and strawberry rounds for eyes.

"Darius?" Juniper's voice drew him back to the table. "Everything okay?"

She wrapped her fingers around his the way she used to, back when their biggest concerns were hungry bellies and happy hearts, and not necessarily their own… not *usually* their own. Darius squeezed her hand once before drawing away to pick up his fork, but his appetite curled into the pit of his stomach and refused to come back out.

"Yeah," he said, not really feeling it, not meaning it, but the consistent tug of Lindsay's Virtue above his head made him smile anyway. "Yeah, it's just been a wild couple of days."

Juniper's face lit up, and her eyes glistened. "I know what you mean."

It didn't matter that years had gone by and both of them had thought the other long since dead. Darius and Juniper quickly and easily fell into a familiar rhythm, the pattern of old friends chatting like no time had passed at all. Only time *had* passed, and the stories they shared were less about life and laughter and more about death and tragedy.

Juniper recounted the same story Saul had told, but shorter, without detail or design, like thinking about it was hard enough and talking about it downright miserable. Even her time with the Cochranes was treated with a certain distance, and Darius didn't push her to share more. She only seemed interested in what he'd been going through anyway.

So, he told her everything—every single moment between finding Thad dead on the threshold of the orphanage to knocking on David and Michelle's door thirty-five hours ago. They talked about Alan Blaine and the Martyrs, Teresa Solomon and the Virtues, Autumn Hunt and the Sins, but mostly, most *importantly*, they talked about Eva.

"I can't believe she's gone," Juniper whispered. "Ever since that woman told Saul she knew where she was—"

"Thorn?" Darius supplanted.

Juniper's cheeks went pink, and she looked at her half-eaten plate of pancakes. "Yes, her. Ever since then, we'd been holding out hope. Saul must be devastated…"

Darius nodded, and suddenly, he found himself waking

up after that car crash, sorting through a whirlwind of memories: Eva's blood saturating her blouse, Thorn's hand wound around his, and hearing those four crushing words:

"Eva didn't make it."

His heart broke all over again.

"It was really hard," Darius murmured. "Eva was all I had. I didn't know how to function for a while."

Juniper glanced back up, considering him from beneath blonde lashes. "It sounds like you two got… close."

"Yeah," Darius said. "We did."

"How close?"

The question sank in with an old bitterness Darius hadn't heard in years. His jaw clenched, and he consciously worked to relax it.

"June," he said quietly. "Don't do this. We—"

"I think I'm done," she cut in. She gently pushed her plate away until it clinked against Darius's. "I'm sure you're busy, so I'll find my way back to my room…"

Juniper got to her feet. Darius leapt after her.

"Wait." He took her by the wrist. Her lips pressed tightly together. "I don't have anything to do until four in the afternoon. But up to then, I'm yours."

Juniper frowned, lingering in her doubt a moment before she said, "You sure?"

"Positive." Darius smiled and opened an arm to indicate the courtyard. "I want to show you around, let you see what we've been up to these last few years. This place means a lot to me, and I want you to be a part of it."

Her expression brightened, pinching the corners of her eyes, but the joy didn't quite fill her face. She raised her hands at her sides and let them slap back against her thighs with an anticlimactic shrug. "Well… okay! Where do we start?"

Darius laughed. "How about with making sure you don't get lost again?"

So, the tour was off. Darius helped Juniper figure out the best way to navigate the hallways, explained how the grid pattern worked, and directed her to the nearest bathroom and central laundry room. On the way back to the courtyard, Juniper only took one wrong turn, and she playfully punched Darius on the arm when he teased her about it.

Next, he showed off all the amenities the Underground had to offer, from the pool to the gym, the fitness studios to the industrial kitchen. Juniper marveled at its floor-to-ceiling pantries and walk-in refrigerators, stocked with enough food to feed a small army. Along the way, they met a handful of Martyrs—Seth Graves doing jump squats on the mats, Skylar and Raquel enjoying coffee beneath a leafy vine, and Kenia loading dishes into the machine, all the while gushing about that sweet child Virtue. Soon, Juniper's apprehension disappeared, replaced instead by appreciation.

"It's like a little village," she said as Darius led them out of Cain's art studio, which was currently full of TAC agents adding the final details to their cavalry of crow masks. She held one in her hands, a tiny, delicate thing painted canary yellow that Cain had made for Lindsay while they'd been visiting. "Is there anything you *don't* have?"

Darius let out a laugh that was more about dispelling grief than expressing humor. "A therapist."

Juniper cast him a curious look as he reached for the door to their next stop. He pulled it open, and they froze on the threshold.

Christmas decor dominated the break room. Every card table housed a tiny tree, glistening with fake snow and colorful baubles, and string lights circled the walls. A couple of uneven snowflake banners draped from the ceiling, so low in some areas that anyone taller than Darius might run face-first into paper flurries. Mackenzie stood on a stool just inside, where she was hanging a sprig of mistletoe over the heads of unsuspecting Martyrs—which, right now, were Darius and Juniper.

He swooped it away and ducked inside. "What's all this?"

Mackenzie's eyes lit up. "Jones!" She leapt from her

perch and threw her arms out. An elf hat threatened to fall off her bleached hair. "Perfect timing! C'mere!"

She grabbed him by the wrist before he could protest and dragged him toward a cardboard box sitting open on a central table. Juniper followed nervously on their heels, eyes darting around at the handful of Martyrs already gathered here. Marcus Boseman, the head of Thorn's Cleaning Crew, leaned back on the couch, his eyes locked onto the news as he frowned behind a neatly manicured beard. Seated in a couple of chairs behind him, Julien and Remy Harris curled over a handheld video game, headphones in their ears and smiles on their faces. Near the far wall, Alexis Claytor threw Mackenzie a disgruntled look as she walked around the pool table. Darius was surprised to see her here. Alexis's position in the city made her a rare sight in the Underground, and Darius was caught off guard by how rough she seemed— her eyes tired, platinum pixie cut sloppily put together.

Mackenzie either didn't notice or didn't care.

"I know this may come as a shock," the Irishwoman said as they reached her decorating station, "but I have little fuckin' legs." She let go of Darius to dig through a menagerie of red and green tinsel, ornaments, and all kinds of other shiny things. The box was so large that it nearly swallowed her arm whole as she reached for something at the bottom. "I need someone tall to help me put *these* at the tops of those giant trellises in the courtyard. Look!"

She yanked out a package of obnoxiously sequined tree topper stars, creating a miniature explosion of glitter, and thrust them into the air. Darius laughed.

"Wow," he said, raising his brows. "That's… a lot."

"*I know!*" Mackenzie bounced on the balls of her feet, her pixie-like face stretching into a grin. "Let's go!"

She tossed the stars back into the box and moved to pick it up, but Darius laid a hand on her shoulder.

"As much as I'd love to help you terrorize the Underground with holiday cheer," he said, "I'm showing June around all afternoon."

He gestured to the woman at his side, and Mackenzie's eyes shot wide. "Oh, my god, I'm such an ass—hi!" She brandished a hand, flaunting chipped blue polish and a colorful array of band bracelets. Juniper tentatively took it. "Mackenzie McKay, Discovery Director. This guy's told us all kinds of stories, but it's nice to meet you in person."

Mackenzie nudged Darius with an elbow, and he shook his head with a chuckle. "I didn't tell *that* many stories," he corrected.

"Well, the ones you did tell were lovely," Mackenzie said. "Anyway, I've gotta hurry up and get this done before Wolfe has a fit because I'm not 'logging crow movements in the city.'"

She threw up a pair of finger quotes and rolled her eyes with such a dramatic flourish that the irises disappeared entirely. Darius smiled through a sudden rush of intense emotion. "I thought all that was more important than decorating the Underground," he said.

Mackenzie's expression softened in an instant, and her tongue piercing clinked against the back of her teeth once before she shook her head. "Nope. You were right. Decorating *is* the most important thing."

Alexis scoffed from the back of the room as she chalked the tip of her cue stick. Her icy eyes landed on Darius. "So, *you're* to blame for all this shit?" She gestured around, at the large television mounted to the wall, the community computers plugged in at nearby desks, and the floor-to-ceiling shelves stocked with books, movies, and board games. They were all decked out in similar holiday fashion with bells and lights.

Mackenzie propped her hands on her hips, brows furrowed beneath her bright yellow hair.

"Don't be such a Scrooge," she snapped. "There's a wee little one in the Underground now! If you think for one second I'm not going to make that little girl's first Martyr Christmas the most magical Christmas that's ever... *Christmased,* then you're raving mad. I want this place *puking* red and green before she's discharged from the hospital."

Alexis's back went rigid. "Right," she muttered. "Better make sure her childhood is fucking *great* since we're raising her like a lamb for slaughter."

The entire room went quiet, all except the sound of the news program droning and the Harris boys, completely unaware, laughing over their game. Mackenzie's jaw dropped before snapping back together. Her tongue piercing clattered against her incisors as Juniper stared, and even Marcus's head tilted in their direction. Darius's stomach swirled.

He couldn't believe he hadn't considered this complication, too. Thorn wasn't the only Martyr with a personal interest in Lindsay's Virtue. There had been only two options for which Sin she might be destined to destroy: Wrath, the one who had possessed Thorn and made her life a literal waking hell, or Greed, the one who had possessed Alexis's father fourteen years ago and ordered her and her family killed. Alexis and Caleb had been the only two to survive. Now, all Alexis had left was the husk of a man she'd once called Dad, trapped so far beneath Greed's violence and hatred that there was a chance he didn't exist at all.

Mackenzie snapped out of her stupor first.

"Jesus, Claytor, that's not what's happening," she said. "She can grow up to be whatever she damn well pleases!"

Alexis rolled her eyes and returned to her solo game. "You know as well as I do that living *here* will make it fucking impossible for her to do anything else." She thrust her stick forward, and a clattering of balls rattled in Darius's ears. "But go ahead and keep pretending any of us has a choice."

"We do have a choice," Darius said, "and you acting like we don't is an insult to all the sacrifices people have made. Not just the Virtues but everyone else. Jeremiah. Lina. Caleb."

Alexis threw him a cold fire glare.

"We've been running ourselves *raw*, Jones," she snapped. "And for what? It sure as hell isn't some bullshit 'work-life balance.' Fuck, I drove all the way out here for my weekly game with Conrad, and he couldn't be bothered to show up because TAC is too busy painting those stupid masks for this suicide mission against Edith Froschlin."

Darius's hands ached to ball into fists, but he steadied them with a breath. "They're just ready to end this."

"What makes you think they *can* end this?" Alexis asked. She laid her cue across the table and faced him again. "Froschlin has more people, more connections, and more *money* than we do. She's also a better leader. Ours is a fucking basket case who went out there and made herself the *wrong kind* of famous."

"And Froschlin is the *right* kind of famous?" Darius argued.

Alexis huffed. "At least her *face* isn't all over the goddamned news."

Her eyes darted over Darius's head, and he glanced back. The local station was doing a rundown on the string of crow-related incidents. That still of Thorn holding one of them up by the throat flashed across the screen, with the words, "Who is Jane Morgan?" sitting above her head. Darius's lip curled.

"You like taking bets, McKay," Alexis went on. "How many months do you think it will take for Rose to drive this thing straight into the—"

"That's enough," Darius snapped. His voice boomed, a firm, crushing beat, but inside, he was shaking. A simmering anger bubbled up his windpipe, and he clenched his jaw to keep from shouting again. Now, everyone stared at him, Juniper and Mackenzie wide-eyed, while Marcus turned around to watch from the opposite side of the room, and the Harris boys finally took out their earphones to tune into the real world. Alexis, however, glowered, her sharp features twisted. She crossed her arms.

"Are you trying to censor me?" she hissed. "Afraid others will agree? God forbid anyone criticizes your *favorite* Forgotten Sin."

Juniper stiffened, casting Darius a look. He swallowed

his rage.

"A couple of years ago, you tried to talk to Alan about *saving* your father from Greed," he started, keeping his voice as level as possible. Alexis balked. "If he managed to get out, would you be this critical of *him* after everything he's gone through?"

Alexis didn't respond, didn't shrink under his gaze. If anything, she stood taller. Darius shook his head.

"I'm not saying you can't have your concerns," he went on, "but I *am* saying that if you can't have any of the same grace for Thorn that you would have for Anton Claytor, maybe you should think about leaving."

Alexis scoffed. "Is this a fucking joke? No one here could rebuild what I've done!"

"You're right. It would be tough," Darius said with a resigned nod. It didn't seem to be what Alexis expected to hear, and her lips fell open. "But I don't want you to stick around if you're so miserable. We're dealing with enough already, and we don't need Martyrs tearing each other down on top of it. I think we're above that, don't you?"

Alexis's face seared a bright, sunburned shade of red. Darius raised a brow.

"Should we start working on an exit plan?" he asked.

She forced her gnashed teeth just far enough apart to spit, "No."

"Glad to hear it," Darius said. "Next time you have criticism you'd like to share, make sure it's constructive."

With that, he placed a hand on Juniper's shoulder to guide her from the room. When they reached the courtyard, neither spoke, and that silence stretched to the elevator. It wasn't until Darius hit the button and the doors slid closed that Juniper finally asked, "Is it true? What that woman said about Thorn?"

Her voice trailed off, and Darius's teeth gnashed.

"No," he insisted. "It's not."

But it didn't matter. Not if the rest of the Martyrs believed it was.

Thorn stood alone, surrounded by the dead.

The memorial hall glittered in obsidian and ivory. Thorn had drawn the curtains shut, closing out the bright light and murmuring sounds drifting in from the courtyard. The dinner rush filled the kitchen with people, making the rest of the Underground feel empty by comparison, and Thorn didn't have it in her to be a part of it tonight.

She walked down the center aisle, boots sinking into the plush carpet that led to the front. A dais waited there, home to statues of a peacock, a fox, a bat, and a macaque, all intricately carved from solid blocks of black marble. Behind them, backlit alabaster slabs paneled the wall, and overhead, a pair of onyx and crystal chandeliers shone at their lowest setting, casting the room in a dim, ghostly glow. Rows upon rows of chairs had been removed, replaced by two large, circular benches dressed with black and white glass flowers. Thorn settled onto one of them, her Familiar wrapped around her throat.

Usually, she only set foot in this cursed place through obligation, attending funerals for people she hadn't been able to save, Paul Kwan and Tamera Osborne the most recent. Their names joined the others, carved carefully into the granite plates fixed to the left and right walls, preserved forever in a piece of fucking stone so that maybe someone would remember they existed another century and a half from now.

No. Thorn *hated* coming here, but where the hell else could she go? She wasn't safe in New York, not until her history stopped dominating local minds, and that didn't look like it was happening any time soon. Jay and the patrons of The Cross weren't the only people who had known her under some alias or another. Familiar faces of others she'd associated with started hopping on interviews with Rebel Truth's latest channel to talk about the woman they'd met with her face and a different name.

Those old lives flashed through Thorn's memory: her time as a traveling nurse in Lower Manhattan, a decade as a building inspector for a fictitious company in Harlem, even that brief stint as a security guard thirty years ago that had allowed her to kill District Attorney Chuck Reeves and take out that iteration of Greed. Those revenants crawled from the grave, burying Thorn in a mountain of freshly turned earth, and she figured...

What did it hurt to surround herself with the dead when they were coming for her anyway?

Sparkie sighed, winding more tightly around Thorn's neck. She laid a hand over him.

A rustling sound made them both jump. They jerked around as the black curtains drew open. Sounds from the courtyard broke through as Cain froze in the entrance. His bright, half-empty eyes widened at the sight of her. Beside him, Crescendo's spine arched, fur standing on end.

"I apologize," Cain began. "I didn't realize you would be here..."

Then he took a small step to the right, as though to obscure something. Thorn frowned and looked beyond him. A great stone beast hovered there. Her breath caught.

A wolf. But not just any wolf.

Alan's wolf. His Familiar. His *soul.*

Cain cleared his throat. "Again, I apologize. I... I can do this another time."

He began pushing the wheeled platform the other way. Thorn got to her feet, heart pounding in her ears.

"Wait!"

Cain glanced back. She swallowed against a chalk-dry mouth.

"Let me help."

His lips slipped open, and he blinked at her once. Then, he smiled, and he nodded.

Placing this memorial statue with the others wasn't really a two-person job, not when both of those people were Forgotten Sins, but Thorn and Cain worked in tandem as though it were, as though reuniting Alan with his old friends and comrades was a rite of passage. They each took one side, delicately positioning Rae at the center of the dais before rearranging the other four around her. Cain had rendered the wolf on her feet, regal and proud, with eyes just as sharp in stone as they'd been in real life. Once satisfied with the setup, Cain drew a polishing cloth from his back pocket and ran it across the Familiar's face, taking care to dip into every curve, every crevice, from the tip of Rae's shining nose to the points of her perfectly carved ears.

Then, he stepped back and considered the monument in its entirety, silent with reverence. A pool glistened within his eyes. Thorn's jaw clenched, and Sparkie chirped a quiet, mournful sound.

"These last few days must have weighed heavily for you to come here," Cain said after a moment. His silky voice sang through the room. "Would you like to talk about it?"

A lump grew at the hollow of Thorn's throat. She scoffed to loosen it. "There's not a lot to talk about. Chris has a plan to take on Edith Froschlin, David Cochrane is completely cancer-free, and Lindsay should be out of her burnout period soon. Things are… looking up."

She made her way back to the bench. As she settled onto it, Cain lowered beside her. Crescendo and Sparkie sat upon the back, his Familiar watching hers as the lizard staunchly refused to look back.

"Yes," Cain agreed with an ancient, knowing rise to his voice, "and much of the Underground is celebrating." Thorn felt his eyes on her, measuring her. "That child is quite remarkable, don't you think?"

Thorn didn't respond right away. She was too busy forcing her face to remain neutral. Finally, she simply said, "Yes. She is."

Cain nodded, considering the dais at the front of the room. Thorn did, too, and once again, just the sight of Alan's Familiar was enough to make her empty chest hurt. Cain's rendition was so perfect that the only way to differentiate the two had they been standing side by side would have been Rae's ice blue irises. Thorn drew a slow, collected breath.

What would Alan have thought, how would he have *felt*, if their positions had swapped? If Thorn had died and he was stuck here, missing her?

Would he be this conflicted?

Thorn released a sigh.

"When we were going over to meet Lindsay," she began, pulling Cain's attention in again, "do you know what I was most afraid of?"

She glanced at him, and he replied swiftly, like there could be no other answer. "That she would not be Patience."

"No." Thorn let out a short, bitter laugh. "That she *would* be. Lindsay's not even seven yet, Cain. Just a fucking *child*. And all I could think was… what if *my* soul can only be saved if this *little girl* gives hers up?"

Cain frowned. "But she's *not* Patience…" he murmured, and Thorn shook her head. His brows drew closer together. "So, why aren't you more relieved?"

"Because it doesn't matter," she said. "Patience, Charity, whatever, it *doesn't matter*. She's *still* a Virtue." Thorn's voice caught, and she glanced at the hands wrapped in her lap, fingers laced so tight that each knuckle strained. She finished in a whisper. "No child should be dragged into this fucking mess."

Beside her, Cain let out a resigned breath.

"That may be true," he agreed, "but war spares no one. Throughout the millennia, war has claimed more childhoods than we can fathom, more childhoods than it has claimed *lives*. This one is no different."

Thorn's eyes slashed to him, her lip curling. "So, you're saying I shouldn't care?"

"Of course not." Cain waved his hand. "What an absolute travesty it would be to stop *caring*. But the world is not so black and white. We exist in the messy gray, my dear."

He leaned forward, holding her with a gaze so earnest it made her want to turn away, but she didn't. "You can care *and* celebrate," he murmured. "You can rage and revel. You can grieve… and live."

Then Cain offered an open palm and tilted his head toward the cluster of cold energy collected in the courtyard. A soft smile lit his face.

"Let's go live, if only for one meal."

A nervous hole opened up in Thorn's stomach, a pinprick of a feeling eating into her psyche, but all the same, she lifted her hand, ready to give herself over to Cain and let this happen—

Her phone buzzed, and she reached into her pocket instead. A notification from Holly hit her like a tranquilizer, numbing her from the crown of her head to the soles of her feet. Half of the auras outside the kitchen suddenly moved toward the stairs. Cain frowned at the closed curtains.

"What's happening?"

Thorn's tongue felt like sandpaper in her mouth as she said, "Edith is staging another attack."

Cain blanched. "Well," he said, a sudden edge of anxiety shortening the word, "I suppose it's time to put those masks to the test."

CHAPTER TWENTY-TWO

Rockefeller Center swarmed with people, not a single one in a crow mask.

Not yet.

The winter night had long since chased the day away, but New York was a world upon itself, with its own sun, its own sky, fueled by the kinetic energy of millions of people piled atop one another like cold bodies in a mass grave.

That's all Thorn could see. Long lines circling the pop-up hot cocoa stands, crowds gathered outside restaurants and storefronts, clumps of skaters twirling in the sunken rink beneath the ninety-foot Rockefeller Tree—they were all living corpses. Her stomach ossified into a hard, jagged stone that scraped against her insides.

Edith would happily kill every civilian here if it meant ending just *one* Martyr life. Thorn had brought forty. She breathed through the apprehension climbing the crags of her spine, one vertebra at a time.

"Any sign?" Chris's voice chimed through the com unit in Thorn's ear. She jumped, covering the reflex by touching her fingertips to the device.

"None," Gabe confirmed, "or of her followers."

"Same," Chris said. "Thorn? What about your team?"

Thorn glanced around again, eyes floating over the four TAC agents at her back. They planned to come at Edith from three angles within the flock itself, but to do that, they had to *find* the flock. The plaza stretched out in a rainbow mosaic of humankind—vibrant scarves, patterned hats, and puffer jackets in every color—but no black beaks or feathered cloaks. Thorn shook her head. "Nothing."

Gabe exhaled a short breath. "You're sure we got the right location?"

"Positive," Chris said. "Holly entered it in herself."

"Well, maybe Froschlin made a mistake," Gabe replied.

Thorn's teeth clenched. Edith had calculated every single move she'd made so far, taking her time to come in for the fucking kill—a mountain lion sizing up a marmot. They were about to find themselves skewered upon her claws and trapped between her teeth.

"She didn't," Thorn said. "The coordinates pointed right to the rink." She looked down onto the ice. It glistened in a multicolored expanse of reflected Christmas lights, like stars glowing from the sky. "Froschlin will be here."

"All right," Gabe conceded. "Then what now?"

"We wait," Chris said. "Gabe, fall back to the Channel Gardens. Thorn, keep your team by the rink, and I'll take mine to the ComCorp Tower. We have ten units in full gear stationed up and down 50th and 49th, and the medical team is disguised as a choir van behind St. Patrick's Cathedral. Everyone's on the lookout for strange behavior and influxes of people, so we should spot Froschlin and her crows as soon as they arrive."

The medical team. A gut-churning sensation made Thorn's body feel distant as Sparkie circled overhead before gliding to the east. Cathedral spires stabbed into the air far below where he hovered at skyscraper height, and the central roof created a massive black cross that dominated the city block from 5th Avenue to Madison. From his aerial vantage, Sparkie spotted a black van at the head. Though they couldn't see Darius hidden inside, just knowing he was there, knowing he was *so close* to where Edith Froschlin would soon show her masked face, made Thorn want to agree with Gabe—insist instead that the Raven *had* made a mistake, and they should just go home.

But she knew better, so she kept her mouth shut.

They moved into position. Thorn led her team around the walkway, circling the rink until they found an open spot at the northern wall overlooking the Prometheus statue. Thorn frowned down at it.

A series of floodlights glowed upon the titan, making his gold finish so radiant in the night that he somehow outshone the massive Norway spruce looming over his shoulders. Even in the dead of winter, jets shot cascades of water around his base. Skaters twirled before him, and all the while, the figure glowered down upon them, observing the civilization he brought to life by stealing fire from the heavens.

But that was only part of the myth, wasn't it? The *palatable* part.

Thorn wondered if it had been worth it—having his liver torn out day after day—knowing that he'd saved mankind and all it took was sacrificing a little bit of himself in the process. Did it feel like having his soul ripped to shreds?

"I hope the bitch shows up soon," Conrad Carter grumbled. Thorn glanced up as he pulled a tin of chewing tobacco from his pocket and pressed a pinch behind his lip. "She has no clue what's comin'."

The rest of the team—Carter's partner, Charlotte Davis, as well as Madison Lewis and Lucas Olsen from Unit Twenty-Seven—glanced at him. Like Thorn, they all wore winter jackets over plain clothes to blend into their surroundings, but slim-fit bulletproof vests still covered their chests. Each of them carried a bag—either a tote or a backpack—with their crow disguises tucked safely inside. Thorn had taken extra precautions, hiding her long hair beneath a hood and her face behind a red scarf.

"Careful what you wish for, Carter," Thorn growled

through the fabric.

He snorted. "I ain't scared of her."

Lewis's bright eyes darkened. "You should be," she muttered.

A knot tied up Thorn's windpipe as she scanned the walkway around the rink. Her attention snagged on every blonde head. Every black hood. Every iridescent gleam of green or purple. Sparkie returned to the skies above to search for a raven in the black of night. Neither of them saw anything.

Minutes passed. Thorn leaned against the concrete banister, acutely aware of the cold pressure of human souls around her while the rest of her team talked. Before long, Olsen disappeared to get them all hot chocolate, insisting it was so they could more easily blend in while they stood watch, but Thorn suspected the blue tint to his lips had something to do with it, too. She sighed into her scarf, hot air trapped against her face, and pulled her phone out to check the time.

Six twenty-seven.

Edith had given them an hour warning, and that hour had come and gone. Thorn's teeth ground together, vibrating inside her skull with crushing pressure that made the muscles at her temples sting.

Maybe Gabe *had* been right.

Lucas Olsen's voice rang out in Thorn's com device.

"Amoretto," he breathed. "I just saw Connor Amoretto."

What?

She snapped up and scanned the plaza again. Olsen was less than twenty yards away, walking back from the hot chocolate cart with a pace that betrayed his nerves. He cast a glance over his shoulder. Thorn followed the look. Her body went numb, like her muscles had been pulped by a blade stabbed through her *Peccostium*.

Lust loitered outside a restaurant near the south entrance to the promenade. He stood out in the crowd, not because he was particularly tall or imposing, but because he commanded a charisma Thorn was positive had more to do with Influence than authentic charm. His navy peacoat cut a crisp line from his shoulders to thighs, highlighting an athletic build but not the toxic core beneath it all. When he smiled at an attractive woman on his arm, deep dimples pinched his cheeks, and his blue eyes shone hungrily. With a quick, suave motion, he brushed his thumb against her lower lip, revealing a broad palm and two missing fingers at the center of his left hand. The memory of those fingers jammed down her throat made Thorn's stomach clench—and the memory of cutting them off filled it with new fire.

"Lust?" Chris asked. "Can anyone else confirm?"

"Yes," Thorn said. She nodded at her team to act nonchalant as Sparkie kept an eye on Amoretto from the air. Across the rink, the blonde TAC director's head peered over the banister. "He's just across from you. By the French bistro."

"What the hell is he doing here?" Chris asked. "Helping Froschlin?"

Gabe offered a terrifying alternative. "Or getting off on her work…"

Amoretto appeared in flashes through the busy plaza, blonde hair bright under the artificial lights. He laughed, looking at his watch. Then, others turned away from him as though pressured by some invisible force. Amoretto dipped his hand into his jacket to draw out…

A mask.

Thorn's stomach plunged.

Suddenly, all at once, all around them, black feathers and billowing cloaks materialized—to the left, the right, even on the rink below. Thorn gaped.

They hadn't just found Edith's flock. They'd found themselves *inside* of it.

"Move!" Chris commanded. They donned their costumes, swapping out one communication system for another. As Thorn placed her mask over her head, she slipped the attached earbuds into place and hid it all beneath a hood. She exhaled a breath from deep in her lungs, which clung to her chin in a hot mist behind paper mâché.

Fuck, she felt crippled.

The thing cut into her field of vision, giving her a narrow tunnel instead of the full range she was accustomed to fighting in, and she couldn't see her team at all without twisting around. Instead of Martyrs, she found herself face to face with black birds. Her mouth ran dry.

God, this better work.

A hush trickled through Rockefeller Center as the crows began to move. Civilians outnumbered them six to one, but the strangeness of the scene reduced them to whispers. Shrouded figures walked up from the gardens, in from the streets, out of the nearest buildings until they surrounded the rink. Those on the ice skated to the wall near the stairs. Together, they all looked *up*. Thorn did, too. Her jaw clenched.

The Raven stood on the concrete banister above Prometheus, her raised arms and black cape cutting a silhouette against the rainbow lights from the Christmas tree at her back.

"Close in," Chris ordered. "Look for an opportunity to take her out—*without* civilian casualties!"

Thorn's hand wandered to the firearm at her back, but she didn't draw it. Not yet. She was too far to the left, and any shot at Edith would land on the street beyond her. Thorn shifted slowly, trying not to raise suspicion as she found a better angle. Her team followed.

A figure approached Edith's side, and though she couldn't see his face through the mask or read his aura in the crowd, Thorn had the sinking feeling she knew the man behind it all.

He raised a megaphone, and her barista's voice screamed out of it.

"We won't be lied to any longer!"

"Nevermore!" the crows screamed.

"The Martyrs think they can *murder us*, but we're done hiding!"

"Nevermore!"

"It's time to take back our city!"

The crows screamed. No, they *cawed*. Hundreds of voices sang in unison, reverberating off nearby buildings and out to the heavens, where even Sparkie couldn't escape them. Thorn ducked between bodies, but the pressure of so many auras made it feel like clawing through ice.

The barista held out his megaphone. Edith Froschlin took it, and the plaza stilled.

Thorn stood still among them.

"Hello, my darlings," Edith cooed. "My, my, look at *you*. What a *powerful* force we have become together. I am… so *proud.*"

She raised a hand, palm up, delicate fingers held perfectly straight as she indicated her congregation. The crows shuddered as though they'd heard the word of God.

"Though, I suppose I shouldn't be," Edith went on. Even without being able to read her face, Thorn heard the wry smile in the words. "Pride is a *Sin*, after all."

Her flock laughed, individuals elbowing each other and nodding in shared amusement. Thorn stepped closer, but she couldn't push to the banister.

"So, too, is *wrath*," Edith continued. "And I am afraid I am *full* of that, as well. Wrath at the *violence*, at the *injustice*, and at the *guillotine* Jane Morgan and her Martyrs have held over this city's throat for more than a century."

Rage echoed around Thorn and took root in her stomach, where it flourished into a briar. As the crowd howled, Thorn's palm hovered over her weapon.

Chris's voice whispered through the earpiece. "Oh my god…"

Commotion behind Edith stole Thorn's attention. Movement in the lower branches. She thought for a moment someone was coming in for the kill, to end Edith's grab for power right on top of Prometheus himself, but she quickly realized it was a mannequin being hoisted up by a noose around its neck. She frowned.

And then she gasped.

The mannequin was *her.*

A grotesque image of Thorn's face had been 3D rendered and applied to the thing's plastic head. A black wig flew wildly around its shoulders, making it an unmistakable imitation. It even wore a pair of elbow-length fingerless gloves.

Thorn's chest caved in.

"Jane Morgan has killed your people," Edith cried.

"Nevermore!" her crows responded.

"She has stolen your future!"

"Nevermore!"

"She has corrupted your city, but NEVERMORE!"

The last word rang not just from her mouth but the mouths of hundreds of souls around her. Every single one felt like a bullet to the heart, and Thorn could do nothing but sink into the sound. Hatred and loathing flowed through these people as potently as though Wrath herself had planted it inside their minds—a bottomless well of vitriol and violence.

But Wrath hadn't done this. *They* had.

And it was all directed at Thorn.

"I have a clear shot!" Carter shouted into his mic.

Thorn's lip curled. "Take it."

The crowd was so loud that the blast didn't register. Carter's weapon went off just feet to Thorn's right, ringing in her ear and the ears of those around her, but the rest of the congregation didn't react until Edith toppled off the banister and disappeared beneath the hanging mannequin's feet. Then a hush. Thorn forced her way to the front, fingers splayed along the half-wall, a knot in her throat.

Edith stood again. She pressed a hand to her collarbone, drew it back, and revealed a bloodied palm.

"Fuck," Thorn hissed.

The plaza erupted. Crows and civilians devolved into

pandemonium. Black cloaks and winter coats exploded around Thorn as people ran. Another gunshot screamed by, but this time, it struck the banister to Edith's side in a concrete powder burst. She ducked beneath it.

"Move in!" Chris commanded. "To the tree!"

Thorn pushed through the crowd. All the while, sights and sounds and sensations bombarded her. The flash of panicked faces. The cry of terrified people. The weight of cold souls. Thorn called orders to her team, alerting them to her location, keeping them at her back. They turned the corner at the far end of the recessed opening to the rink below and sprinted to the tree. Thorn kept her eyes down to avoid looking into her own lifeless face suspended in the branches. At the same moment, Chris's party closed in. The two of them met beneath bright lights and glistening tinsel. Even though Thorn couldn't see Chris's face behind the black feathers, she knew what mortified expression lay upon it.

Edith was gone.

Chris's hand moved to her ear to tap into the coms again. "We lost her," she shouted. "God damn it, we lost her!"

"Split up!" Gabe called. "Track her down!"

They ordered their units apart. Thorn sent Carter and Davis in one direction, Lewis and Olsen in another, while she dove back into the plaza alone. The rink congested with people trapped on the ice in a bottleneck trying to get out while others swarmed down the central walkway through Rockefeller Center. It emptied out—it *should* have emptied out—but more than half of Edith's followers stayed behind, and an unnatural number of civilians joined them, plastic and expressionless in a clear sign of Influence. Thorn's stomach soured.

"Lust is still here," she said. "He may try to help her!" She scoured the crowd, hunting for his aura, but the crows were packed so tightly together she couldn't make one soul out from the others. "Check the Puppets—"

"Mercenaries!" Chris said. "Coming in at the south and

north entrances!"

Thorn twisted around as a troop of six men in black and beige stormed onto the promenade from West 49th. A fire sparked in her gut.

"I got the south side!" she shouted, and she loosed her gun from its holster. "Carter, Davis, back me up! Lewis, Olsen, take the north!"

"With pleasure," Carter growled.

As they searched for Edith, Chris called their backup into the fight. Sirens wailed to life down the block, and Thorn sprinted toward the oncoming mercs-made-Martyrs. She raised her weapon.

And shot.

The bullet found its mark in the lead mercenary's belly, doubling him over before he had a chance to draw. He hit the ground, and Thorn expected the others to hesitate, to avoid attacking the crows for fear of hitting their own disguised men.

But instead, they fired back.

The second mercenary pulled his trigger and missed. Another blast grazed Thorn's shoulder, and someone behind her screamed. The sound of pain and panic made that flame of fury unfurl into Thorn's throat.

They were killing people under *her* colors, using *her* face, further sullying that cursed *fucking* name. A vise of hatred crushed her lungs, and with a horrifying, vengeful irony, she thought just one word.

Nevermore.

She shot again. And again. Carter and Davis joined her, and soon the Martyrs dressed as crows and crows dressed as Martyrs lobbed bullets like bombs, back and forth until one, two, three more mercenaries went down. Thorn took another hit to the same shoulder, and blood dribbled down her arm to pool in her jacket at the elbow. She shook it off, feeling the pleasant sting of cut flesh coming back together.

Charlotte Davis went down.

One of the rounds smashed into her armored chest and

sent her flying. Carter roared past her, taking out the man who'd shot her with a blow to the leg and another to the throat, vaporizing his aura in a red-speckled spray. The final mercenary pointed his gun at Carter's masked head, his finger tightening—

Thorn hit first, smashing the butt of her pistol into his chin. The bone dislocated in a disorienting pop, and Thorn silenced his screaming with a strike to the head that rendered him unconscious.

Carter fell to his knees at Davis's side and propped her up on the concrete.

"I've got a man down over here," a different TAC agent screamed into the com line.

Thorn tapped her earpiece as she helped Carter heave his partner up from the ground and pulled Davis's arm around her shoulder. "Us, too," she said. "Bring them back to the medic van! Darius, get—"

A gurgling sound sent frigid chills down Thorn's throat, like she'd swallowed a vat of liquid nitrogen. A new voice came through the Martyr channel.

"Too late, Mourning Dove," Edith Froschlin cooed. "Four down."

The plaza vanished. Thorn's vision faded in and out until everything was gray and empty. Icy energy swirled around her, but Thorn was hardly aware of that. Edith let out a belly-deep laugh that cracked Thorn's skull open and set the birds upon her thoughts, plucking all other feelings free until they devoured everything but horror.

"It's so good to see you again," Edith went on. "After our last date, I thought I might have come on too strong, but it looks like you just can't stay away…"

Thorn went numb, starting with her toes. Her fingers. Her face. A light tone chimed, and Chris's voice joined Edith's—quieter, quicker—as she tapped into a private channel between just the two of them.

"She's by the gardens," she said. "We're on our way. Keep her talking!"

Thorn's vision careened back into focus—not from her position on the ground but her place in the skies. Sparkie dove closer, scanning the plaza for one specific raven mask among many.

"Clever, dressing your people up like mine," Edith continued. "Though, I should hardly be surprised. Great minds *do* think alike, and even you must admit, Thorn, we are *very* much alike."

Disgust coiled around Thorn's throat. "I'm nothing like you," she hissed.

Edith chuckled. "Darling, you even *look* like me now. Tell me, that little birdie slung around your shoulder... How badly is it wounded? Do I get to claim *another* kill?"

Thorn's grip tightened around Davis's wrist as she threw her attention up, but there was no indication of Edith's Familiar in the black expanse. Sparkie finally spotted Edith at the eastern edge of the Channel Gardens, one of the Martyr masks around her head. A dead TAC officer lay in the water, a dark cloud of black fabric and red blood seeping out around her. Another knelt at Edith's feet, her blade at his throat. A ring of crows surrounded them, cultists or mercenaries protecting their messiah. Chris and her team wouldn't be able to break through, not easily. Thorn passed Davis off to Carter, ready to fly in herself.

Edith clicked her tongue. "Ah, ah, ah," she said, and then, her masked face raised heavenward, as though she could spot Sparkie's silhouette in the sky. Her knife drew closer. A thin line of red dribbled down the Martyr's neck. "No cheating."

Before the meaning had fully formed in Thorn's head, a deep, croaking cry assaulted her, and a black mass took a swing at her Familiar. The raven fell upon him, wings wide, talons gleaming in the Christmas glow. Panic jolted in the link between Thorn and Sparkie, forcing her to stutter to a standstill while he bolted through the air. The disorienting pressure of wind against her face and icy drafts zipping down her spine left her breathless. All she could hear for a frantic moment was the beating of powerful wings at her back. Her vantage disappeared, and suddenly, she was blind and alone in the middle of the plaza—surrounded by civilians, crows, and casualties.

Chris's voice broke through the noise. "The police are almost here!" she cried into Thorn's private channel. "Pull out!"

But Thorn hardly heard her. Up above, Sparkie darted into the Rockefeller Tree and scrambled desperately through high branches and bright lights as the raven clawed after him. Edith cackled. Thorn heard a distinct yelp. A murky thud. A cooing voice.

"Five down."

Thorn's hand balled into a fist around her firearm until her bones themselves ached. "I will tear you to fucking *pieces*," she whispered.

"You'll have to find me first, Mourning Dove."

Edith's line disconnected with a crunch that roused the monster in Thorn's gut. She abandoned Carter and Davis at the edge of the plaza as she sprinted toward the gardens. People pushed in—mercenaries or cultists or goddamned innocents, it didn't matter. They invaded Thorn's space, blocked her path. She couldn't see, couldn't think.

She'd never catch Edith. Not like *this*.

So, Thorn reached into that deep, dark place again, into the link she shared with Wrath, to tap into the Influence she tried *so* hard not to use. A net of panic cast out around her. With every ounce of her power, tying her very *soul* into the command, Thorn parted the crowd like a screaming red sea. Civilians floundered under the pressure of Thorn's will, and mercenaries faltered, holding their heads against the pressure of ideas that never belonged to them being forced into their skulls. Finally, Thorn spotted Edith Froschlin across the promenade. She lurched forward—

And Wrath's Influence came down like a plastic bag over her head.

The feeling blinded, deafened, muted her, an invisible

rope winding through the air with the horrifying pull of one body toward another. Wrath was everywhere all at once, capturing four dozen lives in a web that stretched from the massive Christmas tree to the emergency vehicles screeching to a stop on 5th Avenue. A horrifyingly familiar aura broke from the crowd at Thorn's back. She twisted around with a sob lodged in her throat.

A woman pulled her crow mask free and revealed a smiling face Thorn hadn't seen in seven months.

"Hello, Rose," Autumn Hunt said. "Or can I call you *Jane* again?"

Time slammed to a standstill. Thorn froze, wholly and completely. Wrath's lips cut a wide grin, somehow leaving her teeth sharper, whiter, more menacing. Her gray eyes glinted, blade sharp and bloodthirsty, as she took a step forward.

Thorn stepped back. Her lungs seized, sucking in tiny mouthfuls of air that made her mind go fuzzy. Sensory details muddled her brain. Frigid energy pressing in, tree branches ripping down her spine, harrowed cries from people all around, and the raven calling at her back. The space flickered, transforming from a wide-open courtyard to a dingy warehouse. A cold night and Christmas lights to warm sun through broken glass. Panicked civilians to Caleb Claytor, agony ripping out of his throat in a scream.

Hands trapped Thorn now the way ropes had then, and she couldn't move. As Wrath's Puppets grabbed her wrists, her arms, her hair, her *throat*, Hunt herself drew in. Every inch closed between them felt like a knife digging deeper and deeper into Thorn's chest.

"Let me see you," the Sin whispered.

She reached out. Thorn recoiled with a feral jolt, but the wall of cold energy held her fast. Wrath hooked her pinkies beneath the base of Thorn's crow mask and ripped the thing off. It scraped against her cheeks, smearing through tears she hadn't realized were streaming down her face.

Hunt leaned forward. Dark brown hair fell in wild

strands around her cloaked shoulders as she threw Thorn's mask to the ground. One hand grabbed Thorn's face. Her stomach twisted.

"Mmm…" The Sin traced a single thumb in a circle at the hard line of Thorn's cheekbone, gliding against the tears as though they were blood. "You look like *shit.*"

Thorn's nose curled, and despite the water still pouring freely from the corners of her eyes, she rasped out two words: *"Fuck you."*

Hunt arched a brow before she threw a glance around the plaza, where the chaos of the crowd seemed dull and distant compared to the hell inside Thorn's head.

"Impressive," Hunt murmured, "what you've accomplished." She stood so close that her breath pattered against Thorn's nose with every syllable. "Driving the Martyrs straight into the ground. Alan would be… *so proud.* I know I am."

Thorn's diaphragm hitched in shallow gulps as Alan's final moments played on repeat in her mind, so vividly that the wretched stink of his blood caked the inside of her nostrils. Wrath's smile widened until it devoured her entire face. She came even closer, her cheek sidled up along Thorn's, and her voice rumbled against her hair in an icy whisper.

"Do you know what a flock of ravens is called?" Hunt asked, the question thick and joyous. "An un*kindness.* Isn't that *great? Un*kindness."

She laughed into Thorn's ear canal, and pain stabbed through her head from one tympanic membrane to the other, but Thorn hardly registered that. She hardly registered anything. She held her breath, her heart, her *sanity* deep in her chest.

Until Hunt spoke again.

"Which brings me to my next question… Where *is* Darius Jones?"

Thorn's knees buckled at the sound of that name in Wrath's mouth. She would have collapsed to the ground if not for the Puppets snared around her. An old threat echoed within the confines of her skull: Hunt's voice a murmur and a scream all at once.

"How many times have I told you that I will kill everyone you love?"

Her mind spun with thoughts of *him*, but not the good ones. None of the good ones. She saw Darius broken and bleeding in the middle of that intersection after getting thrown from the car. Saw him tethered to machines and wasting away after giving up so much of himself that he almost didn't make it back. His face, wide-eyed and horrified, after watching her beat Alan within an inch of his life—after seeing the kind of monster Wrath had forced her to become.

A torrent of bile bubbled into Thorn's gaping throat.

"Stay away from him," she breathed, barely, with a scratch like shattered glass.

Wrath laughed again, and she brushed Thorn's hair away from her face. Her nails traced a sharp line at the crest of her forehead.

"Oh, *Jane...*" she murmured. "I can't do that. And you know why?"

Thorn didn't get to hear the reason. A cylindrical item sailed overhead, and before Hunt could utter another word, a splitting sound blast rocked the plaza. Thorn's eyes slammed shut, her teeth gnashing, as the Puppets crumbled in a single motion and dragged her down with them. Her hands covered her ears, which rang so loudly she couldn't make out a goddamned thing around her. The heels of her palms slipped against trails of blood leaking to her jawline.

A massive figure grabbed Thorn by the arms and yanked her up. Conrad Carter. He tugged her away, shouting something she couldn't make out through her healing eardrums, but the meaning was clear.

Run.

And they ran.

Carter dragged Thorn away from Wrath and the circle of unconscious Puppets thrown around her like debris from an impact crater. Though Thorn's mask was gone, Carter pulled her hood back over her head to preserve a little of her identity as they dove into a force of enemy crows, but no one looked at her. They turned, instead, to the plaza.

Wrath's power blanketed Rockefeller Center in cold vengeance. The crowd, already howling, riled into a volatile storm. Chants turned to jeers. The sound of breaking windows cut through the night. People flooded into storefronts and restaurants, trampling onlookers and setting awnings on fire. Crows surrounded the massive Christmas tree piercing the night sky.

As Carter forced Thorn forward, she craned her neck back, watching the Norway spruce. The hanged mannequin version of her swung on the lower limbs as a troop of crows pushed against the trunk. A pair of bolt cutters glinted in the lights.

Snap!

One of the guylines broke with a deep, dangerous twang that rang out so loudly it floated above the sound of the riots. Another followed. The crowd roared as the tree began to sway.

Then, they screamed.

A splintering crackle blasted across the rink and sank deep into Thorn's bones. Edith's raven vaulted from the branches, and Sparkie scrambled up the trunk, barely clearing the crystal star at its peak before…

The tree began to fall.

Thorn stopped dead, Carter beside her, and helplessly watched as ninety feet of timber roared toward the earth. The crowd beneath it—full of cops and cultists and cornered skaters who hadn't been able to climb off the ice—howled as twelve tons of tree consumed them whole and struck the ground with such a seismic force that it sent a tremor across the plaza. A mass of energy extinguished, and Thorn was left choking on the horror, gasping for breath.

Carter grabbed her again.

"Go!" he shouted.

She had nothing left to do but follow.

They sprinted toward 5th Avenue, darting through the Channel Gardens and hordes of people. A line of emergency vehicles lit the street with strobing red and blue flashes. Carter banked left. Thorn had no idea where they were going or where their evacuation was stationed, so her eyes darted around the block, and her Familiar scoured the streets from the sky. Carter led her between passing cars, across 50th, through crowds gathered on the sidewalk. An unsettled tickle crawled down Thorn's spine as they reached the Atlas statue. She glanced to the right.

Her heart stuttered, and she tripped over her own two feet, right into Carter's back.

He glared back with a growl. "What the hell are you—"

The complaint died alongside the chew pressed behind his lip.

A cloaked figure rushed up the steps across the street, right in front of St. Patrick's Cathedral. That iridescent cloak and intricate mask, distinct from all the others, were unmistakable.

Edith Froschlin.

Carter's disguise hid his expression, but the way his entire body hardened into a hunk of muscle was enough for Thorn to know he was fucking pissed—pissed enough to do something stupid.

Before she had the chance to say anything, *do* anything, he tore across the street. Thorn's jaw dropped.

"Carter, *don't!*"

He ignored her. Carter bolted between gridlocked cars on 5th Avenue with a fury. Thorn followed, her pulse thundering. He broke to the far side, a firearm in his palm before he stepped foot onto the sidewalk. Edith's back was turned, black cape billowing down the steps as she headed toward the open cathedral doors, as though seeking sanctuary from the very damnation she'd brought down upon them all.

Carter's mouth split. "Hey, bitch!"

Edith turned. Her raven mask glistened under the orange glow of church lights.

He pulled the trigger.

A bullet slammed into her chest with a thud and a grunt, sending her sprawling onto the concrete stairs in a furling lump of black fabric and feathers. For a moment—gravity-defying and awe-inspiring—Thorn thought he'd done it. Her lips slipped open.

Then, the lump jolted to the side. Carter shot again, but this time, it crashed into the cement and sent up a blast of dust. Edith spun around, crouched on all fours, and Thorn caught the distinct impression of a kevlar vest behind the folds of her cloak. She said nothing—just angled that masked face in Carter's direction. He sprinted up the stairs to meet her on the top level and raised his weapon again.

A black beast descended upon him.

Thorn slammed to a stop as the raven's claws gripped Carter's shoulders, and it ripped the hood from his head. He flailed with a guttural cry, waving his arms to get the thing off of him, but the creature batted them away with its massive wings. The mask flipped off, exposing Carter's face—ruddy and raving—to the night air.

Then, the bird plucked at his eyes. Wild, howling screams echoed into the night as that sharp beak came in again and again, breaking skin, exposing bone, puncturing the soft, scleral tissue until it left Carter's face awash in crimson runnels. Thorn reached for the holster at her lower back and, with a sickening, sinking horror, found it empty.

She'd lost her gun.

A soundless bullet from a distant sniper's perch slammed into Carter's thigh and brought him to his knees. Thorn stared from her position at the bottom of the great, concrete steps, as still and silent as the statue of St. Patrick himself, watching the sins of man unfold before her without raising a finger to stop them. Part of her knew she had to run in, to help, to do fucking *anything* other than bear witness to this unjust penance, but her body wouldn't move— *couldn't* move.

Except backward. One step. A single *fucking* step.

Edith approached Carter, a brass sign pole in her right hand. At the top, in bold, gothic print, the words "SAVE US, O LORD" stared down at him in glistening, gold ink.

Carter didn't see her—he couldn't. Both of his eyes had been reduced to raw, red craters, and he bellowed a sound that was more a plea for mercy than a battle cry. The raven vaulted from his shoulders and landed upon the cross high above the doors, where it loomed over this unholy retribution. Carter's body hinged at the waist, dipping him into gruesome genuflection.

Edith didn't speak, didn't say a goddamned word, as she swung that sign into Conrad Carter's head.

Crack!

Thorn gasped. Dread spilled down her spine, wet and viscous. A red spray coated her vision, and Mayor Bently's lower jaw came clean off his face.

Edith struck again.

Crack!

Carter sprawled on the ground. His blood poured down the steps in scarlet falls.

Crack!

Another skull shattered. The vibration of the hit rattled up Thorn's arms, into her joints, making her entire skeleton ring like a chime of bone and sinew.

Crack!

A soul flicked out in a burst of cold energy. Splatter painted Edith's sign and dripped down the metal stand. Thorn's palms bathed in it.

Crack!

Alan called her name, over and over again. Those black eyes looked at her, right fucking at her, and at the steel pipe in her grip—

Crack!

Someone grabbed Thorn from behind.

She spun with a scream, a sob, a supplication. Her fist flew out, the instinct to protect herself at all costs making her vision spin and her stomach buckle. A pair of warm hands wrapped around her wrists—just below the *Pec-costium*—before she had the chance to strike.

"Thorn!" Darius shouted.

She gasped, and then, she gagged.

Fuck. Not *him.*

She couldn't do this, couldn't be here, couldn't hurt Darius again because she knew if she did, nothing could stop her from throwing herself off the Brooklyn Bridge a second time, a third, as many as it took for the death to stick. Thorn tried to yank away, and Sparkie landed upon them, trying to come between Thorn and Darius, but Darius's grip wouldn't give.

"Come on!"

He dragged her toward the street, where a Martyr van disguised as a choir transport had pulled halfway onto the sidewalk. Skylar Fulton beckoned them inside with wild, sweeping gestures. Knowing she was about to be locked in that metal box with people she cared about made Thorn's whole body convulse.

Darius didn't let go. Not as they reached the vehicle. Not as he lifted her inside. Not as Skylar closed the back, and the TAC team at the helm ripped them away from those cursed cathedral steps. Darius didn't let go of her for a single moment. His strong arms wrapped around Thorn so tight she had no choice but to succumb.

And she did, completely.

The panic she'd fought so hard to stamp down since seeing Wrath's face erupted in a fit of haggard breathing until Thorn was reduced to trembling in tears. As her muscles gave out, her Familiar uttered a cry, and Darius knelt on the floor with them. One hand moved to cradle Thorn's head directly against his beating heart.

"I'm here," he murmured into her hair. "I'm here. I've got you."

She pressed her eyes closed against an onslaught of grief, and then, it annihilated her.

CHAPTER TWENTY-THREE

By the time they pulled into the Underground, Thorn had composed herself.

But Darius knew better.

He sat in a seat against the wall, buckled in and ill at ease as he watched her stare out the window. After breaking down, shaking and sobbing in Darius's arms, Thorn wiped her face, smoothed her clothes, and hid at the back of the van. She didn't say anything, hardly moved, and the red, puffy skin around her eyes healed so quickly Darius wasn't sure it had been there to begin with. Even Sparkie betrayed little to her emotional state, laid across her shoulders like an accessory instead of a living, breathing thing.

So, when the car wash opened and Thorn went rigid as a sculpture, Darius's breath caught. Skylar, sitting beside the mounted surveillance station, cast him a nervous glance. Then, the door closed, swallowing them in darkness.

The other units had already arrived back. SUVs, coupes, and sedans lined the loading area outside the hospital in a haphazard array, some of the electric engines still engaged and doors gaped open. On the other side of the wall, warm auras bustled in the triage room, making Darius's stomach swirl with new anxiety. Chris stood outside, armor off, arms crossed, and jaw set. When they parked, she pulled the medical van open, and Darius stood to help.

She held a hand to his chest.

"Elijah and Lamar have it under control," she said. "I need to talk to you."

Something in her voice held Darius in a dangerous grip, and her expression matched the mood—bullet-smooth and volatile. Skylar stepped out, followed finally by Thorn. She caught Chris's eye, and for a moment, the two women stared at one another. Chris's brow tightened so subtly that it might have been a trick of the dim garage lights. *Both* of you," she finished. "Now."

Sparkie stiffened on Thorn's shoulder, and her lips parted as though she intended to argue or, at the very least, question why, but she didn't. She simply followed Chris to the conference room. Darius entered last. He paused at the threshold.

Mackenzie and Nicholas were already there, grim expressions painted across their faces. They hadn't taken their seats but instead stood behind them, and Nicholas's hands gripped the back of his chair so tightly that his knuckles pressed against his skin. Chris closed the door and walked to the head of the table, but she didn't sit, either. She exchanged a tense look with Nicholas and Mackenzie before all eyes turned to Thorn. Thorn's spine snapped into a straight line. For a deafening moment, they hovered in a silence only broken by Mackenzie's tongue piercing clicking against her teeth.

Darius frowned. "What's going on?"

Chris squared her shoulders and held Thorn's gaze. "You're suspended from TAC."

Darius's jaw dropped, and he glanced at Thorn. Whatever semblance of control she'd managed to scrape together fractured in cracks around the corners of her eyes. "What?" she hissed. "Why?"

"Why?" Chris echoed. She flung an arm toward the door, hand shaking in anger. "What happened when I ordered you

to get out of there? Did you head to the nearest evac? Get your team out of danger? Or did you run right the hell back in, *just* like you did when we went after Lust last May?"

Thorn stared as though thrown back to that fateful day seven months ago. "I had an opportunity to go after Froschlin."

"You could have gotten yourself killed," Chris snapped. "We lost *six* people tonight, and we're lucky it wasn't more. You're off the team, Thorn."

Thorn exhaled a short, hostile breath. Sparkie's wings frilled beside her head. "You *can't* kick me off," she said, quiet and dangerous. *"I'm* the Martyr commander."

Chris's teeth gnashed, the muscles along her jawline bulging. "If that's how you feel, then *I'm* stepping down as the Tactical director."

Weight descended upon them, the pressure of an entire ocean above their heads. Mackenzie and Nicholas shared a glance, not half as surprised by the threat as they should have been, and Darius realized with a sinking feeling that they'd already talked about this.

Thorn's eyes never left Chris's—dark versus light. "You wouldn't."

"I would," Chris said. "If you're just going to override every call you don't like, I can't do my job. Either you respect my authority, or you find someone to replace me."

Thorn's eyes sharpened, and her hands balled into fists at her side. She glanced to where Nicholas and Mackenzie lingered behind Chris's back. Darius shook his head and stepped forward. "C'mon, there has to be another solution—"

"There's not," Nicholas interrupted.

A sound escaped Thorn's throat, something between a scoff and a sob. The air around her charged with staticky anger. "You can't do this," she said, voice trembling. *"You can't."*

"Yes, I can," Chris responded quietly. "You left me no other choice."

The bridge of Thorn's nose wrinkled, and her eyes gleamed. "This is my life, Chris. My whole *fucking* life!"

"Thorn—"

"It's all I have left!" Thorn cried. "You can't take it from me, too!"

Chris's jaw clenched. Over her shoulder, Mackenzie ran her fingertips beneath her lash line. Thorn shook her head. The motion was more of a jerk.

"Please," she whispered this time. "Don't... Don't make me *beg.*"

"My decision is final."

Thorn's lower lip quaked, and her gaze flashed around, looking for an ally in a room full of wolves. Mackenzie came forward. "Thorn, just listen—"

"To *what?*" Thorn barked. Her hands flew into the air as Sparkie screeched. Darius winced at the sound. "To my own goddamned people plotting against me?" She paused, swallowing hard, as though to steady the tremor in her vocal cords. "You all have a death wish! I'm the best soldier we have!"

"We don't *need* a soldier!" Chris replied, shouting now. "We need a *leader,* but more than that, we need to know you're okay enough to be one, and you *clearly* aren't!"

Thorn's mouth gaped open in a gasp, and she took a step back toward the door. Darius was convinced she was going to turn and bolt, but instead, she rooted to the spot. Her Familiar vanished behind her hair.

"So, you're willing to let Edith Froschlin—"

"God *damn* it, Thorn!" Chris closed in and glared up at Thorn with a furious, terrified gleam in her eyes. "I don't *care* about Edith Froschlin! I care about *you!*"

Quiet settled, so hard and whole that even Mackenzie didn't dare tap her piercing. Darius gawked as Thorn shrank under Chris's adamance. Chris, on the other hand, drew taller.

"If I had the power to restrict you to the Underground, I would do it in a *heartbeat,*" she said, "because I can't *stand* the idea of watching you lash out and get yourself hurt again, but all I can do is take you off of TAC." She shook her head and finally, quietly, let out a weary sigh. "Darius was right. I never should have let you be involved."

Darius's guts turned to gravel.

Thorn's attention cut to him in a single, sharp stroke. The betrayal written across her face was almost as painful as Sparkie's mournful cry. She stared at him for a moment, which stretched to a minute, and soon consumed everything until it was all Darius could do to stop himself from apologizing. His lips slipped open, searching for the right words to fix this.

There weren't any.

"You… *all* feel this way?" Thorn asked.

She turned to the rest of the room again, from Chris to Nicholas to Mackenzie. The Irishwoman nodded with a quick bob of yellow hair as Nicholas sighed.

"No one's happy about this, Thorn."

Thorn's jaw crushed closed, and her eyes glistened. She glanced back at Darius with a look that cleaved hearts.

"No," she muttered. "I'm sure you're not."

She twisted on her heel and stormed from the room. The door slammed behind her with a crack of thunder.

For a few seconds, the rest of them stood there in silence. Cold anger seethed up Darius's windpipe, and his mouth tightened against his teeth as he glowered at the others.

"You couldn't have warned me? Let me weigh in on all of this before you ambushed her?"

Chris propped her hands on her hips in a way that reminded Darius distressingly of Thorn. "Why? So you could try to stop us?"

He threw a hand out. "It's not like that!"

"Yes, it *is*," Nicholas said, shaking his head. "Look, I know you're worried about her—"

"We're *all* fucking worried," Mackenzie interjected.

"—but avoiding these hard conversations is *not* a

kindness," Nicholas went on. "If anything, it shows you don't trust her to make the right call." He paused, and his dull, blue eyes narrowed. *"Do* you trust her?"

Darius scoffed, and a frustrated heat rose to his cheeks, but his throat closed around his answer like his subconscious wasn't sure it was honest. "Of course I do."

Nicholas frowned. "Good." Clearly, he didn't believe it, either. "Now, prove it."

Darius waited at the edge of the courtyard, wishing the room felt less dead.

The despondence following the tragedy at Rockefeller Center lingered over the Underground like the promise of plague from a vengeful god. Even Mackenzie's Christmas decor, which stood out in a gaudy contrast to Cain's funeral drapes, did little to brighten the mood. Martyrs spilled from the memorial hall in a trickle of warm souls and black cloth as they headed toward the dining area, where Kenia had set up a reception of modest appetizers and cheap wine.

Darius moved through the crowd, shaking hands, sharing hugs, and extending condolences. He'd done this so damned often in the last few months that the effect had worn off, the grief grown thin. Nurses, TAC agents, and maintenance staff wandered off to find empty tables. Once everyone was settled, Darius stood alone in the room and exhaled a weary breath.

A warm hand slapped onto his shoulder. He turned to meet Saul's somber but smiling face. Like the first four funerals, he came in a nice suit, sharing his respect for a dead Martyr he'd never met, but Darius knew that Saul was really here for *him*.

And, god, he was grateful for it.

"C'mon," Saul said. "June saved you a seat."

They weaved between tables full of sullen faces. Conrad Carter's service was the eighth since Edith Froschlin had started hunting Martyrs for sport, and his death the most horrifying at her hands. Darius hadn't seen the Underground so dejected since they'd laid Alan to rest. The Harrises sat in bleak silence, hardly lifting their heads as Darius walked by, and even Lamar didn't seem to find a silver lining to peel back as he and Naomi whispered over glasses of merlot. Alexis sat on the fringe of the room, alone and aching, with pink rings around her eyes that betrayed the tears she'd shed.

And far beyond her, walking toward the eastern block of rooms, Darius spotted Thorn. His stomach wrung like a wet rag with nothing left to give.

When Chris removed her from TAC three days ago, Thorn hadn't immediately fled the Underground. In fact, as far as Darius knew, she hadn't left at all. He hated how shocked he was by that—and hated more that he couldn't believe she'd made it to every single celebration of life since. She put on a simple dress, sat in the front row, and stayed until the bitter end.

Then, she promptly vanished. While the rest of the Martyrs mourned together, forcing finger sandwiches between their teeth to slake an appetite they didn't have, Thorn retreated to her quarters.

This evening, she paused in the ingress, haloed in a wide rectangle of yellow light, and turned in a delicate half-circle as she looked across the room. Her dark eyes landed on Darius, and his heart fluttered. He raised a hand and provided a soft smile, neither of which Thorn returned. Instead, her gaze cast toward the ground, and she walked away. When her heeled shoes clicked around the corner, Darius slumped into the chair beside Juniper, feeling small and worthless.

"Why doesn't she ever stay?" Juniper asked. Two fine, parallel lines creased between her brows as she stared at the place where Thorn had been standing. "It's the least she could do."

Darius pinched the bridge of his nose. "She's been through a lot, June."

"You've *all* been through a lot," Juniper muttered, "but *she* is the only one who sulks in her room while you do all the hard work."

She prodded at her plate. Even the food looked flat and unappealing, like prepping for a fifth wake in forty-eight hours had drained Kenia of her culinary magic. Darius considered Juniper before glancing at Saul, who shrugged in return.

"She *is* working," Darius said, hoping to hell Juniper didn't challenge him on it. She threw him an arched look. Still, he pressed forward. "A *lot* has happened since that last incident. We're all swamped."

That much, at least, he knew was true.

He glanced around the room. Mackenzie hadn't joined them, instead standing with Cain near the kitchen, talking animatedly with arms flailing around her head. On the opposite side of the dining area, Nicholas sat with Skylar and a handful of researchers, heads down as they pored over what Darius could only assume were *more* LymeLite feeds. Chris and Gabe shared a table nearby. More than anyone, these funerals had taken a toll on her, and she exhaled a deep breath as Gabe drew her hands to his lips and kissed her knuckles. She smiled, murmured something—

And then her green eyes flashed up. The second they spotted Darius, a blush darkened her cheeks, and they both turned around.

Fuck, they had to fix this—had to be *better* than this. The Martyrs couldn't afford a rift in their leadership, but Darius wasn't sure how to stop it from growing.

Juniper grabbed his forearm and tilted toward him. Wisps of long, orange hair draped in soft sheets around her face. "Is there anything we can do to help?"

He smiled, or tried to, but his cheeks felt fatigued from the very act of feigning happiness. "I don't think so," he said, "but thanks."

Saul thumped a comforting hand on Darius's shoulder while June's mouth pressed into a line. Darius gently pulled out of her grip to take a chance on Kenia's little sandwiches. The three of them sat there, entombed in the murmuring quiet of a room in mourning. Darius kept glancing at the hall to the eastern wing—and kept pretending he didn't notice Juniper throwing him a dark look every time he did.

Until, a few minutes later, something tugged at him from above. Lindsay's Virtuous aura entered the elevator and made its way toward this level, so powerful it nearly drowned out those of the people sharing the car with her. An idea sparked in Darius's brain.

"Actually," he said, the suddenness of his voice making both Saul and Juniper's eyes snap to him, "maybe there is something you could help me with."

Juniper touched him again, this time a palm to his leg. "Anything."

"Lindsay's family," he began. "How are they doing with all of this?"

Juniper and Saul shared a grim look. Darius's heart skipped.

That wasn't a good sign.

"Look, man," Saul said, giving Darius the distinct impression that he was about to soften a hard blow with a cushion of logic. "They knew this place dealt with some heavy shit, but seeing all of those wounded people come in was a *big* reality check. Why do you think they asked to be out of the Underground for the funerals? Michelle and David don't want to scare Lindsay."

Darius groaned and pressed his fingertips against his eyelids. Lindsay's burnout period ended two days ago, which meant she and her family had been in the hospital ward when the disaster at Rockefeller Center dropped a room full of bleeding Martyrs at their feet. The Cochranes had front-row seats to the pandemonium that followed. While he'd been in and out healing people, he'd spotted David peering through a crack in the door only to snap it shut the moment he caught Darius's eye. He'd talked to them, but how could he explain *this* in any way that was less than horrifying?

That damned tree may as well have crashed through their roof instead of onto the ice.

"The last thing I want to do is freak them out…" Darius muttered, glancing at the elevator doors as it crawled ever closer. "I wonder if we can fix some of the damage. Make them feel more comfortable here…"

Juniper frowned, finally pulling her hand back to lace her fingers in her lap. "How can *we* help with that?"

"As far as they're concerned, I'm the guy who helped them find their daughter only to come back years later to take her away again," Darius said. Admitting it aloud carved his heart from his chest. "I think they'll be happier talking to people they trust…"

The elevator dinged and opened behind Darius's back. He lifted his sandwich with a sigh.

"God knows we need a little more happiness around here."

A sudden shift crackled through the courtyard—bodies bending toward the elevator as a burst of murmurs and whispers came to life. Darius glanced up, but he couldn't see past the wall of bodies now standing out of their seats. Suddenly, Mackenzie let out an ear-shattering shriek.

"OH MY GOD!"

She bolted from the kitchen, piercing the crowd like a needle through skin. Darius tried to sense beyond the Martyr auras, but that proved even more impossible with this many people jammed so tightly together, especially the closer they were to where little Lindsay's Virtue drowned them out.

With a frown, he got to his feet and started walking through the memorial crowd, gently pushing between crammed shoulders, until someone in a color other than black caught his eye. Michelle's mustard yellow blouse stood out like the first bloom of a spring flower, backed against David's sky blue shirt with Lindsay in a polka-dot dress between them. She gawked at the gathered Martyrs as though watching a wave ten stories tall crashing toward the shore, and a glisten of sweat speckled her young face. Darius was about to call for everyone to sit back down and give her some space.

A familiar voice beat him to it.

"Hey, Lindsay's new to this Virtue thing. Let's back off a bit, yeah?"

Darius's heart skipped, and he shoved between the last rows of people until he finally saw Abraham Locke.

He stood with Cain, Mackenzie wound around his middle in a crushing embrace like a child reunited with her favorite uncle. Other old guard Martyrs had come in to welcome him home, and they gradually pulled back to open space around the little girl. Darius stilled, and Abraham looked right at him. His kind, brown eyes softened.

A strangled laugh escaped Darius's throat. "Abraham!" He strode forward, grabbed Abraham's palm in a desperate grip, and pulled the man in for a hug. "What the hell are you doing here?"

He chuckled. "Hey, Darius," he said. "I'm sorry I missed the service."

* * *

After a few minutes of fanfare and emotional reunions, Darius and Abraham extricated themselves from the rest of the Martyrs and headed upstairs to talk privately. They stood outside Darius's office, and Abraham considered the name plaque, which had once read "Locke," as Darius opened the door.

"Come on in," he said.

Abraham paused over the threshold, a pensive look across his face. "Hmm. It still feels like home."

He glanced at Darius, who sheepishly ran his fingers through a crop of hair he hadn't cut in far too long. "Yeah, I didn't change much," he said. Abraham's focus fell to the open area by the couch, where a glass coffee table once sat.

Darius's cheeks burned. "Except that. It's a long story."

A sad smile settled onto Abraham's face. He seemed older than he had when he'd left a year and a half ago, with more gray mixed into his brown curls, but healthier, too, like time had more power to heal the spirit than a Virtue ever could. He walked to the chair and settled into it. It fit him like an old leather glove that had molded to the shape of its master's hand.

"There are a lot of long stories I've missed out on," Abraham said.

Darius hesitated before he took the couch and blew out a puff of air. "God, I don't even know where to start."

"I think I have the basics," Abraham said. When Darius frowned, the old counselor chuckled. "Stefan Brandt unloaded on me as soon as I walked into the convenience store above ground. You've managed to find all but *one* of the Virtues?"

Darius nodded. "All but Patience."

Abraham's smile flickered. "I met Lindsay and her family. They're very sweet. I imagine it's complicated for you to be reunited with one of the children you cared for this way, on top of... everything else." Abraham leaned forward. "How are you holding up?"

The last seven months crumbled around Darius and buried the question beneath piles of rubble. Something about sitting here again, with the same man who'd helped him process so much, made it hard for Darius to hold it together. His jaw flexed, throat tightened, eyes *stung*, and before he even tried to speak, Abraham sighed.

"I'm sorry it took me so long to come back," he said. "I left for a good reason... and I wasn't sure I could handle being here again, especially with everything circulating LymeLite. I'd be lying if I said it wasn't a selfish decision."

He drew a phone from his pocket but didn't turn it on. Instead, he fidgeted with it between his knees, eyes downcast. Darius shook his head. "What made you change your mind?"

Abraham glanced up, his thick brows drawn together. "When I saw the footage from St. Patrick's Cathedral, I knew I had to."

A cold rush drained the blood from Darius's face. He hadn't sought out the videos himself, but he'd heard whispers about them. No camera could have possibly caught the carnage in its full, excruciating detail the same way his mind had committed the moment to memory. "Yeah," he murmured. "What happened to Conrad was… awful."

"It was," Abraham said with a nod, "but that's not what I'm talking about."

Now, the counselor turned on his phone, opened a file, and turned the screen toward Darius. The sound was muted, and the footage cropped close, thank god, so they couldn't hear or see Edith crushing Conrad's skull into the concrete. Instead, they focused beyond all of that, in the background.

Darius's heart dropped.

He remembered *this* moment in excruciating detail, too.

Thorn stood at the base of the steps, hood askew, face open to the cold air. Darius could practically feel the wind, hear the screams, sense the warm auras rushing in as people sprinted by. Thorn didn't move—didn't even register the world around her moving—and her eyes went distant in a way that reminded Darius of the night Alan had died. Every time the Raven drove that church sign down, Thorn's body convulsed like she herself was struck.

Then Darius appeared in the scene. Thorn spun and took a swing at him, which he managed to catch. At that point, the camera view flung toward the ground, and the screen went black.

Darius and Abraham sat in silence.

"I knew losing Alan would be hard on her," Abraham finally said, "but I didn't expect *this.*"

"I don't know what to do, Abraham," Darius admitted in a whisper. "Every time we start to make a little progress, something happens, and she falls right back into that hole again. It's starting to…" He faltered, searching for the right thing to say—the right *way* to say it. "The others have their limits."

Abraham frowned. "But *you* don't?"

He zeroed in on Darius with a calculating look, and Darius balked. It wasn't that he didn't have limits of his own, but being asked the question so directly made him realize he had no idea where those limits lay.

How much could Thorn do—how far could she go—before he finally had too much?

Abraham saved him the trouble of answering by speaking himself. "I wish I could give you something more concrete to work with, but this is what healing looks like. We all want it to be a straight path, but it's more like a steep mountain trail. Every single step takes tremendous effort, and occasionally, the ground gives way and drags us backward again." He shrugged, a gesture that could have been so defeating but somehow, on Abraham, felt like a comforting arm around Darius's shoulders. "Just because her progress is hard to see doesn't mean she's not making any."

Darius nodded, and then, he let out a tight laugh. "God, Abraham, it's good to have you back. But…" He paused and considered their counselor with a serious look. "Are you *sure* this is where you really want to be? After what happened with Lina and Jacob—"

Abraham cut him off with a raised palm. "It's not your job to worry about *my* decisions," he said. "Darius, I promise you, I wouldn't be here if I weren't absolutely sure. Though, it *does* look like I'm going to need a new office…"

He glanced around with a soft smile. Darius frowned. "No. No, *this* is your office. I don't have much stuff here. It will be easy to—"

"No, I couldn't—"

"*Please,*" Darius cut in, silencing Abraham's argument before it escaped his mouth. The counselor's lips froze half-open as Darius shook his head. "You have to. It's already set up, minus a table, and it never really felt like mine. Please, take it."

Abraham didn't respond right away, his lined forehead creasing in concern. "Where will you go?"

Darius smirked. "I don't need an office to heal people."

"No," Abraham agreed, "but you're more than a healer now, Darius."

Abraham's cold energy hovered overhead, positioned in the space Thorn recognized as his office from years upon years of sensing that exact aura in that exact same spot. In the past, it had hardly registered—just part of the constant background noise of the Underground.

Now, though, that office belonged to *Darius*, and though he was invisible to her, Thorn knew he'd be there, too. Knew he and Abraham must be talking.

And she couldn't help but wonder—but *worry*—that she was the topic of their conversation. Of *every* conversation.

"Darius was right. I never should have let you be involved."

Thorn tore her dress off and threw it onto the floor before pulling on a pair of red lounge pants and a black camisole, teeth clenched the entire time. Those words had haunted her for three goddamned days, and no matter what she did—swimming laps in the pool, abusing the punching bag, even running circles around the convenience store at two in the morning—they wouldn't fade. She'd thought she couldn't feel more useless, more *worthless*, than she already did, but here she was.

No one, not even her closest friends, believed in her. And the worst part?

She didn't fucking blame them.

With a muffled scream that turned into a groan in Thorn's throat, she flung onto the bed and laced her fingers over her eyes. Sparkie curled into a scaly ball on her breastbone, rising and falling with the pattern of her breath. They lay there, wishing the chaos in their shared mind might calm down to match the silence around them.

Then, a sharp, cold aura drew Thorn's attention. Her stomach twisted.

God damn it. She didn't need this.

Mackenzie moved with a purpose, the vibrant allure of her energy navigating the hallways in the most direct path right to Thorn's door. Before she'd even raised her hand to knock, Thorn was already bristling. Then, a series of sharp raps rattled her brain.

"Thorn?"

The Irishwoman tried again, this time louder, and the sound drove spikes into what little sanity Thorn had left. Sparkie raised his head to watch the brass knob. It wiggled but didn't open, and Mackenzie grumbled on the far side. The thunk that followed sounded like she'd used her forehead instead of her fist.

"C'mon, Thorn."

"Get lost, McKay!" Thorn shouted.

"You know I won't do that," Mackenzie went on. She'd scooted to her right, and her voice came through a little louder as she spoke directly against the closed seam. "I'm not leaving until you open this door, and if you *won't* open it, I'll have Holly give me a key. Normally, she's all about preserving 'personal privacy,' but she bet me ten bucks you wouldn't let me in. I'm sure she'd happily bend that rule just to watch me pay up. It's up to you."

Thorn exploded from the mattress. Sparkie slithered to her shoulder, claws digging into her flesh to prop himself up, as she thundered across the room. When her fingers hit the lock, Mackenzie's energy leapt back, like she knew she was playing with a loaded weapon.

The door slammed open, and Thorn stormed through.

"What the fuck are you—"

Mackenzie's arms swung around her, smothering her anger in an immediate, desperate hold. The sensation of a cold soul and hot body pressed against Thorn's chest made her want to simultaneously crawl out of her skin and sink further into the embrace. But she didn't. She didn't move at all.

She stood still as stone, her heart beating wildly within her chest, unsure of what to do, how to *feel*. Mackenzie squeezed tighter, and Thorn drew a trembling breath.

This time, she whispered. "What are you doing?"

"Aggressively loving you," Mackenzie said. Her face pressed into Thorn's collar, muffling her voice. "Just like you've always loved me, so shut up and take it like a woman."

Seconds passed, then minutes, Mackenzie gripping Thorn in the open doorway while Thorn scrambled to sort out her scattered thoughts and feelings. She was so ready to fight that she had little sense to do anything else. Her arms hung rigid at her sides, and her breath came in short, shallow gulps. Mackenzie sighed against her skin, and goosebumps trickled down Thorn's spine.

"I know shit is hard," Mackenzie murmured. "I know you're angry, and hurt, and probably scared as hell, but we're here for you."

Sparkie let out a keening cry as the corners of Thorn's eyes prickled. "Is that what that little intervention was?" she managed to ask, but whatever venom she tried to push into the question dissolved on her tongue, poisoning her instead. "You all *being here* for me?"

"Yes." Mackenzie drew back, planted a palm on each of Thorn's shoulders, and held hard. Her blue eyes flashed earnestly beneath a brush of yellow bangs. "That's *exactly* what that was."

Thorn's lips slipped open, a thin breath pulling between them, but she said nothing. Mackenzie scoffed.

"Jesus Christ, what the fuck do you expect us to do?" she went on. "Sit back and watch you self-sabotage until you have *nothing* left to lose?" Thorn's throat tightened, and Mackenzie shook her head. "You're not chasing Edith Froschlin, Thorn. You're running from your own demons, but here's the thing… Those demons will *always* catch up unless you turn back and face them. I should know. Mine almost killed me."

Mackenzie finally pulled away completely, and, to Thorn's shock, she ached for that touch again—for the feeling of those palms against her skin, that support in her soul.

"I don't care what you do, who you talk to, how you work it out," Mackenzie said. Her voice broke, and she swallowed hard. "But you deserve to heal, so please, please, *please* start caring about yourself enough to heal."

Then she spun around, but not before Thorn caught the glistening of tears shining behind her lashes. She watched the Irishwoman walk down the hall until she slipped around the corner. The second Mackenzie vanished, Thorn's eyes drifted to that spot on the far ceiling where she could sense Abraham Locke.

CHAPTER TWENTY-FOUR

It took less than two days of having Abraham Locke back in the Underground for it to feel like he never left at all.

Darius hadn't been exaggerating when he said he didn't have much in the office. Other than logging the computer into his account, filling an empty shelf with books from the late Humility's estate, and accidentally shattering the glass table with good intentions and bad ideas, he hadn't changed anything. Within an hour, their old counselor was behind the chair again, and now, warm energy pulsed through his door like commuters on the subway.

As Darius walked down the corridor, he glanced at the wall where David and Michelle Cochrane's auras sat with Abraham now. A smile settled across his lips.

God, they'd needed this for a long, long time.

He opened the R&D headquarters and walked into the room. His smile quickly vanished.

The Research and Discovery Department was always busy, but that had become even more pronounced since Edith Froschlin had been in the picture. People filled the wall of desks to Darius's left, and both circular tables in the center of the room crowded with Martyrs on laptops, heads down and earbuds in. Every screen looked out with different versions of the same harrowing topic: the tragedy at Rockefeller Center. Clips of screaming mobs. Footage of a tree as tall as a building barreling toward the ground. Still shots of casualties in the chaos—civilians, crows, cops, Conrad. As Darius made his way through, the drone of clicking and typing slowed until it stuttered to a stop, all eyes following him. When he reached the back, Nicholas glanced up, closed the open task on his monitor, and came around the side.

"So," he said, crossing his arms, "back to being a drifter."

"Looks like it," Darius replied.

"Why don't you move into Alan's old office?" Nicholas asked. "It's not doing any good sitting there empty."

An icy draft poured through the room as though Nicholas had pissed on the man's grave. Darius frowned, surprised at the suggestion, but the look on Nicholas's face made it clear he had more points to bring to the argument if Darius pushed harder.

So, he shrugged.

"I don't need an office," he said. "I got along just fine without one before."

Darius sat at the other workstation. Nicholas sighed and returned to his chair as Darius settled in.

This was Mackenzie's typical spot, and the surface was a testament to a scattered brain he couldn't even begin to fathom. Bright notes in various colors stuck to every surface, scribbled in what Darius could only assume was some foreign language she'd made up herself. The screensaver was the identification photograph they'd taken for Nicholas when he joined the Martyrs. She'd doctored it with some cheap art program, doodling grumpy eyebrows, a curly mustache, and a variety of fake tattoos all over his face in black pixels. Darius chuckled before he logged out of her account and into his own. The rest of the room started rattling away again.

"Are we still trying to get videos from this last attack flagged for removal?" he asked.

Another lull in activity drew Darius's attention, and he glanced up to see the rest of the researchers not watching him but Nicholas. Nicholas hesitated for a moment before running a hand over his beard.

"We haven't had to do a lot of removing," he said.

Darius shook his head. "You're just leaving that footage of Conrad out there?"

A smirk twitched onto Nicholas's mouth. "That's not what I mean. I mean that we haven't *had* to pull most of it down. Dan, can you load up that RebelTruth clip?"

Daniel Park thrust a thumbs-up into the air from his station along the wall, and soon, the big screen filled with that AI-filtered face Darius had grown to hate so much. The sound was muted, but the title said it all:

Is The Raven More Dangerous Than Jane Morgan's Martyrs?

Darius's eyes shot wide, and his mouth fell open. "He's turning on Edith?"

"It might be premature to say he's *turning*," Nicholas said, "but it's a start. This video was taken down within an hour, and we had nothing to do with it. Clearly, some other party doesn't like this line of thinking. I wonder who *that* could be?"

Nicholas's smirk evolved into a fully-fledged smile, but Darius was still too stunned to share the joy. He stared at the screen. Nicholas glanced at Daniel again, gave him a signal, and the display shifted to *The New York Times* website.

An image of the Rockefeller Tree felled in the plaza dominated the first page.

"Edith Froschlin grossly overestimated her power," Nicholas went on. "She thought she was untouchable, that she had the Sins in her back pocket, but this proves otherwise." He held a palm out. "Lust isn't even *trying* to Influence the media away from telling the truth this time. This shit has been linked directly to the Raven and her flock."

"But *Edith* has linked herself to the Sins," Darius said.

"Why wouldn't Amoretto cover it up?"

"Because it's gone beyond his reach," Nicholas answered. "Lust's Influence in New York City can't stop national outlets. The most famous Christmas tree in the goddamned country just killed twenty-four civilians and wounded hundreds of others."

"Basically, the Raven elevated herself to god-level fame overnight," Naomi said from her position at the nearest circular table. She glanced at him, peering between chunks of scarlet hair framing her face. "And the Sins *don't* like publicity."

"Exactly," Nicholas agreed. "Edith Froschlin is learning an important lesson in being a god: once you stop serving your people, they stop serving *you*. There's a reason the Sins gave up on the divine game. As far as they're concerned, they'll hop on board when Froschlin is doing well, but they're not afraid to feed her to the sharks the second her ship starts to sink. There's blood in the water now. She's panicking."

Darius slowly nodded as the elements arranged themselves in his mind. "And since she can't do a damn thing about *traditional* media, she's trying to make sure LymeLite doesn't turn against her."

"That's what I think," Nicholas said. "But she's got her work cut out for her. RebelTruth isn't the only account saying shit like this. The dam has burst."

An indignant breath burst from Darius's mouth. "I can't believe it took this long."

Nicholas leaned back in his chair. "She's had a pristine image," he said. Darius cast him a dubious look, and Nicholas laced his fingers behind his head. "*We* know better, but as far as everyone else is concerned, it's been the *Martyrs* killing civilians... until Froschlin beat a man's skull in with a 'Save Us O Lord' sign in front of God, Jesus, and the whole internet. This is a PR nightmare for her—and a dream for us."

With that, he grinned at his team, who met him with

short smiles before turning back to work. Darius stared at his screen, where an open LymeLite tab flashed a distracting array of moving color.

"If you're not taking content down," he said, "then what *are* you doing?"

Nicholas didn't look up as he said, "There's more to my job than playing internet hall monitor. Froschlin is smart. She's got to be working out some plan to salvage her image. We're trying to figure out what so we can get ahead of it."

Darius shook his head. "How the hell can you do that?"

"We're pretty sure there's a private group on LymeLite or some other forum where her followers communicate under the radar," Nicholas said. "So we're hunting it down. If you want to help, Dan can give you the details on what to look out for. Dan!"

Nicholas waved Daniel over, and within minutes, Darius was digging through dozens of comment feeds, social platforms, and personal profiles for mobs in black masks, communicating under false accounts and false pretenses, to see if he could infiltrate a cybernetic stronghold.

The chlorine had long since rinsed from her hair and sluiced off her body, leaving Thorn naked and raw beneath a scalding spray. Water burned down her scalp, her shoulders, and the canyon of her spine, hot enough to burn before healing, burning, and healing again. This cycle wasn't *healthy*, but Thorn didn't quite know how to break it yet. The first step was easy: turn off the shower.

But then she'd have to go out *there*.

Voices echoed through the locker room, down the tile hall, and into the dressing alcoves until they reached the shower stalls. A group of TAC agents prepared for weekly combat training, laughing and joking in friendly banter that clashed with the thoughts and feelings swimming about within Thorn's skull. Sparkie perched atop the frosted door, and he watched the crowd swell as more people filtered in to change.

Thorn tried to time her workouts when the gym was empty, but that was starting to feel impossible. Most of TAC was stuck indoors. They were still down to half their standard capacity, even less in the last five days, ever since—

Crack!

Conrad Carter's eyeless face interrupted her thoughts, blood streaming like tears down his cheeks. Suddenly, the laughing felt like screaming, and Thorn couldn't bear the sound. She shut off the water and grabbed her towel. Her locker sat in the center alcove, and the women hushed as Thorn made her way to it, like her presence was a dark cloud that smothered light and warmth. She dressed quickly, oddly disconcerted for the first time in her immortal life to be nude in front of others, as though her trauma was just as evident as the scars on her arm. As she walked out, chatter resumed, but this time in quiet tones. No more laughter. Fucking great.

Thorn stepped into the gymnasium, and another room went silent around her.

This one was emptier, just a couple of over-achieving agents who had shown up in their workout gear rather than needing to change into it. Saul was among them, wearing a pair of navy sweats and a white tank. He and the rest spread across the mats to warm up for the training ahead. On the opposite wall, Chris and Gabe talked, no doubt discussing the day's routine. When Thorn appeared, they stilled. Chris's green gaze flashed up, met hers, and a pink heat tinted her cheeks.

Thorn's heart leapt, tugging her forward, urging her to go over there and apologize for all the ways she'd fucked up, to beg for Chris's forgiveness, but more than that, beg for her *help*, because Mackenzie was right. She was going to lose everything if she didn't make some kind of change…

But Thorn didn't move, and Chris turned away. She pulled a loose strand of blonde hair behind her ear as she talked to Gabe again. He cast Thorn a hard look, those cognac eyes narrow. Thorn had never considered herself a coward, but as she strode across the gym without so much as a final glance in Chris's direction, she thought the title fit.

The courtyard stretched out before her, and the sense of disjointed reality became even more pronounced. Thorn paused.

Since the funerals, Mackenzie had leaned full tilt into Christmas, more than Thorn had ever seen. She'd enlisted Stevie Arias's help, and the entire maintenance staff had transformed the open space into something resembling a tacky mall Santa setup. There were giant boxes painted to look like wrapped gifts, a length of red carpet leading to a hideous upholstered chair, and draping string lights Thorn was certain Mackenzie had stolen from Raquel and Skylar's wedding decor. A massive artificial tree stood in the center of the room.

Thorn's stomach twisted as she approached. This plastic pine held nothing to the grandeur of the Rockefeller Tree, but all Thorn could see was the carnage at the plaza when the larger one fell. She walked in a slow circle, taking in the steel rod branches, polyethylene needles, and fiber optic bulbs glowing in a rainbow array. A bunch of ornaments dressed the thing, not nearly enough to fill it, and most of them took up the lower limbs like they'd been hung by an overzealous child.

"Hi, Thorn!"

Her chin flicked up.

Lindsay sat at a nearby table, waving wildly with one hand while Lamar Verrette delicately held the other, a tiny nail polish brush pinched between his fingers. Thorn hadn't known they were there—couldn't sense the purity of their Virtuous souls—and the sight of the child made her heart ache just as vividly, as viscerally, as it had the night they'd first met. Juniper Foster sat across from her, back to Thorn. She glanced over her shoulder, and the muscles along her neck tightened as Thorn drew closer.

"Hey, Lindsay. Juniper," Thorn said, putting on her best customer service voice. Adopting a false persona, something that had always come so naturally in her work outside of the Underground, felt suffocating within it. "How are you feeling? Getting the hang of those new superpowers?"

Lindsay wrinkled her nose. "Not really. I still don't know how to *use* them," she said. "Everyone just feels all… warm. Except you. And that guy with the beard. And—"

Thorn interrupted her with a laugh, and Lamar chuckled as he brushed a layer of clear polish over Lindsay's thumb.

"You healed your dad, didn't you?" Thorn asked with a shrug. "That's the best superpower of all, and you did it by just following your heart. If you do what feels right, you can't go wrong."

Lindsay turned to Lamar. "Is that what *you* do, Mr. Lamar?"

He nodded, tight locs bouncing. "That's right. A Virtue's instincts are *never* wrong. Well. *Almost* never."

Lamar winked, Lindsay giggled, and Thorn couldn't help but smile. Then, she considered Juniper. "How are you all settling in?"

Juniper loosened a quiet sigh. "Just fine, thank you." She lifted a glass of water to her lips without looking at Thorn. Lindsay, however, beamed.

"It's *so* fun here," she chirped. "I got to help that nice lady with the ring in her eyebrow put up the tree, and now Auntie Juniper and me are getting our nails did while Mom and Dad talk upstairs." The little Virtue thrust a hand forward. "Look!"

The grin on her face glowed with the flawless glisten of freshly fallen snow, clean and untouched by the corruption of the world. A strange, melancholy bulge tightened in Thorn's throat, but she managed to swallow it down as she held a palm out. The girl plopped her fingers into it. Her soft skin sent a heartbreaking warmth through Thorn's chest—a warmth she associated with holding her own son's hand decades ago when he, too, had been too young to understand the curse he'd been born into—too young to comprehend how hard his life was destined to be. Her breath caught.

Lindsay's voice dragged Thorn back to the present. "They're *Christmas lights!* See?"

Thorn squinted, and Sparkie tilted his head from her shoulder. She supposed, if she tried hard enough, she could make out the shape. Lamar had painted a backdrop of white, upon which red and green ovals sat in the center of each nail. They were so tiny that he hardly had enough space to add a golden stroke near the cuticle and a sloppy black line to represent the cord linking them all together. Thorn cast him a look, her lips curling into a smirk. "I see *something*, all right," she teased.

Lamar laughed, but Juniper's spine stiffened.

"I think they look wonderful, Lamar," she said, casting Thorn a reprimanding glare. Thorn's brows twitched together, and Sparkie's wings flared.

"Pure *artwork*," Lamar said, "if the artist is Pablo Picasso."

Lindsay's face scrunched. "Who's Pablo Pi... Pissaco?"

"Picasso," Thorn said. "He was a painter. Considered one of the greats."

"I don't know if I'm great," Lamar said, delicately applying a final stroke to Lindsay's pinky before he popped the topcoat brush back into its bottle. "What do *you* think, sweetie?"

This set matched the other—an abstract representation if Thorn ever saw one, but perfect in a way she couldn't explain, in a way that felt like a cup of warm cocoa beside the hearth and freshly baked cookies on the table. Like childhood, but not the one Thorn had. The one Thorn had deserved, that *all* children deserved, free from horror and hate.

Lindsay squealed. "I *love* them!" She bounced in her chair before leaping to her feet and throwing her arms around Lamar's shoulders. "Thank you, Mr. Lamar!"

"You are *so* welcome," Lamar said, ruffling her brown hair with his own set of painted nails—a simple gold with silver glitter. "Just be careful! They're still wet."

She flopped back down and laid her hands flat upon the wrought iron table, fingers splayed as wide as possible. Her beautiful, round eyes caught Thorn's again. "Do you want *your* nails painted, too? Auntie Juniper got green, and you could do red! Then we'd all be matching!"

Juniper shifted in her seat and laced her fingers in her lap, making it clear she had no interest in sharing any common ground with Thorn. A tingle of annoyance bolted up Thorn's spine and settled into her clenched teeth. She was tempted to sit her ass in the chair across the table and let Lamar do his best just for the pure spite of it.

But these were Darius's friends—his *family*—and she cared about him too much to sink to that level. Juniper wasn't ready yet. Maybe she never would be. Thorn knew her rough edges scraped some people raw.

So instead, she shook her head.

"I can't," she said. When the girl wilted, Thorn laid a palm on her shoulder. "Next time."

Lindsay lit up. "You promise?"

Thorn smiled. "Promise."

"She'll even let you pick the color," Lamar said. He threw Thorn a coy look from beneath his lined lashes. "Glitter pink will go great with all that black. What do you think?"

He winked at Lindsay, who giggled wildly. Juniper's cheeks darkened to their own shade of magenta, and Thorn took that as her cue to go.

"Pink it is," she said, stepping back. "You can even paint Sparkie's claws. He'll love it."

Lindsay let out a thrilled gasp as Thorn chuckled and turned away. Her Familiar slipped behind her hair to peer back, and while Lamar and Lindsay dissolved into conversation, Juniper watched Thorn with a high-caliber glare that could pierce through armor.

The upper level of the Underground swelled with cold energy. Combat agents getting ready to trade out patrols lingered in the tactical lockers, hospital staff hummed around the medical ward, and the R&D headquarters was so full of people that the entire room felt like a block of ice. Like the gymnasium, it was harder to avoid people up here lately, too. Thorn's gaze slid toward the doors to the garage, where the dark shape of her motorcycle lingered beyond the glass.

She could leave. It would be easy. Grab her satchel from her office, take the keys from her top drawer, and vanish into the anonymity of New York.

Though, she supposed she didn't have anonymity in New York. Not anymore.

With a sigh, Thorn headed away from the garage and down the hallway. As she turned the bend leading to the alcove of director offices, one of them opened. Thorn paused as Michelle and David Cochrane stepped out.

"Thank you, Mr. Locke," Michelle murmured through a sniffling nose. Red rings swallowed her eyes, and she clutched a crumpled piece of tissue in shaking fingers.

"It's my pleasure, Michelle." Abraham's voice followed the couple into the hallway, and the shape of his aura leaned against his doorframe. "And please, call me Abraham."

"Same time next week?" David asked.

"That's right," Abraham replied, "but if you need me before then, you're welcome to come by any time."

"We will," Michelle said, nodding fervently. "Thanks again."

They turned together, David's arm draped over his wife's shoulders. The moment they spotted Thorn, their backs went rigid, as though the sight of her was enough to dredge up the host of shitty feelings they'd just spent the better part of two hours working through. She pressed her lips together in a hollow smile, and the Cochranes returned it with just as empty of an acknowledgment before they brushed past her and disappeared around the corner. Thorn didn't move.

The door to Abraham's office stood wide open.

A shiver tickled down Sparkie's spine. Thorn drew in a slow, low breath, lips open just enough for it to whistle past them like a breeze. Her first step thunked onto the tile like her feet were made of lead. The second, too. She was certain Abraham must have heard her coming, and she wondered what would be more awkward: her pretending not to notice him as she walked by or him pretending not to notice *her?*

But… did either of them have to pretend at all?

Thorn stopped in the doorway. Abraham looked up from his desk. Silence bounced between them. Thorn broke it first.

"Welcome back," she said.

Abraham smiled as he got to his feet. "Thanks. It's… been a crazy couple of days, but I'm glad to be here."

Thorn nodded. "There's a lot going on. I…" She paused. Abraham didn't fill the space. He simply watched her. Waited for her. Her mouth ran dry. "I'm sorry I didn't come by earlier."

He closed his eyes and waved a hand. "Don't worry about it. Like you said, there's a lot going on. Besides, you're here now. That's all that counts, right?"

His smile softened and somehow filled with more warmth. Abraham hadn't changed much in the sixteen months he'd been gone, not *physically*, at least. A few more gray hairs. A few more fine lines.

But something about his *spirit* felt different. More secure. Thorn shifted her weight, and Sparkie vanished behind her hair.

"Right," she murmured.

Abraham stepped forward, looping his thumbs into his pockets. "Would you like to sit down?"

His chin tilted toward his couch. Thorn's blood suddenly pulsed like syrup through a straw.

She wanted to sit down, to rip her ribcage open and bear

the scars on her soul, to admit to Abraham that she'd descended into hell on that very same fucking couch weeks ago only to wake up screaming with the stench of death caked inside her nostrils. She *wanted* to sit down for a good talk and an even better cry.

Instead, she pressed her lips shut, shook her head, and promptly walked out of the room.

Abraham called after her. "My door's always open!"

Thorn bolted through the lounge and into her own office so quickly she didn't even turn on the lights. For a few seconds, she sat in the dark, her spine pressed against the wall, breath shallow.

Her phone buzzed in her pocket.

She drew the device out to the same deluge of unanswered texts. Darius, checking in like he did every single day. Mackenzie, inviting the entire Underground to a party in the courtyard on Christmas morning. Gabe, giving Thorn the TAC updates Chris used to send her. And Abraham...

He'd sent her a LymeLite video.

She frowned and opened the link. An older woman filled her screen, dressed in a sleek tank top, arms coated in tattoos, standing before a bookshelf full of monochromatic titles. The caption above her read, "How To Manage Your PTSD Triggers At Home."

Thorn glanced at the wall over her shoulder, where she could make out the cold shape of Abraham settling back at his desk. She looked at her phone, read the caption again...

And hit play.

CHAPTER TWENTY-FIVE

Darius was six when he stopped believing in Christmas magic.

Garret Jones had lost another job and coped the only way he knew how: with whiskey. Jack Daniels wasn't a therapist, but it *was* cheaper, more accessible, and didn't make the man think too hard about the bad decisions that led him here. Instead, he escaped from them.

Unfortunately, his paychecks escaped with him. Santa brought Darius nothing more than a new pair of shoes, bound together with ribbon, and a stocking full of overripe oranges. While Garret's hangover kept him in bed, Ayda had helped Darius tie his laces and walked him to the corner store, where they counted out enough change to buy a tube of cookie dough. They baked them right when they got home, laughing and dancing to the neighbor's holiday music coming through the thin walls until Garret yelled to keep it down. Then, they shared their cookies over whispered stories and dreams. Darius never even realized they hadn't had dinner that night, too full of sugar to care. As far as he was concerned, it was the best Christmas ever.

Until he went to throw his paper plate away and found the box for his shoes buried in the trash, a sale sticker slapped on the side.

It all came crashing down like a boot on a cockroach. Suddenly, he understood why there were never any gifts under their little, plastic tree with his mom's name; why the kids at school bragged about video games and fancy toys when he was lucky to get a book; why his mother always insisted Santa would prefer they leave out carrots for the reindeer so Darius should eat the gingerbread they made himself.

He glanced back at the couch, where she was staring at an old screen, watching a show on silent to not disturb her husband, and he realized…

Santa Claus wasn't some big man in a red suit. Santa Claus was here, in this room, doing it all alone. All for him.

After Ayda Jones had died, Darius quit celebrating Christmas altogether.

Then he'd come to the Underground, and *this* was beyond anything he'd seen yet.

When Darius stepped into the courtyard, his lips slipped open.

"Whoa…"

Mackenzie usually set up a handful of decorations and called it good, but this year, she'd sent out multiple Underground-wide invitations (marked as "URGENT" and "MANDATORY") to every Martyr in the system. As far as Darius could tell, they'd *all* shown up.

People packed in, from the break room to the kitchen, the elevator to the huge tree in the center of the wide, open room. As Darius walked closer, the smells of fresh waffles, maple sausage, and hot cocoa wafted to him, and his mouth watered like he hadn't eaten in days. The wrought iron tables had been pulled together and draped in overlapping red and white linens, giving the illusion of candy cane stripes down the dining area. Souls gathered so closely together that they felt like one massive, beautiful life.

Except Mackenzie. Her aura tucked into the kickboxing studio on the eastern wall of the courtyard. Darius frowned and approached the room. The door had been left ajar, and Nicholas's voice erupted through.

"I am *not* wearing that."

"Awe, c'mon!" the Irishwoman pleaded. Her energy leaned forward, and Darius felt the warm shape of her hands come together, as though presenting a holy item with adoration. "The kids *need* a Santa Claus!"

Nicholas scoffed. "The kids? Mackenzie, there's *one kid!* I'm not wearing the suit!"

"Just the hat, then."

"No!"

Darius smirked and stepped away. Their argument instantly vanished in a burst of cheerful noise. Overhead speakers buzzed with holiday music, both classic and contemporary, while jokes and stories and conversations spilled into the beats between numbers. More than half the Martyrs hadn't bothered changing out of their pajamas and the ones that had still wore comfortable, casual clothing. The warmth, the *normalcy*, left a strange ache in Darius's chest— an uncomfortable blend of joy and guilt that he should feel this joy at all. When he looked around, he couldn't help but notice the people who *weren't* here today—the empty spaces left like gaping wounds between the living.

But he smiled anyway, not for him, but for *them*. For Parker and Marcus Boseman, who held up mugs of cocoa as Darius passed by. For John Waters, who sat with the other Recon agents back from assignment in the city just for today before getting back to it. For Gabe and Chris—especially Chris, who got up from her chair to wrap Darius in a warm hug like all the hurt in the last week wasn't worth holding onto anymore. Gabe shook his hand, and Darius started to think things could go back to normal, or they could carve a new kind of normal out of the rubble. He saw Daniel Park helping Kenia make the next round of breakfast, Raquel and Skylar kissing under a sprig of mistletoe, and even Samira and Leroy Khoury sitting at the edge of the counter with Abraham after flying down to surprise him late last night.

This room was full of love.

Darius glanced around again, searching the sea of people one last time for one last face, but he knew he wouldn't see her. His heart twinged, and he twisted back, seeking out another.

Lindsay's Virtuous allure drew him toward the western edge, where fewer Martyrs had gathered. She wedged between Michelle and David, dressed in snowman-themed, footed jammies. Two squished Frosty faces kicked to and fro beneath her as she devoured a plate of peppermint waffles. When Darius materialized through the crowd, Lindsay's beautiful, brown eyes were already on him. The little girl thrust her hand into the air.

"Hi, Darius!" Smears of syrup stretched from the corners of her mouth, making her grin seem wider. "Sit with us!"

He smiled and settled onto one of the empty chairs across from the little family. Michelle and David glanced up, but the smirks they shared felt more like a force of habit than real happiness.

"Merry Christmas," Darius said. "How's your first holiday in the Underground?"

"It's great, thank you," Michelle answered. She cast a glance around the courtyard. "It's... very elaborate."

Darius chuckled. "It's usually not," he admitted. "Mackenzie went all out this year."

David frowned, and Darius cleared his throat. He didn't want to dig too much into it—to have to explain how the Underground reveled over their daughter's Virtue while David and Michelle were still clearly grieving everything it would cost her. So instead, he turned to the child.

"What about you?" he asked, brows high. "Looks like you made out like a bandit!"

Lindsay's face lit up. "Yeah!" She wiped her sticky fingers against her pajamas before dragging her modest pile of presents closer. "Wanna see?"

Darius threw his hands up. "Heck yeah, I wanna see!"

She dove in, pulling each item out with the same enthusiasm as the one before it. A winter jacket and warm boots. Gloves with plush faux fur lining. A four-pack of assorted hot cocoa mixes. New shoes. A frog-shaped toothbrush. And, her favorite, a brand-new teddy bear with dandelion yellow fur and a bowtie the color of lilacs. She'd named him Sunny.

Darius watched patiently, listened earnestly, but he couldn't help but notice everything matched the kind of gifts he'd gotten as a kid—more "must-have" than "for-fun" items.

"Ho, ho, ho!"

Darius looked up as Mackenzie stomped toward the table, and he grinned.

The Irishwoman wasn't wearing pajamas or other comfortable clothing but a full-body reindeer onesie, complete with limp antlers and a light-up red nose affixed to the hood, which draped over her freshly-dyed emerald hair. She'd done her makeup to match, painting the underside of her nose and upper lip in brown liner to give herself a distinctly cervine look. Over one shoulder, Mackenzie slung a big, golden sack. Over the other, Nicholas rolled his eyes beneath a Santa hat's fur rim.

"Look who it is!" Mackenzie exclaimed. She dropped the sack at Nicholas's feet so she could use both hands to gesture at him with car-salesman gusto. "Old Saint *Nick!*"

A chorus of snickers roused from Martyrs at nearby tables. Nicholas heaved a sigh. The red suit sagged around his shoulders and waist. "Jesus Christ. Did you rope me into this for that damned joke?"

Mackenzie elbowed him in the ribs, winking at Lindsay. "Don't mind Santa. Some naughty elves sprinkled reindeer droppings into his hot buttered rum last night, so he's feeling a little grumpy." The girl snickered, and before Nicholas could open his mouth to show just how grumpy he could be, Mackenzie dropped to her knees and plunged shoulder-deep into the bag.

"But he *did* come bearing gifts. It's just... in... here... gah! Hold on... Ah hah!"

After a dramatic show of digging around, she pulled out a white, lidded box bound in red ribbon. Lindsay clambered onto her knees as Mackenzie placed the present on the table. The girl untied the bow, popped open the top, and peered inside.

"Art stuff!" Lindsay squealed. She shoved her hands into the box and pulled out paints, brushes, and plastic pallets. Darius peeked over the rim to see boxes of colored pencils, fancy drawing paper, a small easel, and more, clumsily organized inside. Lindsay beamed. "Thank you, Mr. Nicholas!"

"Old Saint Nick," Mackenzie corrected to a groan from Nicholas. "And you're very welcome, sweetheart."

"How did 'Old Saint Nick' manage to pull this off?" Darius asked as he cast Mackenzie a dubious look.

Nicholas scowled. "He's been wondering that himself."

Mackenzie waved them away. "Christmas *magic,* obviously." When Darius and Nicholas responded with raised brows and crossed arms, she grinned. "Magic to the tune of an anonymous benefactor who generously donated time, materials, *and* money from his personal account. Emphasis on 'anonymous,' so shut up and have fun."

She flounced off in a manner that made her look like an awkward deer trying to prance. Darius frowned and considered the collection of art supplies now laid out in front of Lindsay.

An anonymous benefactor? Who could have...

His eyes shot wide, and Darius searched the sea of Martyrs until he found Cain Guttuso.

The Forgotten Envy stood near the counter, a glass of red wine in one hand, the other pressed into his pocket, while he talked with Colette Harris. His Familiar sat upon a stool by his side, tail flicking, bright orange gaze observing the courtyard like a proud teacher at graduation. That gaze caught Darius, and Cain looked up. He smiled, raised his glass, and Darius melted like a patch of ice under the sun.

He supposed Mackenzie was right. There was Christmas magic at work, right in this room, with salt-and-pepper hair and half a soul.

"Darius?" Lindsay asked. He turned back. She clutched the box of colored pencils, and he noticed she'd placed two pieces of paper on the table, one for herself and one for him. "Will you draw with me?"

Darius's heart soared into his throat as he remembered every other child who'd ever asked him something like that.

"I would *love* to."

They drew whatever Lindsay's little brain could come up with—squirrels and school buses and squat little dogs chewing on sticks. Darius's sketches were a mess, but they made the little girl smile, which made him feel like the most talented artist alive. Minutes later, Saul and Juniper joined them, and the courtyard filled and flourished. As people finished breakfast, they brought out board games, and Holly set up an old projector and screen to show holiday movies near the tree. A bunch of TAC agents sat in front of it, dragging chairs over to create a makeshift theater. Darius glanced up as a recent retelling of *A Christmas Carol* flickered on the screen. The ghost of Yet To Come descended into the room, face shrouded, shoulders cloaked in black satin, and for a heart-stopping moment, Edith Froschlin interrupted his thoughts.

Saul's voice drew Darius back to the table.

"What's that?" he asked, leaning over to look at Juniper's drawing.

Michelle and David had gone to talk to Samira, leaving the three of them with Lindsay. The girl sat to Saul's left and peered over at June's paper, too.

"What do you mean, what is it?" Juniper defended with a smile, but a brush of pink colored her nose beneath the freckles. "It's a snake!"

"A *snake?*" Saul raised a playful brow. "Which end is the head?"

He grinned, and Juniper rolled her paper up to smack

him on the shoulder with it. Saul took cover beneath his arms before pulling Lindsay in front of him like a little human shield. She dissolved into giggles, and then, all three of them were laughing with her. For a wonderful, isolated moment, Darius traveled back more than three years to a life he'd cherished, a life he sometimes still visited in his dreams, without Sins and Virtues and destiny. A hard life, but a simple one.

"All right," Saul said once the revelry settled. He placed Lindsay back onto her chair. "What next, *princesita?*"

She tore another four pieces of paper from her new pad and handed them out. Her lips pressed together in a thoughtful frown before her eyes lit up. "Sparkie!"

Darius's heart skipped while Juniper froze. "I'm sorry, sweetheart," she began as Saul reached for the box of pencils. "...*What* do you want to draw?"

"Sparkie," Lindsay repeated. She grabbed some crayons and started scribbling. "You know, Thorn's baby dragon. He's *so* cute!"

Juniper's face went a deeper shade of pink, which only Darius seemed to notice. She tucked her hands beneath the table as Saul tilted his head in Lindsay's direction. "Is he a dragon or a lizard?"

She shrugged. "He *looks* like a dragon."

Lindsay got back to coloring as though that settled the matter, and a moment of silence followed while she and Saul worked. Darius drew the colored pencils toward himself, thumbed through them until he found a deep blue and blood red, and slid the box to June. Then he dragged the blue across his empty canvas in a single, gliding stroke he imagined would make up the Familiar's spine. A gentle tingle ran up his own back.

Jesus, why did this feel so... *intimate?* Sketching out the bared open part of Thorn's soul?

He tried not to focus on that—to approach this latest piece the same way he had the others—but with every line committed, he thought about the creature itself. The sudden thud of Sparkie's body slamming into his chest after he'd woken up from that coma. The chilling sensation of his head nuzzled beneath Darius's jawline when he'd held Thorn in his arms. The way he'd felt damn near lifeless in Darius's palms while Wrath tortured Thorn, and the dizzying relief when he'd finally woken up—when *she'd* finally woken up. It all flooded out, pigment to paper, and Darius found himself so engrossed in what he was doing that he didn't notice a shadow looming over his shoulder until he finished filling in the Familiar's beady, black eyes.

"I didn't know you were an artist, Jones," a quiet voice murmured.

Darius jumped and spun to see Thorn standing behind him. He couldn't tell if there was a pink tint to her cheeks or if he was imagining a mirror to the way his own stung. He glanced back at his sketch—at the off proportions, scratchy line work, and uneven color—realizing suddenly just how *awful* it was and mortified Thorn had seen it at all.

"We're drawing Sparkie!" Lindsay exclaimed as she held up her paper. "I made him a dragon! Look!"

Lindsay's rendition took a lot of creative liberties, giving the lizard a long neck, extra legs, and a ridge of black spikes down his spine that looked remarkably like thorns. She'd also added a plume of fire spouting from his open mouth. It didn't matter if the lines were messy or the colors bled past them; it was a masterpiece if Darius ever saw one.

Thorn laughed. "I see that."

Her eyes took in the table, from Saul's version, which was black and white and crystal clear, to the blank sheet in front of Juniper, and then Darius's. She leaned over him, shrouding him in sandalwood and vanilla as she reached for his page. Her long hair flowed around the crook of her neck and brushed against his arm, sending electrical currents through his skin with every single strand. Sparkie appeared, and together, the pair considered Darius's work. Seeing the real thing side by side with his monstrous attempt made him even more self-conscious. When she glanced at him, his breath caught.

"This is great," Thorn said.

Darius didn't think his face could flush any hotter. He scratched the back of his neck with a chuckle. "Well, then it's yours. A Darius Jones original, the first *and last* of his best work."

Thorn tilted her chin, one slender brow arched in a delicate curve. "How thoughtful. And I didn't get you anything."

A smile slid across her face in that gentle, teasing way that made Darius's chest come to life. Without stopping to consider the audience, the implication, or the consequence, he said, "You're here. That's the best gift I could have asked for."

Thorn's smile vanished, her lips parting just enough to expose a flash of white teeth. Now, he was certain of the light dusting of color across her cheeks. Sparkie disappeared down her back as she drew her hair behind an ear and cleared her throat, tearing her focus away.

"Well, I just wanted to wish you all a Merry Christmas." Thorn looked around the others before eventually landing on Darius again. She held up his drawing. "Thank you."

She made to leave, but Darius jumped to his feet. "Wait." He touched her arm. "Why don't you join us?"

A subtle frown knitted her brows, and her gaze flicked to Juniper before she shook her head. "I haven't eaten yet."

"Neither has Darius," Saul suddenly chimed in. They turned to him, and he barely managed to hide a grin behind a row of curled knuckles as his shoulders rose and fell in a half-shrug. "Go get some food."

His brown eyes flashed to Darius, gleaming and clever, while the coldness of Juniper's mood washed off her as clear as an aura.

"But we're spending time with Lindsay," she said.

"Right, and next up, we're drawing a toad in a tutu." Saul curved toward the little girl, one elbow propped upon the table as he lifted his pencil. "What do you think, *princesita?*

A big, pink tutu."

Lindsay giggled. "Yeah!"

She vaulted to the middle of the table for a green crayon, tongue pinched between her teeth. Saul boomed a laugh from the pit of his belly. Then, he and Lindsay were lost in their art, and Darius and Thorn stepped away. As they headed toward the kitchen, he cast a final look over his shoulder just in time to catch Juniper hissing something to Saul before storming to the western wing of rooms.

"I'm sorry," Thorn said. She watched Juniper's retreating back, too. "I never meant to cause so many problems for you."

"You aren't," Darius insisted. She glanced at him, a pair of matching, vertical lines creasing between her brows. He nudged her with an arm. "I'm exactly where I want to be."

Thorn considered him, holding his gaze until Darius thought he might tumble right into it and fall endlessly through those bottomless, black eyes. Then she turned away, rolled his sketch up, and tucked it behind her back. By the time they reached the kitchen, both it and her Familiar had disappeared.

"Thorn!" Mackenzie called out. Her reindeer hood had fallen, exposing her vibrant green pixie cut and a pair of round, tearful eyes. She threw her arms open. Darius was sure she intended to wrap them around Thorn, but by some miracle, she kept them to herself. When she spoke, the words came breathlessly, as though she were pushing them through a gale of emotion. "I wasn't sure you were going to come!"

A soft, uncomfortable laugh passed Thorn's lips as she glanced around the courtyard. "You took over the Underground. I'm not sure it was possible *not* to come."

Mackenzie grinned so wide that it wrinkled the bridge of her nose and tugged her eyes into half-moon slits. "Yeah! That was kind of the point. C'mon! Lamar's making peppermint grasshoppers!"

She grabbed Thorn by the hand before she could argue

and dragged her toward the far end of the dining area. Darius chuckled as he trailed after them. A handful of stools stood off to the side. Naomi sat upon one while Lamar danced behind the counter, a cocktail shaker rattling in his palm. A smile burst to life on his face.

"Well, well," he said, propping one hand upon his hip. He'd traded his signature blue makeup for a brush of golden eyeshadow that made his warm eyes feel alive as he winked. "Would you look at that? My favorite customers."

He tilted the contents of his shaker into a Collins glass, its edge rimmed in chocolate shavings. The drink itself was white, but he'd drizzled red syrup along the inside, giving the whole thing a distinctly holiday feel. As Mackenzie tugged Thorn closer, he handed it off to her.

"It's not scotch," the young Virtue said, "but it *is* good."

"And you'll hurt his feelings if you don't drink it," Naomi added with a dry shrug, pulling a strand of vibrant, scarlet hair around her shoulder.

Lamar poked out his tongue. "It's true. I'm a *very* sensitive man."

Thorn took a sip. Syrup clung to her upper lip, tinting it in a brush of red that made Darius's cheeks catch fire. She licked it clean, and he cast his attention to the floor.

"What do you think?" Lamar asked.

Thorn nodded. "Not bad."

Lamar clapped his hands together. "You heard it here, folks! *Not bad.*" He tossed Thorn an impish look, which she responded to by rolling her eyes. Then, he turned to Darius. "What about you, hon? I have a virgin batch in the back…"

Darius laughed. "Sure."

With a twirl, Lamar sauntered away from the counter, vanished inside the industrial refrigerator, and returned with a pitcher of some pre-mixed solution the color of freshly fallen snow. Mackenzie leapt onto an open stool, and Darius pulled one out for Thorn before settling beside her. As Lamar prepared Darius's glass, an aura-less figure appeared at his shoulder.

"What the hell are you making, Lamar?" Nicholas asked. "And can you make it a double?"

Lamar glanced up, a playful smile upon his face. "For you, handsome? Absolutely." He poured Darius's mocktail, slid it over, and began to put the ingredients for Nicholas's drink into the shaker. "Where's the suit?"

Nicholas scoffed as he dragged a stool around and wedged himself between Mackenzie and Darius. He'd traded the oversized jacket and baggy pants for a white cable knit sweater and black slacks. He'd kept the hat, though, wearing it askew over his blonde hair.

"Fuck that suit. The thing was a goddamned tent."

A delicate brow arched on Lamar's head as he strained the cocktail into a prepared glass. "Mmm. Well, I like the new look." He held the peppermint grasshopper out. "It's very… *Daddy Claus.* "

Naomi snorted. Nicholas glanced at her with a frown. "What the hell does that mean?"

"It means," Mackenzie said, propping her chin into one palm as the other hand reached toward his face. Her nails trailed down Nicholas's cheek, dragging through the beard from his temple to his jaw at an agonizing pace, "that you're a *sexy* Santa."

She winked, and Lamar and Naomi burst into howling laughter. Nicholas turned so bright red that his freckles all but vanished upon his skin, and he downed half of his drink in four deep gulps. Darius grinned, and even Thorn broke into a pure, stunning smile that made her eyes light up like a sea of stars on a deep, moonless night.

The afternoon carried on, Lamar making more drinks as other Martyrs joined in until the length of the counter resembled a bar. Kenia packed uneaten food into containers as Cain helped Lamar hand out alcohol, but where Lamar crafted more beautiful cocktails, Cain simply poured generous glasses of wine Darius imagined must have come from some secret collection. Soon, Saul wound his arms around Darius and Thorn's shoulders before he scooted a chair over to join them. Darius laughed and looked around.

He had *never* seen the Underground like *this*.

The Harris family grabbed a nearby table, the boys sucking down a couple of the same mocktails Darius and Mackenzie were enjoying while their parents sipped zinfandel. Parker, Amelia, and Skylar converted the movie screen into a karaoke stage, which John Waters and Madison Lewis used to rouse the crowd into a toneless chorus of an old Christmas duet. Martyrs created a makeshift dance floor around them, bouncing to the beat. Leroy and Samira twirled along, him spinning her wheelchair in circles while she held Lindsay on her lap, and the child bubbled with laughter. Away from the throng, tucked quietly behind a trellis, Chris and Gabe whispered below a net of golden lights. Gabe smiled against Chris's mouth, wrapped a hand behind her head, and pulled her in for a passionate kiss.

Darius took it all in, the love and light, until his heart expanded into every dark corner of his chest, chasing the shadows away.

Then, the tickling sensation of eyes upon his back made him turn.

Thorn watched him, spine curved in a gentle arc toward the counter where she palmed a tumbler of neat scotch. Sparkie had returned and wound around her throat. While the courtyard pulsed, the air between Darius and Thorn stilled with a sudden, heated silence. He smiled and extended his hand.

Without a breath of hesitation, she released her glass and took it. Her fingers laced between his, soft and sacred. Darius's stomach vaulted skyward with a pair of newfound wings.

He saw it now—the little steps, the forward momentum, the peak of that mountain still in the distance, but not so far that it felt insurmountable. A flood of relief washed down his back and threatened to bring him to his knees before her, and god, what a privilege that would be.

Suddenly, a plate of warm chocolate chip cookies landed

beside them, matching nine others lining the counter.

"All right, ya filthy animals," Mackenzie screamed over the noise. "One per person! Don't get greedy! It's fuckin' Christmas!"

A new wave rushed the kitchen. Thorn and Darius tucked together as people pushed in on all sides. Before he knew it, her palm landed upon his thigh, his arm hooked behind her back, and the tempting scent of sandalwood and vanilla made his mouth water. When the crowd pulled away, Thorn didn't, and Darius couldn't move for fear of losing the feeling of her pressed up against him.

Lamar appeared with a stack of plastic cups and a gallon of milk. He poured them all and held his up, gold nails catching the light. "Cheers!"

He broke his cookie in two and dipped it into his milk. Mackenzie did the same. Nicholas took a bite and then a sip. Mackenzie paused with a soggy cookie halfway to her mouth.

"The *fuck* are you doing, Wolfe?"

He frowned. "What do you mean what the fuck am I doing?"

"I mean *that*," she said as he took another bite before tipping more milk through his lips. "You're supposed to *dunk* your cookie. Not... whatever *that* blasphemy is!"

Nicholas arched a brow. "And ruin a perfectly good glass of milk?"

Mackenzie's eyes shot wide, and she slammed her cup down like he'd insulted her religion. "Ruin? You mean *improve!* Drinking the cookie milk at the end is the best part!"

Nicholas scoffed. "Only a sociopath likes lukewarm milk with crumbs at the bottom."

A rumble of chuckling rolled through the Martyrs, but before Mackenzie could argue, Darius's phone buzzed in his pocket. Thorn's must have, too, because she extricated herself from his hold to take it out. Down the counter, Nicholas and Mackenzie did the same, and a nervous, dangerous sensation prickled up Darius's spine. He turned on his screen to a message from Holly.

"We have a Froschlin situation."

Darius's body numbed, and suddenly, the happy voices dancing around him sounded canned and distant. He looked up to Thorn. She'd gone white, and the pupils in the center of her black irises tightened into sharp points. Those eyes met Darius's before glancing at Nicholas and Mackenzie.

They all moved at once, getting to their feet, floating through the Martyrs in a straight shot to the elevator. Chris met them halfway. Abraham, too. The six directors stepped onto the lift, and Mackenzie's hand trembled as she tapped the top floor button over and over again until the doors slid shut.

Thorn called Holly on speaker. The security lead picked up on the first ring, and Thorn spoke before she could say a word. "What's going on?"

"There's an attack at the Winter Village Market in Bryant Park," Holly said.

"How long did she give us?" Chris asked. "I can have people there in—"

"You didn't hear me," Holly cut in. "There *is* an attack. Right now. I'm sending the livestream to the conference room."

Darius shook his head. "Edith didn't text the burner?"

"She did." Holly's voice took on a dark timbre. "It said, 'Merry Christmas, Mourning Dove.'"

Thorn's eyes sharpened, and her fingers tightened around her phone. The second the elevator stopped, she sprinted through the upper level and burst into the conference room, where she froze on the threshold.

"Oh my god," she whispered.

Darius and the others squeezed around her. Chris gasped, and Abraham covered a gaping mouth with his palm.

A woman who looked like Thorn—*exactly* like Thorn, from the black hair, dark eyes, and fingerless gloves— opened fire on the crowd. Piercing screams rang through the speakers as Christmas day shoppers stampeded between glass-paneled booths. A host of people lay strewn down the pathways, motionless beneath bulky winter coats.

"Obviously, this is some kind of deepfake," Holly said. Thorn took a stuttering step backward, and her phone tumbled from her hand. Holly was still speaking as it hit the ground. "They must have scanned a hundred pictures of your face to get a filter this accurate."

Nicholas swore and spun from the room, disappearing down the hall. He slammed the door to the R&D Headquarters with a bang like a gunshot. Thorn's body jerked. Mackenzie snatched her phone off the floor.

"But you said this is *live*," she shouted. "I thought you couldn't make live deepfakes!"

"You can," Holly said, "but they're easier to discredit. Other people can have footage proving it's fake—if there's anyone alive to *take* footage."

The Thorn on the screen drew a baton from a sheath at her back and swung. It crashed into a man's skull. The sound of bone breaking crackled through the room. As he crumbled into a crimson heap, she cackled. Darius caught a sense of the person behind the digital mask. Those mannerisms. Those movements.

They belonged to Edith Froschlin.

"She's making *Thorn* the monster," Abraham breathed.

Chris blanched. "We need to get down there."

She ran from the room, too. Mackenzie shook her head furiously. "What the fuck do we *do*, Holly?"

Sparkie let out a wailing scream as Thorn's spine collided with the doorframe. Darius watched the mountainside crumble beneath her, dragging her into hell all over again. Her eyes pooled, hands shook, chest heaved in great, gasping breaths. She lurched into the hall. Darius chased after her.

"Thorn!"

She ignored him, or maybe she didn't hear him. Thorn moved through the hallways like a phantom—all haze and horror—until she reached her office. When she tried to slam the door behind her, Darius shouldered his way in.

"Thorn, wait—"

"Wait for *what?*" She spun around. Every muscle in her body trembled. "For Edith Froschlin to kill more people wearing *my fucking face?*"

Sparkie screeched from her shoulder before diving beneath the couch. Darius's heart drummed a furious rhythm against his sternum.

"We'll fix it," he said. "Nicholas is already—"

Thorn barked out a scoff. "How can we *fix it?* I'm *stuck* down here, fucking *useless*, and even if I weren't, it doesn't matter! They *hate* me!" Even her voice shook now. She dragged her fingers through her hair, twisting them, pulling like she meant to rip her scalp straight down the center. A sudden rush of tears flickered behind her lashes, and her arms dropped. "Abraham is wrong. Edith isn't *making* me a monster. I already am one!"

Darius came closer. "Thorn, stop—"

"No, Darius, *you* stop!" she shouted. Sobbed. Every syllable she spat pierced between his ribs like a bullet. "Stop acting like it didn't happen! Like you didn't see what I did! They *should* be scared of me! You should all be fucking scared—"

"Thorn!" He couldn't do it anymore—couldn't stand here and watch her carve pieces off of herself for another goddamned second. He cleared the space in four steps and wrapped his hands around Thorn's face. His fingers cradled the back of her skull as she gasped, and his thumbs smoothed against the tears now streaming freely down her cheekbones. Her fists met his chest, but not to push him away. They curled into his shirt right above his pounding heart.

"I am *not* scared of you!" Darius said. "I have *never* been scared of you. I'm scared of *losing* you." Thorn's breath rattled against him, and his throat constricted. "God, Thorn, I'm fucking *terrified.*"

Her body went rigid then fluid in a sudden stroke, and her eyes—those deep, endless, *perfect* eyes—melted into his. Her grip loosened in the fabric, and she began tapping her thumbs to each and every fingertip. Darius let out a short, wrenching laugh. He tilted forward until their foreheads pressed together just to savor the cool warmth of her soulless skin.

Thorn's tapping stilled. Her hold relaxed.

Then, it twisted back into his shirt, and she closed the gap between them.

Her lips met his with a fury, intimate and insatiable. A stunning starburst of sensation spiraled through Darius, from his face to his fingertips, his gut to his groin. Thorn's hands clawed their way around his neck, where her nails dug into the skin just below his hairline, and a chilling current trickled down his spine. She taunted his mouth open, teasing him with the tip of her tongue and a sigh in her throat.

Then she drew away just enough to hiss a haggard word against his teeth.

"Fuck…"

Darius's stomach dipped.

Fuck.

He needed to taste her again.

Darius buried his fingers into Thorn's hair and pulled her chin back. Her lips parted with invitation, and she pushed against him so forcefully that he stumbled. His thighs crashed into her desk, and one palm flew out to steady him, sending a flurry of loose paper fluttering to the carpet. Thorn pressed her body into his, and the swell of her breasts grazed his heaving chest. He felt every touch, every curve, every *movement* with excruciating clarity. The silken glide to her skin. The sweet sting of her teeth. The sultry heat in each stuttered exhale. When she slipped one of her legs between his, he gasped.

Thorn caught it. Her tongue entangled his in a masterful dance, and Darius responded with an animal need he couldn't stop even if he'd wanted to. The front of his slacks grew tight, and he grabbed her by the waist to crush her closer. Thorn rocked her hips, pinning him to the wood, and he let out an involuntary moan right into her open mouth. She breathed it down with another kiss, this one rougher than the last, like she'd been trapped underwater, and he was the first surge of fresh air to enter her lungs in a century.

Then her fingers trailed a fervid line down his sternum, his navel, his pelvis—and she grabbed a handful of him. A husky sound bubbled from Darius's chest.

"Thorn," he managed to get out.

She hummed along his throat before marking a series of searing kisses from his jawline to the dip at his clavicle. Her palm explored the length of him with just enough pressure to make his head swim and knees buckle. His lower back arched into her touch, grinding himself against her. Thorn pinched the button at his waistband. It popped open with a snap.

Darius grabbed her wrist. "Thorn, wait," he rasped. "We can't—"

"We can." She silenced him with another hungry kiss and dragged her nails down his zipper. Darius turned his face away.

"No," he said. The word burned in his mouth. "Not now. Not while you're—"

His voice slammed to a stop. She froze. "While I'm *what?*"

He didn't know how to say it, but with his senses tumbling into order, he knew he was right. Thorn's black eyes glittered, but salt-stained trails streaked her porcelain skin beneath them. The pattering of frantic energy around the top level of the Underground forced his mind out of this moment. He swallowed hard.

"With what Edith is doing—"

"This has *nothing* to do with her!" Thorn growled.

She drew away, and the pink flush across her cheeks deepened. Darius exhaled a sigh.

"Doesn't it?"

Thorn bristled. Sparkie scurried out from the couch to climb upon her shoulder. "You think I'm using you as an *escape?*"

Darius's heart fractured behind his ribs as she voiced it aloud because...

"Yeah," he admitted quietly. "I do." He shook his head. "And I want *more* than that, Thorn."

She choked out a scoff, took another step back, and stared at him. But she didn't speak, didn't even try to defend herself, which almost hurt more. Darius wished she'd say something, *do* something, to make him feel wanted.

But she just turned around and vanished through the open door.

CHAPTER TWENTY-SIX

He lingered for hours.

His touch. His taste. His tantalizing scent, rich and earthen and *intoxicating.* Thorn couldn't escape the memory of his lips pressed to hers, the satisfying scratch of his stubble grating her chin, the way he swelled into her palm. Ready for her. *Wanting* her.

But his final words hung like a noose around her neck.

"I want more *than that, Thorn."*

More than hot kisses, rough hands, and a hard fuck on an office desk. More than sex without sentiment, than passion without connection, than *lust* without *love.*

More than she'd dared to offer anyone in a lifetime.

Thorn wanted more, too. She'd wanted to say so, to shout it with her whole fucking chest, to scream until her throat ripped so wide her accelerated healing wouldn't be able to fix it.

But instead, she'd said *nothing,* because that was all she had. All she was. He wanted *more,* but even giving him all of herself meant giving him an empty husk, a broken vessel with deep gouges that couldn't hold water, let alone a human heart.

A howl built up within Thorn's chest, scraping for a

release, but she didn't let it out.

She couldn't risk waking the Underground.

It was cemetery silent at three in the morning. Thorn passed through the courtyard like a ghost. Sparkie glided overhead, searching through Christmas decor for any movement without an aura, but all he saw were empty glasses, skewed chairs, and debris from a party no one had bothered to clean up yet. Cold energy circled them, Martyrs in their beds, deep in the residential wings. Thorn reached the door to the stairwell and pulled it open. Its hinges hissed, and she drew a slow inhale to match. Sparkie landed on the backpack across her shoulders with a dull thump. When Thorn closed them inside, she held the handle down so the mechanism didn't click.

Then, they made their way to the lowest level.

When Thorn had left Darius in her office, she returned to the conference room to find the attack had already ended. Local news reports replaced Holly's livestream, and a casualty count at the bottom of the screen kept ticking up as more dead were discovered. Her face, or the digital replication that looked so fucking close even she couldn't tell it didn't belong to her, flashed by. Thorn hardly heard Nicholas say he'd managed to get the video flagged for removal, or Chris announcing that a couple of TAC teams were on their way to do damage control. All Thorn could think, the *whole* damned time, was that Darius was right.

She *was* trying to escape—from Edith, from Wrath, from *all* of it.

And this wouldn't end until they were dead.

Thorn bolted through the basement. Humid air pumped around her, creating a dewy film of moisture at her hairline and along the back of her neck. Down here, the constant drone of water pipes and HVAC systems masked any sounds she could make, so she ran. As she approached the far end, Sparkie launched into a ventilation grate. He tore it down, slipped inside, and scurried through the ducts.

Her Familiar reached the security room before Thorn

did and unlocked the door from inside. A blast of cold air punched her in the gut as she stepped through.

Contrary to popular belief, Holly Andrews *did* sleep, and she didn't do it on a cot under her desk. All her major security systems had automated programs to alert her to red-level threats in the middle of the night. Thorn was grateful that unauthorized access to her office wasn't one of them. Holly's desk sat nearest the entrance, its surface an organized mess of reports, fidget-style toys, and task lists a mile long. The top drawer opened easily. Holly hadn't locked it. She probably didn't think she had to.

She *shouldn't* have to.

Thorn reached inside, pulse pounding in her fingertips, and grabbed Edith Froschlin's burner. Its weight in her palm sent a cascade through her nervous system—a high like injecting methamphetamine right into her brainstem. She ran a thumb across the screen. Turned it on.

"Merry Christmas, Mourning Dove."

The screams from Bryant Park echoed in Thorn's head as she scanned weeks' worth of texts. They spanned the whole spectrum of cybernetic terror. Coordinates and time stamps. Veiled threats and accusations. Taunts. Jeers. *Images.* Edith had sent pictures and videos and goddamned audio recordings of Martyr and civilian deaths in a twisted menagerie of snuff porn that made Thorn want to vomit. And that wasn't the worst part.

A dollar amount. A number for each one of Thorn's people. A cost so high she could hardly comprehend it.

The monstrous fury in Thorn's soul threatened to consume her entirely.

But she stamped it down and shoved the phone into her pocket before closing the desk. There would be time enough for this later, a moment to release the beast and let it sharpen its claws.

Now, she had to get the fuck out of here.

Thorn had already grabbed the essentials: clothes, toiletries, some personal weapons. She could get more from their tactical lockers in the city, but she had to be careful. The system would log her information the second she unlocked the door, and this whole thing would fall apart if they found her. She'd have to leave her helmet and crow mask behind. They came with embedded tracking devices, and Thorn needed to be untraceable.

Which left one more thing…

Her office hummed with an onslaught of scorching emotion. Thorn walked over a collection of papers still strewn about the floor—papers Darius had knocked over when she'd crushed him against her desk. It was all she could do not to think about that—about the way his moans tasted on her tongue, how his fingers carved divots into her waist, and that growing heat pressed against her hip, making it clear that even Virtues had carnal needs. A warm sensation trickled down Thorn's belly, pooling in liquid fire. She picked up the papers, stacked them neatly onto the corner, and grabbed a blank one from the stack.

Figuring out what to write took the longest—longer than planning, than packing, than breaking into Holly's room all combined—and in the end, it didn't feel like enough. Just seven words:

Darius,
I'm sorry. I'll be back.

-Thorn

She stared at her own script, trying to convince herself this wasn't just *another* goddamned escape from the torture her life had become. That it was the right call. For him. For the Underground. For New York City.

Thorn set the pen down, moved the sheet to the center of her desk, and laid her phone upon it. Sparkie whined from her shoulder.

Then, she threw on her motorcycle jacket, hurried into the garage, and walked up the ramp. Her admin override codes opened the car wash from the inside. Thorn stepped into the frigid air, wrapped a scarf around her face, and started walking.

Before the sun even crested the Atlantic, before the first Martyrs cracked open their eyes and yawned into a new day, Thorn had disappeared.

***

News of the Bryant Park incident chilled the Underground like an ice storm.

Darius and the other directors tried not to raise panic, keeping the situation as close to the chest as they could, but Nicholas needed researchers; Holly, her tech team; and Chris sent Gabe's unit into the city to see if there was anything they could do to minimize the damage. All it took was one person, a single whisper, before every Martyr knew. By the time Kenia served Christmas dinner, the magic was gone, and instead of joy and revelry, the courtyard settled into a heavy fog.

That fog followed them into the next day.

Darius sat in the break room at a card table with Juniper, Raquel, and Saul, eyes locked onto the massive television mounted to the wall as news footage rolled by. Every seat was taken by off-duty TAC agents, nurses, and other staff. Stevie and her maintenance crew were supposed to be tearing down the decorations, but instead, they stood along the walls, arms full of tinsel and lights as they watched.

A screenshot of Edith wearing Thorn's image appeared at the corner of the display. Darius's heart plunged.

"The NYPD is on the lookout for this woman, who has gone viral on LymeLite these last few weeks under the name Jane Morgan," the anchor said in a droning, emotionless tone. "Morgan has gained attention through platforms like TruthRebel, where viewers claim she is some supernatural and immortal being. However, I think we can all agree that she is more likely the human kind of monster."

A nervous shuffle hissed through the break room, and Darius's chest bloomed with fire. He propped his elbows on the table and laced his fingers together, pressing them against his lips.

"Concerns have been raised that the video of the attack at Bryant Park was fabricated using advanced AI technology," the anchor went on, "but what was *not* fabricated were the casualties. Over eighty people were killed in the Winter Village Market shooting, many of them children, and dozens of others are in critical care, so that number is expected to rise. Whether Morgan is responsible or not remains to be seen, but until we know more, she is presumed to be armed and very, very dangerous."

Juniper dabbed her glistening eyes with her shirt sleeve. "My god..." she whispered.

Saul cast Darius a serious look. "How's Thorn handling this?"

Darius's breath caught. The imitation of Thorn dominated the screen as details on who to call with information of her whereabouts scrolled down the side. His cheeks flushed red as he thought back to the last time he'd seen her.

"She's not okay," he admitted quietly, but just *how* not okay, he didn't know. He'd texted her when he woke up, asking to talk, but she hadn't responded. Somehow, this one stung worse than every other ignored message.

"How could she be?" Raquel asked. "They used *her face...*"

"Is there anything we can do?" Saul leaned forward, brows pinched together. "To prove she *didn't* do this?"

Raquel offered a hopeless shrug. "Skylar said they're looking for other videos from the incident, which wouldn't have the deepfake filter applied, but so far, they haven't found any, and there's a good chance they won't. Remember how Froschlin was removing clips from Rockefeller Center? She's probably taking all these down, too."

Saul groaned and looked back to the news. *"Puta madre..."*

"You said it," Raquel agreed with a sigh.

"Jones!"

Darius glanced up. Holly stood in the doorway, eyes furious behind thick-rimmed glasses. She waved him over, and Darius got up from the table. Saul and Raquel continued to watch the screen, but Juniper's warm aura moved with him, sticking to his heels like a shadow.

The second he stepped into the courtyard, Holly shouted.

"You *have* to do something about Thorn! I am done dealing with this bullshit!"

Darius hesitated, shaking his head. "What happened?"

"Froschlin's burner!" Holly yelled. "It's gone! She broke into my goddamned office and fucking *took it!*"

The accusation stung his face like a slap, and his jaw dropped.

"How do you know it was Thorn?" Darius asked.

"Because I have it on camera!" Holly pulled out her phone, opened a surveillance app, and selected one of the newer files. A video filled her screen, showing Sparkie tumbling from the ceiling before unlocking the door. Thorn stepped in, pulled out the drawer, and snatched the burner from inside. For a few seconds, she thumbed through the messages before shutting the desk, locking the door, and leaving again. Darius squinted, leaning closer to the screen.

Thorn had a backpack over her shoulders. A big one. And it looked full.

A cold rush plunged down his back. Juniper hovered in the doorway behind him, but he ignored her. "Where did she take it?" he asked Holly.

"I don't know," she said, "and I removed the GPS chip, so I can't trace it! I did try texting the damned thing, but it immediately bounced. Looks like Froschlin set it up to only receive contact from her."

Darius's mouth went dry. Holly went on.

"I need you to go talk to Thorn," she snapped. "This is absolutely unacceptable—"

"What about Thorn's phone?"

Holly's anger flickered toward confusion, and she frowned. "What?"

"Where is Thorn's phone?" Darius asked.

She navigated her device to a tracking app, which showed a glowing green dot for Thorn in the Underground. "Here. She's probably barricaded in her office, antagonizing Froschlin."

"No," Darius murmured, a grip of fear constricting his throat. "Shit. I need to check something. Can you call her? And keep calling until someone picks up."

Holly's eyes narrowed. "Until *someone* picks up? What do you—hey, where the hell are you going?"

Darius bolted toward the elevator, shouting over his shoulder.

"Just call her!"

He ran across the courtyard. Juniper caught up to him.

"What's going on?" she breathed.

Darius's teeth clenched. "Thorn's in trouble."

They reached the stairwell, and Darius vaulted up. Juniper struggled to match his pace, and by the time he burst onto the top level, she was nearly a whole flight beneath him. The rooms here shifted with the normal pattern of energy, but right now, it all felt distant. He sprinted down the hallway, turned the corner, and crashed into the lounge between Thorn's and Alan's offices. When he grabbed her handle, he hoped he was wrong—hoped that she'd locked it.

But it pulled open. Her phone buzzed on the desk, Holly's face glowing from the screen. Darius raised the device, stared at the paper beneath it, and a vise nearly pinched his heart in two.

He answered as Juniper came into the room.

"Holly," he said, lifting Thorn's note in a shaking hand, "she's going after Edith. Check the other security feeds to see what else she did and what time she left. Maybe we can catch up to her."

Darius hung up and stared at Thorn's phone. A list of unanswered calls and texts lined the lock screen. Unanswered not because Thorn was ignoring them.

Because she'd left them.

He slammed the device onto the desk.

"God *damn it!*"

Darius hovered there, hands flat to the wood, chest heaving with panicked breath as he tried to think, just *think*, but his brain wasn't firing right. It flashed backward and forward, ricocheting between that warehouse in Hunts Point to some unknown street in New York City where Thorn had unrestricted access to a psychopath in a raven mask. An unfamiliar blend of rage and fear boiled in his belly.

Juniper spoke tentatively from the doorway.

"Are you okay, Darius?"

He took a slow breath.

"No," he began evenly. Then, he stood bolt upright and raked a hand through his hair. "No! Thorn is going to get herself *killed!*" He started pacing a sloppy line in front of Thorn's desk. His pulse leapt, making his head feel fuzzy. "There are almost fifteen *million* people in New York City, June, and she has a century of experience disappearing there. If she doesn't want to be found, she damn well won't be. Fuck, I don't know what to *do!*"

He stopped pacing. Stopped talking. Nearly stopped breathing. His fist still clutched Thorn's note, and he shakily opened it to read that familiar cursive again.

I'll be back.

She'd said that before... and then she'd walked right into Wrath's open arms.

God, he was going to be sick.

"Why do you have to *do* anything?" Juniper asked.

His head jerked up, brows smashed together. Juniper came further into the room and offered a cold shrug. "She's the one who abandoned the Martyrs."

"She didn't abandon us," Darius started, but Juniper interjected with a scoff—a cutting sound that pierced like the point of a blade.

"She *literally* did," she said. "I don't care what excuse she had for it. She left you alone, *again*, to hold this place together while she goes off and does whatever the hell she wants. She doesn't care about what it does to *you*. She's *self-ish*, Darius, and she doesn't deserve—" Juniper abruptly stopped. Her throat constricted, blue eyes glistening. "She doesn't deserve your loyalty."

Darius shook his head. "What the hell are you saying, June? That I should just let Edith rip her to shreds?"

Juniper's chin tilted up, the "yes" written all over her face in unyielding, almost *emotionless* lines. Darius's lips slipped open.

"What happens to her is *not* your problem," Juniper said. "If Thorn wants to jump off this bridge, maybe you should let her."

The image of Thorn's body tumbling toward the East River slammed into Darius's psyche. For a moment, it was all he could do to just stare at Juniper—at this woman he hardly recognized as his oldest friend anymore. His fists clenched at his sides. "That's an *ugly* thing to say," he managed.

"I'm just telling you what no one else is brave enough to tell you," she replied, drawing nearer. The warmth of her human soul suddenly felt bitter and biting. "She's bad for you."

Juniper reached out and traced a light circle on his arm. Darius tore away from her.

"*That's* what this is about," he muttered. "It's not about the Martyrs. It's not even about Thorn. It's about what you think is happening between Thorn and *me.*"

Her lips curled down. "*Is* something happening?"

He didn't respond. Juniper swallowed, and the next question crawled across her lips like she was terrified of the answer.

"Are you in *love* with her?"

Darius was going to ignore her, but as the question dug

into his brain, it exhumed every memory of Thorn. The way she'd smoke alone on the balcony at Teresa Solomon's estate. Bonding over Chinese food in Georgia when she told him about her scars. Her breath hot against his ear as she demanded a dance, and how the feeling of her in his arms consumed his dreams for weeks after. Every thread of who Thorn was—her secrets, her fears, and her passions—lit up inside his skull. Darius drew in a reverent breath as he admitted to himself for the first time that, fuck…

"Yes," he whispered. "I am."

Hopelessly and completely.

Juniper's eyes filled with tears. "More than you loved me?" she asked, stepping back toward the door. "More than *Eva?*"

Darius pinched the bridge of his nose, choking on a sigh. "Jesus, June, it's not about *more* or *less*. It's just… *different.*"

She nodded, but in that way that meant she completely misunderstood. "It should be *me,*" she murmured, every syllable scraping her throat. "She doesn't love you like *I* love you. She wasn't there for you like *I* was there! She doesn't *deserve* you, but *I do!*"

By the end, Juniper was sobbing, and Darius gawked. He didn't know what to say—didn't know what he *could* say.

"She *left you*, Darius," Juniper continued, "but I never did! Not once! Not after you knocked me up! Not after those drugs Max gave us almost killed me. Not after you *ended it* so you could focus on the orphanage. I stuck around! I helped build that dream—for *you!* Hoping you'd see me again! Hoping you'd *love* me again, but you never did!"

Juniper shook her head. A fresh wave of furious tears crawled free from her lash line, and orange hair fell loose from her clip, wild about her head like strands of flaming filament. Moments flooded back to him—of being nineteen and terrified as Juniper curled up on a ratty towel in a back alley by the market, hemorrhaging so much he was sure she was going to die. He hadn't slept for days, *weeks*. Darius swallowed against a throat as dry as scorched earth.

"I'm so sorry, June," he managed to say. "I never realized you were so angry about our decision—"

"I'm not angry about *my* decisions," Juniper snapped. "I'm angry about *yours.*"

Darius gaped. "I was *a kid!* I was afraid it would happen again, and I didn't want to risk—"

"What about what *I* wanted?" Juniper choked out. "I wanted *you!*"

Silence fell, the sound of his beating heart pounding hard in his ears the only thing Darius could hear.

"Let's leave," Juniper whispered at last. "Please. You're living in a *graveyard*, Darius. Falling in love with ghosts. That little hovel we had in Alphabet City was a hundred times more alive than this cold, dead place. We can start over. Build it again. Build it *better.*" She stepped closer. Grabbed his hands. Brought them together and pressed a kiss against his knuckles. *"Please."*

The feeling of her lips on his skin made Darius ill. He pulled gently out of her grip. She gasped like he'd struck her.

"I can't go," he said.

That withering look contorted her face again. "Because of *her?*"

"No," Darius said. "Because of *me.*"

Juniper withdrew. Her jaw trembled as she backed away, and new rivers flowed down her cheeks.

"Then I'm leaving without you," she muttered tearfully, her voice creaking from her mouth. "I can't wait for you anymore."

He nodded.

"You never should have."

CHAPTER TWENTY-SEVEN

Thorn stood at the edge of a dilapidated parking lot on the southern tip of Manhattan, head high, hood up, and cracked conscience leaden within her chest. A winter storm surged toward the shore, gray clouds and thick fog rolling off the ocean with ominous inevitability, so dense that the boundary between sea and sky disappeared. The old Staten Island Ferry depot jutted into the mist, a scar of broken glass and warped metal on the horizon. Thorn didn't understand why the city hadn't torn it down after Hurricane Annie had slammed into it all those decades ago. Maybe it stood as an homage to better times…

Or maybe, as an omen to worse ones.

A dangerous tickle ran down Thorn's back, making every hair stand on end. She stilled as a cold aura approached.

"Yo, lady!" a man called. "You here for the car?"

Thorn turned around.

He was a scrawny little fuck, no taller than Thorn, but he held himself with an ego big enough to fill out the heavy coat his skin and bones could hardly handle. A hand-rolled cigarette burned between his lips, the glowing cherry at the tip the only color in this gray, dead neighborhood. He thrust a thumb to his left, where a battered old truck with missing plates and chipped paint was parked fifty feet away. Another man leaned against the vehicle. His thick arms and barrel chest made the first guy look like a goddamned child. Clearly, he was here for intimidation.

Thorn dug through her bag of false personas, piecing together the right identity for this particular flavor of fuckery. Her tone remained low and flat as she said, "Sure."

A wormy smile split the first guy's mouth, revealing a straight line of nicotine-yellow teeth. "It'll be six grand."

Thorn frowned behind the red scarf covering the bottom of her face. "Your contact said four."

He snorted. "Yeah, well. Rates just went up." A pair of squinting eyes moved down her body. "That's my offer, sweetheart. Take it or leave it."

Thorn raised a brow and looked around. The fog made it hard to see, but she didn't need to. This area was as empty of human aura as her own soul. Sparkie swooped in and out of the clouds overhead and confirmed what she already knew.

They were alone.

She scoffed a low, lethal laugh.

This was how it always turned out, wasn't it? Wherever she went, someone came for her, and every single encounter deteriorated into a violent haze—a pissing match between the hero and the villain.

And she was always the fucking villain.

"Tell you what." Thorn reached into her satchel, where a wad of cash she'd withdrawn from her Gray Unit account sat like a block of uranium against her thigh, slowly irradiating her. "I'll give you three."

The man's nostrils flared wide enough that he could have shoved two whole blueberries up there and lost them inside his skull. "I ain't here to *negotiate*. I provide the merchandise. You provide the money. No money, no merchandise. And would'ya look at that? Rates just went up again. *Seven grand.*"

Thorn withdrew a fistful of folded hundred-dollar bills. The money may as well have been a baggie of crystal meth for the way it made both men freeze on the spot. Thorn began counting. "I don't have seven," she stated as she flipped through eight, nine, ten crisp, new notes. "How about one?"

She splayed the cash like a winning poker hand. The scrawny guy sneered and jerked his chin. His buddy stepped away from the truck and strode toward them, ham hands clenched.

Thorn smiled. God, she half-wished they could see it.

"I don't think you understand the *situation* you're in here," the little one said. He cracked his neck in a deliberate show that was supposed to be threatening but just made him look pathetic. "I want *seven thousand*... But if you don't have it, there are other ways a pretty little thing like you can pay..."

His narrow eyes raced down Thorn's figure, molesting her with a gaze as foul as the gunk between his teeth. He jerked his pelvis forward. An erection bulged at his groin. Her smile vanished.

That's all she was good for, wasn't it? Fucking and fighting. Because the second you become a victim, these assholes smell it on you forever, like the stench of cigarette smoke embedded in your clothes.

She wanted to cry.

She wanted to *scream*.

"On your knees," he said as his partner closed in. "Put that mouth of yours to work..."

The muscle lunged. Thorn struck the second he came within reach—a cold clock right to the side of his head with the very same fist she clutched her cash. He dropped, and his cohort went flaccid with a yelp.

Thorn grabbed him by the collar before he could bolt.

"How about this, *dickhead?*" she growled behind her scarf. "I'll take this piece of shit off your hands for *free*, and I won't throw you into the East River." She lifted his sneakers from the concrete, left his legs *dangling*, and dragged him so close that her words hissed against his slimy face. "That's my offer, *sweetheart,*" she mocked. "Take it or leave it."

The man shook so hard that his teeth rattled. Suddenly, the warm stink of piss wafted up from his crotch. "I-I take it!" he stammered. "I-I fuckin' take it!"

He dug in his pockets and gave her the keys. Thorn didn't so much drop him as toss him away. He crashed onto the concrete next to his buddy and curled into a fetal position. Thorn walked over, glaring at him.

She had nothing left to lose. Not out here, at least.

Thorn stomped on his ribcage just for good measure. She told herself it was to teach him a lesson, but her throat soured nevertheless as he cried out. When he finally looked up, she was gone, and the truck's taillights glowed like red eyes through the fog.

A dreary, gray haze coated Manhattan, like even the weather knew what a bleak occasion this all was.

Darius sat awkwardly in the front seat of a Martyr sedan, staring out the window while Juniper's malcontent aura hovered behind his back. He hadn't planned on joining when Cain drove her into New York City, but the old Forgotten Envy insisted that he'd regret not having this final chance to say goodbye, so… here he was.

"We're almost there," Cain announced. He glanced into the rearview mirror, but Juniper's energy didn't move. "You're *certain* this is where you would like to be let out?"

He turned down another road, and Darius's heart ached at the familiar streets north of the Williamsburg Bridge Street Market.

"I am, thank you," Juniper replied.

Cain's chin tilted in Darius's direction, and Darius was sure he was trying to catch and trap his gaze. He refused to glance back.

They maneuvered through cramped side streets until Cain found a place to pull over. There was no such thing as an empty block in New York, so a handful of pedestrians wandered by as Cain double-parked by a broken-down taxi and unlocked the doors.

"Just one more thing before you embark on this next chapter of your life…" He unbuckled his seatbelt and turned around. "Programming."

Darius's stomach iced over, and he peered around his headrest. Juniper sat rod straight, a green coat draped over her lap, a rolling suitcase of essentials on the bench seat beside her. Crescendo curled up on the deck beneath the rear window, eyes closed but ears pricked forward.

"Obviously," Cain said, "I'll install a series of Programs to cover much of your time with the Martyrs. Nothing personal, such as the people you met or the experiences you had, but any pertinent details of the war with the Sins. That includes the name and location of the Underground. You understand this necessity—and it is non-negotiable."

His lips curled into a half-smile. Juniper nodded at him, staunchly refusing to acknowledge Darius at all. "I understand."

"Very good." Cain cleared his throat. "I also want to ask if that's *all* you would like to cover… I could hide the *entire* experience, obscure unpleasant memories, mask particular people you may rather forget…"

His voice trailed off, and Darius's heart skipped a painful beat. Juniper's eyes flicked his way at last. A pink flush crossed her cheeks.

"The basic Programming is fine," she replied. "I would like to keep the rest of it to remember *why* I ended up here again."

Cain's smile vanished, and his Familiar peeked out from one slitted lid, but he maintained his composure better than Darius would have. His guts twisted into knots as he turned toward the front of the car. The Programming took a couple of minutes, and all the while, Darius stared out the windshield, furious he was here—and more furious Cain thought he needed to be.

"There we go," the Forgotten Sin said at last. "That should last you the rest of your life—or, at the very least, the rest of mine." He chuckled to a dead audience before clearing his throat and moving to exit the vehicle. "Let me help you with your bags—"

"I've got it," Juniper interrupted. Darius watched in the mirror as she removed her fingertips from her temples to get her suitcase. She dragged it onto the street, pulled her winter coat over her shoulders, and slammed the door before Darius had even made up his mind on whether or not he was going to get out to say goodbye. Her figure disappeared in a flurry of softly falling snow.

"Well," Cain muttered, shifting the car into drive and pulling back into traffic, "that was less painful than I anticipated."

Darius bit his tongue because he knew if he said anything, it wouldn't be kind.

Snow drifted from a colorless sky. Heavy clouds blotted out the sun, turning the heavens so opaque that darkness devoured the afternoon. The peaks of the tallest buildings vanished in the overcast. Metal and glass faded, consumed not all at once but in that slow, creeping decay you don't see coming until you've dissolved entirely.

Thorn didn't recognize this city anymore. She recognized herself even less.

How long had it been since she'd peeked beneath the clouds?

High Line Park stretched in a winding, barren ribbon north and south from where she sat on a bench near the West 19th overpass. Naked tree limbs boxed her into a wooden cage while the snow clung to flower beds full of brown, dead things, hiding the rot beneath a layer of crisp, clean white. It was fucking freezing, that *damp* kind of cold that snaked through your skin and settled in your bones, so Thorn didn't see a lot of other people up here. A handful of joggers now and then, or the random pedestrian with their head poking out of their puffer jacket neckline like a frightened turtle. Thorn kept her face down, staring at the burner in her hand as she pretended to read, but the screen showed an empty home page with no new notifications. She'd realized pretty quickly that it didn't allow for communication outside the chat with Edith, which had remained silent since Thorn had stolen the thing, but that didn't matter. Right now, her focus was someplace else.

Two places, actually.

First, on the white sedan parked on the street below. It had been there since Thorn arrived, and she knew it wouldn't leave any time soon. Hell, it was probably prepared to camp out overnight if it came down to it.

A TAC team.

They were no doubt standing guard over the weapons locker fortified within the old, brick building halfway down the block. They hadn't even tried to be subtle about it, setting up right outside the rolling garage door like they expected someone to come by and loot the thing. Thorn focused on their auras, trying to identify them—to *name* them.

To her humiliation, and her relief, she couldn't.

She knew the cold sense of their souls, but for the life of her, she couldn't attach more than that. Not even a *face*. In a way, that made it easier. Less personal. Like robbing a bank instead of robbing her own people—her own *family*.

Thorn bit the bitterness back and turned her attention to the *second* place of interest—which wasn't here at all.

Four blocks north, Sparkie squeezed out from a gap in a dryer vent in a thirteenth-floor apartment.

Alexis Claytor's apartment.

Cain drove them home in dense silence, but at least now Darius didn't have the looming pressure of a warm soul and broken heart creeping up his spine. Crescendo perched upon the center console, his tail flicking nervous patterns.

When they reached Freehold, Cain pulled off the interstate.

Darius frowned. "What are you doing?"

"You've had a hard couple of days," Cain replied without looking his way. "I thought we could stop for a quick glass of wine. You know. Take the edge off."

"I don't drink," Darius said.

"Ah, right." Cain's hands strangled the steering wheel. "More for me, I suppose."

Cain stopped at an open pub. The parking lot was nearly empty, which, given the holidays, didn't surprise Darius. They walked into a dimly lit building that reeked of cigar smoke and whiskey. Cain approached the counter, ordered three bottles of their most expensive wine, and whisked Darius to an isolated table in the corner of the room. The bartender proffered two glasses, but Cain left Darius's empty as he filled his own to the brim. He took a deep swig and let out a low, satisfied hum.

"Mmm. This is delightful," he muttered, more to himself than to Darius. "Are you *sure* you don't want any?"

"Cain." Darius leaned forward. "Come on, man. Thorn's missing, the Underground is a mess, and I just lost one of my oldest friends. I don't have time for this. If you need to drink, we have wine at home."

He stood, but Cain simply poured another gulp of merlot into his mouth. "Yes, well," he said, "we also have prying eyes and listening ears, *neither* of which I want accompanying us for this conversation."

Darius's brows came together as Cain drained his glass and topped it off again with trembling hands. An anxious tickle ran down Darius's back. He settled into his seat. "What conversation?"

"One I should have had ages ago," Cain mumbled

irritably. He flicked his wrist, shaking his head. "No, in fact, it's one *Alan* should have had, but the coward went and got himself *killed,* so now I have the great pleasure of doing it myself. The secrets we take to our graves are the ghosts that haunt our memory. Alan's memory is very haunted indeed—"

"Cain," Darius interrupted. "What the *hell* are you talking about?"

"I am *talking,*" Cain breathed through an exasperated sigh, "about *Patience.*"

───────

Sharp, metal edges scraped along Sparkie's back, and Thorn winced as he flopped onto the dusty tile behind the unit. Puffs of loose lint fluffed up around him and clung to his wings. He ruffled them with no effect and sneaked around the edge, peering through the gap to make sure the dark studio was as empty as Thorn assumed it would be.

Alexis's shift shouldn't end for another couple of hours.

Silence proved her right. The room settled in a terminal quiet, devoid of even the rattling drone of a heater or a neighbor's muffled voice. Sparkie scampered into the open, but before he'd made it four inches, something caught his eye.

Flickering light.

Thorn's heart pounded against the emptiness in her chest, and she tried to convince herself it was the *nerves,* not the guilt, making her pulse so wild. Sparkie made a beeline for the living area. The blinds were drawn, and a pair of sun-starved succulents sat dead on the sill. Alexis's television glowed upon an empty couch piled with a nest of blankets and one well-worn pillow. Takeout boxes littered the coffee table, and the stale, greasy odor of days-old food made Thorn's nose wrinkle from a quarter mile away. On the other side of the room, the bed sat immaculate, as though no one had slipped beneath its covers in months. A dusty photograph looked out from the side table.

Thorn's stomach plunged when she spotted *him* within the frame.

———

The bar hung with a bold, cigar-smoke fog that pressed against Darius's brain and made him wonder if he heard Cain correctly—if he *understood* correctly.

"Wait…" he began. "Are you saying that Alan *knew* where Patience was?"

"Yes," Cain said.

Darius's hands curled into fists. Nails bit skin.

"And you?" His pulse pattered in his throat, the threat of anger looming on the horizon. "Do *you* know where Patience is?"

Cain watched Darius over the rim of his wine as he drew it to his lips and took a sip. When he set the glass down again, he swallowed hard. "No."

The fog thickened within Darius's lungs. "But you clearly *did*," he said. "*Alan* did. And neither of you *ever* thought to tell me? To tell *Thorn?*"

It wasn't a question so much as an accusation, which Cain responded to with a silence that screamed guilt. The corner of Darius's lip curled.

"Jesus, Cain!" The bartender glanced up with a frown, and Cain threw him a nervous look. Darius arched forward and hissed, "Thorn has been searching for Patience for *years!* Decades! And you two knew where they were, and you *never told her?*"

A pink flush scorched Cain's cheeks. "It's compli-cated—"

Darius scoffed. "How the *hell* is it complicated?"

"Because there is a very real, very *terrifying* possibility that Patience could never destroy Wrath."

———

Alexis kept an old family portrait—god, Thorn didn't even know she'd grabbed one when they escaped the house—of herself, her brother, and their parents. It had been taken years before Greed had possessed Anton and ordered the rest of them killed. The kids were young. Maybe twelve and fourteen. Their mother looked at the camera with the bland smile of all pretty women who married for money, but Anton's arm wrapped around his daughter's shoulders like she was the only thing in the world he cared about. On his other side, eyes sad...

Was Caleb.

Looking into his face—even from a distance, between both space and time—filled Thorn's lungs with lead.

She crushed her eyes closed as Sparkie twisted back and made his way to the television screen. He slipped behind it, found the fiber optic cable tethered to the Martyrs' system, and chewed through it. Then, he vaulted to the bathroom and landed on the counter with a soft thud. As Thorn got to her feet, her Familiar stretched up the tile backsplash to the mirrored medicine cabinet and jammed his nose into a button tucked under the lip.

Inside the apartment, nothing happened.

But back at the Underground, Thorn knew Holly's security alerts were bright red and blaring.

Sparkie squished himself back into the dryer vent, and Thorn made her way to the High Line Park exit at West 20th. The TAC guards burst with sudden movement, and before she'd even reached the street, they were tearing away from the curb. The moment that white sedan turned the corner, Thorn broke into a run.

Fifteen minutes. She guessed she had just *fifteen minutes* before the Martyrs reached the apartment and climbed to the thirteenth floor. Fifteen minutes before they told Holly Andrews that somebody had tampered with her communication line, making it impossible for her to tap into the unit from the Underground.

Fifteen minutes before anyone thought to check if any

weapons had been checked out of the vault's inventory system, which would happen automatically as soon as those items crossed the threshold.

And by the time those fifteen minutes were up, Thorn was gone, along with a duffle holding two handguns, a pair of holsters, a battle belt equipped with smoke flares, additional pistol magazines, three boxes of ammunition, and a tactical vest with bulletproof inserts.

She walked two blocks to her stolen vehicle, which she'd bartered for with stolen money, and unlocked it with a pair of stolen fucking keys. As she threw the duffle onto the passenger seat, the TAC car screeched to a stop outside the locker. Sparkie watched them from the crest of the building, and Thorn slammed the door, teeth gnashed together before she turned the ignition.

The truck didn't start.

Thorn roared and punched the dash. The engine rolled over with a whine, and she adjusted the mirrors. She paused when she caught her reflection.

God, she didn't know the woman looking back.

The air stilled. For a moment, Darius was deaf to everything but the rushing of his blood, harsh in his ears.

"What do you mean?"

Cain sighed and poured more merlot with a shaking hand. Soft light caught his face in an amber glow, nearly filling in the color that drained from it. "I mean that Patience has been tampered with… *damaged.* Maybe irrevocably."

Darius's mouth ran dry. He shook his head. "That's impossible."

A pair of empty, blue eyes flicked up to him. "How can you be so sure?"

Darius stared. His lips softly parted.

"Indulge me for a moment." Cain downed a hearty swig of his wine. "Imagine the first time you met Lamar, or

Samira, or Nicholas. There was an undeniable draw to those people. A *pull*, wouldn't you say? Evidence *directly* of a Virtue at work within their souls, even if they hadn't initiated it. Isn't that true?"

His gaze narrowed. Darius nodded. "Yes."

"Now, imagine *this*," Cain went on as he set his glass down. "Imagine *any* of them, prior to destroying their Sin, *losing* that pull. One moment, it's there, and the next—" he snapped his fingers "—it's vanished entirely. What would you assume?"

Darius frowned. "That the Virtue was gone."

"Precisely," Cain said, but a strange, nearly manic twinkle glistened in his expression. "But… what if—what *if*—a Forgotten Sin still felt whole in that Virtue's presence? What if *you* could not detect them, but a Forgotten Sin *could?*"

Darius's eyes widened, but he said nothing. Cain leaned in.

"Would you still believe the Virtue was *gone?*" he whispered over his merlot, toying with the stem, spinning it in delicate circles. "Or would you believe, maybe, it's been *corrupted?*"

Rickety scaffolding cast the sidewalk in shadow. Thorn walked down the street, blocks away from where she'd stashed her stolen truck, now loaded with a metric fuckton of equipment.

Thorn stopped outside a gaudy storefront display, where strands of neon orange and bright purple lights glowed into the gloom. The window itself was backed in false spiderwebs that highlighted three mannequins dressed in furry boas, sequined skirts, and netted leggings. The central one boasted a pair of wire-framed wings covered in gold feathers and a set of devil horns upon its faceless head.

Instead of a bell, Thorn entered to the sound of a distant scream from a wall-mounted speaker. The narrow room was no wider than two cars parked end to end but stretched out further than Thorn could see. Rows of costumes assaulted her with a technicolor blitz. The checkout counter stood on the left. A young drag queen glanced up from a laptop on its surface. She dressed like she could have stepped into the window and outshined any of the display mannequins, wearing a flashy turquoise dress that cut deep down her dazzling chest piece. She grinned when Thorn stepped over the threshold. A frenulum piercing glinted in front of her teeth.

"Welcome to Mystique Boutique," she chirped, "where you can become whoever—or *whatever*—your heart desires." She winked a set of dramatic, false lashes. "Is there anything I can help you find?"

Thorn shook her head, grateful for the scarf she still wore around her face. She didn't have to fake a fucking smile.

"No. I've got it."

The queen gave an enthusiastic nod. "If you have any questions, let me know."

Thorn walked off without another word. She weaved through racks of vintage clothes, bright spandex catsuits, and accessories of every kind and color until she found what she was looking for. She paused at the end of the row.

Staring into an ocean of dead faces.

Darius drew a shallow breath. "Is that what happened? Could Alan sense Patience?"

"Answer the question."

"But the question doesn't make any sense!" Darius threw his hands up. The tingle of Influence hovered at his temples, and the other people in the room looked away. "How could a Forgotten Sin sense a Virtue but another Virtue couldn't?"

"Forgotten Sins and Virtues interact with one another in very different ways." Cain splashed the last of his wine across his tongue and poured another serving. "Virtues are drawn together like magnets, each attracting the other. Forgotten Sins and Virtues, on the other hand, have no such draw. It is more like… a change in the environment itself…"

He paused, looking into his glass as if it were a goblet of his own blood, his own past, his own broken soul. After a moment, his head jerked to the side in a single shake.

"The Virtue may as well be the sun," he said, "shining life-giving light onto a potted plant. For the sun, the plant is meaningless. Completely irrelevant. But for the plant? The sun is *everything.*"

A short, hopeless chuckle escaped his lips, and he drowned his wine with another gulp. Darius leaned forward.

"You're saying that something could block a Virtue from being sensed by the others," he said, "but *wouldn't* stop a Forgotten Sin from feeling whole?"

"Yes," Cain said. "And if that were the case, if *you* could not sense it, but *Alan* could, is the Virtue *gone?*"

Darius's mouth barely opened to form the word, "No."

Cain's eyes sharpened. Darius sighed.

"But I can't say it's corrupted, either."

"No?" Cain asked. He raised his merlot. "Why not?"

"Because a Virtue *can't* be corrupted!" Darius argued. "Sin power doesn't work on us. We can't be Influenced. We can't be Programmed—"

"Once you are *Initiated,*" Cain interrupted with a casual nonchalance that made Darius feel like he was going insane. *"That's* when your active abilities manifest, but before, you are susceptible to the Sins… or don't you remember your own early interactions with them?"

He raised his brows, and Darius thought back to those first few weeks—to that dinner with Alan and the pressure of Programming wrapped around his skull, and to that night in the rain with Autumn Hunt, with *Wrath.* He felt her poking around inside his brain again, her Influence needle sharp and sniper accurate. She'd teased at his fury, coaxed him out

of that damned car, made him put his own life on the line…
and he'd done so willingly.

But Darius shook his head. "None of that, *none*, corrupted my Virtue."

Cain's lips pressed together. "No, I suppose not. Virtues are attached to the soul, which is *much* harder to reach." He swished his wine. "So… how do you touch the *soul?*"

A phalanx of eyeless sockets followed Thorn like soulless bodies on the battlefield.

The store carried masks of every kind. Some that covered the whole head and others that attached with adhesive to the orbital bones. Some with intricate detail beside clean slate samples, ready to be made into whatever the mind could dream up. Thorn recognized imitations of popular figures, from television or politics or world history, and others she couldn't place. There were caricature masks, horror masks, fancy masquerade colombinas, and any animal she could imagine. Cats. Foxes. Monkeys. Bats.

Crows.

Slow realization crept through Darius, but he dashed it away with a firm shake of his head. The room swam around him. Cain's gaze didn't waver, watching as though he could see the puzzle coming together.

"Darius. How do you corrupt the soul?"

Darius leapt from his seat.

"No…" he whispered.

Cain lifted his chin. "You *possess* it."

Darius raised a shaky palm to his mouth, fingertips crushed against his lips. His empty stomach buckled, and he fought a swell of bile rising in his throat. Memories careened to the forefront of his mind, slammed into him like a sedan crushing his body against a brick wall—words Cain had spoken to Alan months ago.

"Robbing her of what makes her inherently human will destroy her more than being possessed by Wrath ever did."

It all made sense. It *finally* made sense.

Alan's secrecy. His protectiveness. His *fear*. And more than that, *worse than that*, his willingness to give up everything—the founders, the Martyrs, his *life*—for just *one* person, the *only* person who had ever escaped possession by forcing that Sin out, something that should have been impossible.

But not for a...

Warm bar lights cast Cain's face in deep shadow and caught the silver peppering his hair. For a breathtaking moment, Darius saw the weight of six hundred and forty-four years crashing down around him.

"Oh my god. I can't breathe."

Thorn gaped. An entire rack, floor to ceiling, had been dedicated to birds of every color, but the *black* ones dominated the space. An expanse of corvids stretched up the wall, like Edith's flock beheaded before her. They all looked the same, disturbingly generic, a nameless, faceless army.

This was inevitable, she supposed. All she was meant to be—meant to do. The darkness would consume her, drag her into the ever-gazing abyss, obscure her with shadows in the shape of black birds until Thorn didn't exist outside of it anymore.

This was the only way to defeat Edith Froschlin.

Fight fire with fire.

She reached for a crow mask. Her fingers brushed a stiff acrylic feather, firm as a blade.

Dark spots mottled her vision.

"Darius! Stay with me!"

Cain jumped to his feet, eyes darting around the pub, Influence pushing out in a dull wave to keep the patrons and bartender complacent. The world spun so fast Darius could hardly stand up straight, much less make sense of it. He wanted to vomit—felt the acrid burn burbling up his esophagus. He swallowed it down.

"You're wrong." Darius shook his head. A brush of tears he hadn't realized built up behind his lashes rattled free. He scrubbed them away with the back of his wrist. "It's not possible!"

Cain came around the table. A hand landed flat on Darius's shoulder blade. "I'm afraid it is—"

"Stop!" Darius's vocal cords strangled the words. "If *Thorn* were Patience, she'd feel the healing effects of it in her own soul! She'd feel... *me*—have known *me!* And how the hell could Wrath have attached to her in the first place? It would have burned out the second it tried!"

Cain lowered Darius back to his seat, and Darius allowed him to. The pressure of his palm settled like an anchor.

"I'm afraid I don't have a lot of answers for you," Cain murmured. He returned to his chair and tilted the last dregs of merlot into his glass with an unsteady pour. "We always speculated that an Uninitiated Virtue simply wouldn't have the power to obliterate a Sin, even at such a personal level, even *attached* to the same source. As for why Thorn can't feel it, well... No Virtue's healing effects work on *themselves.* Perhaps this is no different, and as a result, the void in her soul remains unchanged."

Darius's eyes stung, and his throat went tight as he made another, more devastating realization.

"And it always will," he murmured. Cain glanced up. "Even if she does destroy Wrath, Thorn will *never* feel whole again... Will she?"

A flash of grief glistened in Cain's irises.

If someone had asked Thorn if it was possible to drown above water, to fall with her feet on solid ground, she would have said no.

Until today.

The sea of horror stood over her, a tsunami wall of black feathers and sharp beaks. Every incident with Edith Froschlin lapped at her consciousness, frothing pink from all the bodies bobbing beneath the waves. Deidre Cummins, Tamera Osborne, *Conrad Carter.*

Thorn lifted a mask. Stared at it.

He'd looked like this in the end—two gaping holes where the eyes belonged.

Her vision spun. Thorn swayed on the spot.

And the burner buzzed in her pocket. The sensation startled her, making her pulse leap, and she drew the device out with trembling fingers to read the first text delivered since she'd stolen the thing.

"Hello, Mourning Dove. It's been a while since I've heard from you, so I wanted to check in… The East River's awfully cold this time of year."

The room went white as Thorn tilted over the edge, a single tear diving free.

Part of Darius thought he must be dreaming—or maybe he wished it.

While Cain popped his second bottle, Darius pressed his fingertips against the sides of his head and willed it to stop pounding. It refused, instead thundering a more furious beat against the inside of his skull.

This was all too insane—and all too *convenient.*

Unless… it wasn't.

The weight of horror in his gut burst into a sudden, raging fire, so hot that Darius's whole face burned with it. His head snapped up.

"Wrath," he stated abruptly. Cain peered over a freshly

poured glass of wine, eyebrows curved in question. The corners of Darius's nose flared. "Wrath knows. It possessed her *on purpose.* That's why Hunt wants Thorn alive. She thinks she *won.*"

A bitter laugh rumbled up Cain's throat. "Heinous, isn't it?" he growled. "To imagine Patience has been rendered *impotent?* Unable to Initiate, unable to move on, effectively making Wrath *indestructible.*"

He poured the whole of his merlot straight into his stomach. Darius stared at him.

And the rage exploded.

"She's *alone* out there," Darius snarled. Now, he kept his tone low, his shoulders hunched, but the words seethed from his mouth. "God *damn it,* Cain! Patience is out there right now, unprotected, where *Wrath* can get to her! This *never* would have happened if you and Alan had just *told* her!"

Shame reddened Cain's expression. "I know," he murmured. "I know, and you're right. I always thought she deserved to know. It was one the largest conflicts Alan and I ever had—the very reason I chose to leave the Martyrs all those years ago. It's *her* life, *her* soul, *her Virtue,* and what she did with that information was her decision to make, not his."

Cain uttered a cold chuckle. He gripped the stem of his wine glass so hard that his fingernails pressed white.

"Now, Alan is dead, the responsibility lies with me, and what have I done? *The same damned thing.* I called him a coward for decades, but it appears I am no better…"

Darius frowned. "What stopped you?"

Cain narrowed his eyes. "Because what if Alan's greatest fears were *right?* What if she chooses to jump off that bridge again?"

Suddenly, Darius saw Thorn crashing into the East River. His lungs seized as though he himself were drowning.

Wind whipped outside Thorn's skull, yanking at her hair, pushing against her face, and screaming so loudly in her ears that she couldn't hear the one pouring from her mouth.

Her senses burned. Her nose, mouth, throat dry and callused, empty of everything, her breath whisked free. And her eyes—all they saw was a nauseating swirl of color, whipping between dark water, blue sky, water, sky, water—

Water.

It streamed down her face, *up* her face, as the pressure of the fall made gravity both the most important law of physics and irrelevant all at once.

But still, as she fell, as she spun, as she plunged toward the *water* with dreadful inevitability, she cried. Pleaded. *Prayed.*

She hadn't wanted to die.

She just wanted the pain to stop.

But instead, she hit that *water*…

It hurt more than that *thing* ripping free. It hurt like cutting herself in two.

Cain released a sigh that sounded like it came from the very cracks in his broken soul. An ancient, wounded sigh.

"Alan believed, with every cell in that bleak body of his, that Thorn's Virtue was whole and intact beneath the corruption of Wrath."

A blood-red ribbon unfurled from the wine bottle's mouth, coalescing into a rippling pool at the base of the glass. Cain raised it delicately by the stem and swirled it once. Twice. Three times. Darius's heart pounded the same rhythm. Cain's lips pressed together.

"But he could never be sure… would *Thorn* believe in *herself?*"

Thorn's head crested the surface.

And she found herself bobbing in that ocean of crows.

Fingers tapped, thumb to pointer, middle, ring, pinky, and back again in a tempo matching her rabbiting heart. She focused on the matte black feathers stretched out before her as the cashier at the front of the store chimed a distant laugh. Her nostrils flared, pulling in shallow breaths that smelled vaguely of cheap plastic. She swallowed hard.

Her feet on solid ground.

A drop of water escaped Thorn's lashes and trailed a path down her cheek. She dabbed the corner of her eye with the heel of her glove and worked through the grounding exercise again, sinking into her senses.

Sinking into *him.*

"I want more than that."

Her eyes stung anew. She looked down at the mask still clutched in her hand. A spark furled to life in her cored-out chest.

She wanted more than this.

"Alan thought she would kill herself?" Darius asked in a whisper.

"What other solution is there?" Cain didn't catch Darius's gaze. Didn't look up from the wine sitting reverently like a sacrifice in his hands. "If *Wrath* is right and Patience is irreparable?"

Darius didn't respond. He knew the answer.

Cain said it aloud anyway.

"To let it be reborn. And the only way to do *that* would be for Thorn's life to end."

Fuck.

She couldn't do it. Couldn't hide behind something that

Edith had so thoroughly violated. Couldn't *beat* the bitch by *joining* her.

So, she replaced the crow, put it in line with dozens of others peering out like mourners at a wake, and took a step back to see the scene with new eyes, a broader perspective, a greater purpose.

"This burden is heavier than I ever could have anticipated." Cain's eyes glistened in the warm pub lights. "I understand now more than ever why Alan was so tortured by it."

He reached for the third bottle but hesitated with his hand around its neck. The muscles along his throat went rigid.

"I love Thorn deeply," he said. "She is *family* to me. And the idea of anything happening to her…"

A tear fell down his cheek, and he swiped it away. Darius's heart clenched.

"What if Alan's fears were *right?*" Cain whispered. "I have lost everyone else. I don't know that I could survive losing her, too."

Darius shook his head. "But what if Alan was *wrong?*" he asked. "What if Thorn *can* and *does* Initiate Patience?"

Something glinted at the edge of her attention, something she hadn't noticed before. A mask, tucked between the others. The hint of light feathers flashed behind a veil of black, bright and blinding.

Thorn lifted it with a frown.

A white bird. A dove?

No.

The plumage shone like a star, silky smooth and glistening. Red and gold accents fringed the crest, bursting to life

in a stunning gradient that made the thing look like it had
been set on fire and left to burn. The beak dipped into a
sharp point, like a golden blade. Thorn turned it over and
read the title on the tag.

Her lips slipped open.

————

Cain refused to look at him. Darius leaned forward.

"We *have* to tell her, Cain," he insisted. Demanded.

"Of course we do," Cain agreed. He popped the cork on
his final merlot. "But first, we have to *find* her."

————

"Did you find yourself back there?"

Thorn glanced up from a can of spray-on white body
paint, a frown behind her scarf. The cashier smiled and gestured to the items Thorn had placed on the counter as she
raised them one by one, scanning each barcode. The paint.
A cloak. And of course—

"Ooh," the queen said, reading the tag on the mask, before she threw Thorn an approving look. "Yes, *slay*, girl!"

New York nipped Thorn with cold fangs as she headed
back into the real world, scarf around her face and a brand-
new identity shoved into the bag at her side. Flakes of snow
struck her cheeks, where they melted upon her skin and
dripped like life-bringing tears.

Thorn always thought she would one day burn to the
ground and choke on the ashes.

But she was wrong.

She hadn't burned.

She'd drowned.

And risen again from the *water*.

A phoenix with liquid wings.

CHAPTER TWENTY-EIGHT

Thorn's office looked exactly as it had the day she'd kissed him. The day she'd *left* him.

He stood in the doorway, hands in his pockets, heart in his throat, and he tried to breathe through the hopelessness crushing his lungs together. It didn't work. Instead, it grew so burdensome that Darius was sure he'd die with this pressure in his chest.

What the *fuck* was he supposed to do now?

The rest of the Underground reeled with the frenetic energy of a hive without its queen. People pulsed in the research department, in tactical, in the courtyard, while Darius hovered like a thing stuck in time, out of frequency and out of touch.

Was this how Alan had felt all those years, with this secret strangling his soul?

Darius looked over his shoulder at the door bearing the name "Blaine" before he closed Thorn's behind him. The room smelled of her. Warm and welcoming. A hint of sandalwood.

Holly's staff was buried in video footage from her facial recognition software, hoping against all hope that they might spot Thorn among the millions of people in New

York City. Half of Nicholas's researchers joined them, while the others continued to run damage control on the Bryant Park shooting. Mackenzie had the Gray Unit agents and Recon teams searching for her with boots on the ground, and for the first time in weeks, TAC found itself back at capacity, with people assigned to every Martyr-owned locker or apartment in the city. This was an all-hands-on-deck situation.

But Darius knew it wouldn't be enough.

Because they knew *nothing*.

He reached Thorn's desk, eyes lilting over the stack of papers now set neatly at the corner, the evidence of their passion tidied up and tucked away like it never happened.

But it *had*. Darius ran his fingertips along the wood, remembering how it dug into the backs of his thighs. When he closed his eyes, he could feel the silhouette of her body molded against his, taste her water-smooth breath dancing on his lower lip. He dragged it between his teeth.

These should have been pleasant memories—the kind he called upon when he wanted to feel good, to feel *warm*, but right now, all they did was open a trap door beneath his stomach and send it spiraling into the dark.

He pulled out Thorn's chair. Sat down.

Maybe being here, where she did all her planning, all her plotting, would give him an idea of what the fuck she was thinking now.

Her phone lay in front of him. He picked it up.

The device was locked, but Holly dug through her logs on the Martyr server and came back with nothing. It turned out, Darius wasn't the only person Thorn actively ignored. She hadn't texted anyone about her escape to the city, and her call logs were just as uninspiring. Darius turned the thing over in his hands, brushing a thumb against the screen. It lit up.

A new notification glowed at the top. He couldn't read the message, but the preview showed who'd sent it. He froze.

Jay Coons. The bartender from The Cross.

A tingling sensation bubbled up Darius's back.

He tapped the device, opened the keypad, and stared at the four-digit passcode input for half a second before mindlessly entering the numbers for Thorn's birthday. It buzzed a failure. Darius frowned, tried the numbers in reverse, and swore when that didn't work, either. Strike two.

What the hell would Thorn's passcode be? Alan's birthday? Maybe her mother's. He considered grabbing that file Cain had wanted him to read to see what he could find when—

The answer hit Darius like a punch of cold air.

"Oh, god…"

He leapt to his feet and ran from the room, darting down the stairs to the main level. Dinner was about to start, so Martyrs filtered toward the dining area. He rushed past them, ignoring the looks that followed as he made his way to an alcove on the opposite side of the courtyard.

The memorial hall.

Cain had inscribed the names of every Martyr ever lost on a set of granite slabs mounted to the side walls. In the garden, the person he was looking for had been the oldest buried, but since moving their mortuary to the Underground, Cain had added those lost before him. Dates spanned over one hundred and fifty years, organized not by when they were born but by when they died.

Darius started in 2024, scanning casualties from January to December, until he found Donovan Rose. Darius's hands shook as he entered his birthday into Thorn's phone: September Nineteenth. Zero nine one nine.

The screen blinked to life. Darius opened the text from Jay.

"Hey, Thorn… Sully might kill a man if he doesn't see you soon."

It was the latest in a long string of unanswered messages, ranging from casual to concerned, but one thing about it, about *all* of them, made Darius's heart skip.

Jay didn't call her Teagan. He called her *Thorn.*

Darius slipped Thorn's phone into his pocket and dragged out his own. He had to go down there, but he couldn't do it alone, and there was only one person he trusted with this… with *all* of it.

He tapped the top number on his speed dial. Chris answered on the first ring.

"You busy tonight?" Darius asked.

"I'm busy every night," she said with a sigh. "Why? What's up?"

"I need your help." Darius glanced at the ceiling, toward the robust figure of her aura sitting in her office. "I have to go into the city, but I don't want to go alone. Security and all that, but it's… confidential. Something I don't trust anyone else with but you."

He could hear the frown in her voice as she asked, "What's it about?"

Darius exhaled a shaky breath. "The last Virtue."

Chris's aura froze. She hesitated just a heartbeat before saying, "You can fill me in on the way."

* * *

Chris didn't speak, and Darius wondered if she'd heard anything he'd said in the last hour. It was dark, the roads through New York slick with gray slush, and as Darius watched her, Chris's eyes remained glued to the road. She smothered the steering wheel with a white-knuckle grip that made the sleeves of her jacket appear a deeper olive under flashing city lights.

As they approached the exit for the Robert F. Kennedy Bridge, Darius finally asked, "You okay?"

A tight, choppy sound that may have been a laugh blustered from her mouth. "I'm just trying to wrap my head around this," Chris said, distinctly *not* an answer. She threw him a harried look. Her green eyes were so wide that the whites showed around them. "I can't believe it. Or… can I?" She shook her head. Loose, blonde hair grazed her shoulders. "When did Cain tell you?"

"Last night," Darius said.

"Last night…" Chris echoed in a whisper. "But he's known since…?"

She glanced at him again. Darius shrugged.

"Forever. Since she was possessed by Wrath. Alan, too."

"Oh my god…" Chris held a shaky palm over her mouth. Her voice crawled out. *"Alan."*

Suddenly, her entire expression changed, warping from awe to outrage. Chris yanked her wheel to the side, abruptly slamming to a stop on the shoulder of the road. Darius grabbed the handle over his head to steady himself as a car blasted by them and laid on its horn. She rounded on him, cheeks flushed and furious.

"Alan knew! He let Thorn hunt for Patience for years. For *decades*… and the whole time, *he knew.*"

Hearing those words, that anger, outside of the echo chamber in his mind was more relieving than Darius could have dreamed. He leaned forward, breathing a sigh as some of the weight lifted off his back, as though he and Chris carried it together.

"Yeah," he murmured. "He did."

"Why didn't he tell her?" she asked.

"He was afraid Thorn wouldn't believe she could do it," Darius said. "That instead of Initiating Patience, she'd end her own life to let the Virtue be reborn."

Chris scoffed. "That's a coward's excuse," she hissed. "If *anyone* can do this, it's Thorn." Chris turned back to the wheel and jerked them into traffic. Other drivers honked. Chris ignored them. "We have to tell her—before the rest of the Underground finds out. She has to know first. She *should* have known first."

Darius nodded. "Yes," he agreed. "She should have. I hope we can find her before she—"

He cut off. Left the statement incomplete, because they both knew how it ended. A messy knot tied Darius's vocal cords together. Chris flexed her jaw, a brush of tears glistening behind her lashes. They crossed over to the Bronx before anyone spoke again.

"What makes you think Jay can help us?" Chris finally asked.

"He knew *this* side of her," Darius said, indicating the city through his window. "The side of her that lived in New York. And… he knew the *real* her." When Chris cast him a questioning look, Darius sighed. "Thorn trusted him with her name. Maybe she trusts him with more."

The Cross was located on the southernmost edge of the Bronx, somehow close to almost all traffic and footbridges crossing the Harlem River without being particularly easy to reach from any of them. Parking presented a similar challenge, and the closest Chris could get them was around the block. They walked down the sidewalk, hands shoved into their pockets. Considering Edith's bastardizing of their TAC uniforms, Chris had insisted they wear plainclothes, but the bulletproof vest under Darius's winter coat worked as a reminder that they were still in enemy territory. He sighed, and a cloud of dense condensation materialized in front of his face.

Halfway down the road, beneath a flickering streetlight and broken Martyr security camera, stood The Cross.

Darius had seen this building once, on a video feed flickering with distant fire from a car bomb that had almost claimed Thorn's life three years ago. In person, it was so much grander.

And more depressing.

The bar had been built into an old, converted church, which Darius was sure had been moved to this location from its original home somewhere less bleak. It wasn't a large structure, but the ornate brickwork spoke to construction with care, and large, stained-glass windows glowed with warm light. A neon crucifix bearing the bar's name blared bright red as Darius and Chris approached. He paused at the bottom of a set of stone steps, staring at the heavy, oak door.

"What's our cover?" Chris asked. She hugged her jacket tighter and cast Darius a look. They'd been so caught up in talking about Thorn that he hadn't filled her in on his plan… or bothered to come up with a better one.

"I don't have a cover," Darius said. "I'm sick of pretending."

He climbed the stairs, leaving Chris behind, eyes wide and mouth open. By the time he reached the top, she'd returned to his side. Darius heaved the door inward.

Sound and cigarette smoke greeted him with a jarring embrace. Warmth crowded in as Darius and Chris crossed the threshold, both from the heaters and the human souls around the room. A dozen people orbited pool tables or sat at booth benches made from repurposed church pews. The deities on the far wall had been traded out for a different kind of spirit, glistening in glass bottles under yellow lights, and a long counter replaced the ritual altar. Jay Coons stood behind it, pouring drinks for a lonely patron sitting on a stool. As the door closed with a thud, his blue eyes flicked up. When they landed on Chris, he froze, and Darius's stomach dropped.

That was right. Jay had seen Chris after Lust stabbed Thorn in the wrist last spring. She'd been the first TAC agent on the scene.

It looked like the moment had stuck with him.

Darius swallowed his nerves and walked across the room. Chris followed, her spine a straight line from sacrum to skull. Men and women scowled at the newcomers in their territory, and no amount of casual smiling or head tilting from Darius softened their expressions. They reached the bar, and Darius took a stool four down from the other man. Chris sat between them, and she unzipped her jacket, more for easy access to the gun hidden at the small of her back than to make herself more comfortable.

Hell, having easier access to her gun probably *did* make her more comfortable.

"What can I get you?" Jay asked. He kept his voice

neutral, clearly having mastered putting on a face for customers at his counter, but his whole aura stilled anxiously.

"We're not here to drink," Darius said. "We're here to talk. About Thorn."

Every muscle in Jay's body tensed, and his facade of nonchalance frayed. He glanced over their heads, and Darius became aware of the room going quiet.

"I don't know a Thorn," Jay said. Suddenly, he didn't seem so approachable.

"Teagan, then," Chris said. "Or Jane—"

"Shh!"

Jay came forward so quickly that Darius's pulse leapt, and Chris's right hand whipped behind her coat. The man on her other side shifted. He wore a pair of sunglasses backward upon his buzzed head, which moved as his face turned in their direction. Jay angled his torso to block the guy out, but it wasn't very effective across the counter.

"Jesus, what the fuck is wrong with you?" Jay hissed.

Backward Sunglasses grabbed his drink and stood up, casting a strange look their way before taking one of the empty booths on the right wall. Jay waited until he settled before shaking his head.

"Not *everyone* here is safe, so be fucking careful."

Darius frowned and glanced over his shoulder. Most of the patrons still watched them, but now there was a different tone. A more… *protective* one. An older gentleman by the pool tables placed his cue stick into the rack and started walking over. Darius turned back to Jay.

"Other people… *know* about her?" he murmured.

Jay bristled as though Darius had taken a shot at him. "I didn't exactly have a choice," he said. "After those videos started going around—"

"*You* told them?" Chris cut in, brows raising.

"Evening, Jay." A deep, gravelly voice boomed over their shoulders. The man from the pool table hovered just close enough to touch, his mouth set into a deep frown behind a bushy, gray mustache. He crossed his arms over a chest the width of a city bus, and though he'd addressed Jay, his narrow eyes homed in on Darius and Chris. "You good?"

Jay lifted a hand. "I got it, Sully."

Sully's nose curled, glare still solidly fixed on the new blood taking up the stools, before he finally considered Jay. "This ain't about… *our girl*… now is it?"

"No," Jay began.

But Darius interrupted. "Yes."

Sully's spine rolled upward, drawing his head higher, shoulders apart, a grizzly bear rising to its hind legs. An urgent tingle climbed Darius's back, prodding his brain alert, and he threw a quick look around the room. More people stared now, but a few busied themselves with drinks or games. Backward Sunglasses kept his nose down, focus glued to his phone. Darius turned back to Sully and Jay. He had to sit sideways on his stool to see both of them, which left him feeling dangerously exposed.

"You're not the only people close to her," he insisted, voice level.

He may as well have told Sully he was a serial killer with a penchant for dark-haired women for all the good it had done. The old man's face reddened, and he worked his jaw as though sharpening his teeth. Jay leaned forward, putting his head right in Sully's laser-focused eyeline.

"They're good, Sul," he said. He considered Chris before looking Darius over more critically, appraising him. Whether he liked what he saw or not, Darius didn't know, but the bartender nodded, and then, he lied. "I've met them."

That did the trick. Sully deflated with a low growl of air exhaled slowly through dilated nostrils. Jay released a sigh of his own. "So, what the hell's going on?" he asked Darius. "I've been trying to get a hold of her for weeks, but she never answers my damn texts."

"She won't," Darius said, and though a sense of relief settled on his shoulders, it didn't calm the hairs tingling at the nape of his neck. He glanced around again. Still nothing. He shook his head. "She *can't*. She left without her phone. We hoped *you* might know where she might be staying."

Jay's blue eyes widened. "She *left?* When? Why?"

"Because of..." Chris tilted closer, lowering her voice. "...what happened in Bryant Park—"

"It wasn't her!" Sully snarled. A couple of auras startled, and Sully continued in a hiss. "I've seen plenty of videos online proving that shit was faked!"

"I know it was," Darius agreed, "but she's—"

"Going after the Raven," Jay whispered. Darius saw his own terror reflected in Jay's face. "To stop her from doing it again."

A lump caught in Darius's throat. He swallowed past it. "Yes. I *need* to find her."

Jay watched Darius for a moment longer, and then, he shared a dark look with Sully before straightening up. He cleared his throat, grabbed a glass from beneath the bar, and filled it with tonic.

"She never shared much about her life," he said, suddenly back in a casual, service-soft voice. "Not with me, anyway. I have no idea where she could be hiding. But... if I hear from her, I'll let you know."

He topped off the fake drink and slid it over the counter to Darius with a napkin. Darius grabbed it, confused at first, until he felt the pen beneath the paper. Jay didn't release the glass until he met his eye again. He gave Darius a hard look. "As long as you promise to return the favor."

Darius nodded. "Of course."

He scribbled his number on the napkin while Jay moved to the back counter, returning moments later with his own details written on a coaster. All the while, the foreboding sense in Darius's brain became more than he could handle. He slipped Jay's number in his pocket and raised the glass with a shaking hand, taking a sip as an excuse to look around one last time.

He froze, and a splash of tonic poured down his chin.

"Shit."

"What's wrong?" Jay asked.

Backward Sunglasses wasn't looking at them, but his phone's camera pointed in their direction. When he noticed Darius watching him from the view on the screen, his eyes went wide. He leapt to his feet.

"Chris!" Darius shouted.

Sully was on the man before he'd fully risen from his pew. A massive paw of a hand grabbed him by the back of his neck, knocking those sunglasses right off his skull. He howled as Sully yanked him backward.

"Get your filthy hands off me, you f—"

Sully silenced him with a punch to the throat that sent the guy wheezing. He collapsed onto his knees, and his phone fell from his hands onto the worn, wooden floor. Darius snatched it up and turned it on. He didn't have a lock on his screen, so it opened up to the last app he'd been using.

LymeLite—in a secret group.

Darius's stomach dropped as he stared at a photograph of Chris sitting at the bar, her side to the camera, the profile of her face barely in focus thanks to the shit lighting, but recognizable enough. The caption beneath the image read, *"Talking about Jane Morgan at a bar in The Bronx."*

He'd posted it five minutes ago and attached a location marker. One person responded—an anonymous user with a black silhouette for a profile photo.

"We're on the way."

Darius looked up. Chris's face washed with white. "It's Froschlin's group," he said. "We can use this."

"We have to get it back to the Underground," she breathed.

"Then ya better hurry," Sully said as he hoisted the guy off the ground, still choking on his own folded trachea. "Go on. We'll take care of this shitbag."

He gestured the rest of the patrons, who were now on their feet. If his heart wasn't so busy trying to rip its way from his chest, Darius imagined it would have felt full. "Thank you," he said as he shoved the other man's phone into his pocket. "For everything."

"D'ya know what the word 'hurry' means, son?" Sully growled. *"Go!"*

As Sully dragged Backward Sunglasses toward the rear exit, flanked now by a squad of other large men with cigarette-stained nails and sinister scowls, Jay rushed Darius and Chris to the entrance.

"We'll cover for you."

"They're dangerous," Chris argued.

Jay barked a cold laugh. "Yeah, I know. I watch LymeLite, too." He opened the door, and a wall of icy air slammed into Darius's chest. Jay turned to them. "Get the fuck out of here," he said, and then, he lingered on Darius. His mouth set into a grim line. "Find her."

Darius nodded. "I will."

They dashed down the stairs and onto the street. The sense of dread stalked Darius back to their vehicle, drenching him in sweat. They'd parked under a streetlight, which he'd appreciated at the time, but now it felt like being caught in the eye of a magnifying glass. Darius jumped into the passenger's side and slammed the door. Chris hurried around the car. Opened the driver's side—

A black SUV rounded the corner. Darius's stomach dropped.

"Get in!"

Chris ducked as a rally of bullets clattered into the vehicle. She popped back up with a curse and hopped in, engaging the engine and smashing her foot onto the accelerator. They shot away with a squeal and the stink of burned rubber. Darius twisted around to see the SUV bounce onto the curb where they'd been parked and skid to a messy stop.

"Shit," Chris breathed as she buckled herself in. Darius did the same, and her green eyes flicked to the rearview mirror. "That was too close."

The SUV screamed into reverse. Its headlights blared

their way as Chris turned a corner. A siren screamed a war cry in Darius's skull.

"It's *still* too close," he muttered.

Chris turned again, and another car shot toward them, crossing lanes on Bruckner Boulevard for a head-on collision.

She jerked the wheel, sending Darius swinging to the right. The other vehicle's driver's side window blew past his. He barely caught the look on a startled civilian's face as their mirrors knocked, both flying sky-high into the dark.

"Influence," he gasped. He turned to Chris as she pulled them toward the interstate. "They were Influenced!"

"Fuck." Chris's cheeks lost their color, and she tapped the panic button on the dash. "Froschlin's here."

They flew up the on-ramp, and Chris sent a distress message to all on-duty TAC units, requesting backup. At this time in the evening, New York's traffic moved quickly, thank god, but not quickly enough. Darius looked over his shoulder again as the black SUV careened after them. Another one joined. Soon, a third.

His heart pounded.

Chris weaved them in and out of other cars, but the flow became unnatural. When she attempted to change lanes, vehicles crowded in. As they reached Randalls Island and tried exiting to Manhattan, a line of drivers blocked them inside. Darius had the distinct impression this was deliberate, as though they were being herded like sheep for slaughter. Chris's focus remained doggedly on the road. A glistening of sweat peppered her brow.

But still, they pulled ahead. Soon, the black SUVs were lost behind a line of civilian cars, the mercenary auras a tiny flicker within a bulk of distant energy, and Darius started to think they could finally breathe. They reached the Robert F. Kennedy Bridge, crossing the East River, and he exhaled a sigh.

More than halfway across the water, a truck three cars ahead of them arced left and t-boned a coupe.

The smaller vehicle launched, tumbling once, twice, three times. The auras inside disappeared with a snap as it slid to a grinding stop on its flank across the center two lanes of traffic. Another car smashed into it, and more followed. Vehicles piled up, the sounds of crunching metal, screaming horns, and breaking glass slicing through Darius's skull. Chris slammed on the brakes.

It wasn't fast enough.

Taillights came at Darius like balls of fire, red and blinding. The collision flung him against his seatbelt, and the rising white wall of an airbag caught him before he struck the dash. They went weightless for a moment, and then, upside down. The SUV smashed back to the pavement face down. Darius sucked in a shattered breath. Before it halfway filled his lungs, their car jolted again, and a warm soul blinked out behind them.

The world settled off-axis in a blur of shouts and dancing light. Darius groaned as the airbag deflated, his head spinning from a sudden rush of blood pooling to his skull. The blaring noise of cars honking and people screaming pushed through the ringing in his ears.

And sharp pain radiated up his right leg.

Chris's energy shifted, and she swore. He heard a sound like a body hitting the ground, and then, a warm hand touched his chest, his neck, his cheek. When he opened his eyes, Chris's face, right-side up, filled his view. Her palm smoothed against his forehead.

"Fuck, Darius!" she gasped. "Are you okay? Can you hear me?"

He nodded. Shook his head. Chris winced as she went to unbuckle his belt, but the mechanism stuck. He tried to pull himself free, but something bit into his ankle—the sharp edge of a crushed door. "I-I can't move," he rasped. "My leg. It's stuck."

Chris swore again and tried to look, but the limp airbag made it impossible to see.

"We'll get you out," she began, but the words died in her

throat. She glanced back the way they'd come as a sudden, subtle pressure tapped Darius's temples. His stomach dropped.

"Oh, *shit,*" Chris murmured.

Influence.

The tell-tale sensation around his skull could be nothing else. All four lanes of traffic had come to a standstill, and the drivers left behind suddenly moved with an all-new, frantic energy, not uniform the way a Sin could Puppet but feeding on the same fear, the way Edith Froschlin could control a crowd.

Wait. Not *all* of the energy. Darius tried to glance over his shoulder, where he could barely make out a line of three vehicles stopped beyond the pileup through their broken back windshield. Two men climbed out of each, their auras a warm light in the night.

Then, someone *without* an aura stepped up to the center—a woman with pale skin and yellow hair pinned so flat to her head it looked plastic.

"Oh, my god." Darius grabbed his seatbelt, yanking at it, trying to rip it free. "It's Froschlin! We've got to—"

Chris took his hand. Darius looked at her, and his breath hitched. In the darkness and chaos, she was difficult to make out, impossible to read, but the truth was written out in a dark red smear. Her left eye swelled, already half shut, and blood soaked her left shoulder through her winter jacket. She tenderly pinned that arm to her side as she drew a gun from her holster and palmed it in her right hand.

Realization stabbed Darius in the gut. "No!" he cried.

"Stay here," she said. "I'll draw them away."

"Wait—*wait!* Chris!" Darius screamed after her. She kicked out the driver's side window. The whole pane thudded onto the concrete. Darius thrashed against his seatbelt and the door pinning his leg. "You can't go out there! They—"

"Didn't see you." She threw him a hard look that made Darius's very soul go cold. "And Froschlin can't sense you, but she *can* sense me, and I'm leading her right to you." She checked her firearm. Loaded the chamber. When her eyes landed back on Darius, they glistened. "There's no way I can get you out on my own. You *have* to stay. Lay low. Wait for backup."

His eyes stung. He shook his head. "You *can't* go!"

Chris smiled—a goodbye kind of smile—and wrapped her hand around his so firmly that her fingertips left the imprint of her heartbeat against his skin. Darius watched helplessly as she crawled out of the mangled vehicle. Her blonde head whipped backward, where Edith's force moved toward them, and then, she disappeared.

As soon as Chris took off running, Edith's men did, too.

Darius held his breath as they bolted past his position—six distinct energies moving with a uniform, trained precision. Soon, gunshots and shouting echoed in his ears, reverberated in his chest. He tried to track Chris, but she darted right and left, up and down, as though climbing, dodging, avoiding obstacles outside the vehicle Darius couldn't see.

But he couldn't focus on her forever, because something dark appeared in his window.

Edith Froschlin sauntered down the road. The bridge lights above sent her shadow across Darius's face, and the LED glow created a halo around her crown of yellow hair. His heart lodged in his throat, the dangerous tingling in his spinal column so intense that Darius ached to get out and sprint as far as he fucking could. Edith walked past the decimated vehicle, following slowly, with the confidence of a predator who knew she could outpace her kill. Then, she vanished, and Darius couldn't tell where she'd gone.

He yanked at his belt again, over and over, until his common sense caught up, and he opened the glove box. An array of items clattered free—a pistol, a holster, a *knife*. He scrambled for it, upside down in the dark. Chris's aura bolted with sharp, precise movements in a deadly dance with the others. Another blast of gunfire echoed through the night.

Darius found the knife, cut his belt, and toppled to the ground. His pinned foot howled in pain as metal dug deeper into his skin, slicing through his shoe. He hung there, gritting his teeth.

A gun fired, and someone screamed.

Not Chris—a man. The howl stretched over distant sirens crying over the river. Darius pulled harder, harder, *harder*, groaning in the back of his throat as he pried his leg out. The shoe slipped off, leaving him with a mangled foot. Blood poured from a gash across his ankle. Darius's head swam at the sight, and he pressed his eyes closed.

Another shot sounded. An aura went down.

Darius crawled across the roof of the car, hands and knees scraping against broken glass and warped metal, and squeezed onto the street. His wounded foot hollered as he dragged himself up and looked around, but he couldn't see anything through the sea of damaged cars.

Except for a dark shape in the sky, silhouetted in the streetlight glow. Darius gaped as a massive raven swooped down.

"Fuck!" he hissed.

He started to run—*tried* to run—but all he could manage was a slow hobble to the shoulder of the road. Chris kept moving, this time retreating to the edge of the bridge. Darius made it to the side railing and slumped against it to stay standing. His head whipped around.

Chris pressed up against the concrete barrier, her legs spread in a fighting stance, one arm raised to defend her head while the other drooped at her side. She didn't have a weapon.

Oh, god.

He pulled himself closer, but he could hardly walk, and vehicles had crashed into the guardrail and blocked the path. Four mercenaries closed in around Chris, two to either side. One took a swing at her, and Chris screamed in pain as she deflected it with a forearm. A massive, black bird swooped at her head. Its talons grabbed clumps of hair, yanking her back until her heels hit the barrier. Edith drew in. A gust of wind caught her cape, unfurling it like a pair of demonic wings. She backhanded Chris so hard that her whole body staggered to the side. As Chris rose to full height, Edith held out that same hand.

One of her men placed a baton in her palm.

Darius's heart lurched, and he vaulted forward. His ankle folded beneath him, sending him to the ground with a yelp. When he got back up, Edith's familiar landed on her shoulder and spread its wings. Chris took another step back as Edith raised the weapon.

And then, the world went still.

Chris's gaze flicked to the left, blood-streaked hair flying wildly about her face. Her eyes landed on Darius.

He saw the decision the second she made it.

No…

The baton came down—a violent, life-ending swing at the side of Chris's skull.

It never made contact.

Because Chris threw herself off the bridge.

Just like Thorn had.

Darius's heart stuttered. He stopped trying to claw his way forward and instead slammed against the guard rail, bent at the waist until he nearly fell over. Chris twisted and tumbled toward the river below, a mass of olive fabric and bright yellow hair. The darkness consumed her before she struck the water, devouring all of who she was in a single cold bite.

Everything but her soul.

That warm light—beautiful and agonizing and full of life—pulled at Darius's psyche.

And then, that light began to flow downriver.

Edith shouted something he couldn't hear over the sirens closing in. She and her mercenaries sprinted toward the opposite side of the bridge. Darius didn't follow because he knew leaving meant losing Chris, meant moving too far to feel her aura.

But even if *he* didn't move, she did. The river dragged her away.

Darius screamed into the night.

"Chris!"

Silence screamed back. Tears rolled down his cheeks, where they froze upon his skin.

Chris's energy jerked with the current, further, faster, *rougher* than Darius could imagine. And soon, *deeper*, as she went below the surface. A sob caught in Darius's throat. Her aura weakened, and he couldn't stop himself from imagining this new hell—frigid water over her head, pouring into her mouth, filling her lungs. He hunted for her in the dark, but there was nothing to see. Nothing to latch onto.

Nothing he could do.

He screamed again.

"Chris!"

But her aura was gone, swept away, leaving another soulless body at the bottom of the river.

CHAPTER TWENTY-NINE

The Martyrs laid Chris Silver to rest on January 1, 2094.

They'd given it time. Searched the shores of the East River for a body to bury, crawled the news for reports of unidentified women fished from the bay. Darius spent every waking moment for over forty-eight hours frantically watching surveillance cameras and listening to Coast Guard feeds, but at the end of the second day, Cain had come to him.

Darius still felt the shadow of his palm against his shoulder, still heard the words he'd spoken like he'd said them in a dream.

"She's gone. It's time for you to say goodbye so others can, too."

Her service was the largest since Alan Blaine's. Cain, once again, opened the memorial hall's accordion glass walls, and two columns of chairs spilled into the courtyard. Non-combat Martyrs filled the front sections, clothed in either black or Chris's favorite color: a deep, forest green. Beyond them, her entire TAC force stood shoulder to shoulder. They took up the last six rows, a solid block of black and beige and bloodshot eyes. Gabe positioned himself at their head, posture at ease, with his hands clasped behind his back, head held high, and amber irises glittering in gleaming pools.

Darius spoke first. He hardly remembered what he said. It didn't seem to matter. There weren't enough words in the English language to describe the kind of person Chris had been, what she'd meant to him. Hell, even if he'd had all the words in all the languages of the world, it *still* wouldn't be enough.

Chris's light transcended voice. It transcended feeling. And now, it transcended them all.

A low murmur of quiet crying served as a backdrop for every tribute. Dozens took to the podium, sharing stories and memories. John. Raquel. Mackenzie. Abraham. Even Noah Montgomery, who had traveled down from the city. Darius watched, and he listened, and he allowed his tears to softly fall, for the grief to overtake him. When Gabe took the mic, the room stilled, but whether it was because others had nothing left to give or because his eulogy, raw and ragged, stole the air from their lungs was anyone's guess. And it didn't matter. By the time he stepped down, leaving the altar empty except for Chris's photograph projected on a screen, the Martyrs had been drained of every drop of water, every gram of spirit, every ounce of faith.

The memorial hall emptied, but Darius didn't leave. While everyone else moved into the courtyard for yet another wake, with more wine and little finger sandwiches he couldn't taste, Darius sat in the same chair he'd sat in for every other service in the last eight months and stared at Chris's face. They'd chosen a picture from Skylar and Raquel's wedding, her smile so radiant and full that Darius almost expected to feel Chris's aura attached to it.

A sob caught in his throat as he sat here alone, in this room without life.

This never should have happened. None of this. The trip to The Cross. The man with the sunglasses. The bridge and the jump. If Darius hadn't insisted they find Thorn—

His breath hitched.

Oh god.

Chris was dead, and *Thorn didn't know.*

His mouth tingled with that sickly-sweet sensation that so often precipitated vomit, and he swallowed an acrid bubble moving up his esophagus. His gaze, blurry and wet with a fresh wall of tears, flicked up to the dais. Five stone Familiars stared back at him with cold, stone eyes.

A numb cloud descended over Darius's head.

There was so much Thorn didn't know. But *they'd* known. They'd *all* known.

His focus shifted to the wolf, standing proud at the center, and for the first time since watching Chris vanish into the dark, Darius felt something other than anguish.

And it burned hot.

A figure moved behind him, a ghost of a person lacking the substance of a soul walking down the center of the room. Darius didn't look up as Cain settled onto the chair across the aisle. He, too, considered the dais, his hands laced in his lap. For a few minutes, they sat there in silence.

Until Darius breathed a sigh.

"What is it, Cain?" He glanced over, and Cain replied with a confused frown. "Are you here to offer some… immortal wisdom? Words of comfort? An allegory I won't understand?" Darius forced a laugh and tilted his face toward the sky, imagining the universe above him. "Whatever it is, I'm not in the place to hear it."

When he looked back, Cain's expression darkened.

"I wish I were," he murmured, "but unfortunately, I have nothing to offer except more bad news."

He raised his hands helplessly at his sides. Darius frowned.

"What's going on?" His heart pounded, and his mind went wild with possibilities, but somehow, he didn't anticipate what Cain said next.

"Envy has claimed a new host."

The conference room felt like a cell.

The white paint, cold silence, and stagnant air dropped an oppressive weight between these walls. The Martyr directors had left the head chair decidedly empty. Darius stared at it, his stomach on fire, as Nicholas shook his head.

"This is just what we fucking need," he said.

He groaned and leaned forward. God, Darius hadn't seen the man this worn out since he'd obliterated Sloth. His blonde hair, normally styled nicely, looked as though the only comb it had seen in the last five days was Nicholas's own fingers. Even his beard felt flat, maybe because Nicholas kept depressing his chin into his palm. He did so again now, dull eyes caught on Darius. "When did this happen?"

"We can't know for sure," Darius said. "Cain said he first felt Envy use its Influence yesterday morning, right before Chris's—" His voice snagged, and he cleared his throat. Gabe, who now sat beside Darius the way she always had, looked down at the table. His energy condensed into a hard, aching mass. Darius forced himself to go on. "He seemed confident that meant the possession was pretty recent. The last couple of days, probably."

Nicholas uttered a soft curse as Abraham sighed. Gabe's brows furrowed, and he looked around at all of them.

"So, what do we do?" he asked. "Look for the new host?"

Mackenzie let out a scoff. She seemed no better off than Nicholas. Her legs were drawn beneath her, and the green dye in her bangs made the puffy bags under her eyes stand out in bright red contrast. *'How?* We're already spread pretty fucking thin between our search for Thorn *and* Froschlin, and at least we know who the fuck to look out for there. Envy's new host could be literally anyone in that goddamned city."

She flung out a hand, narrowly avoiding knocking Nicholas in the jaw.

"That's what the Gray Unit is for," Abraham said. "Who is assigned to watch out for Envy?"

Darius, Mackenzie, and Nicholas exchanged a dark look.

Mackenzie slid her tongue piercing between her teeth as Nicholas drew in a deep breath. At last, Darius said, "Since Eva… no one."

A short pause consumed them. Then, Nicholas exhaled an exasperated sigh.

"All right, this is insane," he said, fingers once again pulling his hair out of place. "We *need* to talk about who's taking over Intelligence operations."

The table bristled, every face around it swiveling to Darius. His heart pattered against his ribs.

"No one is taking over Intelligence operations," he said, willing his voice to stay level. "Thorn—"

"Has been gone a *week,*" Nicholas cut in. Darius's teeth snapped shut. Nicholas, however, swung again. "We have no idea when *or if* she'll be back *and* no way to contact her. The Gray Unit needs someone at the helm."

"And that person should be Thorn," Darius countered.

"I agree, but where the *fuck* is she, Darius?"

Nicholas threw open his arms, indicating the room, the Underground, the whole goddamned state, as far as Darius could tell. And Darius didn't reply. He couldn't.

Because he didn't know.

"I'm telling you," he said in a last, desperate claw for control, "Thorn *will* be back."

Nicholas didn't budge, but his expression shifted from frustration to something closer to calculation, like he could read the words Darius hadn't spoken tattooed behind his eyes.

Mackenzie cleared her throat.

"I'll keep managing the Gray Unit until Thorn comes back *or* it becomes clear she isn't," the Irishwoman said. She put her feet on the ground and leaned over the table with the no-bullshit attitude that made her a good director in the first place. "But I'm not going to put someone on the Envy case. I have *no* idea how to go about that, and quite frankly, I don't think it's a priority. What *is* a priority, though, is stopping Froschlin. We can't worry about finding new Sins *or* the last Virtue until we handle that Rockefeller-Tree-Sized problem."

All of Darius's indignation drowned in a sudden flood of liquid fire, and a shallow breath hitched in the hollow of his throat.

The last Virtue.

Darius's eyes flicked back to that damned head chair.

How many times had Alan sat there, *right fucking there*, in front of a room full of people hunting for a piece to the puzzle that he'd slipped up his sleeve decades ago? How many times did he look Thorn in the face and act like he, too, felt the absence that missing piece left behind?

How many times had he *lied* simply by withholding the truth?

Darius's hands balled into fists.

"Darius? You good?"

He glanced up to see Nicholas watching him again, in that same shrewd, sharp way. Darius's pulse ticked in his neck like a clock as everyone else turned to him, too.

He could have told them. Maybe he *should* have—to share this burden, to not carry it alone.

But he didn't. Thorn *deserved* to know first.

"Mackenzie's right," he said. "We knew Envy would re-possess eventually, and Edith Froschlin is a much bigger threat right now."

"I agree," Gabe said. "I'll worry about Envy when Froschlin stops killing my people."

His eyes glistened, and a rough quiet consumed them all. Darius wanted to scream into it just to feel something other than sorrow for a second. Instead, he locked onto Nicholas again. "Was that phone useful?"

"Yeah," Nicholas replied instantly, as though he, too, was hungry for a different feeling and work was the only distraction he knew how to utilize. "Incredibly useful. We're tapped into her private LymeLite group, and she clearly used it to organize all the past attacks. There are details about every single one of them. When she plans another, I have no doubt they'll talk about it, but we have to be careful."

"Careful?" Abraham asked. "Why?"

"Because we're using a profile for a man who's MIA."

Darius's mouth dropped open before he had the chance to stop it. "What?"

Nicholas grabbed a tablet and laid it on the table. A missing person's report, complete with a photograph of Backward Sunglasses himself, looked up from the screen. "Ace Rodfield. He was last seen by his family in the South Bronx on Tuesday, December 29, the same day you ran into him. Location services tracked his phone until it entered the Martyr vehicle a couple of blocks away and again before someone picked you up on Randalls Island. That's the last sign of him the authorities can pin down."

Darius's mouth went dry. He pressed his tongue flat and tried to swallow. "Are the people from The Cross under investigation?"

"They've been questioned," Nicholas said, "but since his phone *did* ping the satellites a good two miles away, there's not a lot of focus on them. Plus, everyone agreed that he walked out the front door of his own accord at exactly 9:45, and they all have an air-tight alibi. It looks like they're getting away with... whatever they did to him."

A cold block grew in Darius's stomach. He should have been unsettled at the idea of Thorn's friends killing a man, but he wasn't. Ace Rodfield was the reason Chris was gone, and Darius couldn't find an ounce of sympathy in his body to spare for the man.

Realizing *that* felt awful, though.

"So, if he's... *'missing,'*" Mackenzie said, throwing up a pair of finger quotes. A set of bright gold nails caught the light. "Why do we have to be careful?"

"LymeLite tracks login attempts and shows when users are active," Nicholas replied. "Skylar got into the settings and turned all that off, but if anyone looked into the site's user details, they *would* see that he was last active the day after he went missing. Hopefully, no one does the math."

Darius crossed his arms. "Can't we join the group with a dummy account of our own?"

"No," Nicholas said, shaking his head. "It's invitation-only, and we can't *invite* ourselves through a dead man's profile. We've just got to lay low. The next time Froschlin and her fucks start planning an attack, we'll know about it before she ever texts that damned burner."

The thought made Darius's pulse leap, and he tapped his fingertips against his bicep to release some of the energy. "Good," he said aloud, but the rest of his thoughts bounced around his skull like a volley of ricocheting bullets.

Because finding Edith meant finding Thorn—and it was the *only* way to find her. He just hoped they'd be able to reach her before she did something truly stupid and got herself killed.

Suddenly, a warm aura turned down the hall—an aura Darius didn't expect to feel up here at this time of the day. He got to his feet, and when David Cochrane knocked on the conference room door, Darius was already there to answer it.

"Ah, hey." David stuttered over the words, his fist poised mid-air. He threw a look over Darius's shoulder, cleared his throat, and dropped his hand. "Sorry to interrupt, but... can I speak with you? Alone?"

Darius's lungs filled with dread as he nodded. "Of course."

He left the conference room without a goodbye, grateful for an excuse to get out of that goddamned conversation, but he was halfway to his office before he remembered he didn't have one anymore. All of them were empty, and he was sure no one would have minded if he borrowed theirs, but he didn't want to sit in anyone else's space right now.

So, he kept going until he reached the door at the end of the hall and welcomed David into the lounge between Thorn's room and Alan's. Darius flicked on the light.

"Take a seat."

He gestured to the couch on the opposite wall. David

settled on the left-hand side, which meant Darius had a perfect view of Thorn's name plaque over his shoulder. He sat down, too, smoothing his palms over his thighs. God, why did they feel so clammy?

Maybe it wasn't his hands. Maybe it was David. The man stared at Darius like he was looking into an open grave.

"What's going on?" Darius asked.

David hesitated, breathing through a long sigh. "There isn't an easy way to say this."

The bottom of Darius's chest opened up and sucked his heart right into it. David continued.

"But Michelle and I have talked it over, and we're not sure raising Lindsay in the Underground is a good idea."

Darius's head bobbed in a slow, instinctive nod—one that his body seemed to know was the right move to make when his mind was still swimming in a numb gel.

"We knew it was dangerous," David said. He wrung his hands in his lap—hands that were strong with life again since his daughter obliterated the cancer in his body. "We knew it was a risk, but there have been *six* funerals since we arrived, and that was only three weeks ago. Then Thorn disappeared, Juniper left, and now your tactical leader is dead… Lindsay can't grow up in this, Darius. She needs more stability."

"I understand," Darius said. The words tumbled out on autopilot because he *did* understand. It was hard growing up a daughter of the Martyrs. Chris would have known that better than anyone. The corners of his eyes stung. "What do you plan to do instead?"

David's shoulders melted, like he was relieved Darius hadn't tried to argue with him. "We're thinking of heading upstate. Michelle has a cousin up there. We just need to grab a few more things from our apartment and tie up some loose ends. We might call Juniper and see if she won't join us, too."

Darius's throat swelled. He forced a gulp of air down. "I wish I could do more to help," he murmured. Alan would have paid for the relocation—purchased property, prepared assets, put securities in place—but under new authority, the Martyrs hardly had enough money to keep themselves above water.

"You've done more than enough," David said, without an ounce of scorn in his voice. "You helped my daughter realize more of her potential… You saved my life. I get to watch my little girl grow up." His jaw clenched, and a glassy sheen flashed across his irises. "I want to keep in touch. When Lindsay's an adult, she can decide what to do with the gifts she's been given."

David smiled, driving a final spike into Darius's chest, and for a moment, he was as breathless as he'd been the first time he'd lost Lindsay. And the second.

"We'll have to cover some of your memories," Darius said. He couldn't believe how level his voice sounded. "About the Underground. What it looks like, how it works. But the big details can stay."

"That's completely fine," David said. "Thank you."

He reached out a palm, which Darius took. His arm felt distant, like he was watching two different men shake hands.

"Of course," Darius said. "I want what's best for Lindsay. For all of you."

They continued talking, discussing the finer details of when they would leave. Darius committed them to memory, but in the moment, they flicked away. When David left, Darius stood and waved, and then, he stayed behind.

Once he was alone, his ears began to ring. Had they been doing this the whole time?

The lounge lost its color, fading until nothing stood out except the doors to his right and left. Darius glanced at Thorn's first. Her name opened a pit in his chest like half of his soul had been torn out. But Alan… god, just the thought of him was enough to bring back the red.

His office was coated in it. The carpet, the chairs, even some of the volumes on the shelf on the opposite wall— they were all vibrant and angry. Darius walked through this dead space, and every step lit a spark beneath his heel. He dragged his fingers across the desk, slicing new wounds in the dust.

When he looked up again, Alan looked back.

The old military portrait. It sat on a shelf, haunting the room with a shell-shocked stare. Darius looked into those eyes, and he wondered when this photograph was taken— before or after Wrath had started peeling pieces of him away, revealing the raw core within.

Darius lifted the frame. A thumb-stroke patch of cleared dust streaked Alan's face. Someone else had touched this relic recently. His heart fluttered.

Who else could it have been but Thorn?

The embers of Darius's rage suddenly ignited, as though Wrath itself found purchase inside his soul.

God fucking *damn it*.

How much of this could have been avoided? How many lives could have been preserved, memories salvaged, if Alan Blaine had told Thorn *everything*?

Instead, he let her suffer alone.

A series of firing neurons and tightening muscles clenched Darius's fist around the picture before he spun around and pitched it across the room. It crashed into the wall beside the open door, breaking the glass and digging a chip out of the paint. The portrait landed on the crimson carpet with a dull thump, like a two-dimensional body hitting the ground.

It wasn't enough.

A scream built up in his throat. Instead of swallowing it down, bottling it away with the rest of his fucking feelings, Darius opened his mouth and set it free. In a flurry of movement, he threw open the closet, yanked Alan's jackets from their hangers, and tossed them onto the ground in a sacrilegious heap. He turned to the desk, seizing the pair of reading glasses sitting in the dust. They hit the carpet, and he crushed them beneath his heel. Then he pulled open the drawers, ready to upend them, spill their contents like entrails at his feet. He froze.

The folder of Thorn's life sat at the top.

Staccato breaths rocked Darius's chest. He glared around—at the shattered picture frame, the mound of coats, and his own balled hands. The fury flying through his veins hunted for an outlet, something to *do*, and Darius thought, in a distant, dissociated way, that this must have been how Thorn had felt that time she'd destroyed her office.

Darius wanted to destroy more than an office…

He wanted to destroy a pattern. A system.

A lie.

He forced his fingers open, dipped them into his pocket, and pulled out his phone. He dialed a number and held the device to his ear with a trembling hand.

"Hey, Stevie," he said. "Do we have any extra paint lying around?"

CHAPTER THIRTY

A cardboard city filled the lounge, packing boxes stacked like brown skyscrapers. They reached from the cream carpet to the ceiling in a grid so tight that Darius had to squeeze between pillars to reach what had once been Alan Blaine's office.

Darius slid the name plaque free from the door. It was heavy, made of thick bronze, darkened with time. He slipped it down the side of a box full of personal items, including the broken picture frame, the folder, and an envelope with Thorn's name scrawled upon it in Alan's neat script.

Darius considered these items for a numb moment before grabbing his own name plaque from his back pocket. It was made of lighter metal, both in color and weight, but it fit into the bracket as easily as though it had been made for this position—affixed to *this* room. Darius would have stepped away to admire it, but there were too many boxes, so instead, he opened the door and strode inside.

Here, he was surrounded by ghosts.

White sheets shrouded the furniture, which had all been dragged to the center in a lopsided mass. Similar throws covered the carpet, too, leaving the taupe walls exposed and

471

ready for a new layer of paint.

Two buckets of white primer sat in one corner. Darius popped one of the lids, poured some into a tray, and grabbed a brush.

The first stroke felt like slicing a blade through memory, as though he were committing an invisible crime, but every one after became easier until Darius entered a meditative state. His breathing synced with his work, his heartbeat a steady percussion, and all the while, his mind went dormant.

Until the sound of a door gliding against carpet perked his ears.

Darius didn't turn around, but his senses became more alert as a body without an aura squeezed through the cardboard borough in the lounge. They reached the doorway, and Darius could feel eyes upon him as he lined the floorboards on the opposite wall.

"Need help?" Nicholas asked.

Darius's head reeled around. Nicholas leaned against the doorframe, his arms crossed, typical slacks and button-up replaced with jeans and a ratty t-shirt. A moment of shame warmed Darius's cheeks.

He'd expected a scathing comment. Maybe an "I told you so." Something with teeth.

But Nicholas came in with kindness—and Darius felt awful he'd presumed anything else. He nodded his head toward the paint supplies. "Grab a roller."

The next couple of hours passed in peaceful, companionable silence. Nicholas followed Darius, applying a layer of primer over the walls he'd already edged while Darius finished the others and eventually grabbed a roller, too. They finished the first coat twice as fast as he would have on his own. Afterward, sweaty and speckled in little white dots, the two of them sat on the ground with their backs against the covered desk to appreciate the work. Darius took in a deep, filling breath. The chemical scent stung his sinuses, and he thought maybe he should have grabbed a mask, but right now, he was happy that this room didn't smell like it belonged to someone else anymore. It was new. A clean slate.

A fresh start.

"So," Nicholas began, "what's going on?"

Darius glanced at him, and Nicholas's focus sharpened.

"I'm moving into the office," Darius said.

"Yeah, I got that," Nicholas replied with a tone that made it clear he wasn't buying it. "I wanted to know why." He paused, taking Darius in as though viewing him under a microscope. "Does it have anything to do with why you and Chris went to The Cross that night?"

A flutter tickled behind Darius's ribs. "I told you why we went."

"You told me *part* of why," Nicholas challenged, "but if it was just about questioning the bartender, anyone could have gone. But *you* did, with only Chris, and you didn't tell anyone else."

The blood drained from Darius's face, but he said nothing. Nicholas's chin dipped before he turned back to watch the paint dry. A sigh rolled over his tongue.

"It must be bad," he murmured, "to make you clean out his space like this."

Darius's teeth clenched, and his fists followed suit. His nails bit into his palm as he said, "Let's just say I'm *done* doing things Alan's way. It's not working anymore. Hell, I'm not sure it ever worked."

He didn't need to look to know Nicholas's eyes had found their way back to him. The former Diligence nodded. The motion in Darius's peripheral made him feel like he was floating.

"What are you going to do differently?" Nicholas asked.

"I don't know," Darius admitted. "But I'm sick of the secrets. Sick of hiding." He sighed and pinched the bridge of his nose. "Not that we're really *hiding* anymore. Not with Edith Froschlin dragging us into the literal LymeLite."

A sudden memory struck him—an old argument. He turned to Nicholas again. "Maybe that's where we start. We fight back… tell the public what's *actually* going on with Edith and the Sins. Are you still interested in that?"

A righteous grin bloomed through Nicholas's trimmed beard, highlighting the smattering of freckles and white paint sprayed across his cheeks.

"Am I interested?" he repeated with a laugh. "C'mon."

He slapped a palm onto Darius's shoulder, using him as leverage to rise from the ground before extending that same hand to hoist Darius up. Nicholas led the way through the cardboard neighborhood, down the hallway, and into the R&D headquarters. When he opened the door, the room glanced up. When Darius walked through, it froze.

"Dan," Nicholas called. "Pull up Underground Press."

A quiet shuffle vibrated among the gathered auras as they passed one another scattered glances. Daniel Park blinked, his black irises flicking from Nicholas to Darius and back again before he turned to his computer. The screen mounted next to the entrance turned on, displaying a LymeLite profile. Darius frowned as Nicholas raised his hands. "Welcome to the resistance. Take a seat."

He gestured to the nearest table. Darius took the empty chair between Naomi and Parker. The young women exchanged a look behind his back that he couldn't see so much as sense happening. Nicholas approached the display, and Darius took it all in.

The name "Underground Press" sat below a black and white icon that mimicked the *Peccostium* in style, with its sharp points and crisp curves, but instead of a serpent's eye with a slit through the middle, it appeared to be two nested omega symbols inside the basin of a thin, crescent moon. Beneath it, a feed full of content featuring… Thorn?

"What the hell is this?" Darius asked.

"Our counterattack against Edith Froschlin's propaganda," Nicholas answered. He tapped the screen, activated the touch controls, and flicked a finger toward the sky. The feed zipped upward, showing dozens of items. "We've covered everything from what the Sins are to how to identify the work of Influence in your body and protect yourself against it, as well as the truth behind all of the attacks Froschlin's carried out. Recently, we've focused on debunking the conspiracy theories around 'Jane Morgan.'"

He tapped an arrow that dragged the entire profile back to the top and clicked on one of the newer videos. The screen filled with a side-by-side comparison between the Raven, Thorn, and the deepfake version that had attacked the Winter Village Market. Nicholas's voiceover boomed from the speakers.

"We've already covered the digital artifacts that prove this footage was AI-generated," he said. *"So today, we're going to use a different tool: our common sense."*

A pair of red lines moved up the side of each figure, from heel to head, with numbers along the side.

"Jane Morgan stands at around five foot nine inches," the narration went on. *"As you can see in this original image of the Raven taken at Washington Square, she's only five foot three. That's a striking six-inch difference. Now, in the Bryant Park footage..."*

The display changed again, flicking back to the shot of the faux-Thorn with a bloody baton in her hand.

"Our program indicates the woman in this footage is short, matching the Raven's stature, and not *Jane Morgan."*

Nicholas paused the feed and turned to Darius, who didn't realize his jaw had dropped until he tried to speak.

"How long have you been working on this?" he asked.

"Since the end of November," Nicholas answered. "After Froschlin sat down for that first interview with RebelTruth."

Darius gawked. "A *month?*"

"Just over, yeah."

A sound between a scoff and a laugh erupted from Darius's mouth. "How hasn't anyone noticed? Holly's—"

He stopped abruptly, realization hitting him like a bludgeon to the back of his head. Nicholas's smile widened.

"Oh, my god," Darius muttered. "Holly's in on it. Who else knows? Mackenzie?"

Nicholas snorted, and a series of chuckles rollicked through the room. "Of course Mackenzie doesn't know. I'd have to glue that woman's mouth shut to get her to keep a secret like this. No, it's just us and the security team."

He walked back to the table, looking around his staff. A dozen sets of eyes followed him, expressing a range of feelings from nervous to proud. Nicholas's hand landed on Parker's shoulder, and her tawny face turned bright red from the sudden influx of attention.

"Parker's the brains behind our content," he said. "She keeps tabs on what the LymeLite crowd is talking about, what's in the Spotlight, and gets ideas together. From there, it goes to Naomi. She's our lead creative. All the videos you see here? She's the one in charge of editing and aesthetics."

Darius stared, at a loss for words. Naomi offered a shrug, but the smirk on her face was the closest thing he'd ever seen to real joy from her.

"As for how we get our message *out there,*" Nicholas went on as he walked the edge of the room, "we're still lying low. We don't want Froschlin to figure out what we're doing and get our accounts shut down, so most of our strategy revolves around replying to comments with some fake accounts to start a discussion and get people thinking. When they're receptive, we invite them to follow our channel, which is private… so far. Dan and his team have been making that happen."

He held out a fist, which Daniel bumped with his knuckles. Darius, however, shook his head.

"What if you invite one of Edith's followers?"

Nicholas propped his hands on his hips. "That's where the security team comes in. When we find someone we want to invite, Skylar looks into them. It probably doesn't come as a surprise that many of Froschlin's die-hard fans are *not* quiet about it. Even a *whiff* of pro-crow propaganda gets people blacklisted. So far, it seems to have worked. We haven't had our account deactivated… yet."

"How many followers do you have?" Darius asked.

Nicholas grinned again. "Over twelve *thousand.*"

A short, shallow breath rushed from Darius's mouth. "And that's *with* lying low?"

"Yep," Nicholas said with a nod. "Imagine what we can do when we lean *all in.*"

A wild glint lit Nicholas's eyes, filling them with a passion reminiscent of his time as a Virtue. Darius wanted to share the thrill, but all he could think, as he looked over the name, the icon, the videos featuring Thorn's face, was that she would be *livid* when she found out.

But worse than that was the realization that he didn't really care.

"What would leaning all in look like?" Darius asked.

Nicholas crossed his arms, a smug look on his face. "Are you saying you're on board?"

Darius glanced around at a dozen expectant pairs of eyes—at a group of people who believed so deeply in what they were doing that they'd defied direct orders to make it happen. He turned to Nicholas again.

"Yeah. I am."

A switch flicked in the R&D Headquarters. Any inkling of nervous energy disappeared, replaced by a refreshing excitement that gave Darius a sense of optimism for the first time since Thorn had disappeared. While Nicholas returned to his desk, Darius wandered the room and talked to as many people as he could, getting up to speed on what the digital frontline looked like. Parker walked him through a massive content document, full of ideas they hadn't yet put into place, and Naomi showed him the videos she was currently working on, which included more items about the Bryant Park attack, old footage of Puppets, and a walkthrough of what makes someone susceptible to Influence. After that, he sat down with Daniel and talked about distribution.

"Going public is a bit of a risk," Daniel said as Darius scooted his chair closer. "So, we're going to have to be careful."

Darius's brows knitted together. "What kind of risk? Could people get our information? Track the account back to our location?"

Daniel shook his head. "Nah. Holly's routed our network through so many VPNs that we may as well be accessing the internet from Mars. The biggest concern we have is getting caught and shut down."

"By LymeLite?"

"By *Froschlin,*" Daniel clarified. "We know she's getting other creators' accounts banned, just like *we* were doing, so we'd like to avoid that."

"And if we can't?"

"We follow RebelTruth's lead," Daniel said with a shrug. "We have a handful of backup accounts ready, but we'd rather not have to use them, so we're taking precautions."

"Precautions like what?" Darius asked.

"Like blocking the people who could rat us out," Daniel said with a sly smile. He navigated his display to LymeLite, where he scrolled through Edith's secret group from Ace Rodfield's account. "Thanks to you, we now have a list of the Raven's die-hard fanatics. We're making sure *none* of them can access our page."

He continued to scroll, and Darius wanted to be proud, but that final photograph of Chris at The Cross flashed by and doused his good feelings with fresh sorrow. A sudden sting of tears clouded his vision, and Darius cleared his throat to stop it from closing up.

"Have they started talking about any other strikes?" he asked in a clumsy claw for a new topic to keep grief from swallowing him whole.

Daniel shook his head. "Not yet. One user seems to be leading the charge for their public events—someone with the handle Poe_198."

He clicked on the profile photo—an anonymous black silhouette—and loaded the account. There wasn't much. No content, no biography, nothing personal at all, just a list of activity inside Edith's closed group. The most recent item was a comment left on that damned photo.

"We're on our way."

Darius's blood ran cold.

"Whenever the crows have all been called together, Poe's behind it," Daniel continued. "During the first incident at Washington Square, they posted about it thirty minutes ahead of time. Every incident after, they gave a full day's warning, so we expect to have twenty-four hours to prepare the next time they plan something."

Darius nodded, but his mind ran through the calculations. Edith had been making appearances regularly since Halloween night, showing up at least once a week, but since drawing the wrong kind of attention by murdering Conrad Carter, she'd slowed down. Part of Darius worried she would stop altogether, and if she *did*, he wasn't sure how the hell they were going to find Thorn.

His stomach twisted, and a nervous chill trickled down his spine.

The door swung open as an auraless body strode in. Darius spun around with his heart in his throat, imagining, hoping, *praying* against all logic it was her.

Instead, Cain entered the room. Darius's shoulders slumped.

"Excuse my intrusion," Cain said. His eyes landed on Darius. He offered a strained smile and tilted his head toward the exit. "Mr. and Mrs. Cochrane are ready. They wanted to say goodbye."

The rest of Darius's optimism swirled through his chest like water down a drain. He glanced at the wall to Cain's right, where the sensation of a little Virtue hovered in the waiting area.

God, he'd been so caught up he'd completely forgotten Lindsay was leaving today.

Cain held the door as Darius slipped through, and they walked down the hallway. Darius made the distant realization that he was still in a pair of paint-speckled jeans and a dirty shirt, and he wished he'd thought to change, but it was too late now. It was too late for a lot of things.

"Be careful with the Programming," Darius said.

"Yes, I'm well aware of the procedures to remain difficult to find," Cain murmured. "Trust me. No one wants to be caught by Envy less than I do. We are taking an obscure route, and Gabe has kindly assigned a TAC guard to follow us the entire way."

Darius nodded, but he didn't feel any better.

David and Michelle stood by the glass garage doors, a couple of suitcases on the ground by their feet. Saul held Lindsay in a crushing hug. She pressed her face against his until their cheeks squished together.

"Goodbye, *princesita,*" he murmured.

"Bye, Tío Saul. Will you come visit us at our new house?"

"Of course, I will," Saul replied.

Lindsay drew away, eyes bright and mouth open in a grin. "Tomorrow?"

Saul chuckled. "Tomorrow? You won't even have time to miss me by tomorrow!" He gently flicked the tip of her nose with a knuckle, which sent her into a fit of giggles before he placed her back on her own two feet. Before he rose, he planted an affectionate kiss on the crown of her head.

Lindsay turned to Darius, more hesitant now. He dropped to a knee before her.

"Goodbye, Darius."

"Goodbye, Lindsay."

"I, uhm…" She shifted from one foot to the other, glancing at her mom. Michelle tilted her head forward, and Lindsay spun back to Darius. Her hands wrung at her waist. "Thank you for finding me a family."

Darius's chest cracked open in beautiful agony. He let out a short laugh as the corners of his eyes prickled. His nose wrinkled playfully, and he cast David and Michelle a quiet look. "It's a pretty good family, huh?" Lindsay nodded fervently. Darius mimicked the gesture but with much less gusto. "I'm so happy *you're* so happy, sweetheart."

Lindsay passed a lackluster smile. "What do I do about my… you know…" She leaned forward and whispered against his ear. "My Charity?"

He frowned, thinking. "You just… keep it close. It's a secret for you and your parents to know… And then, I guess you…"

His voice drifted off as he searched for the right words.

"Follow my heart?" Lindsay offered.

Darius chuckled. "Yeah. Exactly. Just do what feels right."

"And I can't go wrong," Lindsay completed. Now, her smile shone bright and eager. "That's what Thorn told me."

Darius drew a short, shallow breath, which lodged in his throat alongside his heart. "She did?" he managed to whisper.

"Yeah," Lindsay said. "She knows a lot about Virtues, huh?"

"She does." Darius forced himself to nod. "More than she realizes."

"When she comes back," Lindsay said, "will you tell her bye for me?"

"I will," Darius said. "Promise."

Lindsay threw herself into Darius's arms. He held her close, closing his eyes, appreciating the sensation of her Virtue pressed so closely against his—the magnetic allure of her soul a perfect, beautiful expression of everything good in the world. When she drew back and rejoined her family, he said goodbye to David and Michelle, wishing them well. Cain led them into the garage, and the little family piled into the same sedan he and Darius used to take Juniper into the city a week ago.

It felt like so much longer.

Darius stood by the doors and watched until the vehicle was out of sight, and then, he waited until he couldn't feel the pull of Lindsay's Virtue tugging against his. Saul stayed at his side until Darius finally exhaled a sigh.

"What the hell am I doing wrong, Saul?" he whispered.

"Why is everything *falling apart?*"

The empty room swallowed his voice, and it was like he hadn't spoken at all. Saul didn't reply for a while. His energy shifted, and his brows drew together as he thought.

"I don't think it's falling apart," he answered at last. "I think it's falling together… but that still includes a fall, and the fall's the scariest part."

He caught Darius's gaze with a smirk, and his hand slapped against his shoulder.

"C'mon. Let's go get you a jacket."

"A jacket?" Darius asked as Saul led him toward the elevator. "Why?"

"Because you could use a walk—and not on one of those damned treadmills. You need real sun and fresh air."

Darius shook his head. "It's *January.*"

"Which is why," Saul insisted, "you need a jacket, or do you want frozen *cojones?*"

He elbowed Darius in the ribs, and Darius laughed—a real, heartful laugh that felt like a Virtue's healing touch against the cracks in his soul. Then, Saul forced Darius to do something he hadn't done in months: take care of himself. The two of them wandered through the woods around the gas station above, talking about whatever came to mind—things that mattered and things that didn't. Afterward, Saul dragged him to the dining area and made sure he ate dinner, and then he distracted Darius with a card game in the break room. For once, the news wasn't playing, as though the rest of the Martyrs had also tired of the constant barrage of catastrophe.

When Darius settled into bed hours later, his grief felt smaller, or at the very least, more manageable, and instead of gnawing at his guts from the inside out, it curled up in the corner of his psyche. He shut off the lights and let himself drift off to sleep.

His phone rang at midnight.

Darius jolted up, suddenly wide awake, and whipped his device off the nightstand. Part of him thought it might be

Thorn—who the hell else called this late at night?—but David Cochrane's name glowed on the screen instead.

That was worse.

Darius's stomach twisted as he pressed the answer icon.

"Hey, man," he said. His voice felt horrifyingly loud in the dark. "Everything good?"

A rattling breath shook through the speaker. "D-Darius?"

His face went cold. "Lindsay? Honey, what's wrong?"

Lindsay squeaked. Sobbed. She choked out his name. "Darius, help—"

Then she cried out. Darius's heart clenched. "Lindsay!"

"She can't come to the phone at the moment." Fear slid down his spine like an egg cracked against his skull. "Hello, *Darius Jones,*" Autumn Hunt purred. "I hope I didn't wake you."

Darius's lip curled. "What have you—"

"Ah ah ah," Wrath interrupted. "I don't have time for this back and forth. I have a *child* to take care of, and it's way past bedtime…"

A deep laugh rumbled from her throat like a tiger's growl. Darius's fingers tightened around his phone.

"But I don't want a child," the Sin went on. "I want *you.* So, I'm here to offer a trade. Surrender yourself, and—what was it that you called the little brat? Leslie?"

"Lindsay," Darius hissed through gritted teeth.

"Whatever. *It* goes free if *I* have you."

Darius froze, his pulse pounding, breath arrested in his lungs.

"You have twelve hours," Wrath said. "Noon tomorrow at the Huddlestone Arch in Central Park. Ask *Jane* what happens if you try anything clever… If you can find her."

She laughed again. Darius caught the distinct note of a screaming child before Wrath disconnected the call.

CHAPTER THIRTY-ONE

Darius entered the conference room to chaos. Seven people sat around the table, and their voices slammed to a stop as Darius shut the door. They looked up in a synchronized movement: all the Martyr directors, along with Saul, Holly, and Cain, in various stages of dress. Mackenzie wore nothing but a pair of loose shorts and a tank top, while Cain had at least managed to put on some slippers with his pajamas. Only Gabe managed to show up, arms crossed, in his full TAC uniform.

"Well?" he asked as Darius approached the table. "Has John found David and Michelle?"

Darius exhaled a shaky breath and shook his head.

"They're dead."

Whispers and exclamations and loose swear words flew around the room like debris. Darius waited for the noise to settle before he lowered into the chair at the head of the table.

"What happened?" Nicholas asked.

"I'm not entirely sure," Darius said. The words felt strange, like they'd been drawn from his mouth through a vacuum. "Marcus and his Cleaning Crew are on their way into the city right now, but I don't think they'll be able to do much. John ran over from his apartment as soon as I called him, and he said police were already on the scene."

Nicholas swore while Abraham leaned forward. "What did he see?"

"Not much," Darius admitted. "We'll have to look at the police reports to get the whole story." Holly whipped open her laptop. Like Mackenzie, she hadn't bothered to put real clothes on when Darius woke her up at midnight, and her sweats nearly swallowed her whole. He glanced at her before he went on. "But John did say they pulled two body bags out of the building. We don't technically know David and Michelle were in them, but…"

Darius's voice petered out. Cain cast him a dark look. "We know," he finished.

A blanket of silence fell, broken only by Saul getting to his feet to pace behind his chair. No one had challenged Darius when he'd brought his oldest friend in for this meeting. Maybe they'd all recognized he needed the support—or that Darius was not in the mood to debate about who he wanted in his corner right now.

"It doesn't make any goddamned sense," Mackenzie said at last. Her green hair frayed in a mop of bed-headed chaos, and black smudges rimmed her eyes from makeup that hadn't been effectively washed off before she went to sleep. "How the *fuck* did Wrath find them? They've been gone less than twelve hours!"

"Maybe it has something to do with Envy's new host?" Abraham posited, glancing at Cain. "Could it have felt your Influence when you Programmed them?"

Cain shook his head. "Certainly, it felt my Influence," he said. "That's undeniable. But I was nowhere *near* the Cochranes' apartment when I performed the Programming. We very deliberately took an obscure route through New Jersey and stopped at a cafe along the way. It would be virtually *impossible* for Envy to track them home based on Influence alone."

"And Envy was *not* the one to find them," Nicholas

added. "Not as far as we know, at least. *Wrath* called Darius." He frowned, jaw set beneath his beard. "The question I have is… what else does she know?"

Darius pressed his fingertips against his tired eyelids until his vision swirled with gray spots. "I'm worried about that, too. Something she said makes me think she knows Thorn took off. I figure she tortured that information out of Michelle and David before—" His voice caught, and he cleared his throat, removing his hands from his face to look at the table again. "What else could she have learned? About the Underground? About the Martyrs? About *Lindsay?*"

A pause. Mackenzie's piercing clicked against her teeth. Saul's face went ashen. "If she knows she's a Virtue…"

"Then she's already dead," Darius finished.

His heart clenched, and Saul raised a closed fist to his mouth, as though biting his first knuckle kept him from screaming. Cain exhaled a short, choppy breath.

"I doubt Wrath knows about Charity," the old Forgotten Sin said, though his tone reeked of doubt. "Lindsay is too young for the Sins to sense her aura, regardless of her Virtue. There is no reason to presume she is anything other than an ordinary human child, and the Sins wouldn't ask questions about something they don't suspect in the first place. Even if they *had*, my Programming would have prevented her parents from disclosing such information to anyone who does not already know. They couldn't have spoken the words aloud, even if they wanted to."

Mackenzie let out a disheartened scoff. "What do I always say? Programming makes us *'torture proof.'*"

Cain nodded in her direction. "While minor details aren't covered, the essentials *are*: information about our group, our location, and our secrets. Lindsay is a *hefty* secret."

Then he glanced at Darius, and his eyes narrowed. "Thorn's disappearance, however, is *not*. The Cochranes could have easily let that bit information slip, which is likely why she called *you* and *not* Thorn."

Darius's mouth ran dry. He swallowed hard, looking at

the rest of them. "This brings up another big concern," he said. "Even if David and Michelle couldn't talk, Lindsay *could*. She's an Initiated Virtue, which means you couldn't Program her, could you?"

Cain's mouth pressed into a thin line. "I could not."

Darius held out a hand. "Lindsay may be too young to understand any useful information about the Martyrs or the Underground, but she *does* know what she is. She knows what she can do."

"Which means," Abraham said slowly, the muscles in his neck tight, "that even if Wrath hasn't realized she has a Virtue, she could soon. All it would take is that little girl saying one wrong thing."

The room went quiet for the breadth of time it took a heart to skip. Then, Saul swore. "We have to get her before that happens."

"I agree," Gabe said. "Darius, what *exactly* did Autumn Hunt say?"

"Just that she wants to trade Lindsay for me," Darius said. "Noon tomorrow at the Huddlestone Arch."

Cain sucked in a sudden, sharp breath, and one hand whipped up to cover his mouth. "The Huddlestone—are you *certain?*"

"Yeah," Darius said. "Why? What's wrong?"

The color drained from Cain's face as his eyes moved around the room. "How much do any of you know about what happened to Thorn's son?"

They all shook their heads, except Darius, whose body felt so tense he couldn't do anything. Holly tapped on her laptop again. "I can access the unredacted files," she said, but Cain stopped her with a touch to the wrist.

"Donovan Rose was captured by Wrath," he said. Holly closed her computer, and Saul stood behind his chair, hands clenched along its top bar. "She attempted to use him to lure Teresa Solomon out of the Underground, threatening to kill him if the Martyrs did not surrender their... singular Virtue."

His eyes caught Darius's. A furious heat rose to his cheeks as Cain cleared his throat.

"Alan wouldn't hear it, but instead of killing Donovan, Wrath tortured him. For *three months.*" His voice cracked with a sudden surge of feeling, and he dabbed at the corners of his eyes with his fingertips. "Back then, Alan's protective Programming was much simpler, and Donovan couldn't resist Wrath's Influence, likely because he was saturated in that same power since his very conception. She managed to pull so many vital details out of his brain. Unit assignments. TAC routes. Martyr aliases… Those three months were devastating for the Underground, but no one suffered more than Thorn."

Cain paused for a breath, but the rest of them held theirs deep in their chests.

"Eventually, Wrath contacted her directly. Again, she asked for Teresa. Thorn declined… but she did offer *herself* in Humility's stead. Wrath agreed and instructed Thorn to meet her… at the Huddlestone Arch."

Darius's heart plunged. "Is that where Donovan was killed?" he asked in a murmur.

"It is," Cain said. "Thorn had every intention of giving herself over to save him, but Alan figured out her plan. The second he intervened, the entire operation unraveled. Hunt buried a blade in Donovan's back before Thorn even realized Alan was there… and once she finally had her son, Wrath shot him, too, just to *guarantee* he never made it home. He bled out in Thorn's arms."

Cain's voice faded like a spirit, its essence lingering in the room before leaving it cold. Mackenzie stared, mouth agape, while Abraham covered his with his fingertips. Darius buzzed with a blend of horror and hate, and he understood more than ever why Thorn wanted to end Wrath so badly.

But that thought sent him on a different spiral.

"It can't be a coincidence that she asked me to meet her at the Huddlestone Arch, too," he said.

"No," Cain agreed. "Autumn Hunt may be impetuous,

but she isn't stupid. It's a message to Thorn: Wrath wants to hurt *her.*"

Everyone looked at Darius. His cheeks burned as he said, "Not this time. How can we stop this?"

He glanced around a sea of blank faces. Mackenzie's tongue piercing rattled against her teeth while Nicholas crossed his arms beside her. Abraham and Saul threw their gazes toward the ground, and Holly tapped her fingertips against her closed laptop lid. Gabe, finally, leaned forward.

"The biggest complication is Wrath's ability to sense our auras," he said. "She'll know we're coming before we get close enough to do a damned thing." His amber eyes landed on Cain. "How did Alan do it last time? Did he go in alone?"

Alan's name lit a fiery spark between Darius's lungs. Cain sighed and shook his head.

"As far as I'm aware, no, but I was not part of the Martyrs at the time." His shoulders drew up in an apologetic shrug. "I did speak with Alan later, and while he didn't share specifics, I gathered that he used his rifle to disable Wrath from a distance, which allowed TAC to swoop in. Where they were hiding, how many he brought along, and how effective they were, though, I can't say."

Gabe nodded, and his lips pressed together. "We'll be crippled without an experienced sniper, but it shouldn't be impossible to run a similar play." He turned to Holly. "Bring up a map of northern Central Park."

Her laptop swung open, and before Darius could blink, the paper-thin screen descended from the ceiling on the far side of the room. Saul stepped aside to avoid being in the way. A digital rendering of Manhattan came to life, and Holly zoomed in. A red icon tagged "Huddlestone Arch" blinked into existence.

Gabe got to his feet and walked around the room, squeezing past Saul to point at the marker.

"The arch goes under East Drive. This area is more secluded than other parts of the park, but there will still be plenty of people. Unless..." He frowned back at the table.

"Do you think Wrath will force civilians to leave?"

"She might," Nicholas said. "It would make it easier to catch an ambush—in other words, *us*—but she'd also limit access to potential Puppets."

"She's much more likely to use her power to secure a safe perimeter," Cain said. "Like a bubble, large enough to warn her if someone starts to get too close but small enough that she could easily ensnare passersby into her net, should she need them."

Mackenzie arched her pierced brow. "Random joggers in the park aren't the only things we've got to watch out for. Wrath could bring the other Sins. She could bring mercenaries. Hell, for all we know, she'll Puppet the entire goddamned NYPD and shoot us on sight!"

"Hmm…" Gabe pressed his fingertips to his lips. "We'll need every unit we've got for this."

"That's going to draw a lot of attention," Abraham said with a grimace. "Even from a distance, that many souls will stand out. If they're too far to be sensed, they might not make it to the scene in time to help."

Saul crossed his arms. "Do you guys have, I dunno, drones or something?"

"Assassin drones *would* be nice," Holly grumbled. She slipped her fingers under the rims of her glasses, rubbing her tired eyes beneath the lenses. "But unfortunately, after that IOF extremist group used drones to kill a couple of senators in 2053, jammers were set up all around Manhattan. The second it got high enough off the ground to do any good, it would be forced to land, and the NYPD would have tags on our location."

Saul swore, and Mackenzie said, "There has *got* to be another way. What would Alan—"

"No," Darius cut in, harsher than he'd meant to, but he couldn't stomach the idea of following in that man's footsteps for another goddamned second. Mackenzie's jaw froze open, and she stared at him. "No, we're not doing this the way Alan would have. He might've caught Wrath off guard and stopped Thorn, but her son *died*. We can't risk the same thing happening here."

A pink flush tinted Mackenzie's cheeks, and her teeth snapped back together. Nicholas shook his head. "Then what the hell do *you* want to do?"

Darius drew a deep breath. "I want to make the trade."

Everyone responded at once in a chorus of shock—all but Cain, who considered Darius with narrow eyes and tight lips. Darius couldn't make all the arguments out, and he didn't care to try. Instead, he raised a hand to quiet them. Nicholas, as usual, slipped in a final word.

"This is fucking *insane*, Darius," he hissed.

"It's also our best shot at getting Lindsay back," Darius responded. "My *number one priority* is protecting that little girl—that little *Virtue*. If trading me for her is what it takes, then that's what it takes."

The conference room stilled so completely that Darius couldn't even sense the motion of breath expanding between lungs. He looked at all of them, from Mackenzie back around to Cain. Once he landed on the old Forgotten Sin again, Cain exhaled a sigh.

"There's no guarantee the exchange will protect Lindsay," he said. "We can't trust that Wrath will follow through."

"I think we can," Darius said. "This isn't a battle. It's a *barter*. We have something Wrath wants more than she's wanted anything else in a long time, which means we also have all the negotiating power."

Mackenzie snorted, throwing out a hand. "Negotiate *what?* Give her just a leg, then? Or cut you down the middle?"

"No," Darius said. "We negotiate how the trade happens, where Lindsay goes, all before Wrath has a chance to get her hands on me."

"What if she just kills you?" Saul asked. He stared at Darius from the far end of the room, eyes dark and dire.

"She won't," Darius said.

"How can you be sure?" Abraham asked.

"Because Darius isn't what Wrath is truly after," Cain answered quietly. "She wants to make Thorn suffer. A quick death would be too… unsatisfying." His focus landed on Darius again. "But death *would be* inevitable, and you will beg for it in the end."

Darius forced a numb smirk. "Only if you guys can't manage to save me first."

Nicholas's eyes widened, and he tilted his head back in a dawning realization. "You're not saying we can't come in swinging… You just want to get Lindsay out first."

"If one of us is going to get caught in the crossfire," Darius said, "I'd rather it be me."

Gabe's mouth settled into a frown. "It's risky," he said, "but smart. I think we can do this."

"I think so, too," Darius said as he glanced at the clock on his phone. One a.m. "Now, to figure out how. We have eleven hours."

Mackenzie exhaled a strained puff of air and got to her feet. As she headed for the door, Nicholas called after her. "Where the hell are you going, McKay?"

"To make a vat of coffee," she grumbled. "It's gonna be a *long* night."

Ten hours of planning and panic passed in a blur. The Martyrs mobilized and moved into place, preparing to carry out the most insane plan they'd ever attempted.

Darius's heart pounded as he tightened the tactical vest around his chest. He and Cain geared up in the locker room alone. The scratch of velcro pulling apart scraped against his skull like nails, and his breath caught in his throat.

"You know," Darius murmured. "After what happened last May, I didn't think you'd want to be part of another mission."

Cain uttered a chuckling scoff. "It's not about what I

want to do," he said, tone high and anxious. "I would rather cut off my fingers, reattach them, and cut them off again than be anywhere *near* Autumn Hunt. However, there are things I care about in this world more than myself, and for those, I will walk right into hell."

He threw Darius a guarded look, and shame warmed his cheeks.

Darius smiled. "Well, knowing you'll be there to help makes me feel better. Thanks, Cain."

The bridge of Cain's nose wrinkled. "A foolish sense of comfort, really, but you're welcome all the same."

Darius laughed, which sounded especially out of place in this empty space, and they drifted into silence as they finished up. Minutes later, Cain shut his locker with a snap. Then, he cleared his throat.

"If I'm being honest," he muttered, "something about this situation doesn't feel right."

Darius frowned. "What do you mean?"

Cain breathed a sigh. "Envy has been exceptionally active the last few hours."

Darius's already knotted stomach twisted into an even worse tangle. "That's not a surprise," he answered as he closed his locker, too. "It must be securing the area."

"Certainly," Cain said. "But I can't shake the suspicion there is more to it than that. This whole thing feels… convenient, don't you think?"

Darius's mouth ran dry, but he tried to smile, as though maybe that would ease his nerves. "What are you, a Virtue?"

A blustering sound escaped Cain's mouth. "I don't need to be a Virtue to have a bad read, but perhaps you're right. Perhaps the fact that Envy is here again has me on edge. It's been a peaceful few years without the constant reminder of its presence in my head."

He moved toward the door. Darius fell in step beside him and placed a hand on his shoulder.

"We've dealt with Envy before," he said, "and we can do it again."

Cain's brows drew together in a hard knit as he considered Darius more fully. More deeply. "Maybe this time, we'll deal with it *for good.*"

A cold weight of dread sank into Darius's stomach, through his chest, and left a gaping hole behind. He resisted the urge to place a hand upon his sternum. "Maybe."

They walked out of the tactical lockers and into the waiting area, where Gabe and the last remaining officers stood at the ready. Saul joined them, looking mismatched in plainclothes beside a troop of TAC uniforms. When Darius and Cain arrived, his brown eyes snapped to them. The worry on his expression pulled his brows into a deep furrow, which highlighted the scar cutting beneath the left.

"All ready?" Gabe asked.

"As ready as we can be," Cain grumbled.

Gabe crossed his arms around his ballistic vest. "Lucas's team is in the garage waiting for you. They'll drop you off as close to the arch as possible before getting into position."

Cain's jaw tightened. "Marvelous," he said without an ounce of marvel. He exited the room in the same fashion, like a man walking to his own execution. Darius stared after him, pulse pattering in his throat.

"Is he the last piece?" he asked.

"Besides us?" Gabe answered. "Yes. Ground units are placed throughout the park, and I have cars at all entrances north of the 97th Street Transverse. Once the trade is made, we should be able to intercept their vehicle wherever they try to exit." His focus narrowed on Darius. "How are you doing?"

Darius let out a short laugh. "Nervous as hell," he answered.

Saul grabbed the crook of Darius's neck. "You're gonna be fine," he said. "And so is Lindsay." His jaw tightened, and so did his grip. "Bring her home, yeah?"

Darius raised a hand, wrapping it around Saul's shoulder, too. "You got it."

The darkness in Saul's expression lightened as he pulled

Darius in for a hurried embrace. When they drew apart, Saul's eyes glistened. Darius swallowed hard.

"Let's get this over with."

Gabe's team headed toward the doors, and Darius turned to follow, but the sudden sound of a door slamming open down the hallway caught his attention. He turned as Nicholas stormed into the waiting room.

"Wait!" he called. Gabe paused over the threshold, one glass door in hand. Nicholas stopped on the other side of it, right beside Saul. "We have a complication."

Gabe's heavy brows drew together, carving a deep crease between them. He slipped back into the Underground. "What kind of complication?"

"It's Froschlin," Nicholas said. "Her LymeLite agitator just announced the Raven's next public appearance."

Darius's heart flipped, but Gabe shook his head. "That crisis will have to wait," he said. "We're a little busy with another one right now."

Nicholas's eyes sharpened. "That's exactly my point," he said. "I think it's *part* of this crisis. Froschlin has given her followers a solid twenty-four hours' notice before her stunts. This time, she cut it to *one.*"

The room stilled.

"That's the same time we're doing the tradeoff for Lindsay," Darius breathed.

"You see the problem," Nicholas said. "This *has* to be deliberate."

"But why?" Gabe pressed, propping his hands on his hips. "To make us split up our people? They have to know Lindsay is more important to us than Froschlin is."

Darius's eyes went wide as the pieces settled into place. The Raven, the Martyrs, *Wrath…* Cain's worries needled into his brain, his insistence that something felt *wrong.* Darius understood that feeling now.

And his stomach dropped.

"It's not about Froschlin," he murmured, "or Lindsay, or even me. It's about *Thorn.*"

The others stared at him, but the more Darius considered the information, the more right he thought he was. Thorn wasn't just the most important thing to Wrath. She was the most dangerous. The *only one* who could stop this trade from happening.

Wrath needed her distracted.

Darius's focus landed on Nicholas like a knifepoint. "Where is the Raven gathering her crows?"

"Columbus Circle," he answered.

Darius closed his eyes, picturing the city in his mind and trying to calculate how far away that was. The opposite corner of the park. A good thirty minutes away.

God, it could work…

"We need to send a team down there," Darius thought aloud. "We need to intercept Thorn and bring her—"

"No," Gabe cut in with a decisive stroke. "Absolutely not!"

Darius's heart pounded against his sternum. "But she has to know!"

"Then she never should have left," Gabe argued, and the words stole the breath from Darius's lungs. "We can't afford to change the plan now. My job is to save Lindsay, and I refuse to put it all on the line for a woman who walked away from us."

Darius stared at him, then at Nicholas, and finally, at Saul, who watched back with harrowed eyes.

And he realized—*fuck*—he *was* just like Alan, putting Thorn above everything else, *everyone* else, because he cared about her.

Darius's chest ached as he tilted his chin in a quiet nod.

"You're right," he said, knowing it was true. *Hating* it was true. His teeth gritted, and he turned around. "Let's go."

He stormed from the room, from the Underground, from the Martyrs. As he and Gabe climbed into the last TAC vehicle in the garage, he looked through the glass doors one last time. Nicholas and Saul had both disappeared. Nicholas, Darius assumed, went back to the R&D

department, but Saul's energy headed deeper in, settling in Mackenzie's office.

But he didn't have the chance to wonder about it because soon they were up the ramp and on their way into New York City.

CHAPTER THIRTY-TWO

Christopher Columbus sat behind bars.

He stood upon a stone pillar that was so blatantly phallic Thorn thought it must have been a deliberate dig at the dickhead at its top. This version of the colonizer had been carved from white marble—an exact replica of the original statue that had been destroyed by activists in 2034. Instead of removing and renaming the offensive piece of history, the city had decided to protect it, erecting a goddamned cage around its new deity.

Couldn't have anyone *beheading* America's God of Genocide, no matter how much he fucking deserved it.

Thorn looked around. People swarmed the sidewalks, unaware just how close they themselves were to annihilation.

Her stomach twisted into knots. This location might be the most terrifying yet. Columbus Circle was an infamously busy part of New York City. Even now, in the middle of a Tuesday at the beginning of January, with snow coating the ground, muddy slush clogging the gutters, and temperatures cold enough to make Thorn's breath crystalize against her scarf, hundreds of civilians gathered here. Pedestrians, public commuters, and pop-up food stalls with long lines filled the area with so much energy that Thorn felt like she strode along the shore of the River Styx—a freezing current of death, whisking souls off to Hades right beneath her feet.

It would be hard to fight here. Harder still if Thorn planned on keeping people alive.

Edith had sent a text with coordinates an hour ago, and Thorn got her shit together and arrived on the scene less than twenty minutes later. Since then, she'd wandered the neighborhood to see exactly what she was working with.

The intersection itself was massive—over four hundred feet across at its widest point—and storefronts, five-star hotels, restaurants, transit stops, and tourist destinations ringed the entire goddamn thing. While it lacked the grandeur of anything like the Rockefeller Tree to topple onto the crowds, it wouldn't take much for Edith and her flock to wreak a lot of havoc.

And none of that accounted for the high-rises…

Thorn's gaze cast to the sky, where she counted over thirty buildings tall enough for a sniper's perch with a clear shot of the entire Columbus monument. Sparkie circled, hunting for a flash of black or the glint of sunlight against a scope. So far, nothing, but that didn't mean shit. The gunman could just be lying low like the crows were.

She looked back to the street. Most of the people here belonged—shopping or commuting or simply existing within the ecosystem of Midtown Manhattan. They disappeared, threads of the fabric woven seamlessly into its pattern.

Others, however, stood out like grease stains.

They'd begun wandering in the second Thorn arrived, slinking around, heads turning left and right with nervous glances, like they were carrying illegal weapons inside their backpacks instead of cloaks and crow masks. Howard Poole was among them. Thorn's old barista sat his ass down on the concrete rim of a dry fountain near the edge of Central Park, fidgeting with his phone while he ran his fingers through his receding hairline. Thorn's stomach soured—

not for bitterness or hatred, but disappointment that she had to fight *him* now, too. She passed by without a second glance.

As time passed, others trickled in. Soon, Thorn had her eyes on no fewer than forty people. Something about that number felt *off*… She checked the time on the burner: five minutes to noon. Thorn frowned.

There should have been more of them by now.

She shoved the phone back into her pocket and made a final loop around the circle—one final search for Edith Froschlin, for Lust or Wrath, for *anyone* and *anything* that could be used to make this the most devastating attack yet. The tactical vest around her chest squeezed like a vise, the guns clipped at each hip pressing, hot and hungry, against her body. Her pockets overflowed with an assortment of tools—smoke flares, flashbangs, firecrackers, and more— and she'd strapped enough ammunition to her person that she could land a bullet in every single civilian here if she had to. But Thorn didn't plan on firing her weapons. Hell, her goal was to not kill anybody at all.

Except for one.

She reached the corner by Central Park and glanced at the device again. Edith should make her grand entrance any second now. Thorn's attention swung around the square one last time, but it was Howard Poole who caught her eye first.

Abruptly, with a stiff spine and trembling hands, he got to his feet and started toward the monument. His gaze remained staunchly ahead, almost as though he'd been Puppetted to move, but Thorn knew it was adrenaline making him act so fucking unnatural. Hers spiked, too, but instead of turning her into a lumbering idiot, it sharpened her senses. Honed her focus.

All the people she'd pegged followed the barista's lead, and a crowd gathered in the middle of Columbus Circle. Sparkie hunted the heads for something familiar. Within seconds, he found a petite woman with a long, black jacket and blonde hair pulled into a severe French twist. She glanced up, and he got a full view of her face. Those icy irises, that small nose, and a set of pert lips, pressed into a frown. Thorn's chest filled with fire while panic turned her guts into an icy slurry.

Edith Froschlin.

Images flooded in—of a knife plunging into Deidre Cummins's throat, of Tamera Osborne's chest ripping open in a high-caliber blast, of that monstrous raven plucking the eyes from Conrad Carter's skull like they were a pair of grapes. Flashbacks rolled over her wave after wave. Thorn oscillated between the instinct to bolt and the violent desire to sprint in—the impulse to cower and the insurmountable craving to shove her gun between the bitch's teeth and pull the trigger.

She did neither.

Instead, Thorn drew a slow, even breath, and her thumb tapped each finger. She settled into what she could see and hear, smell and sense right here, right now, until the visions faded, and reality bloomed to life around her. Columbus Circle suddenly seemed crisper than before, and Thorn exhaled her anxiety in a huff. Sparkie quietly landed upon the monument over Edith's head, a tiny stone gargoyle upon the granite. Thorn pulled the burner out and set her plan into motion.

It started with a text.

"You should smile. The show's about to start."

She hit send and moved closer. Edith grabbed a phone from her pocket. A sudden, dangerous smile brightened her face. She snapped up, searching the crowd before looking above. Her eyes passed right over Sparkie, and Thorn's stomach twisted, wondering if she would spot him.

She didn't.

Instead, Edith's gaze moved to the city. Thorn's followed.

A massive raven stepped onto a distant balcony, slipping out from behind red curtains in a hotel room's sliding door.

A man in black followed the beast. He carried a sniper's case.

Thorn's lips twitched up. She sent a second text.

"What's wrong? Don't you recognize me?"

Thorn slipped the burner back into her pocket as Edith furiously responded. It buzzed, but Thorn didn't check it.

Unmasked crows continued to gather. Not a single one paid attention to the tiny blonde standing beneath the pillar, as though they didn't know they were in the presence of their own corrupted god. She looked around one final time, dropped a large bag off her shoulder, and took a knee.

The moment she lowered to the concrete, the pressure of Influence tapped on Thorn's temples. People suddenly shifted, those closest to her tucking in and turning their backs until Edith had a perfect enclave inside a human privacy fence to hide within. Sparkie watched as she drew her mask and cloak free. Iridescent feathers glistened in the sun, flickering with a greasy prism of dark color in her hands. She donned the cloak, set the mask over her head, and lifted her hood. By the time she lowered her Influence and climbed the three concrete steps at the base of the monument, Edith Froschlin had vanished entirely.

And the Raven stood in her place.

She raised her hands. A rush of shocked and joyous shouts filled the air at her sudden, downright *godlike* appearance. Suddenly, forty people adopted crow personas in a swoop of black fabric, and Thorn again had the disconcerting thought that there should be more of them. Howard Poole's cheeks lost their color as he vanished behind his new, downy visage, and then, all at once, each individual disappeared within the murder. The barista pulled one more thing from his backpack—a megaphone—and pressed its handle into the Raven's palm.

"My lovelies!" she bellowed. "What a beautiful day for *retribution!*"

A rousing chorus replied, caws echoing to the heavens. While most of Columbus Circle kept flowing, a handful of civilians glanced up or, worse, inched closer. Thorn joined a group of them as they crossed the street near the 59th Street subway stop. She adjusted the tote beneath her arm, felt the nervous trickle of sweat prickling down her spine.

Edith continued.

"You have read the stories," she called over their heads. "Heard the *lies*. They say we're dangerous, that *we* are the villains. The monsters. The *terrorists*. But that's how those who change the world are seen in their own time. History will recognize us for what we truly are: revolutionaries!"

She punched a fist up, and the rest followed. Half the flock. The others hesitated—just a moment, *just* long enough for Thorn to notice. Howard Poole was one of these, shifting side to side in an awkward shuffle before joining.

"Make no mistake, that's what this is," Edith continued. "A revolution! Against *Jane Morgan* and her *Martyrs*—those mindless sheep who follow her blindly to the slaughter! Her reign of hatred ends today!"

More screaming. A black shadow passed over Thorn's face. She resisted the urge to glance up—to give herself away—as Edith's raven perched upon Christopher Columbus's cage. It spread its wings. Edith opened her arms in unison.

"I will not stand idly by while she rules this city through *fear!*"

"Nevermore!" the flock called back.

Thorn took a knee. The tote slipped from her shoulder, and the glisten of pearly fabric peered through the opening.

"I will not turn a blind eye as she kills *my* people any longer!"

"Nevermore!"

The phoenix mask slid into Thorn's hands, its feathers silky in her palms. She tied it to her face.

"I will tear Jane Morgan down from the pedestal she's built beneath herself, and she will *never. Rise. Again!*"

"Never—"

Crack!

A plume of blinding white smoke hissed into the air. As it billowed away, a woman rose to her feet. She stood all in white, head and shoulders shrouded in a satin cloak that transitioned from ivory to gold to red so seamlessly that it coalesced with every step like it was woven from threaded flame. A mask of captured starlight fanned out from her face, feathers glistening, beak gleaming. The black eyes behind it locked onto the Raven with cold, distant fury.

Why surrender herself to the shadows when she could be the sun that chased them away?

Thorn thrust her fist high, revealing a black, fingerless glove and a crackling flare. Bright smoke furled upon itself, painting Eldrich horrors into the blue sky. Sparkie soared through the stratus like a silver vein in a sea of white granite, scales painted like pearls. The crowd, the crows, the fucking *coward* at the base of that monument stared at her. Thorn's lips slipped into a smile.

"Come and stop me!" she screamed.

Thorn slammed the flare onto the ground, and smoke consumed her.

Frigid air sliced Darius's cheeks, his nose, his ears. No amount of noon sun shining from above soothed the humid cold of New York's winter. Darius shoved his hands into his pockets to steady them, but he was pretty sure it was the nerves, not the weather, rattling him to his core.

Gabe shifted to Darius's left, shaking his head. "She's late," the TAC director muttered. The pair of them stood on a bridge over a frozen creek, facing downstream where ice flowed through the tunnel beneath the Huddlestone Arch. Gabe's amber eyes narrowed as he looked into the darkness, where a semicircle of light revealed an empty walking path on the far side.

Darius nodded. "Of course she is," he answered. Four

other TAC members flanked them, two on either side, and they glanced Darius's way as he exhaled a sigh. "It's a negotiation strategy. Showing up late puts the other party on edge… makes them more likely to make mistakes. I used to deal with this shit in the market all the time."

His stomach twisted, remembering Max Douglas and how he'd screwed Darius over with this exact tactic when they'd bartered for the medication that almost killed Juniper. Darius had been too naive to realize he'd probably laced it with something else. Something cheaper. More dangerous.

He cleared his throat, forcing those thoughts away, as he tapped into his com device.

"Cain," he said, "any sign of Autumn Hunt?"

A sigh filled his ear, so heavy that Darius could practically feel it in the air from where Cain had camped out inside the Harlem Meer Center on the opposite end of the arch. His cat sat atop the stone wall, orange eyes flickering in Darius's direction.

"Nothing, I'm afraid," Cain replied. Background noise distorted his voice—laughter and conversation and music blasting through. "No sign from Envy, either. Its Influence has been quiet for the last thirty minutes. They're close, if not here already, biding their time…"

Darius's insides oozed like slime. "Do we have eyes on the other Sins?" he asked. "Amoretto or Claytor?"

"No word on Claytor," Holly chimed in Darius's ear. Her keyboard rattled. "But we just got a hit on Lust at the Midtown North Precinct. I suspect he's interfering with the police response."

Gabe frowned. "Midtown? They don't have jurisdiction up here."

Holly huffed a dark laugh. "I didn't say he was interfering with the response for *you.*"

Darius went cold. Midtown. Columbus Circle.

Thorn.

Gabe threw him a look like he was thinking the same

thing, but Darius ignored him—and ignored the temptation to pull his phone out and search LymeLite for any updates on what was happening there. Instead, he said, "Good. One less Sin for us to worry about."

"And the time to worry approaches," Cain said. Darius glanced back to the arch. Crescendo was no longer perched upon the retaining wall. Cain prattled on, nerves quickening his words. "I have a sense of Hunt. In a…" Cain let out an indignant scoff. "Well, *that's* something. In a *gold limousine*. It just entered the park from the north. I can feel four others in the vehicle. Two I don't know. Mercenaries, perhaps. Then Anton Claytor, and the last is…" He paused. "No, that can't be right…"

Darius closed his eyes, stretching his senses out. Lindsay's Virtue slowly materialized in the distance, the draw subtle at first but quickly growing stronger as the vehicle drew in. Relief flooded down his spine.

Alongside a sinking, cold sense of dread.

"Cain?" Gabe said. "Who else?"

Cain stammered, but Darius tuned him out, focused instead on the grinding of tires on asphalt down East Drive. The limo crawled over the Huddlestone Arch, its windows so deeply tinted that Darius couldn't see the people within it, but he could feel them. The mercs took up the front seats while another four settled in the passenger compartment. One of these was clearly Lindsay. The powerful sensation of her Virtue nearly masked the other souls entirely.

But Darius could still make them out. His mouth opened in a gasp.

"Oh my god…"

Autumn Hunt's aura sat near the front with one Darius didn't recognize but assumed belonged to Greed because the fourth person in the back was someone he'd never thought he'd sense again.

"It's Juniper," he muttered. Gabe turned to him, aghast. "They have Juniper."

The vehicle continued along East Drive until it reached

the far side of the bridge over the Huddlestone Arch and turned down a smaller road toward a courtyard outside the Harlem Meer Center. It parked, the gold paint on the limo's left side glistening through the tunnel. Gabe went rigid beside Darius, and his hand slipped beneath his jacket to wrap around a weapon.

"You're *sure* they have Juniper?" he asked.

As though to answer, the car doors flew open. A woman spilled onto the pavement—a skinny woman with pale skin, wide eyes, and a shock of orange hair that Darius would have recognized from across a busy market plaza. In her arms, she clutched a child.

Lindsay.

Juniper looked up, and Darius's nerves caught fire.

Fuck.

"FIND HER!"

Edith Froschlin's voice boomed through the megaphone, but Columbus Circle swirled in a tumbling, twisting mass of white smoke, and Thorn was impossible to see.

Her senses screamed at her—ears ringing with panicked shrieks, eyes stinging as tiny particles fought past her mask, nose curling at the distinct scent of gunpowder caked inside her nostrils.

But her mind sank into a crystalline clarity, a certainty, a purpose.

She shut everything else out, inhaled a deep breath, and willed the world to slow down.

Auras dragged around her in a slow-motion gait. Thorn focused on the push and pull of souls scrambling left and right, forward and backward, twisting in a whirlwind of confusion. She closed her eyes. Tracked on those energies. Waited for one to make a move. Instinct coiled in her spine, tingling up each vertebra, stronger and stronger until…

Finally.

A figure in a black cloak and bird mask lunged at Thorn through the wall of fog behind her left shoulder. An arm swung for her head, but Thorn ducked before the stroke hit the apex of its curve. Knuckles sailed past her skull without so much as grazing the feathers framing her face.

Her hand shot up and caught the beast beneath the jaw. A man let out a strangled yelp as Thorn's fingers dug into his carotid. A pair of brown eyes gaped at her through the holes in the mask. Thorn reached up with her other hand until she found his right ear.

A communication device wrapped around the helix.

Thorn smiled. Her grip tightened, cutting off blood flow until the crow lost consciousness in her palm. Then she ripped the earpiece out and let the man crumple to the concrete.

Another shape moved toward her. This one clumsy. Untrained. One of the civilian crows. They raised a weapon—a small, wooden bat—and flailed toward her. Thorn curled her fingers around the com before raising her fist, catching the strike with her forearm, and deflecting it with a quick twist. The bat went flying, and the crow with it. They let out a squeal and tumbled into the haze.

More swarmed in. More like this one.

Edith's brainwashed horde of faithful followers turned the circle into an unwieldy soup of white smog and wild screaming. Thorn pulled another smoke bomb from her pocket, pulled the pin, and tossed it into the sky. By the time it landed on the concrete where she'd been standing, she'd disappeared again. Cold energy danced across the space. Thorn observed it from a distance as she slipped the headphone into her ear canal.

Voices burst to life—a handful of men barking back and forth, calling orders, giving directions, and announcing locations. Thorn walked in a slow circle around the edge of the cold energy horde, listening. Learning.

It sounded like there were six more mercenaries, not including the sniper hiding in the hotel. God, like the crows,

Thorn couldn't believe there were so few. Sparkie, from his silent orbit around the Columbus monument, found them all. While Thorn, in her white cloak and clothing, nearly vanished within the fog, the black figures loomed like shadows and were easy for the Familiar to follow. Thorn tracked his focus, committing the auras to memory, creating a plan of attack.

Then Edith Froschlin's cold, piercing command came through the speaker.

"I don't want to hear excuses," she shouted. "Where the *hell* is Hans? He had eyes on her!"

A smile drew Thorn's lips apart.

"I'm afraid Hans isn't available," she said in a low hum. The com went silent. Thorn couldn't help it. She laughed.

"One down, you sick, sadistic bitch."

Edith screamed, both in the unit inside Thorn's ear and the megaphone blasting overhead. "Find her *now!*"

The plaza shuddered. More energy swarmed in—the ones Thorn pegged as Edith's mercenaries joined by more civilian crows. There were fewer now, but still more than Thorn wanted to deal with—more than she could reasonably take on alone if she got herself caught. The Raven stood watch from her position at the top of the steps while her Familiar circled overhead. The mercenary crows continued to yell updates through the coms, but differently, vaguely, now that they knew Thorn was listening in. A dull, distant pressure at her temples told her Edith had forced Influence into the crowd, rousing them to action. Or, Thorn's stomach flipped to think, it *wasn't* Edith, and another Sin was on the scene.

But not Wrath. Not yet. Thorn hadn't felt the tell-tale draw of Hunt's power here. She was probably lying in wait. Thorn stretched her senses out, feeling through the chaotic mess of human auras for anything familiar, but it all spun together in a chaotic weave of searing cold.

She gritted her teeth and activated more smoke bombs, giving herself the space, the camouflage, to walk about unseen and unheard. Black shapes darted past her. Around her. Shadows in the bright fog. Thorn ignored them—avoided them—like a spirit that only haunted guilty souls.

And one of the damned rose above her.

He skulked through the fog, spine straight and arms raised like he held a gun between his palms. As Thorn slid up behind him, he froze. The hairs along the nape of Thorn's neck stood up on end.

The mercenary turned. Shot. A scream pierced the plaza. Thorn's fist flew up.

Her knuckles crunched against the man's throat. He stumbled away, choking on his spasming trachea, and Thorn crashed an elbow into his temple to send him down for good. He fell into the wall of white. An airy grunt pushed from his lungs as he hit the ground, the sound loud in Thorn's ear canal.

"Two down," she said.

Edith howled again.

Thorn kept moving—kept *hunting*. She released two, three, four more smoke bombs. Soon, the entire intersection was so thickly shrouded even traffic slammed to a stop. Thorn couldn't shake the nagging feeling that something wasn't right. It was silent—no sirens approaching, no police warning. Energy thickened when it should have dissipated. The weight of Influence grew heavier as more people came *in* instead of running *out*. It became harder and harder to move without getting caught—to avoid the bumbling band of confused crows in the smoke. And still, shockingly, *impossibly*, there was no sign of the Sins. Thorn couldn't sense them, and Sparkie couldn't spot them. Unease grew in her gut until it all but consumed her.

But it didn't stop her from taking out another merc. And another. She announced each strike, and each time, Edith grew more angry—more *vengeful*. By the time Thorn caught the next man in a headlock, holding his thrashing body against her chest until he went limp, the Raven was raging.

"Five down," Thorn said.

"When I find you," Edith hissed in her ear. "I will split you open."

She threw her megaphone to the ground and dove into the smoke. Thorn laughed.

The sound strangled in her throat as a shape pulled free from the mass of cold energy, and a fist flew toward her.

Thorn barely avoided the strike. It glanced off the edge of her phoenix mask, throwing the thing askew, and suddenly all Thorn could see was a black-painted interior. Her attacker's aura twisted around and came in for another hit. Thorn ducked this one—

And a person barreled into her from behind. A set of strong arms pinned hers down, and something jammed into the soft flesh beneath her chin. She swallowed hard. Her digastric muscle pressed against a pistol barrel.

"I've got her!" a male voice screamed.

Her heart thundered.

Fuck.

The crowd drew closer, a hurricane of frigid souls coiling in a volatile circle. Edith let out a manic cackle, and Thorn's blood turned to ice in her veins. Influence throbbed harder, full of so much fury and hatred that it was all she could do not to get swept away. The other mercenary jumped for her. Thorn kicked back, flailing her legs to catch him in the chin. He grabbed her foot mid-air and twisted, yanking her out of his cohort's hold. She landed flat on the concrete. Her mask flew free, skittering down the plaza to be trampled under a wave of crows. Thorn stared after it, and a heavy boot came toward her head.

She jerked out of the way. The heel crashed into the ground where her face had been, and a baton whipped toward her. Thorn spun again, this time managing to get her ankles tangled with the mercenary's. He crashed down beside her. She ripped the baton from the man's fingers and slammed it into his temple. His aura vanished as his crow mask came clean off. Blood dribbling down the side of his wide, empty face. Thorn leapt to her feet.

And found a gun pointed at her chest.

***

"Jones." Autumn Hunt's voice echoed off the stone-work through the Huddlestone Arch. "I thought I told you to come alone…"

She glared at him, bright light haloing her in a semicircle of warmth that didn't match the tone of her words. Anton Claytor lingered beside her, one fist wrapped dangerously in Juniper's orange hair. June whimpered while Lindsay said and did nothing. Her body lay frozen in fear, clutched against Juniper's chest.

Darius swallowed hard but forced his breathing to stay even. "No, you told me not to try anything clever, and I'm not. You can see us all, clear as day."

He held out his arms to indicate Gabe and the four TAC agents at his back. Hunt smiled, but it lacked pleasantry, filled instead with hunger. Her chin tilted up, exposing a slender neck over her winter jacket as she considered Darius down a sharp nose.

"You can't come at me for bringing people when you did, too," Darius continued. "Including an extra hostage."

His eyes flicked to Juniper. She whimpered again. A dangerous, anxious dread lapped at the base of Darius's skull.

Hunt's lips pulled into a grin so wide it exposed nearly all her teeth, bright against a tawny face. "If I told you I had both, you'd have come in with the cavalry."

Then she looked away—not to the Martyrs visible from where she stood, but to the naked trees around them, as though trying to catch the whiff of a trap lying in wait.

"You can sense everyone here as well as I can," he called to her. "And we both know you have the upper hand."

Those cold, gray irises snapped to him again, gripping him with an intensity Darius had only ever seen in one other person. He swallowed hard.

"I'm not here to screw around," he went on. "I know

what happened to Thorn's son. I can't take the risk of it happening again. I can't gamble with her life," he said. He glanced at Lindsay and Juniper. Anton Claytor's grip tightened, and June closed her eyes. "With *either* of their lives. I'm just here to make the trade."

A brow arched on Wrath's head. She considered Gabe with a predatory glare. "With *muscle?*"

"With *insurance,*" Darius corrected. "They're here to protect the girls. I think you can understand that."

Wrath laughed. The cackle blasted through the tunnel like the crack of a gun. "Oh… the *girls* aren't the ones who will need protection…"

She considered Darius like a prize—like some kind of rare game she'd spent her entire life aching to mount on her wall. Darius's body rang with warning bells, every atom in his being vibrating an alarm, a systemwide red alert. Lindsay shifted in Juniper's arms, trying to look at him, but Juniper pinned her head to her breast.

"Jesus, can we just get on with it?" Greed snapped.

Wrath cast him a dark, warning look before she stepped closer to Darius. The shadows beneath the arch danced at her toes.

"Here's how this is going to go down," Wrath said. The nearer she came, the more Darius could make out. Her brown hair was pulled back, her jacket zipped up, but it looked thick around the middle, as though it covered an armored vest and probably a firearm. "You saunter your handsome little ass over here, and once I've got my hands on you, these two go free."

She grabbed Lindsay by the shoulder and shook her so hard Juniper nearly lost balance. The little girl cried out, and Darius's chest roiled.

But he kept the fire confined to the cage of his ribs as he said, "No."

Wrath's smile flickered. A glint of rage flashed across her eyes. "Or I could just kill them now."

A knife appeared in her hand and pressed against the

soft flesh at the base of Juniper's neck. A thin line of blood dribbled to the divot of her collarbone. She froze. So did the agents behind Darius. Gabe and his guard went rigid, hands flashing to the pistols at their belts.

Darius raised a palm. They all stilled.

"You won't do that," he said.

Wrath's lip curled into a snarl. "Oh, no?"

"No," Darius confirmed, and he dug into his dusty bag of negotiating tools for every trick, every tactic he'd ever had to use on the market. "Because if they die, your chances of getting *me* alive disappear."

Hunt's expression soured further. Darius shoved his hands into his jacket pockets, hoping to hide how badly they shook.

"Either I get away, and you're out a bargaining chip," he continued, "or I'm killed, and you don't get to dangle me over Thorn's head."

A scoff blustered from Hunt's throat. "You think I care if you die?"

Darius smirked. That seemed to enrage Wrath further.

Good.

"If you *didn't,*" he said, "you wouldn't have worked so hard to make sure she didn't come here to stop you… because *you know* Thorn would stop you. She's the only one who can."

The contempt in Wrath's expression disappeared, replaced instead with wide eyes and parted lips. She stared at him, measuring him, her focus flicking around his face as though trying to decipher him. All he did was smile. Anton Claytor cast a nervous look between them as Wrath finally pulled her blade away from Juniper's throat.

At last, she hissed, "Rose *can't* stop me."

Darius chuckled. Gabe's aura glanced in his direction, and Cain muttered a vague warning. Darius ignored them both as he said, "She can, and someday, she will."

Autumn Hunt gaped at him, and god, Darius wished he could bottle this moment, preserve the horror creeping across Wrath's face. A distant part of him reveled in this. Even if he did die, at least he died knowing he'd rattled this Sin right down to the corruption she called a soul. But a larger, more present part, knew how empty that threat was. His smile faltered.

"But not today," he said, "and I can't take any chances. Not with their lives on the line."

Wrath frowned, and Darius stepped forward. He indicated for Gabe to stay behind. Now, he stood in the mouth of the tunnel, twenty feet from the Sins. Juniper watched him with a whale-eyed stare.

"We walk through at the same time," Darius said. "No guards. No weapons. Then, you and I will leave while my team takes care of them." He tilted his head toward Juniper and Lindsay. "Deal?"

Hunt considered it, her tongue slipping between her teeth to run along the crest of her top incisors. Darius expected her to fight, to claw for *more*, and he readied himself for another round of negotiation.

But instead, she nodded at Claytor.

Then it happened. The corner of her mouth twitched. Almost a smile. Ice crackled down Darius's spine.

"If *any* of you attempt some *thrilling heroics,*" Greed blurted out, his tone wrestling with a malformed sense of confidence, "we will kill *all* of you."

He gestured between Gabe and the other TAC agents. The mercenaries on either side of the Sins propped their hands on their belts, within easy grabbing distance of their firearms. Gabe's nose curled, and he held his chin high.

"Shut up, Claytor," Hunt hissed. Something tightened the word. Worry? *Nerves?*

Darius's gut clenched.

What did Wrath have to be nervous about?

She glanced back. Caught Darius's eye. *Grinned.*

"Well? We're ready whenever you are."

Hunt jabbed Greed in the ribs. He thrust Juniper forward with a disgruntled scowl. She stumbled over her feet but managed to stay standing. Lindsay yelped, and Darius's heart screamed at him to run forward—to wrap his arms around them and drag them back into safety.

But he instead took a single step. Juniper looked at him, the child still pressed against her chest. Darius forced a smile.

"It's okay," he said. "Steady now. Just… keep walking."

They did. Beat for beat, breath for breath, Darius and Juniper strode through the Huddlestone Arch. Within the stonework, flanked by a solid wall to one side and a frozen creek on the other, Darius felt suddenly cornered—caught in a chasm between hell and damnation. Every inch forward made the dread in his bones sink deeper, weigh heavier, until it was all he could do to push against it. Juniper's focus remained glued to him, but in the shadows, he couldn't make out her face.

They met at the center. Darius banked left to give June space to pass on the side without water. Still, she just stared at him.

"It's going to be okay," he murmured. Juniper nodded. The motion drew his attention to the line of blood on her throat.

And his soul ran colder than the ice at his feet.

There was no wound.

Darius's eyes flicked to Lindsay. Hers pooled with liquid fear. Juniper's fingers held so tight to the girl's neck that she couldn't move. At the edge of June's jacket, barely exposed by her sleeve, a sharp, black curve stood out inside her right wrist—a curve he suddenly realized he felt drawn to *touch*…

His breath caught in his throat.

Oh, god…

This wasn't Juniper.

She was *Envy*.

CHAPTER THIRTY-THREE

Bang!

Thorn dove to the side. A civilian shrieked, and flickering energy dissipated behind her back. The mercenary followed her movement. Shot again. A crack tore through Thorn's shoulder in a blossom of red. She swore and swung. The baton crashed into his fingers, and the firearm went flying.

Then the circle stilled. Thorn took a step back. Smoke cleared the intersection and whisked away her last scratch at anonymity. Crows hovered around her, whispering instead of screaming as the final mercenary squared off with Thorn. Her fingers tightened around her weapon. Hot blood poured down her arm and soaked into her glove. Fury and fear battled for purchase inside her skull.

This all felt distressingly familiar. The pain. The people. The pipe, cold in her palms…

Wait. It was a baton, wasn't it?

Panicked breath arrested her lungs as the past overtook her future and dragged her into the darkness. She remembered the crunch of bone, the stink of blood, but worst of all, the way she hadn't been able to stop it. Her eyes flicked to the dead mercenary on the ground, and her thumb tapped each fingertip, pointer to pinky.

"Six," she whispered.

Edith laughed. Her flock fell away as the Raven came for Thorn. A black beast cawed overhead as smoke rose like steam into the sky. Thorn's grip tightened on the baton.

"Stop!"

Thorn looked up as Howard Poole, mask abandoned, hood down, screamed into the megaphone.

"Look at what we've done!"

Corvid heads flicked left and right, taking in the fog on the street, the civilians on the sidewalks, the blood on the ground. Thorn's chest ached with held breath.

Howard looked at Edith.

"You *lied* to us," he said. "You said you were different. That you had the answers! But you don't care about us! You're after *her!*"

A finger pointed right at Thorn.

The crows shuffled—glanced between each other, at the gathered crowd, at Thorn. Her attention, however, caught on Howard, mouth gaping.

"We're better than this!" he shouted. "Better than *you!*"

Edith's shoulders rounded in a dangerous curve. "Stop him!" she screamed—not to her last mercenary or her army of crows, but into the coms, to her one man in the air.

The sniper.

Thorn's heart plunged. "No!"

Sparkie launched toward the sun. A blur of white, followed immediately by an enormous black smear.

"The Raven hasn't made us safer," Howard continued to scream, though his hands shook. "She's fed into our fear! *Used* us to hurt others!"

A distant glint flashed from a hotel balcony. The tips of Sparkie's wings sliced through churning white tendrils, carving sharp lines as he propelled himself forward, upward, onward. Thorn's skull rattled with the percussion of feathers beating at his back.

"I won't do it anymore!" Howard cried.

Thorn reached for a pistol, but the last mercenary lunged for her. A blade flew forward. It nicked her cheek. Thorn wrapped her hand around the man's wrist and wrenched the weapon free.

"And neither should *you!*"

The sniper came into focus. The shape of him crouched by the balcony, and a rifle barrel poked through wrought iron bars. Sparkie caught a gust. Burst closer. Close enough to see his finger curl around the trigger. The raven snapped at his tail. It missed.

Howard thrust a fist above his head. His eyes locked onto Thorn. The mercenary twisted—toward the steps. She jerked him back and sliced the knife up. It caught beneath the mask and carved a deep line from his chin to his cheek. He went down with a squeal.

"Run!" she screamed.

Howard smiled. "I stand with Jane Mor—"

The rifle fired.

A powerful blast of heated air knocked Sparkie off course and made Thorn gasp. Howard Poole's battle cry shattered as a bullet shredded his vocal cords. He clutched his throat. Arterial spray painted his fingers red, and his aura blinked out.

A deafening quiet followed.

The circle stilled, smoke settled, as Thorn and the civilian crows stared at the body slumped against the granite pillar—at the barista who became a rebel and then a *martyr*.

At a man who had been conned by a parasite named Edith Froschlin and lost his life because of her.

A roar ripped from the depths of Thorn's core. She sprinted, all the fury of the last few months exploding from every muscle, every nerve, every cell in her body. Meters above, Sparkie shot like a bolt of lightning to that damned balcony. Edith's raven breathed down his spine.

The sniper glanced up to a streak of white scales and black feathers.

Thorn swung the baton at Edith's skull.

She ducked, deflecting the blow with her forearm in a crunch of splintering bone. Thorn swung again.

Sparkie squeezed through the banister bars. The massive bird barreled after him. It croaked a throaty, angry cry, and the sniper jumped to his feet. He twisted around, back hitting the railing.

He teetered—

The baton crashed into Edith's ribcage. She let out a thick, wet grunt. Thorn whipped around and struck her a third time. This one to the head. Edith's mask stayed staunchly in place, but the woman herself rolled to the ground. Thorn came down to crash the goddamned thing against her shrouded face.

Sparkie thudded into the sniper's vest. His screams echoed in Thorn's skull as he hurtled toward the earth.

Edith avoided the attack. She crawled to her feet with one good arm and sprinted through a formation of crows. Thorn followed, bloodied fingers firm around her weapon, her very soul aflame. Sparkie burst into the sky, white against a bright blue backdrop, and the raven dove after him. Thorn swung, and she pushed, and she *screamed* until Edith's back hit the dry fountain. She climbed into it and up the tiers, moving toward a wall of naked trees and piled snow. She tripped. The whole of her vanished, replaced instead with a black lump on the concrete. Thorn jumped after her.

A gun shot caught Thorn as she leapt, grazing her side just below the hem of her tactical vest and throwing her off balance. Her foot slid on the ledge, and she crashed hard to a knee. With a wince, she pressed a hand against the wound beneath her ribcage.

Sparkie cried out. Plummeted. The raven pulled its wings tight to its body and bolted at him like a poison dart.

Edith shot again.

This one struck Thorn square in the chest, cracking her sternum behind the kevlar. She choked out a painful breath as her back landed hard in the empty fountain basin. Thorn reached for her firearm. A boot crushed her hand to the pavement.

The Raven pointed a pistol between her eyes.

"You see?" Edith's voice carried across a field of gawking crows. "You *see* what kind of beast she is? How she's able to corrupt you? To *brainwash* you?"

She shook her head, that iridescent mask gleaming, and gestured her broken arm to Howard Poole's dead body. Thorn's exposed face bit with cold wind as Sparkie spiraled toward the earth. The raven closed in on him.

"It ends today!" Edith thrust a fist into the air and screamed, "Nevermore!"

Her flock stared in silence.

Edith hesitated, chest heaving, hand shaking, before she looked down at Thorn. Her expression was all but invisible behind the mesh covering the eye sockets, but a thick line of blood coated the side of her neck.

"Goodbye, Mourning Dove," the Raven whispered.

Edith's finger tightened on the trigger. Her familiar opened its maw, reaching for Sparkie's throat.

Something sailed through the air.

A wad of ice crashed into the back of Edith's head. Thorn glanced up. One of the crows crouched by a muddy bank of snow, another white, gritty chunk in one fist. Her aura trembled—with fear, with fury—but she threw again.

Sparkie's wings shot open. They caught air and lurched him upward, past the raven, and then above it. It tried to change direction, but Sparkie was too quick. Too agile.

He landed on its back.

More items sailed at Edith: snow and stones and a random assortment of shit pulled from pockets. Half of the flock swarmed in—not toward *Thorn*, but toward their fallen messiah. Edith screamed. Shot. Staggered away. A crow went down.

More rushed in. The plaza filled with sound. Sparkie tore at the beast's back, ripping feathers from its neck, its spine, the line of its wings. It flailed, but Sparkie wound his tail around the thing's middle and held tight. Thorn rose to her feet, drew her gun, and shouted.

"Get down!"

The crows paused, and then, they dove. Edith stood alone.

Thorn fired.

A bullet crashed into the woman's back and sent her flying. She toppled over a mound of slush and vanished on the far side. Her familiar stalled in the sky and plunged toward traffic. Sparkie took to the air.

Then, the raven's wings opened. It flew off with a furious cry. Thorn scrambled to the top of the fountain.

A cloak and mask lay discarded on the sidewalk, no body beneath them. Thorn cursed as she hunted for a sign—a drop of blood, a piece of fabric, fucking *something*. A dangerous tickle clawed up her spine.

There, barely visible through the gawking crowd. The back of Edith Froschlin's blonde head. Thorn's teeth gnashed together, and she started to run—

"Thorn!"

A voice wrenched into her brain, and she twisted around. Saul and Mackenzie sprinted at her from the street. The ashen look on his face made her stomach turn to lead.

And then, Mackenzie shouted, "Wrath has Lindsay!"

The air evacuated Thorn's lungs in a sudden, horrific exhale.

Oh, *fuck*.

It all made sense now. The lack of crows and mercenaries, the Sins' suspicious absence. *That's* why Hunt hadn't shown up here. This had been a *diversion*.

And Thorn had fallen for it.

"Where?" she asked.

"The Huddlestone Arch," Saul said. "Darius is trading himself to get her back!"

Thorn's world collapsed like a dying star, the gravity of her core so heavy, so intense, that she felt herself falling into oblivion. Her mind flashed back to that cursed place—to

Donovan crying for her as his blood carved sigils of death into plains of fresh snow.

Then Darius replaced him.

Thorn couldn't breathe. Bile lodged in her throat. She swallowed it down.

And she ran.

Saul and Mackenzie called after her, but Thorn ignored them, ignored *all* of it. The crows. The civilians. The searing pain from her wounded shoulder and cracked sternum. Thorn shed her cloak, her jacket, her *hate*—anything that weighed her down and sprinted up Central Park West.

Darius should have known.

The exchange was too easy, the Sins too pliant, almost *eager*. They'd listened to everything. Hadn't fought him at all.

That had been the first sign. Darius's first mistake. If something seemed too good to be true, it usually was. He knew that, but he'd let them get in his head. Let them distract him from the truth.

Wrath hadn't wanted to get her hands on him. She'd wanted to plant someone in the Underground. To plant another *Sin*.

That was his second mistake—not thinking for a single second that it was too much of a coincidence that Envy would find a new host *and* the Sins would capture Juniper in the same week. Too much of a coincidence that Envy's power had been all over the park only to vanish right before the trade.

God. How could he have been so *stupid?*

Darius moved in slow motion, a half-formed plan piecing together. His eyes snagged on Juniper's, recognizing someone else behind them—some*thing* else—he hadn't seen in over three years.

And as he stared, her facade fractured. Feigned horror transformed into a scarier feeling: real, fully-fledged fear.

Darius took a step, but instead of placing that foot in front of the other, he pivoted on his heel. Angled toward her. He reached for the hand she pinched around the back of Lindsay's neck—reached for the *Peccostium* he knew sat below Juniper's right wrist.

The moment Darius's fingertips grazed her jacket sleeve, Juniper whipped around. Darius turned with her, now grabbing for the child in her arms. She thrust an elbow up and knocked his fingers away. He rebounded—threw a punch toward her face.

But the Sin dodged left. Juniper came back around and clocked an elbow against the side of Darius's skull. Then, she thrust him into the wall, back flat to the stonework. He sucked in a breath. Tried to. Air couldn't get past the forearm pressed against his trachea.

"What the hell is going on?" Gabe shouted in the coms.

Darius couldn't respond. His fingers grappled with Juniper's arm, but no amount of scratching, punching, kicking had any effect.

Cain gasped. "She's *Envy.*"

"What?"

Envy glowered at Darius as Lindsay screamed in her arms. She wound a hand into the girl's hair, yanking hard, and pressed closer to Darius. Gray spots speckled the corners of his vision, and he was vaguely aware of warm energy coming in on either side of the tunnel. A gunshot blasted. Wrath's aura ducked behind the arch.

"It's been a while," the thing inside Juniper said. Her lip curled into a vengeful snarl, and her blue eyes wandered around his face like she was seeing it for the very first time. "I don't know what you did to her," she whispered, "but this woman *hates* you. I can *feel* it." Envy chuckled—a cold, dead sound that fluttered against Darius's chin. "What did you *do* to her, *Kindness?*"

Guilt and dread danced in Darius's breathless chest. He drove his nails into Juniper's skin, digging for muscle, for a pressure point, for *some* kind of leverage. He found none.

Her face began to blur…

Lindsay thrust her fingers into Juniper's eyes.

Envy screamed, and her hold on Darius loosened enough for a haggard breath to surge into his lungs. He choked on the winter air—

A beast of fur and fury flew past him.

Crescendo collided with Juniper, all teeth and talons, yowling as he carved deep cuts into her cheeks. The Sin howled and stepped back, one hand still buried in Lindsay's hair while the other swatted the Familiar away—

Gabe grabbed Darius's wrist and yanked him backward. "Go!" he screamed.

Darius didn't want to. He watched in horror as Gabe leveled his weapon at Juniper's head, as Envy wrenched Crescendo off her back, as Lindsay let out a terrified, piercing scream. His chest constricted under the pressure of a tragedy he couldn't stop. Another TAC agent pulled him back the way they'd come, and Lindsay stared after with wide, harrowed eyes.

A gunshot struck stone, showering Gabe with a deluge of dust. He ducked, and Envy tossed the girl into a mercenary's arms. He carried her, kicking and screaming, to the limousine, where Greed had vanished behind tinted windows, and threw her into the back.

"Darius!" she screamed.

"Lindsay!"

The other merc's weapon turned on him. He dove as a bullet sailed overhead. Lindsay's Virtue peeled off with the squeal and stink of burned rubber. The gun's sights landed on Darius again. Gabe hit the man with an uppercut to the jaw and dragged Darius to his feet.

"Get the hell out of here!" he shouted as he thrust him out from the arch. Sunlight blasted against his face, and he winced.

Voices berated him. TAC agents from positions all around Central Park droned in a chaotic jumble. Darius struggled to make sense of it all. Warm auras closed in, the pressure of Influence tapped at his temples, and the dizzying sensation of Lindasy's Virtue ripped up to East Drive—then veered in a violent turn.

"North!" he shouted into the mic. His voice rasped from his aching throat. "They're heading north! Get ready to intercept them!"

Darius sprinted away from where TAC had engaged with the Sins and their mercenaries to scramble up the hillside. He burst onto the road through a naked treeline as a flash of gold paint twisted around the bend.

Cain's voice cut through his earpiece.

"Watch for Puppets!" he cried. Noise cascaded around him—of panicked shouting, items moving, the jumbled rattling of things in motion. "I'm clearing people out, but Envy's grabbing them too fast!"

A chill ran down Darius's spine. He glanced into the basin on the opposite side of The Huddlestone Arch. A horde of mechanical, emotionless civilians exploded out of the Harlem Meer Center, roiling down the sloped drive in an avalanche of bodies. So many. Too many for one Sin to control, especially a Sin as newly possessed as Envy.

But not too many for Wrath.

She stood in the lot where the limousine had parked and glared up at East Drive. Her gray eyes landed on Darius with an icy, blade-sharp precision—a vengeance so palpable that he felt it like a fog.

Oh, *fuck.*

They bolted at the same moment, Darius north and Wrath up the bluff. She clawed through the snowy brush like a plow, throwing obstacles away in a violent rush. Darius's heart hammered in his chest, his throat, his *skull* as his feet pounded the asphalt. A wave of warm energy crashed behind him. Sweat dripped down his spine.

Wrath pulled ahead.

And more joined in.

Hunt plucked people from the park, the skating rink, and the pop-up coffee stands peppering the roadside. Figures shrouded in thick winter jackets veered in from the right and surged onto East Drive.

"Shit!" Darius hissed.

Without breaking stride, he changed direction, dove onto the shoulder to his left, and tucked into a thick line of barren trees.

Silence greeted him. The cushion of branches and brambles coated in snow buffered everything but the voices in his earpiece. TAC units called back and forth.

"They blew right past us! Heading west!"

"We'll cut 'em off!"

"Darius!" Gabe shouted. "Where the fuck *are* you?"

"North Woods," he gasped. A switch whipped him in the face. The thin wood sliced against his cheek with a hot sting. He glanced over his shoulder. People thundered through the undergrowth, wordlessly, soundlessly heralded by creaking branches and crunching ice. God, that was more terrifying than if they were screaming. "Wrath's on my tail with a bunch of Puppets. I'm trying to shake them, but—ah!" He stumbled. Caught himself. Kept running. The mass hedged closer. "There's too many!"

"On my way," Gabe said. "Hold on!"

"Hurry!"

Darius vaulted up another short hill, his legs howling, feet freezing, and slid down the other side. A few more yards, he leapt over a length of knee-high fencing along a walking path. The second his heels hit pavement, he took a sharp right and sprinted toward Lindsay's aura. It dragged further away—so far that it hovered at the fringe of Darius's senses, flickering and indistinct. Shit, they had to be close to the edge of the park now. The TAC agents at the second exit shouted something about the limo blasting by them, too, but Darius could hardly make it out.

Because Wrath's Puppets hit the fence. Half of them crashed onto the path yards behind Darius, while others kept to the trees and ran alongside him. More warm auras drew in from the distance, ahead of him and to his left.

Fuck.

Wrath was collecting others.

He glanced over his shoulder again. His stomach plunged.

Autumn Hunt led the pack—a vicious figure of rage and revenge.

Darius neared a fork in the road, and a man jumped at him. Darius banked right to avoid outstretched arms and dove headfirst into the trees again, hoping to slow them down, praying the wide trunks and narrow gaps thinned the horde.

It didn't. Darius's lungs seared, his heart strummed, thighs screamed under the pressure of running so hard for so long. The world flashed by in a swirl of brown and white, but the pressure of warm souls closed around him. The path opened to a convergence of three separate trails. Hunt's aura crept within lunging distance. If he could just—

She leapt.

Wrath collided with Darius. He toppled forward and slammed to the pavement. His chin knocked the ground, and his teeth sliced through the side of his tongue. Blood spilled from his mouth as he scrambled away.

But Hunt's fingers twisted in Darius's jacket and yanked him backward, refusing to let go. He slipped his arms from the sleeves and slid free, fumbling to his feet.

He froze.

A circle of Puppets closed in—through the trees, on the path, everywhere he could hope to go. The wall of blank faces and empty eyes pressed shoulder to shoulder. Darius swallowed hard and turned around.

Hunt stood opposite of him. The smile she'd worn at the Huddlestone Arch transfigured to a snarl, and malice poured off her body in a thick wave. She threw Darius's coat onto the ground and rushed him.

The first punch sailed at his head. Darius ducked beneath it, tracking Wrath's aura to keep her in front of him. His arms raised in a defensive stance at his face. Hunt roared and threw her fist again. She moved quicker than a human being should be able to move, but Darius had trained with someone just as fast, just as powerful. He deflected the second attack with a sweeping motion that sent her barreling past him. Darius twisted. Held her in his sight.

He didn't have to beat her. He just had to *survive* her.

The Sin came again and again, and Darius fended her off the way Thorn had taught him. Every sparring match flooded his body with muscle memory—the form, the focus, the footwork. He kept the distance. Kept defending.

But Wrath *wasn't* Thorn. Her moves were less predictable, less *practiced*—more the wild, violent clawing of a starved beast let out of its cage. Soon, she landed a hit to Darius's ribs, which sent a torrent of pain into his side despite the armor around his chest. Then, an elbow caught him on the forearm so hard he thought the bone might have fractured. He cried out.

And Wrath's knee came up to his groin.

Visceral, electric pain pulverized Darius's muscles and his mind. He dropped to his knees in an instinctive slump. Wrath grabbed him by the vest, hoisted him to eye level, and shoved his back against a gnarled tree trunk. Her gray irises glinted like a pistol aimed at his head. The Puppets opened space around them, watching with those lifeless gazes.

Wrath struck him. Her knuckles collided with his cheekbone. His head flew to the side, and he gasped in a haggard inhale that was more bile than breath. He choked on it.

Hunt hit him again. Once. Twice. Three more times. His skull rang with strident cacophony—of TAC orders, tinnitus, and the tolling bell of his own pulse. He cried out. Tried to. All that dribbled from his mouth was a blood-soaked groan. Wrath paused.

And then, something pressed against him.

Darius glanced down. Through his swelling eyes, he caught the flash of a knife. The tip of the blade poked his body armor.

Right above his beating heart.

CHAPTER THIRTY-FOUR

The blood drained from Darius's face, from his hands, his feet. He sucked in a breath and held it before it drew too deep and expanded his ribs right into Wrath's weapon pressed against his chest.

Autumn Hunt leaned forward. Her face slid beside his, hair catching the raw, open flesh on Darius's cheek.

"You have been nothing but a *thorn* in my side since the day you showed up."

She hummed into his ear. The com went silent. Energy pulled closer, ensnaring him in a cocoon of human hell. The blade burrowed into his vest. It broke the surface. A shallow, dangerous hole.

"You have fucked up my plans." Wrath pressed harder on the knife. It slid a half-inch deeper into the armor. The force ached through Darius's sternum, and he winced.

"You have *rallied* these Martyr *rats,*" she hissed. The weapon drove further. With a *snick*, it pierced his protection. The metal point dug against his skin. His breath caught as a shadow fluttered across his face.

"But worst of all?" Hunt whispered. "You *know.*" She thrust her hand forward. The blade nipped into his muscle, right between the ribs. Darius clenched his teeth to keep from groaning. "Don't you?"

Wrath stopped moving—stopped forcing her knife through Darius's armor and into his chest to draw back and look him in the face. He took a stuttering breath. Pain shot from the wound, and blood warmed his undershirt. A white blur flashed behind the Sin's head.

"I know," Darius rasped out, the words thick through a slurry of tacky saliva, "that you are *fucked.*"

Hunt's nose curled. She twisted her wrist, and Darius let out a sharp, strangled cry.

"I'll see soon enough," she growled. Her fingers released the hilt as she positioned the heel of her hand against the end—the perfect position to deliver a final blow. "But *you won't.*"

Wrath's expression, her body, her aura all tensed, and the blade crawled another half-inch into Darius's ribcage. He arched back, thrashed his legs, looked for any purchase, any *give*, but found none. His eyes squeezed closed, and Darius uttered a groan that turned to a plea.

Then he fell.

Hunt's grip on his bulletproof vest relented, and his weight suddenly dragged to the ground. Darius caught himself before he crumbled into a bleeding heap. He raised a trembling hand and fingered the edge of the knife still lodged in his chest.

Wrath howled.

She flung her arms up, swinging blindly. A white, winged creature clawed at her face, emitting a throaty, reptilian hiss. A hiss Darius recognized.

Sparkie.

Thorn's Familiar bounded around Wrath's head, her shoulders, her chest. Paint coated his wings and body, making him almost impossible to see in the surrounding trees and snow.

"Darius, you hear me?" Gabe's voice crackled in his ear. His aura flew through the woods with other familiar, warm souls. "We're closing in!"

"I'm here," Darius said. His voice scraped like grit in a glass bowl. Stabbing pain shot through his chest, and he winced. Wrath's line of Puppets closed in, circling tighter—

One went down.

The woman collapsed into a bundle of faux fur and feathers. Then, the man next to her and the one beside him. Darius's heart thundered beneath the point of the blade as he looked up.

A black, white, and red blur crashed toward him, eyes sharp, hair wild. Darius's breath caught, and his knees gave way. He slumped against the tree. It was the only way he could stay on his feet.

"Thorn," he muttered, eyes stinging.

Wrath ducked beneath Sparkie's latest attack and glared at the oncoming storm of vitriol barreling down the path. Her Puppets suddenly streamed toward Thorn, piling over brush, decimating snowy drifts. Soon, Darius couldn't see her. His stomach clenched.

A gunshot rang out. A Puppet fell. Darius looked back.

Gabe DuPont, leading four other TAC officers, flew onto the path.

The woods became a battleground. Wrath splintered her force between the onslaught of Martyrs, and weapon fire filled the air. Darius tried to stand up—to move away from this damned place.

Wrath's voice cut through the chaos.

"YOU!"

She separated herself from the fight, alone at the center of the intersecting paths. Her hair frayed up in a nest, and healed cuts from Sparkie's claws lined her face with remnant blood. Darius's heart skipped.

A pistol pointed at his skull.

She pulled the trigger.

Darius's eyes smashed closed, but the impact never came. Instead, he was overcome with something else.

The smell of sandalwood, vanilla…

And blood.

His breath hitched, and he looked up.

Thorn curled above him, her back to Wrath, arms rigid against the tree trunk over Darius's head. God, she looked like hell. She wore no jacket, and a healing shoulder wound soaked crimson onto her bright white shirt. The fingers revealed by dark gloves were coated in red, and the front of her ballistics vest showed evidence of a gunfight—a hole blasted in the center of her chest that surely matched the one Wrath had just landed in her back. Her face contorted in a grimace, but her eyes darted to the knife in Darius's armor. Her lips slipped open as she pressed a shaking hand against his sternum.

"My god," Thorn whispered.

Wrath screamed obscenities, and the warmth of her aura rushed forward. Thorn twisted around and knocked Wrath's gun away with a sweeping thrust followed by an uppercut to the jaw. The Sin's head snapped back, and Thorn punched again. Wrath spun to the side.

Hunt let out a deep, animalistic snarl as she came for Thorn with rabid hatred. Her army of Puppets regrouped, balling around them in a mindless horde. Thorn vanished within it.

"Thorn!" Darius shouted.

He couldn't see her. Couldn't hear her. Couldn't do *anything*. Darius pushed away from the tree and stumbled toward the writhing mass of bodies. A hand wrapped around his bicep.

"Come on!" Gabe shouted. Blood dribbled down the side of his face. "We have to get you out of here!"

He pulled Darius toward one of the paths, but Darius yanked out of his grip and staggered to one knee.

"Thorn!" Darius cried again.

Two of Gabe's TAC officers picked Puppets off one by one. As bodies fell, Darius caught glimpses of black hair and bruised fists. Sparkie dove with a gut-wrenching cry, but Wrath slapped him out of the sky. He crashed into the woods.

And Thorn hesitated *just enough* for Wrath to smash her knuckles into her chin. She flailed back. The Puppets dove onto her.

Gabe grabbed Darius again. "Darius, come *on!*"

Darius shook his head. "I have to talk to her!"

"Talk to her?" Gabe scoffed. "Talk to her *later!*"

But Darius couldn't take the chance that there *was* no later—that *this* was his only moment to right a century-old wrong. He watched in horror as more Puppets fell, as a Martyr went down under a pile of clawing bodies, as Autumn Hunt wrapped her hand around Thorn's throat and squeezed her airway shut. Thorn's eyes went distant the same way they had in that warehouse. She gripped the Sin's wrist with two hands, and Wrath pressed the barrel of her pistol into Thorn's stomach.

Darius screamed one last time.

"It's *you,* Thorn! *You're* the one!"

Wrath jerked around to watch him now, and so did Thorn. Those black irises connected with Darius's through the trees. Her face flushed a dangerous, breathless red. His eyes burned.

"You're Patience!"

"You're Patience!"

The words barely registered. Thorn heard them through a haze—through a ringing in her ears so loud, so overwhelming, that it was a miracle she could hear anything at all. Wrath's fingers drilled into her neck so hard that her muscles pulped between them, bruising and healing and bruising again. She couldn't breathe, couldn't *focus*, but still, those words hovered.

"You're Patience."

Darius stared at her, green eyes pooling, tears flowing down his battered face and diluting the blood on his cheeks. The knife protruding from his armor heaved with labored movement. Gabe stood over his shoulder, staring at Thorn with a gaping mouth like she was a monster.

Or like she was a—

No.

It couldn't be.

Could it?

A strange sensation tingled up her spine.

"She's trying to break you," Darius shouted, nearly sobbing. "Don't you *dare* let her break you!"

Wrath. The Sin's grip didn't change, but her substance had. Her *stature*. Instead of glaring at Thorn with murder in her eyes, she looked instead at Darius—in fear and in fury, not because what he said was a lie.

But because it *wasn't*.

Thorn's heart plunged.

Oh, god…

It crashed together in a rush of memory—a hundred years of moments with all new meanings. The way Wrath clung to her despite all Thorn's attempts to dispel it. The way Alan had moved heaven and hell to save her, unconcerned with the river of sacrificial blood running at her feet. The way he avoided every conversation about Patience when Thorn asked him what it was like to feel the Virtue— the way he never gave her any real *answers*.

Because *this* was the answer.

Thorn tried to reject it, to *deny it*, but the truth wrapped around the pit Wrath had carved into her soul and wouldn't let go, like the shards of Patience left behind were reveling at finally being recognized—and furious at being fractured. It started in her heart—a noxious swirl of sharp, wounded heat, before it spiraled outward, expanding into her chest, her face, her fingertips, until Thorn was sure she was goddamned steaming out here in the snow. Tears cut down her cheeks as her jaw creaked open. Then, past the fist Autumn Hunt had wrapped around her windpipe, Thorn forced out the words, "What did you *do* to me?"

Wrath leaned in and spat, *"I ruined you."*

Something snapped—Thorn's sanity, her sanctity, or maybe, just her goddamned self-control. She emitted a scream from her shattered core and dug her nails into Wrath's wrist so forcefully that they broke skin. The Sin's fist loosened. Air trickled into Thorn's lungs—

A gunshot went off. It ripped into the soft flesh above Thorn's navel and deep into her gut. She sucked in a gasp as she released Wrath's arm, pressing her palms instead to the gushing wound. Blood soaked her gloves, hot in the winter air. Vaguely, distantly, Darius screamed her name.

Hunt dragged Thorn closer—close enough to whisper in her ear. "And I will continue to ruin you, bit by *agonizing* bit, until that precious *Virtue* inside of you is so fucked up it can *never come back.*"

Her Puppets moved. Half of them swarmed closer while the others rushed toward Darius and Gabe. The two of them vanished beneath a mountain of winter jackets and cold souls. Fire erupted in Thorn's chest, but her vision spun. Sparkie tried to take the air, but vertigo landed him back into a pile of snow. Wrath laughed and stroked a thumb across Thorn's hammering pulse—her *weakening* pulse.

"Say goodbye to your little boyfriend, *Jane.*"

More Puppets came in from the fringes of the park—so many that there was no way they could fend them off. Her people disappeared—Gabe, the TAC agents, *Darius.*

No...

Thorn let herself unravel. Influence shot out of her in a vengeful pulse, and she started cutting consciousness like she was slicing throats. One, three, seven Puppets fell. Their bodies hit the earth with sullen finality. Wrath squeezed harder, her grip so tight around Thorn's windpipe that air stopped flowing entirely. Gray dots speckled her vision. It went dark.

Wait. *Everything* went dark.

A swirl of clouds circled over the western edge of the park, and a gale whipped through the woods. Thorn glanced through the naked boughs to the sky above. A storm spiraled, like a hurricane concentrated on one single point. A tiny point. Human-sized. *Child*-sized. Her heart stuttered.

She'd seen this storm before…

In a strike like they'd all been zapped by the same bolt of lightning, every single one of Hunt's Puppets collapsed. The Influence binding them dissolved, like that power itself had been rocked to its core. Like Wrath's very essence had been attacked.

Like one of the Sins had been destroyed.

Wrath howled.

"No!" She turned to the west, eyes searing, thin mouth cut into a violent slash upon her face. *"NO!"*

A bullet hit Wrath in the shoulder and ripped through her jacket. Her hold around Thorn's throat opened. Thorn collapsed, clutching her belly.

Gabe rose from a pile of fallen civilians and leveled his pistol at Hunt. Her chest rocked as she glanced around—at Thorn, at Darius, at the TAC agents climbing to their feet, too. When Gabe shot a second time, she dove to the side and sprinted north. TAC followed.

Thorn hobbled toward Darius.

Her stomach pulsed, blood seeping through the hole in her abdominal wall. The bullet must have gone far—hit something important. Her legs quaked beneath her, so she staggered, one hand flat against the wound. Darius sat up as she landed on the ground beside him. Thorn and Sparkie reached him at the same time. Her Familiar climbed to his lap while she pressed her other palm to his chest just to feel the comforting rhythm of his heart—evidence that the blade embedded through his armor hadn't pierced deep enough to stop it. "Are you okay?"

"Yeah… yeah, I am." What little of his face wasn't bruised purple went ashen as he looked her over. His eyes caught on the deathly color saturating her white shirt and leggings. "Jesus, are you?"

She nodded a lie. The motion made her head spin.

Darius didn't look like he believed her, but his attention flicked to the west, where the storm in the clouds had vanished as quickly as it came to life. He looked back to Thorn. "Stay here," he ordered. "I'm going to find Lindsay."

He came to his knees. Sparkie tumbled to the earth as Thorn's heart plunged.

"What? No."

"Thorn, you're hurt—"

"So are you," she cut in, indicating the blade in his armor. He grabbed the hilt and, with a haggard grunt, tore the weapon out. Thorn went hazy as he tossed it into a snowbank beside them. "I won't leave you."

He threw her a dark look but didn't argue further before he stumbled to his feet. God, he looked like the walking dead, battered and bruised, as he fumbled out of the underbrush and onto the path. Thorn grabbed her Familiar and came up beside him, but she had to clutch a tree to keep herself level. The bile in her belly mixed with her blood, making her nauseous as well as dizzy.

She shook her head—and she forced through it.

Darius bolted through the park as fast as he could, which wasn't very fast at all, thank god. Thorn wasn't sure she'd have been able to keep up. Gore gushed through her sodden gloves with every step, and more than once, she had to grip a trunk to stay steady. Sparkie had climbed to her shoulder, where his claws dug in so weakly it was a miracle he didn't fall free. Darius didn't look at them, his focus sticking staunchly to some point in the distance she couldn't see—couldn't *sense*. Her eyes, her ears, her *mouth* filled with disorienting sights and sounds and textures. She watched Darius's back distantly, disconnected, as she searched her psyche for some sign, some shred of *evidence*.

A pull. A weight. *Something.*

But god, she couldn't find it.

They trudged forward. Fallen civilians Wrath had Puppetted who had never made it to the fight lay unconscious along the paths, and distant, Martyr energy swarmed toward the northern exits in a whirlpool of cold souls. Darius ignored all of that as he led her in a straight line away from all that chaos. Soon, the endless stretch of naked maples opened up to West Drive. Thorn's jaw dropped.

A golden limousine had veered off the road and crashed into a light pole on the opposite side. Smoke spiraled out from beneath the buckled hood and swirled into the sky. There were no passengers Thorn could feel—no driver, no one in the back compartment. One of the rear doors was left open, and the leather interior glistened like an oil slick. Darius swore and rushed across the blacktop.

Thorn didn't immediately follow. She gripped a branch with a shaking hand. Her fingertips were so cold she could hardly feel the rough bark beneath them.

Fuck. This wasn't good.

"Oh, my god…" Darius murmured. "Thorn, look!"

Dread sank into the pit of her hemorrhaging stomach, and she forced herself forward. When she reached Darius's side, she had to grab onto his shoulder to stay on her feet. Even he felt cold beneath her palm. Fuck, Darius had *never* felt cold before. She swallowed a swell of iron-tinged nausea as she leaned around him to peer inside. Thorn gasped.

The limo was empty except for a pile of ash.

Thorn's lips parted, but her blood-starved body hardly had the sense to do more. Darius tore away from the car, away from Thorn, and she leaned against the door. Her body swayed, and she wound her fingers around the frame.

"Lindsay!" Darius screamed. His voice vanished into the winter air, swallowed by snow and silence. He cupped his hands around his mouth. *"LINDSAY!"*

Deadly quiet followed. Thorn's stomach swirled. Bile climbed into her esophagus.

"Darius!"

That tiny voice shattered Thorn. Her heart fractured into pieces and fluttered into the empty pit inside her chest as she looked south down West Drive. The haunted sound of a crying child bounded up the asphalt, followed quickly by the patter of little feet.

Thorn fell to her knees.

A figure in a tattered dress that must have once been yellow ran toward them, sobbing so loudly that it drowned out the dangerous ring chiming in Thorn's ears. Her skin, her hair, her clothing were gray as war and ruin, gaunt and ghoulish. Hot tears streamed down her cheeks, streaking them the color of ink. Her extended palms, her scrawny arms, her pleading face were smeared with the light, gray powder of human ash—*Anton Claytor's* ash.

Thorn's lungs sucked in a reverent breath.

"D-Darius!" Lindsay wailed again.

Whatever pain he still felt, whatever exhaustion settled into his bones vanished. Darius ran to the child and collapsed before her, pulling her tight to his chest. She rocked in hard sobs as he ran his fingers through her hair.

"I've got you," Darius whispered. Lindsay nestled her face into the crook of his neck. "I'm here."

And Thorn lingered at a distance, heart aching, eyes stinging, stomach gushing blood as she stared at this anguished child. This shattered soul. This empty Virtue—

A *Virtue*.

Her vision blurred. All color disappeared.

"Darius," Thorn murmured.

The park went black.

CHAPTER THIRTY-FIVE

A tingling sensation radiated from the hand pressed against Darius's bare chest, warm and soothing, and sank into every damaged cell. The gash between his ribs, the cracked bones in his face, and even the lactic acid buildup within his muscles eased into the healing power.

But his mind didn't.

While Lamar worked, Darius's gaze flicked over his shoulder to the OR doors. Elijah and Raquel's energy hovered near the center of the room, balanced around the void of Thorn upon the table. Lamar glanced at him.

"She's fine," the young Virtue murmured. "Dr. Harris just wants to kick that healing agent of hers into gear..."

When Darius looked back at him, Lamar's focus had returned to his work, watching the injury stitch itself shut. An uncomfortable knot writhed in his empty gut. He knew Thorn would be okay—had known it the moment she'd regained consciousness in the car before they'd even left Manhattan. Somehow, though, knowing hadn't made him feel better.

Maybe because a bullet to the stomach wasn't the worst wound Thorn had to heal from now.

The silence dragged on. Lamar considered Darius again,

a curious gleam in his mahogany eyes—a gleam that asked questions Darius wasn't prepared to answer. After a moment, Lamar withdrew his palm, and the Virtuous power stopped.

"That's all for now," he said. His umber skin seemed washed out under the sterile hospital lights as he offered Darius an apologetic shrug. "I've got others to heal…"

Lamar gestured to the rest of the hospital ward. Martyrs dotted the room, their warm energy settled behind closed curtains. The hospital staff quietly wandered between them.

Darius sat up with a wince. Though the worst of it had resolved, the puncture wound between his ribs stung as he moved. "Don't worry about it," he said, though his protesting aches begged to differ. "I'm just sorry I can't help."

"Oh, honey." Lamar dismissed Darius with a short laugh and quick flick of the wrist. "Did you *see* you when you came in? I mean this in the kindest way possible, but you looked like *shit*. You shouldn't be worrying about anyone's healing but your own."

He winked, but worry lines knitted his brows together as he glanced at the operating room again. Darius chuckled. That hurt, too, and he laid a palm against his bare chest to soothe it.

"I'll try," he said.

Lamar shook his head with a sigh as he pulled a tablet out and jotted a few notes. "I suppose that's all I can expect," he said. "We'll wrap this up in the morning, mkay?"

"Sounds good. Thanks, Lamar."

"Anytime, sweetie."

While Lamar spun on his heel and pattered down the ward, Darius flung his legs off the side of his hospital bed. His bloodied TAC shirt had been cut off in triage, so Lamar had brought him a standard white tee. He tenderly pulled it over his head and got to his feet, but instead of leaving the hospital ward, he went to the nursing station, where Cain sat, waiting.

As Darius approached the desk, the Forgotten Sin stood.

"Feeling better?" he asked.

"Much," Darius said. "You?"

"Ah, my scrapes were nothing but a minor inconvenience," Cain said, waving a hand.

The tone mismatched the movements. While he worked to keep his voice level, his body practically buzzed with nerves. Darius got the impression that he wanted to speak more about what had happened, but he didn't get the chance. A robust, warm energy approached them from the ward, walking up the central aisle until it stood beside Darius at the crown of the curved desk.

"Well," Gabe said, the word sighing out as he propped his hands on his hips. "That was a mess, but it could have been worse. A lot of injuries, but we didn't lose anyone."

"A miracle, indeed," Cain muttered faithlessly. Darius threw him a short look.

"Yeah," Gabe agreed, but his expression became more serious. "Look, I know there's a lot of other shit going on, but we've *got* to talk about what the hell we're going to do about Envy."

His amber eyes flashed over Darius, and Darius's stomach dropped out. He wound his arms around his chest, ignoring the sting of his half-healed wound.

"What about Envy?" he asked.

One of Gabe's dark brows arched. "She's *been* to the Underground."

"No," Cain said. "The *host* has, but Envy itself has never set foot in this place."

A twinge pinched behind Darius's ribs at that—at the word *host* said so plainly, matter-of-fact, as though Envy had possessed some random nobody off the street. His jaw clenched, and he glanced at the ground as Gabe scoffed.

"What's *that* matter?" the TAC director asked. "They're one and the same now! Should we be on constant red alert? Should we *move?*"

Cain's nose wrinkled as he shook his head. "I assure you, we're still *quite* safe. The Sins and their hosts cannot read one another's minds or memories. They simply share *feelings*. Emotion. Envy could not get that information out of Juniper's brain no matter how hard it tried."

Heat burned Darius's cheeks. The Sin's words echoed in his head:

"I don't know what you did to her, but this woman hates *you. I* can *feel* it.*"*

A frown settled over Gabe's expression, and his eyes narrowed. "You're sure?"

"Positive," Darius said. Gabe and Cain glanced at him. "If Envy knew where the Underground was, they wouldn't have staged a trade. They would have just shown up and turned this place into a morgue."

Gabe's expression relaxed. He placed a steady palm on Darius's shoulder. The warmth, the support, the comfort without words dissolved the anxiety building between his lungs.

Until Gabe spoke again.

"How's Lindsay?"

Darius blanched, and he looked over Cain's shoulder to the collection of private hospital suites. All were empty but one—the one Lindsay had stayed in through her burnout period and recovered from the life-altering experience of accepting her Virtue.

Where *now* she was recovering from the experience of *losing* it.

"I don't know," Darius began quietly, "but she's been through a lot. Her parents are dead, her Aunt Juniper turned into a monster, and she lost half her soul."

Those words settled like lead. Gabe and Cain both looked back at the door, too. Saul and Abraham were there, warm auras on either side of the bed. The shape of Saul exposed his grief—arms outstretched, back curved forward, as though he were holding a small, soulless child on his lap. Distress crawled up Darius's throat like bubbles of bile.

"I can't believe she did it," Gabe said after a long, somber moment. "I can't believe that a *seven-year-old* managed to take out one of the Sins alone…"

Darius's gaze flicked back to the private suite. Abraham's aura shifted. Got to its feet. Cain considered it, too. Gabe followed their lead, staring at Lindsay's door with a frown.

"Whatever happened out there," Gabe went on, "we should be grateful. Without Greed's Influence in play, Noah Montgomery stands a better chance at recovering the assets we lost in the InvestX scandal. Then there's also Froschlin."

God, in all the chaos of the last few hours, Darius had almost forgotten about Edith entirely. She seemed so small now, in light of Linday destroying Greed and Envy possessing Juniper.

Cain sighed. "Yes, she'll be stripped of her power. No longer a *god*…" His half-empty eyes glinted anxiously—maybe even enviously—as he considered Darius before shaking his head. "I suspect the Raven will hang up her mask, and things will go back to normal. Well… as normal as they can. I don't know if the Martyrs will ever fully disappear into anonymity again."

"Maybe not," Gabe agreed, "but at least we'll *just* be fighting the Sins. And now, there are only three of them."

A flutter in Darius's chest made him look up to see Gabe's sharp, amber eyes trained right on him. The apples of Cain's cheeks flushed a rosy pink, and he tapped his fingertips against the tops of his thighs. Darius swallowed hard, but he didn't have the chance to say anything before the door to Lindsay's suite opened, and Abraham stepped through.

"Darius?" he said gently. "Could you come here?"

A complex blend of relief and dread mixed in Darius's stomach as he excused himself and headed over. Abraham stepped out of the room entirely and shut it behind him.

"Is she doing okay?" Darius asked before he'd even stopped walking. He crossed his arms, shoulders hunched forward. The counselor paused before he loosed a shallow breath.

"No, of course she's not," he said. "Grief and loss is one thing, Darius, but I don't have any tools to help someone work through what Lindsay has gone through. The best I can say is… it will take time. And guidance. A lot of guidance."

Darius's throat tightened. Abraham laid a palm on his shoulder. The warm grip of his fingers sent a comforting current into Darius's core.

"She asked to see you," he said. "I think… you can help her more than anyone else here."

Abraham's mouth crooked into a smile that felt more somber than joyful, and he walked away without giving Darius a chance to reply. He watched the counselor join Gabe and Cain at the nursing station before he breathed deep, swallowed the lump in his throat, and walked into Lindsay's room.

She and Saul glanced up.

And, god, Darius's heart shattered all over again.

Lindsay had been cleaned up—her ashy clothing stripped away and body rinsed off, brown hair pulled into a pair of damp braids at the sides of her head. The Martyrs didn't have child-sized clothing to give her, so she wore an overlarge t-shirt over a pair of boxer shorts that made her arms and legs look especially thin. Darius's numb mind fixated on that detail first, scratching notes inside of his skull to place an order immediately, finances be damned. A soft voice drew him back.

"Darius, I did it," Lindsay said. "Just like you said. I listened to my heart."

He focused on her again—truly focused—on the half-smile upon her lips, the red rims around her eyes, and the light in her brown irises, which seemed dimmer now, like part of it had been extinguished.

Just like Thorn's.

He shut the door and gripped the handle to keep himself steady.

"That's right, you did, honey," he said. His voice

cracked, and he cleared his throat. Lindsay shuffled on Saul's lap, and Saul held her close, his jaw clenched shut. Darius sat on the chair beside them. "God, I am *so* proud of you."

He raised a hand. Stroked it along her cheek. She tilted her head into his palm. For the first time, he noticed her right fist clenched at her chest, wound up in the fabric at a spot between her lungs. His own ribcage emptied out.

"Mr. Abraham says I'll feel like this forever," the little girl whispered. The slightest quiver tremored in her lower lip. "Is that true?"

A rush stung at Darius's lash line. He nodded. "Yes. It is."

The trembling grew, and then, Lindsay's face contorted. She softly cried, a quiet, wrenching sound constricting from the deepest parts of her—the part where her soul once lived. Saul choked out a rough, guttural sound as he tilted forward and pressed his head against hers. She wrapped her free hand around his neck.

"I don't want it to last forever," she rasped in a tired, lost voice. "It… it hurts!"

She dissolved further. Saul shook his head, nostrils dilated and irises gleaming.

"Oh, *princesita,*" he cooed. "Come here…"

Lindsay pulled her legs up and curled into Saul's chest, safely cocooned in his arms. Her face pressed into the crook at his throat, and her body rocked in a rumble of deep, aching sobs. Darius arched toward her, around her, embracing her on the other side so that no part of her was left unloved in this cold, lonely place—this *empty* place.

The three of them sat there for a while. Darius didn't know how long. He and Saul waited until Lindsay wore herself out, until she purged all she had left to purge from that little soul of hers and settled in their warmth. At last, when the crying ceased and the tears stopped flowing, she took a slow, shaky breath.

"That man," Lindsay murmured against Saul's skin.

Darius pulled back, and she lifted her head. "The one I touched… was he really bad?"

Darius thought about it for a moment. "The man might not have been," he said, "but something inside of him was very, very bad. You got rid of that bad thing."

"And the man, too?" Lindsay asked. When Darius nodded, her jaw set. "That's sad."

"I know," Darius said, "but it's just how it works…"

"He let me do it," Lindsay continued quietly.

A shock of surprise seized Darius's heart, and his mouth slipped open. "He… what?"

Lindsay's shoulders curved into a shrug. "Something… changed. He started crying and said he was sorry. And when I… grabbed his leg? Where his tattoo thing is?" She raised her left wrist and pointed to the spot where Thorn's *Peccostium* sat. "He let me do it."

Darius's eyes went wide, and he glanced at Saul to see him staring back. An uncomfortable flutter made Darius's stomach uneasy.

If that were true, then Anton Claytor wasn't as passive of a host as they'd thought.

A soft knock at the door made them jump. Darius's heart lodged in his throat as he spun around, sensing no soul on the other side. He got to his feet as the knob slowly turned.

Thorn peered into the room.

God, she looked spent. While all physical evidence of the day's conflict had been erased—her windswept hair brushed, bloodied clothes shed, and healing wounds hidden behind a new shirt—she wore an expression that betrayed an inner turmoil Darius could only begin to fathom. Tight lips. Tighter brows. A pained gleam in her eyes that made his very soul ache. Those eyes snagged on Darius for a breathtaking moment before they flashed to Lindsay instead. Her face softened.

"Hey, Lindsay." She slipped into the suite. The door didn't fully shut behind her. Thorn kept one hand around the wood as though guaranteeing a quick escape. She hadn't put on new gloves, and her *Peccosium* and the scars around it seemed especially vivid beneath the stark hospital lights. "I always knew you were a superhero."

A smile graced her thin lips. Lindsay let out a short, sad laugh and wiped her eyes with the heels of her palms. "I don't feel like a superhero anymore," she muttered.

Thorn's smile faltered. "I know," she said, "but being a superhero isn't about feeling like one. It's about helping people. Saving them. You did that today. You saved *all* of us."

Lindsay lit up, flickering like a solitary candle flame in the dark. She nodded. Thorn did, too.

And then, her endless black eyes landed on Darius again. "Can I talk to you?" Thorn asked.

Darius's heart pounded so hard it made the wound next to his sternum ache. "Of course."

She led him through the hospital ward. It quieted as they entered, the pattering of feet and murmuring of voices stilling in a breath. Sparkie hid behind Thorn's sweeping, black hair, but his head peered out to watch the room as the room watched her. Warm energy tracked their movement until they reached the exit, and Darius was sure whispers broke out the second they were gone. A nervous knot curled into his stomach.

How quickly had the word spread? How many people *knew?*

Thorn strode down the hallway, past the Tactical lockers, the R&D headquarters, and the conference room before turning left to the directors' offices. She didn't stop until she reached the door at the far end, the one leading to the lounge between hers and Alan's. Darius's stomach clenched as she pulled it open.

Thorn froze. Sparkie let out a soft, surprised chirp.

Boxes filled the room, all of Alan's life and legacy packed away in neat parcels. They towered from the floor to the ceiling and took up so much space that Thorn could barely fit between them. She slowly entered, eyes wide, lips parted as she walked through the cardboard city to the door on the right now bearing the name "Jones." Thorn peered inside, taking in the fresh paint and covered furniture before she spun around.

"What did you do?" she whispered.

"With Abraham back, I needed a new office," Darius began. Even he was shocked with how level he managed to keep his voice. "I've labeled everything and pulled all of Alan's personal items aside. Including this…"

He crouched beside one of the boxes, popped open the top, and grabbed an envelope. Thorn's name sat on the outside, written by Alan's hand months ago. Hell, maybe *years* ago. Darius stood back up and passed it over. Thorn drew in a shallow breath as she took it from his fingers.

"I haven't read it," Darius said as he shoved his hands into his front pockets.

By the way Thorn looked at the envelope, with both recognition and surprise, he suspected she hadn't, either. She tore it open, pulled out a thick sheaf of papers, and started flipping through them. Her irises flickered left to right, Sparkie's head upon her shoulder darting back and forth to the same tempo until suddenly, they stilled. Thorn's fingers tightened around the letter until her nailbeds pressed white. She glanced at him.

"Cain knew," she muttered, less an accusation or a question and more as a statement of fact, like she was confirming something she already suspected. "He's known the whole time." When Darius nodded, the bridge of Thorn's nose wrinkled. "Son of a *bitch.*"

She turned away, one hand migrating away from Alan's letter to run through her hair. Black strands slid between her fingers, rippling down her back in a silky wave. Thorn walked into the empty office, looking around, but her eyes didn't land upon anything in particular. Instead, they remained distant, as though she were gazing not into a physical space but an ethereal one, analyzing every moment of her life with a new lens.

At last, she looked back at Darius. A fine layer of tears glinted furiously behind her lashes, and she squared her shoulders before she spoke again.

"How long have *you* known?" Thorn asked.

"One week," Darius replied.

Thorn visibly crumpled. Her spine shrank upon itself, each vertebra curling closer and closer as relief flooded down her back. Her left palm migrated to her stomach and pressed against her shirt as she exhaled a short, pacified breath. Even Sparkie relaxed. His flared wings drooped to his sides and pulled in as close as they could before he disappeared behind Thorn's hair.

Darius stepped nearer, hands still shoved in his pockets. He ached to hold her, to feel the cool heat of her body nestled against his, but he held himself back... waited for a cue that he was welcome. She didn't give him one.

So, he said, "Cain wanted someone else to know. To be honest, I think he's been trying to get me to figure it out for a while..."

Now, Thorn scoffed. She brandished the letter one last time before tossing it on the covered desk. It landed on the sheet with a thump, and she glared at it with sharp, narrow eyes. The tip of her tongue pressed against the edges of her teeth as she shook her head.

"Who else knows?" she asked. Her focus slashed to him again. *"Knew?* Before today, I mean."

Darius's chest caved in, a rockslide of emotion around grief he hadn't fully handled yet. Hadn't had the *time* to handle.

"Just Chris," he said through a dry mouth. Thorn frowned, and her attention suddenly moved past him—to the wider Underground over his shoulder that she could sense with her Sin abilities. Darius kept talking. "After Cain told me, I needed to find you, so I took Chris and told her everything. It was important to her that you were the first to know—"

"Where is she?" Thorn suddenly cut in. Her pitch heightened, her vocal cords strained, and the muscles along her neck moved as she swallowed hard. Her eyes continued to dart around, as though hunting through distinct points of cold energy that didn't belong to who she was looking for. When they landed on Darius again, they were wide. Full of fear and terrible understanding. Her lips parted as she inhaled a shallow breath. "Darius." His name crackled on her tongue. "Where's Chris?"

Darius's teeth clenched, and he forced them apart to say, "We went to The Cross to ask about you." His hands and feet felt numb. Hell, his entire body did. All but his heart, which ached so deeply he thought it might cease beating. "One of Edith's followers was there. He heard us talking and contacted her. We managed to get away, but there was a crash. I got hurt and couldn't get out of the car, so Chris ran off to lure Edith away, and…"

The words caught on a barb of feelings. Thorn's lashes glistened, and her jaw dropped open. Sparkie let out a keening cry that pulled a tear down Darius's cheek. He wiped it away.

"And what?" Thorn whispered.

"She jumped into the East River," Darius replied.

Thorn staggered like she'd taken a bullet to the chest. "But… Chris can't swim."

"I know."

Thorn stared at him, and a rattling breath drew between her teeth. For a moment, that's all she did. Stare. Breathe. Exist like existing was the hardest thing she'd ever had to do. Her hand hovered to her mouth, and shaky fingertips tapped against her lips. She shook her head. Once. Twice. Again and again, in short, staccato motions. A wall of tears built up. Darius took a step closer and placed his palms on her shoulders.

"Thorn, I'm so sorry…"

She tore out of his grip. Sparkie wailed a piercing cry.

"Why did you *look* for me?"

A bolt shot through Darius's chest. "What?"

"You should have left it alone!" Thorn hissed. "If you hadn't dragged Chris out of the Underground, none of this would have happened! She wouldn't be *dead!*"

Thorn walked away from him, raking her nails across her scalp while Sparkie screeched again. Darius watched her with his heart in pieces behind his ribs.

Two weeks ago, he might have folded. Given in. Taken the fall for it all just to keep the peace.

But now, a fire grew in his belly.

"Are you serious?" The words strained out. Thorn twisted around—on the other side of the room now, too far to touch. Darius crossed his arms like maybe that could keep him from falling apart. "You're blaming this on *me?* What about *you?*"

Thorn's mouth slipped open in a choppy exhale. "What *about* me?"

"*You* are the one who disappeared without leaving us a way to reach you," Darius said. "*You* are the one who decided to steal from us, *hide* from us, and take things into your own hands so we couldn't hold you back. *You* are the one who abandoned the Martyrs."

Her eyes went wider now, so wide that the entire iris showed in the middle—shards of onyx sinking into lipid crystal pools. "I was making sure Edith couldn't hurt any more of our people," she argued. "I did it *for* the Martyrs!"

"No," Darius said. His throat constricted, vocal cords raging against him. "You did it for *you.* To make *yourself* feel better, to run away from *your* trauma. And now you're blaming *me*—blaming *Chris?*—for wanting to find you? For wanting to make sure you're okay?" His voice waned to a whisper. "For *loving* you?"

Thorn sucked in a quiet, aching breath. A fresh tear fell from the corner of one eye. She let it roll down her face, along her jawline, to the point of her chin. It dove free and died upon the ground.

"I won't pretend I did everything right," Darius said

through an onslaught of growing emotion—a potent blend of rage, grief, and regret that threatened to collapse his lungs from the inside out. He swallowed hard. "I won't say I didn't make mistakes, and maybe bringing Chris out there was a mistake. But we both know damn well that this is *not* all on me because if *you* hadn't left, I never would have had to make that call. If *you* hadn't left, Chris would have gotten to tell you herself how much she believed in you—how sure she was that you'd prove Alan's fears wrong and fully embrace Patience."

Darius was openly crying now, and he didn't fucking care. Thorn's expression shattered, just as crushed, as desolate as Darius felt. *Jesus*, what he wouldn't give to go back in time, to rewind twelve days to Mackenzie's Christmas party. What he wouldn't trade to hold Thorn in his arms under a sprig of mistletoe and holiday music instead of within a fog of horror and heartbreak. What he wouldn't do to stay with her all night—to *be* that escape he didn't want to be because at least then Chris would still be alive to comfort him through it.

But he couldn't.

And neither could Thorn.

"If we're going to do this," he muttered. "If we're going to pull the Martyrs back together after everything that's happened, we have to *work together.*" His jaw clenched, and his lower lip quivered as he shook his head. "So, if you walk away from us again, I'll clean out your office, too."

He turned away and strode into the lounge, Thorn watching after him. The door slammed shut with a clap of thunder so loud it almost masked the howling inside Darius's skull.

CHAPTER THIRTY-SIX

Inmate 10058 curled on her cot.

The cell stung with icy air. It leaked through the barred window, crept up the concrete floor, and sank into her bones, which already hurt, but god, how it deepened the ache. Fingertips grazed over a fresh welt above her ear, navigating the stubble of her crudely shaven head. She wasn't sure if she'd ever adjust to the baldness—how the cold could grip her entire scalp like a hand.

It had taken two attendants to strap her broken body to the chair when the razor growled to life. Wisps of blonde hair, long like river reeds, tumbled down her clothes. She'd screamed at them. Howled until her throat ran raw and flailed even though every movement was agony. Then tears streamed down her cheeks and pattered onto the yellow coils wilting in her lap. It felt like losing a limb.

And that had been the easy part.

A distant door opened, and her eyes shot wide. Memories of being dragged from this room made her throat sting with bile. Rough hands around her arms. Thick straps binding her wrists. Piercing pain at her temples, digging into her brain, delving for answers.

And those eyes—bright and blue and *cold*—staring her

down without a mask to obscure them.

Her heart vaulted. Sweat broke across her forehead and trickled down her spine. 10058 nearly tumbled over the edge of panic, but she forced her nostrils open and coerced her diaphragm into a slow, intentional rhythm. She had to soothe the terror, manage the fear, before it could be used against her. She had to become less malleable—less *suggestible*.

But the footsteps that trudged into the hall weren't the steady, sure gait of the guard who dragged her off before. They moved slower, sloppier, suddenly joined by a squeaky wheel that instantly filled her with a rush of relief so palpable that her eyes drifted closed.

The dinner trolly.

Thank god. She'd thought it was *him*.

He'd been there when they'd stripped her nude, thrown away her clothing, and powdered her with thick, white delousing agents. A room full of nurses scrubbed her down with a brush so abrasive it made her flesh scream under the lukewarm spray. She had to brace against the shower wall to stay standing.

The guard had leered from the doorway, admiring her scars like they were scorch marks on a perfectly grilled steak.

"Now this one," he'd said, voice hungry, "she was a *soldier.*"

A soldier...

Not anymore.

10058 lifted her head from the mattress as the cart clattered closer. The meal slot in the reinforced door creaked open, and a plastic tray scraped onto the shelf. A guard in a charcoal uniform snapped the grate shut before walking away without looking at her through the tiny, riot-glass window. The squealing wheels echoed further down the ward. Other voices called to him, distant and desperate from within their own tiny rooms.

10058 didn't speak. Didn't do anything. She simply lay there for another few moments, allowing her nerves to resettle and steeling herself before she sat up.

When she did, a guttural, involuntary cry tightened her throat.

10058 gripped the edge of her cot with stiff fingers, clenching her jaw and eyes shut as pain radiated from her right hip. It shot up into her lower back and down to her thigh until the neurons caught fire. For several seconds, she sat there, rigid and shaking, until the sensation eased, and she could breathe easily again. Then, she got to her feet.

Well, one of them.

Every step was agony. When her right heel landed on the cold ground and her weight shifted over it, the pain flared so intensely that her muscles quaked. She clung to her bed and then to the sink and the wall as she hobbled forward. When she reached the door, she stopped to catch her breath. Her hands shook as they held tight to the frame, and her arms ached under the strain of holding her body weight upright. She sank to the floor with a groan. Beads of sweat caught at her hairline.

Fuck. She'd been hurt before, but nothing came close to *this*.

10058 pulled the tray off the little metal shelf, careful not to irritate the scabbed wound on her left shoulder, and lowered it to her lap. In this position, with her right leg curled beneath her and the left stretched out to keep her stable, her hip didn't sear so much as throb. The ache pulsed to the rhythm of her beating heart. She winced, considering her food. The limp slab of processed chicken both smelled and tasted like it had been supplemented with sawdust. The vegetables were marginally better if she pretended they were actually green instead of a highly saturated gray, and the roll was hard enough to use as a projectile weapon. If she had the arm, or the energy, maybe she could use it to get the fuck out of here.

Before *they* dragged her away again.

She knew what they were doing to her before they ever did it. She'd trained herself for it, walked through the exercises, but *nothing* could have prepared her for what it was really like.

The interrogation room had constricted around her again and again. The weight of them digging into her skull, tearing open her *soul*, filled her head with so much pressure she was sure she would erupt.

But she never did.

They kept mining. Day after day. Thoughts that didn't belong to her clogged her mind. First, they attempted to lure her deepest secrets to the surface. When that didn't work, they tried coercion. Starvation. *Pain.*

They'd withheld food. Tased her. He'd even struck her once. That guard from the showers. The back of his hand crashed into her cheek. Split her lip. She glared at him as blood dribbled down to her chin.

Suddenly, it was all she could taste. Sweet and metallic in her mouth, like he'd hit her again.

10058's stomach churned at the sight of this so-called "dinner," and she placed the tray on the ground. Then she lifted a little paper cup from the corner. It held a single orange pill. Ibuprofen, she'd been told.

She didn't take it. Didn't *trust* it. Couldn't risk that it would slow her mind and make her easier to manipulate.

Instead, she tenderly scooted her butt across the concrete until she reached her cot again and pushed the corner of the mattress up. A collection of matching tablets sat on the slab beneath it. She tilted the new one onto the pile and lined them up to count them. Her heart sank.

Twelve.

She'd been here twelve days.

She'd expected to be found by now.

But maybe… she never would be.

A nervous bubble swelled in her stomach.

These people had taken everything.

Her individuality. Her identity. Her *dignity.* They'd replaced language with arithmetic, reduced the person she had been to a sequence of digits sewn into a breast pocket.

10058.

And now, they were coming for the last thing she had left.

Her sanity.

"I don't give a fuck what they called you outside of these walls," the guard had hissed. A stocky finger jabbed against the tag. *"This* is who you are now."

She touched her chest. Felt the ache of bruised skin—and the deeper ache of what she was becoming.

Not a woman. Not even a human being.

A number.

God, she wasn't sure how long she could hold out.

Certainly not forever.

Footsteps returned to the hallway in a heavy, thudding cadence—a cadence she knew. Her entire face went cold.

Shit. It was *him.*

Her hearing went dull and distant as the guard neared, and she stared at the window in the door as though she were looking down the barrel of a loaded rifle. She tamped down her thundering pulse with a second of measured breathing.

But her body still shook as a figure paused outside her room.

"Inmate 10058!" a booming voice called through the glass. "On your feet!"

Her teeth clenched, and she willed herself to recall her training to keep a level head. Getting off the ground hurt more than standing from the cot. She let out a soft grunt as she wrapped her fingers around the mattress and crawled to her feet. Her hip howled, and the wound in her shoulder pounded.

"Now, inmate!" the guard yelled again.

"I'm trying!" she shouted back.

Once 10058 had her weight centered over her left foot, she took a moment to compose herself. Her muscles trembled from the effort, and she hissed a short breath as she hopped back a few paces and turned to face the door. One palm pressed flat to the wall to maintain her balance.

The guard glared at her through the window. His eyes were all she could see, and they narrowed. "Hands out in front of you."

Her lips slipped open. He hadn't made her do this before. "But my leg—"

"Hands out!"

The blood drained from her face. She swallowed hard as she shifted again, touching her right toes to the floor to offer a little support as she released the wall. At first, she swayed, and even that was enough to send a fresh, agonizing current up her spine, but somehow she managed to stay upright. With a wince, she clenched her fists and thrust them forward.

The door swung open. A mountain of a man filled the doorway, so vast that both shoulders nearly touched the frame as he strode through. He wore the same dark gray uniform the food delivery guard had on, but the stripes proudly pinned above his breast pocket made it clear he was much higher ranked. He sneered at her. The expression highlighted a stitched wound from his chin to his cheek that cut both his bottom and top lips to the left of his center line. She frowned.

That was new. And *fresh.*

"What are you staring at, *inmate?*" he growled.

She didn't reply. Didn't have the chance. The guard roughly grabbed her by the arm with that horrible, familiar grip. The force knocked her off balance, and she instinctively shifted onto her right foot. Her hip roared, pain going supernova in her bones. It arrested her nerves, burned through her muscles, and she crumpled with a cry. The guard came down upon her, pinning her to the ground with a knee to the gut as he cuffed her wrists together. The pressure of his weight against her pelvis felt like she was being torn in two. She screamed again as hot tears melted down her skin.

"Looks like I'm gonna have to teach you some *manners,*" he said, but she hardly heard him. The storm of agony turned her mind to mush, her stomach to shreds. She buck-led as nausea filled her throat then her mouth with a slurry of bile. The guard returned to his feet and grabbed her by the bicep to pull her up, too, but she couldn't stand.

"I'll drag you out of here if I have to," he snarled.

He had to.

The guard forced her from the room, holding her up by the arm on her uninjured side, which made it all but impossible for her to walk on her own. Every time her right heel hit the ground, the pain rebounded, growing with every step, every stumble, until she was blind with it. Her vision spun, her guts churned, her ears filled with so much static that she hardly heard the voices chasing them down the hallway. Men and women pressed their noses against the glass windows in other cells, as though starving for a glimpse of another human face, but the guard kept such an excruciating pace that she caught nothing more than a flash of them.

A locked door stood at the far end of the ward. Another man opened it before they got there, and the asshole with the fucked up face shoved her through ahead of him. When he released her arm, she crashed onto the ground again. This time, with her hands bound, she couldn't catch herself, and she went down hard. The injury on her shoulder tore open, and a hot trickle of blood flowed into the dip at her clavicle. She let out a high, grating yelp.

"Jesus, you're fucking *pathetic.*"

Hands found her again, lifted and jerked her to the other side where at least she could use her left leg a little easier. Hallways branched out, opening to rooms and people. She expected to turn left, to go back to that dark room where they'd tie her to a chair and pry into her mind, but instead, he yanked her to the right.

Into new territory.

10058 looked around, logging as much information as she could. A kitchen. A laundry area. Offices. Occasionally, she spotted other officers in gray, but mostly, people wore blue uniforms. At first, she thought they were all men, but as they turned a final corner and entered a blindingly white room, a woman with a buzzed head caught her eye. Her stomach dropped.

But she didn't have time to think about it. The guard guided her through what appeared to be a medical reception area. An older woman in a lab coat got up from the desk. She'd drawn her dark hair off her shoulders in a tight clip, and threads of silver laced it with bright strands, making her nearly glow under the fluorescent lights. She smiled with teeth. Too many teeth.

"You're late," the woman said, tone sharp enough to cut skin. A nametag on her breast read Dr. Maya Singh, and her dark eyes glossed over the woman with little interest. "I asked you to be here at exactly seven o'clock, Mr. Armstrong."

"I apologize," Armstrong said. "I had a little trouble with the inmate."

He shook her. The motion sent a rippling pain down her leg, and she let out an involuntary cry. Dr. Singh's penciled-in brow arched, casting a range of creases up to her hairline.

"Of course you did," she snapped, crossing her arms. "The woman's *hurt,* you idiot. She can hardly stand! Let's get some images. See if we can't salvage her…"

Salvage? A stone caught in her throat, and 10058 gritted her teeth as the doctor led the way from the front desk to a ward in the back. More men and women in blue uniforms dotted the beds, but neither Armstrong nor Singh stopped at any of these. Instead, they headed to a separate room. Singh looked the inmate over, the corners of her lips turned down in disgust, as they walked through the door. "Get her up here."

She slapped her hand upon a large metal table. A massive, ceiling-mounted X-ray machine loomed overhead. Without warning, the guard lifted the prisoner beneath her arms and sat her ass down hard on the table. She winced, fingers instinctively digging into his shirt for support. He chortled a laugh that made her feel sick.

"Lie down, inmate," he ordered while forcing her to do so anyway. Fire licked through her body. Her vision went gray.

"Excellent," the doctor said. "That will be all, Mr. Armstrong." The guard stiffened, his thick fists clenching at his sides. Singh's lips pursed into a tight frown. "Is something wrong?"

"I'm not supposed to leave the inmate unattended, ma'am," he said. "Protocol states—"

"Protocol states that you must be in the room for *dangerous* inmates," Singh interrupted, casting an open palm toward the woman on the table. "Does *she* look dangerous to you?"

Armstrong's jaw flexed. "Her file says she is."

The doctor waved him away and opened a door on the opposite wall. It led to a control booth. "If she tries anything, I'll walk at a brisk pace to the nearest security terminal," Singh said. "How does that sound?"

A deep, angry flush colored Armstrong's cheeks. He strode toward the exit, but Singh called to him.

"Oh, one last thing… I heard that Mr. Douglas arrived this afternoon."

The guard hesitated, a frown tightening his features, before he said, "Yes, ma'am, he did."

Singh nodded, her mouth a thoughtful pout. "If he's still on campus, bring him to me. Immediately."

Armstrong's eyes narrowed, and he threw a final glare at the inmate on the table before saying, "Of course."

Then he strode into the ward, and the door clicked closed again.

Leaving 10058 lying in dim silence.

The doctor hummed a keyless tune as she entered the control booth and shut it behind her, which swallowed her voice with a snap. A low hum filled the room, and the machine's primary imaging sensor glowed to life. As it hovered toward her chest, the woman on the table looked around. There wasn't much. The machine took up so much space it didn't leave room for anything else. A small cabinet and sink resided in the back corner, but the drawers would certainly be locked, and even if they weren't, she didn't stand a chance of getting over there and finding a weapon before Singh called the guard. 10058 considered her options as the sensor caught snapshots of her entire body, from her torso to her toes. It emitted a chorus of buzzing and clicks, each image announced with a beep that felt like a needle in her ears.

A sudden knock made her jump. She glanced at the exit as Dr. Singh popped her head out.

"It's open!" the doctor called.

The door swung inward, and 10058 winced as a bright light poured across her face. A man the general shape and color of a peeled potato stood over the threshold. He wore a suit with a bright yellow tie, which he held against his chest with a squat hand as he tilted forward.

"Is it safe?" he asked. His deep-set eyes flicked over the X-ray machine before landing on the woman below it. The sight of her made a sneer stretch across his mouth.

"Of course, it's safe," Singh said without an ounce of sympathy. "Come in."

He did, quietly closing the door and swallowing the light before he made his way across the suite. The inmate watched until he disappeared, and he considered her the entire way, as though trying to decide if he knew her. She didn't recognize him, not personally, at least, but something tugged at a thread of memory she couldn't quite place.

Once he reached the booth with the doctor, the man closed them inside. Or, he intended to. But the door didn't click, and a crack remained between it and the frame. Muffled voices leaked through. 10058 turned her head to listen.

"Have a seat, Mr. Douglas," Singh said.

"Please," he said in a soft, cloying tone, "Maya, how many times have I asked you to call me Max?"

"As often as I have told you to call me Dr. Singh," came an icy reply. *"Sit down."*

Max Douglas. A nauseating weight grew in the inmate's stomach. She twisted on the table to look back toward the wall, but a jolt of pain in her back made her grimace. She bit her cheek to stifle a cry.

Max breathed a sigh as a chair scraped across the tile. "So, to what do I owe the pleasure, *Dr. Singh?*" he asked with a heavy hand of scorn. "I was just heading out when Keegan said you needed me. He didn't look too happy about it…"

"No, I imagine he wasn't," Singh replied. The sensor clicked overhead, beeped, and shifted down. "Mr. Armstrong is worried Inmate 10058 might try to hurt me." She let out a dead laugh that made the woman on the table squirm.

"That doesn't seem very likely," Max muttered. "Are these her X-rays?"

"Yes," the doctor said. "According to her file, she was injured when she came in. A gunshot wound to the shoulder and obvious impact trauma in her pelvis, but I wanted to see just how extensive it is. Luckily, the shoulder seems to be intact. Just a muscle laceration. It should heal up on its own just fine. The hips, however…" A pause hovered in the air. The distinct clicking of a keyboard drifted through the crack. "Her SI joint is severely dislocated, and there are fractures along the right iliac crest. No wonder she can't walk, and if it doesn't get addressed, she may never be able to again."

The inmate's heart pounded, and the corners of her eyes stung.

"Well, that's not ideal," Max said. "But there must be something we can do to salvage her?"

There was that word again. *Salvage.* Her mouth went dry.

The doctor sighed. "It depends on what that means to you, Mr. Douglas," she said in a short, matter-of-fact attitude. "Can we repair the hip? No. Not here, and not within my scope of expertise. It will require a specialist, as well as a significant sum of money."

"I'm… not sure that's possible," Max replied. "Can't we just… I don't know. Give her crutches and put her to work? She doesn't need to walk to fill pill bottles."

"No, I suppose she does not," Dr. Singh replied, but the tone of her voice made it clear this was nothing more than a distraction from the topic she really wanted to discuss. "Though I am confused on one matter…"

"Oh?"

"Why *exactly* are we moving this inmate now?"

"What do you mean?" Max asked. The words dripped with nerves, so much so that the woman on the table could practically sense the humidity rise as he poured sweat.

"I mean," Singh replied, "that Inmate 10058 was supposed to be in solitary for a month, but it's been only two weeks since she arrived in Falkenrath. Her file *does* say she is to be relocated to the SPEC block, but what it doesn't say is *why.*"

The inmate's lips slipped open, and her pulse pounded so hard against her eardrums that it dizzied and disoriented her.

Falkenrath.

The prison.

Fuck.

"It's simple," Max answered. "She's already undergone four rounds of mental manipulation, which showed that she knows absolutely *nothing* valuable. The boss wants to get her into the workforce as quickly as possible. She's a waste of resources stuck in that cell."

The boss. 10058 imagined those dead eyes again, and her temples pulsed with reimagined pain.

"Just *four* rounds?" Singh pressed. "I'm surprised she gave up so quickly…"

A tense silence followed, and the inmate strained her ears.

"Is there something you want to ask, *Dr. Singh?*" Max asked.

The doctor let out a low, dark sound. "I don't think I

have to ask it to know the answer. The rumors are true. Edith Froschlin has—"

Max cut her off with a rough hush. "Quiet! There are ears *everywhere!*"

Another heavy silence. 10058 craned her neck upward, holding her breath.

"Does Neema Davis know?" Singh asked at last.

"*No one* knows," Max replied. "And Miss Froschlin would like to keep it that way, so I'd appreciate your *discretion* in this matter…"

"You'll have it," the doctor answered. "The last thing we need is to incite a riot. If this gets out—"

"It would be disastrous," Max cut in irritably—impatiently. "Now, if you're done, let's hurry. Another one of *them* has taken an interest in us."

"Another one like *Anton Claytor?*" Singh asked. Max made a noise of confirmation. "Who?"

"A woman named Autumn Hunt."

Panic flooded down the inmate's spine. She froze where she lay, and her ears pounded so hard with the sound of her own racing heart that she nearly missed what Max said next.

"She'll be here tomorrow to inspect the operation. We want everything running as smoothly as possible."

Autumn Hunt. Here. *Tomorrow.* 10058 rolled onto her side. Her right hip howled in pain, and she bit her cheek as she forced herself into a seated position. Her head nearly knocked the X-ray sensor.

She had to get out of here—*now.*

10058 lowered herself off the table. Her bare feet hit the tile without a sound. She centered her weight over her left, steadied herself, and hopped toward the door.

The control booth swung open. The inmate froze where she stood, barely balanced on one foot as Singh and Max stared at her. His eyes and mouth were wide, but a cruel smile stretched across Singh's lips.

"Where do you think *you're* going?"

The next few minutes were a blur. They called

Armstrong back into the room, and he slammed her hard into the wall in a gratuitous show of control. Pain kept her senseless as he dragged her back into the central infirmary ward. A single crutch materialized out of thin air, thrust into her hands, and she was expected to use it with her wrists still chained together. She refused, standing still in the center of the room until Armstrong grabbed her by the bicep and thrust her forward. She stumbled and fell, crashing into the tile with a yelp that made the other prisoners on their cots cover their ears. He pulled her roughly back to her feet and hissed, "Move, *inmate*, or this is going to get a lot worse for you."

She hobbled into the hallway, the guard on her heels. From there, he guided her down another and another, each impossibly longer than the last, or maybe it was just the screaming in her hip that made her think so. Finally, he stopped to open a door.

To another goddamned hallway.

This one, though, moved in an arch around a guard's control station, which had easy visual on a horseshoe of doors. Doors that led to cells. Her mouth went dry.

Each was closed and locked tight, with bright yellow paint in stark contrast to the gray concrete walls. Narrow, vertical windows offered her little clarity on what waited inside, but they hardly had to. Like in solitary, faces pressed against the glass, curiously watching as Armstrong reached a cell in the far left corner. No one peered out of this one, but she caught a glimpse of a buzzed head with black fuzz lying on the bottom bunk.

"Welcome home, 10058," the guard grumbled as he turned a key in the lock. Even as it clicked open, the inmate inside didn't move. "Door's locked until 0800. I hope you got enough dinner."

He chuckled as he removed her cuffs, pulled the door open, and shoved her over the threshold. She barely managed to catch herself on the crutch, but still, a whimper escaped from the depths of her throat. Then, the door

slammed shut at her back. The telltale clicking of the bolt sliding into place made her heart skip.

As Armstrong's footsteps moved away, the other person in the cell looked up.

And she froze. She had ocean-blue eyes, which went narrow as they took 10058 in—from her face to her shoulder to her leg. In a flash, she leapt to her feet.

"Did they do this to you?" she demanded, and before 10058 could stop it, she ran a tender hand down the side of her cheek. The contact nearly made her gasp.

"No," she managed to say. "No, I came in hurt."

The memory of that night came at her in violent flashes and cold plunges. She closed her eyes.

"You're bleeding," her cellmate said. She huffed a frustrated breath through her nose and grabbed her by the elbow. "C'mon. Sit down."

She guided 10058 to the bottom mattress. When that elicited a sharp cry, her brows pinched in.

"What happened?" she asked as she pulled a box from beneath the bed. Inside sat an array of items, including magazines, spare clothing, playing cards, and a baggie of personal hygiene products. "You get hit by a car?"

10058 shook her head as her cellmate got back to her feet, already opening a menstrual pad. "Not a car," she replied. She winced again as the other woman moved her neckline to press the absorbent side to her reopened shoulder wound. "I got hit by a river."

The cellmate paused. Her grip tightened, sending a soothing current down the other's spine. "By accident," she muttered, "or on purpose?"

God, that was a hard question to answer…

"Accidentally on purpose," 10058 settled on at last. Her cellmate cast her a look. "It's a long story."

"Well," the cellmate sighed, "I'll have plenty of time to hear it. Looks like we're roomies." She crossed her arms and cocked a brow, a half-smile quirked upon her lips. "Don't worry. I'll move to the top bunk."

She laughed, and 10058 couldn't help but laugh, too. It had been so long since she'd last laughed. So, she laughed harder, and harder…

Until she broke.

Sobs poured out of her, one bounding on the heels of another in a stampede of hurt and heartache that threatened to trample her until it wasn't just her hip that was broken. The crutch clattered to the ground at her feet as she dipped her face into her palms. A sudden weight collapsed onto the mattress beside her, and an arm wound around her back, pulling her close. She expected the other woman to speak— to share some platitudes that had helped her cope with her own slice of shit—but instead, she remained quiet. Nothing but a comforting presence. A strong front to lean against.

And she waited until the sobs began to slow before she uttered anything at all. When she did speak, she said just three words.

"What's your name?"

"Inmate 10—"

"Not your *designation*," her cellmate said with a sneer. "Your *name*. Who you *really* are. Not who they told you to be."

She drew away, leaning forward with fingers laced between her knees. The inmate swallowed hard and ran a hand over her scalp, which had once flowed with bright, yellow hair. She imagined all the scars that marked her and remembered how she got them—and how she didn't. A palm cupped her cheek as she recalled a knife slicing through her skin.

Then she clenched the fist that had grabbed that same knife—had torn it right across the monster's throat.

"Christine," she said at last. "But you can call me Chris."

ABOUT THE AUTHOR

MC Hunton is a bright personality with a shockingly dark taste in the stories she writes. She graduated with her bachelor's degree in Creative Writing in 2010 and has been working on her debut series, The Martyr Series, since 2005. The first book, Resurrection, won first place in the fantasy category of Writer's Digest's Best Self-Published E-Book Awards in 2022 and took home the win in the paranormal category in the Indie Reader Discovery Awards in 2023. She has a penchant for fast-paced action, deeply-rooted sociopolitical and spiritual themes, and emotionally driven plot and character development.

Check out what she's up to by visiting her website:
www.MCHunton.com